Sun City, Arizona: where old people go to die.

At least that's what Milo, a retired border patrolman, thinks when he first arrives in the palm- and orange-tree-lined retirement community. He takes up photography to wile away his remaining days.

Before long, he is fighting and flirting with Claire, a young widow who is working through her trauma while volunteering at the zoo. He meets Sax, a former cop and the bartender at the Brass Monkey, and Sax's favorite barfly, Sondra.

Unable to turn off their suspicious natures, Milo and Sax see danger and intrigue simmering just beneath the serene picture-postcard settings of Arizona. And life will never be the same for any of them!

The Brass Monkey Series

Wild Life

Charmed Life

Night Life

New Life

By

Susan Wells Bennett

Published by Inknbeans Press

Cover: Nikki McBroom, Trident Art

The Brass Monkey Series © December 2012
Susan Wells Bennett
and Inknbeans Press

ISBN-13: 978-0615742045 (Inknbeans Press)

ISBN-10: 0615742041

Wild Life © 2011 Susan Wells Bennett
and Inknbeans Press
Charmed Life © 2011 Susan Wells Bennett
And Inknbeans Press
Night Life © 2012 Susan Wells Bennett
And Inknbeans Press
New Life © 2012 Susan Wells Bennett
And Inknbeans Press

This is a work of fiction. Names, characters, places, organ-
izations, businesses or incidents portrayed in this novel are the
product of the author's imagination, used fictitiously or with
permission given to the author for use

Table of Contents

Wild Life

Susan Wells Bennett

book one
of the BRASS MONKEY series

Milo Crosby is a retiree with too much time and too many women on his hands. He's the thorn in a zoo volunteer's side, an easy mark in an aging actress's sights, and the co-conspirator in his doting granddaughter's life. When all four paths intersect, Milo discovers just how WILD LIFE can get.

Wild Life
Book One of
The Brass Monkey Series

Susan Wells Bennett

PUBLISHED BY:
Inknbeans Press

Wild Life

In memory of my grandfather, John Dallas Truedson, who was, at various times in his life, a Border Patrol agent, a photographer, and a cantankerous old man.

From At the Zoo

The monkeys stand for honesty,
Giraffes are insincere,
And the elephants are kindly but
They're dumb.
Orangutans are skeptical
Of changes in their cages,
And the zookeeper is very fond of rum.
Zebras are reactionaries,
Antelopes are missionaries,
Pigeons plot in secrecy,
And hamsters turn on frequently.
What a gas! You gotta come and see
At the zoo.
-- Simon and Garfunkel

Wild Life

Sly Fox

"Anything in your pockets?" asked the muscular black man who guarded the entrance to Monkey Village like a bouncer at a hot nightclub.

Milo had been through the routine before. "Hello, Zareb. How are the monkeys today?"

He raised an eyebrow, eyeing Milo suspiciously. "Anything in your pockets?" he repeated.

Milo did his best to look innocent and offended. "Zareb, don't we know each other better than that by now?" He flashed his antique Kodak folding camera and smiled. "I'm just here to try out my new gadget. Only thing in my pocket is some extremely expensive film."

Zareb gave him a smile. "You really should invest in a digital camera, Milo."

Milo shrugged. "Photographs mean so much more when it costs something to take them."

"Maybe," the baritone man acknowledged, "but when you take a bad shot you don't have to feel so guilty."

"So am I cleared for entry?"

"You swear you don't have any peanuts?"

He held his right hand up. "So help me God." The dried peas rattled in his pocket as he walked past Zareb; luckily, the man was already talking to the young mother behind him.

The zoo had nearly twenty squirrel monkeys in the exhibit. They ran across ropes and trees with enviable agility, barely noticing the humans who gawked at them from the ground below. Milo knew the zoo had a strict policy against humans hand-feeding the monkeys. Last week, when he had casually poked a few peanuts through the hole in his pocket in an effort to lure a monkey or two down from the trees, the beige woman had reprimanded him before picking up all of the nuts and expelling him from Monkey Village.

The beige woman – he couldn't help thinking of her like that. She had blonde-gray hair and pale skin without a hint of makeup. In her beige zoo polo shirt and tan khaki pants, she looked like she was all set to hide out in the Sahara.

4

Wild Life

He opened his camera and focused it on the area just beyond the ropes where he intended to lure the monkeys with the dried peas. After some internet research, Milo had discovered that two-thirds of all female squirrel monkeys see in color, just like humans. He hoped that the sharp-eyed little primates would be attracted to the flash of bright green when he tossed a pea into the area.

He saw the beige woman approaching in his peripheral vision and straightened up, glancing at her badge before meeting her eyes. "Nice to see you again, Claire," he said genially.

"Mr. Crosby."

"I don't believe we've been properly introduced. Milo Crosby. And you are?"

"I'm a zoo volunteer. That's really all you need to know." Her expression remained neutral and forbidding.

"My reputation precedes me."

"I asked around." She crossed her arms under her ample bosom.

Milo's eyes dipped involuntarily. He might be fifty-seven, but he wasn't dead.

"You threw apples to the orangutans."

"They looked hungry."

"You taught the macaw to say "So's your old lady.'"

"It seemed appropriate."

"And, as I recall, the last time you were here you were smuggling peanuts."

"I didn't realize there was a hole in my pocket."

"Look, I understand there's no way for me to get you banned from the zoo, but that doesn't mean I can't watch every move you make in this exhibit. You are a menace to the animals and a bad example to every child you encounter."

His lips twitched as he tried to contain his prideful grin. "Call me Milo."

She turned on her heel and walked back to the other woman patrolling the exhibit. He couldn't hear her words, but she was pointing at him, apparently instructing the younger black-haired volunteer to keep her eyes on him. He smiled and gave the girl a friendly thumbs-up, causing her to slide her eyes quickly away.

Wild Life

Another stream of visitors flowed past him, providing ample cover as he slipped a hand into his pea-filled pocket. Waiting until a solid line of people separated him from both Claire and Zareb, he flicked the pea into the foliage a few feet outside the human boundary. One of the monkeys in a nearby tree followed it with her eyes. Milo had her interest; she ran closer to the boundary.

Slipping another pea from his pocket, he flicked it out to land next to the first one. The curious monkey jumped lower in the tree, her eyes moving from the peas to her benefactor and back. She dropped to the ground and moved into the frame Milo had preset with his camera.

"Monkey!" squealed a toddler next to him as she dove under the rope meant to separate the humans from the primates.

The squirrel monkey picked up both peas and paused just a moment, skittering away as Milo took the picture, leaving what Milo knew would be a blur of tail on the negative. "Damn," he muttered.

Claire was swimming upstream through the crowds, attempting to catch the attention of the toddler's mother. "Ma'am? Your little girl, ma'am," she called.

Milo reached out and pulled the child gently back under the rope.

"Get your hands off my child!" the indignant mother snarled at him, finally distracted from her conversation with her equally inattentive friend.

"She was outside of the ropes," he tried to explain. The woman just glared at him. He let go of the girl, who wrapped her arms around her mother's legs and looked back at him accusatorily.

Claire finally reached them. "Ma'am, I know the monkeys are tempting for small children, but it's very important that your daughter stay behind the ropes. The monkeys are wild and will bite."

"This man touched my daughter," the woman announced stridently. "He should be ejected."

"I was just trying to keep her out of harm's way, ma'am." Milo stepped toward Claire, his hands held out in supplication. The contents of his pocket rattled drily and Claire glanced downward, frowning.

Wild Life

"Ma'am, I'm sure Mr. Crosby didn't mean any harm."

The woman exchanged a doubtful glance with her friend. "What kind of adult man goes to the zoo alone?"

"I'm a photographer, lady," Milo said, abandoning any pretense of charm.

"Milo," Claire asked, "would you mind clearing the aisle so that the rest of the patrons can see the monkeys?"

Milo tipped an imaginary hat at the unpleasant young mother and her spoiled progeny before moving toward the open space at the center of the exhibit. He could feel the eyes of the other attendant on him, but every time he looked at her, she shifted her eyes away. While winding his film forward to the next frame, he watched as Claire escorted the two women and the brat out of the exhibit and pointed them toward the front of the zoo, no doubt instructing them to file a report against Milo if they really believed he had assaulted the girl.

While she was distracted, Milo pulled another pea from his pocket and tossed it toward an open space. The same female who had gotten the first two peas made a dive for the third one, this time sitting prettily in just the spot Milo had hoped she would. He steadied the camera and snapped the photo well before she finished her snack. He folded up the camera and stood back to let the other visitors get a closer look, glancing toward the entrance. Claire was chatting with Zareb now. The dark-haired girl was answering questions about the monkeys. The monkey who had retrieved the dried peas inched closer to the human-monkey boundary and met Milo's eyes. With a quick glance toward the occupied attendant, he reached into his pocket and liberated a few more peas, which he tossed just a few inches inside the human territory. The monkey held on to one of the iron stakes with a hand and reached for the peas with the other one. Another of the monkeys noticed what she was doing and scampered fully into human territory, stealing the peas and running away. The older, more cautious female chased after him, chittering angrily at the other monkey's audacity. The crowd laughed, drawing the zoo attendant's attention away from her interviewers.

"What's going on?" she asked Milo, since he was the nearest adult to her who had been watching the animals.

7

Wild Life

Milo swallowed hard, as if he were a schoolboy caught doing something wrong. "Nothing. The monkeys were just playing."

"Which ones? Where did they go?"

He pointed toward the stream. "One was chasing the other."

She waded into the crowd and tried to spot the monkeys, who by now had moved into the trees. Milo, certain he was in the clear now, sauntered up the path at what he considered an unsuspicious pace. Halfway to the exit – his goal – he felt something tug his pants leg. Expecting to see a child at his feet, he was shocked to find a monkey reaching into his pants pocket.

The cold blast of water from Claire's spray bottle turned his shock to stunned stillness. The monkey, its hands full of dried peas, sprang off his leg and into the greenery surrounding them.

Chagrined, he met Claire's eyes.

"Lucky it's so warm today, Milo. That wet spot will be dry before you know it."

He looked down to see the sizable stain spreading across his crotch as it soaked into his chinos. "Thanks."

"I know you just forgot that you had a pocketful of dried peas. You really should be more careful, though. These monkeys are wild animals and they have an amazing sense of smell."

Zareb was laughing as Milo walked out of the enclosure.

"Look, Mommy," a little boy said, pointing at him. "That old man isn't potty trained." His mother shushed him and rushed him past Milo with an apologetic grin.

"See you soon, Zareb," Milo said with a half-salute.

Zareb, still laughing, waved.

8

Wild Life

A Horse with No Name

"We need one of you to go work the stables." Mr. Rodriguez, his dark-blue suit in danger from the monkeys traversing the tree limbs and ropes above, glanced up with apprehension.

"Why don't you go, Isobel?" Claire prompted.

"I don't know anything about horses."

"You don't need to," the zoo manager said, stepping backward in an effort to save his suit. "You can flip through the information binder to learn the horses' names. Most of the information is on the wall anyway."

"Where's Jim? Doesn't he usually handle the horses?" Isobel crossed her arms and stood her ground.

"Jim called in sick."

"Claire, you know more about horses than I do," Isobel pleaded. "And you're not afraid of them."

"Zareb!" Claire called. He turned and she beckoned him over.

He shook his head to indicate he couldn't leave his post.

She rolled her eyes.

"Claire, please." Mr. Rodriguez glanced at his watch. "I don't have time to find someone else. I'm late for an interview as it is."

"Fine. I'll go." She unhooked the spray bottle from her pants and handed it to Isobel. "Take care of this for me, okay?"

"Thank you, Claire. I owe you one."

"Whatever."

She stalked out of Monkey Village and turned toward the Children's Zoo. She split a class of field-tripping kindergartners like a log splits a stream, the two halves coming back together on the far side. The teachers smiled at her, but she avoided direct eye contact with them and trudged onward, her feet taking her where her mind never would go willingly.

She remembered the first time she saw a rodeo. Grandpa Harry took her as a special treat when her mother was in the hospital giving birth to Beryl. She was ten at the time. The trick riders captured her imagination and made her want to ride horses.

At least Mr. Rodriguez wasn't sending her to the riding ring. At the stables, she wouldn't have to do more than stand and watch the people and two or three old horses that hadn't carried a rider in years.

The red barn loomed ahead and she tried to paste a smile to her face – the children would expect it. A girl of eight or nine was petting the white streak of a horse in the middle stable. The sign above read "Mr. Ed."

"How old is he?" the girl asked.

"Don't know exactly, but he's at least twenty," Claire answered as she headed toward the bin where she expected to find the horse information binder.

"Is that old for a horse?" The girl left Mr. Ed and followed Claire.

"Pretty old."

"How long do they live?"

"Usually around thirty years."

"That's as old as my mom!"

"Where is your mom?"

"She's in the bathroom. She told me to wait here."

"Don't tell her that thirty is old, okay

The girl smiled. "How old is that big horse?" she asked, pointing at the draught horse to the right of Mr. Ed.

"Probably twenty or so."

"Are all the horses here twenty?"

"No, I don't think so."

"You don't know much about them, do you?"

"No, I'm afraid I don't. But I can get the answers." She lifted down the milk crate Jim had stashed in the overhead cubbyhole. The white binder slid off the top and landed with a slap on the concrete behind her. Distracted by the falling book, she over-compensated and the contents spilled to the ground around her. Exasperated, she sat down on the now-empty crate – the sun-brittle plastic cracked and she dropped through the top of it.

The little girl laughed like she had just seen the best Charlie Chaplin routine ever.

"Hope?" A woman in red-check shorts and a white t-shirt was speed-walking toward the barn.

Wild Life

The girl couldn't stop laughing to answer her, so Claire called out, "She's over here."

"My goodness, are you okay?"

"I've been better."

"Do you need some help?"

"That would be nice."

The woman put out both hands and Claire grasped them, planting her feet on the ground. A moment later, she was on her feet again and towering over her rescuer. "Thank you so much. That could have been much more difficult."

"Not a problem. Glad I was here to help. Hope? Are you ready to move on?"

"Can we wait just a minute, Mom? She was going to tell me how old the horses are."

Her mother sighed, exasperated. "Does it really matter? We're going to miss the Giraffe Encounter."

"Who cares about giraffes? Horses are much smarter...and you can ride them."

"You have one at home. You don't have any giraffes at home."

"How old is your horse?" Claire asked, suspecting the girl's ulterior motive.

"How old is Matilda now, Hope? Seventeen?"

Frowning, the girl shrugged.

"I think she's worried about Matilda getting too old to ride."

"Is that so?" The petite woman looked at her daughter, who was only an inch or two shorter than she was.

"I just want to be sure we're not hurting her."

The woman smiled apologetically. "My daughter's a bit of a worrier. I've been planning to get the kids riding lessons, but it's hard to find someone to come all the way out to Tonopah these days. You don't give lessons, do you?"

"I don't ride."

"Oh. I just assumed since you work with the horses—"

"I don't, normally. I'm usually in the Monkey Village." Claire stooped and picked up the white binder, flipping it open. "Hope, Mr. Ed is twenty-eight. The draught horse, Godzilla, is eighteen. And the pony is thirty-five."

"What's the pony's name?"

"Apple."

11

"Sweet!" The girl skipped over to the gray-and-white-speckled pony.

"Do you know if the regular attendant teaches riding?"

"I'm sorry, but I don't."

The woman smiled. "Thank you for humoring my daughter."

"Not a problem." Claire turned away from the woman and kneeled to gather the contents of the now-destroyed box.

"Come on, Hope. Let's go see some animals we don't have at home," the woman called to her daughter.

Left alone with the scattered horse brushes, treats, and Jim's personal objects, she tried to relax, even as her mind was flooded with memories of Grandpa Harry and Dorian.

"You don't give that child enough love."

Just ten years old, Claire hid around the corner as Grandpa Harry reprimanded her parents.

"Nonsense," her father said. "Nanny Helga takes excellent care of the girl."

"I didn't accuse you of neglecting her physical requirements, Ted. But the girl needs affection."

"She's difficult, Daddy," her mother whined. "She's not naturally affectionate like I am."

"You're about as naturally affectionate as a scorpion with everyone but that baby in your arms."

Claire chanced a peek around the corner. Her mother was bouncing baby Beryl in her arms. Claire was certain her mother had never done that when she was an infant.

"Now, Daddy—"

"Never you mind, Olivia. I'm just glad you and Ted have settled your differences and come to an amicable relationship after all these years. That you've got another baby to prove it is so much the better. I guess it's too late for you two to take an active role in sweet Claire's life, so I'll do it. I'm buying the girl a horse."

"A horse? Isn't that dangerous?" her father protested.

"Don't be ridiculous, Ted. Olivia was riding her own horse by the time she was eight."

Claire's mother swelled with pride. "I took second place in a jumping competition when I was twelve."

"There's so much I never knew about you," her father sighed.

Claire's stomach turned. She rolled back around the corner and silently planted herself against the wall.

"I think learning to ride a horse would be good for her," her mother said.

"Absolutely. I've already found the perfect mount – a yearling with champion bloodlines. He'll be delivered to the ranch tomorrow. You two should drive Claire out."

Her mother demurred. "We're having pictures made tomorrow."

"That's okay," her father said. "We'll have Helga drive her over."

The next day, Claire met the love of her young life – a silvery gray colt who answered to the name Dorian. Her grandfather hired an Olympic bronze medalist as her riding coach, and Helga drove Claire to the ranch for lessons every day after school.

Her grandfather wanted her to be a jumper like her mother had been, but that one rodeo she had attended with him had given Claire a different idea.

"Barrel racing?" Her grandfather ran his hand straight back through his thick white hair. "Seems a mite undignified, sweetheart."

"I can't jump in a rodeo," she answered. "There's no competition for that."

"Well, no. But I just expected you'd compete in show jumping. You can't go to the Olympics as a barrel racer."

"Who cares about the Olympics? I want to be a rodeo rider."

Grandpa Harry smiled and shook his head. "If I'd known that, I would have found an old cowboy to train you."

Vicky, the bronze medalist, turned out to be something of a rodeo aficionada herself; she studied barrel racing and adapted her lessons to fit Claire's goal. Dorian proved to be a willing and easily trained barrel horse. Claire entered her first competition with Dorian when she was thirteen and soon built a reputation in the Bible Belt as a contender, frequently placing in the top three and winning more and more competitions as she gained experience.

Using the excuse that they wanted her to have a better education than the small-town schools near their home could provide, her parents bought Helga a home in Oklahoma City when Claire reached high-school age and enrolled her in Bishop McGuinness Catholic High School. Neither of her parents had taken the fact that they were nominally Baptists into consideration when selecting the school. Helga, the only actual member of a congregation – Lutheran – had tried to intervene, but her half-hearted objections were silenced with the promise of a happy retirement in a home of her own as soon as Claire was successfully through school.

Claire had tried to blend in with the crowd, but after three years, she still had no real friends at school – and certainly no boyfriends. She consoled herself with the fact that she had more than enough going on outside of class to keep her busy. Training for the rodeo circuit occupied nearly every afternoon, and her weekends were fully booked at least once a month.

It was at one of these rodeos that she first met Dorsey, a Native American and soldier at nearby Fort Sill. She had been riding for seven years by then, and Grandpa Harry told her she was growing into a beautiful young lady – though she didn't believe him. Meeting her at the gate after a race, Dorsey's soulful gray eyes and sweet slow smile drew her to him even before he asked for her autograph.

"I don't have a pen or paper," she answered, blushing.

"I have a pen right here, ma'am," he answered, pulling a blue marker from his pocket.

Taking the pen in hand, she said, "I've never been asked for an autograph before."

"I've never asked for one."

Glancing toward the stadium seating, she spotted her grandfather slowly making his way toward them. "Have you got something for me to sign?"

He unsnapped the pearl buttons of his shirt until he could expose the right side of his chest. "Here."

She giggled nervously and backed up a step. "I can't do that!"

14

"Sure you can."

"What's the point of signing there, anyway?" she objected. "You'll just wash it off the next time you shower."

"That's where you're wrong. Your name is already tattooed on my heart. After you do this, I'm going to make it official."

Her grandfather was just ten stairs away when she leaned forward with a wicked grin and drew a large "C" on his hairless pectoral muscle.

"Claire!" Her grandfather's stern tone made her pull away before she could finish writing her name.

"Yes, sir!"

"What are you doing?"

Dorsey answered instead, turning to face the stately old man. "Sergeant Dorsey Combs, sir." He gave a brief salute. "I asked Miss Turner for an autograph, but I didn't have any paper."

"Do you think this is funny, young man?"

Claire, who couldn't see Dorsey's face, hoped he wouldn't make the mistake of smiling.

Dorsey cleared his throat. "Of course not, sir."

"Are you aware that she is only seventeen?"

The silence that followed dropped Claire's heart to the dirt beneath her feet. Finally finding her voice, she said, "It's okay, Grandpa Harry. He just wanted my signature."

Grandpa Harry pushed a finger into the center of Dorsey's chest. "Stay away from her, son, or I'll be down to speak with your commanding officer."

Dorsey turned and smiled sadly at her before taking off at a jog. Watching him go, Claire felt a yearning pull inside her for the first time. She turned it into anger. "Why did you do that? I'm a big girl!"

"He's nothing but a dirty Indian, Claire. You are better than that. I can't believe you actually touched him. I thought you were raised better."

Her eyes widened. She had never heard her grandfather say anything hateful about anyone before; he was the most genial person in her short life. Turning on her heel, she led Dorian, who had been patiently waiting at her heels, toward the horse trailer. As she brushed him down, she let her tears flow, heartbroken twice in one day: she would

15

never see Dorsey again and she would never love her grandfather as much as she had before.

She was wrong about one of those nevers, though: Dorsey was in the stands at the next rodeo she competed in. In fact, he always appeared in the stands, no matter where she competed: Kansas, Missouri, Oklahoma, or Texas. For the next year, every time she rode out into the arena, she spotted him in the front row. In all that time, he never talked to her; she was glad he was there, just the same. Once, as she and Dorian trotted out of the arena, she came close enough to him to make eye contact. He cupped his hand in a "C" shape and held it to his chest. Her heart thudded in response.

A year after their first encounter, Dorsey waited just outside of the arena as Claire exited. Her grandfather, who had lowered his vigilance after Dorsey made no further attempts to contact her, was still high in the stands. "You're eighteen now, right?"

Claire nodded. "Why?"

"I just wanted you to know I wasn't lying." With that, he reached up and pulled the snaps of his dark blue cowboy shirt apart, revealing a red-ink "C" on his right pectoral.

An incredulous smile spread across her face.

"I'd like to take you out on a date."

"Grandpa Harry—"

"I'd prefer that it just be the two of us."

"He won't like it."

"Doesn't matter. Where can I meet you?"

"I go to McGuinness High School in Oklahoma City. You know where that is?"

Glancing behind him, he saw her grandfather bearing down on him. "I'll figure it out. See you on Friday. Great riding, by the way." He turned and jogged away.

"Who was that?" Grandpa Harry asked, shading his eyes and squinting after the young man.

"Just a fan," she answered.

That Friday, she told Helga not to worry – she was going to the main library to research her English term paper. As she waited by the school gates, she wondered if she shouldn't just go to the library. As the parking lot emptied and the clock ticked past four, she prepared herself to be stood up.

Wild Life

A few minutes later, though, a dented old Ford truck – its main color rust – rolled in and pulled up next to her. Behind the wheel sat Dorsey, his black hair freshly trimmed in a high and tight and his soft lips curved in an apologetic smile. "I'm late," he said matter-of-factly.

"A little."

"You mad?"

"No. We didn't set a time."

He leaned over and popped the passenger door open. "Get in."

She slid across the vinyl seat, pulling the door closed behind her. He drove them to a little diner and asked, "Is this okay?"

"I've never been here."

"You'll like it. They make great waffles."

"But it's almost dinner time."

He shrugged. "Get a burger, then."

He hopped out of the truck and ran around to her side, opening the door with a flourish. "My lady."

She giggled and blushed, sliding out in her red plaid skirt.

"May I say, you look slammin' in that outfit."

She rolled her eyes. "It's my school uniform."

"Never really understood the whole Catholic schoolgirl thing before now."

They took a table and the waitress, a gum-chewing redhead Claire's mother's age, got their order: a burger for her and waffles for Dorsey. When she left their table, Claire and Dorsey sat in uncomfortable silence for a few minutes. "Um...how long have you been in the service?" Claire asked.

"I'm coming up on six years in a few months."

"How old are you?"

"Almost twenty-five."

"Wow."

"I'm trying to decide what I'm going to do: re-enlist or go home."

"Where's home?"

"Arizona. You ever been there?"

"No." She sipped her cola. "Why not stay in Oklahoma?"

"I don't have anything here."

17

She bit her tongue to keep from making a fool of herself.

"In Arizona, I have some land and an idea. You ever heard of hydroponics?"

For the rest of the date, she listened as he expounded on the glories of soilless farming – and she wasn't bored. Just watching his mouth form words fascinated her.

A few months later, she stopped loving horses. It wasn't Dorsey's fault – he loved that she barrel raced. Even after they started seeing each other, she kept up her practice and competition schedule. Dorian, now nearly ten years old, understood her every mood and move. Though her coach spent more time with him than she did, Dorian would have followed her anywhere if he had been able.

Right before high-school graduation, she and Dorian won a competition in Kansas. Vicky was thrilled – Claire had beaten her stiffest competition, practically guaranteeing a prize-winning summer. When she showed up for practice the following Monday, though, she found her coach in tears outside Dorian's barn. She grabbed Claire's hand and dragged her down next to her. "I have to tell you something," she whispered hoarsely.

"What's wrong?" In all the years she had known Vicky, she had never seen her like this. Panic zipped through her body, slicing her heart in pieces.

"It's Dorian." Huge tears rolled down her cheeks, stopping her voice.

"Dorian?" She tried to stand up, but the coach wouldn't let her go. "Dorian!" she screamed, willing the horse to stick his head out of his stall like he always did when she called his name. The stall was ominously empty. "Where is he? Where's Dorian?"

"He's sick."

"What's wrong with him?" Fat tears were dropping like summer rain on her white blouse.

"The doc says it's colitis-X."

Colitis. Claire had known other riders who had lost their best friends to it. Her legs turned to jelly and she collapsed next to her coach. "I don't...how?"

Vicky shook her head slowly. Her tears had slowed and her voice was restored. "He was sick when I got here this morning. I called the vet right away, but he suspects Dorian was sick most of the night. He just laid down about an hour ago." She strangled again, but wrapped her arms tightly around Claire's shoulders. "Go…be with him," she whispered.

Claire hugged Vicky briefly and, unable to stand, crawled toward Dorian's stall. Pulling the gate open, she saw her beloved horse raise his head to look at her. She rubbed his nose and her tears fell in rivulets. "It's okay, Dorian," she said. "It's okay." Inserting herself into the foul-smelling space, she took her dear friend's head in her lap, caressing him as his life ebbed away.

While she sat with Dorian, Vicky called Grandpa Harry. Looking more worn out than she had ever seen him, her octogenarian grandfather arrived not long after Dorian succumbed. With his still-strong arms, he lifted her from the stall and pulled her close. "I'm so sorry, my darling girl. So very sorry."

She collapsed anew against him and he led her away from the barn. Grandpa Harry arranged to have Dorian buried in a pasture on his ranch. Claire's grief was so overwhelming that her high school principal agreed to let her miss the last week of classes and still graduate. Claire didn't even consider that Dorsey wouldn't be able to find her; she could think of nothing but how horrible Dorian's death had been.

At the celebratory lunch after graduation, her coach said, "We need to get you back on a horse. Your next competition is in two weeks!"

They were sitting in a steakhouse with Helga, Grandpa Harry, and Beryl, her adoring younger sister. Their parents were in Paris on what they called a second honeymoon; Claire suspected it was just another way for them to avoid celebrating any triumphs in their oldest daughter's life.

"We can't get a horse trained that fast," Claire answered in a monotone. "I'll have to withdraw."

"Nonsense!" boomed Grandpa Harry. "I've already found the perfect horse. He's a trained barrel racer."

Claire frowned.

"He really is a great horse, Claire. You'll love him." Vicky sliced a bite of prime rib and dipped it in horseradish, avoiding Claire's gaze.

"You've already seen him?"

"Yeah. I didn't have anything else to do, so I drove out to Kansas last week to take a look."

Claire played with her mashed potatoes, flattening them against her plate. "I just don't think I want to ride another horse. Not yet, anyway."

"You're one of the best barrel racers on the circuit. This is your summer! Come on – everyone here has faith in you. Dorian would want you to keep riding, don't you think?"

"He was a horse, Vicky. I'm pretty sure the only things he thought about were when he was getting a brush down and his next meal."

Beryl set her fork down, folded her arms, and looked at her older sister. "Grandpa Harry was going to take me to your next rodeo, Claire. I really wanted to go."

Claire's parents hadn't allowed Beryl to come to any of her competitions in the past. They considered the rodeo to be a working-class event. Beryl was going to be their debutante daughter – they didn't want her exposed to anything rough. Especially not Claire. But with their mother and father out of the country, Grandpa Harry was free to take Beryl wherever he wanted.

Claire decided she had to ride at least once more – so that her sister could see her. "Okay."

The white-and-black paint horse her coach and Grandpa Harry had located was like a machine. He ran the clover-leaf barrel pattern with a grace and speed that would have shamed Dorian. Claire climbed into the saddle and just held on for the ride – the horse didn't need anything but a nudge to start him running.

"That's amazing!" Vicky raved on the fourth day of practice. "You just beat your old record with Dorian. This horse is going to bring you a lot of wins this year."

Claire patted the horse, but he didn't lean in and nuzzle her affectionately the way Dorian used to.

A few days later, she waited at the gate for her chance to race. From her vantage point, she spotted her sister and Grandpa Harry holding a sign that read, "We love Cowgirl Claire." She waved at them and they waved back. The gate opened and her horse started running. He made the first turn and headed for the second barrel. Claire, gripping the saddle, glanced up and recognized Dorsey in the front row straight ahead. He had a sign, too: "Marry me, Claire." Shocked by what she read, she whipped her head around to read it again as the horse flew around the second barrel. That one gesture was enough to pull her off balance, and the horse beneath her didn't compensate for her shift in weight. A second later, she landed with a thud, pushing the breath from her body while simultaneously causing the crowd to inhale sharply. The horse finished with what would have been a winning time had he arrived with a rider.

Dorsey was at her side before anyone else. "Claire! I'm so sorry!"

"Yes," she said. "My answer is yes."

"Are you okay?" Vicky was kneeling on the other side of her now. "Is anything broken?"

"My left leg hurts a lot."

She felt them skim her jeans up her leg and screamed as they tightened just above her knee.

Vicky squeezed her hand. "Don't move, Claire? I'm getting help. Stay with her, okay?" she said to Dorsey.

"Of course."

"My leg's broken, isn't it?"

"Looks like it."

"The horse is okay?"

"Yeah, he's fine."

"Good for him."

Dorsey chuckled at that.

The coach was back with a stretcher. "Careful, guys," she instructed the two rodeo clowns who came out to help her.

"Where's Grandpa Harry?" Claire asked, wincing as the clowns prepared to lift her.

Vicky frowned and scanned the crowd. "Can you handle this, boys?" An urgency had taken hold of her. Claire struggled to see whatever her coach had seen, but the men gathered around her blocked her view.

"Go on. We've got this."

Vicky sprinted away.

"Where's she going?" Panic seeped into Claire's voice. "Where's Grandpa?"

Dorsey spun to look at what Vicky had seen. He turned back to Claire and said, "Everything's fine, baby. Don't worry. Let's take care of you right now." He helped the clowns carry her out of the arena.

Now, as Claire eyed the old draught horse, she couldn't help but hate him. He never did anything to her – she had never even ridden him. She hadn't ridden since the day she broke her leg – the same day Grandpa Harry died of a heart attack in the rodeo stands.

Wild Life

Southbound Pachyderm

After Milo left Monkey Village, he headed to the elephant enclosure, taking a seat where he could watch the zoo's two Asian elephants as they lumbered around their yard. Milo had always been partial to African elephants himself, but he supposed an elephant was an elephant.

There's an old saying: elephants never forget. Because of his remarkable memory, Milo's colleagues back in Minnesota used to give him elephants for his birthday. Because he thought of the creatures as imposing, intelligent, and charming, he liked that people thought of him that way.

He liked to watch children's reactions to these animals. Most were enthralled by them; some would begin imitating the hypnotic sway of their long trunks. Occasionally a child would show fear at their massive size, not realizing how gentle most of these giants were.

He rolled his film to the next open frame and focused on an area about ten feet inside the elephant pit. He had been to other zoos where the elephants were in a slightly recessed area, and he had been up close and personal with a few circus elephants. The closer he could get to an elephant's eyes, the more connected to them he felt.

He remembered taking dead Alice to a circus, back when they were dating. It was before most of these animal rights activists were even born and not even a handful of laws regulated the treatment of these beasts. They had seemed happy enough. He could tell when an animal wasn't happy. There was a jaguar at the zoo who spent most of her time pacing the length of her cage – that was a miserable cat.

He had always loved animals. When he was in high school – way back in the Sixties – he wanted to become a veterinarian. His parents didn't have much money, though, so he planned to work in his father's bakery and save his wages for college. What he didn't count on was the draft. All of his college plans went by the wayside when his number came up. He had been dating dead Alice for a few months at the time. She had been beautiful then, even if she was a little bossy. He liked her a lot, and she offered him comfort as he prepared to leave for boot camp. When he came home on furlough before shipping out to 'Nam, she had a little surprise for him – a slight baby bump. Being an honorable sort, he took her right down to the courthouse and married her the same day, thanks to a sympathetic judge who waived the five-day waiting period since Milo was only home for four days.

When he came home from the service, he found a cranky, dissatisfied woman and a toddler he couldn't distinguish from any other white boy he might meet on the street. He knew his career plans would have to change – he had a wife and child to support.

Drawing on his military service, he found a position with the United States Border Patrol – in International Falls, Minnesota, one-hundred-and-forty-three miles of the safest border in the world. He spent his days stamping passports and making small talk with the travelers.

He developed a reputation, though. Milo never forgot a face. Because of this unique gift, he made more busts in one year along the Canadian-U.S. border than had been made in the previous ten years combined. Yet despite his stellar record and numerous requests for a transfer to the Mexico-U.S. border, his supervisor always managed to keep him in International Falls. Though he suspected some meddling on dead Alice's part – she was good friends with his supervisor's wife – he could never prove she was putting the kibosh on his career aspirations. As the years passed, the job's sheer repetitiveness dulled his keen observational powers. He knew most of the people who crossed his piece of the border by name, and spent a large part of each day waving people into and out of his country.

He was an honorable man. He lived up to his vows, staying with dead Alice through nearly thirty years of marriage despite the ever-widening canyon of dissatisfaction that yawned between them. When she died a few years back, he felt like he was able to breathe again. No longer distracted by the misery of his home life, he threw himself into his work, looking to score a big win and finally get that transfer to Arizona – hopefully with a promotion too.

It wasn't long before Milo noticed something odd in the travel patterns of one Vaughn Wagner. Wagner was a frequent border crosser, often visiting the United States for a week at a time. He tended to dress in western shirts that made him look like a Texas rancher and he had a penchant for cowboy hats. And he was young – not more than forty, if that. Milo couldn't help but wonder how a young Canadian man had so much vacation time. The thought niggled at his brain, always just on the edge of his consciousness – something wasn't right. The next time Milo saw him, he pulled him in for an interview.

"Good afternoon, Mr. Wagner. I'm Officer Crosby." He stood, hands behind his back, appraising his quarry.

"What's this about, ay?" Wagner asked, drumming his fingers once on the metal table of the interrogation room.

"Your travel patterns, Mr. Wagner. They're odd."

"How so?"

Milo placed both hands on the table and leaned forward, squinting. "Tell me, Mr. Wagner, what do you do for a living?"

"I'm a square-dance caller."

Drawing on his own limited knowledge of the activity – he vaguely remembered learning how to allemande left in grade school – he scoffed. "Either you're full of shit or you're starving to death."

Wagner pinched his lips together in silence.

"Which is it, Mr. Wagner?"

"I do just fine, thank you."

"Would you like to hear my theory, Mr. Wagner?"

Wagner raised his eyebrows briefly, indicating Milo should continue.

"I think you're a drug smuggler."

The man seated at the table giggled incredulously. "Where am I smuggling them? In my boxers?"

Milo smiled in a way that usually rattled his preys' nerves. "That's what you're going to tell me."

Wagner calmed. "I'm afraid you're wrong about me, officer."

"Look, I'll give you one chance to fix this. Be honest with me."

"What kind of drugs do you think I'm smuggling, anyway?"

Milo eyed him up and down slowly. "You're smuggling prescription meds."

"What?"

"That's right, Mr. Wagner. I've got you dead to rights on this. I've studied your travel plans for the last two years. Almost

25

without fail, you've traveled to well-known retirement destinations: Phoenix, Orlando, Southern California. You're peddling cheap prescription drugs to old people."

"I was calling at square dances."

"You honestly expect the United States government to believe that you are supporting yourself on what you make calling at square dances?"

"Yes! Check the dates."

"Oh, I don't doubt there were dances on those dates. You're using the square dancing as a cover for your little smuggling operation."

Cal, one of the other officers on duty that afternoon, opened the door. "Milo? Can you step out for a minute?"

"You think about what I've said here, Mr. Wagner. Do yourself a favor, okay?" Milo stalked out the door to where the other officers stood gathered around Wagner's half-disassembled car.

"There's nothing here," Cal said.

"There's got to be. It's too suspicious to be nothing." Milo, supporting himself on an open door, bent as low as he could to see underneath the car. "You check the wheel wells?"

"Yep," answered one of the other officers, a new guy named Steve. "And the spare-tire compartment."

Milo frowned and scratched the back of his head, ruffling his fluffy white hair.

Steve smirked.

"Put the car back together." Milo turned on his heel and went back to the interrogation room. "You're working illegally in the United States."

"What?" Vaughn Wagner raised his head from the table.

"You heard me. You're an illegal worker. As such, you're banned from entering the country for the next five years."

"That's ridiculous. I'm an entertainer!"

"Do you have a work visa?"

"No. I don't need one." He enunciated slowly, "I'm an entertainer."

"I don't find you the least bit entertaining, sir. Get yourself back to Lac du Bonnet and don't even try to cross the border until 2012."

"You're insane. You can't do that!"

"I'm the judge and jury here, Mr. Wagner, and I say you're banned."

Sternly, he pointed Mr. Wagner toward the door. They marched through the office and out to where his car, now reassembled, waited.

"I'm going to file a formal complaint against you, Officer Crosby." The man stood straight as a baton and looked up into Milo's eyes. "I promise you that, sir."

"Go ahead." Milo turned on his heel and left the troublesome Canadian. His fellow officers applauded him as he walked triumphantly back to his post.

"Great catch, Milo," Cal congratulated.

"Thanks, Cal." Milo knew it wasn't enough to get him the promotion and transfer he dreamed of, but it was a good start. Wagner was the first in a streak of successful detainments. By the end of the month, he had broken his own record and was starting to believe he was unstoppable. When his supervisor – the same one who was married to dead Alice's best friend – called him in for a meeting, he was sure that good news was in the offing. He strode into the meeting with his chest puffed up and a prideful smile.

"Milo, we've got a problem."

He deflated like a bad tire – loudly. "What?"

"Now, now, no need to take that tone."

"Dave, I've been on the hottest streak of my career – and I've had some hot streaks. What could possibly be wrong?"

"Vaughn Wagner."

"The drug smuggler?"

"The square-dance caller."

Milo shrugged. "So he says. In any case, he needs a work visa."

"He's appealing your ban. Did he actually tell you that he was paid for his work as a square-dance caller?"

Milo searched his memory. "Not in so many words."

"Our attorneys have done a little research. None of the square dance festivals he called at are admitting to paying him."

"That's because he's actually a drug smuggler."

"We can't prove that."

"Come on. You know it's true. Give me a chance to—"

"Let me stop you right there, Milo." The beefy ex-Marine leaned forward on his desk, his forearms forming a fleshy barrier. "Our attorneys have determined that the best way to keep this from becoming an international incident is to allow Mr. Wagner back into the country."

"But—"

"Look, Milo, he hasn't done anything wrong so far as we can prove. I'm sure you understand."

Milo melted back into his seat, defeated.

"Our attorneys are advising one other thing."

"What? Should we give Mr. Wagner a ticker-tape parade every time he crosses?"

"No." His boss shifted uneasily in his chair, causing Milo to wonder if the man had a hemorrhoid. "I understand Brian lives in Phoenix."

"Yes." Milo had a difficult relationship with his son Brian. He chalked it up to not being around during the boy's first few years. Just thinking about Brian made him squirm a little. He had failed at fatherhood.

"You've never been a big fan of the cold weather, have you, Milo?"

"Not particularly."

"Look. I know the last few years have been difficult. I can't imagine how I'd feel if I lost my wife. Maybe I'd start spinning out of control too."

Milo frowned and grunted his disagreement.

"You've been with the Border Patrol for, what, thirty years?"

"Thirty-three this fall."

"Well! That's a long career on the front lines, Milo. It's one thing to be sitting behind a desk at our age. It's totally different when you're out there, every day, facing the dangers—"

"We're on the Canadian border."

"Still."

Milo leaned forward, his hands on his knees. "Let's stop beating around the bush."

"Fine. Our attorneys recommend that you retire. You're well past your thirty years of service. We're even offering you a generous golden parachute. All you have to do is apologize to Mr. Wagner and pose for a few pictures in front of the local press."

"What?"

"Just say you're sorry, Milo. Say you're sorry and move to Arizona."

He grimaced. "This job is my life."

His boss sat impassively across from him, his eyes unreadable.

"Can I take a day to think about it?"

"What's there to think about? Either you apologize and retire with your golden parachute or you don't."

"So I don't have to retire?"

His boss chuckled for the first time; meeting Milo's eyes, he hid the laugh behind his fist and pretended to cough. "No," he said when he regained his composure. "Either you apologize and get the golden parachute or you don't apologize and we force you to retire anyway."

"I'd still like to think about it, if I could."

His boss glanced at his watch. "Take your time. The press conference doesn't start for another ten minutes."

The trouble with having a memory like an elephant is this: when you do something you aren't proud of, you can never forget it. The memory of Vaughn Wagner's clammy handshake and the blinding camera flash sent a chill of revulsion down his spine every time he thought of it. Try as he might, he couldn't shake the memory. As he took down pictures that had hung in the house for decades and packed up dead Alice's china, his mind repeatedly flashed on Wagner's hateful grin – the one that told Milo he had been right all along. The guy was a criminal.

The real estate agent he contracted with to sell his home was thrilled with the house. "Mr. Crosby, this is an absolute gem! Of course, the wood floors need to be refinished and the walls need paint, but it's still a fantastic home!"

"Thank you, Mrs. White."

"I can get you at least...oh, let's say...eighty thousand for it?"

He and dead Alice bought it for twenty thousand right after he started with the border patrol. He smiled for the first time in days.

Wild Life

Despite an essentially lifelong estrangement from Brian, Milo still expected that moving to Arizona would repair their relationship. Brian, however, seemed less than thrilled when Milo parked a U-Haul truck in his driveway. "How long are you staying?"

"Indefinitely," Milo repeated. "It's high time I got to know my grandchildren better, don't you think?" He glanced toward the surprisingly pasty boy and girl and winked.

"Children, go to your rooms." As if on cue, they rose and disappeared, leaving Milo alone with Brian and his sour-faced chestnut-haired wife who looked very much like dead Alice, in Milo's opinion.

"What are my children's names?" Brian queried.

"That's just bad parenting, Brian. You ought to know your own children's names."

Brian closed his eyes and took a deep breath. "I do know their names. The question is: do you?"

"Oh." Milo swallowed uncomfortably. "I know what this is about."

"Do you?" Brian cocked an eyebrow at his father. His wife scooted closer to him, laying a calming hand on his knee.

"Of course. I've never forgotten that day. I'm normally so good with faces..."

"You couldn't recognize me in a crowd of children."

"To be fair, Brian, you were all wearing the same uniform."

"I'm your son!"

"And Minnesota does have a large population of towheaded children."

"Name my children."

"Alice Marie and Eric Thomas.

"You see, darling? Your father knows their names. He just wants to be part of the family."

"Why thank you, Millie."

She frowned. "Marla."

They let him stay on the pullout sofa. He wasn't allowed to sleep past seven o'clock in the morning, because Marla had OCD and couldn't leave the house without the living room tidied. Brian worked long hours as a DEA agent and Marla spent her days volunteering for the children's school. Unable to sit and watch television for hours on end,

Wild Life

Milo wandered the new city, boredom always at his heels. He visited the museums, the botanical garden, and the zoos. When the civic amenities were exhausted, he took to the antique stores. Before long, he developed a passion for film cameras. He identified with them on a subconscious level — they, too, were obsolete.

He emptied the contents of the U-Haul truck into a storage locker, wondering the whole time why he had bothered to bring the forty-year-old furniture and decorations with him. When he accidentally dropped a box full of knick-knacks and heard them crash to pieces, he looked around guiltily for dead Alice. She wasn't there. He sighed with relief and dumped the whole box in the garbage without even opening it to see if anything was salvageable.

He stayed with Brian and Marla until his house in Minnesota finally sold — nearly a year after he arrived. The housing market — suddenly suffering the effects of the recession — made selling more difficult than Mrs. White had anticipated. Though he hadn't wanted to settle for less than four times what he paid for the home, his discomfort as a houseguest finally prompted him to take the offer of sixty-five-thousand dollars.

He found a reasonably priced duplex in Sun City and happily removed himself from his son's house. Only his granddaughter was sad to see him go. He consoled her by taking her to the zoo.

"What do you want to see today, Alice Marie?" Her small warm hand in his made him happier than he had been since he left the Border Patrol.

"The elephants!" The white residue of the sunscreen her mother had smeared on her face and arms made her look even pastier than normal.

"Then we'll start with the pachyderms!"

"No, Grampa, I said the elephants!"

He laughed and swung her into his arms and up onto his shoulders. He couldn't remember sharing a moment like this with his son, but he swept the twinge of guilt away. "Pachyderm is another name for elephant."

"Pack-e-derm," she repeated slowly, sounding out each syllable.

"That's right!"

She wrapped her arms around his head and squeezed. "I love you, Grampa."

"I love you too, Alice Marie." His dead wife's face flashed through his mind and, for just a moment, he was glad he married her.

Wild Life

Swan Dive

Whenever she had petting zoo duty, Claire always stopped by to see the black swan. He was a little off the most convenient route to her assignment, but she felt he looked forward to her visit as much as she did. He had lost his mate a year or two before and the zoo had yet to obtain a single female swan for him to bond with. She heard a rumor in the volunteers' lounge that Mr. Rodriguez had decided not to find the swan a mate because he was already twenty-two years old and not likely to live much longer.

All in all, the swan seemed content. If he was lonely, he didn't seem to show it. Claire would wait by the fence that separated her from the bird until he noticed her. When he did, he would walk to where she was and honk at her in a gentle way, almost as if he were talking to her. If anyone else approached the fence when she was there, he would run aggressively toward him or her, honking angrily. One of the keepers told her that meant the swan had chosen her as his mate. The first thought that crossed her mind when she heard that was *I can't wait to tell Dorsey that*.

Dorsey hadn't been the jealous type. From the very beginning, he had seemed confident that she belonged to him and no one would ever steal her away. The day she was thrown from the horse he became a permanent fixture in her life, holding her hand whenever he was close enough to reach her.

With Vicky's help, Dorsey contacted Claire's parents to tell them about the accident. Claire knew they didn't fly home because she broke her leg – they returned because Grandpa Harry was dead. Within a week, Claire stood at the edge of her grandfather's grave, supported by crutches and Dorsey. On the opposite side of the trench stood her mother and father, both of whom shot her hateful stares – as if she had caused the man's death. Of her whole family, only Beryl hugged her that day.

Claire couldn't shake the feeling that her parents were right. Her sudden isolation did nothing to alleviate her guilt. Vicky, a constant companion for nearly eight years, accepted a new position somewhere in the South. Helga, her nanny, considered her contract with the Turner family complete now that Claire had graduated from high school; she served Claire with what amounted to an eviction notice. Her parents, never affectionate, were decidedly chilly toward her now.

Dorsey, his Army days at an end, made taking care of Claire his primary concern. He took a month-to-month lease on a two-bedroom apartment and moved her in with him. They planned their escape from Oklahoma as soon as Grandpa Harry's estate was settled. Dorsey convinced her, despite her guilt, to stay and receive what Grandpa Harry had wanted her to have.

On the day the will was read, Dorsey drove Claire to her parents' mansion. As they pulled up to the top of the half-circle driveway, Dorsey said, "I'll wait in the truck."

"I want you to come in with me."

He shook his head. "That's not a good idea, baby. Your family doesn't like me."

She stared at her lap. "They don't like me, either. Please."

With one finger, he turned her chin to face him. "You sure?"

She nodded.

He walked around and opened her door. Reaching into the back of the truck, he produced her crutches. Together, they navigated the steps leading into the massive house.

Her mother opened the door. "Claire. I'm sorry, but this is for the immediate family only."

"Dorsey is family, Mother. We're getting married."

Olivia Turner's eye flicked over the muscular man disapprovingly; her lips tightened into a perfect pink rosebud of distaste. She walked away from them, leaving Dorsey to close the door behind Claire and himself. Following the clacks of her mother's heels toward the library, she took in the entry hall. Portraits of her parents and Beryl lined the walls. She spotted only one photo of herself – a small framed picture of her with Dorian. Seeing the horse made tears well in her eyes and blurred the hall before her.

"You okay?" Dorsey whispered.

She nodded and kept moving. Her mother's footsteps were no longer audible, but she knew the meeting would be in the library.

Her mother and father were already seated to one side of the great mahogany desk, which her father had ceded to the attorney for this occasion. The attorney, a bluff man whom Claire had met a few times before, smiled at her as she entered the room. The man's frown appeared when Dorsey came into view. "Claire. Good to see you. I'm sorry for the circumstances, of course."

"Mr. Handlemann. This is my fiancé, Dorsey Combs."

"Please," he said, gesturing to the chair opposite her parents, "have a seat. Dorsey, if you could pull one of those chairs from against the wall..."

"Yes. Thank you." He pulled a chair even with Claire's and took her hand.

"Let's get right to it, shall we?" Mr. Handlemann pulled his spectacles from his breast pocket and smoothed the document spread before him.

"I, Harold James Smithson the Third, being of sound mind and body, do hereby proclaim this to be my last will and testament...."

As the attorney droned on – he wasn't the most interesting of speakers and he didn't lend any color to the document before him – Claire studied her parents. Intuitively, she knew this was likely to be the last time she would ever be in the same room with them. In the last eight years, she had spent less than a week's worth of hours in their presence. They didn't hate her; it had been worse than that. They simply didn't care about her. The only family members who did care about her – or had cared about her – were Beryl and Grandpa Harry. That same intuition that warned her she would never see her parents again whispered that it would be years before Beryl would be free to contact her.

Dorsey nudged her, breaking her gaze. She tuned into the lawyer's words again.

"...granddaughter, Claire Elizabeth Turner, I leave five-hundred-thousand dollars, to be held in trust until her thirtieth birthday, provided she does not marry prior to that date. Should she marry, this trust is to be divided between

Claire and her sister Beryl and distributed on the occasion of Beryl's thirtieth birthday."

The whole room held its collective breath, waiting for Claire to speak. Dorsey let go of her hand and leaned slightly away as if preparing to dodge a physical blow.

"Do you understand what that means, Claire?" Mr. Handlemann asked.

"Yes. It means Dorsey won't be marrying me for my money." Her lips twitched in an ironic smile.

"This is serious, young lady," her father intoned. "You have a responsibility to your family. You can't just marry some half-breed G.I. who didn't even have the respect to ask for your hand."

Dorsey clasped her hand and stood up. "I'd ask your permission to marry Claire," he said to her parents, "but the only approval I need is hers."

In a surge of adrenaline, Claire grabbed her crutches and raised herself from her chair. "I'm marrying Dorsey. He's a good man – probably better than any I've met in my life. Don't worry – we're not staying in Oklahoma. No one will know that I've shamed you." She let go of Dorsey and balanced on her crutches.

"You're still our daughter—"

"I'm eighteen. You're rid of me – be happy."

Dorsey waited for her at the library door, smiling proudly.

Together they walked down the long hall to the main door. At the stairs, Claire stopped and shouted, "Beryl!"

The house was silent.

"Beryl!" she called out again.

Her mother's clacking heels came running down the curved hall, the woman herself appearing within seconds. "Stop that, Claire!" she whispered angrily, her eyes blazing.

Hearing a door open upstairs, Claire yelled again, "Beryl!"

Her sister appeared at the railing just as their mother reached her. "It's time for you to go, Claire."

Ignoring her mother's words, she looked up at her dark-haired, sweet-faced sister. "Beryl, I love you. Don't forget me, okay?"

36

"Where are you going?" She scrunched her face, concerned.

"Arizona!"

Her mother pushed against her shoulders harshly, throwing Claire off-balance. Dorsey caught her and pulled her to him.

Beryl was panicking. "Take me with you!"

"I can't. I'll be in Arizona! Come find me!"

Her father rounded the corner now. "Leave this house. You aren't welcome here."

"It's your fault Daddy is dead!" her mother spat.

Stunned, Claire let Dorsey lead her from the house and helped her into the truck. As the house shrank in the rear-view mirror, she let her tears flow.

"Are you sure about this?" Dorsey asked again.

"This is what I want." She took his hand. "You are who I want."

They loaded their belongings in the back of the truck and drove to Phoenix.

One morning, as Claire was reading the news and drinking her coffee, she found an article about a black swan that was brutally stoned to death by some unthinking teenagers. The dead swan's mate was now mourning her and attempting to save their egg.

Silent, salty tears slid down her cheeks as she read the story. Her dog, sensing her distress, came to her side and, putting his small tan paws against her leg, stared up at her with worried brown eyes. Reaching down, she lifted the substantial pug into her lap and hugged him. "I'm okay, Taz." Her voice didn't match the sentiment. The dog lapped up her tears.

When the phone rang, she set the dog back on all fours and reached for the receiver. "Hello?"

"Claire? It's Beryl."

"Hi."

"You okay?"

She hiccoughed another round of sobs. "Not really."

"Are you sure you don't want me to come stay with you for a few weeks? Rory and the kids will be fine without me."

Wild Life

Claire pictured Beryl's perfect family – her handsome husband, two boys and two girls. She and Dorsey wanted kids, but it never happened. All Rory had to do was look at Beryl lustfully and nine months later – pop! She dried her tears with the back of her hand. "I'll be fine. I just need some more time."

"It seems like every time I call, you're crying. Are you getting out of the house, at least?"

Claire let out a short laugh. "I promise I don't cry all the time."

"Are you still volunteering at the zoo?"

"Yes, Mother." She pushed back her chair and walked to the sliding-glass doors of her condo, determined to get some air.

"I can't help it – four kids would make any woman into a perpetual mom."

Claire laughed for real now, taking in a deep breath of fresh air and scanning the Phoenix skyline. She did enjoy city living, despite missing the farm.

"So? Are you better now?"

"Yes."

"May I ask what happened?"

"I read an article about a dead swan."

"The one in Australia?"

"Yeah."

"Maybe you should stop looking at the news for a while."

"Beryl, I'm going to cry sometimes. I think it's normal."

"Maybe so." She sighed heavily, sounding like an obscene caller for just a moment. "What are you doing today?"

"I'm working the petting zoo."

"That'll be good. Children lighten the soul."

"Really?" she deadpanned. "Is that what you're going with?"

"Come on! I have a light soul, so it must be true!"

Turning back to her apartment, she caught a glimpse of herself in the large mirror over her sofa. "When did I get old?"

"You're not."

"I am. And I'm very…beige."

"How can you be beige?"

"I'm about as colorless as a person can be. Beige hair, beige skin, beige clothing..."

"Put on some lipstick."

"Then I'll be a set of red lips surrounded by beige."

"Do you have to wear beige shirts?"

"No. The zoo has purple shirts too."

"Wear purple."

"I didn't say I owned any of them."

Her sister laughed. "Figures. Buy some today."

"That's a waste of money. I have plenty of zoo shirts."

"Live a little, Claire. I doubt your light bill will go unpaid if you buy a few purple shirts."

She knew Beryl was right. "Okay."

"Good. I'll call you tonight."

"You don't need to do that."

"Fine. I'll call you in the morning."

"Thanks."

"That's what sisters are for. Love you."

"Love you too." She hung the phone up without saying goodbye, as she always ended calls with her sister.

Leaning over the sofa, she gazed into the mirror again. She wondered if it was possible that all the color in her body had drained out, like hair loses its pigment. Fluffing her hair with both hands, she tried to find the Claire she used to be. Unfortunately, the old woman reflecting back at her refused to move out of the way.

Reaching down, she ruffled Taz's fur. "I'll be home around two, boy."

The dog cocked his head to one side before dropping it between his paws in what looked like despair. She pulled the door shut and locked it. The hallway was quiet and she rode the elevator to the parking garage alone.

The drive to the zoo was almost peaceful. With the summer came earlier hours, and she found herself in the parking lot by six-thirty. The gift shop didn't open until after seven; she would have to buy her new shirts on her way out.

The siamang gibbons were still quiet, a sure sign that their keeper wasn't on their island habitat yet. Once the keeper showed up, the siamangs would begin their morning concert – a noise that always drew large crowds of visitors to stand along the banks of the mainland and watch as the animals inflated their large throat pouches to create their distinctive, resonating songs.

The black swan spotted her as soon as she rounded the corner. He waddled over and spread his feathers in what she knew was a courtship display. She thought again of the dead swan and her mourning mate as she walked slowly along the edge of the enclosure. If she could keep this animal from suffering, she would.

Wild Life

Hunting Bears

Milo stood as quietly as possible, obscured by the bamboo and hoping his greenish shirt served as additional camouflage. His camera of choice for today's hunt was a large-format Horseman camera he stumbled across on Craigslist a few weeks earlier. The widow of a photography hobbyist had been anxious to rid herself of her dead husband's collection. He picked up a couple of good lenses, two tripods, and the camera for only five-hundred dollars. His guilt for underpaying was assuaged by the knowledge that the widow would have a hard time finding a buyer to pay top dollar in the current digital and recessional age.

The zoo had two spectacled bears, but whoever designed the enclosure for them had clearly been working in the bears' interests, not the visitors'. Spotting the small South American beast in the wilderness of grass and rocks was nearly impossible. In all the visits he had made to the zoo over the last year, he had yet to get a decent picture. He talked to the keeper and the volunteers assigned to the animals, but they shed no light on the bears' habits.

"Oh, you know, they just wander now and again. One of them likes to nap over there," the last volunteer had said, pointing at a spot covered by grass on one side and obscured by a boulder on the other.

"I'd like to get a picture of him if I could," Milo had prompted.

The volunteer, an old man who was probably the same age as Milo, scratched the back of his head and squinted. "If I were a photographer, I think I'd set up behind that bamboo fence." He pointed across the compound. "Of course, you can't get there right now."

"Why not?"

"Zoo's got that half of the trail fenced off. They're making some repairs back there."

"Thank you," Milo had answered.

The next day, he returned, wearing a pale green Guayabera and carrying the Horseman camera and a tripod. He headed up the trail and loitered around the macaw and the howler monkeys near the barrier – just a sawhorse with a no-trespassing sign – until he was alone. Slipping past it, he walked around to the bamboo and waited for the bears to make their appearance.

Milo had never been much of a hunter. When his friend Cal and their fellow border guards – avid sportsmen all – questioned him about it, he always blamed his urban upbringing. "I was taught to duck when I heard gunfire," he would say, and his colleagues would laugh and slap him on the back. He took in stride the occasional razzing he received.

In truth, he didn't hunt because he couldn't stomach killing a wild animal. While he didn't have any sentimental attachment to cows, pigs, or chickens, he found the idea of killing a moose or an elk repugnant.

When Brian was a teenager, though, he asked his father to come with him on a father-son camping and hunting trip. "Please, Dad. I don't want to be the only one without a father there."

Milo had looked to his wife for help, thinking she would come up with the right words to get him out of it. Instead, she said, "You have the weekend off, Milo. Don't worry about me – you and Brian could use some quality time together."

"I don't know, son. I don't really like the taste of game animals. And I believe that you should always eat what you kill."

"It's okay, Dad!" the boy exclaimed. "Whatever you kill, I'll eat!"

He felt like a moose caught in the crossfire – nowhere left to turn and certainly nowhere to hide. He grimaced, but agreed.

He borrowed a tent, some sleeping bags, and a couple of rifles from a chuckling Cal. "Does your boy know how to set one of these up?" he asked as he helped Milo load the camping necessities into his truck.

"I don't know."

"Maybe we should do a dry run just to be on the safe side."

"Are you suggesting I'm not capable of setting up a tent, Cal?"

Wild Life

The rugged outdoorsman shrugged, not meeting Milo's eyes. "Not exactly. But it's not as easy as it looks."

"Brian's been in the Boy Scouts since he was eight," Milo grumbled. "Something tells me he'll be able to help me out."

"Suit yourself. Your boy ever shot a rifle?"

"Yes. He's got his merit badge for that."

"What about you?"

"I've shot my share of guns."

He gave Milo a long look. "I'm going to grab you a couple of safety vests." The lanky man loped back into his garage.

Milo leaned against his truck, enjoying the unseasonably warm October afternoon. Halloween was still two weeks away and Indian summer hadn't abandoned Minnesota to Jack Frost yet. Cal's wife leaned out of their house and waved. Milo waved back at the pretty brunette.

"Where's Cal?" she called.

"In the garage." He pointed with his thumb just in case she couldn't hear him across the yard.

She smiled and waved again, disappearing back inside. Milo wished he had held out for someone undemanding and sweet-tempered instead of Alice.

Cal reappeared, two bulky orange vests over an arm and two orange caps in his other hand. "Be sure to wear these, okay?"

"Yeah." He took the garments from his friend. "Your wife was looking for you."

Cal glanced at his watch. "Dinner time," he said with a smile.

"You're a lucky man."

"Don't I know it!"

On Friday afternoon, Milo and Brian piled into the truck and followed the map to the planned campsite. The ride was uncomfortably silent, mostly because Milo never knew how to get Brian talking.

"How's school?"

"Fine."

"Your grades good?"

"Good enough."

"What does that mean, exactly?"

43

"Mostly As and Bs."
Silence.
"How's football going?"
"I didn't go out for it this year."
More silence.
"You got a girlfriend now?"
"I'm not gay, Dad."
Milo gave up.

Three other sets of fathers and sons were already at the campsite when Milo and Brian arrived. Brian jumped out of the truck before it even rolled to a stop and ran over to his buddies, high-fiving all around. Milo casually saluted the other fathers, each of whom nodded or saluted in return. He recognized two of them – one from his favorite pre-shift breakfast spot and the other from the local hardware store. They all looked more at home in their current environs than Milo felt, but he straightened his back and did his best to look like a seasoned camper.

He pulled the gear from the back of the truck, piling it about ten feet from the established campfire ring. The man he recognized from the diner walked over and stuck out a hand in introduction. Milo met his handshake.

"So you're Brian's dad. Have to admit, I didn't know that before today."

"Milo, please. My job keeps me away more than I'd like. I'm with the Border Patrol."

"Dangerous work." Milo thought he saw a smirk, but the guy hid it well. "I'm Frank."

"Nice to meet you."

"You too, you too. You do much camping?"

He let his pride get in the way of his common sense. "Enough," he answered, pushing out his chest in an aggressive manner.

"Okay. Good to know. Me and the other guys, we thought you might be a city slicker. Brian told us you're from Chicago."

"I was in the army."

"Vietnam?"

"Yeah." He had been there, briefly. His powers of observation had landed him on the security detail of a high-ranking officer rather than the front lines. He spent his tour of duty traveling as an aide-slash-bodyguard and he never passed a single night outside.

"Me too. Spent two years in-country." He knocked on his head. "Once a Marine, always a Marine. I'll leave you to it," he said, gesturing at the pile of gear. "We're taking our boys down to the lake to catch some dinner. You want us to take Brian?"

"I didn't bring my fishing tackle." He didn't own any.

"I've got an extra pole he can use."

"Good. Thanks. I'll just get our campsite set up."

"Sure thing." Frank walked away, shouting, "Gather up!"

They huddled on the far side of the fire pit, and Frank shared his plans with them. When they broke apart, Brian held up a fishing pole and waved at his father.

Milo waved back and watched as the group disappeared into the trees. He opened the tent sack and pulled out the mind-boggling array of poles and canvas pieces. Standing back from the collection, he rubbed his neck. "Come on, Milo," he said to himself. "Anyone can put up a tent."

The ground seemed a little on the hard side, but he supposed the sleeping bags would provide enough cushion. Knowing there had to be some kind of floor to the tent, he picked up the most neatly folded piece of cloth in the jumble. A few brittle pine needles fell from between its folds as he shook it out and settled it on the ground.

After that, he was lost. He had never been one of those guys who went full speed ahead with assembling anything – he figured the instructions were there for a reason. He picked up the other canvas piece. Its shapelessness didn't lend itself to an easy interpretation of how it should look assembled. He picked up one of the flexible poles and recognized that it had a female connector piece attached to it. A quick survey of the rest of the poles showed that many of them also had connectors.

He spread the canvas cover out on the ground as flat as he could, unzipping any zippers that proved troublesome to his goal. Deciding that the tent must be a dome, he began assembling the poles into something like a symmetrical half-circle. The pieces didn't fit together properly in that form –

some of them were too long and others were too short. Frustrated, he sat down on a nearby log, his head in his hands. When he heard the nearby crunch of twigs, his spirit sank even lower, knowing his ineptitude would embarrass Brian.

"You okay over there?"

Milo looked up and saw that only Frank had returned. "I thought you were fishing."

"We are. I just came back for some elk jerky to share with the boys. You want a piece?"

Milo shook his head no.

Frank crossed the campsite. "You look like you could use some help after all."

"I borrowed this tent setup from a guy at work. He didn't include the instructions."

Frank looked at the tent canvas and said, "I've set one of these up before. My brother-in-law had one just like it." He pulled the poles apart. "I'm sorry about earlier."

"What do you mean?"

"Making light of your job. It's not like I've got a particularly manly one myself."

"You own the diner, right?"

"Chief cook and bottle washer." As he talked, he reassembled the pole framework in a different order than Milo had done. "Always wanted to own my own business. Never thought I'd end up in the kitchen, though."

"You serve good food. You've got something to be proud of."

"Maybe," he acknowledged. "Grab up that canvas there, okay?"

Milo obliged and helped him pull it around the frame. "Thanks. I owe you one."

"Don't mention it."

They hammered the stakes into place and Milo crawled in to spread out the sleeping bags.

"Come on down to the lake. We're going to fish until dusk," Frank said, picking up his bag of jerky again.

The rest of the day went smoothly enough. Brian caught a couple of good-sized bass. Though he didn't talk to Milo, he seemed glad that his dad had come on the trip. Milo noticed that none of the boys talked to their fathers much, which made him feel less like a bad father and more like a typical parent.

He talked to the other fathers. Lindon, the man from the hardware store, was a talented carpenter, though Frank's compliment seemed to discomfort him.

The third father, Sweeney, was a big talker who dominated what little conversation they shared while their lines were in the water. "I pulled a thirty-five-inch walleye from this very lake, boys."

Out of Sweeney's line of sight, Frank rolled his eyes and gave his head a slight shake.

"You sure about that?" Lindon asked.

"Damn straight!"

"Why ain't it stuffed and hanging over your mantel, then?"

"Who's to say it's not?"

"I woulda noticed the last time I called on your wife," Lindon drawled, drawing a hearty laugh from Frank and a scowl from Sweeney.

As the sun sank low in the sky, the men and their sons trudged back to the campsite. Lindon lit a fire while Sweeney and Frank taught the boys how to clean the fish. Milo opened a few cans of beans that he had brought along just in case the hunting didn't work out too well and poured them into the old tin pan Cal had included in the camping kit. Before the moon rose, dinner was on the fire and they were gathered close around it. The other men started telling stories about hunting trips they had taken in years past and kills they had made.

"Went bear hunting once," Frank said, popping open a can of beer.

"Really?" Brian asked, awed.

"Yep. Got me one, too."

Frank's son beamed with pride as the other three boys sounded their admiration.

"How big?" Sweeney asked.

"Nearly a three-hundred pounder. Taller'n I was."

"That's nothing," Sweeney scoffed. "I shot me one twice that size."

Even Sweeney's son looked doubtful.

"What about you?" Lindon asked Milo. "Got any trophies at home?"

Brian answered for him. "The only trophies my dad has are plaques from work."

The others laughed and Milo pinned a smile to his face.

When the food was gone, Frank stretched and stood up. "Well, boys, I think we'd all better get some sleep now. The early hunter gets the bird, so to speak."

The father-son pairs each headed in a different direction, crawling into their respective tents. Milo zippered Brian and himself into theirs. "You have a good time fishing?"

"Yeah. Frank's a cool guy, huh?"

Milo nodded. "Seems like."

"You don't think so?"

He turned around and saw his son's hurt expression. "I just don't know him well yet, Brian. I'm sure he's a good man."

"He's always around for Scott."

"Working at the diner can't leave him a lot of spare time."

"You'd be surprised."

Milo took off his boots and jeans before crawling into his sleeping bag and turning off the flashlight. "Good night, Brian."

"Why don't you love Mom?"

Milo rolled over to look toward his son. "I do."

"She thinks you don't love her."

"She say that?"

The silence lasted so long that Milo considered turning the flashlight back on. Finally, Brian answered, "Not in those words exactly, but...close enough."

"Your mother's a good woman, Brian. I'll never leave her."

"But you're not happy together."

"Happiness is overrated. I made a commitment to your mom, and I don't break my promises."

"Yeah. Whatever."

Milo didn't know how to respond to that. As he tried to think of something worth saying to his only child, Brian's breath fell into the steady rhythm of sleep. Milo couldn't rest so easily after their conversation.

That pheasant hunt was the only time Milo went hunting with his son. Brian went to Arizona State University a couple of years later and never came back to Minnesota. He married the paler than pale Marla, went to work for the DEA, and never seemed to remember to call on Milo's birthday or Father's Day. After Alice died, he never called at all.

He shook his head and wiped away the wetness accumulating at the corners of his eyes. This is why he hated the quiet – with a memory like his, he could never keep the sadness at bay. Hearing the rustling of foliage, he put his eye to the viewfinder and scanned the grass bed where he had last seen the bear. He caught the tail-end of her lumbering just out of the shot. Excitedly, he spun the camera to where she would soon be if she continued on her current trajectory. Just as she appeared in the frame, a tap on his shoulder made him jump. "What the—!"

"Mr. Crosby. What a surprise." The beige woman was behind him, though slightly less beige in a purple polo shirt today.

"Claire, right?"

She raised an eyebrow. "You're not supposed to be back here."

"Really?" He feigned innocence. "I didn't see a sign."

"Goodness. A blind photographer. You really are a wonder."

"How'd you find me?"

"I looked across the enclosure."

"I think I'm pretty well camouflaged for bear hunting."

"Maybe – if you only need to hide from the bears."

"Don't you usually work in Monkey Village?" he asked, attempting to change the subject.

"I work wherever the zoo needs me. Today, they needed me here. What a lucky coincidence. What kind of bear treats did you bring?"

"I resent your implication."

"Of course you do."

"You know you just cost me the shot I'd been waiting for, don't you?"

She smiled slyly. "It's time to go, Mr. Crosby."

"Fine. I understand."

"The signs are there for a reason. It's dangerous back here."

"What? Is this where the zoo is keeping the alligators?" he scoffed as he folded his tripod up and stowed his camera in his gear bag.

"The area is being renovated. The workers shouldn't have to watch out for idiots." She waved him in front of her.

Looking back, he said, "I'm going to assume you mean that in the most affectionate way possible."

"You do that."

It was hot and the sun was getting too high in the sky for him to get any decent shots anyway. He walked out of the park and to his car, deciding to find some lunch.

One of his favorite places to eat was a little bar called the Texaz Grill. They served a great chicken-fried steak and the place was nice and dark – the perfect environment for licking his wounds. His bear hunt bore a striking resemblance to his hunt for his son's love: it was always just out of reach.

He had been hurt when he realized that Brian kept in contact with his friend Scott's father. One Sunday while Brian and his family were at church, Milo made the mistake of snooping. In one of Brian's desk drawers, he found Christmas cards from Frank and his wife calling Brian their "second son" and telling him they were proud of him. One of the cards from a few years before referenced a hunting trip Brian had made with Frank and Scott. All Milo had to do was look around the office to know that Brian hadn't lost his taste for blood. Trophy mounts of birds, deer, a Bighorn sheep, and even a bear surrounded him. His son was better at everything than he was: a better law enforcer, a better provider, a better man.

"Everything okay, sweetheart?" The buxom blonde waitress slid an olive-topped salad in front of him and set the large plastic tumbler of ice tea to one side.

Shaken from his reverie, he cleared his throat. "Yeah, I'm fine. Thanks."

"No problem. Your lunch'll be up soon. Let me know if I can get you anything else in the meantime."

Forcing himself to think about something other than his miserable relationship with Brian, Milo focused on the zoo volunteer who seemed to have it in for him: Claire. She must

Wild Life

be a miserable old thing. One of those women who really needed to get laid. He chuckled lightly to himself and stabbed a forkful of lettuce. He suspected he was on the zoo's unofficial "watch list." For months now, every single time he handed his membership card to an attendant at the gate, he or she would scan the card, do a double-take at the screen, and greet him by name. When it first started happening, he thought the zoo had put some kind of customer service initiative in place, like the stores do sometimes. He hated those little signs at the bank: "If I don't call you by name during our transaction, I owe you a dollar." What if he didn't want to be called by name? Milo preferred a certain level of anonymity. Once people knew your name, he thought, they started just walking up and talking to you in the middle of grocery stores or in movie theater lines. He hated that. Back in International Falls, it had been virtually impossible to go anywhere without someone coming up and starting a friendly conversation. After dead Alice's funeral, he spent months being consoled in public by people he barely knew and didn't care to know. What damned business of theirs was it how he was getting along without her?

And, of course, he had gotten along just fine – which just gave the neighbors something to gossip about, as if surviving the death of a spouse were intrinsically wrong. Especially a spouse as long-suffering and saintly as dead Alice was supposed to have been.

No, despite his irritation with the way it had happened, leaving Minnesota – or at least International Falls – was the best possible thing that could have happened to him.

Phoenix was a huge metropolis, home to nearly one-and-a-half million people. He could go just about anywhere in the city and be treated with the polite but distant friendliness he treasured. Even here, at the Texas Grill – a restaurant he visited at least twice a month – the waitresses never gave him more than the fleeting attention he deserved. So why was it that he couldn't visit the zoo without feeling as if he were the bear and the volunteers were the hunters?

"Here you go," the waitress said, deftly replacing the emptied salad plate with a heaping portion of chicken-fried steak and mashed potatoes.

Hardly remembering a bite of the salad, he frowned.

Wild Life

"Isn't this what you ordered?" she asked anxiously.

"Yes, yes, of course. My mind was wandering."

"Shew," she said, wiping her forehead with an exaggerated motion. "For a minute I thought I'd just heard what I wanted to hear. After all, this is your regular order!"

As she walked away, Milo ground his teeth in frustration and vowed to add more restaurants to his rotation of favorites, even if he couldn't bring himself to remove the Texaz Grill from the list.

Wild Life

Coyote

Whenever she had a chance after one of her volunteer shifts, Claire liked to walk over to the Arizona exhibits. After living so many years in the desert east of the city, she missed seeing the roadrunners, desert tortoises, and javelina in their natural habitat. The zoo insisted on calling their javelina "collared peccaries." Dorsey would have found that amusing. In all their years together, they had never visited the zoo. The farm was too all-consuming for vacations – or even daytrips.

Her favorite exhibit by far was the coyotes. People, particularly those who grew up east of the Mississippi, think of coyotes as solitary animals howling at the moon. South-westerners are slow to disabuse them of this falsehood, instead capitalizing on it by selling those tacky, pastel-painted carvings of the animals with bandannas tied around their necks. The coyotes themselves perpetuated the myth, because every coyote pack seems to have an insomniac. While the rest of the pack sleeps away the daylight hours, the insomniac goes wandering. At least two or three times a week, Claire would see a lone coyote trot across the far reaches of the farm, looking more like a family pet than a dangerous predator. Nevertheless, she made sure Taz was always under her watchful eye when they lived there – she knew even a solid twenty-pound pug was no match for the deceptively scrawny coyote.

The zoo had an insomniac too. Claire could always spot the lump of fur that comprised the rest of her pack sleeping toward the back of the exhibit. The insomniac, dubbed Sleepy by the regular keeper, made circles around the enclosure, forever checking to make sure the perimeter was secure. It made sense to Claire that Sleepy was the oldest female of the pack. She was a worried mother watching for danger, a huntress on the prowl, a protector. Claire saw the same behavior in Beryl. Though she had never visited her sister's home in Oklahoma, she had no trouble picturing Beryl as she trekked through the house, checking each of her sleeping children's bedrooms several times each night. She imagined Beryl making solitary journeys to the grocery store, coupons in hand despite the family's multi-millions. Her sister – the protector and huntress.

The long, lonely years in the Arizona sun made her realize just how important a sister could be. When, after years of trying to conceive, she and Dorsey learned that they were destined to be childless, she wished she could call her sister.

Not that she hadn't tried. Over the years, she sent birthday cards in care of Grandpa Harry's attorney and directly to her parents' house. She always called at Christmas, hoping that the holidays might soften her parents' hearts just enough for her to speak with her sister. It was rare that her parents answered, though, and after caller ID came into vogue, no one even bothered to pick up the receiver.

Nearly a decade passed, but Claire wasn't surprised when Beryl contacted her. She had been watching the calendar for months, her fingers crossed, as Beryl's eighteenth birthday approached. Beryl had been a smart kid, and she was devoted to Claire. At the time, Claire had tolerated her sister's adoration, though it set her teeth on edge. Grandpa Harry had told her repeatedly that someday she would be glad to have Beryl's love. Knowing that Grandpa Harry had been wrong less than five times in his life – by his own count, anyway – Claire believed him.

She was washing dishes at her kitchen sink, watching one of those lone coyotes tour the back twenty acres, when her phone rang. Drying her hands on a kitchen towel, she reached for the receiver. "Hello?"

"Claire, is that you?"

She had known Beryl's voice instantly, despite the years. "Beryl. I'm so glad…" She found her voice choked off by the lump of time stuck in her throat.

"I've missed you so much. I tried to get Mr. Handlemann to give me your contact information sooner, but he wouldn't until I was legally an adult."

"I've missed you too."

Beryl was, by nature, a maternal sort, even at eighteen. She met her husband Rory in the spring semester of her freshman year of college. She majored in Philosophy, telling her sister that she had no intention of doing anything at all with her degree other than raising a passel of children.

54

"Why haven't you and Dorsey had kids?" she asked idly during one Sunday afternoon conversation.

Claire remembered the painful fact of her infertility, an agonizing but imagined cramp digging into her womb. "We can't."

"Why not?" she asked in that dumbfounded way younger women always seem to have, as if bearing children were a God-given right and not a physical function.

"I can't carry a baby." The phone line went silent. "Are you still there?"

"Yes. I'm sorry."

"It's okay," Claire lied.

"Have you been to a specialist?"

"Yes."

"There must be something they can do."

"Dorsey and I are okay with things the way they are. Can we not talk about this anymore?"

"Sure. Sorry."

A few years later, when Beryl and Rory brought the first of their children – a little girl they named Clarice in her honor – to visit them in Arizona, Rory confided that Claire's infertility had frightened Beryl. "She broke up with me, you know."

He and Claire were sitting at her kitchen table on the farm; Dorsey and Beryl had already given up for the night. Claire was cradling her namesake in her arms. "No. I didn't know that."

"She knew how much I wanted a big family, and she was certain she wouldn't be able to have babies."

"I can't believe she never told me that. I was under the impression you'd been together all through college."

"We were." He smiled and Claire could see why her sister loved him – his chiseled jaw and model good looks were warmed to a steady glow by the joy within him. "I refused to let her leave me. I told her we'd adopt if we couldn't have kids of our own. She was the most important part of my future."

At that moment, Claire knew Beryl had married well – as well as she herself had. In the years that had passed since then, Rory had never given her reason to doubt that knowledge. When Dorsey left Claire, Rory was the one who packed Beryl's bag and drove her to the airport, promising to take care of their little ones until Claire was okay.

Claire hadn't been able to attend to the details of selling the farm; Beryl took care of everything. She helped Claire find the twenty-first-floor condo on Central Avenue, remembering that her sister had always loved a panoramic view and wanting to remove all traces of sadness from Claire's life. Beryl boxed up and brought from the farm only those items she felt certain Claire was going to want someday, even if she didn't want them now: photos, an antique tea set, a broken wristwatch. As she slid it under Claire's bed, she said, "This is for later."

"I told you not to bring anything but my clothes." Her voice was muffled by the pillow, but she didn't bother to turn over in the bed.

"Have you eaten anything today?" Taz's head popped out of the blanket at the sound of "eat" and Beryl let out a gasp of surprised laughter. "I wondered why he didn't greet me at the door."

"He hasn't left my side all day."

"He's worried about you. Animals know when their masters aren't well."

"I'm fine."

"Physically, maybe. Mentally, you're still a mess."

"Thank you, Dr. Freud."

Beryl sat down on the edge of the bed, causing Claire to roll until her hip hit her sister's thigh. She opened her eyes and winced at the brightness of her sister's smile. "It's so nice to see your face."

"I don't want to get up."

"You don't have to."

"Good." She let her eyes slide closed again.

"You remember that song Mom used to wake us up with?"

"Mom never woke me up with singing. In fact, Mom never woke me up at all."

"Really?"

"Beryl, I know you're younger than me, but didn't you ever notice the way our parents treated me?" She opened her eyes again, searching Beryl's face for any sign of understanding.

Beryl shrugged, unconcerned. "I think everything you remember is colored by what happened when you left. Mom and Dad love you as much as they love me."

"Of course they do. Which is why Mom's here taking care of me, right?" Even to Claire, her voice sounded harsh.

"Mom knows you don't want her here. You've never tried to make amends with her and Dad."

"I don't see them trying to apologize either." She sat up against the headboard. Taz stood up, stretched, and walked across the bed to lay down with his head on her thigh. His big round eyes gazed up at her. She put one hand on his head and scratched behind his ears. "They never loved me the way they loved you. After you were born, they didn't even try to love me anymore. I was Helga's problem and you were their pet."

Beryl frowned. "But you weren't even home! You were gone all the time at your rodeo competitions. And then you went to high school in Oklahoma City. That's what really drove a wedge between you and our parents."

"Did Mom and Dad tell you this?"

"No. I pieced it all together myself."

Claire couldn't fault her sister for wanting their parents to be kind, good-hearted, and decent. They had obviously done a good job raising Beryl and, surprisingly, they had never said anything negative about her to her sister. Claire wagered they had never even said her name again after she left with Dorsey. "Do they know about...what happened?"

"You mean, to you and Dorsey?"

"Yes."

"Of course. I called them."

"And?"

"And what?"

"What did they say?"

"Mom told me to take good care of you and not to worry about Rory and the kids. She'd help out – at least until they left on their Australian cruise. Now, let me get you some lunch."

They didn't talk about Mom and Dad again. Claire couldn't see any point in bringing it up: Beryl wasn't going to change her opinion, and neither was she.

Wild Life

The farm's location turned out to be fortuitous. Dorsey had purchased acreage adjacent to one of the country's largest hydroponic vegetable farms. Where Dorsey and Claire's produce went to farmer's markets – frequently sold in stalls manned by the couple – their corporate neighbor sold their crops directly to grocery chains. As the corporation grew, they bought up more and more of the land around the Combs farm. Though neither Dorsey nor Claire had been particularly cognizant of the fact, the green giant had surrounded their little farmhouse on all sides for the last several years. Despite the sluggish real estate market, the conglomerate bought the farm for much more than Dorsey had paid for it; the sale was closed in just a few weeks. Claire had enough money that she wouldn't have to work if she chose not to. Considering that Claire didn't even want to get out of bed, the money was definitely a blessing in her mind. Beryl didn't agree.

"You've got to do something." Beryl had managed to coax her older sister from her bed to have a Belgian waffle in the dining room. She only succeeded by refusing to bring the breakfast to the bedroom for her.

"No, I don't." She was waiting for the butter to melt in the pockets of the warm treat.

"You don't have to work, but you should find something else to do. I saw a horse rescue over by South Mountain was looking for volunteers—"

"No horses."

Her sister frowned and sipped her tea thoughtfully. "But you have so much experience—"

Claire cut her off with just a glare.

Beryl tried again. "The veteran's hospital always needs help."

"I don't want to be around people." Focusing on the plate in front of her, she cut into her waffle.

"You need to socialize, Claire. Otherwise, you'll just spend the rest of your life in this condo. You haven't left the building since you moved in."

"I'm not ready." She reached up and probed gently along her cheekbone, her fingers smoothing across the line of stitches and the painful greenish-purple skin.

"The bruises are nearly gone."

"They're deeper than they look."

Wild Life

Beryl set the cup on the table and walked to the sliding-glass doors, opening them. The cool morning air rushed in. "I don't even know what you like to do anymore."

Her stomach clenching and her hunger abandoning her, she slipped a piece of the waffle to the patiently waiting pug at her feet. "I don't want to talk about this."

"You need something outside of this building to keep you busy."

"I like animals," she volunteered.

"The horse rescue—"

"Not horses. Animals. Elephants and monkeys, things like that."

"I didn't know that about you." Beryl smiled wistfully. "I wish we'd gone to a zoo together when we were young."

"Animals can't lie to you. They are what they are, and you can tell just by looking at them. And you can't hate them for being animals."

"Those people were animals, Claire," Beryl said quietly.

She looked at her sister with dead eyes. "No, they weren't. They were humans, the same as us. Animals – even vicious ones – are honest."

"Why don't you volunteer at the zoo?"

Pushing her plate away, Claire considered her sister's suggestion. "Don't you have to be qualified to work with animals to volunteer?"

Beryl, ever the optimist, shrugged. "Seems to me anyone could volunteer. They probably need as many people as they can get." She retrieved her laptop from the guest bedroom and brought it to the table. "Let's see...there are a few zoos in the area. Have you ever been to any of them?"

"No. We were too busy with the farm."

"This one's been around for almost fifty years. That's a long time out here, right?"

A colorful webpage filled the screen, drawing Claire's eyes. "Yeah."

"Look at this! You can apply to be a volunteer right here!" Beryl started typing.

After a few minutes of Beryl's intent clicking, Claire pushed away from the table and went back to bed. She soon drifted into sleep, the only respite she could get from the bleakness of her future.

Days passed swiftly. Beryl moved through the apartment like a helpful ghost, only materializing for a few moments each day. Claire split her time between the quiet condo and dreams of Dorsey and the farm. Sometimes she was certain the condo was the dream instead of the other way around.

"Claire? Are you awake?" A sliver of light pierced the darkened room from the doorway. Taz jumped off the bed and went to Beryl.

"Yes."

"I need to talk to you."

"Maybe later."

The door opened wide, flooding the room and silhouetting her sister's plump frame. She had a box balanced on one hip. "Now would be better."

Sighing, Claire pushed herself to a sitting position and clicked on the brass lamp on her bedside table. "What's in the box?"

Beryl walked in and sat down next to her on the bed. "These are Dorsey's ashes."

Claire's eyes widened in horror. "What? Why...?"

Beryl set the box to the side and took her sister's hands in her own. "You remember, don't you? We talked about this. You didn't want a funeral because you were the only one mourning. You wanted him cremated so you could spread him on the land that he loved."

Panic overtook her. "But I don't own the land anymore!"

"It's okay. The buyers agreed to let you spread his ashes there anyway. It was one of the terms of the sale."

"I'll never see him again." Tears welled up and slipped silently down her cheeks.

"I saved the photo albums. They're in the box under the bed."

"No. I'll never see him – he'll never hold me again. We had each other, no matter what. Now I have nothing." Her heart ached.

"Listen – I'm going home soon."

Claire wiped at her eyes, trying to clear the blur from them. "What? You've only been here—"

"A month and a half," her sister interrupted.

"That can't be..."

Beryl nodded. "I need to get home. Mom and Dad are on their cruise and Rory is all alone with the kids. He's not complaining, but that's only because he's a good man. He's drowning on his own."

"Six weeks? Really?"

"I received a call from the zoo's volunteer coordinator today. They're holding a volunteer orientation on Monday. What do you think?"

"About what?"

Beryl let go of Claire's hands. "It's time for you to rejoin the world. I can't stay here forever and I don't think you want to come back to Oklahoma with me. Volunteering at the zoo will give you a reason to get out of bed in the mornings after I'm gone."

"I'm too ugly to be out in public. Especially at the zoo. I'll scare the children."

Beryl laughed. "Have you even looked in a mirror lately?"

She had. That very morning, she had examined her reflection when she stepped out of the shower. The limp she obtained from that ill-fated rodeo years before was more pronounced than it had ever been. The tan she had earned through years of working with Dorsey had faded, leaving her skin paler than porcelain. The scars on her face made her look like a shattered dish that had been glued back together. She nodded. "I'm a mess, and I'll never look right again."

Beryl put a hand on either side of her sister's face. "You look fine. You could use a little sun – right now I think you'd pass for a vampire – but otherwise, you're beautiful."

"Don't lie to me. I can see the scars!"

"What scars, Claire? You have one little scar along your cheekbone, but it's practically hidden by your hair."

"What about the ones around my nose? And above my eyes? The huge gash under my lip?"

Beryl leaned away, her eyes worried. "You're seeing things. I promise you, there are no other scars." She dropped her hands to her lap. "I think you should talk to someone about what happened."

"I told the police all about it."

"I know. But I think—"

"I don't really care what you think."

"That's clear." She stood up and walked to the door, where Taz sat patiently with his leash at his feet. "I've booked my ticket home. I'm leaving on Tuesday." Leaning down, she picked up Taz's leash; the dog danced in a circle. "Come on, buddy," she said, clipping the leash to his collar. "I'm done, Claire. It's time for you to face the world again." Her sister disappeared with the dog and she heard the door open and close.

Pushing herself to a standing position, she made her way to the bathroom mirror. She ran hot water over a washcloth before holding it to her face. When she pulled the cloth away, she examined her image again. She was certain she could still see the shadows of the bruises on her face, but the angry red lines she thought had been there that morning were gone. The only mark she saw, the one along her cheekbone, was pinkish but not nearly as noticeable as she had thought. She wondered if she were going crazy. Her legs wobbled beneath her and she collapsed onto the toilet seat. A calm, rational thought rose from deep within her: if she didn't get some kind of exercise, she would spend the rest of her life bedridden.

When her sister came back from walking the dog, Claire was dressed and sitting in the living room. Shocked, Beryl dropped the leash. Taz, ever full of joy, ran and jumped in her lap, licking his mistress's cheek and making her smile.

"I'm sorry," Beryl said, closing the door.

"For what?"

"I shouldn't have been so harsh with you. I don't have any idea what it's like to go through what you've been through."

"Has it really been a month and a half?"

"Yes."

"Dorsey would be so disappointed in me. He used to call me his tough little cowgirl, did you know that?"

Beryl smiled. "Yeah. I remember him saying that when Rory and I were here years ago."

She looked up with tired eyes. "Not so tough now."

"Even cowgirls get the blues," Beryl smirked.

Claire rolled her eyes and laughed, surprising herself with the sound. She sucked in a breath. Beryl froze, wide-eyed. Taz broke the silence with a tiny whine and Claire let herself smile again.

"So, what's the plan?"

"Maybe we could go out to dinner. You've been cooking since you got here." Claire stroked Taz's tan fur and the dog rolled over, exposing his belly for a rubbing.

"That would be great."

A few hours later, Claire stepped out of the building for the first time since she had moved in. They walked across Central to the chain restaurant on the corner. Claire was self-conscious at first, certain that the patrons were staring at her. Soon, though, Beryl succeeded in distracting her by pointing out some of the stranger-looking people in the place.

"Do you suppose she knows that her hairstyle recently made a comeback?" Beryl asked, nodding her head toward an older woman with a beehive.

"It did?" Claire was astonished – she had never seen anyone younger than her mother wearing the style.

"Yes! Haven't you seen Amy Winehouse?"

"Who is that?"

"It's like you've been living in a cave somewhere. Didn't you and Dorsey ever watch television?"

"Not really. There was never anything good on and we both liked to read."

"You had a computer. Did you surf the internet?"

"Not much. We really only used the thing for business-related stuff."

"I think we should buy you a new computer tomorrow."

"Is that really necessary? I don't have a business anymore. And I still have the old one, right?"

"I took it to Goodwill."

"What? Why? That thing cost us three-thousand dollars!"

"When did you buy it? The late 1980s?"

Claire bristled. "Early '90s, probably. It was top-of-the-line technology."

"It was junk. Sorry, but the only thing it was good for was scrap metal. You could go gray just waiting for it to boot up."

"Fine. Why do I need a new one?"

"You just do. Trust me."

"I don't have money to throw around, you know."

"Actually, you do," Beryl mused. "With your half of the trust fund and the proceeds from the sale of the farm, you're pretty well set. And, of course, your future is secure – you'll receive half of Mom and Dad's estate."

Claire rolled her eyes. "You have such faith in them as parents."

"Even if they don't do the right thing, I will. You have my word."

Claire softened. "A new computer, huh?"

"Yes. Definitely."

Attending the volunteer orientation at the zoo hadn't been as horrible as she had feared. The other attendees were split in two groups: retirees looking for something to keep them occupied and young college graduates seeking to move from volunteer status to zoo employees. She didn't really fit with either group, but she wasn't an outcast, either. She took two shifts a week to start.

By the time Claire drove Beryl to the airport on Tuesday, she felt like a butterfly that had fought her way free of a cocoon. Beryl had insisted that Claire buy a good computer and a flat-screen television, which they mounted on the living room wall. They had also gone to Ethan Allen to purchase a well-designed computer desk and arranged for cable internet and television installation. Beryl left a list of websites and instructions for Claire to follow once the internet was connected.

Claire parked the car and walked in with Beryl, despite her objections.

"I want to spend a few more minutes with you if I can. I haven't been a great hostess this visit."

"Don't be ridiculous," Beryl said, wrapping an arm around her older sister's waist. "I was here to help you, not to be entertained."

Claire jumped every time someone in the flowing sea of people brushed against her. "Maybe we could find a table and sit down for a few minutes," she suggested.

They made their way to a bagel shop just outside of the security gates. Claire got a table while Beryl stood in line for bagels and coffee. The small table was along the edge of the café's boundaries, but the short railing made Claire feel more secure. She glanced at her watch while she waited; Beryl's plane wasn't leaving for another ninety minutes.

"They were out of cinnamon raisin," Beryl said, setting the small plates and the styrofoam cups on the table. "I got you a cinnamon sugar one instead."

"Thanks."

Beryl settled in across from her, dropping her blue duffel bag and computer case onto the empty seat between them. She focused on Claire. "Are you going to be okay when I'm gone?"

Claire gave her sister a weak smile. "Eventually."

"I know Dorsey wouldn't want you to waste the rest of your life."

"We had big plans, you know."

"What do you mean?"

She gazed into the middle distance, seeing not the crowds but the future they had planned. "We were going to sell the farm in a few years and buy a travel trailer. We wanted to see the country. We hadn't taken a vacation in all the years we'd been together." She met Beryl's eyes. "The only thing that made it bearable was that we spent every day working shoulder to shoulder."

"You can travel for the both of you."

"What's the point? Without him, it just seems like a waste of time."

Beryl chewed her bagel thoughtfully. When she swallowed, she said, "You're still young. Maybe you'll meet someone new."

"I'm pushing fifty pretty hard. All the good men are married. Only bad husbands are single in their fifties. Besides...Dorsey was the love of my life. Wouldn't it be greedy of me to expect to win another man's heart?"

"All I'm saying is don't close your eyes to the possibilities. You never know when Mr. Close-Enough-to-Right will stumble across your path."

"If something happened to Rory, would you look for another man?"

She smiled mischievously. "He'd be the one pushing up daisies, not me!"

"You're awful."

"Awful cute to be single!" She popped the last bite into her mouth and slurped down the rest of her coffee. "Seriously, though, call me if you need anything. I'm just a plane ride away. I still think you should talk to someone, too. What you went through…it doesn't make you weak to need a little support."

Claire held up her watch and tapped the face. "You've got less than an hour to get to your gate. You'd better get in the security line."

The sisters stood up. Claire gathered the plates and cups to throw them away, while Beryl shouldered her bags. Together, they walked along the edges of the crowd toward the line.

Beryl turned and hugged Claire. "I love you. Don't forget that."

"I love you too. Give the kids kisses from Aunt Claire and tell Rory thank you for letting you be with me."

And now, almost a year later, Beryl still called her every morning, "just to check in." It made her smile, thinking of Beryl as an insomniac coyote. Claire sat down on the bench under the awning that shaded the coyote viewpoint. The heat made her sluggish, but she was in no hurry to get home. Only Taz waited for her, and he was incredibly patient. The zoo's shorter summer hours meant more hours alone in her condo. Alone in the zoo felt better than alone in her home.

The night before, she had finally unpacked the box Claire had slid under her bed so long ago. Inside, she found pictures Dorsey had taken of her and the farm, of Taz, and of some beautiful sunrises they had shared together. There were only a few pictures of Dorsey, his cap tilted back and a wide grin on his brown face. He kept his black hair short – just a little longer than a military cut. Finally, there were a few photos of them together: one taken by his brother at their courthouse wedding, another about ten years later at a party his family gave them for their anniversary, and, finally, a studio portrait. The portrait had been Dorsey's idea – he said he wanted them to have a nice photo for their twentieth anniversary. One day after a farmer's market, Dorsey surprised her with an appointment at one of those Glamour Shots places. The stylists had taken over and made them both look more like movie stars than farmers. They put

Wild Life

Dorsey in a whiter-than-white dress shirt – unbuttoned to the middle of his chest – and hung a bright red tie around his neck, as if he had just come home from a business meeting. They moussed his hair and tweezed his brows. They even put a light coat of lip-gloss on his already attractive mouth. They found a red sweetheart bodice to wrap around Claire. The stylist had pulled her hair into a French twist while the makeup artist reddened her lips and outlined her eyes in charcoal grey. The result was a portrait that looked nothing like them, yet made them both happy. They hung it in their bedroom, where no one saw it but them – and that was fine. Seeing it in the box was a shock. Even though she had known – intellectually, anyway – that Beryl had been in every room in the old farmhouse, she hadn't been prepared to realize that Beryl had been in that room.

When Beryl called that morning, Claire asked, "How could you go in our bedroom?"

"I didn't have a choice. It had to be cleaned."

"Why didn't you hire someone to do that?"

"Cleaning is very therapeutic for me; I didn't mind."

"But all the blood—"

"There wasn't that much, and it was dry."

"I still think you should have hired someone."

"Well, you were in no condition to share your opinion at the time."

Claire could hear the exasperation in her sister's voice. "I'm sorry. Thank you for saving the pictures for me."

"You're welcome. What about the other things? Did I get the right stuff?"

The antique tea set had belonged to Dorsey's white grandmother. Dorsey was half Navajo and half white. Grandma Combs had been partial to Claire from the moment Dorsey introduced them. She gave Claire the tea set as a wedding gift, and Claire had treasured it, especially after the sweet old woman passed on. Dorsey had worn the broken watch every day, even though it hadn't worked in years. Claire offered to have it repaired, but Dorsey refused, telling her that it was broken for a reason – time shouldn't be counted in hours or minutes, but in memorable moments. "Yes," she told her sister. "You saved just the right things."

Wild Life

So many other things in their home – and yet, Claire didn't miss any of them. What she missed was the view from her kitchen window, where she used to watch the insomniac coyote worry her way across their land.

Wild Life

Prairie Dog Town

Milo liked to watch the prairie dogs, especially during feeding time. The volunteer would come around with a five-gallon bucket half-full of lettuce and carrots and toss them around the small open-air exhibit. The prairie dogs would all pop to the surface, munching happily on the free greens. Occasionally, the shadow of a bird would soar overhead and all of the rodents would scamper into their holes, unaware that netting above kept them safe from the winged predators. Milo thought it was particularly cruel to keep the vultures in the pen next to them – their presence had to keep both species in a constant state of vigilance. Of course, that could have been the point.

The prairie dog town reminded him of International Falls. Back there, people always seemed to pop up to chatter about other people's business. Of course, he didn't know of any polygamists back in Minnesota; that aspect alone had to make living as a prairie dog – at least as a male prairie dog – much more appealing. He smiled at the thought.

Glancing at his watch, he noted that it was already one-thirty. The zoo would be closing soon. Reluctantly, he turned toward the exit, making the loop around the desert bird gardens and past the snake exhibits. As he exited through the large metal doors, he spotted Claire. A few weeks had passed since she caught him behind the bear exhibit. She was tanner than before, making her pale blonde hair more striking. He realized for the first time that she was actually an attractive woman, if a little sad. He noticed her limping and wondered how she hurt herself. "Claire!" he called out, waving. Immediately, he wondered what had possessed him and frowned.

"Mr. Crosby. What a coincidence." She smiled tightly but stopped walking just the same. "Which animals have you been tormenting today?"

He gave a half-hearted laugh and a fake smile. "Good to see you, too."

Her smiled widened and she laughed a little. "I'm sorry. That was rude. I didn't even catch you doing anything wrong today."

"Headed out?"

"Yes. As much as I don't want to, I should go home."

"I'll walk with you." They took a few steps before he asked, "What happened to your leg?"

"Long story."

"I've got time."

"I fell off a horse."

"Was that the abbreviated version?"

"Yes."

"So...you from around here?"

"I grew up in Oklahoma but I've been here most of my life now. You're a transplant too, aren't you?"

He nodded. "I'm from Chicago originally, by way of Minnesota."

"Why'd you move here?"

"My son and his family."

"It's good to have family around." She stopped walking.

When he realized she wasn't beside him anymore, he turned around. "What's wrong?"

She narrowed her eyes. "Why are you buddying up to me? What's the goal here?"

"I don't know. I just – I thought you looked like you could use a friend."

"Well, I can't. I'm fine on my own."

"Jesus! Someone sure as hell worked you over, didn't they?" His exasperation bubbled out of him like hot lava.

Her face set in anger, she walked quickly toward the exit, her limp more pronounced than ever.

"I'm sorry," Milo said as she passed him. "I didn't mean it."

"Ha!" came her one-syllable reply.

"Okay, you're right, I did mean it." He jogged to catch up to her. "But I shouldn't have said it." He kept pace with her as they made a beeline for the bridge that led into and out of the zoo. "Please accept my apology."

She sped up.

"Talk to me, please. I didn't mean to hurt your feelings."

As soon as they passed under the iron gate that officially marked the entrance to the zoo, she whirled on him.

Wild Life

"You are a real pain in the ass, did you know that, Mr. Crosby? If there were a way to revoke your membership, it would already have been done."

"I shouldn't have said that back there."

"No, you really shouldn't have." She folded her arms over her chest and glared at Milo.

"Let's start again. Can we do that?"

"No, I'm afraid we can't."

"We can try, can't we?" He stuck out his right hand. "Hello. I'm Milo Crosby. I'm glad to make your acquaintance."

Her expression faltered for just a moment before hardening again. "Goodbye, Mr. Crosby." She turned on her heel and left him standing there. He walked slowly to the bridge rail and looked down. A huge carp swam below him. He couldn't quite make sense of his life anymore. Even back in the prairie dog town of International Falls, he had been liked and respected. His job may have seemed like a joke to many of the locals, but they still treated him like a human being. Maybe they did all pop out of their homes to gossip, but they waved when you drove by, too.

The anonymity he had craved suddenly seemed like a punishment. Walking slowly to his car, he decided to try again with Brian and Marla.

He knocked on the door, a pound of See's candy behind his back.

"Milo. What a surprise. We weren't expecting you," Marla said, her hand resting on the door. "The kids and I were just about to leave. Alice Marie has a ballet lesson."

He gave her his most charming smile. "Oh, dear. I didn't realize. I brought you a little something, my girl." He pulled the box of nuts and chews from behind his back.

She stepped away. "Are you trying to kill me? I'm allergic!"

"To chocolate?" His face fell.

"To nuts!"

"Oh. I'm so sorry. Next time I'll bring you creams." He turned on the step to leave.

Alice Marie slipped around her mother and wrapped her arms around his legs. "Don't go, Grampa!"

He looked down at his sweet granddaughter and put a comforting hand on her head. She was dressed in a pink leotard and ballet slippers. "It's okay, my darling. Grampa should have called first."

He glanced back at Marla. "Can the kids have these?"

She looked at him worriedly. "Is everything okay, Milo?"

"Just a bad day. I'm a little…under the weather."

His daughter-in-law frowned for a moment before stepping aside. "Come in. Brian will be home in a bit. Do you mind watching Eric for me? He really doesn't like to go to ballet classes with his sister."

"Thank you, Marla. You're a gem among women."

She smiled indulgently. "Eric!" she called. "Grampa is here. He's going to stay with you while I take Alice Marie to her dance lesson."

They waited a few moments before receiving an answer: "'Kay."

"Come down here and visit!" she admonished.

Some movement upstairs suggested he was doing as his mother commanded. She smiled at Milo. "We'll be home in a couple of hours. Why don't you stay for dinner?"

"I'd like that."

Alice Marie squeezed his legs again. "Bye, Grampa. See you later!"

"Goodbye, sweetheart."

Marla closed the door behind them and Milo settled onto the living room sofa. No more sounds came from above, but that didn't surprise him. His grandson was a surly sort who hadn't warmed to him. The boy was probably playing a video game and resented the idea that he still needed someone to watch after him.

His son's living room was one of those places that was mostly for show. The overstuffed sofa had a crunchy feel to it, as if human weight were actually crumbling its structure. The room had no television – only nature paintings and a few of Brian's hunting trophies. The end-table lamps had started life as duck decoys. At some point, a decorator had thought it was a great idea to drill a hole through the middle of them and skewer them with metal rods – no doubt to create a "conversation piece." Milo generally thought that if you were reduced to talking about the furnishings of a room, you probably didn't have a whole lot to say.

72

Wild Life

Unable to get comfortable on the sofa, Milo wandered through the main level of the home. He hadn't been in the house since he had moved out several months earlier. The few times he had picked up Alice Marie for a day at the zoo or some other outing, Marla had met him at the door and sent the girl out to him. He had only seen the whole family together in restaurants, where they were gathered to celebrate his or Alice Marie's birthday. He hadn't been invited to Brian's birthday, though he had sent a card with a cash present through the mail. When he called to wish his son a happy day, Marla informed him that Brian was on his annual birthday hunt with some old friends. Milo didn't probe any further, reluctant to know if the "old friends" were from Minnesota.

The house hadn't changed much, though he was able to locate a new trophy – presumably from the birthday hunt. The massive moose head dominated the den's fireplace. The deer head it had supplanted was nowhere to be found, at least on the first floor.

Milo sat down in Brian's favorite chair, a brown leather recliner that had seen better days. He wondered where he had gone wrong with his son. This man – half him, genetically speaking – was a mystery. Milo had always thought of his empathy for other living creatures as something he inherited from his parents. Could dead Alice's lack of empathy have so easily overwhelmed that aspect of his person? And who was he to say that she was wrong? After all, she had lived her life exactly as she wanted it, orchestrating everything from their marriage to their lifestyle and even their location. Never mind that they had never been passionately in love – they had all the trappings of success and happiness, and that was more than enough for her.

He thought back to his time in the military. He suspected the real reason he had served as a personal aide to a general instead of on the front lines was because he flinched. One day he was part of a platoon – the next, he was reassigned, serving as the personal secretary to an officer. He wasn't opposed to shooting bad guys, but he didn't want the blood of innocents on his hands. In Milo's mind, animals were as innocent as children – he could no more kill them than strangle a child.

Wild Life

The one and only time he hunted with his son, he discharged his gun early, scaring the game into flight before the other hunters were ready to shoot. Only his son succeeded in bringing down a bird in that first premature flush. Milo was shunned for the rest of the weekend, while Brian earned kudos from the other fathers and sons. He still felt badly about that pheasant.

Milo heard the garage door engage. He considered staying in Brian's chair, but since he wanted to reconcile with his son, he moved to Marla's instead.

"Dad?" Brian called out from the kitchen entrance.

"In here, Son."

Brian's head swiveled and found his father in the adjacent den. "What are you doing here?"

"I came to make amends."

"Are we fighting? I didn't realize."

"Not openly, we aren't. But I think we have things to discuss." Realizing he still had the box of chocolates in his hands, he held them out toward his son, who was walking through the kitchen toward him. "Candy?"

Brian grinned and grabbed the box. "I love these." He pulled off the top and inhaled the aroma. "I shouldn't eat them, though."

"Why not?"

"Marla's allergic."

"But you're not."

"Doesn't matter. If I eat one of these and then kiss her, I could kill her."

Milo smiled, thinking how much different his life would have been had dead Alice been allergic to nuts. "Can't you just brush your teeth after?"

"You'd think so, but it's not that easy to get rid of the nut oils."

A dirty thought crossed Milo's mind: did she use her nut allergy to avoid giving blow jobs? He bit his tongue to keep from blurting out the joke. Brian didn't have much of a sense of humor when it came to Marla.

Brian narrowed his eyes. "What are you thinking about, Dad?"

"Nothing important."

"Does Marla know you're here?"

74

"Yes. She invited me to stay for dinner. Is that all right with you?"

He masked his frown, but not quite fast enough – Milo caught it. "Of course. Always nice to see you."

"Sit down, son. I'd like to talk to you."

Brian reluctantly sat in his old chair. "What's going on, Dad? Is there something I need to know? Have you been to the doctor?" His eyes widened. "That's it, isn't it? God, Dad – is there anything they can do?"

"Jesus, Brian, can you not put me in the grave just yet? I'm only fifty-seven!"

"Mom died—"

"I know," Milo cut him off. "I'm healthy as a horse, as far as I know. No major malfunctions yet."

"Good. Glad to hear it."

Milo grimaced at the lack of emotion behind the words. "You know I've never been one to talk about feelings much," he began.

"Or about anything at all, really." Brian had crossed his arms over his chest. Suddenly, he looked more like his sullen son Eric than an almost-forty-year-old man.

"Yes. Well. I'd like to fix that, if I could."

"It's a little late for that, isn't it, Dad? Our relationship – it's pretty well set. And I'm okay with that. I know what I can expect from you, and I thought you knew what you could expect from me."

"I moved all the way down here from Minnesota to get to know you better."

Brian laughed. "Not exactly. You moved down here because the Border Patrol forced you to retire."

"It's not like they ran me out of town on a rail. I could have stayed there."

He shrugged.

Milo pushed on. "I'm sorry I was never the father you needed me to be. I'd like the chance to fix that." Brian looked away from him, locking his eyes on the picture window instead. Beyond the wall lay a swimming pool and barbeque pit – all the trappings of a happy life, Milo thought. He was so much like his mother that it was difficult to see anything of himself in his son.

Wild Life

"You're my father and you'll always be my father. I want you to be around for my kids. They'll never know their grandmother." He leaned forward, his elbows on his knees, and locked eyes with Milo again. "Honestly, I think that's a terrible thing. If I'd had to pick a parent to be around for my kids, it would have been Mom."

His words struck Milo like blows to the jaw. They left his mouth hanging open and scattered all of his thoughts. He leaned back on the sofa and stared out at the picture-perfect life his son had created.

The front door swung open and he heard his granddaughter's ballet slippers swish across the carpet. "Grampa!" she cried, throwing herself into his arms. "I missed you!"

"I missed you too, my darling."

Marla rounded the corner and turned into the kitchen. "I bought fried chicken for dinner. Is that okay with you, Milo?"

He hugged Alice Marie to his chest and stood up. "I'm sorry, Marla my dear. I need to get home."

Marla's forehead creased. "Are you sure? I know Alice Marie really wants you to stay."

"Grampa, you promised."

"Did I?" He pulled her away from his chest so that he could see her face.

She giggled.

"No, I didn't. But I'll promise you this: I'll be back on Saturday to take you to the zoo, if that's all right with your mom and dad."

"I don't know—" Marla started, her eyebrows scrunched together.

"That would be great, Dad."

Milo, feeling his son's hand on his shoulder, frowned. "Okay. I'll be here early – the zoo opens at seven to beat the heat." He walked out from under his son's touch, hugged Alice Marie tightly, and lowered her to the ground. "I'm sorry I can't stay, Marla. Thank you for the invitation, just the same."

"Maybe another time."

He let himself out the front door, looking back for just a moment to see Alice Marie waving goodbye.

Wild Life

Wild Life

Elephant Ears

Milo picked Alice Marie up at a quarter before seven on Saturday. He didn't even have to walk up to the door – the little girl came bounding out of the house in a yellow sundress with all of her exposed skin slathered in sunscreen. As she leapt into the car, he briefly lamented the oily residue that was bound to bond itself to the upholstery.

"Where are we going for breakfast, Grampa?" she demanded.

He immediately forgot his irritation. "Where would you like to go?"

"Can we go to the bakery?"

"Which one?"

"Oh, I don't know," she breezed, "the one with the elephant ears?"

He smiled. "Your wish is my command."

He whisked her away from the house, gladly listening to her chatter about her friends and ballet classes and her summer so far. They had just pulled to a stop in the bakery parking lot when she turned to him and very seriously asked, "And what have you been up to, Grampa?"

He smiled at the dark-haired, pale-skinned girl. "Why do you ask?"

"Mom is worried about you," she said matter-of-factly.

"How do you know that?"

"I heard her tell Daddy that you seemed sad."

"Don't you worry about me. I'm fine."

"Daddy says 'fine' is code for 'your life is about to suck big-time.'"

Caught off guard, Milo gasped out a laugh. "I swear that I'm okay."

"Do you have any friends?"

"Just you!" He reached over and tickled her; she giggled and squirmed away. "Let's go in and get our breakfast." He opened his door and she did the same. They met at the back of the car, where she slipped her small hand into his. They walked into the family-run bakery and stood in line behind four other groups.

"What do you want today?" he asked, looking down at her.

"Two elephant ears!"

"Two? Don't you think that might be too much breakfast?"

"One for now and one for later," she answered.

"We can get snacks at the zoo if you get hungry."

"They don't have anything as good as elephant ears there," she pouted.

"What about the kettle-corn?"

She contemplated that for a few moments. "That is yummy."

Only two customers were ahead of them now. "It's one or the other."

"Why not both?"

"Because if I bring you home on a sugar high, your mother may never let you come with me again." Her giggle warmed his heart and made him glad that he moved to Arizona. He had spent the last few days wondering if he had made a mistake coming here. He even considered moving back to International Falls and all the gossipy neighbors he thought he had left behind forever. At last, he had resolved that if Brian was unwilling or unable to reconcile fully with him, at least he could wage a campaign for the heart and mind of Alice Marie.

"How may I help you?" asked the pleasantly plump woman behind the counter.

"What have you decided?" he asked his granddaughter in turn.

"One elephant ear, please," she answered politely.

"What an adorable little girl!" the woman cooed. "So polite. Is she yours?"

"He's my grampa!" Alice Marie said, looking up at Milo adoringly.

"Well, he's a very lucky grandfather indeed!" she said to the girl. "Will there be anything else?" she asked Milo.

He ordered a couple of Boston creams and two milks. The shop only had a few tables, but, luckily, one was free. They sat down and Milo doled out the donuts and the pastry for them.

Alice Marie crossed her arms and leaned on the table. "What about her?"

"What do you mean? Her who?"

"The lady behind the counter. Could she be your friend?"

"I'm sure she's very nice, my darling, but I don't think she would want to be my friend."

"Why not?"

"I don't know exactly. I just...don't think she would."

"Maybe you should ask her on a play date."

"A play date? What's that?"

She sighed and rolled her eyes at him as if he were a complete idiot. "It's a date where you play, silly!"

"Play what?"

"Whatever you want!"

He laughed and said, "I'll think about it."

"You've got to have more friends than just me, Grampa."

"I do have more friends."

"Promise me?"

"I promise."

"Good."

"Where do you want to start when we get to the zoo?" he asked, biting into his first donut.

"The elephants, of course!"

They spent the rest of their meal discussing the animals they had to see that day. When they were finished, Milo gathered up the crumbs and papers and carried them to the trashcan. The two then headed back to the car and off to the zoo.

On her way to see the black swan in the children's zoo, Claire spotted Milo sitting on a bench by the elephant enclosure and instantly felt ashamed of herself. Even though Milo Crosby was a bit of a thorn in her side, she was certain he didn't deserve the dressing down she had given him earlier in the week. She considered staying out of his line of sight, but she knew that eventually she would run into him again – even if it wasn't today. "Mr. Crosby?" she called out and waved.

He turned decidedly away from her.

"Mr. Crosby," she tried again as she advanced toward him.

"Not today, Claire," he said irritably.

"Look, I just wanted to—"

"Stop! I'm with my granddaughter, so if you don't mind—"

"Grampa, is this your friend?" a little girl asked, running toward them. She was pasty pale with dark hair, reminding Claire of Wednesday Addams from the television show of her childhood.

"Hello," she said, "My name is Claire. What's yours?"

The girl held out her hand and said, "I'm Alice Marie Crosby."

Claire shook her hand and smiled. "It's very nice to meet you."

"Likewise," she said, and Claire smiled at the incongruity of a child using the word. "Are you Grampa's friend?" she repeated.

Claire glanced at Milo, who looked miserable. "Yes," she answered.

"Grampa! Why didn't you tell me you had a friend at the zoo?"

"I didn't know..." he said slowly, "that she'd be working today."

"Actually, I'm not working yet. The keepers don't put the orangutans out until nine o'clock, so I'm free until then."

"You work with the monkeys?" Alice Marie asked excitedly.

"Sometimes. I've been allowed to scratch Duchess's belly through the bars once."

"Which one is Duchess?"

"The grandma. The one with the big potbelly." Claire held her hands in front of her, miming the orangutan's gut.

Alice Marie giggled. "You're funny."

With a straight face she said, "Funny looking, maybe."

"I like her, Grampa. She's a good friend for you."

"Thanks. I'm glad you approve. Are you done watching the elephants?"

"Not yet! Just a few more minutes – please!"

"Okay. Go on."

The little girl skipped away.

"Thank you." The man looked drawn and tired for the first time since Claire had made his acquaintance.

"Is everything okay?"

"I appreciate what you did just now, but I know you don't want to be friends."

"I came over to apologize. You caught me off-guard. It was my anniversary and I was sad."

"You're awfully young to be a widow."

"You're awfully old to be a troublemaker."

He smiled mischievously. "Life is no fun if you always obey the rules." He shifted his eyes to find his granddaughter. "You don't have to stay here."

"I know. Why don't you and Alice Marie come with me? I was on my way to say good morning to my boyfriend."

The disappointment registered on his face for only a second. "Why not?" he said. "As much as I love elephants, fifteen minutes is more than enough time spent watching them." He pushed up from the bench. "You're not limping today," he noted.

"I am, but not like I do after a long day."

"Alice Marie!" he called.

The little girl came running, slipping herself between the two adults and holding each of their hands. "Where to next, Grampa?"

"We're going with Miss Claire."

"Where?"

"To see my boyfriend," Claire said, squeezing the girl's hand.

"Okay!" As they took the winding path into the children's zoo, the siamang gibbons began their haunting two-pitch call. Alice Marie's eyes widened and she looked up at Claire. "What's that?"

"That's the gibbons on the island over there." She pointed toward the jungle-like space in the lagoon.

"I don't see anything!"

"They're probably in their cages or up at the top of the trees."

"It sounds like two different animals talking to each other."

"I know, but it's not. The siamang gibbons make both noises at the same time."

The girl frowned doubtfully and shifted her gaze to her grandfather. "Grampa, is she lying?"

"Why would she lie to you?"

"Adults always lie to kids," she stated simply.

"When?" Milo asked.

"All the time," she shrugged. "Like when Daddy says the animals just come and volunteer to be a part of our house."

Claire met Milo's eyes. "What does she mean?"

"My son has a lot of trophies in his home."

Her eyebrows rose in understanding.

"He thinks I'm dumb," Alice Marie continued, "but I know he hurts the animals."

Milo grimaced and Claire wondered why he was uncomfortable. She decided to rescue him. "You're right, Alice Marie. But your dad is actually doing a good thing when he hunts."

"How can hurting be good?"

"If one death could save a hundred lives, would you think that was a good or a bad thing?"

"I guess it would be good for everyone but the one who had to die."

Claire grinned. She would have wanted a child like this one. "Hunting for certain animals thins the herd and makes the food more plentiful for those remaining. The rest of the animals are able to get enough to eat so that they don't starve to death."

Alice Marie frowned; Claire worried that she hadn't explained the hunter's role well enough. After a few moments, though, the girl's face cleared and she smiled brightly. "So Daddy's doing a good thing?"

"Yes," Claire answered definitively.

"Grampa?"

Claire hadn't been watching Milo through this exchange; now she looked up to see a pensive expression. She smiled encouragingly at him.

"Yes, Alice Marie. Your daddy is doing a good thing."

They were almost to the black swan's enclosure now. Just out of sight from the bird, she said, "You two wait right over there. My boyfriend is a little jealous and I don't want him to come at you."

The girl's eyes widened and even Milo looked alarmed. Claire broke away and walked along the front edge of the enclosure and the swan, upon spotting her, waddled quickly to her side. Together, they walked from one end to the other before turning to head back the other way.

"Can we come over now?" Alice Marie called.

The swan, hearing her voice, looked toward the girl and her grandfather. He spread his wings menacingly and squawked in their direction.

"I'd say that's a no," Claire answered.

Milo grinned broadly. "That's your boyfriend, huh?"

"Yes. The keeper says that he seems to have bonded to me. He doesn't know exactly why."

"Maybe he just knows a beauty when he sees her."

Claire, embarrassed, turned away. Alice Marie came over to stand next to her, causing the swan to puff himself up even more and honk threateningly at her.

"Oh, shush," the girl admonished. "You can't get to me, so you might as well get over it."

Claire and Milo both laughed and Milo joined them at the edge of the enclosure. "Perhaps we should move along. I'm afraid we're giving your boyfriend a heart attack."

They walked on through the various bird exhibits, including the great horned owls. Circling around, they made their way into one of the zoo's shaded areas featuring life-size cast versions of some of the animals around the park. Milo and Claire found a bench and sat down while Alice Marie explored the metal creatures.

"Alice Marie seems like a wonderful little girl," Claire said.

"I wish I could take credit for that, but I'm afraid I haven't spent much time with her until recently."

"Oh. Right. You just moved here from Minnesota."

"About a year ago or so."

"You're retired?"

"Yeah."

"What did you do before?"

"I was a Border Patrol agent."

Claire's eyebrows shot up. "Really?"

He nodded. "You seem surprised."

"Only because...well, honestly...I didn't know we had Border Patrol in Minnesota. It seems a little...well...low priority."

"What is it with you people? You think only the Mexicans are trying to cross the border?"

She held up both hands. "I'm sorry! It's just that the only time I remember hearing anything at all about the northern border it was Americans fleeing to Canada, not the other way around."

"I'll concede that it wasn't particularly dangerous, but it's still a border and someone has to guard it."

"Did you enjoy it?"

He shrugged. "To be honest, it could be a little dull. Other guards would get complacent. You see the same people crossing day after day, week after week. After a while, everyone starts to look the same if you aren't vigilant." He straightened a little. "I have a great memory for detail, though. I caught more bad guys than anyone else along my stretch of the border."

"Seems like they'd want someone like you down here," she observed.

"You'd think." He slouched against the bench. "You ever going to tell me the long version of how you hurt your leg?"

She smiled, remembering who she had been all those years ago. "I was a barrel racer when I was a teenager."

"Like in a rodeo?"

"Yes. I had this great horse – his name was Dorian. My grandfather named him that because of his color – gray."

"Dorian Gray," Milo chuckled. "Witty."

"Especially for an Oklahoma oilman."

"Okay, go on."

"Anyway, Dorian and I were finally gaining ground in the ring. We'd just won a major competition when he died of colitis."

"You didn't know he was sick?"

She shrugged. "One day he was fine, the next he was gone. That's how colitis is."

"So you limp because your horse died?" He flashed an incredulous smile at her.

85

"Dorian and I were supposed to compete in a big rodeo just a couple of weeks later. My riding coach and Grandpa Harry went and found me a replacement horse that had been trained exclusively for barrel racing. The first time I rode him, we almost beat my fastest time on Dorian."

"What was the horse's name?"

"I don't know."

"You've forgotten the name of the fastest horse you ever rode?"

She shook her head. "I never knew it."

"But—"

"Dorian had just died. I didn't even want to ride. I didn't care what the horse's name was." Across from the bench where they were sitting, the golden lion tamarin jumped from rope to rope to the wire mesh of the cage, endlessly bouncing and climbing and running. If she could have an exotic pet, she would want it to be a monkey.

"Claire? I'm sorry. Please finish your story."

"That's it, really. I went to the competition, rode on the back of a horse I didn't know, leaned the wrong way, and ended up on the ground. I broke my leg in three places and I never rode again."

"You gave up on something you were good at because of a broken leg?"

She shrugged, unwilling to tell him the rest of the story.

"You don't seem like a quitter to me."

"Just like that horse, sometimes life takes you in a different direction than the one in which you expect to go."

Alice Marie swung around the side of the enclosure. "Let's go to the petting zoo, Grampa!"

"Will you come with us?" Milo asked Claire.

"What time is it?"

"I'm not wearing a watch. You are, though."

She smiled. "It doesn't work." She pulled her cell phone out of her pocket and checked the time. "I'm afraid I need to get over to the orangutans now."

"I guess we'll see you later then."

Alice Marie ran over to Claire and threw her arms around her shoulders. "Thank you for introducing us to your boyfriend," she said with a giggle. "I wish you could stay with us!"

"I wish I could too," Claire answered. She squeezed the little girl in a quick hug. "It was great to meet you."

Alice Marie pulled away and took her grandfather by the hand. "Let's go, Grampa!"

Milo pushed himself up. "Thanks again," he said to Claire.

"You're welcome. It was good talking to you."

"And to you."

As Alice Marie walked away with Claire's former nemesis, she heard the girl ask, "How about a play date with her?"

She couldn't hear Milo's answer.

Wild Life

Brass Monkey

The Brass Monkey looked like a dive from the outside and the inside matched. The glass of the two windows at the front were painted to match the interior – a deep midnight blue – as if the painter had been blind drunk when he was rolling the place and simply hadn't noticed the windows at all. An air conditioner kept the temperature an even sixty-eight degrees all the time. The bar was trimmed in brass fixtures, and a two-foot-tall brass monkey that the patrons called George sat on the counter behind the bartender, a retired New Jersey cop who went by Sax.

Milo had passed the small bar every other day for months before he finally went in. Located in a seedy old strip mall right on the edge of Sun City, the Brass Monkey was the kind of place Sun City women were always trying to get shut down and Sun City men were constantly sneaking off to visit. Milo hadn't gone in before because it looked like the kind of joint he had initially hoped to avoid – a place where, if you visited once, the other denizens recognized you forever. After spending Saturday at the zoo with Alice Marie, though, he thought that might not be such a bad thing after all.

He pushed open the door and walked into the bar. Standing to one side while he waited for his eyes to adjust to the gloom, he swore he heard the sound of a dozen old necks popping as they swiveled to give him the once-over. A moment later, the swoosh of all those necks returning to their original positions told him he wasn't likely to get thrown out. He must look like he belonged there.

His eyes adjusted, he walked toward the bar and took a stool a few seats down from a man with rheumy eyes and a dour expression.

"What'll it be, mac?"

"Beer."

"Which one?"

Milo, who hadn't ever been much of a drinker, asked, "What's good?"

"I'll get you a Bud," the bartender said before turning away. Milo thought he detected a little irritation in the man.

Wild Life

Milo scanned the room and quickly determined that most of the clientele were likely long-term alcoholics – not that Milo had a problem with that. International Falls had more than its share of heavy drinkers. He had always thought that had more to do with the weather than anything else. Why shouldn't the coldest place in the contiguous United States prefer a beverage known to give people the warm fuzzies?

"Here you go. That'll be a buck-seventy-five." The burly man set a mug of light-gold beer in front of him.

Milo dutifully pulled out his wallet and handed over two dollars.

The bartender grunted and took the bills, heading toward the till at the other end. He didn't come back with the change, but Milo figured that was okay: the bartender would deserve more than a quarter tip if he nursed his beer along for a few hours.

Over the bar, a muted television was tuned to a local news program. Milo watched the scrolling text as it unwound over the solemn news anchor's hands:

As some of our viewers will recall, a hydroponic farmer was killed and his wife savagely beaten nearly one year ago. Dorsey and Claire Combs, longtime residents of Gilbert and well-known merchants at most farmers' markets, were allegedly attacked by Rafael Santos and Damon Dreyer, both of whom are associates of a suspected smuggling ring. In the opening statement today, the prosecutor suggested Santos and Dreyer targeted the Combs farm because they mistakenly believed Combs was growing marijuana in the eight hydroponic tents located there. Claire Combs, who survived the deadly attack, is expected to testify tomorrow.

As the anchor talked, pictures of the defendants flashed. Santos looked muscular and thuggish, but Damon Dreyer looked like your average white teenager. To Milo's disappointment, the program showed no pictures of Claire and Dorsey Combs. His investigative sixth sense had kicked in as soon as he saw the name "Claire" on the screen. Just like back in his old Border Patrol days, he could almost see the pieces of a puzzle coming together.

He had been so focused on the television that he hadn't noticed the woman who took the stool next to him until she tapped him on the shoulder. "Hey, handsome, slide that bowl of pretzels this way, will you?"

He glanced to his right and found a thin woman with brightly dyed red hair and cigarette lines around her mouth. Milo slid the bowl her way, noting that she used to be beautiful – he could see it in her bone structure if not in her actual face. Now, she was merely attractive. "Here you go."

"Hey, Sax!"

"Yeah, Sondra?" the bartender answered.

"This gentleman wants to buy me a drink. Whiskey sour, sweetie."

Sax raised his eyebrows at Milo, looking for confirmation.

Milo smiled and gave an affirming nod.

"I'm Sondra Lane," she said, turning herself to offer her hand for him to shake.

"Milo."

"You're new here."

"Yes."

"You live in 'sin city'?"

He recognized the unofficial moniker of his retirement community: Sun City had recently been outed as having a surprisingly large number of people carrying sexually transmitted diseases. "I take it you're not?"

"Not yet." She smiled seductively. "Where are you from?"

"Illinois by way of Minnesota. You?"

"California. I was an actress."

He sipped his beer and nodded.

She gave him her most beguiling smile, seemingly unaware that the years had taken their toll on it. "You may have seen me in *Siege of the Moon*. That was my biggest role. I played Sunrise Aeon, the leader of the Martian battle forces."

"I'm afraid not."

She shrugged. "It's a crapshoot. About one out of every ten guys I meet recognize me. Women usually remember me from my recurring role on this old soap opera back in the Seventies."

He looked at her again and instantly knew who she was. "Carmella Savage!"

She drew back and gave him an appraising look. "You don't look gay."

He chuckled. "I'm not. My wife loved *Scions of Beauty.*"

"Apparently the audience was housewives and every gay man in America. I could sign an autograph for you to take to her..."

"She died a few years back."

"I'm so sorry."

Milo thought that, for an actress, her delivery of the line was a little too upbeat. Sax finally arrived with her drink. She inhaled it like a camel that had spent a week too long in the desert. He signaled Sax to bring her another, digging a twenty out of his wallet. "Why'd you move to Arizona?"

"I had to get out of L.A. The city was killing me. My daughter lives here and she asked me to come and stay with her for a while. You?"

"My son's family."

"Sometimes I wonder what the draw is," she said. "I mean, what brings all these people to this God-forsaken dustbowl of a city?" She sucked a long ice cube slowly into her mouth, her eyes meeting his over the rim of the glass.

Discreetly readjusting himself, he answered, "People always think they're going to love the heat."

She released the poor, melted ice cube and it dropped, exhausted, to the bottom of the glass. "Do you?"

"I'm adjusting." He hadn't thought of sex in a very long time. He knew that for a man to so completely sublimate sexual urges was unusual, but, between his high-blood-pressure medicine and his lack of desire for dead Alice, he had taken all of his sexual energy and diverted it into his work. In fact, he was currently experiencing his first hard-on since 1987. He had forgotten just how much blood was required to maintain an erection and wasn't exactly sure why he couldn't seem to focus on anything other than the not-quite-lovely Sondra.

"I only come here because they keep their air conditioner set so low. My daughter doesn't want the air in her house any cooler than eighty degrees. It's so hot I just want to walk around in the nude!"

Milo reached up and wiped the sweat from his upper lip. His brain was no longer able to form complete sentences. "My house cool."

Sax put another drink in front of Sondra and gave Milo a look that seemed to say *you poor bastard.*

"I just bet it is." She picked up the drink and downed it in one long pull. "Why don't we have a drink at your place?"

"No booze," Milo said.

"That's all right," she answered. "I'm sure we'll think of something to do."

Milo left the twenty and a half-full glass of beer on the bar.

Not indulging in sex with anyone for more than twenty years, Milo approached the project with a great deal of enthusiasm. He dared to allow his hands to roam over Sondra's body and was both surprised and pleased when she didn't push him away from any part of her. He even went "south of the border" – a place he had never wandered on dead Alice. Of course, dead Alice's "south" had been wild and wooly. Sondra, by contrast, was like a desert sand dune – smooth and just waiting for a bolt of lightning to turn it into glass.

The actual moment of copulation had moved more swiftly than he remembered. Thankfully, Sondra seemed satisfied as he rolled off her, a smile on her face that he was certain was matched by his own.

"That was fantastic," she cooed.

Flattered, he said, "Thanks. You were too."

"No, really. I've had my share of lovers, and you're quite good. Men your age almost never do what you did."

He wasn't sure which particular act she was referring to. He rolled onto his side, propping his head up with one arm. "What—?" She interrupted his thought by stepping out of the bed and allowing the bedclothes to fall away from her well-shaped body. For a woman who had to be pushing sixty, she was amazingly toned and had none of dead Alice's modesty. Of course, dead Alice had a body about which one should be modest. Milo was surprised to feel himself hardening again. He wondered if he had forgotten to take his blood-pressure pill the night before. "Where are you going?"

"I'm thirsty, and I could really use a ciggy. Mind if I smoke?" she asked over his shoulder as she walked toward the bedroom door.

"Uh...no. Not at all. There's an ashtray on the end table in the living room." He had never used it; he hadn't smoked since he left the army. Dead Alice always kept the bright-orange remnant of the 1970s on an end table back in Minnesota, and he had brought it with him to Phoenix out of some sense of nostalgia for a life that had been perfect on the outside.

She paused at the door, flicking a few strands of her overly red hair over her shoulder, and asked, "Can I bring you anything?"

"Just you, baby. Hurry back," he said, feeling like the leading man in a cheesy B movie.

She flashed a toothy grin at him and disappeared.

He lay back on the pillows behind him and laced his fingers beneath his gray head. Unlike so many other men he had known over the years, Milo had never been a womanizer. His father had raised him to respect women and the bond of marriage. Alice, a Baptist minister's daughter, had thrown herself at him. He remembered when he told his parents that dead Alice was pregnant. They were both so disappointed – they were Lutheran and hadn't liked the idea of her much – but they had agreed that marrying her was the right thing for Milo to do. So dead Alice had snagged him and that "perfect" life she aspired to.

Sondra was the second woman that Milo had...well, "made love to" didn't really fit, because, of course, he didn't love her. He had sex purely for the pleasure of it, he barely knew the woman, and he didn't know if they'd see each other again. He smiled broadly; a laugh escaped.

"Did you say something?" Sondra called from what sounded like the kitchen.

"No," he called back loudly, "I coughed."

Not hearing an answer, he sank back into his thoughts. Sondra was nice enough, but he doubted they had more in common than the Brass Monkey and a shared memory of a long-defunct soap opera.

She appeared in the doorway again, this time with a glass in one hand and the ashtray with a pack of cigarettes in the other. He wondered if she waxed her nether regions because she didn't want to dye them to match her hair. "You look lost in thought."

"Just contemplating my navel, so to speak." He patted the bed next to him. "Come and join me."

She smiled and sauntered to the bed, setting the ashtray and the glass down before tapping a cigarette from the nearly empty package. "You want one?" she asked, tilting the pack toward him.

"No, thanks. I don't smoke."

"I suppose you don't have a light, then, eh?"

He rolled toward the nightstand on his side and, opening the drawer, produced a lighter he kept there for lighting candles in case of a power outage. Rolling back, he flicked it and lit her cigarette for her.

She took a long draw and breathed out her thanks on a haze of smoke. At last, she sat down, one leg curled beneath her. She made no move to cover her body and Milo's blood flow once again migrated south. "What do you like to do, Milo? Besides me, of course." A throaty laugh followed her words.

He looked away from her body. Conversation definitely seemed unlikely if he continued to look at her. "Photography."

"Are you offering to help me with my portfolio? Because that's usually how you get a woman like me into bed – not something you say after sex."

He liked her sense of humor and her easy self-confidence. "Actually, I prefer photographing animals."

"Really? That's fascinating. Have you made the switch to digital photography?"

"Um…no. I prefer film."

"A traditionalist. Endearing." She nodded once, as if giving her stamp of approval to Milo's choice.

He shifted toward her. "Do you still act?"

"Now and then. I'm rehearsing for a musical right now. I've been cast as Adelaide in a local production of *Guys and Dolls*."

He wondered if that was why she had her hair dyed so garishly. "You're a singer too?"

"Not by Broadway's standards," she laughed, "but around here I'm a star." She glanced at the clock. "Don't feel badly if you're not, but are you up for another round before I go?"

He glanced pointedly at the tented sheet. "I do believe I would enjoy that."

"Virility is so sexy," she purred as she stubbed out the cigarette and pounced on him.

The next morning, with Sondra long gone, he awoke to find he had slept in later than normal. Humming to himself, he pulled on his discarded boxers from the night before and padded to the bathroom. After relieving himself, he studied his grizzled face in the mirror. He wasn't certain, but he thought he looked ten years younger. Dead Alice must have been spinning in her grave. He had sex with another woman – and it was much better than he remembered.

Back in the bedroom, he picked up the orange ashtray with its three cigarette butts and walked down the hall toward the kitchen. As he emptied the tray, he realized what tune he was humming: "Take Back Your Mink." Sondra's rendition of the song after their second round had led to a third – a record for Milo. Afterwards, he diligently took his blood-pressure medication, certain he had forgotten the day before.

He emptied the ashtray in the bin under the sink, rinsed the ashy residue from the bottom of the tray, and carried it back to its spot on the living-room end table.

Standing back from it, he looked at his living room. The ashtray wasn't the only item that was dated – his sofa, another Minnesota refugee, must have been covered with the toughest fabric ever created, a roughly woven brown, green, and orange acrylic. Dead Alice had picked it out, and he never really liked it. He couldn't sit on it unless he was fully dressed or it made him itchy. He had suggested that maybe they should look at something else.

"Nonsense!" dead Alice had said. "We're getting this one because it will last forever."

"You're right," he had answered. "Things that don't get used always last forever."

Forty years later, the damned thing looked brand new. In fact, the whole living room looked like a layout for a late

1970s home magazine. He didn't have to live like this anymore. He had never been a big fan of the earth tones that dead Alice preferred. And he didn't need to be careful about his money – no matter what he thought of dead Alice, she had been one heck of a good money manager. Between the savings account balance and the price he got for his International Falls house, he had enough to get rid of this furniture for good. The only problem was he hadn't a clue how to decorate. He frowned as he contemplated this new problem.

Dropping into the one comfortable chair in the whole house – his dark-green leather recliner – he thought about the night before. Sondra had done something for him that he hadn't known he needed: she brought him back to life. And now that he was ready to stop dying and start living, he knew something else: as grateful to Sondra as he was, he had his heart set on someone a little pricklier.

Wild Life

A Wolf at the Door

When Claire asked for two weeks off, the volunteer coordinator didn't question her. Claire was grateful for that – she had been certain that the gossipy woman would pry. In preparation for such an event, Claire had rehearsed a vacation story that seemed plausible: she would be visiting her sister in Oklahoma.

In reality, it had taken all of Claire's considerable will to convince Beryl not to come back to Phoenix to stay with her during the trial.

"You shouldn't be alone," Beryl argued.

Claire sighed. This was the fifth time in as many days that they had hashed over this subject. "You don't need to worry about me. Stay home, take care of your kids and Rory, and I'll talk to you every morning."

"Are you sure? If you don't want me there, do you have any friends who could stay with you instead?"

"Relax. I'll be fine."

"I don't think you realize how hard this is going to be on you," she fretted. "Reliving that day could tear you apart."

Claire understood her sister's fear: she knew that the moment of reckoning had finally arrived.

Beryl was still pleading to visit that Tuesday morning. She dressed herself carefully, the words of the prosecutor still in her mind: she needed to look like a grieving and sympathetic widow to the jury, and that meant somber colors – but not black – for her outfit and subdued, tasteful makeup and hair. She hated shopping, but she went to the mall to get just the right clothes for her day on the stand: a sage-green pantsuit and a pair of brown-leather low-heeled pumps. She found some light mauve lipstick and some waterproof eyeliner and mascara. She pulled her hair away from her face because the attorney said the jury would want to see her eyes. Studying herself in the mirror, she thought this version looked even less like the Claire Dorsey had known – too tame by far.

On the drive to the courthouse, she tried not to think about the trial ahead of her. Her mouth was dry and she feared her body was saving all of its moisture for the inevitable tears.

97

Wild Life

She parked her car on the second level of the garage and walked carefully down the stairs in her new pumps. She had never liked carrying a purse; she used to rely on Dorsey to have his wallet with him. The purse she gripped was the only one she owned: a smallish black handbag that she had picked up at a yard sale. She shifted it from left to right, flexing her free hand in an effort to get the blood moving again.

She could hear only the click of her heels against the pavement as she walked toward the courthouse doors. The people around her were like ghosts barely glimpsed; she couldn't spare a thought for them. Inside, she laid her purse flat on the conveyor belt and walked through the security arch. It buzzed loudly, and a female security guard moved in front of her, asking that she raise her arms and spread her legs. When she did, the woman waved her wand along Claire's limbs and torso. The guard, satisfied, waved her through.

Reclaiming her purse, she walked to the courtroom where the men who murdered her husband were on trial. She hadn't come the day before even though the prosecutor asked her to be there. The gallery was surprisingly full – she assumed the murder of a Native American farmer would draw a much smaller crowd.

A door at the side of the courtroom opened and two men in orange jumpsuits were led in. She saw the white one – Damon – scan the crowd. Rafael just shuffled along, his head down. She doubted his slumped shoulders had anything to do with defeat or remorse.

The judge, a Hispanic woman, banged her gavel and called the court to order. Claire couldn't hear anything but her heart beating. She watched the prosecutor closely, hoping he would look at her when he called her name – otherwise, she might not know when to go forward. When he actually did, though, she heard it: "I would like to call Claire Combs to the stand."

Claire was in the house that morning, listening to NPR. A reporter was talking about the relatively slow success of a program designed to reintroduce Mexican wolves into the wild. She was dusting; she had to dust twice a week on the farm, because the fine silt of the desert always seemed to locate a crack or seam that let it inside.

The knock on the door startled her. She and Dorsey didn't get many visitors, and, if someone planned to drive out, they usually called first – no point driving ten or twenty miles only to find that they weren't home.

Leaving her dust rag on an end table in the living room, she opened the door. "Yes?"

"Good morning, ma'am," said the lanky youth on the other side. "My car broke down about a mile back. I was hoping I could use your phone."

Claire ran her eyes over the boy, thinking he couldn't have been more than twenty-two, if that. He had an earring, but otherwise he looked clean-cut. He resembled a popular actor, but she couldn't put her finger on which one. Brad Pitt? Owen Wilson? In any case, he looked trustworthy enough. "Come on in," she said, standing to one side. "The phone's in the kitchen."

The smile he flashed made her shiver: something predatory behind his eyes. She led him to the kitchen. "There's the phone." She picked up the walkie-talkie that kept her in contact with Dorsey.

"What's that?" He had stopped in the middle of the kitchen, staring at her instead of going to the phone.

"I'm just going to let my husband know we've got company." She pressed the button and raised it to her mouth.

"I'd rather you didn't."

"Why not?" She kept her finger on the button, but lowered the device.

The leering youth took a step toward her. "Well, you see, my buddy is out there right now trying to get the drop on your old man. If you call him, you might tip him off."

"Run, Dorsey!" she shouted loudly.

He backhanded her across the face; she fell against the wall, dropping the walkie-talkie.

He pushed his hand around her throat, pressing her into the wall. His breath, laced with the disconcerting smell of peppermint, was hot on her cheeks. "I should have known you would be a troublemaker. Women always are, aren't they? It's just something you bitches can't help."

Wild Life

Taz, who had been sleeping in his bed on the second floor and hadn't heard the knock on the door, ran down the stairs, apparently alerted to the trouble by the sound of Claire's body hitting the wall. He scooted to a stop and began barking with alarm when he saw the strange man in the house.

Without removing his hand from her throat, the intruder turned and growled menacingly at Taz, who, being at heart a coward, turned and ran back up the stairs with a whimper. "Not much of a guard dog, eh?" The man laughed.

Claire couldn't see a weapon on this horrible man; she suspected she could overpower him. His slap had just caught her off-guard. As accustomed to work as she was, she was likely to be stronger – and he was in the perfect position for her knee to disable his ability to function temporarily.

A noise on the back porch distracted him, and Claire took her chance, raising her knee sharply into his crotch. The shock caused his hand to release her; a second later, he was bent double. Adrenaline flooded her body as she ran for the back door. Flinging it open, she found herself face to face with Dorsey. The intruder's partner was behind him. "Step back, missus," the stranger said, "or your man might get hurt." He was ugly in a way that Claire had never encountered: an ugliness that radiated from his mean little eyes.

She backed up.

"You okay in there, Damon?" called the new guy.

Damon groaned.

"What did you do to my homes, lady?"

Claire closed her jaw tightly and moved back to let him pass.

"You first," he said, not moving.

She stepped back through the kitchen doorway to where Damon still lay writhing.

"What the fuck, man? She's just a woman," chided Damon's friend.

Damon choked. "She surprised me, that's all."

"Get up. I can't do this part alone."

Damon rolled to his hands and knees, still breathing heavily.

Claire glanced down. Damon was close enough to kick.

100

"Don't even think about it, missus," the dark, ugly stranger said, showing her the gun he had at Dorsey's back.

She took a step away from the injured man.

"You got some rope around here?"

She stared at him defiantly, flicking her eyes over the length of him. His silver-tipped boots glinted in the sunlight streaming through the kitchen window. Without his gun, he would be as easily overpowered as Damon.

The gunman had Dorsey's left arm pulled up behind his back. He wrenched it further and Dorsey grimaced. "Lady, this can go easy or hard – it all depends on you. Cooperate, and things will be easy. Don't, and...well..." He yanked Dorsey's arm again, causing him to grunt in pain.

"What do you want?" she asked.

"Rope, at the moment."

Damon finally pushed himself to his feet. As soon as he was upright, he charged Claire, pushing her back against the wall, this time standing too close for her to raise her punishing knee.

Claire shifted her eyes to Dorsey, hoping for some sign from him that everything would be okay.

"Let her go." Dorsey's voice was low and threatening.

"Or what? You going to stare me to death?" Damon's hateful smirk made Claire struggle against him.

"I don't need you two alive," the gunman threatened. "If you don't cooperate, I'll just kill you both and move on."

Dorsey closed his eyes, cutting off communication with Claire. "There's some duct tape in that drawer," he said, nodding his head in the direction of a nearby cabinet. "We'll cooperate. Just don't hurt her."

"Get the tape, Damon," the gunman said.

"No fucking way, Rafe. I'm not letting this bitch go for even a second. You get it."

"She's not going to try anything now," Rafe reasoned. "She doesn't want anything to happen to her man, now does she?"

"No," Claire coughed.

Damon carefully pulled back, releasing her neck. "Don't move, bitch. I'll be right back." He walked sideways to the bank of drawers, never taking his eyes from her. "I've got to look in the drawer now. You watch her."

"Don't worry. She's not going anywhere."

Claire had forgotten the radio was on; now, as she stood completely still, she heard the announcer's voice saying that it was nine o'clock. She had been certain an hour had passed since she had let this threat into her house; it had been less than fifteen minutes.

Damon dug through the drawer, drowning out Diane Reems as she introduced her guests. "Found it!" he announced triumphantly, holding up the ring of silver tape.

"Tape her hands and then let's take them upstairs," Rafe said.

"Turn around," Damon instructed Claire. "Put your hands behind your back."

With one more glance at Dorsey, she did as the boy commanded.

"Up the stairs," Rafe said. "You first, missus."

With questionable balance, Claire mounted the stairs. Because of her limp, she was in the habit of using the handrail for extra support. Without it, she took each step slowly, making sure she placed both feet solidly on one stair before attempting the next.

"What's the problem?" Rafe asked impatiently before she had gone up five steps.

"She has a lame leg," Dorsey answered. "It throws her off-balance."

"Help her out, Damon," Rafe commanded.

A moment later, Claire was swept off her feet and carried to the top, where Damon dropped her to the ground. Taz came running out of the bedroom, frantically barking.

Rafe let out a surprised laugh. "A clown dog!"

"What?" Damon asked, perplexed.

"That's a clown dog," Rafe repeated.

"What the hell does that mean?"

"Never mind." A shot rang out; Taz yelped and ran.

Claire saw droplets of red leading away from where he had been just a moment before. Tears instantly sprang to her eyes and, gasping, she struggled to get to her feet and pursue her dog. Damon kicked her over. "Why? What did he do?" she cried.

"He was yapping," Rafe said with a shrug. "Damon, find him and make sure he's dead."

"I'm not killing a dog," Damon objected.

"You don't want him to suffer, do you?"

Claire watched as Damon's brow creased with worry. "No."

"You're doing the right thing. Just put the dog out of its misery."

"What about her?" Damon hesitated, pointing at Claire, who was stuck on her back at his feet.

"I'll watch her."

"Give me the gun." Damon held out his hand.

Rafe shook his head. "I need it to keep control here. Use your knife."

Damon cringed. "You do it."

"Hell, no. I'm not leaving you here to watch them. You couldn't overpower the missus by yourself – what are you going to do against both of them?"

"She's tied up now," Damon reasoned. "Leave me the gun—"

Rafe pointed the gun at Damon. "Go. Kill. The. Dog."

"Whatever, man," Damon said, holding up his hands and backing away. "I'll take care of it."

Damon disappeared; the force of Claire's tears doubled. No noise but her crying passed between them for what seemed like five minutes.

"Look, lady, I'm sorry I shot your dog," Rafe finally said, "but he was going to alert the neighborhood."

"What neighborhood?" she sobbed.

Rafe still stood at the top of the staircase; Dorsey was just in front of him. Suddenly, Dorsey slammed his head back against Rafe and they both tumbled backwards down the stairs. The gun went off with a muffled pop. Claire screamed.

"What the hell?" Damon ran back to the top of the stairs. His hands were bloody. Claire squeezed her eyes closed. "Rafe? You okay?"

A moan emanated from below.

"Yeah, man," Rafe answered. "I shot the guy, though. Come help me drag him upstairs."

"You've got to call 9-1-1," Claire sobbed. "Please, you've got to..."

Damon looked at her like she was speaking Portuguese. "Stay there," he said, and ran down the stairs.

They were going to die; she understood that now. She knew their names, Dorsey was shot, her dog was dead – she was certain that this was the end.

The phone rang.

"Should we answer that?" Damon asked. Claire could just see his head as they dragged Dorsey upstairs.

"What the fuck's the matter with you? No, we shouldn't get that," Rafe said.

"What if it's someone who, you know, is checking up on them?"

"They'll know something's up if we answer, dumbass."

"We could get the woman…make her answer."

The ringing stopped.

"See?" Rafe said. "Nothing to worry about."

They were at the top of the stairs now. They laid Dorsey down and Claire scooted toward him. His eyes were open and he grimaced as he hit the floor. "You're alive!"

"Just a flesh wound," he said, reforming his face with a half-smile.

She smiled back at him before letting her eyes wander downward. About a third of the way down on his right side, his shirt was soaked with blood. She looked up at their tormentors. "Please! It's not too late. You haven't killed anyone yet…"

Rafe kicked Dorsey's legs. "Why couldn't you just fucking cooperate, man?"

"I'm sorry. You're right."

"Damn straight, I'm right."

"What do you want from us?" Claire asked.

"We heard through the grapevine that ya'll have the largest crop of weed anywhere in the state. We're here to take that burden off your hands." Rafe raised an eyebrow and stared at Claire.

"What?"

"Marijuana, missus. We're here for the drugs."

"And the money," added Damon. "Don't forget the money."

"Like he said."

"What?" Claire asked again.

"You go deaf or somethin'?" Rafe advanced on her and she shrank back.

Dorsey sucked in a breath. "We grow tomatoes, not weed."

"Bullshit. We have it on good authority that you've got a hothouse full of pot."

"Your authority can't tell the difference between pot and tomatoes, then."

"For fuck's sake! I'm going to kill Marcus, man." Rafe kicked Dorsey again. He tried to curl his legs out of the way, but that just seemed to infuriate Rafe, who delivered two more kicks, bloodying the silver tips.

"They're lying." Damon paced behind them, jittery. "Why should we believe them over Marcus?" The phone rang again. "Rafe, we better answer that, man."

"I told you, we can't."

"I got a bad feeling..."

"Shut the fuck up, Damon. You and your bad feelings." Rafe dropped his head to his chest moodily. "I should have told Sol to run his own damned raid."

Damon laughed like that was funny. Claire grasped Dorsey's hand and prayed. His own clasp on her hand was weak and the bloodstain was growing.

"I'm gonna go out and check the crop." Rafe pointed at Dorsey and Claire. "If you two are lying about the pot, I'm going to come back in here and make sure you learn the importance of honesty." To Damon, he said, "You stay here and watch them. And don't answer the fuckin' phone!"

The three of them listened in silence as Rafe clomped down the stairs and out the back door.

"Please, Damon, call an ambulance. You don't want a dead man on your conscience, do you? By the time Rafe checks all the greenhouses—"

"Your man brought this on himself. Everything would have been fine if you two had just chilled."

She studied his face – her initial evaluation of his age seemed high now. He must be eighteen or nineteen. "What would your mother think of what you're doing here? She must be so disappointed in you."

He frowned. "Don't talk about my mother."

"Why not?"

"Because."

"Because you know I'm right?"

"Stop it," Dorsey breathed. Claire turned to look at him; when she turned back, she saw Damon's fist flying towards her. When it connected, she heard the crunch of bone; she wasn't sure if the sound came from his body or hers. Instantly, her cheek was throbbing.

"I told you not to talk about her." Another blow came to the side of her head, followed by a kick to her ribs.

Defiantly, she raised herself up and stared at the boy. "Brave man, beating up a woman."

"Shut up!" he shouted. This time he punched her in the nose. The blow knocked her into Dorsey, who grunted in pain. A spray of blood ran wetly over her lips and down her neck. She wished she had a hand free to wipe it away. Knowing she was leaning against Dorsey's wound, she pushed herself off him.

"Stop," Dorsey breathed again. "Please, don't hurt her. Please stop."

Damon stepped back. "Oh, God! What the hell have I done?" He stared at his bloodied hands.

The phone began ringing a third time. "Who the fuck is calling?!" he raged, grabbing Claire by the shirt and dragging her to her feet. "Who is that?"

"My sister," she answered. Then she spat in his face.

Enraged, he walked her backwards to the edge of the stairs and pushed her. She felt each bump and bounce; she imagined she looked like a child's toy as she flopped down them. And she remembered: the first time she rode Dorian; the first time she met Dorsey; holding her sister's hand; hugging Grandpa Harry; falling from the nameless horse; twenty-five years of happiness. She closed her eyes and drifted away.

When she opened them again, the house was dark except for the strobe of red and blue lights that seemed to cut through the living room walls. Someone's hand was against her throat; she turned her head to see a young man in a paramedic's uniform.

"You're going to be okay," he soothed. "Lie still. We're getting the gurney for you."

"Dorsey?" she croaked.

"Where is he?"

"Upstairs."

"We'll take care of him. Don't worry, okay?"

Someone found the light switch and Claire squinted at the brightness.

"You probably have a concussion. Did you fall down the stairs?"

"Pushed."

"Who pushed you?"

"Damon."

Someone called out from upstairs. "We've got a body. Gunshot victim."

Claire's heart clenched and she couldn't breathe. The paramedic took her hand. "Calm down, okay? You need to relax."

She looked into his eyes. The world around her fell out of focus until all she could see were his eyes. And then they were gone, too.

When she finished giving her testimony, she walked off the stand and out of the courtroom. The prosecutor wanted her to stay for the whole trial, but she couldn't. She didn't want or need to hear the details again.

More than a year had passed. She had pieced together the order of events that day. Beryl had been the one calling. Even though Rory told her not to worry, she had a premonition that something was wrong. After three tries, she called the police. And then she called them again and again until they sent out a patrol car. By that time, the sun was setting. The police officer had knocked several times and had a look around the farm before finally trying the door handle.

Inside, he nearly stumbled over her body at the foot of the stairs. He immediately called for backup and an ambulance. Since he was alone, he backed out of the house to wait for reinforcements; he feared the assailant may have still been inside. Ten minutes later, the paramedics and another police car arrived on the scene. Together, the three officers re-entered, guns and flashlights drawn.

Upon determining that the first floor was empty except for Claire, they called the paramedics inside and headed up the stairs. They found Dorsey in the master bedroom, propped up on the bed. Someone had bound his wound with duct tape in an effort to keep him from bleeding out. The coroner later determined he had been dead about an hour before the police arrived.

The most shocking discovery was the dog. His legs and nose were bound with tape and he was lying in the bottom of the master bedroom closet. He had been shot in his right back leg, but someone, presumably the same someone who tried to save Dorsey, had bound the wound with duct tape. Despite the notoriously inferior breathing ability of pugs, Taz survived his ordeal with little more than hair loss – pulling the tape off him had proved something of an ordeal, according to Beryl, who had retrieved him from Animal Control as soon as she arrived in Phoenix the next morning.

Claire had been able to give the police artist a detailed description of Damon, right down to the four-leaf clover tattoo on his left forearm. The police picked up prints from him on the duct tape found on the dog and on Dorsey. He wasn't in the system, though.

Her description of Rafe was less accurate; she only remembered he was ugly, with a pronounced brow, and he wore silver-tipped boots. The police didn't find any evidence of him except for a couple of hairs on Dorsey that must have transferred to him in the tumble down the stairs. The police were at a dead end. They gave the sketches to the local news channels and told Beryl they were doing everything they could.

When she pulled into the zoo parking lot, Claire hardly remembered the drive from the courthouse. She pulled into a space and rested her head against her forearms on the steering wheel. She laughed at herself. She was hardly dressed for a zoo trip. The leather pumps were causing her feet to sweat and the polyester fabric of the pantsuit was hardly a hot-weather outfit. No matter – she pushed open the car door and hiked into the park, her feet carrying her along without a conscious plan.

The police had caught Damon and Rafe not because they devoted great resources to catching them, but as a result of a drug-house raid. Damon was hauled into the police station and left in an interview room for an hour. When the detective entered the room to question him, the boy simply broke down and confessed.

Wild Life

The irony was if Damon had kept his mouth shut, he would have been in the wind before the cops realized he was a wanted man. They weren't going to hold him – the others who were picked up had already told the cops that Damon was just a friend who had stopped by for a visit, not a producer or a customer. At first, the detective thought Damon was some kind of nutcase; nevertheless, he couldn't ignore a confession. They ran his fingerprints through the system and – ding! – they had a winner.

Damon told them where to find Rafe, and both men were in custody less than four hours after the drug bust. When the detective called Claire to give her the news, she remembered thinking that he had sounded as surprised as she felt that they had caught the guys.

Standing at the wire-mesh fence that separated her from the Mexican wolves, Claire thought it was unfair the way humans characterized nasty human beings as animals. "The wolves are at the door." "She's a barracuda." "What a pig." Animals are just animals – humans are the real monsters.

She had watched a show about the evolution of dogs – dogs whose ancestors looked very much like these caged canines. She wondered if the descendants of these wild animals would one day be spotted puppies with trusting eyes and wagging tails. She wondered why no one had ever tried to domesticate humans.

Wild Life

The Man Who Stole a Leopard

Milo sat on the bench in front of what used to be the clouded leopard enclosure. The cat, a beautifully plush animal, was gone. He fingered his camera, frustrated that his intended subject was nowhere to be seen. Without the cat to photograph, he had no excuse for continuing to hang around; he didn't want to leave, though. He hadn't spotted Claire yet.

Today was his third day in a row of staking out the zoo in an effort to find her. He didn't dare ask about her — besides, his reputation as a troublemaker guaranteed that none of the volunteers wanted to talk to him. He wished he had asked for her phone number the day he and Alice Marie were with her.

He knew that he would have a better chance of spotting her if he stayed close to the front of the park. But standing on the bridge or sitting on the bench next to the koi pond was too conspicuous. He didn't want to look like a stalker, even if he were behaving in stalkerish fashion.

Three older women speed-walked past him. One of them winked at Milo; he smiled and tipped an imaginary hat at her. Ever since his encounter with Sondra, he had noticed that a lot of older women seemed interested in him. He felt as if the scales had been plucked from his eyes. Just knowing that ladies were looking at him added a swagger to his walk and the confidence to pursue the prickly hearted zoo volunteer.

He pulled a well-used zoo map out of his camera case and studied it, wondering if he should move on to the orangutan exhibit. The animals wouldn't be out for another twenty minutes, but at least he wouldn't just be sitting around staring at an empty cage.

Why the zoo hadn't put out some kind of notice regarding the big cat was beyond him. He worried that the animal had died. He didn't know how old she had been; death was certainly a possibility. He smiled at the thought that some young man had become so entranced with her that he had freed the animal in a misguided attempt to save her — a romantic and fanciful thought. He wondered where thoughts like that were coming from — decades had passed since he had thought of anything so ridiculous. His career had completely absorbed his imagination; for years, he only envisioned possible crimes, not fairytales.

Yet his mind continued to wander down this path. He imagined the young man and the lonely leopard running off together. Perhaps he was transformed into a leopard himself, and they were hunting side by side in the forests north of the city. Milo, the warmth of the summer sun against his face, allowed his eyes to drift shut as he pictured their life together. Shadows crossed in front of him, darkening and then brightening the show that played on in his mind: the leopards hunting, thriving in the mountains, building a population of wild cats among the canyons and pines of Arizona.

A shadow lingered in front of him too long, and he opened his eyes. The outline of a woman stood before him. "Claire?" he asked.

"Hi, Milo. What are you doing here?" She sat down next to him.

He held up his camera. "I came to photograph the clouded leopard."

"The zoo moved her to San Diego last week."

"With no warning?"

"Not too much, actually."

"Why did they do that?"

"They traded her for another animal. How is Alice Marie?"

"Fine, just fine. I didn't bring her today."

"I noticed that."

"How have you been? I haven't seen you around recently."

"I had some...stuff...to take care of."

Milo remembered the slice of news he heard in the Brass Monkey and wondered again if that Claire and his Claire were the same. Approaching the subject delicately, he asked, "May I ask what happened to your husband?"

She hesitated. "Why do you ask?"

Instead of answering her directly, he said, "I lost my wife a few years ago. Heart attack. She just fell over one day while she was out shopping. I only just made it to the hospital before she died."

"I'm sorry."

"Don't be. You didn't know her. The only thing I'm sorry about is that I didn't love her the way I should have."

She narrowed her eyes. "Did you cheat on her?"

"Never!" He gave her an indignant glare. "My parents taught me that fidelity was important."

"I'm sorry. I didn't mean to offend you."

He stared at the empty cage.

"How long were you married?"

"More than thirty years. I always figured she would outlive me."

"Dorsey used to tell me that I'd outlive him."

Milo, whipping his head toward her, caught her wistful smile. He knew she was Claire Combs now – how many men named Dorsey could there be? And how many of them were married to Claires?

She turned and met his eyes. "Have you been following the trial?"

"I caught a clip of it Monday night on the evening news," he admitted.

"I really don't want to talk about it."

"Okay." He fumbled with his camera for a moment. "May I take a picture of you?"

"Why?"

"I don't know…because you're here and the leopard isn't?"

"You really know how to flatter a girl," she said sarcastically.

He let the camera drop to his lap. "I'm sorry. You're right."

They sat in awkward silence for a few minutes. At last, she pulled her cell phone out of her pocket and read the time. "I need to go now. I'm supposed to be in Monkey Village in just a few minutes."

"Maybe I'll see you there."

"You're not smuggling peanuts today, are you?" She gave him a half-smile.

"Not at the moment. The leopard wasn't partial to them."

She laughed and stood up. "I hope you'll stop by, then."

Wild Life

He smiled and waved her off. As she walked away, he snapped a photo of her with the light streaming through her hair. When he developed it later, he thought it was one of the most beautiful photographs he had ever taken.

Sondra found herself at the Brass Monkey most nights. The silence of her daughter's house was overwhelming, especially after Epiphany – or Fanny, as she preferred – got home from work. Sondra nursed her whiskey sour and pouted. After all the trouble she went to in naming her daughter something unique and suitably Hollywood, the girl had gone and shortened it to something that made her sound Jewish.

She wasn't having a good night – she had paid for her own drink. Usually, some old gent would take an interest and send her one; if not, she wasn't shy about taking the initiative with a handsome stranger. That usually worked, too. Tonight, though, no one showed an interest and no one caught her eye. She had tried to wheedle one out of Sax, but the old grump had insisted she pay up front, just to be on the safe side.

Once upon a time, a Hollywood star – the father of Epiphany – had compared her to a leopard. He had meant it in a complimentary way, not in that harsh way that older women are called cougars today.

A cougar is such a common cat, really, and not a beautiful one at all. She found it appalling the way women had embraced what was essentially an insult. To describe an attractive woman as a predator seemed, well...sexist. Older men had been pursuing younger women for millennia and no one was particularly put off by that. Hell, she had benefited from lustful older men for her entire career.

She was no cougar, though. She preferred to hold onto her lover's fondly bestowed designation. She was beautiful, adaptable, and fast. She smiled languidly and rolled the glass on its bottom edge, remembering the night he first called her his leopard. The ice clinked, drawing the bartender's attention.

"Another?" Sax asked, leaning one arm against the bar.

She tilted her head and jutted her chin out in an effort to tighten the skin of her neck, then she spun the barstool slowly around, scanning the room for newcomers. Seeing no one, she came back to face Sax. "One more."

He laughed knowingly and sauntered toward the bottles. "Where's your date from the other night?"

"Don't know. Have you seen him around again?"

"Can't say that I have. Seemed like a nice enough fellow. Handsome, too." He poured the whiskey and lemon juice into a shaker and added some ice. "Maybe he decided this place was too dangerous."

She rolled her eyes and brushed her hair back with her right hand. "You're just mad that he wasn't interested in you."

Sax shrugged nonchalantly. "I never have trouble getting a date when I want it." He slid the drink in front of her and went back to the other end of the bar, where he had spent most of the evening chatting up Bob Kovich, the director of the local theatre where Sondra was a regular player.

Up until a few years ago, she had always been able to get a date when she wanted one. In Hollywood, she was a legend. Thanks to her years hanging onto that old Hollywood star, she was well known among the hoi polloi. She had been on the cusp of real fame right at the end of the golden age of Hollywood – back when movie stars shone as brightly as their astronomical counterparts. Even after her movie-star lover died, she had still been on all the party guest lists. Of course, somewhere along the way her escorts had changed from handsome men who were interested in her into beautiful boys who were interested in each other, but that hadn't mattered – much.

But then the party planners stopped calling. No one wanted to hear the stories she could tell about – well, who even remembered anymore? She had packed her bags, left the movie star's mansion – hers to live in until she died, but not hers to sell – and moved in with her daughter, Epiphany. Fanny. She tipped her head back and took two long swigs of her drink, draining it.

Fanny wasn't much to look at. Considering she was the offspring of a Hollywood he-man and a B-movie queen, she was downright homely in Beverly Hills. Sondra had tried – oh, but she had begged – to get Fanny bigger breasts and a smaller nose. The girl would have none of it. As soon as she was able, she packed up and left California, choosing instead to attend some lesbian-creating college in the Midwest. Sondra was certain that was what was wrong with her daughter: she was obviously gay, her ten-year marriage and boring son notwithstanding. Of course, both the husband and the son were long-gone now. The husband had left Fanny for a secretary and the boy was off at some college on the East Coast, obviously as desperate to escape Fanny as Fanny had once been to escape her mother.

Bob stumbled off his barstool and out the door, presumably to his golf cart waiting in the parking lot. With any luck, the old man would weave his way home without hitting a palm tree.

Sondra flashed Sax a knowing smile, to which he responded with a shrug. "I'm not in the mood tonight, anyway." He made his way back down to her end of the bar. "How are rehearsals going?"

"How did you know?"

"Bob's a talker."

"Before or after sex?"

"I don't kiss and tell, Sondra. You know that."

She rolled her eyes. "As if I cared."

"This is still a small enough town that discretion matters." Picking up her empty glasses, he asked, "One more?"

"No, thank you. Two's my limit."

"Since when?"

"Since I need to get myself home."

"I could give you a lift."

"Thanks, but no. I'd take a water, though."

He filled a glass with ice and tap water. "On the house," he said, sliding it in front of her.

"You're a gentleman and a scholar."

Sax had recognized her the first time she walked into the Brass Monkey, which was what kept her coming back. If he had been straight, she would have been more than happy to go to his bed. Even though he was pushing seventy pretty hard, he was a fine-looking man with a full head of silver hair. Unlike a lot of ex-cops, Sax worked hard to keep his body in fighting trim; she knew this because, the few times she actually made it to the gym before eleven in the morning, she spotted him pumping iron while she was using the stair-climber.

Of course, his sexual preference had been as obvious as his bulging muscles to her the moment he called her Carmella. As a rule, straight men had no memory for short-lived 1970s soap operas about the cosmetics industry.

"So, what was that guy's name?" Sax asked, leaning on the bar in front of her. The crowd had thinned to the point where she was the most interesting person left.

"Which one?"

"You know – the Guayabera guy from the other night."

"Milo," she answered, lingering on the "mmm" a little longer than necessary. She had to admit, he had been a yummy snack.

"You sure he wasn't batting for my team?"

"Positive." She held up three fingers and raised her eyebrows suggestively.

"Really?" Sax grunted his admiration. "Must've been younger than he looked."

"He was sixty if he was a day."

Sax let out a low whistle. "I bet he was a real powerhouse in his prime."

She shrugged, annoyed that he had overlooked the inspiration she had clearly provided to Milo.

"You're not getting any younger, Carmella." He waggled his eyebrows at her. "Maybe you should sharpen your claws and go on a hunt."

"Don't call me that. It's been thirty years, you old queer."

"You'll always be Carmella to me." He suppressed a laugh. "You know what I mean, though. Maybe it's time for you to settle down. He'd be quite a catch."

"He doesn't seem that interested," she pouted. "He hasn't been back here."

"You know where he lives, don't you?"

Finally grasping his line of thought, she smiled. "That's a little forward, don't you think?"

"No one has ever accused you of being shy."

Wild Life

Wild Life

Slow Cheetah

When the doorbell chimed, Milo jumped about a foot in the air. In the six months he had lived there, no one had pressed the doorbell button – at least, not when he had been home to hear it. Plus, it was late for Sun City; the sun had already set, which meant it had to be near eight o'clock.

He set the book he had been reading – a photography technique manual – on one end of the tough old sofa and pushed himself out of his easy chair, wondering if he should answer the door. There had been a string of home invasions in the retirement community: young thugs preying on the elderly. As an extra precaution, he opened the closet and pulled out a golf club one of his Border Patrol buddies had given him as a retirement gift. He put both hands on it and gave it two abbreviated practice swings as he waited to see if whoever was at the door would simply go away.

The doorbell rang again; this time, he was less startled, but still a little uneasy.

"Milo?" a woman called. "You home?"

"Sondra?" he answered, perplexed.

"Yes, it's me!"

He leaned the golf club against the wall and opened the door, feeling ridiculously feeble for even considering the golf club as a weapon. "What are you doing here?"

"May I come in?" She had a bottle of whiskey in one hand. "I thought we could share a nightcap."

Frowning, he stepped back; she flowed past him and through the living room to the kitchen, calling, "I'll just get us some glasses."

Closing the door, he scratched his chin. "Don't you usually have a nightcap after an evening out together?"

"Usually," she answered. He could hear ice cubes clinking against the sides of glasses. "But I was out alone. I hoped you'd show up at the Brass Monkey, but apparently you're more of a homebody."

Liquid was being poured into the glasses now. Realizing she wasn't going to leave, he sighed and took off his reading specs. He stuck his makeshift bookmark – a flattened film box – into the manual and set it on the end table

118

next to the ashtray. He heard the swish of her capri pants and the slap of her thongs as she sashayed back into the room. Turning to look at her, he was briefly reminded of Mary Tyler Moore when she played Laura Petrie – though he was fairly certain she had never been a redhead. He took the drink she held out to him.

"To new beginnings," she said, holding her glass out expectantly.

"New beginnings," he mumbled, clinking his against hers.

She let her eyes wander over the furniture and decorations. "This is very...comfortable," she said, finally settling on a word.

"You haven't sat on the sofa yet."

"Today's generation would call this retro – Seventies Chic, or some such thing."

He let himself laugh. "Why don't you sit down and relax."

"I'd love to." She walked directly to the sofa and sat on the middle cushion. It barely responded to her weight, crunching ever so slightly under her. Her eyes widened. "Sturdy."

"Remarkably so." He sat down in his easy chair again and sipped the whiskey. It wasn't his usual drink, but then he had never really had a "usual" anyway. It wasn't bad, if you didn't mind the burn. He rested the glass on the arm of the chair. "What brings you by?"

"Like I said – I've been expecting you to show up at the bar. I got tired of waiting."

"I only stopped there on a whim. I'm not much of a drinker."

"So I gathered. Sax told me you hadn't been in before or since."

"The bartender, right?"

She nodded and raised the glass to her lips, sipping the drink.

"How are rehearsals going?" he asked.

"Very well. I want you to come and see it next weekend. I'll put a ticket on hold for you at the box office."

"I don't—"

"I'll put aside an extra one so you can bring your granddaughter," she said, gesturing to a photo of Alice Marie that he had framed and hung on the wall.

"How do you know she's my granddaughter?"

"It's either that, or you're some kind of pervert. I've known my share of pervs, though, and you just don't seem the type." She laughed lightly and Milo found himself chuckling with her.

"That's Alice Marie. She's seven."

"What an old-fashioned name! So sweet."

"She's named after my wife."

"You should bring her to see the play. I firmly believe that all children should be exposed to the theatre at an early age." She attempted to lean back; Milo heard the cushion behind her crunch as she winced and sat up straight again. "Mind if I smoke?" she asked, already digging in her purse.

"No, of course not."

She frowned, glancing at the cushion next to her. Finally, she stood up, grabbed the ashtray, and lowered herself to the floor in front of the ancient, itchy piece of furniture. Patting the floor next to her, she said, "Join me."

"I'm not really comfortable on the floor."

She narrowed her eyes, studying him. "I don't think you know that for sure. When was the last time you were down here?"

"Fair enough. But I'm definitely comfortable up here."

She shrugged, acquiescing. "Something has been puzzling me about you. You said your wife was a fan, but you knew my character's name. Why is that?"

Just the hint of the low growl in her voice was enough to arouse him, but the mention of dead Alice killed the mood. "I broke my leg in a car accident in 1978. I was at home recuperating for most of the summer, and I was at her mercy regarding what we watched – we didn't have a remote control and I couldn't get to the TV without help. By the time the summer was over, I was hooked on three soaps: yours, *Days of Our Lives*, and *Guiding Light*."

She laughed. "If you don't mind my saying so, your wife sounds like a bit of a bitch."

"She wasn't always easy to get along with," he agreed.

Wild Life

"You must have loved her a lot to stay with her for so many years." She tilted her head back and drained the glass.

He paused, studying the golden liquid in his glass. Dead Alice had despised alcohol, calling all forms of it "devil's brew" – one of the many lifetime restrictions she picked up from her devout parents. He had stayed away from it more out of fidelity to her than any repulsion on his own part. "Not as much as I should have."

She set the glass to one side and got on all fours, slinking toward him, reminding him of a cat stalking its prey. "That's good to hear," she purred. "You must have a lot of love left to give."

A week later, he took Alice Marie to see *Guys and Dolls*. After the performance, Sondra invited them backstage, where all the actors and actresses – most of them grandparents in their own rights – signed Alice Marie's playbill and made her feel like a VIP. The little girl was beaming from ear to ear by the time they left, Sondra in tow.

They went to dinner at the IHOP, because that was where Alice Marie wanted to go. After ordering their meals, Sondra asked, "Did you have a good time tonight?"

"Yes! I want to do that someday," Alice Marie answered.

"What? Act?"

"No. Sing!"

"Are you a good singer?"

"I don't know."

"I bet you are," Sondra enthused. "You just look like a good singer."

Alice Marie pulled back and gave Sondra a skeptical look. "You can't tell if someone can sing just by looking at them."

Sondra choked a little on her beverage.

"Are you all right?" Milo asked.

"She's a smart kid," Sondra answered.

Alice Marie's eyes narrowed. "I'm right here."

Sondra's expression hardened and Milo wondered if dinner was such a good idea. "I can see perfectly well, thank you."

Alice Marie turned to her grandfather. "I like Claire better," she said pointedly.

"Who's Claire?" Sondra asked.

Milo fought the urge to slap a hand over his precocious granddaughter's mouth. "Now, Alice Marie, be nice."

"She's Grampa's friend at the zoo."

Sondra laughed patronizingly. "What sort of animal is she, dear?"

Milo winced.

"Human. What sort are you?"

Sondra's mouth dropped open. When she realized her jaw was hanging, she pulled it back up and clamped her lips shut.

"Alice Marie! That was rude. Apologize."

"But—"

"No buts, young lady. Sondra is my friend, and you need to apologize."

The girl muttered something incomprehensible.

"What was that?"

"Sorry," she said again, more or less audibly.

Sondra smiled and said, "Apology accepted."

The rest of the meal seemed to drag on much longer than it should have. At the end of it, Sondra hugged Milo good night and went to her daughter's house. He and Alice Marie drove to his home.

The hour was still early, especially for a summer night: only nine o'clock. That was one of Milo's complaints about Sun City: everything happened so damned early in the day, leaving hours before a reasonable person could consider going to bed. He flipped on the television and Alice Marie squished herself into the gap between Milo and the side of the easy chair. They liked to watch nature programs together, so he turned on the Discovery Nature channel.

During one of the commercials, she turned and looked up at him. He muted the television so that he could hear what she had to say.

"Do you really like Miss Sondra?" Her tiny eyebrows were scrunched together.

"She's nice."

"She reminds me of a cheetah."

"How so?"

"She's pretty to look at, but you wouldn't want to cuddle up to her."

Milo laughed. "Why not?"

"Grampa! Have you seen what cheetahs do to gazelles?"

Milo had barely blinked and Sondra was living with him. He didn't remember inviting her, but neither did he block her from taking up residence. His failure to act led to his tacit approval of her invasion.

The scratchy old couch was gone, as was his easy chair and several other pieces of furniture, all replaced with new and comfortable pieces – though no more to his personal taste than the old stuff. The whole experience left him standing, befuddled, in the middle of his living room.

Sondra came up behind him, wrapping her sinuous arms around his middle. "You like?"

"It's...nice. When did you do all this?" He had only been at the zoo for a few hours that day; he had been looking for Claire, but he hadn't seen her.

"I told you I was going to freshen things up a bit. Remember?"

He did remember. She said something about wanting to get rid of the couch; he had given her a credit card and told her to do it. After all, he was no interior decorator – that was something women and gay men were good at. "But my easy chair..."

"You're going to love the new one, I promise. It's real leather and softer than anything you've ever sat on before." She took him by the hand and led him to the new chair, gently turning and pushing him into the fluffy-looking burgundy seat.

He had to admit it was comfortable. The old easy chair's padding had long ago developed a permanent dent where his butt landed for thirty years and the stuffing, once thick, had thinned to less than an inch in some places – he had been able to feel the wooden frame of the chair if he sat down in the wrong position.

She sank into the new sofa, a tan-suede sectional with built-in end tables. A new carpet lay at their feet – an abstract of brown, green, burgundy and tan ovals. New art – also abstract – adorned the walls. He frowned.

"You don't like it," she sighed, disappointed.

"It's not that, exactly. How did you get all of this done?"

"I can send it all back. I knew you should have come with me."

"No...no. It's good." He had to admit it was better than what he owned before. He tilted his head, attempting to calculate the cost of the new living room. Finally, he shook the thought away and smiled.

She beamed a smile at him. "I'm so glad. And don't worry – I didn't max out your credit card." She pulled the plastic out of her pants pocket and handed it back to him.

He made a mental note to check the balance later on the computer.

"So...did you see your friend at the zoo?" Ever since that one meal with Alice Marie, Sondra always asked that question. She had been inside the closet he had converted to a darkroom, and she had seen the photo he had taken of Claire. Milo felt self-conscious enough that he had taken the photo off the wall.

"No."

"You don't have to lie to me Milo. I'm not jealous. After all, I've got you!"

Suddenly Milo felt very much like a gazelle.

Wild Life

The Union of the Snake

Milo didn't usually stop to look at the snakes, even though they were a large part of the exhibits he passed on his way to the prairie dogs. It wasn't that he feared them; he just didn't like them very much.

The next time he was at the zoo, though, he detoured into the hallway lined with their terrariums. Claire was at the far end, staring into one of them. He walked swiftly to the other end and stood a foot or two behind her, following her gaze. She was eyeing a large rattlesnake.

"When I first moved here, I lived in fear of meeting one of these," she said.

"How—?"

"Saw you in the glass."

"Sorry."

"Not at all. It's been a while, Milo."

"Yeah. I've been looking for you."

"I took some time off."

He focused on her outfit, noting that her pants were the same as she usually wore, but her top was a maroon button-down instead of her usual polo. "Are you working today?"

"No...just visiting."

"I read about the trial." The jury hadn't come to an agreement.

He watched her reflection as she closed her eyes and pressed her lips together.

"Paper said the D.A. plans to retry them."

"So they say."

He put a comforting hand on her shoulder; she reached up and pressed her hand over his. "You want company?" She hesitated just long enough for him to lose hope. He pulled his hand back. "No problem. I understand." He turned to leave the snake house.

"Wait." She walked a few steps until she was even with him. "How's Alice Marie?"

He smiled. "She's great. She keeps bringing you up."

"I can see a lot of you in her."

"Don't tell my son that. He'll never let me see her again."

She smiled widely. "Not a fan, huh?"

"He feels the same way about me that you do."

"He misses you?"

"No. He thinks I'm a jerk." They reached the prairie dog exhibit and he turned to look at her. "You miss me?"

She nodded. "Strange, isn't it?"

"I've got a girlfriend," he blurted, his face reddening.

"Okay," she said, raising an eyebrow and smirking at him.

Clearing his throat, he pointed at one of the dogs poking its head out. "Animals never have problems like us, do they?"

"I don't know. Male prairie dogs usually have at least three _wives.' That can't be easy."

"Good point."

"I wonder what it's like to have a big family like theirs."

"I wouldn't know. I came from a small one. Alice and I only had Brian."

"I have a sister. She lives in Oklahoma with her husband and four kids."

"You didn't have any?"

She shook her head once. "I have a dog that might as well be my kid, though."

"What kind?"

"A pug. His name is Taz."

"I never had a dog."

Her eyes brightened. "Then you've really missed out. What are you, a cat person?" She spat it out as if it left a bad taste in her mouth.

"Alice was. She had this tabby that I thought was never going to die. She got it while I was in 'Nam. I didn't know I was allergic until I came home and started sneezing. That damned thing didn't die until after Brian left for college."

She giggled; the sound of it caught him off-guard. He added his own chuckle. "What about when you were a kid?"

"My parents didn't like indoor animals, and we lived in an apartment."

"I didn't want the dog," she confessed. "Dorsey brought him home. Told me someone gave him the puppy and he didn't have the heart to take it to the pound." A smile creased her face, revealing a dimple. "He knew I never wanted another animal after what happened to my horse, but he was counting on the cuteness factor to win me over."

"Must've worked."

"It did." She looked longingly toward the gates leading to the rest of the animals in the Arizona exhibit. "I came to see the coyotes. Come with me?"

"Sure." As they walked, he asked, "Why the coyotes?"

"I miss seeing them. I used to watch for them out my kitchen window."

"They don't come around anymore?"

"Oh, they probably do come around the farm. I live in a high-rise condo downtown now, though."

"That doesn't sound like your style."

"It was Beryl's idea. My sister. She didn't think I should stay out there by myself, and I was in no condition to argue."

"Was she wrong?"

Claire shrugged. "Probably not."

They walked to the edge of the enclosure; both of them leaned against the wall, their eyes searching the desert below for the coyotes.

"I don't see them," Milo said first. "I never can spot them unless I'm here early in the morning."

"There's one who is always out carving a trail during the day. I think she's looking for a weak spot in the fence."

He watched as she scanned the perimeter. Again he was struck by how attractive she was, particularly when she was least aware of herself. He remembered Sondra and looked away.

"There she is." She pointed toward the back fence. "She'll be around this way in a couple of minutes. See the trail?" She indicated the well-trod path a few feet from the wall. "Do you mind if we wait?"

"No, of course not."

They walked to the bench under the awning and sat.

"Why did you leave the Border Patrol?"

"I would have been forced to leave when I turned fifty-seven, no matter what."

"But you retired earlier?"

"My boss was rather insistent."

She laughed. "Let me guess – you were a rule-breaker even then."

"Nope. I walked the straight and narrow. No one wanted to be my partner – I was too honest."

"And now you sneak food into Monkey Village." She folded her arms over her chest and looked at him.

"Fine. Don't believe me."

"Look! There she is!" She pointed to the left and they watched as the old coyote trotted toward the front of the enclosure.

"They're such solitary creatures," Milo commented.

"They aren't, actually. They live in packs."

"I've never seen more than one at a time in the wild." Occasionally they trotted through his backyard in Sun City; Sondra had pointed one out just a few days earlier.

"I think the ones we see during the day are insomniacs."

He smiled at the concept. "So they just decide to take a trot instead of lying there not sleeping?"

"Makes sense to me."

He smiled broadly. "You know that's a classic case of anthropomorphism."

"Have you ever wondered what it's called when an animal assigns animalistic behaviors to humans?"

"Not until now."

She returned his smile. "What have you got planned for the day? You have a hot date?"

Sondra was out shopping with Fanny today. He knew this because she had asked to borrow his credit card again – this time because she wanted to buy him a few new things to wear. His old boxers were an eyesore, or so she said. She had mentioned something about cooking dinner for him, but he wasn't counting on it. So far, he had seen no evidence that she even knew how to turn on the stove. "Nothing. No dates. Why?"

"I'm hungry and I still haven't gotten used to eating in restaurants alone. Do you like Chinese?"

"Yeah."

"I've got just the place for us to go. It's practically on your way home. Have you ever been to the Abacus Inn?"

Claire jotted down directions and her cell phone number on a business card he handed her and they walked toward the parking lot. He was talking about something – rambling really. The buzzing in her head made it hard for her to concentrate on his words. What had she just done? She gave a man her phone number – a man she hadn't even liked until she met his grand-daughter. Lots of men have grandchildren, she thought as they walked. The ability to procreate doesn't make you a good person.

At the end of the bridge, Milo stopped. "Where are you parked?"

"Hmm?"

"Your car. Where are you parked?"

"Oh. Right over there – under the baboon." She pointed to the light-post sign.

"I'm by the mountain lion. I'll see you there, okay?"

"Great."

As she stepped into her car, she considered driving straight home instead of to the restaurant. But that would be rude. Why did she give him her phone number? If she had taken his number, she could call him right now and cancel. He had a girlfriend. Is that what she was now? A woman who steals other women's men?

Milo found the restaurant, which was located in a west-side strip mall, without a problem. Painted on the window was a Buddha holding an abacus; the image amused him. Claire wasn't waiting outside; he thought he might have beaten her there. It was too hot to wait in his car, so he headed inside.

A small Chinese man with a slight accent greeted him. "One today?" he asked, picking up a single menu.

"I'm expecting to meet someone," Milo answered.

"Come this way." The man bowed slightly and led him into the main dining area. Claire was in a booth along the far wall. She smiled as he approached.

"I thought I'd gotten here first," he said as he slid into the booth.

"I thought you'd stood me up."

"How long have you been here?"

"Almost ten minutes." She flipped open the menu.

"I'm sorry. I guess I should have taken the freeway." Opening the menu, he scanned through the lunch specials. "To be honest, I'm not very familiar with Chinese food."

"You don't like it?"

"Dead…I mean, my wife didn't like it."

She looked at him curiously. "What were you going to say?"

He groaned. "Dead Alice."

Her eyebrows shot up. "Dead Alice? That's how you think of her?"

"Alice Marie was born not long after she died."

"So you think of them as _dead Alice' and _live Alice'?"

Indignant, he exclaimed, "No! Of course not!"

"Then, what?"

"Dead Alice and Alice Marie." He grinned sheepishly. Claire laughed.

"Are you ready to order?" A thin, older woman stood at the edge of the table.

"I am," Claire answered. "Are you, Milo?"

"Why don't you order for me?"

"I have no idea what you like!"

"I trust you."

"Two lemon chicken lunches, please."

"Egg drop or hot and sour soup?" asked the waitress.

"Egg drop."

"Any drinks?"

"Just tea for me," Claire said.

"That sounds good," Milo echoed.

The woman nodded and moved away from them.

"What year were you born?" Claire was studying the placemat.

Milo looked down at his own and saw the Chinese zodiac. Quickly scanning it for 1953, he exclaimed, "I'm a snake!" Then he frowned. "That's not very flattering, is it?"

"Snakes don't have the same image problems in the Eastern hemisphere as they do in the West." She looked up at him. "Don't be offended, but I wouldn't have guessed we were the same age."

"You were born in 1953?"

She blushed. "No. Not until 1965."

"I wouldn't have thought we had that large of an age gap."

"Thanks a lot. Maybe we should change the subject."

"I'm sorry." Seven years alone had softened his memory of how hard most women took the aging process. "I didn't mean to hurt your feelings. I'm sure the stress—"

"Just stop there, Milo, okay?"

They stared at each other in awkward silence. Milo wondered if he should just leave.

"Your soup," the waitress said, setting two cups of soup and a plate of fried wontons on the table and distracting them from one another. "Enjoy!"

When the waitress left, he dared to look across the table again. Claire was smiling. "You are a beautiful woman."

"You don't have to say that."

"I know. But it's true. When we were at the zoo, there was this moment when you were completely lost in searching for the coyotes and you just..." He searched his mind for the right word: "glowed."

She reddened again and broke eye contact, raising a spoonful of soup to her lips.

Milo grabbed some of the wontons and added them to his soup.

"What are you doing?" Claire asked.

"I like croutons in my soup. I figured these would work."

She shrugged as he pushed the crunchy pieces under the viscous yellow liquid. "The prosecutor says that the hung jury is my fault."

"What? How?"

"I didn't stay for the trial. He says the jury likes to be able to gauge testimony by the reaction of the victim or the victim's family."

"But there was DNA evidence, wasn't there?"

"Rafe and Damon's attorney—"

He frowned and she stopped talking.

"What's wrong?"

"You're calling them by their first names."

"Yes. Is that odd?" She frowned. "That's how I thought of them, you know...by their first names. I didn't know their last names until they were caught."

"They told you their names?"

"Like I said, just their given ones."

He put down his spoon. "You weren't supposed to survive."

"That's what the prosecutor says, too. But if that's true, why did Damon let Taz live?" Milo shot her a puzzled expression. "You haven't followed the trial very closely, have you?"

"No, I'm afraid not. The last few weeks have been a bit of a whirlwind."

"Rafe told Damon to kill my dog, but Damon couldn't do it. He just taped the dog up and laid him in the bottom of our closet with the door shut. Why would he do that?"

"Maybe he's an animal lover."

She snorted and grinned. "Maybe." She sobered. "They found his fingerprints on the tape used to bind Dorsey's wound. I think he knew I wasn't dead...and I think he is genuinely remorseful."

"So you won't go to the trial."

"I can't. I just don't think I can look angry enough."

"What do you want to happen?"

The waitress interrupted before she could answer. "Lemon chicken," she said, placing a plate for each of them on the table. "You done with soup now?"

Claire pushed hers away and gave the waitress a cursory nod. Milo wished he had slurped faster, but did the same. The waitress took the soups away, and they pulled their meals in front of them.

"Looks great," Milo said.

"I'm never disappointed here."

They each took a few bites in silence, savoring the tangy-sweet lemon sauce and succulent chicken.

He had almost forgotten the question by the time she answered.

"I want justice. I want Rafe to get the death penalty. It's his fault that Dorsey is dead." The hurt in her eyes was like white heat searing Milo.

"What about Damon?"

"He didn't kill anyone. He couldn't even kill my dog."

"So...he should go free?"

She slowly chewed another bite. "No. But he shouldn't die."

"What's the defense saying?"

"They admit that Rafe and Damon came to steal from us. But they say all the injury done to us – including Dorsey's death – was accidental."

"I'm surprised their lawyers are insisting on a joint trial. Damon's attorney must know that he could take a plea and get a reduced sentence for testifying against Rafe."

"They don't have separate representation."

Milo squinted at her, certain she was wrong. "But that's ridiculous. No defense lawyer in his right mind—"

"Mr. Orton – he's the prosecuting attorney – tells me that their lawyer is in the pocket of someone much bigger than Rafe and Damon. Orton thinks that their boss is paying the tab on the lawyer fees and calling the shots. Rafe is more important than Damon. They can risk Damon if it might save Rafe."

"Let's go back to the beginning. Why did they target you in the first place?"

"Some moron saw our young tomato plants and told Rafe's boss that we were growing a huge crop of marijuana."

Milo laughed, certain she was joking. She didn't smile. "You're serious?"

"Before they bear fruit, tomato plants vaguely resemble marijuana. Of course, by the time Rafe and Damon showed up, anyone could see they were tomatoes. If Rafe had just looked inside the hydroponic tents before he attacked Dorsey..."

Milo realized he was staring at her. He swallowed hard and moved his gaze to his meal.

"I don't have to talk about this," she said. "How about them Diamondbacks?"

"Sorry. I didn't...I'm sorry. Does Orton know who their boss is?"

"I think so, but he's not saying. All I know is the guy has his fingers in every form of trafficking – from drugs to humans and everything in between. Orton says the best thing we can do is make sure that his lieutenant gets the death penalty. A jail sentence isn't good enough. The death penalty might scare off potential replacements."

"Are you sure you're not suffering from some kind of belated Stockholm Syndrome? Didn't Damon beat you up?"

"You could be right." She stabbed a piece of chicken and scooped up a little rice with it. "So, you have a girlfriend?"

Taking the hint, he let the trial details wander out of his mind. "Yes. Sondra."

"When did you meet her?"

"A bit more than a month ago now."

"Is it serious?"

He cocked his head and smirked at Claire. "Why do you want to know?"

She smirked back. "I can't imagine anyone who's enough of a masochist to choose you."

"Ha!" The loud laugh turned heads at the other tables and Milo felt heat rising in his cheeks. "I think it might be serious."

"You don't know?"

"She moved in."

"After a month?"

"No. After three weeks."

Her widened eyes told him everything he needed to know.

"Too soon, huh?" He pushed his food around his plate, his appetite waning.

"Only you can know that."

He sighed, perplexed. "I'm still not sure how it happened. I just looked around the house one day and realized she wasn't leaving."

"Wow."

"Yeah."

"How did you and dead Alice" – she smirked – "get together?"

He told her about the pregnancy and the rushed wedding.

She leaned back and let out a low whistle. "You're a gullible fish, aren't you?"

He set the fork down and pushed his plate away. "My granddaughter said something similar."

Grinning broadly, Claire said, "I knew I liked that kid. What'd she say?"

"She said I was a gazelle. She also told Sondra that she liked you better than her."

Claire laughed silently. "She's too smart to be seven. Are you sure she's not a midget?"

The waitress came back once more, this time collecting the plates and leaving fried wonton-wrapped bananas drizzled with honey.

"I've never been to a Chinese restaurant that served any dessert other than fortune cookies," Milo said, picking up his wonton.

"That's one of the best parts of eating here, in my opinion." She bit into the treat.

When the treats were gone, he pulled a twenty out of his wallet. She reached for her purse. "No," he said, "this one's on me."

"Don't be ridiculous. I invited you!"

"Maybe so, but I had been trying to work up the nerve to ask you out. I mean, as friends, of course."

She smiled and put a hand over one of his. "Of course."

He cleared his throat and withdrew his hand with a nervous smile, uncomfortably aware that Sondra might consider this lunch an infidelity. "May I borrow your pen?"

She dug it out of her handbag, handing it across the table.

On the back of a receipt, he wrote his name and phone number. He passed the pen and paper back to her. "Friends should have each other's phone numbers."

She slipped both items back into her purse. "Thank you."

"Has Orton said when the next trial will start?"

"He wants to push it to the fall. No matter when it is, he wants me to commit to attending every day."

"If you need someone to go with you, I'll do that."

"It's sweet of you to offer, but I probably need to face this on my own."

"If you change your mind, call me."

Wild Life

Wild Life

Barracuda

The carport door opened and closed, followed by the clatter of car keys on the kitchen counter. Milo appeared around the corner, an unusually joyful smile on his face.

"Where were you?" Sondra was making an effort to look preoccupied. Curled in the corner of the sectional, she had a fashion magazine in her lap and a nail file busily attacking the fingers of her left hand.

"At the zoo," Milo answered. As soon as he met her eyes, the smile slipped away.

"I thought the zoo closed at two." She glanced at her watch, which read five o'clock.

He shrugged. "I went to lunch."

"You knew I was cooking for you! I hope you didn't spoil your dinner."

His brow creased and he backed up a few paces to look into the kitchen.

She set the magazine aside and folded her arms. "I wasn't sure when you would be home, so I didn't start cooking."

"All's well that ends well, then," he said brightly. "Why don't you cook for me tomorrow instead?"

"Why weren't you answering your phone?"

He patted his pockets absent-mindedly. "Shoot. I must have left it in the car. The heat probably killed the battery."

One of Sondra's eyebrows shot up. Having spent most of her life in Hollywood, she had dealt with unfaithful lovers before. She tilted her head to one side, narrowing her eyes. "Let's see...the zoo closed at two, correct?"

He nodded, a worried expression plaguing his eyes.

"And it takes forty minutes to drive home?"

"Normally, yes," he conceded. "The detour to the restaurant added about twenty minutes."

"That leaves two hours for lunch. Did you have a book with you?"

"No."

"Two hours spent just...what? Watching the other patrons?"

His jaw clenched and his eyes closed.

Years of experience told her a confession was forthcoming. "That must have been very relaxing." She smiled, her teeth showing, as she pushed off the sofa and sauntered toward him.

"I was—"

"No," she said, cutting him off. "Don't worry about it. You're a big boy and I trust you. I'm sure you had a very nice...lunch." She wrapped her lean arms around his neck and pressed her lips to his ear. "Maybe you're in the mood for some dessert," she said, her husky voice blowing across his ear and neck. He shivered and she let out a low, husky laugh before pulling back.

"Since I didn't know when to expect you, I made plans with Fanny. I need to be there in a few minutes." She walked past him into the kitchen, where her red-leather shoulder bag lay on the counter.

"Do you have some cash?" he asked, pulling out his wallet.

"I've got a bit," she answered, even as she held out her hand for the money she knew he would give her. He laid a twenty in her palm and she smiled sweetly. "Thank you, baby," she cooed.

"Drive carefully," he said as she dug her keys from the bottom of her purse.

"I will."

"Are you going to drink?"

"I don't know yet. You know how Fanny can be." Sondra knew he didn't, but it made for a good cover story, just the same.

"Call me if you're too drunk to drive. I'll come get you."

"You're such a sweetheart. Don't worry about me, though." With the key ring around her index finger, she reached up and put her hand alongside his cheek, pulling him in for a chaste kiss. A second later, she was out the door and climbing into her old red sports car, a bewildered Milo waving her goodbye from just inside the house.

She drove carefully through Sun City to the Brass Monkey, where, just to be on the safe side, she parked the car in the back. Though she doubted Milo would be going out after the curve ball she had just thrown him, there was no point in tempting fate. She slipped inside the bar, found a seat at the far end – two stools between her and her nearest neighbor – and flagged Sax down with Milo's twenty. "The usual, sweetheart, and keep'em coming."

Sax smiled as he took the twenty. "You got it, Carmella."

She rolled her eyes and laughed.

A few minutes later, he was back with her drink. "You okay? Haven't seen you around in a few weeks."

"I took your advice, Sax. I went fishing."

"How'd it go?"

"I caught me a big one...but I think the line's gonna break."

He pulled back and studied her. "I wouldn't nibble your bait, sweetie, but I know a lot of guys who would willingly let you set the hook. What's the problem?"

"I didn't know it, but someone was already baiting the water before I got there."

Sax squinted. "Wait a second. Are we talking about the same fish? Guayabera man?"

"That's the one."

"He's handsome enough...but you're Carmella Savage, for god's sake!"

She drained her glass in two gulps, banging the empty container against the bar. "I think I've lost it, Sax."

"Lost what?"

"It. My sexiness...my allure. I'm just an old woman now." She hung her head, staring into the thickly lacquered dark wood of the counter. The lights were dim enough that she could almost fool herself into believing she was young – the creases and folds caused by bad habits and hard living were barely visible. She sensed that Sax had moved away, taking her empty glass with him. She sighed dramatically and closed her eyes.

Someone sat down next to her and put his arm around her shoulders. She leaned into him; when the flesh didn't give, she recognized her comforter as Sax. "What am I going to do?"

"The way I see it, you've got two options: keep fishing or cut bait."

She gurgled a laugh. "What does that even mean?"

139

"Either fight to keep him or let the other fisherwoman take him. Milo is your fish to win or lose; I guarantee you've got the better tackle box."

"You don't know that. You've never seen the other woman."

"Have you?"

She pulled back, frowning. "Just the back of her."

"How's that?"

"Milo took a picture of her walking away. It was hanging in his darkroom when I moved in."

"Is it still there?"

She shook her head, considering. "No, he took it down after I commented on it."

"Maybe you should get a look at the competition before you make a decision."

"How?"

"What do you know about her?"

"Her name is Claire and Milo's granddaughter likes her better than me."

"Are you sure you don't know anything else?"

"She's a zoo volunteer."

"So go to the zoo."

"And what? Stalk her?"

He clucked. "No. Ask questions. Track her down."

"Stalk her, in other words."

"Investigating is not the same as stalking."

"Would you go with me?"

"You don't need backup to ask questions about a zoo volunteer."

"Please? You were a cop, after all. You know how to do this sort of thing."

"You are a bigger pain in the ass than any drag queen I've ever met."

She smiled broadly and batted her eyelashes.

"You know that shit won't work on me."

"I'll skip my refills and let you keep the balance of the twenty."

He sighed. "What time?"

The next morning, Sondra picked Sax up at the gym. "A pink tank top? Really?"

Sax glanced at her and laughed. "I guess we should have called to coordinate outfits."

Frowning, Sondra looked down at her own matching tank top. "I can't very well go home and change with you in tow."

"Why? I doubt Milo would be jealous."

"No, but he would probably be suspicious."

"Then own it, girlfriend," Sax urged.

"Fine." She put the car in drive and headed for the freeway.

"Was Milo upset when you got home last night?"

"No. He was asleep."

"Oh. Did he actually admit to seeing someone else?"

"I didn't give him the chance." As they pulled onto the freeway, a blue Honda cut her off. She laid on the horn. "Hey! Watch it, asshole!"

"You seem to be suffering from some anger this morning," Sax observed.

"No. I'm fine."

"That's a 'girl' fine, isn't it?"

She saw an opening and cut across two lanes of traffic to get in the fast lane. Sax grabbed the handgrip above the door with his right hand, using his left hand to secure the seatbelt around him. "I wouldn't say that."

"Yeah, okay. I won't say it again."

She glanced over at Sax, who had his head down and his eyes closed. "What are you doing?"

"Praying."

"I thought you were a lapsed Catholic."

"I just re-upped."

"Oh, relax," she said, pressing the gas pedal a little harder. "I did some stunt driving in my day."

"I don't remember seeing you in anything that involved driving."

"They shelved the project after my co-star was killed."

Sax swallowed audibly.

"Maybe some music will help you relax. What do you like, show tunes?"

"How stereotypical do you think I am?" he huffed.

"I've got the soundtrack for *Funny Girl* in the CD player."

He reached over and turned it on. Barbra Streisand's remarkable voice filled the air. Before she had finished one verse of "People Who Need People," Sondra and Sax were singing along.

They arrived at the zoo a little after seven. As she pulled into a space near the front of the park, Sax asked, "Milo's not going to be here today, is he?"

"I don't think so. He said something about doing some darkroom work and weeding the yard." They emerged from the car into the early-morning heat. "Good Lord, why did I move here?" Sondra asked, shielding her eyes from the metallic glare of sunlight on car tops.

Sax shot her a sly smile. "Because you didn't want to slowly burn out in L.A. You wanted to be a star again." He pulled a pair of silver-rimmed sunglasses out of the pocket of his loose black shorts and put them on.

"You know me too well. What is it about gay men? Why do you have such a read on women?"

"Not women, darling," he said, coming around the back of the car and putting his arm through hers. "Divas. We know how divas think because, at our very core, we are divas, too."

She laughed as they strode toward the entrance. One middle-aged grandmotherly type eyed her with something like recognition before her grandson tugged her pant leg and drew her attention away. As they passed a couple of fortyish men with a little girl between them, the more masculine of the two stared at Sax's rear until his scarf-wearing partner, a flamer if she had ever seen one, whacked him on the shoulder. Otherwise, they passed unnoticed into the sea of mommies and toddlers.

Swept through the gates with speed and efficiency, Sax and Sondra soon found themselves standing in front of a koi pond.

Noticing the look of disgust on her friend's face, she asked, "What's wrong?"

"This Milo is a strange character. What is he, a pedophile?"

"Of course not!"

"Are you certain? Who else would voluntarily spend so much time in a place with so many children?"

"He's an amateur photographer. He says animals make the best subjects because they never pull their faces at the last second."

Sax pursed his lips. "Hmm."

"Where should we start?"

"Does he have any favorite animals?"

"How do you mean? Like friends or something?"

He drew the next few words out slowly, as if she were suffering from brain damage. "No. Does he take a lot of photos of any particular animals?"

She gave him a dirty look, then realized he couldn't see the irritation in her eyes because of her sunglasses. "He takes a lot of photos of the elephants."

He pulled a small notepad and a pencil from his other pocket. Flipping it open, he jotted something on the page.

"What are you writing?"

"Elephants. Anything else?"

"There's a whole collage of birds in the spare bedroom."

"That's not really helpful."

"Monkeys! He mentioned something about visiting an animal town – Apeville, Orangutown, something like that." She could feel Sax staring at her. She shrugged and brushed imaginary lint from her arm. "I was only half-listening."

"What was the other half of you doing?"

"Flipping through an interior decorating mag," she mumbled.

He sighed. "Is it really any wonder the man's eyes are wandering? You've been together all of a month and you're already ignoring him."

"Not 'ignoring' – multitasking."

"Don't you listen to the news? Science has proven that humans aren't good at doing more than one thing at a time."

"Fine, Dr. Einstein. I'll be sure to put on my 'listening ears' next time."

Sax wasn't listening to her, though. Instead, he was intently studying the map that the cashier had given them after they paid for their tickets. "There's a Monkey Village. Could that be it?"

"Excellent deduction, my good man!" she said, doing her best Holmesian impression.

"Stop that. This is serious."

She smirked. "Yes, I think Monkey Village is probably a good place to start."

They followed the map through the middle of the zoo – past the Komodo dragon and the orangutan house – and were soon standing before a flotilla of strollers at the entrance to Monkey Village.

Sax nudged her and pointed discreetly at the handsome black man standing guard at the entrance. "I'll question him; you chat up one of the other volunteers."

"This isn't *The Dating Game*, Sax."

"Give me a little credit, will you? He mans the gate – he's like the Monkey House bouncer. That means he probably knows Claire – he might even know Milo."

"Plus, he's hot as hell."

"That too," he smirked.

"Fine. But he's probably not gay."

"Sweetheart, my gay-dar is a finely tuned instrument and right now it's beeping like there's no tomorrow."

"When I talk to the volunteers, what should I say?"

"Be casual. You've done improvisation before, right?"

"Not since my acting classes back in the Seventies."

"It hasn't changed."

"I need a character to play."

"Okay. You're an old friend of Claire's and you're trying to find her."

She took a deep, cleansing breath.

"What in the hell are you doing?" Sax was looking at her over the top of his glasses.

"Getting into character."

He shook his head.

"Should we split up?"

"We're dressed like the Bobbsey twins. What do you think?"

"Right. I'll go first." She left Sax's side and approached the gate.

"Do you have any food in your bag, miss?" intoned the African gatekeeper. His deep voice was tinged with a slightly English – mostly something else – accent.

"I'm sorry?" she asked, though she had heard him perfectly well. His name tag read "Zareb."

"No food is allowed inside Monkey Village. These clever little creatures will sniff it out and steal it if possible. You are welcome to leave your bag here, if you would like."

"No, thank you. I don't have any food."

"Good. Please refrain from touching the animals. They are wild and will bite if provoked."

"Are they dangerous?"

A deep rumble of a laugh poured from him like lava from a volcano. "Not at all, as long as you follow the rules." He ran through a list of other warnings and allowed her to pass into the exhibit. She walked along the dirt pathway, mindful not to stand under the ropes or tree limbs above. Zareb had mentioned the possibility of "rainfall," and if there were one thing she would like to avoid in life, it was being peed on by a monkey.

Safely navigating her way to the wide circle at the end of the walkway, she saw two zoo volunteers, both wearing hats and each armed with a spray bottle.

The older of the two was busy pointing out squirrel monkeys to the children, while the younger one was surveying the area like a jailhouse warden during visiting hours. Deciding it would be easier to engage the dark-haired Hispanic girl in conversation, she said, "This must be a great way to spend your summer."

The girl smiled politely. "I love animals, so this is the place to be."

"Like Simon and Garfunkel said, it's all happening at the zoo." She glanced at the girl's nametag: Isobel.

"Who?" she asked, one arched penciled-in eyebrow raised.

"Simon and Garfunkel. Paul Simon? Short guy, popular singer?"

"I prefer rap," the girl said with a shrug. She returned to surveying the trees.

Sondra grimaced. She looked for the older volunteer, who was now cooing over a toddler. She tried Isobel again. "How long have you been a volunteer?"

"About a year."

"What's it like?"

145

"Fun."

Giving up on the small talk, she launched into her story. "I have an old friend who volunteers here. I was wondering if she might be around. Her name is Claire; she has grayish-blonde hair and is about my age. Do you know her?"

"You're a friend of Claire's?" The girl perked up. "She is awesome! She must have been so cool when she was younger."

"Oh, she was!" Sondra enthused.

"You should tell her you're here."

"I really wanted to surprise her. She loves surprises!"

Isobel's smile disappeared and she stepped back a bit. "Maybe we're thinking of two different women. What's Claire's last name?"

"Goodness...I can never remember," she improvised. "It was different when we were girls, you know. And I never really liked her ex-husband."

"Sorry...must be—"

Someone tapped Sondra on the shoulder; she turned and Sax was standing there. "You ready to go, sweetheart?" he asked. He was giving her a look that she couldn't decipher.

"Um...no, darling. I haven't really had a good look at the monkeys."

"Don't you want to see the orangutans?"

"There's plenty of time for that. This girl knows Claire."

"No, actually, I was about to say—"

"Did someone call me?" Pulling off her hat to wipe her forehead, the older woman approached them.

She wasn't beautiful – not the way Sondra remembered having been once. Instead, she was handsome, the way women who have spent too much of their lives outside often become. She stuck out a hand and said, "I'm Sondra. It's nice to meet you."

Her eyes widened slightly with recognition and a slight smile played on her lips. "My pleasure, I'm sure." She met Sondra's hand and squeezed firmly. "Isobel, I'm going to take a short break, okay?"

"Is everything all right?" Isobel looked warily between the two women.

"Fine. Don't worry. I'll be back soon." She headed down the exit path; Sondra followed behind, leaving Sax and Isobel in the circle. There was a lull in the crowd, and Zareb opened the gate for them both to pass through. "Thanks, Z," Claire said. "I'll be back in a few minutes."

Sondra could feel Zareb's eyes on her as they exited Monkey Village.

"Will this bench be okay?" Claire asked, gesturing toward the first one they came upon.

Sondra gave her head a brief shake and pointed to one another thirty feet away. They approached it in silence. Each woman sat on her end, as close to the edge as she could get. "So you're Claire."

"And you're Sondra. Milo didn't mention that you were beautiful."

"He's barely mentioned you at all," she answered, taking a peremptory swipe at the competition.

"We're just friends...barely that, actually."

"Then you won't mind if I ask you to stay away from him."

"Don't you think Milo should make his own decisions about that?"

"He's a man. Men are like fish – they only swim forward. If you were to just...stop putting yourself in his path, he'd forget all about you."

"It's not that fish can't swim backwards, you know. Most can – they just choose not to."

"And your point is?"

"Milo's a particularly persistent...fish. Even though he has you at home to swim towards, he keeps coming back here. What do you think that means?"

"Stay away from him. I caught him and I'm keeping him."

"Good luck with that." Claire stood up and walked away.

Wild Life

Don't Wake the Lion

One morning a few weeks after his lunch with Claire, Milo walked into the zoo feeling out of sorts. Nothing seemed right to him anymore – Sondra had invaded his home, Claire was avoiding his calls, and, just that morning, Vaughn Wagner stared up at him from the Culture section of the newspaper, under a headline reading, "You don't have to be square to like this dance." According to the article, the internationally known square-dance caller was in town to put Sun Citians through their paces. He was instructing a week-long Beginners Square Dancing seminar at the recreation center right down the street from Milo's house, starting Monday evening.

He had taken the paper into the living room, where Sondra was painting her nails over yet another magazine. The woman seemed to have an insatiable need for periodicals. "I'd like for us to do something together this week."

"Such as?"

"I want to go to this square-dancing workshop."

She laughed without looking up.

"I'm serious."

She met his eyes, perplexed. "Why on earth would you want to do that?"

"According to the article, it's supposed to be good exercise and an excellent way to make new friends."

"But didn't you tell me that the reason you don't like to go to the Brass Monkey is because you don't like crowds?"

"I don't like crowds of drunks. These people will not be drinking."

"Give me that," she said, reaching out a hand for the newspaper. "Careful of my nails!" she warned.

He held the article out to her and she took it gingerly, her candy-red polish standing out like ketchup stains against the black-and-white paper. He watched her eyes move rapidly back and forth across the page. "I'm not doing this," she answered bluntly.

"But this is a couple's activity, Sondra. I need a partner or I'm going to stick out like a sore thumb."

148

Wild Life

"No way. Besides, tryouts for *Hello, Dolly!* are Tuesday night."

"Couldn't you just—"

"No! I'm not giving up my shot at the lead! I've played the secondary female in every play since I got to this crummy town. No one else in Sun City has the range I have – this is my part. All I have to do is show up and take it!"

"Fine."

She laid the newspaper, magazine, and nail polish aside and hopped to her feet, fingers spread wide. Milo thought she was about to burst into song. Instead, she stepped into his arms and hugged him. Her arms felt short to him; he realized she still had her fingers stretched apart and extended outward in an effort to save her fresh coat of polish. "Thank you for understanding, darling. Maybe we could do something else together. You haven't been to the zoo much lately. We could do that."

"That's a terrific idea."

She pulled back and smiled brightly. "Great! I'll just—"

"No," he said, cutting her off, "I wouldn't want to trouble you. I'll go alone." He stalked off to the bedroom, relieved when she didn't follow. He dug out a pair of black-and-white plaid shorts and a black Guayabera shirt, found a comfortable pair of walking shoes, and gathered his keys, phone and wallet. A few minutes later, he walked through the living room on his way to the door. "I'll see you later."

"Are you sure you don't…"

He didn't hear the rest of her question; the sound of the door closing blocked it out.

Now, he stood in front of the lion exhibit. The female was up and touring the edge of the enclosure; her brother was sound asleep on a rock at the middle. Apparently bored, the lioness approached her brother and batted him with her paw. He rolled to his feet and roared, a rumbling sound that shook the earth.

Milo knew how the lion felt: unsettled and irritable, certain that nothing could ever satisfy him. His companion was a selfish bitch and all the tasty human treats were just out of reach – frustration must fill his soul. Just as the lion stood and paced the top of the enclosure's hill eyeing his human visitors as if they were lambs walking upright, Milo

149

paced forward, his mind focused on his desired, but unattainable, prey: Vaughn Wagner.

Going to a square-dancing seminar alone would inevitably draw unwanted attention to him – it would be like going hunting in a neon-orange suit. He couldn't let this opportunity pass him by, though – he knew Vaughn Wagner was up to something other than calling square dances. There simply wasn't enough money in traveling around the country entertaining such a small segment of the population. Maybe he could—

"Milo."

He stopped walking and turned toward Claire's voice, smiling. "Where have you been?"

"Oklahoma. Are you okay? I called your name three times before you answered me."

"I'm sorry. I'm mulling something over."

"So it would seem. Here alone?"

"Yes."

He began walking again and she fell into step beside him. "I met your girlfriend."

"What?"

"Sondra. She came by the zoo looking for me. Her and some muscle-bound guy – they were wearing matching pink tank tops."

"Why would she do that?"

"My best guess is jealousy. She asked me to stay away from you."

"Is that why you haven't been returning my calls?"

"Not exactly. I really was in Oklahoma."

"Visiting your sister?"

She pushed her hands into her pants pockets. "My father's sick. Cancer, as it turns out."

"You never mentioned him before."

"I'm not very close to my parents. They didn't approve of Dorsey. Honestly, I was surprised when Beryl called and told me they wanted to see me."

"I'm sorry."

"Don't be. I didn't expect I'd ever see either of my parents again, to be honest."

"Why did you go?"

She shrugged. "What else could I do?"

They were in front of the baboons now. Milo found a bench and sat down, patting the space next to him. She joined him. "You still could have called."

"I was a wreck. I didn't want to talk to anyone – not even you. It's a strange thing...talking to your parents for the first time in your adult life. I never realized how much I missed them. And to know I'll be losing my father so soon after finding him for the first time..."

He put a comforting hand on her shoulder and she met his eyes with a smile. "What are you doing today?"

"I'm volunteering. I'm supposed to be throwing out treats for the baboons and taking visitor questions in a few minutes."

"After that?"

"They'll probably send me to Monkey Village or the orangutans."

Remembering his morning encounter with his past, he asked, "Would you be interested in taking a square-dance class with me?"

"Square-dancing?" Her eyebrows pulled together and he prepared for a negative reply. "I'm not sure. Are you asking me on a date?"

"No." He frowned. "I don't think so. I still have a girlfriend."

"Good. That's good. So...we'll just go as friends, all right?"

"You'll go with me?" He broke into a bright smile. "That's fantastic! Sondra wasn't interested."

"What the heck. Beryl tells me I need to get out into the world more."

"I think I love your sister."

She laughed. "When does it start?"

"Monday night. I'll call you to make the arrangements."

She reached across the bench and hugged him. He was so surprised that he didn't hug her back, just wondered at the sensation of her body against his. He was certain the spark that flew between them could have lit up the sky, had it been night. When she pulled back, her cheeks were rosy. "I've got to get back to work."

She rushed away from him and to the side of the exhibit. A few minutes later she returned with a headset microphone and a five-gallon bucket half-full of chopped vegetables. "Good morning, everyone!" she said, addressing the crowd. Several children rushed to stand in front of her as she launched into her presentation; the baboons gathered on the ledge behind her, awaiting their treats. "The animals behind me are Hamadryas baboons, and they are found in the Horn of Africa and the Arabian Peninsula. The climate is similar to that of Arizona, which is why our baboons are so happy here. Now, can anyone tell me which one of the baboons is male?"

The kids' hands all shot up at the same time.

"What about you in the blue shirt?" she asked.

The little boy – a bit younger than Alice Marie – pointed toward the largest and grayest of the baboons. "Him!"

"Very good! Yes, he is the harem leader. He is very old for a baboon – nearly forty!" As she continued to interact with the group around her, she threw some of the vegetables into the enclosure. Milo, grinning, watched as the baboons eagerly sought the scattered treats.

Sondra had visited the zoo and tracked down Claire. And she brought a friend. Milo puzzled over that, wondering when exactly this visit had taken place. Sometime after their lunch but before Claire left for Oklahoma, that much was certain. He hadn't pegged Sondra for a particularly clever sleuth. No, he thought, the detective had to be her friend in the pink tank top. What sort of man wears a pink tank top? A gay one, that's who. But where would she have met a gay man? He could only think of two possibilities – the theatre or the bar.

Sondra wasn't in the current production at the theatre; nevertheless, he decided to start his counter-investigation there. Stepping into the dimly lit auditorium, he recognized one of the actors to whom Sondra had introduced him when he had brought Alice Marie to see *Guys and Dolls*. He was rehearsing a monologue that might have been from *Death of a Salesman*, but Milo couldn't be sure. He hadn't seen the movie since he was a kid. When the guy stopped talking for a few seconds, Milo called out, "Nathan!"

The man on the stage let out a surprised gasp and put his hand to his eyes in an effort to see out over the footlights. "Who's here?"

"Milo Crosby. Sondra's boyfriend."

"Milo...what are you doing here? Sondra's not in this one."

"I know," he said, walking toward the stage. "She's psyching herself up for the *Hello, Dolly!* auditions next week. Nice job on the monologue, by the way."

"She might as well give that up. Mildred Kovich has her eyes on the lead."

He remembered Mildred from *Guys and Dolls* – she had played the part of the Salvation Army gal. Even in his current state of irritation with Sondra, he had to admit that Sondra was ten times better than Mildred. "She's got a shot, though, don't you think?"

The actor raised his eyebrows and said in a deadpan voice, "The director is Bob Kovich."

Milo winced, wondering if Sondra knew that.

"Exactly. Listen, I need to get back to rehearsing this speech, so if you don't mind—"

"Listen, Nathan, I need a favor."

"Chuck."

Milo felt the heat rise. "I'm sorry, Chuck. I should have known that."

"That's all right. It's actually flattering to be confused with my character. It's a sign that I acted well."

Since he needed Chuck's help, he didn't disabuse him of that notion. "Sondra's birthday is coming up pretty soon."

"Not until October."

"I like to plan ahead."

"Okay, sorry. Go ahead."

"As you know, we haven't been together very long. I'd like to plan a party for her, but I need a list of her friends."

"I'm afraid I can't help you there – I could only tell you a handful of them. And, as my granddaughter would say, they're mostly 'frenemies.'"

Milo was surprised that Chuck had ever procreated. He would have thought the guy swung the other way. "What does that mean?"

Chuck sighed dramatically. "It means that most of the theatre people are rivals, not friends. They put on a good act, but at the bottom of it, there's just hate and discontent."

"I know she has this one friend, but we've never been formally introduced and I don't know where to find him. Big guy, muscular, gay…I think he might be a detective."

Chuck stiffened and eyed him suspiciously. "Sondra said you met at the Brass Monkey."

"We did."

"Then why don't you know where to find Sax?"

Milo stopped at the Brass Monkey on his way home that afternoon and found Sondra's red sports car parked in the back lot. He knew from his previous experience that sneaking into the bar unobserved was impossible. His only advantage would be to catch Sondra and Sax colluding by shining the harsh light of day on them. He opened the door and stood in the frame, late afternoon sunlight shining around him and obscuring his features from the patrons. Just as he had hoped, the muscular bartender was leaning on the bar in front of his soon-to-be-erstwhile girlfriend. They both looked toward the door. He watched as her eyes widened with recognition.

"Sondra. I need a word with you," he announced from the door.

She slid reluctantly off her barstool and walked toward him. "Yes, baby?" She attempted a coo, but it came out as more of a quaver.

"Outside, please." She glanced back at Sax and Milo shifted his eyes to the big guy. "I don't recommend that you interfere," he said calmly.

Sax held up his hands, a grayish bar towel in one of them. "As long as everything stays civil, you'll have no problems with me."

"Thank you." With Sondra now past him and in the sunlight, he let the door swing closed.

"I can see you're upset," Sondra began, placing a calming hand on his arm.

He brushed her away. "I ran into Claire at the zoo today."

"Oh. Really? How is she?"

"She seems to think that you don't want her to talk to me."

Sondra looked down and bit her lip.

"Look at me, Sondra."

154

"You're the one who was cheating!" Tears burst from her eyes with such force that Milo felt a mist hit him.

"No, I wasn't," he answered softly. "I don't cheat."

"Every man cheats, Milo. It's programmed into your DNA."

"Not me. Never have, never will."

She looked up hopefully. "Then you...you want to be with me?"

It was Milo's turn to look away. He stared out at the cars driving past. "I spent more than thirty years of my life with a woman who thought of me as a piece of furniture – necessary to complete the perfect domestic picture, but not much use for anything else." He forced himself to look at her. "After she died, I breathed a sigh of relief. Not because I hated her, but because I had a chance to be my own man for the first time. What did I do with that freedom? I allowed you to usurp it with barely a murmur of protest."

Sondra looked stricken; the color drained from her face. "I thought you liked me."

"I do!" he reassured her. "I just don't love you. And I don't think you love me, either. And, between you and me, I'm too old to settle for something that isn't wonderful."

She took a deep breath and stood a little straighter. "I guess I should move out."

His next words took both of them by surprise. "Only if you want to."

She snorted with derision. "Listen, buddy, I'm Sondra Lane. I'm not staying around as some kind of second-rate harem girl—"

"Of course not," he cut in. "As a roommate. You can have the second bedroom. The fact is I like having you around for company. Plus, you've got a real talent for redecorating."

"I don't know, Milo. That might be weird. What if I want to bring home a boyfriend?"

"Do what you want. You never know – I might bring home a girlfriend someday."

"Claire?"

He shrugged. "I can't predict the future."

"Okay. We'll see how it works." As she turned to go back into the bar, she hesitated. "Have a drink with me? My treat."

"Yeah," he answered, "why not?"

The next morning, nursing a slight hangover, he remembered to call Claire with the square-dance class information. By Monday, Sondra had set up the second bedroom to her liking and they were easing into a friendship. Milo found Sondra much more pleasant to be around now that she wasn't trying to control him; Sondra seemed much more at ease in their surroundings.

As he prepared to leave for the first night of class, he found her at the kitchen table studying the audition scene for *Hello, Dolly!* "There you are," she said as he came around the corner. "Would you mind running lines with me? I think I have my part memorized, but I need to test myself."

"I'm on my way out right now. Maybe tomorrow?"

"Where are you headed?"

"Square dancing."

"Seriously?" She laughed. "I thought you were kidding."

"No, I meant it."

"You never really struck me as the country type."

"I've got my secrets."

She hopped to her feet. "Well, as a friend, I'd be happy to go with you. After all, this is couple's activity, right? I can't have you out there on your own."

"Sit down, Sondra. Study your lines. I've got a partner."

"Who?"

"Claire said she'd meet me there."

"Oh. I mean, good. That's good. I prefer to save my making a fool of myself for the stage anyway."

Remembering his conversation with Bob at the theater, he said, "You do know that the director's wife wants the part of Dolly, don't you?"

"Of course I know that," she answered nonchalantly.

"Don't you think it would be smarter to go for another role? One you have a shot at getting?"

A slow smile spread across her face. "I'm not worried. I'll get the role of Dolly."

He frowned. "I wouldn't be so sure if I were you."

"Yes, you would. I'm a great actress – definitely better than Mildred Kovich. And I know something about Bob that he'd prefer Mildred didn't know." She winked at Milo. "Have a good time tonight. I'll see you in the morning."

Shaking his head, Milo walked out the door.

Wild Life

Eye of the Tiger

He found Claire waiting at the entrance to the recreation center, wearing jeans and a western-cut shirt. "How do I look?" she asked, giving him a quick twirl.

"Like a regular cowgirl," he beamed.

She shook her head at his signature Guayabera. "You're not going to blend in that shirt."

"I don't have to blend – I just need to look like an average guy."

She shot him a curious look. "What's going on? Are we here to learn to square dance or for something else?"

Another couple was approaching the entrance; Milo pulled her to one side, out of anyone else's earshot. "A little of both," he whispered.

"I don't understand."

"You remember me telling you about being forced out of the Border Patrol?"

She nodded.

"The man leading this class is the reason that happened. He's a Canadian citizen who crosses into this country several times a month. He always goes where a large population of retirees live. I suspected he was smuggling prescription drugs in from Canada."

"Is that illegal?"

"Of course it is! Even crossing the border to get a supply of meds for you alone is illegal – but that goes on all the time. The government has chosen to ignore that activity because to enforce it would mean the prosecution of thousands of grandmas and grandpas. No one wants that."

She shrugged. "That does seem a little extreme."

"But this guy is smuggling in meds for more than himself."

"Allegedly."

"What other reason could he have for visiting areas with an above-normal senior population?"

"I can think of one," she said, her eyebrows raised. "He's a square-dance caller. How many young people have even heard of square dancing?"

He grunted his grudging agreement. "Just keep your eyes open. I don't know if there's anything to see, but if there is, I want to see it."

They made their way into the large hall. Vaughn Wagner stood on a low stage at the far end; probably fifty or sixty other people were milling around. A few couples were decked out in traditional square-dancing outfits: tight-bodice dresses with flared skirts and petticoats for the women, matching western-style shirts for the men.

Claire pointed discreetly toward the front of the hall. "That's the guy?"

Milo nodded in affirmation, watching the smallish man with a gut bulge set up his equipment.

"I gotta say, he doesn't look like a drug smuggler."

"He's not pushing meth to adolescents, Claire. He's selling meds to the elderly."

"Prescription medicine."

"You think he checks their scripts before he sells to them?"

She laughed. "What do you think he's peddling – little blue pills?"

He was about to answer her when a sweet-looking older couple in traditional square-dance attire approached them. "Welcome! I'm Rhonda and this is my husband, Howard. We love to see young folks interested in learning to square dance."

"Nice to meet you. My name is Claire and this is Milo."

"Lovely. Aren't they lovely, Howard?"

"Eh?"

"Aren't they lovely?" the woman asked again, this time pulling him down so that his ear was just inches from her mouth.

"Oh. Yes, very nice. I need to replace the batt'ries in my hearing aid before the dance begins, Rhonda."

Rhonda either didn't hear him or wasn't paying attention. "You two should be in our square, my dears. We'll help you learn the ropes."

"How long have you been square dancing?" Claire asked.

"Goodness me – forever and a day. I met Howard at a square dance."

Wild Life

Vaughn Wagner's sound system popped to life and sent a buzz of white noise through the room. "Howdy!" he called, putting his hand to his ear.

"Howdy!" half the crowd called back.

"Oh, now, that was just sad. I said, 'Howdy!'"

Now three-quarters of the crowd answered, including Claire. Howard was still occupied with replacing his hearing-aid batteries, and there was no way Milo was going to shout *Howdy*, no matter how many times Wagner asked.

"Ya'll are here to learn a dance that is part of the American heritage. Did you know that more than twenty states claim square dancing as their official state dance?"

Impressed oohs and aahs filled the air around Milo.

"You may wonder why you need a Canadian to teach you a dance that is so entrenched in American culture." He paused dramatically here and eyed the crowd. "You need me – and men and women like me – because this traditional dance style teeters on the edge of extinction."

Those dressed in square-dancing attire gasped and tsked at these words, shaking disbelieving heads. Milo was starting to think that this was a revival meeting for the Church of the Square Dancers. He glanced at Claire to see if she was sharing his disbelief, but she looked like she was on the verge of converting.

"Tonight you will take your first steps toward rediscovering your roots as Americans, and I will be honored to lead you there!"

A rousing shout of joy, accompanied by enthusiastic applause, followed his words. Claire looked rapturous.

"Square up!" Vaughn said.

The experienced couples pulled the newcomers into groups of eight dancers – four couples each. Howard and Rhonda pulled in two other couples and Milo soon found himself designated, along with Claire and a couple he estimated to be in their mid-fifties, a "side." Howard and Rhonda insisted on being the "head" couple that faced away from the caller since they already knew how to dance. The other "head" couple included an Indian man and his wife, who was dressed in a sari.

"Circle to the left," Vaughn commanded. Following the lead of Howard and Rhonda, they clasped hands and began circling to the left. Before long, they had learned to left allemande and swing. Despite his initial misgivings, Milo was enjoying himself – especially when he got to press Claire close and spin her in a circle.

After an hour of instruction, Vaughn asked the experienced dancers to square up and show the newcomers what a square dance should really look like. Kami and Saura, the Indian couple, sat down next to Milo and Claire for the exhibition. "How are you liking it?" Kami asked Milo.

"It's fun."

"We are liking it very much. We are anxious to learn these American customs."

"How long have you been in Arizona?" Claire asked, leaning around Milo.

"We are being here just a few months now. Our daughter and her husband are living here for many years though. They say we must assimilate. So we learn folk dancing!" As Kami spoke, Saura nodded enthusiastically.

The music started and the dancers began circling and spinning, their dresses flaring out to the point where the women's ruffled bloomers were visible. Milo, amused, glanced at the Indian couple, both of whom had darkened a few shades at the display. He nudged Claire and said, "I think Kami and Saura think those are the women's underwear."

She turned to look at him, but her eyes were caught by something else. Milo followed her gaze and saw the back of Saura's colorful dress heading out the door. "I think you're right."

"That's too bad. They seemed nice."

"They saw mice?" she asked worriedly, picking her feet up off the floor.

"No, nice!" he said louder. "They seemed" – the music stopped – "nice!"

Everyone turned and looked at him – even the dancers across the floor.

"Very nice!" Claire said loudly, standing and applauding. The others around them did the same and Milo's embarrassment was somewhat abated. He stood and applauded with the rest and the dancers beamed.

"The applause is appreciated, but not necessary," Vaughn intoned. The crowd obediently dropped their hands.

"Soon, you too will be spinning and twirling with the best of them. See y'all tomorrow at six-thirty."

Milo and Claire lingered as long as they could without arousing the suspicions of the other dancers. They watched as a queue of old men formed, each one apparently shaking Vaughn Wagner's hand and slipping him a tip.

"I guess square-dance calling is more lucrative than you thought," Claire commented as they sipped coffee and waited for their dinners at the IHOP later.

Milo shook his head. "That can't be all that's going on. I just don't believe it. There's got to be more to this than meets the eye."

"Sometimes a cat is just a cat," she shrugged.

"And sometimes it's a tiger," he parried.

"Are you saying you've got a tiger by the tail?" She smirked as he rolled his eyes. "Let's talk about something else. How's Sandra?"

"Sondra."

"Po-tay-toe, po-tah-toe."

He gave her a short laugh. "She's fine. We broke up, though."

She frowned. "It wasn't because of me, was it?"

"Not entirely."

She pushed back into the bench cushion, biting her lip. The waitress delivered their meals a moment later. When she was gone, Claire said, "I'm not ready for anything serious."

"I understand that. I broke up with her because of what she did."

"Her visit to the zoo?"

"Yeah. That wasn't okay. Like I told her, I spent most of my life married to a woman who thought I was more possession than person. I'm too old now to waste my life in unhappiness."

"So...this still isn't a date?"

"No. We're friends. That's it."

She relaxed and picked up her fork. "Friends." She smiled and dug into her food.

Tuesday morning, Milo helped Sondra rehearse her audition scene and listened to her sing the *Hello, Dolly!* showstopper, "So Long, Dearie," several times.

"So, what do you think? Have I got a shot?"

"You're perfect for the part," he conceded. "I'm not sure that's going to be enough, though."

She smiled slyly. "Like I said, as long as I'm better than Mildred, I'm getting the part."

"What do you have on Kovich?"

"It's a secret."

"Who am I going to tell?"

She glanced around, as if looking for eavesdroppers in their empty home, and then stage-whispered, "Kovich is a closet case."

"You mean…?"

"He and Sax have a little something going on, and I'm certain Mildred doesn't know."

"So if he doesn't give you the part, you're going to out him?"

She shrugged. "Probably not, but I'm going to let him think I will."

Milo laughed. "That's devious."

"I'm an actress. Deviousness is a natural talent." She lowered herself gracefully into the corner piece of the sectional and asked, "How was the square dancing?"

"More fun than I thought it would be."

"I thought you wanted to learn. Wasn't that the whole point?"

"Not entirely. I've got a history with the guy from the paper."

"I saw him at the Brass Monkey last night. He walked in like he owned the joint and took up residence in a booth at the back. Sax was pissed – said the guy was a lousy tipper. He's got quite an attitude for a square-dance caller."

"Was he alone?"

She shrugged. "No women, if that's what you mean. I thought about hitting him up for a free drink, but he's a little short for my tastes."

"What about men?"

"A Mexican guy in cowboy boots sat with him for a while. They seemed to be friends. Did Claire show up for the lessons?"

"Yes. She had a better time than I did. She really seemed to buy into the Church of Square Dancing."

Sondra raised her eyebrows in surprise. "Church?"

"I'm telling you, Sondra, it was like an old-fashioned revival meeting at the beginning. I was half-expecting the crowd to erupt in 'amens.'"

Her lips puckered like she was sucking on a lemon drop. "Wow. I really dodged a bullet there. I've never been much for revivals – except, of course, the Broadway kind. Why did you stay?"

"It's just something I've got to do."

"Suit yourself, Milo. If Claire gets carried away by their cult, don't say I didn't warn you."

At six-fifteen, Milo found himself waiting outside the hall for Claire. The couples were just starting to arrive; he watched the parking lot fill up with Buick Rendezvous and Ford Crown Vics. Most of the dancers were familiar from the previous night. One face caught him off-guard: a man he had only seen in mug shots on fleeting television news broadcasts. Damon Dreyer hopped out of the passenger side of a Cadillac Escalade carrying a brown-leather briefcase and sauntered into the recreation center with all the confidence of a Sun City resident.

A moment later, Claire tapped him on the shoulder and he jumped half a foot in the air.

"You okay?"

"Not really, no. Stand behind me."

"What's going on?"

"I'm not sure yet. See that black Cadillac?"

"How could I miss it?" she asked sarcastically.

"Don't let the occupants see you."

Her eyes widened and she stepped fully behind Milo. "Why?" she asked in a low, nervous voice.

"I think I just saw Dreyer walk into the hall."

"No. That can't be right. Why would he be here?"

"That's what I'm worried about."

"Who do you think is in the car?"

"Could be anyone – Santos, someone higher up the food chain...maybe even that guy Orton wants to take down."

They waited, watching the door. "Maybe he's not coming back out," Claire whispered. "Maybe he's here to see his grandparents dance or something."

"He had a briefcase with him. It could have had anything in it. Maybe a gun."

"You think he's here for me."

"It's a possibility." He reached back and offered his hand. She took it with both of hers. "Don't worry. I'll protect you. Just stay behind me. We need to get to one of our cars. Mine's on the far side of theirs, though. Where is yours?"

"About fifty yards behind us."

He nodded. "That's where we're going. I'm so sorry I put you at risk—"

"Look!" she said, squeezing his hand. "Isn't that him leaving?"

Milo focused on the emaciated body of Damon Dreyer loping toward the Escalade, sans briefcase. As soon as the Cadillac pulled out of the parking lot, he slumped against the side of the building. He felt a couple of beads of sweat congeal and gain enough weight to roll down his forehead.

Claire pulled a pack of tissues from her purse and handed them to him. "You said he had a briefcase."

"He did."

"What did he do with it?"

"I'm not sure."

She laughed nervously. "Why would they try to kill me now? They already hung the jury once – they must know they could do it again."

"I just can't believe that this is a coincidence. What are the odds? They must be after you."

"They don't know who you are," Claire reasoned. "Why don't you go inside and see if you can spot the briefcase."

"Will you be okay out here?"

"I'll be fine."

"Why don't you wait in your car? Just to be safe."

She reluctantly turned and walked to her car. Milo watched her until she was safely inside before entering. Inside the hall, couples were just squaring up for lessons. He walked the far side of the room, carefully scanning the possessions left behind while their owners prepared to dance. There wasn't much: a few purses, a couple of books, and someone's gym bag spread across two seats near the stage. Hoping that Vaughn Wagner had long since forgotten what he looked like, he chanced a walk in front of the stage. There, at Vaughn's feet, was a brown-leather briefcase. The wheels in Milo's brain whirred and clicked like a computer trying to process a huge file with too little RAM available. He froze and stared. Vaughn walked to the foot of the stage and, muting the microphone, asked, "Are you okay?"

He pulled his eyes from the case and plastered on a smile. "Yeah. Fine. Sorry. Just lost in thought."

Vaughn gave him a puzzled look before asking, "Have we met?"

"I was here last night."

"Of course! In the back with the tall blonde, right?"

"Yeah. Good memory."

Vaughn tapped the side of his head. "Requirement of the job." With a wink, he straightened and, turning on the microphone again, said, "Let's start with a review of last night's moves. Circle left!"

The six groups began circling. Milo, now certain that Claire was in no danger, walked swiftly out to her car and knocked on her window.

She jumped, looked up with a panicked expression, and rolled down her window. "All clear?"

"All clear. Let's get inside or we'll miss the lesson."

"You're sure?"

"One hundred percent."

She smiled with relief and stepped out of her makeshift armor, closing the door behind her. "Great. Let's go."

The second night of lessons flew by. Milo found that the more Claire enjoyed herself, the more fun he had as well. During a break, they walked over to investigate a table full of flyers for the various square-dancing clubs around the valley.

She turned to him and said, "I think I might like to join a club after these classes. What do you think?"

He picked up a flyer for a club called Valley Singles. "Here's one for single dancers."

She frowned. "It's in Mesa."

He put it down. "Yeah, that would be a bit of a drive."

"Maybe if I had a regular partner..."

"That would probably be better. You could find a club that met closer to home. I haven't noticed – have you seen any other singles here?"

She was staring at him, one eyebrow arched. "Um, no, not really."

Vaughn called out, "Square up!" and the conversation was dropped.

At the end of the night, Milo again lingered at the back of the hall, feigning deep conversation with Claire. Sitting down so that he could see Vaughn, he told her, "Just talk about anything, okay?"

"I'm having a really good time with you."

"Mmm hmm," he said, staring past her at the line of old men patiently waiting for their moment in front of Vaughn. The briefcase was gone – Milo had noticed that after the intermission. He cursed his stupidity at not keeping an eye on the caller the whole night. Again, the men appeared to be tipping Vaughn; tonight, though, Vaughn was handing each man something the size and shape of an envelope.

"When I was in Oklahoma..." She continued talking, but Milo couldn't focus on her words.

Howard was walking toward the exit, a bounce in his step and a tune on his lips. When he saw Milo watching him, he gave a jaunty salute. "See you and the missus tomorrow night!"

"Wait," Milo said, but Howard's hearing aids must have been due for some fresh batteries – he didn't even hesitate.

"I think Vaughn's a dealer, Claire," he said under his breath.

"Isn't that why we're watching him? Because he's selling meds?"

"Yeah, but I think I had the product wrong."

She frowned. "Not Viagra?"

167

"Not even Cialis."

"What is it then?"

"I'm not sure yet, but I've got an idea."

Milo and Sondra were the first patrons in the Brass Monkey the next day. Sondra, fresh from what she was certain would prove to be a lead-winning audition, practically floated into the bar. "Sax, my darling, you remember Milo."

"Afternoon," he nodded warily, pulling himself to his full height.

"I'm sorry about the other day, Sax. I shouldn't have made a scene."

"You're right."

Milo cleared his throat. "Sondra tells me you're an ex-cop."

"Yeah?"

"We've got something in common."

"You were a cop?" Sax ran a skeptical eye over him.

"Not exactly. Border Patrol."

"No offense, Milo, but you don't look the part."

He grimaced. "In Minnesota."

Sax unsuccessfully suppressed a smile. "That I believe."

"Look, I've got a lead on something and I need some investigative assistance."

"Sorry, can't help you. I'm a bartender now." He slung a dishtowel over his shoulder for emphasis.

"You're telling me you didn't get a charge out of helping Sondra track down Claire?"

He picked up a dry glass from the dish drainer and began polishing it with the rag. "How'd the auditions go?" he asked Sondra, pointedly turning his back on Milo.

"Fantastic!" she gushed. "I nailed it, Sax. There's no way..." She caught Milo's glare and smiled apologetically at him. "Milo could really use a good detective on this with him."

Sax sighed irritably. "What is it you think I can do?"

"You ever hear anything about the drug trade around Sun City?"

He shrugged. "A little. A fair portion of the newer residents are old hippies who still enjoy a joint now and then."

"You okay with that?"

"Live and let live, I say."

168

This was going to be harder than Milo realized. He sat down on a barstool. "Do you know where they get their supply?"

"This is Phoenix, man. Most of 'em probably buy it in Mexico." Milo stared at Sax until the muscular bartender shifted uncomfortably. "Look, I may have been a cop, but I'm no rat."

"How long were you on the force?"

"Thirty years."

"You ever have a guy you knew was guilty walk?"

"Name a cop who hasn't." The longer they talked shop, the straighter Sax stood. Any vestige of homosexual mannerisms disappeared behind his lifelong law-enforcement façade.

"Mine was a Canadian who crossed the border three or four times a month. He claimed to be an entertainer, but I'd never heard of him. He was always headed for senior citizen hotspots – Florida, Arizona, Southern California, Texas. I studied his patterns for several months. Finally, I thought I had enough to hold him. I was sure – I mean, one-hundred percent sure – that he was smuggling prescription meds into the States."

Sax let out a single loud note of a laugh. "Seems kind of minor, to tell you the truth."

"I know, it's not as glamorous as busting a guy with ten kilos of coke, but it was big – especially for International Falls."

Sax nodded thoughtfully. "So what happened?"

"I detained him and had his vehicle searched. It turned out the guy was a square-dance caller. My men turned his car inside out, but they couldn't find anything. I had to resort to banning him because he was working in the U.S. illegally."

"You could do that?"

"Yeah...sort of. The ban didn't hold up at appeal and my boss asked for my badge."

"Hmm. That's crap. But what's it got to do with me or the local drug trade?"

"Vaughn Wagner's the one that got away."

"You mean that little Canuck who's been drinking here the last two nights?" Sax asked.

"The very same," Sondra answered.

Sax leaned against the bar, resting his chin on his palm. "He's a big talker and obviously thinks he's hot shit, but I doubt he's a drug dealer. He just doesn't look the part."

"That's what makes him so perfect!" Sondra enthused. "He's got to be an extremely talented actor to pull off this scam."

"But I thought you said he dealt in prescription meds," Sax objected.

"I was wrong. I don't know how it works, exactly, but I have reason to believe he's selling marijuana supplied by a local cartel." Milo told Sax about seeing Damon Dreyer at the recreation center. "If I'd realized I was witnessing a drug drop-off and not a potential hit, I would have cornered Dreyer right then."

"What's Dreyer doing out of jail? Aren't they holding him for re-trial?" Sax's towel and glass were abandoned now, pushed off to the side.

"Guy must have made bail. Probably with the help of Wagner's supplier, if I had to guess."

"How are we going to get him?" Sax asked.

Milo's next stop after the Brass Monkey was Brian's office. When he was in the parking lot, he called Brian's cell phone.

"Dad! Is everything okay?"

They hadn't spoken since the day Brian told Milo he didn't want to fix their relationship. Milo swallowed hard at the sound of his only child's voice. "I'm in the parking lot, son. Have you got a minute?"

Brian hesitated. "I was just getting ready to head out for lunch. Is this important?"

"Yes, I think so. I need your help."

"I'll be right down."

A few minutes later, his son exited the building, his suit jacket folded neatly over his arm. Milo beeped the horn and Brian turned toward the car. Opening the back door, he dropped his coat on the rear seat, and then stepped to the front door and pulled it open. "You look good, Dad. Where have you been lately?"

"Keeping myself busy. How are Marla and the children?"

"Fine. Alice Marie had a good time at the play a while back." Milo looked away from the accusing glare Brian shot him. "She misses you."

"The last few weeks have been complicated. I'll call Marla and set up a zoo date for Alice Marie and me."

"Listen, Dad, I've been meaning to apologize. Marla says I was too harsh with you—"

"No, no. You were right. I wasn't around for you when you were a kid. It's ridiculous for me to expect you to want me around now."

Brian was staring longingly at his office building. A few of his coworkers exited and walked together to a car on the opposite side of the lot. "What's this visit about?"

"I need your professional advice. I think I've identified a drug dealer."

"Where?"

"He's dealing out of a Sun City recreation center."

Brian laughed. "Have you been buying from him?"

"No!" Milo said indignantly.

"Dad, Sun City isn't exactly the crime capital of Arizona."

"Why is it that young people always think their generation invented vice?"

"I'm sorry. Go on."

"The guy is using his cover as a square-dance caller to sell drugs to old people."

"Wait. Is this that poor guy you persecuted up in Minnesota?"

"It's not persecution if the guy's dirty."

"Dad. I know how frustrating it can be to think you know something—"

"Just tell me – can I call you when I have the proof?"

"It would have to be very convincing."

"You know about the Combs murder?"

"That East Valley farmer and his wife who were attacked by the drug dealers?"

"Yeah, that's the case. I think I can tie the murderers to Vaughn Wagner."

"Jesus, Dad...I hope you're wrong." Brian shook his head. "I hope to hell that this is all in your imagination. But call me if you need backup." Brian reached into the back seat and retrieved his jacket before stepping out of the car. "Be careful."

Milo watched as Brian jogged to the car that was waiting for him.

He called Claire and got A.D.A. Orton's phone number. His secretary told Milo he was in court all afternoon. Milo left a message asking the attorney to call him. With nothing left to do but wait, he headed back to Sun City.

Wild Life

Except for Me and My Monkey

He arrived at the recreation center even earlier than before, this time pulling into the parking lot at six o'clock. Claire pulled in behind him, right on schedule. He walked to her car and opened the door, giving her a quick hug as she stepped out. In her ear, he said, "You know what you have to do, right?"

"Yeah, I've got it."

"Howard and Rhonda were just getting out of their car when I got here. Let's go find them."

They walked into the hall arm in arm, doing their best impression of a happily married couple. Howard and Rhonda took the bait, approaching them immediately.

"How'ya doin'?" Howard said, giving Milo a hearty slap on the back. "We're so glad you keep coming back for more! We need young folks like you to help keep the traditions alive."

Rhonda clasped Claire's hand affectionately. "You remind me of myself when I was younger. You're going to look great in a square-dance dress."

Claire put an arm around the older woman's shoulders and moved her away from Milo and Howard. As they went, Milo overheard her ask, "Where can I buy a dress?"

"May I ask you a question, Howard?" Milo asked, leading the older man toward the chairs that lined the dance floor.

"Let me guess," the old man said, putting his fingers to his temples like a bad psychic act. "You want to know how to keep the spark in the bedroom with your pretty wife." He let out a lecherous laugh. Milo attempted to mask his discomfort and laughed along.

"Actually, I was thinking today about how relaxed you are. There are days when I get so wound up with tension that I just want to hit something, you know what I mean? I used to get a break – I got to go to work for sixty hours a week and get away from the house. Now I'm just going nuts. I don't know if retirement was such a good idea."

Howard backed away and gave him the once-over. "What did you do for a living?"

Sensing the truth was the wrong answer, he said, "I was an accountant. I love numbers. I find them very soothing."

Howard nodded sympathetically. "I understand completely. I was a teacher for thirty years. There's something simple about dealing with other people's children."

"Really?"

"Oh, yeah. So much easier than dealing with your own. I pretty much left our kids in Rhonda's capable hands. Of course, she's never really forgiven me for that." He tapped a finger alongside his nose. "But I have my ways of mellowing her out."

"How's that?"

"I like to bake."

Milo smiled, confident in the turn the conversation was taking. "How's that help?"

"Rhonda loves brownies. Especially mine." He winked conspiratorially.

"You drug her?" Milo couldn't keep the incredulity out of his voice.

Howard looked at him like he had just fallen off the turnip truck. "No. I add an extra helping of Dutch cocoa to the batter. She doesn't know the secret, so she's extra nice to me when the brownies run out. The secret is to keep 'em wanting more."

Milo's shoulders dropped a bit, defeated. "I'll try that," he said, scanning the room for Claire. She was checking out the club fliers again, this time with Rhonda's help.

"Why would I waste a dime bag on her?" Howard muttered, shaking his head.

Milo thought he had misheard. "What was that?" he asked.

"Your hearing aid on the fritz, Milo? Need a battery?" He pulled his keychain from his pocket, the small container of batteries dangling off it.

"No, thank you. I don't wear hearing aids. What—?"

"Maybe you should look into it," Howard said, cutting him off. "I thought Rhonda muttered all the time – turns out, my hearing was seriously damaged from years of sitting too close to the marching band during football games."

"They can tell that from a hearing test?"

Howard laughed. "Heck, no! That's just a guess. I was good friends with the band teacher. I did more than my share of chaperone duty for him."

Milo decided to stop hedging around the subject. "Do you know where I could get my hands on some weed?"

Howard eyed him warily. "Afraid not. My dealer's pretty particular."

The music started and Vaughn Wagner called out, "Square up!"

The conversation was over, but Milo hoped Sondra would have better results.

Sondra was in character before Vaughn walked through the door that night, sitting at the bar wearing a red dress that Sax told her made her look like Norma Desmond. Sondra, who was a fan of the movie for reasons having more to do with the male lead than the film's quality, was flattered. Deciding that her character was more of a gin-and-tonic girl, she ordered one from Sax, who gave her a strange look. "You ever have one of those before, Sondra?"

"Please, Sax. Tonight, my name's Norma."

"Okay, Norma, but you know this guy has no idea who you are."

She straightened her back and pushed out her chest. "He will soon," she said in her best Mae West.

He shrugged, threw the ever-present bar towel over his shoulder, and went to make her drink. Sondra crossed her legs alluringly and wished Arizona allowed her to smoke in the bar. She believed that Norma would smoke, but some things couldn't be helped.

She glanced at the television and saw that the nine-o'clock news had started. As Sax slid the drink toward her, the short Canadian in cowboy boots walked in and headed for the booth he had claimed as his own a few nights earlier, ordering his drink as he passed the bar with a cursory "Usual" and a finger point. The guy didn't seem to have noticed Sondra at all, despite her attempted come-hither pose.

She sighed, slumping just a little and rolling her eyes at Sax.

He walked back to her. "What's the plan?"

"Bring his drink to me. I'll deliver it."

"You got it."

Sax quickly poured a seven and seven and carried it back to Sondra, who slid off the barstool and balanced on her sexiest high heels, thanking the gods for her agelessly sexy legs.

"Good luck."

"Thanks, but with all this, who needs luck?" She gave him her most confident smile and tottered across the floor, her drink in one hand and his in the other. Sliding into the booth across from him, she set his glass down and asked in a sultry voice, "Mind if I join you?"

"Actually, I do," he answered without looking up. "I'm expecting someone."

"Are you sure you're not expecting me?"

He raised his eyes and a slow half-smile crinkled one side of his face. "Perhaps I am," he conceded. "Vaughn Wagner. And you are?"

"Just call me Norma." She sipped her drink and stifled a choke.

"You okay?"

"The drink's a little strong tonight."

"I'm surprised. The bartender doesn't look like the generous type."

"He probably got distracted while pouring."

"If he was looking at you, I can see how."

She swallowed a laugh. "So, what do you do, Vaughn?"

"I'm an entertainer."

"A country singer? I like the cowboy boots, by the way." She left her lips slightly parted with the bottom one pushed out just a bit. Fanny's father, that old-Hollywood star, had once told her it was her most attractive expression – a cross between innocence and wanton lust that the average man was powerless to resist.

"Sort of," he answered. "I'm a square-dance caller."

"How fascinating!" she purred, flashing her eyes at him. Beneath the table, she slipped a shoe off and began gingerly seeking out one of his legs to caress with her stocking-clad foot. As soon as she found it, his eyes widened in surprise. "How long are you in town, Vaughn?"

"Um..." He cleared his throat. "Just until Sunday, actually."

She smiled. "That's plenty of time for us to get to know each other, don't you think?"

Vaughn's eyes shifted away from her and toward the entrance. "I'm afraid I really am waiting for someone, and he's here now."

She swiveled her head and saw a distinguished old man with a cane walking toward the table. "Of course," she purred. "Maybe we could continue this tomorrow night?"

"That would be excellent."

The older man was at the table now. "Good evening, Vaughn. I see you have company. I'm sorry to interrupt."

"That's fine. I was just leaving." She retracted her foot and pushed it into her shoe, stretching one finger down to pull the strap into place.

"Solomon Parr, my dear," the older gentleman said, lifting her free hand to his lips. "Sol, to my friends. And you are?"

"Norma."

His eyes narrowed quizzically. "I wouldn't have pegged you for a Norma. You look more like a Naomi."

She attempted to laugh but it came out more like a giggle.

"Charming, my dear. Absolutely charming. Thank you for allowing me to interrupt your...date?"

"Not at all, Mr. Parr," Vaughn answered. "We were just getting acquainted."

Sondra pushed herself out of the booth and, with Sol's help, steadied herself in an upright position. Once she stood and faced the door, she could see that another man had entered the bar at the same time: a beefy Mexican with silver-tipped cowboy boots and a humorless expression. He stood not far from the entrance, his hands clasped in front of him. Something about him struck her as familiar and terrifying at the same time. Turning back to Vaughn, she said, "I'll see you tomorrow." She picked up her drink and tottered back to her barstool.

"How'd it go?" Sax asked.

"Could have been better. He was waiting for that guy to show."

"From this angle it looked like he was interested."

"I thought maybe, but I'm not certain."

"I guess you won't be getting the evidence tonight."

"No, it doesn't look like it."

"Who do you suppose that guy is?"

"Said his name was Solomon Parr."

Sax's eyes widened. "That's Sol Parr?"

"Didn't I just say that?"

"Sondra – that guy is supposed to be dead."

"I think that would be news to him. Who is he?"

"He was the head of a massive smuggling empire back east before he went missing a few years ago. Everyone in Jersey and New York suspected he'd been Hoffa'ed."

"Maybe he just retired."

"If that's the case, he must have decided the leisurely life wasn't for him. I bet he's Vaughn's supplier."

Milo woke up as soon as he heard the carport door open. Stretching, he called out, "Is that you, Sondra?"

"What are you doing up?" she asked as she tottered around the corner in her red dress and heels. Milo thought she looked every bit the vixen he had asked her to be.

"Waiting for you. What happened?"

"My seduction was interrupted."

Milo's face fell.

"Don't worry! I made a date for tomorrow night."

"You're a miracle worker." He grinned from ear to ear. "I'd better get to bed."

"Wait! Don't you want to hear the rest?"

"There's more?"

"You ever heard of someone called Solomon Parr?"

Milo shook his head.

"Well, Sax had. Apparently, he was well known in Jersey before he disappeared a decade or so ago. He ran a huge smuggling ring."

"Okay."

"That's who interrupted Vaughn and me tonight."

Milo slapped a hand against the arm of his recliner. "That's who Orton wants!"

"Orton?"

"The A.D.A. in charge of Claire's case."

"Have you talked to him?"

"Not yet. He was in court all afternoon. I'm hoping he'll call me back tomorrow." He hesitated, frowning. "I'm not sure I want you to pursue this any further, Sondra. This may be more dangerous than I thought. Brian seemed to think—"

"Don't lose your nerve now, Milo. I think you're going to get your man – and after all these years!"

He smiled, deep in thought. "Maybe so." He pushed out of the chair, intending to head to bed. Remembering Sondra's audition the day before, he asked, "Any word on casting yet?"

"Not yet. Bob's supposed to post the list on Saturday morning."

"I've got my fingers crossed for you."

"Thanks, but I think I've got this one in the bag."

When Milo got up the next morning, he knew he was running up against the clock. The lessons were almost over, and he didn't hold out much hope of cornering Howard again tonight. Even if he could, he doubted he would get enough information to go to his son. Brian wasn't going to be easily swayed. He wondered if it was too early to call Orton again. Running his hands back and forth over his scalp, he decided to wait until after breakfast.

He padded to the kitchen, passing Sondra's bedroom door on the way. He could hear her soft snores coming from inside. She was such a night owl; he knew she had been up until at least midnight. If she were anything to go by, the celebrity stereotypes were all true.

He started the coffee and retrieved a bagel from the freezer, popping it in the microwave for a quick defrost. When his cell phone, plugged into a kitchen outlet for a charge, started ringing, he looked at the clock; it was just past eight.

He didn't immediately recognize the phone number and almost let it go to voicemail because of that. After a brief internal debate, he pressed the send button and said, "Hello?"

"Good morning. Paul Orton here. Is this...Mr. Crosby?"

"Yes! Good morning, sir."

"My secretary says you left me a message regarding the Combs murder case."

"Yes, I did. I'm a friend of Claire Combs's."

"Lovely woman. Though she can be a bit...shall we say prickly?"

"An apt description."

"She has been through quite an ordeal, of course."

"Indeed she has."

Orton cleared his throat. "I hate to rush this along, but I've got a number of cases to prepare for—"

"Of course. The reason I called is that I think I have a way to tie Dreyer and Santos to Solomon Parr." The utter silence on the other side of the line told Milo that Orton had muted the call on his end. He waited, smiling at the knowledge that this man recognized the name. Finally, he heard a barely audible click.

"I'm sorry, Mr. Crosby. Could you repeat that?"

"I can tie Mr. Combs's killers to Solomon Parr."

"Who are you, exactly?"

"My name is Milo Crosby and I am a former Border Patrol agent."

"What do you know about Mr. Parr?"

"I know that he was the head of the largest smuggling operation in the country before he disappeared more than a decade ago."

"Fifteen years, to be exact. I think you'd best come in and talk to me. Can you be here by nine?"

"Mr. Crosby?" Paul Orton, a bespectacled young black man, held out his right hand as he approached Milo, who had only just taken a seat in the waiting area.

"Yes, good morning again," Milo answered, meeting the handshake.

"Thank you for coming down so quickly. I've secured a conference room where we can discuss this matter. Just follow me."

Milo fell in behind the man, who was a good three inches taller and much thinner than he was. Once in the room, he found himself in the company of two humorless women as well as the attorney.

"Have a seat, Mr. Crosby. I'd like to introduce Detectives Marshall and Frayne. They're with the organized crime taskforce." They nodded; Milo nodded in reply and sat. "Now, Mr. Crosby—"

"Please call me Milo."

"Milo. May I ask how a former Minnesota Border Patrol agent came across a man like Solomon Parr?" The attorney smiled patronizingly and the detectives both clicked their pens.

Milo tried not to show his uneasiness. "I've been investigating someone—"

"For whom?"

"As a concerned citizen."

"Go on."

"I suspected this person of selling prescription meds from Canada to local senior citizens."

One of the women – Milo thought she was Frayne – swallowed a chuckle with a half-smile. The other one said, "The U.S. government has turned a blind eye to the prescription drug trade, as I'm sure you are aware."

"Only too aware, thank you. But I was wrong." He laid out the rest of the tale for them – the suspected drug drop involving Dreyer and Wagner, the old men queuing up to give the square-dance caller money, and Sondra's encounter with Solomon Parr. By the end, the three of them looked considerably more concerned than they had at the beginning.

"If what you say is true, Milo, we might finally be able to topple Parr's empire." Orton leaned back in his chair, steepling his fingers in front of him.

"What I don't understand is why Parr was presumed dead."

"He cut a deal," Marshall answered. "He told the DEA and the FBI everything he knew and brought about the collapse of a huge organized crime syndicate in New York and Jersey. In exchange – presto! New life."

"Wouldn't he have a new name, too?"

"He did, but apparently it didn't carry enough clout for him," she answered, one eyebrow raised critically.

"Let's cut to the chase, Milo. What are you proposing?" Orton asked, leaning forward.

"This is a one-party-consent state, right?"

"You're going to have your friend tape her conversation?"

"That was my plan."

"This Wagner guy could be dangerous. Are you sure you want to put her in that situation?"

"Before today, no one believed me when I said Wagner was a bad guy. What else could I do?"

"Now we have options. You say Wagner had drugs on him at the square-dance classes?"

"He did on Tuesday night. I don't know about tonight."

"If you're amenable to pointing out the men who gave Wagner money as they leave the dance tonight, we'll pick them up and see if they'll roll on Wagner." This came from Frayne, whose half-smile had long since become a full frown.

"What about Wagner? He's supposed to go back to Canada on Sunday."

"How good of an actress is Sondra?"

Claire showed up at the recreation center right on time that night and found Milo waiting in his usual spot. "So? Any news?"

He looked at her sheepishly. "I've got good news and bad news."

"Uh-oh. What's the bad news?"

"We've taken square-dancing lessons in vain. I don't think we'll be welcome at any of the clubs after tonight."

"Oh, no...really?"

"I'm sorry."

She sighed. "I understand. What's the good news?"

"After tonight, I don't think you'll have to worry about a new trial – at least, not for Dreyer."

"What? Why?"

"If everything works out right, the A.D.A. is going to offer him a deal – he testifies against Wagner and Parr about the drugs and against Santos for the murder, he can plead out to second-degree manslaughter. Orton says he'll recommend the minimum sentence."

"Why would Dreyer do that?"

"Because he has a conscience. He couldn't kill your dog and he tried to help Dorsey."

The knot in her stomach loosened for the first time in more than a year and she smiled.

Milo beamed back at her. "You're so beautiful when you smile."

182

Wild Life

Blushing, she broke eye contact and stared out at the parking lot. "What about the other one?"

"No breaks for Rafe."

"Good. Will there be another trial?"

"Unless he pleads guilty to first-degree murder, yeah."

She nodded. "Justice."

He held out an arm for her. "Shall we dance?"

"I'd love to."

Wild Life

Kiss that Frog

Milo had waited his whole life to have something work out exactly the way it should. His patience was finally rewarded early Friday morning.

Each and every old square dancer, including Howard, readily confessed to buying drugs from Vaughn Wagner. In exchange for their testimony, they each received what amounted to a slap on the wrists and a promise from the cops that they wouldn't call the men's kids.

After a revealing evening in Sondra's company – in more ways than one, as it turned out – Vaughn Wagner was picked up for possession with intent to sell. Citing professional courtesy, Detectives Marshall and Fraynes invited Milo to ride along to witness the arrest. Nothing had given him more pleasure since he realized he had outlived dead Alice, especially when Fraynes led Vaughn Wagner to a waiting police car in a wife-beater and boxers, leaving a smug and fully dressed Sondra standing against the doorjamb with her arms folded over her bosom.

Wagner, scared out of his wits and certain that he was about to end up a prison bitch (he was a small guy, after all), quickly took the deal on the table: finger Solomon Parr as the ringleader and got deportation and permanent expulsion from the United States.

Solomon Parr never saw it coming.

As soon as Claire woke up, she knew that her life was better – she could feel it in the air around her. She bounced out of bed, leaving Taz in a disoriented fog. Reluctantly, he followed her into the living room, where she was already opening the blinds and letting in the morning sunshine. It was a beautiful early autumn day and she was truly glad to be alive. When the phone rang, she answered it with enthusiasm.

"What's got into you?" Beryl asked. "You sound chipper!"

"And it's about time I did, don't you think?" Claire laughed and Taz jumped. She sat down on the sofa and called the pug to her, scratching him behind the ears.

"Did something happen with the case?"

"Unless my friend is very much mistaken, I think I'm done being unhappy."

"You're being cryptic. Explain, please."

Claire's phone beeped. "I've got another call. Hold on, Beryl." Switching calls, she answered, "Hello?"

"Good morning. May I speak with Claire Combs?" a nasally woman asked.

"This is Claire."

"Please hold for Mr. Orton." Easy-listening music filled the line for thirty seconds before the attorney picked up. "Mrs. Combs, I have some good news. Damon Dreyer has flipped – I think we can get Rafael Santos on Murder One."

Claire smiled. It was going to be a great day.

After her success with Vaughn Wagner the night before, Sondra was even more certain of winning the part of Dolly over Mildred Kovich. Determined to celebrate both Milo's victory over Vaughn Wagner and her inevitable casting coup, she planned a dinner celebration. Sitting down at the kitchen table, she formulated a guest list before Milo was out of bed. A quick glance around the house was more than enough to convince her that reservations were in order. After calling the restaurant, she began inviting her guests.

At seven o'clock that evening, the motley assemblage gathered in the courtyard of the upscale seafood restaurant Sondra had designated. No one, not even Brian Crosby or Paul Orton, had the courage to refuse her invitation. Milo, the man of the hour, was the only one who had given Sondra any trouble at all – and that, of course, had been half-hearted at best. Despite his protests, he was secretly pleased to be celebrating this victory.

Alice Marie ran into his arms as soon as she spotted him. "Grampa!" He picked her up, and she wrapped her arms around his neck and squeezed. A moment later, she pulled back and scolded, "Where have you been?"

"Getting the bad guys!"

"Really?"

"Cross my heart."

Her tiny frown deepened as if she doubted him, but soon disappeared. "As long as you promise."

"I do."

"Where's Claire?" she asked, looking around expectantly.

"I don't know if she's coming."

"She is. Sondra told me so."

Sondra, who was within hearing range, gave him a gracious smile and nod.

"Dad," Brian said as he approached from behind.

Milo set his granddaughter down and turned to meet him. "I'm sorry about the other day, Brian. I put you in an awkward pos—"

"No," he said, cutting Milo off. "You don't owe me an apology. I owe you one. Actually, more than one, according to Marla. I know we haven't always been on the same page, but I'd like to fix that...if you'd still like to."

Milo grasped his son with both hands and pulled him into a hug. Choking back tears, he said, "Of course I'd like that." Milo felt his son's arms hesitantly wrap around him; Milo squeezed tighter. The last time he had a hug from Brian was when the boy was nine years old. This didn't fix everything between them, Milo knew, but it was a start.

"Claire!" Alice Marie shouted, running toward her as she came through the brick archway.

Claire bent down and caught the girl in her arms. Milo released his son with a pat on the back and strode through the crowd to get to her. His beige woman was full of color for the first time – like a rose blossoming, he thought. Then he drove the thought away with a roll of his eyes. Who did he think he was, Shakespeare?

When he reached Claire, she set Alice Marie on the ground and wrapped her arms around him, planting a warm, if chaste, kiss on his surprised lips. If the others noticed, they had the good taste to pretend they didn't.

"What was that for?" he asked when she pulled back.

"For bringing me back to life."

Alice Marie, who was still standing next to them, asked, "Like Sleeping Beauty?"

Claire laughed. "Yes. Just like that."

Alice Marie looked up at Milo thoughtfully. "I think it's more like the Princess and the Frog."

"Thanks, kid. You're a real ego booster." Milo joined Claire's laughter.

Wild Life

Sondra slept later than usual the next morning, having indulged in one too many mojitos at the celebratory dinner. Upon leaving her room, she wasn't surprised to find that Milo was already gone for the day. Claire had said something about working in the orangutan house today and Alice Marie had been determined to hold Milo to the promise of another day at the zoo.

Looking at herself in the mirror, she considered cutting up the cucumber in the vegetable drawer and putting slices on her eyes – the bags she was carrying around were big enough for a European vacation. Then she remembered – it was Saturday morning. Bob Kovich had promised the cast list for *Hello, Dolly!* would be posted at nine o'clock sharp.

She slipped into a red-and-white wrap dress she had snatched from the *Scions of Beauty* costume department nearly forty years before, thankful that the figure-flattering garment had come back into style. A pair of matching red strappy sandals made her feel like the movie star she would have been if she had been born two decades earlier. Sunglasses and a white silk scarf completed the look.

She grabbed the keys to her car and headed for the recreation center, cursing the line of golf carts poking along ahead of her. Finally pulling into the lot, she parked haphazardly – if a star couldn't take two spaces, who could? – and walked with confidence and purpose into the building.

She felt the eyes of others on her as she strode through; she straightened her back and pushed out her chest. She remembered this feeling – the adoration of the masses. She had missed it, but now, finally she had it back. At the cast list, she realized that she should have brought her reading glasses. The sunglasses weren't going to cut it. Taking them off, she squinted at the page before her, then backed up a step. When she was certain she had read it right, she deflated ever so slightly.

"Well, shit."

Wild Life

No animals were harmed in the writing of this novel.

Susan Wells Bennett

book two
of the BRASS MONKEY series

Aging actress Sondra Lane hasn't had a good break since the disco era. Now past sixty, all she has to show for her years in Hollywood are a B-movie credit and a vintage red convertible. With no love and no audience, where is the Charmed Life she once believed was her destiny?

Charmed Life
Book Two of
The Brass Monkey Series

By

Susan Wells Bennett

PUBLISHED BY:
Inknbeans Press

Charmed Life

For LeAnne Martinson, who is still my best friend after all
these years.

Charmed Life

Puppet Master

As she watched Mildred Kovich – a goy if ever there was one – warble the part of Dolly Levi in what was clearly going to be a disastrous version of *Hello, Dolly!*, the woman who was born Sarah Lansky seriously regretted changing her name for the first time in more than forty years.

Perhaps, Sondra thought, if she were more obviously Jewish – and maybe a bit more threatening – Bob Kovich would have given her the lead. As it was, he had cast her in a small walk-on part and the unenviable position of understudy to Mildred. Understudy! Sondra's eyes rolled involuntarily every time the hateful word passed through her brain.

"Line!" snapped Mildred. Trussed up as she was in her period corset, her breath control was even more atrocious than usual.

"A widow has to earn a living," Sondra called out from her seat in the third row. Bob sat a few rows behind her, but otherwise, the auditorium was empty. All of the actors – the ones with actual lines – were in the wings or down in the green room, awaiting their cues.

Mildred closed her eyes, put her hands to her temples, and recited, mantra-like, "A widow has to earn a living, a widow has to earn a living, a widow has to earn a living." She took a deep breath and stepped back to her former position. "I mean, I'm racking my brain, trying to think of something that's made me happier, but I just can't come up with a thing, because this is just too wonderful."

The actor playing Horace Vandergelder stepped down off the prop ladder and looped his fingers around his suspenders. "Well, it's all your fault, you know. You put me into this marrying frame of mind with all your introductions and scheming."

"A girl has to make money," Mildred said.

Sondra groaned.

"Wait...that's not right, is it? I don't know why I'm having such a hard time with that line."

"Maybe you need to be widowed," Sondra muttered under her breath. When she heard the seat behind her squeak she flinched away, anticipating a blow. However, Bob paced toward the stage.

Charmed Life

"Millie, we've been hard at this for a few hours now. Maybe we should call it a night."

Sondra glanced at her cell phone for the time: seven-thirty. She was amazed they had stayed in rehearsal this long; normally, the internal curfew alarm of the cast members went off about fifteen minutes before dark.

Mildred smiled at her husband gratefully. "Yes, Bob. Let's go home. You can run lines with me."

"You're doing fine, sweetheart. You've just got a few trouble spots to work out." The lithe man swung himself onto the stage and called out, "Gather up, everyone!"

Though the play featured characters as young as their late teens, the youngest actor among them was a forty-eight-year-old woman; she was only allowed to participate because her husband was age-qualified to live in Sun City. The group, either irritated or simply exhausted, shuffled to the stage with a pitiful lack of enthusiasm.

"We're going to call it a night. Great job, everyone. Remember, the next rehearsal starts tomorrow at four o'clock sharp. We'll be working on the second act."

The group clapped for their director and began shuffling away.

Mildred sneezed and Sondra looked back to see if she might be on the verge of pneumonia. No such luck, though. "Just dust, Sondra," the woman said with a saccharine smile.

Returning an equally sweet smile, Sondra said, "Take care now, Mildred. Wouldn't want you to get sick."

"I'm sure you wouldn't."

As she drove to her favorite bar, Sondra wondered again how she had fallen so low. Parking her beloved red convertible behind the Brass Monkey, she tried again to pinpoint the exact moment when she took a wrong turn on the road of her life.

"Where are you from, sweetheart?" the director asked, pushing his sunglasses down just enough that Sondra could see his eyes. The script lay on the table in front of him and the casting director was already sorting through the other headshots. She had flubbed the audition.

"Nevada." Being from Las Vegas proper held a certain allure to some, but Sondra always sought to downplay her connection. The daughter of a Jewish bookmaker and a former showgirl, she had seen enough of the seedy side of the town to find its bright lights more garish than glistening. She smiled innocently at the director, who was clad in a brown polyester leisure suit, a gaudy gold chain around his neck. He reminded her of the men her father called business associates. Her stomach was turning, but she was a good actress.

"Listen, sweetheart, you're not right for this part. But you might be right for another project we have in the pipeline. I'm having a party tonight for some of the investors, and I'd love to show you off. You free?"

"No, I'm pricy. But I'd love to come to the party."

"Cheeky. I like that in a girl. I'll send my car for you. Just leave your address with my girl out front."

She left the movie lot with a bounce in her step. She had only been in Hollywood a few months, but until a few minutes earlier she had been on the verge of going the way of Peg Entwistle. Every young starlet knew what happened to her: in despair over her lack of success as an actress, she climbed the "H" in the Hollywoodland sign and jumped to her death. Ironically, a letter asking her to star in a movie about a suicidal young woman arrived at her home the next day. When a girl was down, others were always quick to remind her not to give up – she didn't want to be the next Peg Entwistle!

"I'm home!" Sondra called as she entered the apartment she shared with another young actress.

"How did it go?" Cindy bopped out of the kitchen, a bottle of Pepsi in her hand.

"Not too bad. You got another one of those?" she asked, pointing to the bottle.

"Sure. Help yourself."

Sondra went to the kitchen and pulled a cold soda from the fridge.

"What was the part?"

"Nothing special. A screamer for a horror flick."

Cindy pulled a disgusted face. "I hate those things. And they're always looking for a blonde. I could have told you that you didn't have a chance."

Sondra shrugged and fell into the worn-out sofa, one leg thrown over the arm. "Got a party invite out of it," she said nonchalantly.

"What? From whom?" Her friend moved to the edge of her seat. "And can you bring a friend?"

"A party invitation. From George Miller, the director. And no, I don't think so."

"George Miller?" Cindy's eyes widened. "He's directing a slasher flick?"

"Yeah. Why?"

"Just seems like kind of a comedown."

"From what?"

"He wrote that sitcom in the fifties – you know, the one with that actress."

"Too vague, Cindy. I need more than that."

"The one about a widowed mother living with her parents. *That Donnelly Woman.*"

"Doesn't sound funny."

"Everyone says it was way ahead of its time. The network only gave it two seasons."

"George Miller's a fairly common name. Maybe he's a different guy."

"Could be, I guess. Where's he taking you?"

"He didn't say. Apparently, it's a gathering for a new project. He says I'd be perfect for the lead female."

"Just be careful," Cindy smirked. "Make sure he didn't say 'laid female.'"

Sondra rolled her eyes. "I need to get ready. What should I wear?"

"What about that pageant dress in your closet?"

"Gosh, I don't know. It's three years old and I haven't worn it since Miss Nevada 1970."

"You're a starving actress these days, Sondra. If anything, it's going to be too big."

She laughed and chugged the remainder of her soda. "Not if I keep drinking these!"

"But that's all you drink. And we haven't had more than a box of macaroni between us in weeks."

The phone rang. "I'll get it," she said, pushing off the sofa.

Cindy waved her away. "No. You get ready. I'll field the fans."

"Okay."

She heard Cindy say, "Hello?" as she closed the door to the bedroom. Stripping down to her underwear, she did a quick scan of her body. She didn't think she looked any thinner. Her curled red hair made her feel like a female version of Bozo the Clown – Bozette. She laughed at herself. Digging in her dresser drawer, she located a matching set of black underwear and ditched the mismatched set she had worn to the audition. Wearing mismatched or old underwear was a trick she had picked up from Cindy, who believed doing this would keep her off the casting couch. "I want to be discovered for my acting talent," she told Sondra, "not my performance art." Tonight, though, Sondra thought she might consider a little "performance art" if the occasion arose.

Pulling the golden-yellow spaghetti-strap evening gown over her head, she was shocked to discover that it was, in fact, a size too large. It hung on her limply instead of clinging to her curves. "Cindy!"

"Yeah?" Her friend poked her head around the corner. "Oh, no. That's not good at all."

"What am I going to do?"

"Don't worry – that dress is probably too formal anyway."

"You think so?"

"What did Mr. Miller say, exactly?"

"That it's a party for people involved in a new project."

"He didn't say where it would be?"

"No. Just that a car would pick me up."

Cindy crossed an arm over her chest and tapped her pouting lips with one finger. "What about that green-and-white checked mini-dress you brought home last week?"

"The one I bought at the Goodwill?" Sondra frowned.

"This is Hollywood, chickie. Just because you found it at Goodwill doesn't mean it's not perfect. What do you think the high and mighty of this town do when they run out of closet space?"

"So, you're saying that dress may have been Natalie Wood's?"

She shrugged. "Maybe not. I think I saw Goldie Hawn wear something like it on Laugh-In, though."

"I don't know if that's a good thing."

"Trust me – wear the mini-dress. What time is the car coming?"

"Six."

"What about your hair?"

With Cindy's help, she looked chic by the time the car arrived. When she stepped out in front of the modern white chateau in the Hollywood hills, she was glad she decided against the yellow chiffon number. The few people who were making their way up the drive were wearing leisure suits and subdued polyester dresses.

On the other side of the open front door, a crowd was already gathering in the spacious but low-ceilinged living area. Three stairs led down to a conversation pit where she spotted George Miller with each arm around a beautiful young woman. When he looked up, he smiled and beckoned her in. "Sondra, come here. I'd like to introduce you to a few of my friends."

She took the steps carefully, doing her best to show her legs to full advantage. She felt the appreciative eyes of a few of the men and gave them her best come-hither glance. One of them looked familiar – someone famous, she was certain.

"Gentlemen," Mr. Miller said, "This is Sondra Lane. She is the perfect Julia Stark."

"I don't know, Bud," piped up one of the men. "I didn't picture Julia as a redhead."

"Are you kidding? Of course she's a redhead! What else could she be?"

"I agree with Mick, Bud," the older, vaguely famous one said. "She's supposed to be an archeologist. Shouldn't she have serious hair? Brown or black?"

"Are you saying my hair is a joke?" she blurted, self-consciously reaching up to pat the locks Cindy had spent the last two hours straightening.

"Forgive me, my dear," the man said. "You are lovely, but you don't look like an archeologist to me."

She stared at him a second too long, still trying to place him.

He held out a hand to her. "Bill."

She put her hand in his and he brushed it against his lips in an old-fashioned genteel gesture. "Sondra Lane."

"So I gathered. Now, if you'll excuse us, we'd like to finish up our business so that we can all enjoy the party."

Turning to look toward her benefactor, she saw him give her a little head nod to indicate she should step out of the conversation pit.

If she had driven herself that night, her life might have turned out differently, Sondra thought as she slammed the door of her old car and stalked toward the Brass Monkey. Not having a ride, she had instead discovered the wonders of the whiskey sour. The next morning, she found herself wrapped in a black satin sheet, her matching bra and panties discarded. Next to her lay the equally exposed and snoring "Bud" Miller. She skipped right over the casting couch and into the director's house. In that moment, she realized that while Cindy's method kept her pure, it also kept her poor. Cindy was looking for a new roommate before the month was out.

She walked directly to her preferred stool toward the far end of the bar. A moment later, a whiskey sour slid into her hand.

"How were rehearsals?" Sax asked. The muscular bartender was already in his late sixties, but you couldn't tell it by his body. If he weren't gay, Sondra would have already snapped him up.

"Mildred sucks as Dolly." She raised the drink to her lips and inhaled it.

"Bob said she was improving."

"Bob's an idiot."

"Don't, okay? He's a good guy."

"Why couldn't he have just given me the part? I even gave him a good excuse to give it to me," she whined.

"Blackmail isn't a good excuse."

She jutted out her chin. "He shouldn't be cheating on Mildred. Especially not with you."

He rolled his eyes and leaned his arms against the bar, bringing his face down to her level. "You're not exactly the leader of the moral majority."

"I never cheated on anyone. And, believe me, I was in Mildred's shoes way more than I like to think about."

"Then tell her."

"What's the point? I won't get the role and the rest of the cast will suffer."

"What do you mean by that?"

"You've never done a play, have you?"

"Do I look like an actor?"

"Yeah, actually you do." She sucked down the rest of her drink. "Do you know how many actors have parental issues? Most of them. And the director is like a daddy figure to everyone on that stage."

"These are old people, Sondra, not children."

"Doesn't matter. An actor is an actor is an actor. They never really grow up."

"What about you?"

"Who says I'm grown up? I'm still out there, seeking the director's approval, hungering for the crowd's applause. An actor—"

"Is an actor," Sax finished.

"Right. So I'll wait. I'll tell her after the *Hello, Dolly!* run."

The door swung open and Bob Kovich entered the bar, settling at the opposite end. Sax lit up.

"You really like him, don't you?"

"Yeah," he admitted. "Probably more than I should." He tossed his bar towel over his shoulder and sauntered to the other end, leaving Sondra to stew over her drink.

As she watched the two men covertly flirt with one another, she settled her cheek against her palm. She wondered if anyone ever got more than one shot at true love. If they didn't, she was destined to spend the rest of her life alone. She took heart in the knowledge that her roommate's girlfriend, Claire Combs, had found true love twice. Claire was happily married for more than twenty years before her husband died. Now, she and Milo mooned around like teenagers who just learned how to kiss. More than once, she had walked in and found them necking on the sofa. In fact, she was hanging around the bar just so that she wouldn't catch them making out tonight.

She lifted the empty glass to her lips and attempted to separate the last drops of alcohol from the ice cubes.

Charmed Life

Dudes

Holding his coffee cup in one hand and the saucer in the other, Sax watched as Bob let himself out the front gate of his patio home the next morning. His black-silk kimono hung open, revealing a pair of black briefs, but Sax wasn't worried about the neighbors seeing him – he had chosen the walled-in home specifically because his privacy was important to him. From his picture window, he could see only his Asian-inspired front garden and the six-foot wall that surrounded it. Even the gate was obscured by a sculpted bush, which was trimmed to resemble a Ming vase.

Turning away from the window, he experienced that nagging sensation of dissatisfaction with his life. He had always been a fan of Asian culture, despite his decidedly Anglo-Saxon heritage. He was certain that a mix-up had occurred in the assignment of his soul; somewhere in Asia, a petite grandmother had spent her life wishing she could play football.

Sax had spent much of his life claiming he was married to his job – he was a New Jersey cop – while simultaneously cheating on his spouse with a string of random and equally unfaithful husbands. When he was fifty-five, one of the jilted spouses caught up with him while he was on the job, leading to his retirement back in the mid-nineties. At the time, he was devastated – being a cop was the only thing he thought he knew how to be. His partner – one of the few who had always known Sax's predilections – suggested a fresh start was in order.

He used his nest egg to move not to San Francisco, which was too pricy in his estimation, but to Arizona – Sun City, to be exact. He had heard rumors of a growing gay scene in the desert and decided that a little sun might be just the right thing for him.

He rented a former restaurant housed in the far end of a decent strip mall on the edge of the retirement community, moved a four-foot-tall simian statue inside, and named the place after it. For the first few weeks, he sat in the bar alone, wondering what kind of disaster he had created for himself. But then the long, hot summer ended and the old men who had once frequented the restaurant he replaced returned from their summer homes in places like Minnesota and Kansas and decided to give the bar a try. More than ten years had passed, and now he had a respectable crowd no matter what season or night.

It was already after eight in the morning. Normally, Sax would have been at the gym pumping iron by six o'clock; his unexpected houseguest had altered his schedule. Bob rarely stayed the night. He was married, after all, and the neighbors were prone to talk about old men who didn't find their way home before sunset. Mildred, however, had insisted that Bob go out to the bar. Later, when he decided to go home with Sax, he sent Mildred a text message saying he was having a nightcap at Sax's house. At least, that was what Bob had said the night before.

Sax didn't like to pry into the particulars of their relationship. Back in Jersey, he never worried about what the wives thought their husbands were up to – he didn't see it as his problem. Now, he worried, guilt-ridden and fearful.

"Sax, buddy, there's a woman waiting at the desk for you," his partner called out as he entered the locker room.

"What's she look like?" Sax asked.

"Why?"

"I need to know if I should freshen up first." His comment drew laughs and catcalls from the other guys getting ready for their shifts, and Sax received a couple high-fives from the men closest to him.

"She looks married, judging by the rock on her finger. Don't get no ideas." Ken was always good about playing along with Sax's "manly" innuendoes. Sax knew he was lucky to have such an understanding buddy on the force.

"Got it. No cologne. But if she jumps me anyway, how could her husband blame me?"

More laughs followed him out to the desk. The officer behind it pointed to a petite, homely brunette sitting in the waiting area, her purse held snugly against her body. She didn't look familiar to Sax, who walked right up to her. "Ma'am? I'm Officer Ridley. May I help you?"

She didn't look up right away. Sax later remembered how her body tensed. "My husband is cheating on me."

"Ma'am, I'm afraid that's not a police matter. You need to see an attorney."

He backed up a step when her eyes met his, their intensity scorching him. "My husband is cheating on me," she repeated, "with you." Her hand slipped into the purse in her lap.

Sax's years of training deserted him; his hand didn't even move to his holster as she pulled out the gun. His partner later told him the desk sergeant saw the gun a second before she pulled the trigger. The sergeant's bullet took her down neatly – the coroner said she was dead before she hit the floor.

The bullet from her gun tore through him, just missing his heart and his left lung. An inch difference in any direction and he would have been dead, according to the surgeon who saved his life. Sax wished she hadn't missed.

Even as the ambulance pulled away with Sax, the detectives were starting their investigation. Before Sax was out of surgery, the whole department knew his secret. One hesitation had cost him his life.

The gym was full of women – young and old – by the time Sax got there that morning. Usually, the ladies stuck pretty close to the cardio machines, though there were always a couple who thought they should be doing weight training, too. In his years in Sun City, he had seen a shifting demographic – one that he had been on the cusp of. People used to think of Sun City as God's waiting room; now, though, most of the younger residents were actively working at extending their lives. He figured the trend was an excellent indicator of future property values. Even though he had no intention of leaving his private oasis, it was nice to know that he wouldn't lose money on it if he were forced to leave.

"Sax! Buddy! I was starting to worry about you," the desk clerk exclaimed as he came through the door. "You're late."

"Overslept. I had a late night," he answered as he scanned his card.

"Trouble kicking the stragglers to the curb?" All of the gym workers knew that he owned the bar at the end of the strip mall; some of them were even regulars, though they tended to drink tonic water or, worse, light beer. Sax wouldn't even stock the stuff if the gym rats weren't around.

"Something like that." He headed for the weights, soaking up the sweat from his jog with his gym towel as he walked. If it were still summer, he wouldn't have attempted the jog after eight o'clock in the morning. As it was, he worried that he wouldn't have time to jog home and shower before the Brass Monkey's opening time. He kept an extra set of clothes at the bar for just such an emergency, though he would miss the second half of his cardio routine. Maybe he would run home after closing – the streets were deserted at night, and he could cut across the golf course. On the other hand, he thought, Sondra or Bob would probably be around to give him a lift if he needed one.

"Sax!" someone called from the vicinity of the exercise bikes.

In his peripheral vision, he saw Sondra flagging him down. He hesitated for less than a second before continuing his route to the weights.

"Sax, you fairy queen! I know you saw me!" she shouted. Everyone under forty giggled and looked away; everyone over forty inhaled sharply and stared at Sondra, which only encouraged her bad behavior. She was incorrigible. If she had been raised Catholic, she would have spent her childhood in the mother superior's office.

Sax stopped and turned to look at her. "What?"

"Come here, will you?"

He tapped his watch. "I'm running late. No time!"

By now, the whole gym was watching this interaction like a tennis match.

"Please!" she wheedled.

The crowd stared at him, awaiting his volley. Instead, he tanked the match and walked toward her; the spectators returned to their regularly scheduled workouts. Coming to a full stop in front of her bike, he asked irritably, "What?" Then he remembered he might want a ride tonight; he added a smile.

"Geez. What's put you in such a foul mood? You were fine when I left last night."

"Personal stuff."

She shrugged and waved it away. "We're friends, right? You can tell me anything."

"I'm not a real sharer."

"I've noticed."

"What did you need?" he asked again.

"I was hoping you could put me up for tonight."

"Why? Haven't you got a perfectly good bedroom of your very own at Milo's?"

"His granddaughter is coming to stay the night," she explained.

"I thought you and Alice Marie had put your animosity behind you." Milo's granddaughter hadn't warmed to Sondra initially, but Sax new she had come around a bit since.

"We have, but Claire is going to be there, too. The three of them are taking a road trip this weekend. I thought it would be nice if Alice Marie had an actual bed to sleep in so that she's not too cranky on the road tomorrow."

"That's remarkably thoughtful of you."

She rolled her eyes. "Claire suggested it."

"As it happens, I was going to ask you for a favor, too."

"What's that?"

"Could you give me a lift home tonight?"

"For a free whiskey sour, I could probably do that."

"I'll tell you what," he said, hopping on the stationary bike next to her to finish his cardio for the day, "You can have a free drink or a free bed. Your choice."

"You drive a hard bargain, mister. You know, you'd think that you'd let your own personal celebrity run a tab in your establishment."

"If anyone besides housewives and old fags recognized you, I would."

"Ouch."

"The truth hurts."

They chatted and pedaled alongside each other for the better part of an hour, after which Sondra left and Sax proceeded to the free weights. He still had a good forty minutes to exercise. Fridays were always lower-body days for him. He figured his torso and arms got more than their fair share of attention just working the bar on weekends. Even though the Brass Monkey served a retirement community, traffic was still heavier on Fridays and Saturdays than any other part of the week. Old habits – like Friday night beers and Saturday night cocktails – died hard.

"Hey, Sax," said one of the other regulars in the gym. "That your old lady?" The guy's eyes were glued to Sondra's tight rear end as she exited the building.

He shook his head. "No. She's a free agent."

The guy's gold wedding ring glinted in the fluorescent lights. "Mind if I ask her out?"

"I don't," he answered, "but your wife might have a problem with it."

"We have an understanding," the guy said, hefting twenty-pound dumbbells in alternating triceps lifts.

"What's that?"

"I understand that she doesn't want to have sex anymore and she understands that I don't want to have it any less."

After a lifetime spent as a cop and a bartender, Sax knew that heterosexual men more than rivaled the promiscuity levels of their homosexual brothers. That's not to say that faithful straight men weren't out there – just that an equal number of faithful gay men existed. He put three hundred pounds on the leg press and began his routine.

At ten-fifty, Sax let himself into the bar and made his way to the dimly lit bathroom at the back. Last year, he had a waitress for a while – not that he actually needed one. The joint was small enough he could tend the whole place alone, even on a busy night. He hired the waitress because he hated cleaning bathrooms; he assigned toilet duty to her. When she quit a few months later, she told Sax that she couldn't make enough tips even on the best night at the Brass Monkey – old people were cheap even when they thought they were being generous. Sondra later told Sax the real reason the girl left: old men couldn't hit the toilet if there were air traffic controllers guiding the piss in. After Sondra told him this, he briefly considered having a urinal installed; the cost of the plumbing was more than he was willing to spend on a rental space. If he ever bought a building and moved – which, he had to admit, was unlikely – he would make sure the men's bathroom was already fitted out with one.

In the meantime, cleaning the toilet fell to Sax. He hadn't even been able to induce Sondra to clean the john in exchange for a free drink every night. As he stood in the compact one-holer and changed out of his gym clothes, he could feel the sting of ammonia in his nostrils and knew that today was a toilet-cleaning day. His mood soured to the consistency of curdled milk.

Charmed Life

The Warriors

As an actress, Sondra understood that, above all else, women were rivals. No matter what the relationship – sister, mother, daughter, friend – in the end, the best that could be expected was competitiveness.

Claire was a different sort of a woman from those Sondra had spent her life around, and her differentness confused Sondra. Despite knowing that Sondra and Milo had enjoyed a brief fling, Claire seemed determined to befriend her.

That Friday morning, Sondra awakened to the delicious aroma of fresh-brewed coffee – a beverage that Milo avoided for the most part. In his opinion, Arizona was no place for hot beverages. Therefore, she knew before she even set foot outside of her bedroom that Claire was in the kitchen. Still, the aroma was too strong to resist. She pulled her short pink-satin robe around her and walked quietly toward the kitchen, hoping to get a cup and get out before Claire could catch her.

"Good morning!" sing-songed the relentlessly cheery Claire. "I was just pouring you a mug of coffee!"

The first time Sondra had met Claire, the woman had been dour in the extreme and more than a little careworn. When Milo's and her affection blossomed, though, Claire developed a glow that made Sondra want very much to kick her. But, she reasoned, that would be like kicking a puppy – people frowned when one did things like that. "Thank you," she said, smiling stiffly and taking the mug.

"There's an amaretto-flavored creamer in the fridge."

"I know. I put it there."

"That was you? I thought it was Milo."

"Milo doesn't drink coffee."

"I know. I thought he bought it for me." She sipped from her mug. "I'm afraid I used some of it."

Sondra seethed, grinding her teeth as she poured a bit of the creamer into her cup.

"I'll stop and buy a replacement bottle today. Do you want more amaretto or would you like one of the other flavors instead? French vanilla maybe?"

The anger she had been fostering dissipated, just as it always did where Claire was concerned. She never did enough wrong in sequence to allow Sondra time to build up a good head of steam. She tried to look on the bright side: soon, Claire's unfailing goodness would be enough to raise her blood pressure. It was like living with Glinda the Good Witch. "French vanilla sounds good," she answered. "And feel free to use as much of the creamer as you like."

"Thank you so much, Sondra. You are so wonderful – I feel like I gained a boyfriend and a good friend when Milo and I started dating."

Sondra sat down at the kitchen table and sipped her almond-flavored coffee.

"How are rehearsals?"

"Not great. Mildred Kovich makes an awful Dolly Levi."

"I'm sorry to hear that." Claire sat across from her at the small café-style dining set. She set her cup down and stared thoughtfully at Sondra.

"What? Do I have something on me?"

"No, no. I'm just…well. I have a favor to ask."

She kept from rolling her eyes, but only just barely. "What do you need?"

"You know we're going on a little trip this weekend."

"Yes. Tombstone, right?"

"Right. Alice Marie's writing a paper about the Old West and Milo thought it would be good for her to see some history."

Sondra smiled, thinking of the sweet man who shared his home with her. "He's a good grandfather."

"The best. Anyway, Alice Marie is sleeping here tonight, and I thought maybe you could stay at your daughter's house so that Alice Marie would have a bed to sleep in."

Breaking eye contact, Sondra picked up her mug and took a long drink.

"Of course, I know this is short notice…"

She set her mug back down with more force than she intended, startling Claire and herself. "I pay rent to live here, Claire."

Claire nodded. "I understand that, but you have to admit Milo's given you an excellent rate."

Sondra paid three hundred dollars a month to reside in the second bedroom of the old Sun City duplex. She could have lived rent-free with her daughter Fanny; however, she could live with Milo guilt-free – at least until today. "Fanny and I don't get along that well when we live in the same house."

"It's just one night, Sondra. Surely you can spend a single evening with her."

"Okay. I'll make other arrangements for the night." After all, she thought, she would have the house to herself for the rest of the weekend. Maybe she would even invite over a houseguest tomorrow – if someone struck her fancy.

"Thank you," Claire sighed. "I just can't imagine dealing with a cranky eight-year-old all the way to Tombstone. The talent for childcare must die when it isn't used."

"I was never particularly good at it," Sondra confided. "And I didn't do any better at being a grandmother. Maybe if I become a great-grandmother I'll get another shot."

Taz, Claire's pug, trotted into the kitchen, his tail wound in a tight curl. She reached down with one hand and the dog walked his head under it so that she could scratch his ears. "Milo must be up."

"I think I'm going to throw on some clothes and go to the gym."

"You want some company? I could use a good walk."

"I ride the stationery bikes."

She shrugged. "I could use a treadmill while you cycle."

Milo appeared around the corner, his distinguished white hair tousled from the night in bed. "I hoped we could take a walk together this morning, Claire."

"Oh! In that case, I guess you're on your own, Sondra."

"Don't worry about me," she said happily. "Good morning, Milo."

"Morning, Sondra. How are rehearsals?"

"Ask Claire. She'll fill you in." She pushed away from the table and headed for her room to get ready. Once there, she picked up her cell phone and dialed Fanny's number.

"Hello?"

"Fanny? Are you okay? You sound funny."

"This isn't Fanny. She's in the shower."

"Oh. Who is this?"

"Who is this?" the voice countered.

Sondra couldn't tell if it was a man or a woman. Finally deciding that the voice must be her grandson's, she asked, "Hunter?"

"You don't sound like I expected you to, Hunter."

"No, I'm not Hunter. Aren't you?"

"Look, lady, why don't you just tell me who you are and I'll let Fanny know you're on the phone."

"Why are you answering her phone?"

"How is that your business?"

"I'm her mother!" She heard the click of the line as it disconnected. Infuriated, she redialed; no one answered. She dropped to the bed and let out a cry of frustration. Fanny always seemed slightly disapproving of Sondra's lifestyle. That disapproval had manifested itself in extended stretches of silence when she lived with her daughter. The silence invariably pushed her out the door, like an invisible but aggressive poltergeist. She had spent more evenings at the Brass Monkey than at her daughter's home when she lived there. Fanny wasn't one to pick up strange men and bring them home; that was Sondra's modus operandi. So who had answered her phone? She took a deep breath and redialed.

"Hello?"

"Fanny!"

"Hi, Ma. What's wrong?"

"Who answered your phone?"

"What? What are you talking about?"

"You know exactly what I'm talking about, young lady!"

"Ma, I'm forty. I can have houseguests if I want to."

"Do you know how dangerous—?"

Fanny laughed, cutting her mother's words short. "I guarantee you I know Reuben a damn sight better than you've known the last dozen men you've slept with."

"And he's Jewish?!"

"So are we, Ma."

"You are three-quarters Gentile."

"I'm converting. Reuben wants to marry me."

She had never been a big fan of gyms, but she discovered their finer points as she aged. She was forty-eight before she set foot in one, lured there by one of her more effeminate escorts, a slight man named Adam who resembled Liza Minnelli at certain angles.

"Sondra, my love," he said, taking her hand in his softer one, "you simply must begin to tone your body."

"Why should I go to the gym? I swim every day. I'm in perfect shape!" She had been living alone in the big mansion Fanny's father left her for almost twenty years by then. The dinner invitations had slowed, but she still had an active social calendar. Adam, the latest in a string of escorts, was the first who had to "act" straight. The others had been less flamboyant. Still, she was fond of the beautiful boy.

He had taken her to one of the glitterati gyms – a place where the up-and-coming hung out with had-it-and-lost-its. She felt conspicuous, but Adam assured her that no one was staring. When she finally believed him, depression sapped most of her energy.

"Sondra?" asked a young woman in a leotard.

"Yes." Sondra, glancing up, saw her name badge read Mitzi. Mitzi was all of twenty, with buoyant breasts and platinum hair.

"A young man standing outside the dressing room asked me to check on you. Are you okay?"

"Fine. Just facing mortality."

"In the locker room?"

"As good a place as any."

"You look familiar."

"I'm Sondra Lane. I was Carmella Savage." Fans still recognized her for her role on Scions of Beauty now and then.

"Why did you change your name? Carmella Savage has real verve, you know?"

"No. I played...never mind."

"Wait! I've got it! I know who you are!"

"Great."

"No, really...you were in that god-awful sci-fi flick that Elvira featured last Friday night. What was it called...Siege of the Moon!" The girl doubled over in laughter. "You were painted pale green and they put you in that stupid deep-V bodysuit. You looked like the love child of John Travolta and an alien!"

Fully succumbing to her failure as an actress, she crept from the locker room while the girl was still recovering from her laughing fit. "Let's go," she said to Adam.

"But we haven't worked out yet," he pouted.

"Pick out the machines you think we need and have them delivered to the house."

Peddling away at the gym on the edge of Sun City, she was seldom recognized. Even when she was, retirees were, on the whole, much less cruel and much more discreet than L.A. starlets moonlighting as gym employees. She pushed her memories of gyms past out of her head and concentrated on her current dilemma. The earlier argument with Fanny made staying at her place unattractive. As an actress, she had any number of acquaintances – half of whom she feared would take backstabbing literally if given the opportunity. Not that she wouldn't be similarly tempted...she let herself drift into a fantasy where she prepared a special oleander tea for her most persistent rival. She stood over her convulsing body, cell phone in hand, just waiting until the last of her death throes.

"Sax! Buddy!" the desk clerk exclaimed, pulling her back to reality. Continuing to pedal, she watched for him to finish his conversation and walk in her direction. "Sax!" she called, waving at him as he passed her. He didn't stop, though she saw him miss a beat. "Sax, you fairy queen! I know you saw me!" she shouted. The women on either side of her giggled; Sondra was pleased to have an audience.

Sax finally turned around. "What?"

"Come here, will you?"

His eyes had a panicked look to them. "I'm running late. No time!"

"Please!"

Resigned, he walked to her bike. "What?"

"Geez. What's put you in such a foul mood? You were fine when I left last night."

"Personal stuff. Sorry I took it out on you."

Still pedaling, she shrugged. "We're friends, right? You can tell me anything."

"I'm not a real sharer."

"I've noticed."

"What did you need?" he asked again.

Within a few minutes, her plans for the night were secured: she would give Sax a ride home and, in return, he would give her a bed for the night. They exercised side by side for the better part of the next hour.

When she retrieved her purse from her locker, she was disappointed to discover that Fanny had not attempted to call and make up with her. Their relationship had always been tricky, but it had only broken off completely once before. In Sondra's estimation, Fanny's failure to apologize was a bad omen.

"You can't stop me from going to college!" Epiphany screamed. "I have scholarships! I don't need your approval!" She turned and stomped away, an action that failed to have much effect on the ultra-plush white carpeting.

Adam, who was beside her on the treadmill in the recently created home gym, arched an eyebrow at Sondra, who continued pedaling away on the exercise bike. "This is why homosexuality is superior – no offspring."

"I just don't know what to do with that girl anymore," Sondra said, flipping the page on the script she was perusing. "I offered to get her a nose job and new breasts for her high-school graduation and you would have thought I had informed her she would be locked up in the guest house for the rest of her life."

"She's not a bad-looking girl the way she is, Sondra."

"Maybe not, but she could look better, don't you think?"

Adam, ignoring the question, asked, "Why don't you want her to go to college?"

"I don't care if she goes to college. I just don't want her to go to the one she's picked."

"Why not?"

"It's a girls' school."

"So?"

Sondra squirmed slightly, dropping her pace on the bike.

"Keep pedaling," Adam commanded. "What's wrong with a women's college?"

"You should see the class photos. They're like gatherings of ugly female lumberjacks."

Adam laughed, almost tripping on the treadmill. He grabbed the handrails to steady himself. "You think she'll turn gay?"

"Well…"

"Sondra. Come on, girl. You know homosexuality isn't contagious."

"Maybe not, but what if she's already leaning that way?"

"Fanny? A lesbian?"

"I hate it when you call her that. Her name is Epiphany."

"She hates that name, and you know it."

"She just hasn't seen the beauty of it yet. It's a perfect Hollywood royalty name."

"But she's not Hollywood royalty," he pointed out, his eyebrow arching again.

"Of course she is. She's the daughter of a revered actor and a talented actress."

"She the illegitimate love child of an aged actor and his B-movie mistress, sweetheart."

Sondra winced. "I made the choice not to marry him. It was the Seventies. Marriage was out of style."

"No matter what the reason, the result is still the same." He stopped the treadmill and dabbed lightly at the beads of sweat glistening on his forehead. "None of which is important. 'Epiphany' has no intention of staying in Hollywood."

"I just don't understand why she would ever want to be anywhere else." The bicycle beeped and she stopped pedaling, putting her fingers to her wrist.

Adam, looking at his watch, said, "And go!"

They each counted their pulses in silence for ten seconds. "Twenty-two," she said, picking up her towel.

"Excellent."

"Are you going to the premiere with me tomorrow night?"

"I don't know…I have an audition tomorrow afternoon."

"For what?"

"A sitcom called Bob."

Sondra blinked rapidly. "The new Bob Newhart vehicle?"

"I don't know. Maybe."

"Oh, my God! I want to go with you."

"It's a cattle call for young men, darling. I hardly think you're a good fit for the part."

"Maybe not, but Bob's characters are unfailingly married men. They must need a wife-slash-comic-foil."

"Don't you suppose that part has already been cast?"

"You don't know that for sure."

Sighing, he put his hands on his hips. "Fine. You can come with me."

She bounced on her toes and smiled widely. "You have to admit: I'd be perfect opposite him!"

"I'll come by and pick you up at noon. Be ready. I don't want to be late."

"Of course, darling. Afterwards, we can attend the premiere to celebrate. Bring your tux with you and we'll leave it here."

He hugged her. "You are my favorite starlet, Sondra." He released her and said, "I've got a date tonight. I'd better go now if I'm going to be ready in time."

"Have fun, darling. See you tomorrow." He gathered his workout bag and headed for the door, showing himself out. Sondra jogged up the spiral staircase to Epiphany's room, where she found her daughter stretched out on her pink double bed reading.

"Go away," she said, without raising her eyes from the book.

"Epiphany—"

"Fanny."

"That's not what I named you."

"I'm having it legally changed in two months."

"What?!"

"I'm done, Ma. I'm not going through life with a name that makes people giggle."

"No one in Hollywood giggles."

"That's because they have names like Chastity, Zowie, and Sunshine. Do you know what my college roommate's name is?"

Sondra, leaning against the doorjamb with her arms crossed, shook her head.

"Melissa."

Sondra wrinkled her nose as if she smelled garbage.

"It's a beautiful name! It means 'honey bee.'"

"Your name means something too."

"Yeah…it means that you had an 'epiphany' and realized the only way you could find success was as a rich man's whore!" Fanny's hand flew to her mouth, too late to stop the words.

Sondra staggered back as if Fanny had hit her. "Don't…talk about your father like that," she said weakly. She willed herself to reach her bedroom before the tears poured out. Closing the door firmly, she slid down and leaned against it, sobbing. After a while, she tipped to one side and curled into a fetal position. She cried until exhaustion dragged her under, into a deep slumber.

A tentative knock awoke her.

"Ma? Are you in there?"

Sondra didn't answer.

"Ma?" The girl's voice was louder this time.

"Yes," Sondra answered hoarsely.

"I'm sorry."

"Go away."

"Ma, I'm really sorry. I never should have said that." Her daughter was crying now, her voice thickened.

"I don't care where you go, just don't stay here."

Fanny was like a ghost after that day; a few months later, she was gone, attending the women's college in the Midwest, leaving Sondra completely alone for the first time.

She was restless, unable to settle anywhere. Every time she stopped moving, her mind flew back to the morning's argument with Fanny. From the gym, she had gone to Starbucks, indulging herself in a chai latte and a croissant and engaging a gentleman in a brief flirtation. When his girlfriend showed up, she smiled at the man and left the shop, not wanting to cause him discomfort – or, worse, have him introduce her.

She drove back to the house and showered, determined to wash away the miserable start to her day. Claire and Milo were both gone, though the dog was still there, curled in a dog bed Claire had installed in one corner of the living room. She was reminded once more that she should look for somewhere else to live. It seemed inevitable that Claire would take up permanent residence with Milo. Though she considered Sax a good friend, she doubted he would be inviting her to share his house on a regular basis – in fact, tonight would be the first time she had ever seen his home.

She puttered around the house for a while, making her bed and cleaning her bathroom. Mile and Claire had left a few dishes in the sink; Sondra washed them. When Taz heard her rattling around the kitchen, he roused himself enough to walk in and sit on her right foot, just in case she had some food to share with him.

She patted him on the head, wondering why she had never let Fanny have a pet. Why had the plush white carpet been more important than her daughter's happiness? She couldn't imagine now.

Overwhelmed by the silence, she tried to think of someone – anyone, really – with whom she would enjoy sharing a meal. Finally, she dialed the number of one of her theater friends, a woman who was also in the *Hello, Dolly!* cast.

"Hello?"

"Hello, Liz? It's Sondra."

"Sondra? Is everything all right?"

"Of course! I was just wondering if you were free for lunch."

"I'm afraid I've already eaten."

"Oh. Maybe tomorrow then."

"Tomorrow's Saturday."

"Yes, it is."

"I spend the weekends with my family. If you just want the company, I could—"

"No, no. Don't worry about it. Will you be at rehearsals tonight?"

"Have I ever missed a rehearsal?"

Sondra laughed weakly. "Of course not. I'll see you later, then."

"See you later."

Charmed Life

Sondra hung up the phone. Flipping through a stack of fashion magazines on an end table in the living room, she found one with an article about Karl Lagerfeld. She met him at a party once. Stuffing the magazine into her purse, she left the house and drove to the nearby Chinese restaurant.

The place was half-full, as usual. She took one of the red booths under the windows and waited for the waitress to bring her a menu. The nearby tables had a mix of clientele: an old couple, a manager from the Safeway located in the same parking lot, a couple of greasy-looking men. She ordered the orange chicken lunch and spread her magazine on the table in front of her. Instead of reading, though, she eavesdropped on the old couple.

"Why don't you want to visit the kids in Oregon, Howard?" the woman was asking. "There's a festival up near Medford in the fall, isn't there?"

"I think it's cancelled this year, Rhonda."

"We could still see the kids."

Sondra studied the old man, wondering if he were one of the men caught up in the square-dancing pot ring Milo had brought down some weeks before.

The woman's eyes shifted away from her husband. "What are you staring at?" she asked Sondra, dropping her fork to her plate.

"I'm sorry," Sondra said smoothly. "I thought I recognized you from somewhere."

"Do you square dance?"

"No, I'm afraid not."

"Then you don't know us."

Sondra smiled graciously and concentrated on the soup the waitress had just slipped in front of her. She kept her eyes on the Lagerfeld article after that, but she smiled to herself, knowing exactly why Howard didn't want to go to Oregon – he was on probation and not allowed to leave the state.

It was almost three when she finished eating. Rehearsals wouldn't start until four, but the theater would be open. She drove to the building and parked near the entrance, pleased to have a prime spot.

The theater was still dark, which meant none of her fellow performers had come in early for extra rehearsals. That was fine with Sondra – she simply wanted to soak up some of the theatrical atmosphere. She had always been fond of green rooms and the Hollywood equivalent, trailers. She never had one of her own, except on Siege of the Moon, the movie that was supposed to launch her career. She had the largest role – the female Martian explorer leading a troop of women warriors as they attempted to claim the moon for Mars. The deeper meaning of the script had been a condemnation of the European tactics for claiming the Americas. Sunrise Aeon was Columbus with a conscience, according to George Miller. Unfortunately, the green makeup and disco-era clothing obscured that message.

She descended the stairs to the green room and settled into an overstuffed sofa that occasionally doubled as stage furniture when the play mandated it. It was all wrong for *Hello, Dolly!*, though: more late 1980s than mid 1890s.

On the wall across from the couch were framed programs from the last fifty years of productions – everything from Death of a Salesman to Victor/Victoria. It was impressive, given the shoestring budget the place ran on these days. Sondra had supplied her own wardrobe for every play she had been in, and the set designers frequented the estate sales for furniture, knickknacks, and the like. When the theater staged The Glass Menagerie two winters before, Chuck's now-deceased wife Valerie had spent a week of Sundays perusing the dusty collections of many a dead woman to acquire enough glass-blown animals to set the stage. The glass sculptures were now wrapped individually and contained in a labeled plastic bin: "animal knickknacks." The bin stacked on top of it contained twenty matching bowler hats from the production that followed: A Chorus Line.

But those containers weren't in the green room, thankfully. Sondra allowed her eyes to drift close as she rehearsed Dolly Levi's lines. No matter what else she might be accused of, Sondra was a devoted actress. Though she knew Mildred wasn't going to have so much as a sniffle as long as she had the lead role, she still diligently learned the script and attended the rehearsals.

Footsteps, ending at the green room entrance, stopped her recital.

"I thought I heard a voice," Mildred Kovich said, gliding into the room. If nothing else, she had mastered the art of walking like a lady.

"Mildred. How are you?"

"I'm fine, Sondra. You're a bit early, aren't you?"

"Indeed."

"Any particular reason? You knew Bob and I were coming in early to rehearse."

"You were going to do that here? I thought you planned to work at home."

"I gave Bob the night off. He really needed a beer."

"I bet he did."

Mildred came closer, crossing her arms and leaning against the wall like a premenstrual teenaged girl. "What's that supposed to mean?"

"Did you learn the lines yet?"

"I think I've got it now."

"Good. You know, I never realized how much time theater folk got to rehearse their lines."

"Well," Mildred said saccharinely, "we don't have teleprompters like the soap operas do."

Sondra's eye twitched involuntarily. "I never used the teleprompter."

"As I recall, you never had a lot of lines on Scions of Beauty."

"Which do you think is worse, Mildred? Being a soap actress or one of the bonbon-eating housewives who kept the show afloat for so many years?"

Mildred's eyes flashed. "I wasn't a housewife. I was a theater actress, reciting some of the most brilliant words ever written! I played Juliet—"

"In Tuscaloosa." Sondra watched as Mildred's face flushed red with hatred.

"You bitch! I'll have Bob kick you out of this production! You'll never get another part here as long as I'm alive! What do we need with a damned B-movie actress, anyway?"

"You just try it!"

"Watch me!" She stomped out of the green room. "Bob! Bob! Where are you?"

Sondra stayed on the couch.

Charmed Life

Charmed Life

Silent Rage

Sax glanced at the clock when Sondra walked into the bar. She was three hours early – rehearsals should have just started.

"Whiskey sour, Sax." She took up residence on her favorite stool at the far end of the bar.

She looked like she needed a few minutes to cool off; he took his time shaking the whiskey, lemon juice and sugar. A muted game of Jeopardy filled the television screen. A regular – a washed-up old guy the other patrons called the Professor – was answering the clues over his third beer and basket of peanuts, sounding like a head case with every question he formed. "Who is Peg Entwistle?"

"Just another girl who couldn't hack it," Sondra mumbled from her corner. "Sax, where's my damned drink?" she said louder.

"Right here, sweetie," he said, sliding the drink into her hand. "What's up?"

"Bob kicked me out of the play."

"What? Why would he do that?"

"Mildred."

"You didn't."

"Didn't what?" She looked at him, confused for a moment. "Oh! Nah – I didn't rat out Bob. What would be the point?" She lifted the drink to her lips and sucked down three-quarters of it.

The woman could drink when she had a mind to, Sax mused. "But aren't you the understudy?"

"Ha! As if that bitch would ever be sick enough to miss a night!" She set the now-empty glass back on the bar. "I did some research. Did you know that she has never missed a single performance? The guild has a nickname for her: Mighty Mildred. Directors used to say that she might not be the best actress, but she was certainly the most reliable. She's played every theater from here to Alaska and from California to Florida."

"Impressive."

"And what have I done? I'm just some two-bit actress who only saw her name in lights one time." She pushed the glass toward Sax. "Refill me?"

223

"Who's going to drive us home?"

"Ah, come on, Sax – it's four-thirty. Don't you think I'll be sober again by eleven?"

"Not if you keep drinking them down like the last one."

"I'll slow down, okay?"

He gave her a curt nod and took the glass to refill.

"Who was George Miller?" the Professor said.

"A stinking louse, that's who," came Sondra's reply.

"You knew George Miller, the writer and director?" Sax asked as he poured the lemon juice into the shaker.

"I worked in Hollywood, didn't I?"

"Yeah, but—"

"Who do you think wrote that piece of shit that killed my career?"

"Siege of the Moon was one of his?"

"Yep. Everywhere I went, I was the laughing stock. Him, though…he just swept the whole thing under the carpet. What is he remembered for? The That Donnelly Woman television series and half a dozen decent movies."

"To be fair, that was a great series – way ahead of its time back in the Fifties."

She laughed. "Everyone's always telling me that. I don't even remember the darned show."

"They run it on Nick at Night every couple of years."

"Figures."

"He still alive?"

"Not sure. He was when I left Hollywood; I heard his daughter had to put him in a home, though. Alzheimer's."

Sax clucked. "Too bad. Terrible way to go. I can't think of anything worse than forgetting a whole lifetime of memories."

"Maybe. But don't you sometimes wish you could cherry-pick the best of them and let the rest fade away?"

"It doesn't work like that, Carmella," he said with a wink.

"I'd keep those memories: all those years as Carmella Savage. So what if it was a soap opera? People all over the world recognized me. What's Mildred got that compares to that?"

"Ah. I think I understand what happened now." He watched as she picked up her drink and downed the remainder. "Did she call you a hack?"

"Something like that," Sondra muttered.

224

"And how did you respond?"

"Doesn't really matter. Suffice it to say that she took offense at my retort."

"Give her a few days to cool off," Sax advised. "Bob will help her to see reason and you'll be welcomed back."

"I doubt it." She pushed the empty glass toward him. "One more?"

"Only if you promise to stop at three – at least for a few hours. You can hang out in my office if you want." Sax had a small office in the back, behind a locked door. Furnished in early transient, it wasn't the ritziest place to spend an evening; however, Sondra didn't seem up to sitting on a barstool for another seven hours.

"And that's how I know that you like me more than you let on," she purred. "You'll let me into your sanctuary."

"Are you kidding?" he scoffed. "That's more like a monk's cell than a sanctuary."

"Does it have a sofa?"

"No, but it has a recliner and a TV."

"Sold."

The place was starting to fill up with regulars – old men who had already dropped their wives off after indulging in an "early bird" dinner out, a few widows hoping to snag a date with a lonely older man, and some office workers who showed up on Fridays to celebrate the end of the week. Sax prepared Sondra's third drink of the afternoon, but couldn't stay with her while she drank it.

Someone turned on the jukebox and strains of the Doobie Brothers filled the bar. An old couple got up to dance in the small bare spot near the front and so did a few of the younger patrons. The Professor slid off his stool and headed for the door; Sax hoped the guy was walking. People around Sun City tended to think golf carts weren't cars and, therefore, one could drive a golf cart while drunk. The cops, on the other hand, disagreed.

At some point, Sax noticed that Sondra's stool was as empty as the glass sitting in front of it. He scanned the crowd but couldn't find her anywhere. Remembering he had offered her the office, he checked the drawer where he kept the keys and found they were gone. He was about to check on her when one of the tables full of widows flagged him down and ordered another round.

Bob showed up a little after eight, squeezing in between another old guy and one of the office workers. "Sax!" he called out.

"Hey, Bob. Everything okay?"

"Super duper. You heard about Sondra?"

"Yeah. She's been here all afternoon."

"She shouldn't have gotten into a pissing match with Mildred."

"You can't blame it all on Sondra."

He shrugged. "What else can I do? Mildred is my wife. We vowed a long time ago to always back each other up. I can't stop now."

Sax pulled a mug of Bob's favorite beer and slid it in front of him. "Don't you ever think...well, what if you divorced her?" He said it quietly, almost in a whisper.

"I told you a long time ago that I was married for life – mine or hers."

"But times have changed, Bob. We – I mean, men like us – can live our lives the way we want to."

"How would that be fair to Millie? She's stood right by me through thick and thin for forty years. We have children together—"

"Adopted children."

"Still...they are our children. And it would rock their worlds to discover that I" – he looked cautiously left and right before leaning in toward Sax – "bat for the other team."

"I don't think you're giving your kids enough credit."

"Maybe, maybe not. Doesn't matter. Mildred and I are married, for better or for worse."

"You be sure to give her a hug and kiss from me later."

He tilted his head and smiled slyly. "I thought we could hang out again tonight."

"Sorry. I've got plans."

"With whom?"

"Someone who isn't married." Sax turned his back on his boyfriend and walked away. Several customers anxiously shouted orders over one another. By the time he had filled them all, a fiver and an empty mug were all that remained to tell of Bob's presence.

The crowd finally began thinning around ten. By closing time only one couple, a widow and a man Sax knew to be married, had to be pushed out the door.

He wiped down the bar and gathered the last of the glasses to be washed. He considered knocking on the office door and seeing if he could convince Sondra to help him with cleaning up, but decided it would be easier to take care of everything himself. He took the TV off mute and turned up Letterman as he worked.

When the tables were wiped down, the floors swept, and the dishes cleaned, he held his breath and pushed open the men's room door. One glance told him he was going to want to wait until the morning to clean it up – he just didn't have the energy to mop the floor tonight. Maybe putting in a urinal was worth the expense even if he didn't own the building. Maybe he could even work one into the lease renewal come April and convince the building management to pay for it.

The women's room was cleaner, despite the used paper towels strewn across the floor. If the men couldn't hit the toilet, the women seemed unable to hit the waste basket. He had seen the germophobic women attempting three pointers from the bathroom entrance, the door propped open with one foot. He let the women's room door fall shut and made a mental note to buy an extra trashcan to set outside the bathroom.

He turned off the TV over the bar and rapped on the office door before trying the handle. It was, of course, locked. He knocked again. "Sondra? You okay?"

She opened the door, rubbing her eyes and yawning. "What time is it?"

"Almost midnight."

"Wow. I guess this day really took it out of me." She walked back into the office and retrieved her purse. "Ready to go?"

"Yeah. You want me to drive?" Sax had been in her car when she was wide awake behind the wheel – that was terrifying enough. Even on the relatively empty streets of late-night Sun City, he wasn't looking forward to experiencing her driving skills when she was tired.

"You do know the way," she said, digging in her bag for the keys. "Just be careful with my car."

"I'll treat it like it's my own." He took the keychain from her hands. "What about the office keys?"

Slipping a hand into her pocket, she extracted them and dropped them in the drawer behind the bar. "I could do with a nightcap. There's no hurry, is there?" she asked, slipping onto her stool.

"I'll make you a drink at home," he said, slipping a hand under her arm and pulling her along.

"You're a stick in the mud, Sax," she pouted.

"And you're an old lush." He steered her toward the door and they found themselves in the pleasantly warm evening breeze. Sax inhaled deeply, happy to breathe air not infused with alcohol for the first time in hours. The rest of the strip mall was dark and quiet; above them, a harvest moon hung heavily. He loved fall even more now than he had when he was a kid. In New Jersey, it had signaled the coming of the holidays, starting with Halloween and going right through to New Year's Eve. Here, it heralded eight months – give or take a few weeks – of beautiful weather.

Sondra sighed. "Why am I alone, Sax?"

"You're not alone. You've got your daughter."

She began to cry. A little burst of tears slid down her cheeks, followed by the sound of a deep sucking-in of air. "She hates me."

"Don't be ridiculous. Your daughter loves you."

"No. She wishes I had died and her father had lived." She leaned against his chest.

With consternation, he felt her tears soak his shirt. He put a hand on each of her shoulders and tried to move her away from him. She was surprisingly strong for her size. He found it was easier for him to back up. "Sondra, what's going on?"

"My daughter is converting to Judaism!"

"Why?"

"She's marrying a Jew!"

He studied her face. "How long have you been coming to my bar? Five years? In all that time, I never thought you were prejudiced."

She sobered a bit. Choking back her tears, she said, "I'm not a racist. I'm Jewish." She walked around the side of the building without another word, leaving Sax confused.

He unlocked the car and she got in on the passenger side in silence. When he turned the key, the sound system sprang to life, Neil Diamond's voice pouring from the speakers. Sax didn't adjust the volume; he simply drove the car toward his home as the singer crooned "Sweet Caroline."

He parked the car in the driveway and opened the gate for Sondra to walk through. If she was surprised by the garden home, she didn't say it. Sax was a little hurt that she seemed unimpressed.

Inside, he slipped off his shoes, as was his habit. After a brief hesitation, she shed her shoes as well. The dining room to the left of the entrance had tatami mats on the floor; these drew her interest and she crossed in front of Sax to look inside. He was proud of the room – its low table and cushions were modeled on the tea rooms he had seen years ago during a vacation in Japan.

"I haven't seen a tea room since I was in Hollywood," she commented.

"Why don't you make yourself comfortable? I'll fix us a snack and we can talk."

"I thought you were tired."

"I am, but how often will I have a slumber party with a Hollywood star?"

She gave him a grateful glance from under her long eyelashes and entered the dining room, taking the cushion that gave her a view of the garden they had just walked through.

Sax went to the kitchen. He filled the kettle and set it on the range to warm before locating some tea biscuits and fruit. He knew that she would prefer alcohol to tea, so he opened a small bottle of sake he had been saving for a special occasion. He added loose mint-infused green tea to the bottom of the teapot, pouring the heated water over it to steep. He filled his serving tray with the tea, sake, fruit, and tea biscuits before walking carefully back to the dining room, where Sondra was inspecting the collection of Asian pottery that filled the shelves along the far wall. "The tea is ready," he said, interrupting her reverie.

"I guess I should have recognized your appreciation of Asian culture. George is a dead giveaway, isn't he?"

The brass monkey that adorned his bar was a gift from a long-ago boyfriend – the one relic of his past he hadn't been able to leave behind. His patrons had dubbed him George in honor of the famous children's book character, but Sax would forever think of him as Dong, the name his boyfriend had assigned the statue. "Sit down, Sondra. I've brought you a bedtime snack."

She came back to the cushions and elegantly lowered herself onto one. "I'm sorry about earlier. I don't know what's the matter with me."

"Don't worry about it. You've obviously had a bad day."

"Why don't women like me, Sax?"

"Don't be ridiculous."

"I'm not. First Claire, then Fanny, then Mildred...all day long, I've been assaulted by other women."

"You're being a bit of a drama queen, my dear."

"You too? Have I no friends left?"

"Of the four of us, even you would have to admit I'm the only one who really qualifies as a friend to begin with. After all, where are you sleeping tonight?"

Sondra, pouting, poured herself a cup of sake and selected a stem of grapes and a few apple slices.

"Claire is your ex-boyfriend's girlfriend. That's got to be awkward."

"Surprisingly, not as uncomfortable as you'd think. Claire is a nice woman who seems to be gaining in niceness with each day." She frowned. "It's more irritating than anything else."

"Excessive goodness?"

"Exactly. If you can't find the salt, the sugar is too sweet." She popped a grape in her mouth.

"Mildred is a 'frenemy.'"

"I think we can drop the F-R now."

"You don't want to call her an enemy, Sondra. You can't win against her – not with Bob, anyway."

"I just don't get their relationship," she complained. "What kind of in-the-closet gay man is he? He should be willing to die to protect his secret."

As much as he wanted to clue her in on the nature of Bob and Mildred's marriage, he knew it wasn't his place. He popped a biscuit in his mouth to stop his tongue.

"I always thought my daughter and I would be friends. I tried to give her everything she could possibly want—"

"No. You tried to give her everything you wanted. Did you ever ask Fanny what she wanted?"

"A mother just knows." She inhaled the cup of sake. "I don't usually like rice wine, but this is good...really smooth and sweet."

"A friend brought it to me from Kyoto."

"You have a lot of friends, don't you?"

"I used to, back in Jersey. They don't talk to me anymore."

"None of them?"

"I left the force abruptly."

She poured herself another cup. "You know so much about me, and I know nothing about you. Why is that?"

"Because it's all about you?"

She laughed lightly. "Usually. But I'm tired of talking about me for now. Tell me something I don't know."

He poured some green tea into a cup and stirred in a little sugar as he thought over her request. "Okay. What do you want to know?"

"When did you know you were gay?"

"I don't remember. Next question."

"What do you mean you don't remember?"

"I was so young. I just knew I preferred boys."

"Were your parents okay with that?"

He smiled patronizingly. "What do you think?"

"I would have been okay with Fanny being gay. After her father died, I spent most of my time with gay men."

"Openly gay or closeted?"

"It was Hollywood. Everyone was...flexible, so to speak."

"Everyone?" He waggled his eyebrows at her.

"The men, anyway. Though I knew my share of lesbians, too."

"In the Biblical sense?" He was teasing her now, pleased to have steered the conversation away from himself.

"Wouldn't you like to know?" she purred.

"Actually, no, not so much."

She laughed and a bit of the sake lapped over the edge of the cup, spilling on the small plate containing the apple and grapes. She attempted to soak up the liquid with her fruit, but it wasn't very cooperative. "Pass the biscuits." He held them out to her and she selected one, setting it in the liquid. The alcohol quickly bonded to the cookie and Sondra ate it.

"You're a problem solver," he said admiringly.

"No point in wasting it. Did Bob come in tonight?"

"Yes.

"Did he say anything about Mildred? Am I welcome back to the theater?"

"Maybe you should just track her down and apologize tomorrow."

"She's the one who owes me an apology."

"Maybe so, but she wasn't banned from the theater."

"You have a point." Her words slurred together. She reached for the sake once more, but Sax snatched it away. "Pour me another one, barkeep."

"I think it's time to pour you into bed instead. It's after one."

"I used to party all night."

"So did I, Sondra, but neither of us are young anymore."

"Speak for yourself, old man."

He laughed. "The sake hit you pretty hard, didn't it?"

"I'm fine. Stone cold sober." She hiccoughed. "Well...maybe a little tipsy."

He helped her to her feet, where she swayed and almost fell back to the cushion. He caught her around her waist, placing one hand on each hip to steady her.

"My hero," she cooed, leaning in with eyes half-closed and lips pursed.

Horrified, he released her as if her body were suddenly a hundred degrees warmer. Off-balance, she fell forward, landing hard on the tatami floor.

"God, I am so sorry, Sondra!"

From her face-down position he heard her say, "No. That was clearly my fault. I don't know what I was thinking." The fall seemed to have sobered her. She pushed herself to all fours.

"Let me help you up again."

"I'm probably safer down here."

"You can't crawl to the bedroom."

"Why not?"

"It's not..."

"Dignified?" she supplied.

He blinked at his guest, who seemed determined to stay down.

"Lead on, Sax. I haven't been dignified in years."

Charmed Life

Siege of the Moon

Sondra was grateful for the plantation blinds that kept the morning sun out of Sax's guest bedroom. Before last night, she hadn't enjoyed a cup of sake in decades – not since that Japanese producer wanna-be had wormed his way into the Siege of the Moon project back in the Seventies. The hangover currently circulating through her was a painful reminder of Yasuo Oota. She groaned and rolled over, noticing that the bed on which she was lying was very plush. She could have been sleeping on a cloud, were it not for the brick-like weight of her head.

The bedroom door pushed open slightly and Sax asked, "Are you decent?"

"I'm covered, if that's what you mean."

He pushed the door fully open, and sunlight streamed in from the hallway. Sondra squeezed her eyes closed and slapped both hands over them. "Too bright! Too bright!"

She heard the door click closed and Sax said, "It's okay now. You can open your eyes."

"I've got a doozy of a hangover going. Remind me not to drink sake again."

"I brought you some water and a couple of ibuprofens."

"Do you have anything stronger? A Vicodin maybe?"

"No, I'm sorry. I had to dig to find these."

"What kind of freak are you, Sax? Everyone needs painkillers once in a while."

"I meditate when I'm in pain."

"That works?"

"For me, it does."

She took the pills and drank the water. "Could you bring me a refill?"

"Sure." He took the empty glass and walked back to the door. "You'd better roll over before I open this."

"Yeah. Good point." She turned on the bed and closed her eyes, pulling the extra pillow close to her. Thoughts of Yasuo Oota pulled her back in time.

Charmed Life

"I've got a part for you, baby."

She rolled over in the black satin sheets and looked at her benefactor. Sondra had been living with Bud for almost three years now. He had used that line on her every time she packed her bags to leave – and it always worked. This time, though, she hadn't been packing; she had been lazing about in the afterglow of passably interesting sex, having decided that George "Bud" Miller was probably as good as she was ever going to do. She was just as stuck in her career as she was with Bud. Ever since she took the role of Carmella on Scions of Beauty, she had been dismissed from casting call after casting call as "too recognizable," "too dark," or "too slutty." "Are you serious, Bud?"

"I'm always serious. You know that."

"I mean, do you think I really have a shot at the part or is someone else going to trump your casting?"

"Bill's already on board with me for this one. That's a lot of pull in your corner."

"I thought Bill didn't like me."

"Bill adores you! He just didn't see you as an archeologist."

"Or a dancer, or a lawyer, or a housewife—"

"He sees you as Sunrise Aeon."

She pursed her lips in confused disgust. "What kind of name is that?"

"A Martian one."

"According to whom?"

"The writer. Better known as me."

"You wrote something?" She knew it had been years since he had put pen to paper – he claimed Hollywood gave him a bad case of writer's block.

"What can I say? You are the antidote I've been looking for."

She rolled onto her back, carefully keeping the sheet in place over her bosom – she didn't want to distract him before she had all the details. "What's the story?"

"Your character is the leader of a band of warrior Martian women. Sunrise is mated to a Martian man, but Martian men are clingy and needy, barely able to function without their women. The population of Mars has grown to a point where they need additional planets to support their numbers. When their scientists spot Earth's moon, they see it as a perfect fortress for their eventual invasion of Earth. Sunrise's troops are sent forth to take and hold the moon. Once there, she encounters a settlement of humans. She meets and falls in love with their leader, the handsome Rick Rice."

"Who's going to play him?"

"We're in talks with Steve McQueen."

Her eyes widened. "Really? What's the budget on this one?"

"Big. Bigger than I could have hoped. After Star Wars, everyone wants to jump on the science fiction bandwagon."

"And Bill wants me to play Sunrise?"

"He says he can't imagine a better person. He envisions all the Martian women as redheads."

"Finally! He sees a part for a redheaded woman!"

Bud chuckled. "Yeah, he does seem to have a problem with red hair generally, doesn't he?"

"Who else is producing?"

"We've got a Japanese businessman on the line. Yasuo Oota. The guy's a big fan of Bill's – wanted to produce a movie with him in it."

"So? Why doesn't he?"

"You know Bill – stubborn old coot says he's retired. He won't do another film unless Shakespeare himself rises up to write it."

"Who else?"

"That's it. Bill and this Oota fellow."

"And you're directing?"

"Of course. I wouldn't have it any other way. This is a real message film, Sondra. I don't want some hack muddying the waters."

"What's the message?"

"It's a condemnation of the European approach to settling the new world. And in my version, the natives fight back and win."

"I don't get it."

"At the end of the film, your character is shot dead by Rick Rice's wife."

"What about Rick?"

"She takes him back."

"Not really seeing the triumph here."

"Trust me: it's there."

She leaned over Bud to check the time. "Shit. I'm late."

He twisted around to see the clock. "Not yet you aren't."

She hopped out of the bed and ran for the shower. "I was supposed to come in early. The writers want to meet with me. I think they're going to bulk up Carmella's part."

"Bad timing," he called out. "You need to ask for a two-month hiatus to shoot the film."

"That's still months away, isn't it?" She shimmied out of her underwear and stepped into the space-age shower with its many jets. Twisting the knob, she shivered as the lukewarm water made contact with her skin. If he answered her, she didn't hear him. By the time she was out of the shower, he had fallen asleep.

The door opened again. "Sondra? Keep your eyes closed."

Even with her head turned toward the wall and her eyes closed, she still felt the flood of light throb against her brain. When the door latched again, she rolled back to face Sax. "Thank you," she said as she took the glass.

"No problem." He sat down in the ivory-lacquered armchair in the corner of the room.

Sondra pushed the worried thought that the chair wouldn't support him from her mind. "I'm sorry about this."

He shrugged. "You had a bad day yesterday. It happens."

"You shouldn't have to play nursemaid."

"I'm thinking about taking the day off."

"It's Saturday. Isn't that your biggest day of the week?"

"It doesn't get busy until after four normally. Want to go to a movie with me?"

"I'm not much of a movie fan."

"How's your head?"

"I'm down to a dull pound now."

"You need to eat. Ibuprofen is hard on an empty stomach."

"Give me a few more minutes of darkness."

He pushed out of the chair and went to the door. "I'll knock when your food is ready."

"Coffee, too, please."

"Yeah, of course."

Yasuo Oota was a few inches shorter than Sondra and three times as thick. He spoke remarkable English. She later learned he had been sent to American boarding schools almost as soon as he was weaned. His father owned a huge manufactory near Tokyo; Yasuo was the second son, and, therefore, the one to receive a foreign education. Unfortunately, this education hadn't resulted in a savvy young businessman who understood the largest of Japan's foreign markets; instead, Yasuo was a fame-hungry playboy with an appetite for movie production.

His older brother, who had been raised in a strict Japanese environment, found Yasuo to be useless. Wanting nothing more than to save face for the Oota family, he gave Yasuo a sizeable allowance as long as he stayed far away from Japan.

The short, round man had a tall, willowy young starlet draped over him. Lianne was as tall and thin as Yasuo was short and fat. Sondra couldn't help but imagine them dressed as a hot dog and hamburger the first time she met them.

"I'm a huge fan!" Lianne gushed as she shook Sondra's hand. "You so should have won that Emmy last year."

Sondra smiled stiffly. "Thank you. Would I have seen you in anything?"

"Oh, goodness me, no. Yasuo – the darling – is plucking me from obscurity to play Kay Rice."

The little man smiled and nodded. "She is a natural, though, do you not think?"

"I'm sure." Sondra flicked her eyes up and down the girl and imagined she was a natural – at some things.

She felt a hand on the small of her back. "Bud—"

"Sondra, darling, how have you been?"

Taken aback to find Bill standing by her side, she struggled to find her tongue.

Lianne found hers first. "Oh, my goodness! Joe Gill—"

"Please," he said, taking the girl's fluttering hand and lifting it to his lips, "Call me Bill."

"I could never..."

"Of course you can, my dear."

Oota's blank expression showed his displeasure with Bill's charming greeting. A second later, he dropped the girl's hand and bowed slightly to Yasuo. "A pleasure to see you again, Mr. Oota."

"And I, you. Have we secured Steve McQueen for the male lead?"

"Please, Yasuo, this is a party. Let us leave business for tomorrow. Tonight, we are friends."

Remembering her role as hostess, Sondra said, "Of course. Let's move out to the patio. I'm certain that's where Bud has disappeared to."

She led the small group outside, where the rest of the guests had already migrated. Leaving Bill with Yasuo and Lianne, she approached Bud and stood to one side as he chatted with an up-and-coming director – Steven somebody. Sondra slipped her hand into Bud's and squeezed.

He took the cue. "Have a lovely time tonight. Excuse me, please." They turned from the young man and walked to a spot where they were, for all intents and purposes, alone. "What is it?"

"Yasuo is asking about McQueen. Bill put him off, but—"

"Don't worry, darling. I have someone just as good lined up for the part. Steve will live to regret his decision. This is going to be huge."

"Did you screen-test Lianne? Can she act?"

His head bobbled from one side to the other. "Her part is small, Sondra. She doesn't have to be great. And, by casting her, I got Yasuo to commit another fifty thousand to the project."

But Yasuo Oota wasn't done meddling with the production. "Sunrise Aeon and the rest of the Martian women should be green, shouldn't they?" "The Martian costumes would look better in silver lamé, don't you think?" "If we are going to properly convey the strength of Earth women, shouldn't Lianne's role be bigger?"

By the time filming started that summer in Death Valley – the closest local approximation of the barren moon landscape – Sondra's part had been reduced to something straight out of a Fifties' horror flick. Sunrise and Rick no longer had a passionate relationship; instead Sunrise kidnapped Rick and made him her love slave. She was transformed from a doomed heroine to a villainess. Kay Rice – Lianne's part – was the heroine of the film now.

"I want out!" Sondra stormed at Bud after reading the revisions.

"You signed a contract already," he reminded her.

"This isn't even the same project, Bud!"

"Yes it is. This is still Siege of the Moon, your character is still named Sunrise Aeon, and you still receive top billing, side by side with Lianne and Todd."

"That's another thing – Todd Gibson? Who the hell is he? I've never heard of him. How is he even comparable to Steve McQueen?"

"Granted, he's not a big name, but wait until you meet him. He's fantastic."

"I thought we'd at least have a screen test together," she groused.

"No point! With all the changes in the script, your chemistry together is unimportant. In fact, the less chemistry, the better."

Sondra glanced longingly out the window at her brand-new red convertible. She had given it to herself as a gift for her first movie. All she wanted was to leave this tin box of a dressing trailer and drive back to L.A. Without the money from this movie, though, she would never be able to afford the payments. "I'll never forgive you for this, Bud."

"Sure you will, baby. When this is the biggest hit of next summer, you'll be falling all over yourself to forgive me."

"How about a wager? If this thing flops, you marry me."

He laughed heartily. "I'll tell you what: when this movie tops Star Wars, I'll marry you. If it flops, I'll pay you palimony." He opened the trailer door and the heat rushed in through some kind of high-speed osmosis. "We're filming the

240

kidnapping first – as soon as the sun goes down. You need to be in makeup by six."

The soft knock pulled her back to the present. "Breakfast is ready, Carmella," Sax said with a snicker.

She rolled her eyes even though Sax couldn't see her. "I'll be out in a minute." She found her purse on the nightstand and pulled a pair of sunglasses from it. Slipping them on, she scooted to the edge of the bed and dangled her feet off it. She didn't remember getting into the bed last night, though she did remember crawling toward the room. She wondered if she had passed out before arriving; in which case, Sax must have carried her in and put her to bed. She smiled, remembering all the other nice gay men who had taken care of her over the years – especially Adam. "Adam would know what to do about Fanny!" she said aloud, the epiphany catching her off guard. They hadn't spoken in a few years, though; she wasn't even sure where to find him. The last she knew, he was performing a drag act in Vegas. She made a mental note to search for him online the next chance she got.

"Are you coming?" Sax called loudly from somewhere in the house.

"Yes," she mumbled, "hold your horses." Opening the door, she saw that one side of the hallway was a series of windows and French doors. The doors opened onto a beautiful patio with a small, square pool and a bamboo furniture set. Sondra wasn't surprised at the beauty of the home; in her experience, most gay men had impeccable taste. Opening the French door before her, she relished the crisp fall morning and inhaled the wonderful scent of bacon and coffee. "Mmm...smells wonderful!"

"I've been told I'm not much of a cook, but I make a great breakfast."

Settling into one of the cushioned chairs, she watched as he poured her a fresh cup of coffee. "Thank you," she said. "I don't suppose you have a cigarette around?"

"Sorry, no. I don't smoke. Aren't there some in your purse?"

She shook her head. "I don't bring them into the bar. I'm always afraid I'll light one up by accident after a drink or two."

"How long have you smoked?"

"I started when I was a teenager, but I stopped when I went to Hollywood. For a while I only smoked when I drank. When I moved in with Bud, I stopped completely. He was a health nut and he swore I'd give him cancer."

"Is Bud Fanny's father?"

"Hell, no. You know him as George Miller."

"Wow." Sax seemed impressed.

"He was an arrogant jerk."

"Some people are allowed to be that way."

"He was going to marry me if Siege of the Moon beat Star Wars at the box office."

Sax raised his eyebrows.

"My thoughts exactly."

"Listen…I did a little research this morning, and you'll never believe what I found."

She bit down on a slice of bacon and waited.

"An indie theater in Tempe is showing Siege of the Moon on Monday. Instead of taking today off, I'm thinking of waiting until Monday. You and I can go to see your movie. What do you think?"

She wrinkled her nose. "We'll be the only ones there."

"I doubt it. Apparently, Siege of the Moon is a big draw for sci-fi buffs all over the country."

"You're kidding me."

"Swear on my mother's grave."

"What time is it showing?"

"One showing at seven o'clock. What do you think?"

She chewed her toast thoughtfully. "Yes," she said after a minute, "I think I'd like that."

Halfway through the shoot, Lianne came down with a bad case of prima donna syndrome. Suddenly, nothing was good enough for her – including her benefactor, Yasuo Oota. She flew off the set in a rage one night, slamming the door to her trailer with such force that the rest of the cast felt it before they heard it.

Sondra, who hadn't been in the scene, was startled awake by the noise. A moment later, a soft rap at her door roused her fully. A glance at her clock told her she still had two hours to sleep. She wasn't supposed to be in makeup until midnight.

Stalking to the door, she pushed it open a crack. "What?"

"Did I wake you, my darling?" Bill asked, pulling on the door hard enough that she had to release it or risk tumbling from the trailer.

She pulled her robe tightly around herself. "What are you doing here, Bill?"

"I came down to see how my money is being spent. Frankly, I'd say I've made a piss-poor investment."

"Why? What's wrong?"

"May I come in?" he asked, swaying slightly.

She stepped aside, allowing him to enter. "Have you been drinking?"

"As a matter of fact, I have. Would you like a sip?" He held a silver flask, engraved with his initials, out to her.

"No, thank you."

He fell into the couch and let out a stupendous laugh. "Your co-star seems to have developed a bit of an ego."

Sondra knew immediately whom he was talking about; she had witnessed a hair-raising fight between Oota and his discovery a few days earlier. "Lianne's just young. She'll come to her senses."

"I don't think she has senses to come to. And she's a stiff actress. We could replace her with cardboard and dub in the lines and no one would be able to tell the difference."

"She's not that bad."

"And where is the chemistry between her and Todd? You know, I think that boy is a fag."

She had developed a sort of friendship with the younger man and knew that Bill was on the right track. She shrugged and sat down.

"Have you seen the dailies?"

She hadn't, of course; she had decided to stay on set rather than drive back and forth to L.A. She wanted to save wear and tear on her prized convertible. "Are they bad?"

"You and your troop of Martian women look like attacking Christmas trees! I tried to tell that Japanese son of a bitch — you can't cover a bunch of redheads in green and silver and expect them to look threatening. Or sexy, for that matter."

Sondra swallowed, her leg bouncing with nervous energy. "Can we fix it?"

"My darling, there simply isn't any money to put into fixing this disaster. And now that Lianne has kicked Yasuo to the curb, we'll be lucky to get the funds he promised to finish the flick."

"He can't back out! He's got a contract, doesn't he?"

"Of course. He also has enough money to hire lawyers and let us take him to court. The whole project could be killed simply through delays. All Yasuo wants to do is punish that stupid girl." He took another swig from the flask. "I'm so sorry, dear girl. I thought I was doing right by you. I asked Bud to write a film that would make you a star, and now it's all been twisted around."

"You asked...why would you do that? You don't even like me!"

"On the contrary. I loved you from the moment I met you. If I had been thirty years younger, I would have pursued you. I'm just an old man, though. I have no right...I'm sorry." He looked so sad and defeated as he dropped the flask to the couch. His eyes drooped shut.

In that moment, Sondra saw the matinee idol of her youth and remembered swooning over him, wishing that he would stop aging and wait for her to catch up. She leaned toward him. Her hot breath caused him to open his eyes as their lips met for the first time. They shared a kiss so wonderful that Sondra would remember it with a shiver of pleasure for the rest of her life. He pulled her to him; she was surprised when she felt his tears fall to her cheeks. She probed him with her tongue, seeking confirmation that his professed love was true. When at last they parted, she said, "I'm going to fix this, Bill. Lianne claimed to admire me — I'll talk to her."

He was breathless and distracted. "You can do that later. Stay with me now."

"We'll have time later – after the filming is done. Right now, we need to finish this movie." She gave him a peck on the lips and popped out of his arms. She could see a slight tenting in his pants; that made her smile.

Slipping on some shoes, she left her trailer for Lianne's. Knocking on the door, she demanded, "Lianne? Let me in!"

A moment later, the door flew open and the still enraged Lianne stood before her. "What do you want?"

"We need to talk. May I come in?"

Stoically, the younger woman stood aside. "Did Yasuo send you?"

"No," she answered, settling into one of the armchairs in the living area of Lianne's trailer, which was larger than her own and recently redecorated. "Did you know that Yasuo is threatening to pull his money from the project?"

The girl's eyes widened. "Why would he do that?"

"Why do you think?"

She dropped into the other armchair. "But he can't! He has a contract..."

"Maybe so, but he's a man scorned. He'd do anything to ruin your career at this point."

"But I'm not in love with him. I've fallen for someone else."

"Who?"

She blushed. "Todd. I think we've got a real future together."

Sondra leaned forward and took the girl's hands in hers. "Honey, there's something you need to know about Todd."

After dropping Sax off at the bar around noon on Saturday, Sondra drove to Fanny's house, a squat ranch-style affair in an older section of Peoria.

"Mother," Fanny said as she opened the door. Her naturally curly hair was tied up in a flattering style that made Sondra think of the Roman busts she had seen on a long-ago visit to Italy. Her flowing forest-green dress almost camouflaged her wide hips.

"Fanny, darling, don't you look lovely," she said, stepping toward her to give her the European-style kiss greeting that was their habit.

Fanny stepped out of reach, leaving Sondra suspended on the threshold. "What are you doing here?"

Recovering, she cleared her throat and stood up straight. "I felt horrible about our spat yesterday and I came to apologize."

"This isn't a good time."

"Why not?"

"Reuben's family is here. We are observing Shabbat together."

"No matter how Jewish your nose is, Fanny, you are a gentile!"

"Not for much longer. I started the conversion practice months ago."

"What are you thinking? Converting for a man you just met?"

A slim man with brown hair slid in behind Fanny, placing a hand on each of her hips. "Who is it, dumpling?"

"Mother, meet Reuben. Reuben, this is Sondra Lane, my mother."

"Mrs. Lane. I've been looking forward to meeting you." He held his right hand out for her to shake, snaking it between Fanny's body and her arm.

Sondra ignored it. "How long have you been dating?"

Reuben dropped his hand back to Fanny's side. "We've been seeing one another for almost a year, though we have worked together much longer. I'm an attorney with the firm."

"What, are you his secretary? Is he promising to leave his wife for you?"

"Mother, today is Shabbat. We don't have unpleasant conversations on Shabbat – as I'm sure you must remember."

"Only in my nightmares, darling." She pursed her lips irritably. "I'll be back."

"Call first. But not today. I consider answering the phone work."

As soon as she turned away from the door, it slammed behind her. Muttering irritably, she trudged back to her car, the weight of her heritage pushing her into the ground. She knew what her father would have said about Fanny's outright rejection of Sondra's lifestyle: it was what she deserved.

At Milo's house – she still thought of it as his, after all – she turned on the computer and set out to track down her old friend and confidante, Adam Ross. It wasn't as hard as she thought it would be. Before long, she was at his Facebook page, looking at a recent photo of him. Wearing one of his trademark scarves, he was standing next to a Marlboro-man lookalike; behind them, a lavender semi-truck filled the background. If it weren't for the scarf, she might have continued searching. She clicked the "Add friend" button, certain that he would remember her.

The house was painfully silent without Milo and Claire around. She turned on the television and sat down in Milo's recliner. A second later, Taz, Claire's pug, was in her lap. Absently petting the dog, she flipped through the channels, searching for something – anything, really – that would distract her from her life. Nothing captured her attention.

Restlessly, she pushed the dog from her lap and stood up, pacing from her bedroom to the kitchen and back again. Finally, she slipped her shoes on and drove to the Brass Monkey.

Sax gave her a wave as she came through the door. Someone was in her seat at the far end of the bar, so she slipped into a booth to brood until the intruder left. Sax slid a whiskey sour in front of her a few minutes later. "I thought you were going to enjoy a quiet night alone."

"As it turns out, I don't really want to be alone."

"I have just the thing for you. There's a new guy at the bar. Recently widowed. First time in. Why don't you take a swing?" He moved to one side and thumbed over his shoulder at a sixtyish man in golf pants.

"Eh. I'm just not feeling sexy these days, Sax."

His jaw dropped. "You? Not sexy? That's a sure sign of the apocalypse!"

She gave him a half-smile. "Actually, I think it's just a sign that I'm getting too old. Maybe it's time for me to accept my fate. Stop dying my hair. Forget about shaving and waxing. Maybe even tell Hunter to start calling me Grandma."

"What does he call you now?"

"Mrs. Lane."

Sax winced. "You're not exactly warm and cuddly, are you?"

"Afraid not. You think it's too late for me to change?"

"How old is Hunter?"

"Nineteen."

"You might have missed your window of opportunity with him."

She dropped her gaze to the drink in front of her. "That's disappointing."

"Any chance that Fanny will have more kids?"

"Oh, Christ, Sax. My daughter is almost forty!"

"But you said she has a boyfriend now, right?"

"Yeah, but—"

Someone whistled from next to the bar. "Hey, Sax! Can we get refills, buddy?"

"We'll talk later," he said, turning away from her.

Beads of sweat rolled down the outside of the glass in front of her. She lifted it to her lips, but couldn't bring herself to drink. The warmth and fuzziness she usually desired seemed cold comfort tonight. Pushing the glass to the far side of the table, she turned to watch the crowd.

Saturday nights were good nights for Sax. Years of habit had ingrained the retirees with a strange desire to drink on Saturdays. The crowd was different, too: most of the tables were filled with foursomes, couples out on the town together. Usually, she flirted covertly with the married men, catching their eyes with sly winks and smiles, a small show of thigh or cleavage. Tonight, she stared back at those who dared to glance her direction, challenging their wandering attention with hard eyes.

Women had never liked her much. The closest relationship she ever had with another female was the one she shared with Lianne Morris. And, of course, that relationship had terminated years before.

Charmed Life

Bill's drunken declaration of love didn't evaporate in the harsh light of sobriety. Now that Sondra had shown herself to be receptive, the biggest challenge she faced was keeping the fact of their romance out of Bud's scope of vision.

The film was a stinker; that much was clear. Still, it would be a major motion picture and not one more crappy television credit on her resume. Lianne, refocused after their conversation, called Oota and told him she had just been suffering from awful cramps – a line he bought without question. The next night, he was back on set and the wiser starlet was sure to sit in his lap between takes.

"Cut!" Bud bellowed. "Come on, Sondra, really feel the lines."

"I'm sorry, Bud. The line feels wrong to me. I don't think Sunrise would say that to Rick."

"Which part?"

"'You are so much more powerful than the men of my world. You will make in me a great warrior.'"

"That's what she wants, isn't it?"

"How can she believe he's any better than Martian men? She has him trussed like a lamb for slaughter!"

"Maybe it would work better if he were just caged."

She shook her head. "I don't think so. She still has managed to subjugate him. He's nothing compared to her."

Bud ran both hands roughly through his hair. "Come on, Sondra. It's three o'clock in the morning. Can't you just work with it?"

"What if I said, 'You are so much more beautiful than the men of my world?'"

"Too seductive."

"Wouldn't she be trying to seduce him?"

"No. She would be dominating him."

"Which would mean she sees him as weak."

"Goddamn it, Sondra! Just say the line as it's written. Roll film."

"You are so much more powerful than the men of my world. You will make in me a great warrior."

"You don't understand, Sunrise. I cannot sleep with you," Todd recited stiffly.

"Who will be asleep?"

"Cut!" Bud yelled. "Better, Sondra. Let's wrap for tonight. I don't know about the rest of you, but I could really use my beauty sleep."

Lianne hopped out of Oota's lap, kissing him affectionately on the forehead. "Night, night, baby," she cooed, following on Sondra's heels like an obedient lap dog.

He grabbed her wrist, stopping her progress. "It has been too long since we shared a bed."

Sondra turned back and took Lianne's hand reassuringly. "Oota-san," she said, bowing slightly, "good acting requires purity of the mind and body. For the sake of the film, surely you will sacrifice your own pleasures?"

Oota's lips thinned to a straight line. "Of course, Ms. Lane. You are the expert, are you not?"

"I am," she stated confidently. Oota released Lianne, and the two women walked hand in hand to Sondra's trailer, closing the door behind them.

"Geez, Sondra. I owe you so much. How can I ever repay you?"

"Just be the best actress you can be. This movie may not have a snowball's chance in hell, but we still have to give it our all. A movie can be awful, but a good actress can transcend one bad film."

"My nana told me this would happen." She pushed her palms against her eyes.

"What do you mean?"

"She practically begged me to stay in Texas. She told me no good could come from California."

"Honey, don't be upset. At least you didn't land on some casting couch, spreading your legs for some lecher who still wouldn't cast you."

She shook her head and said, "No, I went right for the producer's couch. Much more effective use of my talents."

A rap on the door interrupted them. "Who is it?" Sondra called.

"It's Bud, baby. Let me in."

"Not tonight, Bud. Lianne's not feeling well and she wants to stay with me."

"Come on, Sondra…it's been more than a week. I'm turning blue."

She laughed lightly to let him know she wasn't convinced. "Just think how good it will be when we can be together again."

Lianne stood. "I can—"

Sondra put a finger to her lips to silence her. The girl sat down again.

Bud's sigh was loud enough to be heard through the metal door of the trailer. "Fine. I understand. Get some rest – we have a long shoot tomorrow. We're doing the solar eclipse scene, so you two need to be in makeup no later than ten tomorrow morning."

"Understood, Bud. See you tomorrow."

They listened as his footsteps trod away from the trailer.

"I don't want to interfere in your relationship with Mr. Miller," Lianne said softly.

"You aren't."

Another knock, this one softer, broke through the silence.

"Come in."

Bill stepped through the door. His joyful grin dissipated to a frown when he saw Lianne. "You're not alone."

"No. But you're welcome to join us for a few minutes."

The actor-cum-producer fell back on his latent skills and became the charming man his persona required. "Of course. How better to spend an evening than with two such lovely ladies?" Bill regaled them with stories of his youth, both before and after he moved to Hollywood.

After an hour, Lianne lost the struggle to stay awake, laying her head on the sofa cushion with her legs pulled loosely toward her chest. Bill, noticing that the younger woman was asleep, moved to sit next to Sondra. "Darling girl, I cannot wait until we can be together," he whispered against her neck.

"Neither can I. But we must – you know how petty Bud can be when he believes he's been wronged." His hot breath against her neck made her body tingle in a way that Bud's had never done.

"I am like a schoolboy – I think about you constantly. When I watch you on the set I swoon with every line you speak."

"Really?"

"Absolutely, my darling. You are the Vivien Leigh of your generation...the next Bette Davis. You are set to take Hollywood by storm. They don't even know what is coming their way."

"But this film..."

"You are greater than this film. You will rise from its ashes and—" Lianne shifted and Bill moved back to the chair with remarkable speed.

"Are you driving back to L.A. this morning?" Sondra said, no longer whispering.

"Frank's expecting me in Vegas in a few hours. He's invited me to stay in his suite for the weekend."

Lianne stretched and opened her eyes. "We'd better get our beauty sleep, Sondra. We have an early call tomorrow."

"I'm afraid she's right, Bill. Thank you for stopping by."

"My pleasure. I'll be back by Wednesday of next week. Bud said the wrap party would be Thursday evening."

"I hadn't realized how close to the finish line we were!"

"Indeed, my dear girls. You are on the verge of becoming movie stars." He bent and kissed each of their hands before leaving the trailer. "Good night and sweet dreams."

Sunday morning found Sondra smoking a cigarette and drinking coffee with amaretto creamer at the kitchen table. Taz begged silently at her feet until she tore her unwanted toast into small squares and fed them to him. Adam hadn't responded to her friend request, and she wondered if she were so easily forgotten.

Despair seemed to be stalking her with every move she made. Sitting in front of the computer felt pointless and she wasn't welcome in the theater or at Fanny's house. The grief that hung around her seemed determined to refresh her memory of every bad thing she had ever done or witnessed.

In particular, Lianne's death was playing on a loop in her head. Though she hadn't witnessed it, the details had been gruesome enough to cause her nightmares for months afterward and periodically since then. At least, Sondra thought, Lianne wasn't remembered as a bad actress in a forgettable sci-fi flick.

If only Bill had lived longer, she might have become something other than a Hollywood star's trophy girlfriend. Catherine Zeta-Jones had transcended her marriage to Hollywood royalty, earning a crown of her very own. But Bill had died thirty years ago and she had become a show pony in the new Hollywood – a relic before her time.

She flipped through a Vogue restlessly. When she lived in California, she had places to wear the dresses found within its fashionable pages. Now, the only place she could dress up was – nowhere. Without the stage, she might as well wear polyester pants and let her hair go gray.

She closed the magazine and pushed it away.

"I think you should sit down." Bill was standing with his hands on his hips in the doorway of the nursery.

"Don't be ridiculous, sweetheart," Sondra answered, stretching toward the ceiling with a roller full of yellow paint. She was fourteen weeks along with their second child. "The doctor said I can do anything, as long as I pay attention when my body tells me that it's tired."

"It's not that, darling girl." He was so somber that she stepped off the ladder.

"What's wrong?"

"I've just had a call from one of the scandal sheets asking for comment on Lianne."

"What's the girl done now?" she sighed, sitting on the second step of the ladder. Only a month ago she had argued – in vain – that larger breasts wouldn't improve Lianne's chances for future roles. Succumbing to what Sondra thought of as Charlie's Angels syndrome, the girl had changed herself from a willowy beauty into a top-heavy trollop. She wasn't the first and she wouldn't be the last. Sondra thanked God that the trend had started after she was old enough to know better.

Bill walked to her and took both of her hands in his. "She's had an accident."

"Oh, my God," she inhaled. "Where is she? Which hospital? Wait – she left for Texas this morning, didn't she? A plane crash?!"

"No. Not exactly."

Her stomach cramped uncomfortably. "For the love of God, Bill, just tell me!"

"From what I understand, she...exploded."

"The plane exploded? Was it a bomb? Who would bomb a domestic flight?"

"Not the plane, Sondra. Lianne exploded. Just Lianne."

She couldn't focus on anything. She tried to stare at Bill's hands, but she kept imagining them covered in blood and gore. "How could...?"

"Her..." he trailed off, searching for the words. "That surgery she had? The...parts...they were defective. They exploded."

It was lucky, really, that Lianne had been on the way home. Her family took care of the arrangements for her burial. With Bill's blessing, Sondra flew to Texas to attend the funeral – closed casket, of course. The story would have made the headlines of the weekly trash newspapers if Jean Seberg hadn't been found dead in the back of her car two days later. Of the two actresses, Jean was clearly better known, having made more than twenty films. In the end, Sondra got more press after she miscarried her baby than poor Lianne, swallowed by obscurity.

Sondra was glad to see Milo and Claire when they came home Sunday night. She hugged them both and cajoled them into staying up. "I'll make a fresh pot of coffee."

The couple exchanged glances, but acquiesced to their needy roommate.

"Was Taz okay for you?" Claire asked, settling into one corner of the angular brown sectional, her legs tucked beneath her and the dog pressed against her thigh.

"He was fine. He's pretty good company – though he spent a lot of time lying in front of the door, waiting for you to come home." Sondra stood in the doorway to the kitchen, keeping her eyes on Milo and Claire. "How was the trip?"

"Fine. Great, really. Don't you think, sweetheart?" Milo asked.

"Wonderful. Alice Marie had a fantastic time."

"What did you do?"

"We saw a re-enactment of the OK Corral gunfight," Milo offered.

"Sounds like fun!" Sondra glanced toward the coffee pot, which was only half full. "What else did you do?"

Claire spoke up, telling her about Alice Marie's first time on a horse. When the coffee pot was full, Sondra said, "Keep talking. I can hear you." She pulled two mugs from the kitchen cabinet and filled them. She carried them in and handed one to Claire before setting her mug next to the sofa and returning to the kitchen for the creamer.

"Don't I get a cup?" Milo called out.

"I thought you didn't like coffee."

"What can I say? Claire's having an effect on me."

Sondra poured an extra mug and gave it to Milo before settling on the chaise longue end of the sectional. She topped off her mug with the creamer and tossed the plastic bottle to Claire, who smiled graciously.

"How was your weekend?" Milo asked.

"Quiet, mostly."

"Did you have a good time at Fanny's house on Friday?" Claire asked.

"I didn't stay with Fanny. She had other plans."

"Oh, no! You didn't get a hotel room, did you? If I'd known you didn't have a place to stay, I would have given you the keys to my condo!"

"That's something to remember if this comes up again. I wouldn't mind playing the cosmopolitan city dweller for a few nights." She sipped her coffee. "But no, I stayed with Sax instead."

Milo smiled curiously. "I didn't know you two were so close."

"Of course we are. I've always had a good rapport with gay men. Sax is no different."

The couple exchanged a glance.

"What?"

"Are you saying all gay men are the same?" Claire piped up.

"Not exactly…but similar, yes."

Milo laughed. "That's like saying you and Claire are the same because you both like men."

"We must have something in common, don't you think? After all, we both like you." Sondra instantly realized her misstep. "Of course, not the same way."

The damage was done, though. Claire's expression became guarded. She stretched and put the coffee mug on the end table. "I'm tired. Aren't you, Milo?"

"Yes. We'll see you in the morning, Sondra."

They were gone a moment later, leaving Sondra with three half-empty cups and her miserable mind.

Sondra was still embarrassed when she awoke the next morning. She stayed in bed until she was certain she heard both Milo and Claire leave. Claire, who volunteered at the zoo four days a week – Monday through Thursday – took Taz with her when she left, a sure sign that she wouldn't be back until Friday. She wondered when Claire and Milo would stop pretending to keep separate homes and ask her to leave. She contemplated her options for that future day. She certainly couldn't move back in with Fanny – not that she would have wanted to, anyway. Maybe Sax would offer her a room – then again, after her behavior Friday night, maybe not. She squeezed her eyes closed against the string of faux pas that had plagued the last several days. In the Seventies, someone would have told her that her biorhythms were out of whack. She wondered if anyone still believed in biorhythms these days.

She finally dragged herself to the kitchen at just past ten. Half of a pot of warm coffee waited for her. She dropped two slices of bread into the toaster and filled her mug while she waited for the appliance to do its work.

Charmed Life

When the toast popped out, she put a cold butter pat between the two slices and shuffled to the kitchen table, feeling every minute of her more than sixty years on the planet. Her sigh echoed in the silent house – she had nothing to show for her life except one lousy film, a couple of years' worth of soap opera episodes, and a Jewish daughter. If being Jewish had been trendy back in the Seventies, she would have hosted Shabbat sleepovers. But even believing in God had seemed passé back then. She bit into the buttered toast, chewing slowly.

Her phone rang and she pulled it out of her robe pocket to see who was calling. Sax's name filled the small screen. She flipped the phone open and grunted a greeting.

"Are you ready for our afternoon out?" he asked cheerily.

"Not really."

"Are you still in a funk?"

"I don't think this is a funk. It's more like a death spiral."

"Over-dramatic much?"

"Seeing that awful movie will probably push me toward suicide at this point."

"Sondra, you've got to cheer up, my dear. I'm telling you, this is going to be a huge ego boost for you. Now, do you have the outfit you wore in the movie, by any chance?"

"Why? Do you want to go in drag?"

"Don't be ridiculous, darling. I want you to wear the outfit, not me."

"That is simply not going to happen. Besides, I don't have the outfit anymore," she lied.

"That's a shame."

"Let's just skip it, Sax. I'm in no mood—"

"We're not skipping it," he said adamantly. "I promise you will be back to your cheery self after this. You might even be better than normal."

"Fine. What time?"

"I'll be by at six o'clock."

Sax arrived right at six, wearing an outfit that reminded her of the earnest tree-hugger garb the wardrobe woman had insisted suited Todd's character – a flannel shirt and body-hugging jeans. Sondra slid her eyes over him skeptically. "Why are you wearing that?"

"All the websites say that the movie is more fun if you get into character."

"I'm not doing that."

"Of course you are! I bet you've got the original Sunrise Aeon costume hanging in your closet."

"That costume was the property of the production team."

"Like that red-and-white von Furstenberg wrap dress you stole from Scions of Beauty?"

"That was severance pay."

His eyebrows nearly touched his hairline.

"I'm not wearing silver lamé to a movie."

"What about green makeup, then? Just for the effect."

"No."

Sax sighed. "Fine. I think you'd have more fun if you got into the spirit of things, though."

She picked up her purse and keys. "You're in plenty of spirit for the both of us. In fact, you could be the Spirit of Movies Past. You're a little old to be Todd Gibson, don't you think?"

"Who's Todd Gibson?"

"The male lead in the movie – the guy you're dressed up like."

He shrugged. "I only saw the movie once, Sondra. Did he make any other films?"

"No. His career was as dead as mine after Siege of the Moon."

"What happened to him?"

"AIDS. He died in 1990."

"And the other female star?"

"Lianne Morris. Also dead."

"So you're the last living star of a cult film classic?"

"Says you."

"Says the internet, sweetheart. Embrace your inner star, Sondra – these people are your fans."

She smiled indulgently at her friend. "This movie was and is a joke, Sax. Siege of the Moon is not an aged wine – it's more like a stale Twinkie."

"At least put on some lipstick and a nice outfit – just in case you're recognized."

"I'd rather put on a hat and sunglasses just to be sure I'm not."

"Humor me."

"Fine." She went to her makeup mirror and smeared on some red lipstick. "What should I wear?"

"Pull out the wrap dress – you still look fabulous in that."

She closed the bedroom door and changed. Examining her reflection in the mirrored closet door, she had to admit she did look fabulous – even if she was old. She flashed her eyes flirtatiously at her reflection and laughed.

In the living room a moment later, Sax was as appreciative as any gay man could be. "You look fabulous, Sondra. Très chic."

"Shall I drive?"

Forty-five minutes later, Sondra pulled into a parking lot near the small theater, splitting a cadre of Sunrise Aeons and Rick Rices with a threatening engine roar and a stern glance over the top of her sunglasses. Sax blew out an exaggerated sigh and stepped from the car on shaky legs. "Are you okay?" Sondra asked, stepping out from behind the steering wheel.

"You have road rage," he accused, pointing at her.

"Nonsense. Everyone in L.A. drives like that. You just have a problem with women drivers."

"You laid on your horn for two solid miles!"

"I just wanted to be sure that bitch knew she cut me off."

"Yeah. I think she figured that out."

A group of Martian warrior women were whispering and pointing at them from the corner of the theater building. "We're drawing attention to ourselves, Sax. Let's just go inside."

Sax turned around and gave the girls a wave. They let out a synchronized gasp before giggling and disappearing. "Strange," he said to Sondra as she joined him.

"I'm sure they are just shocked that a man your age is dressed in costume to attend a movie."

"Don't be ridiculous. I'm blending in with the crowd."

"Not really."

"Bitch."

"Thank you. Better that than a fool."

Sax purchased two tickets from a disinterested box office attendant and the two of them entered the theater lobby, where a crowd of Sunrises and Ricks – as well as a smattering of Kays – parted to allow them through.

"Would you like some popcorn, Sondra?" Sax asked. Sondra noticed a nearby green-colored girl's eyes widen as she turned to whisper to her friends.

"Yes, please. And a soda."

"Your wish is my command." He walked toward the concessions counter, leaving her standing alone as conversations died and all eyes turned toward her. One of the many Sunrise Aeons approached her, pushed forward by her friends. She cleared her throat and said, "Excuse me."

"Yes?"

"This might sound...well...crazy, but are you...by any chance—"

"Spit it out already," Sondra muttered.

The girl, flustered, asked, "Sunrise Aeon?"

"Do I look like Sunrise Aeon?" she countered imperiously.

The girl's friends nodded. Sax was walking back, juggling drinks and a tub of popcorn.

Sondra scanned the crowd, wondering if she was about to be laughed out of the theater. She regretted not wearing a wig and big movie-star shades. "I am Sondra Lane," she admitted, jutting her chin forward.

The crowd inhaled as one and stepped backward, as if she were someone important to admire. The girl before her clapped her hands together excitedly. "Oh, my goodness! Oh, gosh! Sondra Lane! I just love you!"

"What? Why?"

"Everyone does!" she gushed. "You're the original beast! All the best heroines are modeled on Sunrise Aeon – and you are Sunrise!"

Sondra softened her stance and smiled inquisitively at the girl. "What do you mean?"

"Buffy's modeled on Sunrise – a female warrior with a softer side."

260

"Who is Buffy?"

The crowd laughed. Someone shouted, "A pale imitation of you!" A few other voices shouted their agreement.

"You are twice the woman Kay Rice is – Rick totally should have dumped that whiny bitch and ran off with you. Would you sign my glove?" The girl put her gloved arm straight out in front of Sondra.

"I don't have a pen."

"I have a Sharpie!" one of her friends shouted.

"Maybe later, kids," Sax said. "The movie's about to start."

The green girl asked, "Are you the real Rick Rice? Is that why you're here together?"

The crowd sucked in a breath, seconds from exploding into a frenzy.

Sondra diffused the situation, holding her hands up, palms out, and shushing the crowd. "I'm afraid not. Todd Gibson, who played Rick Rice, died a number of years ago."

"I read on the internet that Lianne Morris's chest exploded!" called out a Kay Rice lookalike. "Is that true?"

Sondra winced at the memory. Sax rescued her. "The movie is starting now. Maybe Miss Lane could be persuaded to sign autographs after the show if everyone politely and quietly files into the theater now."

A few grumbles reached her ears, but the crowd began to move toward the assigned auditorium. Sax and Sondra filed along with the rest of the crowd. The green girl and her friends jostled to stay close to Sondra, flanking Sax and her once they were seated.

The theater went dark and Sondra watched her one and only movie with new eyes.

Altered States

Claire poured Milo another cup of coffee and kissed him on the forehead.

"What was that for?"

"Just because you're so wonderful!" she exclaimed, twirling gracefully back to the coffeemaker. "Our life is terrific, don't you think?"

"Yes, my love, it is." Milo, happier than he had ever been, smiled at his girlfriend. He had promised himself that he would never marry again after dead Alice freed him, but Claire was changing his mind on a multitude of subjects. He had even found himself eyeing diamond rings at a mall jewelry store a few days before – though, of course, their relationship still needed more time to grow before he made that leap. And there were still little details that would need addressing. For instance, would they live in Sun City or in her high-rise condo? If they lived in Sun City, would they ask Sondra to leave? How would he break the news to his son Brian and his family? He shook his head, trying to clear the gathering storm clouds away.

"What's wrong?" Claire asked, sitting across from him at the small kitchen table.

"Nothing. Just working some things out." He looked down at the crossword in front of him.

"What's the clue?"

"What? Oh, no...it's not the puzzle."

She frowned. "You can tell me anything."

"I know. But there's nothing to tell. I promise."

She sipped her coffee. "Are you coming to the zoo today?"

"I promised Alice Marie I'd take her out to get her Halloween costume."

"Already?"

"Darling, it's October 22nd."

"Time flies these days, doesn't it?"

"Indeed."

"I need to get going. I'm with the orangutans today." She swallowed the rest of her coffee and stood.

"Say hello to Duchess for me."

"Kiss Alice Marie for me."

"Will do."

Charmed Life

As soon as the carport door closed, Milo heard Sondra's door open. Sondra rarely came out before Claire was gone; Milo suspected that she found Claire's cheery morning demeanor off-putting. She made her way to the coffeepot without looking behind her. Before she could pick up the carafe, he said, "Good morning."

She jumped and turned quickly. "I thought I was alone."

"Sorry about that."

"It's okay. Actually, I'm glad to have some company." She poured herself a cup of coffee, pulled the amaretto creamer from the fridge, and sat down at the table. "How's Claire?"

"She's great. Are you still banned from the theater?"

"Yes. But at least I have the Halloween party next weekend to keep me busy."

"You're throwing a party? Here?"

"No," she answered quickly, "I wouldn't do that without asking first! Sax throws a big Halloween bash every year at the Brass Monkey, and he asked me to help decorate the bar. The party is on Friday night. You and Claire should come."

"Maybe we will. Sounds like fun. Have you got your costume yet?"

"I'm thinking of going as Sunrise Aeon. I have the outfit in my closet."

"Forty years after the film was made?"

She shrugged. "I've kept some of my memorabilia. Did you know the movie has made a bit of a comeback?"

"Really? Didn't you say it was a bomb?"

"So was It's a Wonderful Life when it was released. Tastes change. Sax and I went to see it a couple of weeks ago and the audience recognized me."

Milo caught the hint of excitement in her voice. "That's wonderful."

"It really was! I signed fifty autographs after the movie ended. All these women – and more than a few men – were dressed up like my character."

"It must have been gratifying after all those years of obscurity."

She stilled and said frostily, "A lot of people knew who I was in Hollywood."

He cleared his throat. "I'm taking Alice Marie costume shopping today."

She was irritably tapping her index fingernail against the side of her coffee cup, no longer focused on their conversation.

"Sondra?"

No answer came; it was as if she couldn't hear him anymore.

"Sondra, talk to me."

She looked at him blankly for a moment before smiling. "I'm sorry. My mind must have wandered off."

"I'm sorry, Sondra. That was rude of me."

"No, you're quite right. Not so long ago, the only people who recognized me were sixty-year-old housewives and homosexuals, and most of them weren't in awe so much as in hysterics. The people who knew me in my prime are mostly dead."

Milo drained the remainder of his now-lukewarm coffee. "I need to get going. Alice Marie is expecting me."

"Of course. See you later."

Milo went to the bedroom to find his shoes and put them on. When he came out, Sondra was in front of the computer. "Anything interesting?"

"An old friend sent me a note," she said with a smile. "He's going to be in town next weekend."

"Will he be staying with us?" It would be the first time Sondra had entertained a man since their breakup months before.

"I don't think so. He'll be with his husband."

Milo did his best to pull his eyebrows back down to an acceptable level. "I see."

"He's a wonderful friend, though he makes me look dowdy."

"That seems impossible."

"Just you wait." She went back to the keyboard and Milo left the house.

Forty minutes later, Alice Marie bounced in the seat next to him. "What do you want to be this year?" he asked.

"A princess."

"Cinderella or Snow White?"

"Not that kind of princess, Grampa! A vampire princess."

Charmed Life

"Does your mom know what you want to be?"

She nodded, her big eyes wide with pleading.

"Okay, a vampire princess it is!"

"Yay!" She clapped her hands together excitedly.

"Can you make a scary face?"

She spread her fingers, claw like, and bared her teeth with a hiss.

Milo pretended to be scared. "Whoa! Bone-chilling, Alice Marie!"

She giggled, reverting to her normally pleasant demeanor.

He drove them to one of the Halloween superstores that always popped up around the end of August to fill some of the perpetually empty retail space in the valley. Inside, harried mothers and fathers shepherded gangs of wannabe ghosts and goblins through the aisles of novelties and costumes. He held up a set of fake fangs for Alice Marie to see. "What do you think of these?"

"Cool! Can I have them?"

"Sure! You'll need them for your costume anyway."

She gave Milo a quick hug around his waist and skipped ahead. "I'll be over here!" she called out, pointing in the direction of the giant bat that hung over a selection of monster costumes.

He waved her on while he strolled the row of prank items. He wondered if kids still pulled tricks on those curmudgeonly enough not to hand out treats on Halloween. He had pulled a few when he was a kid – particularly on old Mr. O'Malley, the only one on the block who didn't give away candy. Instead, he always had a supply of toothbrushes. As an adult, Milo could understand the choice. But when he was a kid, it used to infuriate him. He and a couple buddies had left O'Malley more than one stinky surprise on his doorstep.

Shaking his head with a chuckle, he scanned the gags. A small white spray bottle caught his eye. Picking it up, he read the label: Liquid Ass. He burst into laughter – the little boy who maintains a residence in all grown men was amused. A young mother a few feet away observed him curiously. The adult in Milo set the bottle back on the shelf and moved another step down the aisle until he stood in front of the fake vomit. He tried to be interested in the disgusting-looking plastic, but he was drawn to the small white bottle. He knew Alice Marie wouldn't be interested in smelly fart jokes – little girls generally weren't. However, his teenaged grandson Eric would think it was cool. Before he could reconsider, he palmed two of the bottles and went to find Alice Marie.

"I want this one, Grampa!" She pointed to a black-and-red Renaissance-style gown with pointed shoulders.

"Are you sure? We've had a warm fall so far – you might be hot in this one."

She considered his words for a few moments before saying, "This one. Definitely." She found her size and held it against her. "What do you think?"

"Hold up your fangs, too."

She did as he asked.

"Do you need some makeup to go with it? I think I saw a vampire makeup kit."

"I don't think so. I'm pretty pale already, don't you think?"

She had a point. With her dark hair, widow's peak, and pale skin, she would make a perfect vampire princess. He took the costume and laid it over his arm. "Okay. Let's get out of here, Elvira."

"Who's Elvira?" she asked, taking Milo's free hand.

He had taken Alice Marie out for lunch and to a movie that afternoon. When he drove his granddaughter home, Brian and Marla insisted that he come in and have dinner with the family; they simply wouldn't take no for an answer.

"This is lovely," Marla said, praising Alice Marie's costume choice. "You're going to look fantastic on Halloween!"

"I wasn't sure if a vampire princess was an approved costume or not, Marla. I'm afraid I took her word for it," Milo said, settling into the family room sofa.

"Vampires are all the rage these days," she sighed. "I would have rather seen her go as a ballerina, but, as she rightly points out, she already is a ballerina in 'everyday life.' That's not much of a costume."

"I bought a little something for Eric. Is he home?"

"Eric!" Brian boomed. His baritone voice made the windows rattle.

"Yeah, Dad?" The similarly pitched answer surprised Milo.

"When did his voice change?" he whispered to Marla.

"It's still cracking now and then," she answered. "Strange, isn't it?"

"Your grandfather is here and he has something for you." Brian turned to Milo. "He'll be down in a minute."

Milo wasn't holding his breath; in his experience, Eric was a sullen kid who didn't always respond when commanded. When he heard the boy's feet on the stairs, he was impressed.

"Grandpa Crosby," the young man said with a smile. He had grown six inches since the last time Milo had seen him. He was still as pale as his sister, but he was beginning to gain his adult features.

"Eric, my boy! How are you?"

"Good, thank you."

"How is high school?"

"Not too bad, so far."

"Good, good. Listen, I don't know if you still do Halloween—"

"I'm going to a dance this year instead of, you know, trick or treating."

"Well, this might not be such a great gift then." He slipped his hand into the pocket on the front of his Guayabera and pulled out one of the bottles of Liquid Ass.

Eric's eyes widened with delight. "Holy crap!"

"Eric! Watch your tongue!" Marla admonished.

"Sorry, Mom." He took the bottle from Milo. "This is awesome, Grampa."

"What is it?" Brian asked.

"It's stink spray," Milo answered.

"Don't open that in the house," Marla said immediately.

"Awesome," Brian said with a wide grin. "Let me see it."

Eric rolled his eyes, but passed the small bottle to his father, who read the outside of the package. "Man, I wish you'd bought me something like this when I was a kid," he said to Milo.

"Believe me, son, if I had, your mother would have slit my throat."

Brian chuckled. "Yeah, probably. But it might have been worth it just to see her face." He stood up and said, "Let's try it."

"Outside!" Marla exclaimed. "Don't even think of spraying that stuff in here."

"Relax, darling. I wouldn't do that to you. Come on, Dad, let's go sit on the patio."

Milo, Eric, and Brian walked single-file out the sliding glass door. Frowning, Marla closed the door behind them.

Brian pulled the protective cellophane from the bottle. "Eric, go out about ten paces and spray."

"Okay, Dad." He took the bottle and jogged to the middle of the yard. Facing the porch, he pumped the bottle once. They waited with bated breath for a few seconds. Eric smelled it first and retched as he backed up even further.

"Can you smell it?" Milo asked Brian.

"No, not...oh, holy God, that smells like death!"

Milo laughed. When he took his next breath, the full stench hit him: a combination of dead animals and diarrhea the likes of which he had never smelled before infiltrated his nose like a sneak attack of tiny warriors intent on burning every hair from his nostrils. "That is disgusting."

Brian had escaped around the corner of the house for a breath of fresh air. "Wow. That stuff is pungent. I've never smelled anything that awful in my life."

Eric jogged back to the porch. "Oh, man! This stuff is going to kill at the dance."

"Quite possibly," Milo said ruefully. "Listen, I don't think—"

"It's not toxic, Dad," Brian said, coming back around the corner. "It just smells like death, it doesn't cause it." He turned to Eric. "Do not, under any circumstances, use that stuff in a classroom. If I get one call—"

"I won't!" Eric assured him. "I'll only use it in non-educational settings."

"Okay. You can keep it."

The boy gave Brian a quick hug before leaning down to hug Milo. "Thanks, Grampa. You're the best."

"You're welcome," Milo said. A small tear of happiness formed in the corner of his eye – Eric had never hugged him spontaneously before. The boy disappeared into the house and Milo surreptitiously wiped away the gathering moisture. Brian sat down at the patio table with him again.

"The odor lingers a bit, doesn't it?" Brian commented, wrinkling his nose.

"It's potent, that's for sure."

"Thanks for taking Alice Marie out to get her costume, Dad."

"Glad to do it. She's a wonderful girl."

"I like to think so." Brian glanced toward him from the corner of his eye. "So, is everything okay in Sun City?"

"Just ducky."

"Alice Marie tells me you've got another roommate."

"No. Just Sondra. You remember her, of course."

"The redhead who organized the dinner party a few months ago, right? She seemed nice. But Alice Marie says Claire is living with you also."

Milo flushed. "Not exactly. She spends a lot of time there…"

"With her dog?"

"Taz can't be left alone while she's at my place. Besides, my house has a yard. Her condo doesn't."

"So the dog lives with you." Brian smirked.

"Sort of, I guess." He shifted uneasily in the wire-mesh chair. "Now that you bring it up, though, I have been meaning to talk to you about my relationship with Claire."

"Dad, let me stop you right there."

Milo fell back in the chair, deflated. "I'm sorry."

"Don't be sorry. Alice Marie tells me that Claire is wonderful. Marla and I would like to get to know her better. Maybe we could go out to dinner together next week?"

Milo smiled at his son. "That would be wonderful."

It was after eight o'clock by the time Milo arrived home that night; Claire's car was already in the driveway, as was Sondra's. Walking in, he found the two women engaged in conversation on the brown living room sectional.

Claire popped up and walked over to hug and kiss him hello. "How were Brian and his family?"

"Very well. What are you two up to?"

"Nothing much. Sondra was just telling me about an opportunity she's found."

"What sort of opportunity?"

"One of the kids I met at the movie theater tracked me down on Facebook to ask if I would consider appearing at a science fiction convention in New Mexico next month!"

"Why?"

"Because I'm Sunrise Aeon, of course."

"Did you know that there are fansites dedicated to Siege of the Moon, Milo?" Claire asked. "Your roommate is a genuine celebrity!"

"That's surprising."

"I know," Sondra said. "Who would have thought that, after all this time, Bud would turn out to be right? Goodness, I hope he doesn't track me down and try to make good on his promise."

"Who's Bud?" Milo asked.

"George Miller, the director," Claire answered.

"What did he promise?"

"A wedding!" Sondra laughed. "He said he'd marry me when the movie proved to be a hit."

Milo sat down; the bottle of stink spray dug into his hip, and he pulled it out of his pocket, setting it on the nearby end table.

"What's that?" Claire asked, reaching for it. "Liquid Ass. Eww." Her face creased in disgust. "Where did you get this?"

"At the Halloween store. It's for pranks."

"Right. So why did you need a bottle, exactly?"

"You just never know when you'll need a good fart spray."

Claire narrowed her eyes. "Men never really grow up, do they?"

He snickered. Turning his attention back to Sondra, he asked, "Are you going to be paid to appear at the convention?"

"Not too much, but a bit – and they're paying for my hotel and meals."

"Who?"

"The convention organizers."

He nodded thoughtfully. "Sounds like a good deal."

"I think it might be. I haven't committed yet, but I'm definitely considering it."

"What about travel expenses?"

"The young man who got me the gig says I can ride with him if I want."

"I'm assuming his car is newer than your convertible?"

"My car is a classic, Milo."

"Exactly why I don't want you driving across the desert in it. What if you broke down?"

"I'd hitch up my skirt and stick out my thumb," she answered saucily.

"And then you'd use your cell phone to call Claire or me for a ride."

"Thanks for the vote of confidence."

"Look, I have no doubt about your allure – but we're talking about long stretches of desert here. It's not the sort of place where finding a ride is easy."

"Good point." She sighed. "Look, I haven't even decided if I'm going yet. I don't know if appearing at science fiction conventions upgrades or downgrades my celebrity status."

Milo wondered if she had any celebrity status to lose, but let the comment pass with a yawn. "It's been a long day and I'm beat. I'm going to grab a quick shower and head to bed."

"I'll be along in a few minutes, darling," Claire answered.

"Good night, Milo. Sweet dreams."

Shaking his head in amusement, Milo headed for his bedroom.

Charmed Life

Trick or Treat

Stepping into the silver lamé miniskirt and go-go boots without smudging her green makeup was a bigger challenge than Sondra remembered. Of course, on the movie set, the wardrobe women had been there to help her. Short of calling Claire in for an assist, she was on her own.

From her bedroom, she could hear Adam, Steve, Milo and Claire making small talk in the living room. Adam was exactly as she remembered him: flamboyant and friendly. He and Steve had only recently married in New York, though they had been together several years. Sondra thought Milo was doing an excellent job of masking his discomfort around the couple.

Unfortunately, Adam and Claire were both dressed as Cher and Steve and Milo were decked out to resemble Sonny; the costumes were creating much more friction than the sexuality of the parties involved.

"I knew we should have gone as two of the Village People," Adam had said as soon as he saw Milo and Claire.

"No one ever gets that," Steve answered. "We just end up looking like a cowboy and a sailor."

Sondra had excused herself mid-debate to change into her costume. She was certain she had made the right decision in arranging for Steve and Adam to stay with Sax for the weekend. Sax had graciously invited her to stay with him as well, an offer that she had gladly accepted.

Someone knocked on her door.

"Who's there?"

"It's Claire," the woman stage-whispered into the crack of the door.

"Come in…I could use some help."

Claire, complete with a straight black wig and an Indian headdress, pushed open the door just wide enough to come inside the room. "Maybe Milo and I should skip the party," she suggested as she closed the door behind her.

"Don't be ridiculous! You're already dressed!"

"Adam is so upset, though."

"That's not your fault. Just ignore him. He's a bit of a diva." She handed one of the boots to Claire and sat down on the bed. "He's not being mean, is he?"

"He told me I was too busty to be a really good Cher."

"So? He's about five inches too short to be a 'really good Cher.' Don't worry about it."

"He told Milo he looked like Congressman Bono instead of Flower Power Bono."

Sondra couldn't stop the laugh that escaped.

Claire looked pained as she knelt to help Sondra with the boots.

"Sorry. But Steve's too tall and too handsome to be Sonny."

"Adam said he wanted Steve to be Cher, but he refused."

Sondra lifted her foot and Claire carefully fit the unzipped boot onto it and pulled the zipper up before reaching around to get the other one.

"Once we're at the party, the bar will be so crowded that no one will even see all four of you together. Please come."

Claire slipped the other boot onto Sondra's waiting foot. "Okay. But I can't guarantee we'll stay late."

"This is Sun City, Claire. The whole party will break up by ten-thirty, at the latest."

Claire laughed and held up her makeup-smudged hands. "I think I'm green with envy. How is it possible that you look so good in an outfit you haven't worn in decades?"

"Blame Adam. He's the one who convinced me I needed to start exercising." She admired herself in the mirror, turning first one way and then the other. "I look like I'm all set to spend the night at Studio 54." Reaching under her hair at the back of her neck, she pulled the skin tight, causing her neck to smooth. "What do you think? Should I get a neck lift?"

"Can you do that?"

"Of course! But I always said I wouldn't get anything lifted, tucked, or enhanced. Too many of my friends had disastrous cosmetic surgeries. I mean, look at what the doctors did to Priscilla Presley."

"Are you friends with Priscilla?"

"Well, no...we only met a few times at parties. She was nice enough, if a little withdrawn. But have you seen what the doctors have done to her face over the years? That's what happens when a woman doubts her own beauty."

"Why would you consider surgery now?"

"I think if I had my neck tightened, I'd look more like my character, don't you?"

"Sondra, you can't help but look like your character. You played her."

"Still," she said, releasing the skin, "you have to admit I look older."

Claire sighed. "Are you ready?"

"Yes. Let's not keep them waiting any longer."

Rather than piling into a single vehicle, Sondra drove Adam and Steve while Claire and Milo took their own car. The parking lot outside the Brass Monkey was filled with golf carts and large sedans, indicating a crowd inside the bar. Sondra, wanting to make a grand entrance, sent the other four in ahead of her, waiting for the door to stop swinging before she sauntered up to it, pushing it open dramatically. A few heads swiveled, but not nearly as many as she had hoped. She supposed this wasn't really her demographic. Shrugging, she waved at Sax, who raised his eyebrows and waggled a finger at her costume. She shrugged again. Out of the corner of her eye, she saw Mildred Kovich, dressed as a surprisingly plump Cleopatra, scowl at her. She turned and smiled graciously at the woman before proceeding to the far corner of the bar to secure some liquid courage in the form of a whiskey sour.

"I knew you had the costume somewhere," Sax smirked as he slid the drink into her hand.

"Cheers," she said, lifting the glass and draining it in less than a minute.

"What's wrong?"

"Bob and Mildred are here."

"So? I told you they would be."

"I know. Can I get another one?" she asked, pushing the glass toward him.

"Sure thing. I thought you were bringing your friends to this shindig."

"They're around. Just look for the two sets of Sonnys and Chers."

He laughed. "The ones who came in just before you?"

"That's them."

"I didn't recognize Milo under the moustache."

He turned away to get her drink and Adam appeared at her side, leaning back against the bar. "It's great to see you, sweetie."

"Thanks for swinging by. I'm glad you're here – I really needed you."

"Anything for my benefactress, you know that. How's Miss Fanny these days? Does she live in this godforsaken desert, too?"

She shook her head in astonishment. "You always could do that: see exactly what was bothering me."

He shrugged. "You're an easy read – everything is right on the surface with you. That's what made you such a great actress...your expressiveness."

"Fanny is converting to Judaism."

He gasped. "No! Really?"

She narrowed her eyes. "You already knew."

He smiled sheepishly. "And that's why I was a lousy actor."

"How?"

"Fanny is like the little sister I never had – we've stayed in contact."

"Why didn't you stay in contact with me?"

"You had a social network of hundreds to support you. Fanny only had me."

"I've really screwed things up, Adam. Fanny hates me."

"She doesn't hate you, but she does want an apology."

She gave a short laugh. "I owe more apologies these days."

"Uh oh. Who else have you pissed off?"

"You see the clunky Cleo over there?"

"The queen of denial, you mean? Steve and I spotted her right away. She clearly thinks she's twenty pounds lighter and forty years younger."

"Yeah, well, you said it, not me. She's the wife of the local playhouse director."

"Let me guess: Julius Caesar?"

She glanced in their direction. "Hard to tell. He could be Mark Antony."

"I suppose anything is possible. What did you do to her?"

"I may have mocked her a little."

"May have?"

"Okay. I mocked her, she told her husband on me, and they ejected me from the theater group."

Adam laughed silently.

Sax returned with her second drink. "Take your time with this one, will you? I don't want you to crawl to bed tonight."

Adam turned around and gave Sax the once-over with a sly smile. "You couldn't be her boyfriend, now could you?"

"No," Sondra answered before Sax could. "This is Sax Ridley, your host for the evening. Sax, I'd like you to meet Adam Ross-Wright."

"My pleasure, I'm sure," Adam purred.

"It's always good to meet a friend of Sondra's. And, may I say, you're the best-looking Cher here tonight. Of course, Cher herself looks like a man in drag…"

Adam trilled a laugh. "I tried to convince my husband to be Cher, but he didn't want to shave his moustache."

"I understand his reluctance completely. Please relax, have a good time. Can I get you a drink?"

"You make mojitos?"

"Yeah."

"A mojito and a beer, please."

"Coming up."

Adam watched the bartender walk away. "Damn, girl. He's one fine-looking man."

"You're married."

He sighed with a smile. "You're right. Happily, I might add. Steve is a great guy."

"What should I do about Fanny?" she asked, steering the conversation back to her life.

"Listen – she's been dating Reuben for more than a year. She was afraid to tell you about him because she knew your reaction would be exactly what it was. Can't you just be happy for her?"

"She's wasted the gifts God gave her."

"Which ones? The privilege of being Hollywood royalty? Her great looks? Her natural talent?"

"Yes. Those."

"Sondra, face it: Fanny never wanted to be an actress or anything else in Hollywood. As much as you dislike her nose, she thinks it gives her character. And, being the illegitimate daughter of a faded Hollywood star and a B-movie starlet doesn't exactly make you the Queen of Beverly Hills. The best thing she ever did for herself was leave California."

"Have you met Reuben?"

"Steve and I stopped in Phoenix and went to dinner with them a few months ago," he conceded.

Her jaw dropped.

"Before you say anything, Fanny told me you were in the throes of a passionate new affair. I didn't want to intrude."

"It wasn't that passionate."

"What happened to the guy?"

"You met him."

Adam looked flabbergasted. "Milo?"

"Yep."

"But you're living in his house and he's clearly serious about Claire!"

"Wow, Sherlock, you are right on top of the situation, aren't you?"

"Don't be a bitch."

"It's what I'm best at."

He spiked his eyebrows. "True enough."

Sax pushed the beer and mojito toward Adam, who picked up both drinks.

"Where's Steve?" Sondra asked.

"Hustling some senior citizen at darts. Join us?"

"No. I'm going to finish this drink, and then I'm going to go over and apologize to Mildred. It'll be a good practice run."

"Sounds like a plan. I'll see you later, honey." Adam sashayed away from the bar in his long, black wig and bell-bottom pants.

Sondra upended the glass and emptied its contents with two long gulps. She set the glass back on the bar with a resolute thump and pushed herself off the stool, leaving behind a green smudge where her thighs had been.

Mildred had positioned herself so that her back was to Sondra, so only Bob saw her approaching. He shot Sondra a warning look, but she was well past heeding his advice. Tapping the faux Cleo on her well-padded shoulder, Sondra said, "Excuse me, Mildred, could we have a little chat?"

"Go away, Sondra, you old lush. I'm here to have a good time, not talk to your sorry butt."

Sondra straightened, pulling herself to her full height, which happened to put her a few inches above Mildred Kovich. "I merely wanted to apologize for my behavior the last time we met."

"Don't bother. The theater has been ever so much more pleasant without your superior attitude." In a mocking, high-pitched voice, she continued, "Oh, look at me, I was in a movie, I'm Hollywood royalty. I'm so fucking special everyone here should kiss my ass."

The acolytes gathered around the table laughed as supportively as any high-school clique would have. Sondra felt the heat of embarrassment rise to her cheeks.

"A real actress would have gone directly to New York, not California. Everyone knows that California is all about looks and New York is all about talent."

"That must be why you couldn't cut it on either coast and had to scratch by doing regional theater."

Mildred stretched her chubby little arm out and slapped Sondra. Bob stepped between the two women. "That's enough, ladies. This is no way to drum up support for the arts, Millie, and you know it. Sondra, this bar is big enough for you to stay away from us, and I expect you to do just that."

"Get out of the way, you old queen."

The assembled group gasped in shock at Sondra's assertion.

"No one talks to my husband like that!" Mildred screamed, pushing Bob out of the way and coming at Sondra with her claw-like nails. Just before Mildred could reach her, someone hooked his arms under Sondra's and dragged her out of reach, leaving Mildred clawing the air as she lost her balance and fell with a soft whump at their feet. Bob, horrified, was quick to kneel next to his fallen spouse. Sondra, put to rights by her mystery savior, turned to see Steve grinning behind her while Adam beamed with pride at his partner.

"I hate mean, little women like that. They're like yappy Yorkies begging for a swift kick," Steve said. Sondra realized that those two sentences represented the most words strung together by Adam's husband since she had met him earlier that day.

"Thanks for the rescue," she said.

"Not a problem."

"I take it the apology didn't go well," Adam said, sipping his mojito.

"Not as well as I'd hoped."

"I couldn't hear what she was saying, but she seems to have the Greek chorus on her side."

"Yeah," Sondra said glumly. "I'm never getting back into the ensemble, am I?"

"I've got to be honest here, sweetie: it's not looking good."

Her eyes lit up and a mischievous smile curved her lips. "Then I guess there's nothing to stop me from playing a little prank, is there?"

"What sort of prank did you have in mind?" Adam asked.

Steve frowned. "Adam, I think you should stay out of this."

"Don't worry, sweetheart. I'm sure whatever Sondra has in mind is mostly harmless."

Steve looked at her skeptically.

"Mostly," Sondra averred.

"Let me introduce you to our host, Steve. You can catch a ride home with him if Sondra and I don't make it back before the bar closes." He guided a reluctant Steve toward the bar.

Sondra spotted Milo and Claire standing by the jukebox. "Hey," she shouted to Milo over the music, "You two having fun?"

Milo nodded. "You?"

She shrugged. "Not too bad. Are you competing in the costume contest?"

"Yes, I think so. What about you?"

"Actually, I'm taking off. I have something I need to do."

"Tonight? I thought you loved Halloween parties."

"Usually I do. There's a party pooper here, though, and I think she is in dire need of a pranking."

"A spanking?" Milo asked, confused. "I don't think you can legally spank someone."

"Not a spanking! A pranking! I'm going to pull a prank on her."

Milo looked relieved. "Oh! Okay. Need some help?"

"Adam is going with me."

"Be careful!"

279

"We will!" she said, giving him a thumbs up.

Milo smiled and returned the gesture.

Given the narrow width of the bar, she and Adam made as wide of a circle as possible around the theater group, most of whom glared at them as they passed. "Don't meet their eyes, honey," Adam whispered against her ear. "They're like wild animals on the hunt. Don't let them see any fear, either."

Pressed side to side, the duo exited the bar and ran for her car. Sondra jammed the keys in the ignition, fired the engine up, and peeled rubber out of the parking lot.

Adam cackled with glee. "Sitting passenger with you is still a thrill ride! But when are you replacing this car?"

"Why should I? It's a classic."

"It's a forty-year-old convertible."

"That still runs fine."

"It must cost you a fortune to keep it running."

"Not as much as a new car would," she mumbled.

Adam, glancing at her, let the topic drop. "What's the plan?"

"Milo bought some stink spray the other day. I think we should go spray down her costumes. Opening night is tomorrow, so they won't have time to dry-clean them before the show."

Adam squealed and clapped. "Brilliant! Brava!"

Smiling smugly, she drove them back to Milo's house. "Wait here. I know just where it is."

The small cellophane-wrapped bottle still sat on the end table, right where Milo had left it the previous weekend. She slipped the container into her silver evening purse and ran out of the house, locking the door behind her. She started the car again and pulled out of the driveway.

"Where is it?" Adam asked.

"In my purse."

"It fits in your purse? You think there's enough in there to make a real impact?"

"I hope so," she frowned.

"Let me see it."

"Go ahead. Don't spray it in the car, though."

"Give me a little credit, won't you?" Adam extracted the small bottle from her purse and read it. "Liquid Ass. Sounds nasty enough."

"It sounds awful," she giggled.

"Will Milo mind your borrowing it?"

"I doubt it. I think it was an impulse buy."

"What sort of impulse leads you to buy bottled farts?"

She considered his question. "Childhood memories?"

"Straight men will always be a mystery to me." He pulled the tab in the cellophane and the wrapper came away with ease. "Should we smell it first?"

"Why?"

"To get an idea of how powerful it is, maybe? What if it won't stick to the fabric? It could just evaporate into the air."

"I didn't think of that."

He lifted the container, nozzle up, to his nose. "I don't smell anything."

"It probably needs to be primed. We'll be at the theater in just a minute—"

"Holy mother of Christ!" Adam had dropped the bottle and was frantically rubbing the tip of his nose. "Fucking hell! Shit! Damn! Shit!"

"What?! What's wrong? Is there a bee? What the hell—?" The scent hit her like a baseball bat to the sinuses. "Holy crap! Did you spray—?" She retched and swerved to the side of the road, pushing open her door just in time to lose her dinner and two whiskey sours on the asphalt.

Adam, still furiously rubbing at the tip of his nose, had tears flowing down his cheeks, the thick mascara turning the rivulets black. "I can't get this shit off!"

Now that her nausea had passed, the sight of her old friend rubbing his nose and running in tight circles while dressed as Cher suddenly struck her as exceedingly funny; she fell into fits of laughter so extreme that she was unable to catch her breath.

Adam, taken aback by her reaction, stopped running and rubbing, choosing instead to stare at her. "This is not funny, Sondra."

"Yes...it is...fucking...hilarious!" she managed to enunciate between deep inhales and unrelenting laughter.

"I can't get this crap off my nose. All I can smell right now is road kill."

"I guess...it will do...the trick!"

"Get in the car, giggles. I'll drive."

The laughter beginning to subside, she slipped into the passenger seat. "What did you do...with the bottle?"

"It rolled under the seat. We'll get it when we're at the theater." He made one more pass at his nose before pulling away from the curb. "Where to?"

"Turn left at the next stop sign. It'll be on the right." Her heart rate was returning to normal. The terrible odor lingered in the car, so she rolled down her window.

"I guess we should have lowered the top, huh?" Adam said, rolling down his window as well.

"Might have been a good idea, now that you mention it." She flashed a wry smile at him. "I told you not to spray it."

"How could I have known that such an awful smell would come out?"

"It's called Liquid Ass, Adam. What did you think it would smell like? Sunshine and roses?"

"There's no need to be snide."

She rolled her eyes.

Adam turned left and then right into the parking lot. The building was dark. "How are we getting inside?"

"I know the watchman. He'll let me in."

"We can't do that! We'll get caught!"

"Herman won't tell. He hates Mildred almost as much as I do."

"I still say it's a risk."

"It's one we'll have to take if we're going to go through with this. Let's get the bottle out from under the seat." Considerably more sober after being sick, she hopped out of the car and felt around under the seat for the bottle. "Ta da!" she announced, straightening. Out of the corner of her eye, she saw the hunched, thin figure of Herman as he rounded the corner. "Give me my purse! Quick!"

Adam tossed it to her; she dropped the bottle inside and slung the chain strap over her shoulder, walking quickly across the parking lot to intercept Herman. "Good evening!" she called out, waving to him.

"Who's there?" Herman asked.

"It's me, Herman. Sondra Lane."

"Miss Lane? What are you doing here?"

"I need to get something out of the green room. Could you let me in?"

"Mr. and Mrs. Kovich told me you weren't allowed in the building anymore, Miss Lane."

"That's just a silly misunderstanding. Besides, isn't this building owned by the community?"

Herman rubbed his chin. "Now that you mention it, I did think that was a bit odd. You still live in Sun City, don't you?"

"Of course. Not five minutes from here."

"Seems to me the Koviches can't keep you out – and I won't." He chuckled conspiratorially. "Be my guest, Miss Lane." He unlocked the nearest door and ushered her inside. "And take your time."

She held up a finger to Adam, indicating he should wait where he was, and hurried through the opening. "Thanks, Herman. You're a sweetheart. Do me a favor: don't mention my visit to the Koviches. I wouldn't want to upset them."

He laid a finger alongside his nose. "Your secret is safe with me."

She made her way around the back of the stage and down the staircase leading to the greenroom and dressing rooms. Unsurprisingly, Mildred's name – with a gold star – was taped to the door of the largest dressing room. Pushing it open, she met with Mildred's cloying peony-based perfume, a scent Sondra considered only slightly less offensive than that contained within the small plastic bottle now residing in her purse. She turned on the light. Mildred's costumes hung together on a coat rack to one side of the room. Straight ahead, Mildred's makeup mirror and the necessary cosmetics awaited tomorrow night's opening.

Sondra had always loved the theater. Her mother raised her on stories of glamour and excitement, always centering on her long-ago performances as a Las Vegas showgirl. From the first time she smelled the greasepaint, she had known where she wanted to be: in front of an audience. Live or on film, it never mattered to her. She went to California because she could afford the bus ticket there.

Looking around the dressing room, she realized what she was planning to do might ruin the theater for someone in the audience – and she was loathe to do that. She turned to leave – and saw a picture of herself taped to the back of the dressing room door. Someone had added horns and a pitchfork with a black felt-tip pen. Bull's-eyes had been drawn over each of her breasts, and three darts pierced the image. Numerous holes from previous attempts perforated the paper. Fuming, Sondra pulled out the Liquid Ass. Retrieving a perfumed handkerchief from the top of the dressing table, she held it over her nose and mouth as she soaked the costumes with the entire contents of the bottle; only her anger kept the bile from rising up her throat. When she finished, she pulled the door closed behind her and ran for the exit.

Charmed Life

The Car

"I think you may have to replace the car now," Adam said, his nose wrinkled in disgust.

While the handkerchief had kept her from breathing in the concentrated Liquid Ass fumes, it had not provided any protection for the rest of her. She stunk to high heaven. "Maybe the smell will go away if I leave the windows rolled down overnight."

"Maybe. That doesn't solve our immediate problem, however."

"We need tomato juice."

"This isn't skunk spray, Sondra. The whole point of the tomato juice is to break down the oils."

"How do you know this?"

"Rufus. He's got a fatal attraction to skunks."

Rufus, the ugly half-poodle that Steve and Adam owned, was currently in Milo's backyard. "He seemed perfectly fine when I saw him a few hours ago."

"It's going to be fatal the next time he gets sprayed – I'm going to kill him."

"What do you suggest, then?"

He shrugged helplessly. "I've got nothing."

"Tomato juice it is."

She directed Adam, who was still behind the wheel, to the nearest Walgreens, which, by some stroke of luck, had not yet locked its doors despite the clock reading 8:05 p.m.

"We're closed!" called out the old man behind the liquor counter.

"Please," Sondra said, "all we need is tomato juice."

"Don't carry it," a disinterested gum-chewing young woman said from the register to the right of the doors.

"Clamato!" Adam shouted.

"Got that over here," commented the male cashier, "but I already counted my drawer." The cashier made a face as the scent of Adam and Sondra wafted in his direction. "That don't smell like skunk. What you two been rolling in? Sewage?"

Exasperated, Adam asked, "Do we look like we've been rolling in human waste?"

"She's green," the cashier said, considering. "She might'a'been."

"Which one of you smells the worst?" the girl asked.

"I do," Sondra admitted.

"You wait outside. Mister, get your Clamato and bring it over here. There's no alcohol in Clamato...right, Eddie?"

"Nope. Nothing but tomato and clam juice."

"Cool. I can sell it."

Sondra stepped outside and turned until she faced into the crisp breeze. She watched the old man called Eddie shuffle over and lock one of the two entries. He stood in front of the open one, guarding against either Sondra or other pushy late-night shoppers.

A few minutes later, Adam emerged, three bottles of Clamato in hand.

"One each wasn't enough?"

"I don't know, do I? I've never tried to get Liquid Ass off before."

"Don't get snarky."

"Where are we going to do this?"

"Claire will kill us if we bring this stink into the house. The backyard?"

The humiliating experience of undressing to their underwear and dousing themselves in Clamato fortunately was not witnessed by anyone other than themselves and two puzzled dogs. Regrettably, the odor lingered, though it was reduced.

After showering and spraying themselves with Sondra's perfume, they were, at least to themselves, tolerable. Sondra, unwilling to impregnate any of her better clothes with the smell, located an old pair of jeans and a t-shirt. Adam changed into the clothes he had worn earlier in the day, grumbling the whole time about how the odor would probably force him to incinerate the outfit, including the purple silk scarf he wore around his neck.

"Now what?" Adam asked.

"We go back to the party."

"People will wonder what happened to our costumes."

"We'll just tell them we wanted to be more comfortable." She lowered the top on the car and both of them stepped back. "Shit."

"Yep, that's what it smells like."

"Helpful comments only, please."

"Let's leave the top down and go back inside for a while. We can watch a movie while we wait."

"This is instant karma, isn't it?"

"What, like the song?"

"I did something mean, and now I'm paying for it."

He raised an eyebrow. "Are you sorry for what you did?"

She turned back to the house. "Let's see what's on television."

Sondra woke up in front of the television with Claire and Milo staring at her from the living room archway; Adam was still asleep on the chaise longue at the far end of the sectional.

"Where is Taz?" Claire asked.

"Outside with Rufus."

"Is he in trouble? Did he make a mess? It smells like he made a mess. I wonder if he's sick? Does that smell normal to you, Milo?"

Milo sniffed the air suspiciously. "If your dog passed anything that smells even remotely like that, he must be dying." He walked over to the end table before looking directly at Sondra. "Where's my fart spray?"

Sondra swallowed guiltily. Choosing her words carefully, she said, "I may have…borrowed it…for a prank."

"It's pungent, isn't it?"

"And persistent, as it turns out," she said ruefully.

Milo couldn't contain his amusement any longer; his loud guffaws awoke Adam, who frowned with disappointment. "I can still smell it."

"Yes, I know. Claire and Milo can smell it, too."

"Damn it. I think we might have to wait for new skin to grow in order to escape this."

"Naw," Milo said. "I have a trick that will take care of the problem." He disappeared into the kitchen, returning momentarily with two metal spoons. "Run cold water over your hands and rub them with this spoon. That should remove the odor."

"What if it's not my hand?" Adam asked, pointing to the tip of his nose.

"Still should work. Just rub your nose instead."

"Thanks," Sondra said, heading for the bathroom. "I'm going to shower with it."

Milo erupted into another round of laughter as she disappeared behind the bathroom door. After a thorough rubbing with the spoon, Sondra emerged from the shower sans the liquid fart odor. After selecting yet another outfit – the jeans and t-shirt reeked – she found Adam watching the news with Milo.

"Where's Claire?"

"She went to bed. She's hoping the smell will be gone by tomorrow morning." Milo muted the TV. "Adam wouldn't tell me what you did. I think you're obligated to share, since you used my gag."

She crossed her arms and considered his request. "I'll tell you what," she finally offered, "come with me to the opening night of *Hello, Dolly!* tomorrow and you'll see."

Milo grinned. "Fair enough."

Adam's cell phone rang. "Hello?...We're at Sondra's place....I'm sorry, babe; I thought we'd make it back....Okay. We'll be there soon." He disconnected the call and said, "Steve's pissed. He's never been much for crowds – especially when he doesn't know anyone."

"Damn, I'm sorry," Milo said. "I should have offered him a ride back here."

"No worries. You didn't know Sondra and I would be here. But we do need to get over there and pick him up."

"We're staying with Sax tonight," Sondra said. "We won't be able to get into his house until he goes home."

"Steve's already got that handled – Sax gave him the keys to the house. All we have to do is pop over there and give him a ride."

"Milo, do you have an old blanket or a large beach towel somewhere around here?"

"I think there's a towel in the broom closet. Why?"

"I need something to cover the passenger seat so I don't end up smelling like sewage again."

"It's in your car, too?" Milo snickered and shook his head. "You really spread that shit around, didn't you?"

She rolled her eyes. "Be sure to tell Claire how sorry I am about the smell."

"Don't give it another sniff. I'm sure her foul mood will vanish when the air is cleared."

"Funny. You're a regular laugh riot." She picked up her tiny silver purse and immediately dropped it again. "Eww. Not good. I think the purse is ruined."

"I bet your costume is, too," Adam commented. "And mine, for that matter."

"Take the purse outside when you leave," Milo said, turning the TV volume up so that he could hear the weather report.

Grasping the chain between her thumb and forefinger, she walked the purse out the back door. The dogs, smelling the liquid fart aroma, had spread their costumes across the yard. Taz was vigorously rolling on one of Sondra's silver go-go boots. Rufus, tail wagging, approached Adam, bringing with him the foul stench that could best be described as a mix between eau d'outhouse and rotting meat.

Adam gagged. "Rufus! You naughty, naughty boy!"

The dog flattened his ears against his head before rolling to his back in submission.

"I'll help you rub him down with metal spoons tomorrow," Sondra soothed. "Right now, I just want to get to bed."

"Claire is going to kill you," Adam predicted.

"You may be right about that." She dropped the empty purse on the ground. They turned on their heels and left the smelly dog problem for later.

One well-used towel in hand, Sondra quickly upholstered the fouled seat and they were on their way back to the Brass Monkey. The crowd had thinned out to just the usual suspects – a couple of old men and one middle-aged couple lingering at a table in the back. Steve occupied Sondra's regular spot, and he and Sax were debating the merits of various football teams. "I tell you, man," Steve said as they approached, "don't count the Cowboys out."

"You Texas boys never learn, do you?" Sax looked up and waved. "Your ride's here."

Steve shifted his eyes toward his husband coolly. "I'm beginning to understand why Sonny and Cher broke up."

"Don't be like that, babe. I'm really sorry."

"It was my fault, Steve," Sondra offered. "The errand I needed to run took on a life of its own. This was honestly the soonest we could make it back."

"Why is your hair wet?" Sax asked, his brow creased with concern. "And what happened to your costumes?"

"I'll tell you all about it later."

"What kind of mischief have you been up to tonight?"

"We'll see you at your house. Come on, Steve."

"Forgiven?" Adam asked, putting his arm around the bigger man.

"Forgiven."

"Aww," Sax said with a sappy grin. "See you lovebirds later."

One of the regulars looked up and shot them a dirty look.

"You got something to say, Oscar?" Sax asked, his arms folded across his chest.

One glance at the barkeep and the man changed his attitude. "Naw, Sax. Nothin' at all."

The three of them were out the door a moment later and Sondra was readying her keys. Steve got within three feet of the convertible and stopped short. "Do you smell that?" He turned in a circle, sniffing the air.

"Desert air is great, isn't it?" Sondra opened the driver's door and got in the car.

"No, not that. There's something dead nearby."

"People are always squishing bunnies around here."

Steve frowned but got in the backseat of the car. "Whoa. I think you must have been the bunny squisher, Sondra. The smell is stronger in the car than it was outside." His face contorted in disgust. "Maybe a cat got caught in your fan belt."

Sondra gunned the engine and squealed out of the parking lot for the second time that night.

"What's the rush?"

"No rush, honey. That's just how she drives," Adam, turned halfway in his seat, shouted over the wind noise.

The rest of the ride was devoid of conversation, mostly because a car without a top doesn't make conversation easy. In any case, they pulled into Sax's driveway in just over five minutes.

"Pop the hood, Sondra. I'll see if I can clear out the source of the stink," Steve said.

"It's not under the hood, Steve. Pop the trunk, Sondra."

"It's in the trunk?" Steve asked, confused.

"No, but our bags are, and we're going to need them, don't you think?"

"But—"

Sondra put her hands on her hips. "I used this nasty stuff called Liquid Ass to play a prank tonight. Unfortunately, a little bit of it made its way into the car."

"How much?"

"No way of knowing – most of it was probably on me at the time."

"And it all becomes clear," Steve said. "I'll get the bags."

Steve and Adam were suitably impressed with Sax's home. Sondra put the two of them in the room where she had stayed a few weeks earlier.

"Now I wish we had a longer layover," Adam said, falling back on the luxurious bed.

"Flo would kill us if we asked for any extra time. We just took our honeymoon, for Pete's sake!"

"Who is Flo?" Sondra asked. "I thought you were your own bosses."

"Flo is our freight broker. She's wonderful, but she doesn't believe in vacations."

"Ever?"

"It's not that she won't let us take one," Adam explained, "so much as she wants us to take it when there's a lull in business."

"How can you predict that?"

"Exactly," the two men said in unison.

She laughed. "Get settled in. I'm going to make us a midnight snack. I know Adam and I could use it. What about you, Steve?"

"I could eat."

"Great." Sax had told her to help herself, so she went to the kitchen and surveyed the foodstuffs available. Finally settling on cheese and crackers, apples, oranges, and a pot of orange spice tea, she located the serving tray and loaded it up with the goodies. Opening one last cabinet, she found a package of Milanos hidden behind the coffee filters. She added them to the tray and carried it to the Japanese-style dining room. "Adam? Steve? Our snack is ready!" she called. Hearing the door to their room open, she settled herself on the cushion facing the garden window. A moment later, the men emerged, both in pajamas. When she looked at Steve, Sondra couldn't help thinking of Todd Gibson, her long-dead co-star from Siege of the Moon. "Sax won't be home for a little while yet, so we might as well go ahead without him."

"Looks wonderful," Adam said, settling onto the cushion to her right.

Steve took the one directly across from her. "You shouldn't have gone to so much trouble."

"No, I owe it to you both. Thank you for stopping to see me. Besides, all I did was put food on a tray. Sax is the real host here."

"I can't believe this house. I've never seen anything like it." Steve poured tea for the three of them. "Did I see a pool in the back garden?"

"Yes. Totally private – no one can see you swimming." Sondra sipped her tea, savoring the citrus and nutmeg aroma. She pulled a few crackers and some of the cheese onto her small plate.

"Maybe we should move here when we retire," he mused.

"This is all age-restricted, isn't it?" Adam asked.

"Fifty-five or older."

"Not an option for us, then. What if we end up with Maddie?"

Steve nodded solemnly. "Good point."

"Who is Maddie?"

"She's Steve's daughter. Her mother has cancer. It's in remission right now, but Maddie is young and cancer is evil. We have to be prepared to take her in if the time comes."

"How old is she?"

"Four," they answered, in unison again.

Adam chuckled. "Just a sec. I want to show you a picture." Lithe as she remembered him, he jumped to his feet and glided swiftly from the room.

"I thought you two had been together for a while," she whispered to Steve.

"We have. It's a long story."

"None of my business!" she said quickly.

Adam was back with a photo of a dark-haired little girl. "Here's our baby," he said, putting the photo in her hands.

"She's gorgeous!"

"I think she has a future in show business, but Steve and Dina keep objecting."

"She should be modeling. Look at that face – it's perfect!"

The door from the garage to the kitchen opened and closed.

"We're in the dining room, Sax!" Sondra called out.

He appeared in the archway. "I'm just going to change out of this costume – I'll be right back." He disappeared around the corner.

"I didn't realize that was a costume," Adam whispered.

"I think he was Hulk Hogan," Sondra answered, "though, honestly, it's not much of a costume. He pretty much just looks like the guy."

Steve and Adam stifled their laughter. Sondra handed the photo back to Adam, who set it on the floor behind him.

"What will you do if Dina dies?" Sondra asked soberly.

"We'll get off the road permanently." Steve shifted uncomfortably on his cushion. "We can't keep traveling with a preschooler."

"We could too," Adam argued. "Our rig is big enough to add Maddie and still be comfortable. I could tutor her."

"How long could we do that, Adam? Realistically, now."

"A few years, at least."

"You can't have a little girl living with you two in your rig," Sondra said. "You'll be stopped by the police in every city you go through."

"Why would we?" Adam asked.

"Because you're two grown men! They'll think you've kidnapped the girl!"

"That's exactly what I said, Sondra. Thank you." Steve crossed his arms in triumph.

"What did you say?" Sax, dressed in a black silk kimono, glided into the dining room and sat down on the only available cushion, between Steve and Sondra.

Adam waved the question away. "Never mind. You have a beautiful home, Sax. Thank you for inviting us to stay."

"Any friend of Sondra's, as they say." He poured himself a cup of tea and selected some fruit and a few cookies from the serving tray. "I see you found my stash," he commented to Sondra.

She grinned. "I will always find the cookies, even if I can't eat any myself."

"Why can't you eat cookies?" Steve asked.

"I've got to keep my girlish figure," she said wryly.

The conversation turned to Hollywood, and Sondra became the life of the party – regaling her friends with a dozen stories, some from her own experience and others from Bill's. It was well after one o'clock when the four of them finally retired. Sax shared his king-size bed with Sondra, who crawled onto the ridiculously plush mattress and promptly fell asleep.

The windows and doors to Milo's house were all flung wide when Sondra and her friends arrived to pick up Rufus. A furious Claire was scrubbing Taz down in the sink.

"I've used a full bottle of tomato juice on him, rubbed him with a metal spoon, and washed him with his regular shampoo. He still stinks, Sondra."

"I'm sorry, Claire. I didn't mean for that to happen."

"This is what happens when grownups act like children."

Milo sat in the living room, resolutely tuned out of the world around him, choosing to concentrate on a football game instead. Sondra picked up the extra tomato juice and big metal serving spoon and headed to the backyard, where Adam and Steve were already wetting the dog down. Together, they soaked the dog in tomato juice and attempted the spoon trick, which had less effect on dog hair than it did on human skin. Neither Adam nor Steve was particularly

294

talkative, but they didn't seem angry at her. She decided not to worry about it.

After dropping Adam, Steve, and Rufus off at their rig a few hours later, Sondra went directly to the box office located inside the recreation center and bought three tickets for that evening's performance of *Hello, Dolly!* Her car had retained the scent overnight, though it had mellowed somewhat. If she drove with the top down for a few more weeks, it would probably disappear completely. However, she suspected it would take twice as long for the costumes to recover from their dousing. After all, a deliberate skunking was always more persistent than an accidental one.

The windows were still open when she got back to Milo's, but the doors were closed and Claire's car was gone. Once in the house, she could hear that the television was still on. Milo was asleep in his chair.

Picking up the remote from the end table, she turned the TV off. Milo startled awake. "Wha—? Oh, it's you."

"Yeah, sorry about that."

Taz, still damp from his morning bath, wandered glumly into the living room when he heard their voices. Sondra sat down on the rug to pet him.

"No, it's not entirely your fault. Claire and I had a huge fight."

"Over the smell?"

"Yeah. She says it's my fault – and, of course, she's right."

"That doesn't seem like Claire. She's usually so cheerful."

"I don't know what's come over her in the last few days. She's been grumpy and tired."

"Where is she?"

"I think she went to her place."

"Will she be back tonight?"

"I don't know yet."

"That's a shame. I bought this tick—" Reconsidering, she stuffed one of the tickets into her pocket. "Never mind. Why don't you come to see *Hello, Dolly!* with me tonight?"

"That's nice of you, but—"

"No, really...I insist. You'll get to see for yourself how well I put the Liquid Ass to use."

He pressed his lips together as he considered her offer. "Okay. I'll just call Claire and make sure she won't mind if I take you up on your offer."

"Ooh…do you think that's advisable? I mean, if she's already irritated with you…"

He swallowed hard. "Good point. Let me revise that plan. I'll call to apologize and see if she's coming back tonight. If she is, I'll skip the show. If she isn't, I'll go with you."

"Sounds good. I'm going to catch a quick nap – we were up much too late last night."

"I liked your friends, by the way. Steve seems like a down-to-earth fellow. Did you have a good visit?"

"Yes, thank you."

"They could have stayed here, you know."

"I know, but Sax has an extra bedroom. And I didn't want you to be uncomfortable in your own home."

He shrugged as she turned away from him. Stretching out on her own bed a moment later, Sondra found that her brain was much too busy to sleep. Though her apology to Mildred Kovich hadn't worked out as she had hoped, she still needed to formulate a *mea culpa* for Fanny.

The night she told Bill she was pregnant, they had been getting ready for the premiere of Siege of the Moon.

He misheard her. "What? Goodness no, my dear, we can't have a baby. I'm much too old to start another family."

She desperately dabbed at the flood of tears that rolled down her perfectly rouged cheeks. "Then what…I don't know what I'll do!"

The dashing older man took three strides across the room and placed comforting hands on her shoulders. "Darling girl, I had no idea starting a family was so important to you! I must say, though, you picked a terrible time to have this conversation. I want you to walk the red carpet like the star you are…and that means you need to shine, my love."

She dried her tears as best she could and reapplied the rouge, but her sadness could not be contained. Every photo from that evening showed a wan, mournful Sondra on the arm of an increasingly worried movie-star-cum-producer.

The next morning, of course, every newspaper in California blasted the news that their movie was a flop – a headline they ran alongside Sondra's photo. One of the newspapers even had the audacity to caption it: "Film's star sickened at thought of sitting through the film."

Bill awoke to find Sondra bent over the toilet in the master bathroom. Knowing she hadn't taken a single drink the night before, he experienced what he later described to Sondra as an "epiphany": his darling girl was already pregnant. Overjoyed at the realization, he held back her hair until she stopped vomiting and then carried her back to their bed. He brought her a glass of water, a damp cloth for her forehead, and a trash bin for her to use if the urge to be sick came over her again.

He called Lianne and asked her to come over and sit with Sondra while he ran an errand. When Sondra awoke a few hours later, she found her friend curled up on Bill's side of the bed.

"What are you doing here?"

"Bill told me you were sick and he asked me to come and stay with you for a while."

"Great," she pouted, "that's just great. He can't even stay with me when I'm sick. I made a terrible mistake, Lianne. Why did I leave Bud for Bill?"

"Because Bill loves you. What's wrong with you, Sondra? Bill has done nothing but treat you like a princess. Why are you acting like he's an ogre?"

She burst into tears. "I told him I was pregnant last night and he said he didn't want any more children!"

"No...that can't be true." Worry lines creased her forehead as deeply as if she had just heard her parents were splitting up. "Bill would never say that. He adores you!"

"He may adore me, but he hates our child," Sondra said breathily.

"If he does, then he's a monster!"

Sondra sobbed all the louder at her pronouncement.

"I won't let him hurt you like this. You come and stay with me." Lianne had purchased a run-down Hollywoodland bungalow with her earnings from Siege of the Moon, and was renovating it when she wasn't auditioning – which meant that almost nothing had been done to it.

Sondra, glancing around the opulent bedroom, shook her head. "No. I'm staying with Bill – at least for now. But I want him to know how cruelly I feel he has treated me. To ask a woman – practically his wife, mind you – to give up her unborn child...it's inhumane!" Even as she said these words to Lianne, a part of her was relieved. The effect of a full-term pregnancy on her career would be devastating – no one wanted to see a pregnant Carmella Savage on Scions of Beauty.

In a distant part of the house, a door opened and shut.

"That's probably Bill now. I'm going to give him a piece of my mind!" Lianne huffed, jumping off the bed and running out of the room.

Sondra hoped she didn't give him too much – Lianne didn't have much to spare. Sondra was calculating how much jewelry Bill's guilt would translate into when he appeared in the doorway with a small, light blue box in hand.

"Sondra, my darling girl," he began, kneeling at the bedside. "Lianne has just told me how distressed you are. Forgive a foolish old man – I didn't hear you correctly last night." He placed a hand against her abdomen and a single, glistening tear rolled from his blue eye. "Will you marry me?" He opened the box and held out an extravagant canary-yellow diamond ring.

Sondra had an epiphany of her own – it would be better to be Bill's wife than a soap opera star.

Fanny was a beautiful little girl, with her father's blue eyes and the slightest dimple in her chin. People magazine featured Sondra, Bill, and the girl several times in her first few years of life – Fanny was one of the original "celebri-children." When she was six, though, it was suddenly apparent that the girl had inherited neither of her parents' noses, but instead had the nose of her Jewish grandfather. And then Bill died,

Sondra remembered, and People was no longer interested in family photo shoots anyway.

How does one apologize for being a bad mother? Did Hallmark make a card? Maybe something with a verse like: Roses are red, Violets are blue, I was screwed up, But why become a Jew?

She laughed softly to herself. Fanny embracing Judaism wasn't such a big deal, she supposed. Just because believing in a vengeful god didn't work for her didn't mean that it was wrong for everyone. Fanny was still youngish – she might be able to have the family she always wanted. Now that Sondra was older, she could see herself enjoying a grandchild. The problem with Hunter was that he was born before she was out of her forties. No one should be a grandmother before fifty; it's just wrong to be called "granny" before you've admitted to having any gray hair.

Even Sondra had to admit that Reuben was a fine-looking man. And Fanny did look happier than she could ever remember seeing her before – prettier too. She picked up the phone to call her daughter; as she pressed the buttons, she remembered that today was Saturday. Tomorrow, she thought. I'll call her tomorrow. The matter settled in her mind, she fell asleep.

A few hours later, she awoke to the sound of Taz barking. She stretched and pulled herself from the bed, wondering why Taz was here instead of with his mistress.

She walked to the kitchen, where Milo was placating the dog with potato chips. "Why did Claire leave Taz here?"

"She said he still stunk. He smells fine to me. Heck, I can't even smell the odor she said was lingering in the house. I guess my nose has lost some of its aroma-detecting power."

Sondra sniffed the air. "Maybe it's just that we've been in here for too long. I'm going to step outside for a minute and get some fresh air. Maybe I'll be able to smell it after that." She walked quickly past her car to the sunlit front porch. The air didn't seem any different from the air in the house, but the sunshine felt good on her achy shoulders. She lingered a few minutes before returning.

"Can you smell it now?" Milo asked as soon as she had taken a deep breath of the air inside their home.

"Nope. Nothing. Are you going with me tonight or not?"

"Yeah. Claire says she's going to stay at her condo tonight. She's afraid it will still stink here – I'll let her know you can't smell it at all, though. Maybe she'll come home tomorrow."

"Home?" Sondra smirked.

He blushed. "I mean, back here, of course."

"Be ready in about an hour, okay?"

"I will."

Knowing that Mildred would be humiliated in a few hours, Sondra smiled as she applied her makeup and put on her classic red-and-white wrap dress with her red strappy sandals. This was her signature "look" around Sun City – the one that made other women smack their husbands.

Milo drove them to the theater, since the odor from the previous night's escapade still lingered in her car. As the house lights went down, Sondra couldn't help excitedly bouncing in her seat. Milo gave her a stern look; she pressed her back against the chair and took a few deep breaths to calm herself. A moment later, the orchestral preamble to the play began.

She was gratified to see pained looks already on the faces of the other actors in the play even before Mildred appeared. However, when Mildred finally made her entrance, Sondra was shocked to find that the woman herself seemed completely in character and unperturbed by the horrific odor of her clothing. Even in the tenth row – where she and Milo sat – the odor wafted over them occasionally: a combination of Liquid Ass and Mildred's own peony perfume. When Mildred stepped toward any of the other actors, they would – almost subconsciously – step away from her. At first, this odd reaction didn't seem to bother Mildred at all; before the end of the first act, though, worry lines creased her forehead. At intermission, almost everyone who had been sitting in the first five rows left the theater due to the overwhelming scent. Another quarter of the audience left because the play itself stank. Sondra, who had been enjoying the show up to that point, was suddenly overcome with regret.

"What's wrong?" Milo asked as they stood in front of the building, water bottles in hand.

"I did a terrible thing."

300

"You pulled a prank, Sondra. It's not the end of the world."

"Maybe not, but I also ruined a lot of people's evening. I only meant to make Mildred miserable."

"Do you want to go home?"

In despair, Sondra answered, "Yes."

As soon as they were home, Sondra grabbed her keys and drove to the Brass Monkey. Oblivious to the stares and slaps that accompanied her to her seat, she signaled Sax. A moment later, he slid a whiskey sour into her hand.

"You wanna talk about it?" he asked, leaning in front of her.

She drained the drink. "Not really."

"Suit yourself. Does it have something to do with last night?"

"Yes. Didn't I just say I didn't want to talk about it?"

"Yeah, but I've learned not to believe you."

"I mean it this time."

"Fine. Refill?"

"Yes, and keep them coming."

"You're not driving home later?"

"Look," she snapped, "I think I can handle a few drinks without falling off my stool."

He backed away. "Whatever you say, Sondra."

She scowled at him until he slid the refill in front of her. She heard the door swing open, but didn't look up until she heard Sax say, "Bob! What are you doing here? Wasn't tonight the *Hello, Dolly!* opening?"

She snapped her head up to watch the morose director take his usual seat at the other end of the bar. She couldn't hear what the two men were saying to one another, but Bob was wagging his head in a way that told her the second act was worse than the first. She dropped her own head lower over her drink, but couldn't bring herself to imbibe – her stomach roiled with regret.

The next time Sax came close to her, she beckoned him over. "What's wrong with Bob?"

"It's Mildred. Seems she had a bad case of diarrhea tonight, but wouldn't admit it. Instead she went on stage smelling like shit. Put the rest of the actors off and drove away the audience. The cast party was cancelled when dear old Millie locked herself in her dressing room after the show."

She hung her head in shame.

"Does this have something to do with your disappearing act last night?"

"It might." She winced.

He shook his head. "You've made a mighty mess, Carmella."

"I'm going to fix it right now." She pushed the drink away. "I don't suppose you'd take this off my tab?"

"Tell you what: if you plan on being back, I'll save it for you."

"Don't bother," she sighed. "This may take a while. Where is Mildred now?"

"As far as Bob knows, she's still at the theater. She wouldn't come out of the dressing room no matter what he said."

She pushed herself off the stool, briefly wishing she had taken the time to change clothes while she was home earlier. She no longer cared to look glamorous, and the straps of the heels dug into her tender feet like red-hot blades. She tottered toward the exit.

"Sondra! You sure you're okay to drive?"

"I'm fine, Sax. One whiskey sour's all I had."

"You're staggering."

"It's the shoes!"

He shrugged and turned his attention to another patron. She made her way to the car and ditched the shoes in the backseat. A few minutes later, she was at the theater. She parked up front in one of the handicapped spaces just as Herman came around the corner.

"You can't park there, Ms. Lane."

"My feet are killing me, Herman. Can't you make an exception just this once? No one will need this space." She gestured toward the empty parking lot, including the row of unoccupied handicapped spaces that stretched out next to her car.

"Rules are rules, Ms. Lane. If I give in on this one, where does it end?"

"I promise I'm just going inside for a minute. I'm here to pick up Mrs. Kovich."

He arched a bushy white eyebrow at her. "Aren't you two at odds these days?"

"I'm here to make a peace offering."

"Ms. Lane—"

"Please, call me Sondra."

"Sondra," he said. He pressed his lips into a straight line and looked around the parking lot and at the darkened building. Reaching up, he tilted his ill-fitting watchman's cap back and scratched his temple. "Eh, go on. Hurry up about it. Don't get me in trouble."

"Thank you, Herman," she said, scurrying barefoot into the building, which was still unlocked from the evening's performance. As soon as she reached the stairs that led down to the dressing rooms, she could smell the acrid odor of the fart spray mingled with peony perfume. As she approached Mildred's dressing room, the scent increased in strength.

She had expected to hear Mildred ranting or sobbing, but she heard nothing at all until she stood at the dressing room door. From the other side came only the soft snores of the sleeping actress. She knocked three times and waited.

Disturbed snuffling followed by the distinct blowing of a nose came from the room.

Sondra knocked again.

"Come in!" Mildred called.

Sondra tried the door; it was locked, as Sax had said it would be. She rattled the handle rather than answering her back.

"Oh, yes. Just a moment."

Sondra heard footsteps approach the door, a small click as the door was unlocked, and retreating steps.

"Come in!" Mildred called once more.

This time, the door opened easily, revealing Mildred, who posed dramatically in the middle of her dressing room, still wearing one of the offending costumes. "Oh. It's you. Come to gloat, are you?" She dropped her pose and glared hatefully at Sondra.

"No, on the contrary. I'm here to apologize."

"Too little, too late. I won't have you reinstated as my understudy."

"You misunderstand me. I'm not here to apologize for that."

"What, then?"

"For tonight, of course."

"Are you saying you somehow convinced all of my fellow actors and an entire audience to conspire against me?" She frowned in confusion, matching Sondra's own reflected expression.

All at once, Sondra understood: Mildred couldn't smell. Her frown disappeared as her jaw dropped open.

"What's the matter with you?"

"I heard you were terribly ill tonight," she recovered.

"I felt fine until the play went so badly. I've had a sick headache ever since. I suppose you would have been able to pull the whole thing off without a hitch, right? Even when everyone around you seemed to have forgotten their lines."

"No," she sympathized, "I don't think I would have done even half as well as you did."

"You were here tonight?" Mildred's eyes narrowed.

"Yes."

"How did you do it?" she said in a low, threatening voice.

"Do what?"

"Turn everyone against me?"

"I didn't. I swear."

"I don't believe you."

"Can't we just let bygones be bygones? I'll give you a ride home."

"What is this? Did you pull some of your Hollywood strings? Is this an elaborate prank like the one that movie star's husband pulls all the time?"

"No, Mildred. I'm afraid I don't know Demi Moore or her husband."

"Then how did you convince everyone that I stink?" She paced across the narrow room three times, stirring the stench afresh. "Wait – do I actually stink?"

Calling on her own theatrical abilities, Sondra answered, "No. I don't smell a thing. Do you smell anything?"

"Only my perfume – the same as always."

"Are you sure you don't want a ride home? I saw Bob at the Brass Monkey – I don't know when or if he'll be coming back for you."

"He'll come back. He always comes back." She deflated, dropping into her chair. "But...I'd like to go home now."

"I could call him for you," Sondra offered.

"Don't be ridiculous," Mildred scoffed. "Don't you suppose I could call him, too? Do you think only Hollywood types carry phones these days?"

Sondra bit her tongue.

"I'll take that ride, but only because I don't have my walking shoes with me."

"Fine. I'll wait while you change."

"I'll just wear the costume home," she said with a pout. "I need help to get out of the corset anyway."

"I'll help you."

"No, Bob always does that for me."

"What if he doesn't come home?"

"What are you implying?"

"He might stay overnight with…a friend."

"He wouldn't do that to me," she said coldly. "He knows how upset I am. I'm sure he's just having a beer and giving me time to cool off." She turned to her makeup table and picked up her cell phone. "In fact, I'll just send him a text message and let him know you're giving me a ride home."

Unable to argue against Mildred wearing the costume home without arousing further suspicions, she pulled her keys from her bag and said, "Let's go."

As they trudged through the auditorium, Mildred said, "Don't misconstrue this as me forgiving you, Sondra. You've treated me horribly for years now and I won't be easily won over. And where are your shoes?"

"They're in the car. My feet are killing me tonight."

"No doubt from dancing on my grave," Mildred mumbled.

"You aren't actually dead, you know. You just died on stage."

"Isn't that enough?"

Sondra opened the door to the outside and looked for Herman; he was nowhere to be seen, which was exactly what Sondra had hoped for. She walked quickly to the car and got in.

Mildred, however, stopped at the side of the car and frowned.

"What's wrong?"

"I hate convertibles."

"Then I guess you're walking after all."

"Can't you just put the top up?"

Sondra sucked in a deep breath. Doing a good turn for this woman was more trouble than it was worth, but she had gone this far. She stepped out of the car and raised the top. "Can we go now?" she asked as she saw Herman round the corner of the building.

"Yes." The trussed-up thespian got in the car.

Sondra waved to Herman, took one last breath of fresh air, and got behind the wheel.

Charmed Life

The Last House on the Left

"It's that one," Mildred said, pointing to the far left side of the street. "On the end."

Sondra, doing her best to control her gag reflex, pulled into the driveway. Bob and Mildred lived in the only Sun City neighborhood where the homes weren't stacked on top of each other. In the moonlight, Sondra estimated that their home sat in the middle of at least an acre and a half. Clearly, they had been more successful than she had – or maybe they had been better at saving their money. She opened her door to step out of the car.

"You're not coming in," Mildred announced.

"I just want to lower the top again."

Mildred stepped out of the car and walked toward her front door.

"Just a moment, Mildred. If you're not going to accept my apology, the least you can do is hear my complaint."

"Ha! What do you have to complain about?"

"How about this? No woman in the company has even half a chance at a lead role, no matter how perfect they are for it or how miscast you are!"

"I was born to play Dolly Levi!"

"Hardly. I'm Jewish, Mildred! If anyone in the company was born to play that role, I was!"

Porch lights went on across the street and at the house to the right of the Kovich's. "Keep your voice down!" Mildred stage-whispered. "The neighbors will call the police!"

"Why? Because there's a Jew in the neighborhood?" Sondra shouted. "Sic the dogs on me!"

"Don't be ridiculous." She walked closer to Sondra so that she wouldn't have to raise her voice. "They would call the police because you are yelling at me in the middle of my front yard! I have to admit, though: I never pegged you as Jewish."

"No. You just pegged me as a rival. Here's a tip, Mildred: theater companies are like families. If any member is bully, it makes the whole company dysfunctional. You and Bob have turned the entire group into a bunch of ass-kissing sycophants, and I, for one, am glad to be free of you." She turned on her heel and got back into her car, not bothering to lower the top. The car smelled like a whore with diarrhea, but

Sondra was so furious she didn't care anymore. Peeling out of the driveway, she rolled down her window and stuck her hand up and out with her middle finger extended as she hit the gas pedal.

Her cell phone, plugged in next to her bed, began singing "YMCA" to her at five-thirty the next morning. Wondering which of her gay friends had lost his mind, she opened the phone without opening her eyes. "Hello?" she mumbled.

"Sondra? Is that you?"

"Who else would be answering my phone at this hour? Who is this?"

"Sondra, wake up. When and where did you last see Mildred Kovich?"

She pushed herself up against her headboard and rubbed her eyes. "Sax? Is that you?"

"Yes, yes," he answered impatiently. "Did you drive Mildred home last night?"

"Yes. Why? Is she missing?"

"Her house sure as hell is."

"What are you talking about?"

"I'm standing right in front of where it used to be, and let me be the first to tell you that it's gone."

"Houses don't disappear."

"You're right. It's not gone, exactly. But it's certainly not livable. Get dressed. Drive to Bob's house. I need you here."

Sax wasn't in the habit of requesting her presence or help; his words put a sense of urgency to her actions as she hopped out of bed, suddenly wide awake. "Ten minutes," she said before clicking off the phone. She jumped into a pair of jeans and her pink tank top, slipped on a pair of flip-flops, and pulled her keys from her purse. Opening her bedroom door, she walked quickly and quietly out of the house. Her car, which she had left with its top down the night before, had recovered slightly from its odiferous condition. She hoped the brisk pre-dawn air would blow the rest of the scent away.

She drove to the end of the street where she had dropped Mildred Kovich off the night before. There, on the acre and a half of land, stood the charred ruins of a house. Her mouth was dry and the smoke in the air made her throat hurt. With some difficulty, she managed a dry swallow to push back the nausea that threatened to overwhelm her. Spotting Sax and Bob, she parked the car and walked to them. "What happened?"

Bob looked at her blankly, almost as if he couldn't hear her.

"They don't know yet," Sax said, gesturing to the firemen and officers milling around the blackened structure.

The roof was entirely gone and only half-walls remained. She wanted to walk closer to get a better look, but she was afraid the officials would object. "Did a jet hit your house?" That was one of the fears many of the elderly residents had – nearby Luke Air Force Base flew jets overhead day and night.

Bob still seemed incapable of responding. Finally, Sax said, "I doubt it very much, Sondra. First of all, if that were the case, they would probably already know that a jet was missing."

"Good point." She pulled Sax a few feet away from Bob before whispering, "Was Mildred in there?"

"We think so," he answered soberly.

"Where was Bob?"

"He stayed at my place last night."

"Mildred expected him home. She needed help getting out of her costume's corset."

"He got a text from her saying that she didn't need him."

"So he was with you the whole time?"

A fireman walked up before he could answer her. "Mr. Kovich?"

"No, I'm Sax Ridley. That's Bob Kovich."

"I'm sorry," he said and walked toward Bob. Sondra and Sax followed him. "Mr. Kovich?"

"Yes?"

"Mr. Kovich, I'm very sorry for your loss."

Bob's knees buckled. Sax ran to catch him, and the smaller man fell against his chest. "You found her?"

"Perhaps you should sit down, sir."

Sax lowered him to the ground and sat next to him. Bob was rocking back and forth with his hands pressed against his eyes. "What will I tell the children? My God. How will I tell them?"

"Do you know what caused it?" Sax asked the fireman.

"We suspect it was a gas explosion. Mrs. Kovich must have been soundly asleep not to have smelt the gas. She probably didn't feel a thing."

"How do you know she was in there?"

"Besides the neighbors' statements, I'm afraid we've found some...fragments." The fireman winced and whispered the last word. "I assume there were no pets?"

Bob shook his head.

"Mr. Ripper—"

"Ridley."

"Mr. Ridley, it might be best if you took Mr. Kovich somewhere else for a while. The police have already questioned him, right?"

"Yes. I'll, um, take him to my place."

"That would be best," the fireman repeated.

Sax helped Bob into the passenger side of his car before coming back to Sondra. "Are you going to be okay?"

"Me? Fine. It's not like we were close."

"Do you want to come to the house? Maybe you could make some of the calls for Bob. If you wouldn't mind, that is."

"Sure, I can do that. I'll be right behind you. Should I stop and buy us breakfast at the Jack in the Box?"

He blanched. "Not for me. I don't think Bob will be up to eating, either."

She shrugged. "Suit yourself. I'll see you in a few minutes."

She waved at Bob's Cadillac as it pulled away from the blackened pit that used to be his house. Turning back, she saw one of the emergency workers walk toward the waiting coroner's van with what looked like part of Mildred's skull. "Don't go losing your head, Millie dear," she mumbled before laughing silently to herself.

Charmed Life

Charmed Life

Bad Taste

With Bob staying in his home indefinitely, Sax found excuses to go into the bar earlier as late October turned to mid-November. It wasn't that Sax disliked Bob. In fact, quite the contrary: for the first time in a long, lonely life, Sax could imagine a future featuring a "we" instead of an "I." He found it comforting to wake up next to the same person every morning; he just wished that Bob's wife hadn't died.

Before Mildred's death, he hadn't entertained any opinion of the woman, preferring instead to avoid thinking of her. Ever since Patricia Scoville shot him, spouses – even ones who were supposedly well aware of their husbands' proclivities – made him intensely nervous. The fact that Mildred was now in pieces made him feel more guilty, not less.

It didn't help that Sondra was no longer around much. Mildred's death had left a gaping hole in Bob's latest production – one that Sondra had been thrilled to fill.

"You're leaving already?" Bob asked as he shuffled into the kitchen.

Sax, already in his gym clothes, was leaning against the counter sipping his morning jolt of espresso. "I need to get my workout in before I go to the bar."

"You've got hours before the bar opens."

"You know how Fridays can be. I had a big crowd last night, and the bathrooms need some serious attention."

"You should hire a cleaning crew." Bob pulled a cup from the cabinet and added fresh grounds to the espresso machine.

"That's a waste of money. I can do the cleaning."

"You're not as young as you used to be. And you're not alone anymore. I feel like I hardly see you."

"We're both busy," Sax pointed out. "*Hello, Dolly!* still has a week left, and you've been occupied with…Mildred."

"The whole nasty business is nearly behind us now." The espresso machine whined and steamed, filling the kitchen with a fresh burst of the coffee scent. "I think we should both look toward the future, don't you?"

"Of course." Sax drained his cup and dropped it in the sink. "I should get going."

"Fine. We'll talk later."

Sax kissed the smaller man's forehead and headed for the garage. Driving directly to the gym, he hoped that Sondra would be there. However, despite lingering over the cardio portion of his workout for almost an hour, the erstwhile-barfly failed to materialize. Resigned, he concentrated on his weight training until ten o'clock rolled around.

At the Brass Monkey, he threw himself into cleaning. Painting the glass dark blue had seemed like a great idea when he first opened the bar, but now, several years later, he wished he had some natural light. He was certain that the place was never as clean as he thought it should be – especially the bathrooms. By the time he finished scrubbing down the men's room toilet, it was noon and his regular customers were rattling the door.

Tossing the yellow rubber gloves into the empty scrub bucket, he shoved them inside his office and unlocked the front door. Three old men shuffled in and took their regular seats. Sax pulled their beers for them and the day's business was begun.

A little after three, Milo Crosby wandered in and headed for Sondra's regular stool. "Hey, Sax. How are you doing?"

"Can't complain. You?"

"Been better, but not too bad."

"Anything I can help with?"

"Nah. Nothing to worry about. Women get moody, don't they?"

Sax snorted. "You're asking the wrong guy on that one."

"Good point. I'll take a whiskey sour."

"Sondra's rubbing off on you," Sax commented before turning away to prepare the drink.

"Yeah, I suppose so."

Sax poured the whiskey, lemon juice, and sugar into a shaker and gave it a good tumble. Pouring it into a short glass, he pushed the drink into Milo's hand. "How is the leading lady these days?"

Milo frowned. "I hardly see her. You'd probably have a better idea of what's up with her."

"She hasn't been in since she took over the Dolly Levi role."

"Huh." Milo picked up the glass and took a swig, gasping as it went down his throat. "How does she drink this stuff?"

"Lots of practice. You've never struck me as a serious imbiber, Milo."

"I take it in spells."

"When was your last spell?"

"Nineteen-seventy-five."

Sax laughed and Milo joined him, pushing the rest of the drink away. "Can I get you a water instead?"

"Yeah."

Sax swept the drink off the bar and returned with a bottle of water from the mini-fridge he kept next to the sink. "You gonna tell me what's wrong?"

"Claire. She's been so moody lately. I think she's angry with me for allowing Sondra to continue on as my roommate."

"Well, if you love the woman, you probably should ask your ex-girlfriend to move out," Sax answered pragmatically.

"But Sondra's no threat to our relationship! She's just a friend."

"A friend that you've had sex with, right?"

Milo opened his water and took a swig. "I see your point."

"On the other hand, do you know that's what is bothering her? They may not be best buddies, but Sondra says they get along well enough."

"I don't know," he answered glumly. "Claire will hardly talk to me. Maybe I was wrong to think—"

"Think what?"

Milo shook his head. "Nothing important. So, Sondra told me a little about what happened to Mildred Kovich. I don't know about you, but that doesn't sound like an accident to me."

"What else would it be?"

"A gas explosion? Really? Sounds like the perfect way to cover up a murder. How else would the house be so full of gas that it would blow her body to pieces? She had to have already been dead."

"Robert Fisher tried that in Scottsdale a few years back – it didn't work out so well for him."

"Just because he screwed it up doesn't mean it can't be done."

"Who would have done something like that?"

"You were the cop, you know. I was just a border patrol agent. Solving murders was never on my to-do list."

Charmed Life

"I was a beat cop, not a detective."

Milo shrugged. "I guess we'll just leave it to the professionals, then. If they say it was an accident, who are we to argue?"

"Sax!" one of the other patrons called.

He left his friend and took the orders of a few newcomers. When he finished serving them, an empty water bottle and a ten-dollar bill sat in front of the barstool. Sax hadn't even seen Milo leave.

By the time he closed up the bar, it was almost midnight. He drove home in a stupor, anxious to take a shower and go to bed. Bob had other ideas. Two lit candles graced the tearoom table and the scent of barbequing steak wafted in through the patio doors.

"Come and sit down with me," Bob requested, settling on a cushion by the table.

Sax gestured at the clock. "It's midnight, Bob."

"And you don't resemble a pumpkin at all."

"I don't like to eat right before bed. You know that."

"We'll just have to think of something to do besides sleep, then."

Giving up, he sat down next to Bob in the dining room. "How was the play tonight?"

"Excellent, as usual. Sondra definitely has a star quality that Mildred lost long ago. Tomorrow's the last show, you know."

"Yes. What's next on the schedule?"

"The King and I. I was dreading Mildred's rendition of 'Shall We Dance.' Now, it seems we'll have a better singer and dancer to play the lead role."

"Sondra?"

"Perhaps. Perhaps not. She'll audition just like everyone else." Bob's eyes sparkled gleefully. "Oh, Sax, as devoted as I was to Millie, it's such a relief to be free! I had no idea how constraining my marriage was! You must know that I've been in love with you for years now. I want to shout it from the rooftops. I told my son Kent this morning."

Sax filled his wineglass and gulped down a bit of the fortifying merlot. "He must be horrified."

"On the contrary – he says he's known for years. Mildred told him."

Sax briefly considered how a conversation like that would come about before shaking the idea from his mind. "You know I like to live quietly."

Bob put his hand over the one Sax was resting on the table. "I don't want a flamboyant life anymore. I want a quiet, happy home life. As fond of Mildred as I was, I've had enough of her drama queen ways to last me a lifetime. I want the peace we have together."

Sax pulled his hand back as his forehead drew worry lines. "Do you know Milo Crosby?"

"Sondra's roommate? The good-looking guy who wears Guayaberas all the time?"

"That's the one. He stopped by the bar today."

"Huh. I got the impression he wasn't much of a drinker."

"He's not, but that's not the point."

"What is the point?"

"Don't you think it's strange that Mildred didn't smell the gas before it killed her? I mean, if she bumped the stove in her costume – like you suggested – that must have meant that she was awake for at least a while after the gas started filling the house. She should have smelt it."

"She couldn't smell," Bob answered with a shrug.

"You mean her nose was stopped up? She had a cold?"

"No, Sax. She had no sense of smell."

"Who knew that?"

"Besides me? No one. She was a vain woman. She didn't want anyone to know."

"People must have noticed."

"She was an actress." Bob stood. "I think our steaks should be done by now."

"No one knew?" Sax repeated.

"Not even our kids."

As Bob walked out to the patio, Sax recognized that his boyfriend had motive and opportunity. The chill that ran up his spine made him wish he had already hidden a knife under his side of the mattress.

Charmed Life

Charmed Life

Maniac Cop

"Are you closing the bar for Thanksgiving Day?" Bob asked the Monday before the holiday.

Sax uneasily pushed his breakfast around his plate. He hadn't meditated since Bob moved in, and the lack of this ritual was elevating his stress level – that, and the fear that he was sleeping with a murderer. "I usually don't. You'd be surprised how many people don't have anywhere to go on the holiday."

"Maybe you could make an exception. Just this once. After all, this will be our first Thanksgiving together." Bob smiled hopefully.

Sax twitched as his skin itched – he felt as if he were wearing a tight wool suit without the benefit of underwear. He gave a non-committal grunt.

"Kent and Moira would like to come visit. Do you mind?"

"When?" Sax didn't relish the idea of Bob's son and daughter-in-law visiting, but he doubted he could deny Bob's wishes without raising his suspicions.

"They'll be here Wednesday night."

"They're staying with us?"

"We do have the spare room. And our home is so perfect for entertaining."

Sax clamped his jaw closed to keep from reminding Bob that he was only a visitor.

"What do you say, darling? Would you close the bar for me?"

"I suppose."

"Wonderful! You won't be disappointed! I pride myself on creating wonderful holiday meals. One turkey dinner and you'll never complain about closing the bar again."

"I'm sure you're right." Sax pushed the still-full plate toward the middle of the table and stood.

"Are you all right? That's two days now that you haven't eaten your breakfast."

"I'm not much of a morning eater."

"Don't be ridiculous. I've seen you put away half a dozen eggs in the past."

"My tastes have changed," he snapped. "I'm going to work."

Bob silently cleared the plate from the table.

318

"Maybe you should eat it," Sax suggested.

"I made this especially for you, Sax. I don't like my eggs sunny-side up."

Sax grunted again and left the house. After his regular workout at the gym, he walked to his bar. The place remained relatively clean after the thorough scrubbing he had given it on Saturday morning. He sat down at the bar with the local paper and thumbed through it. A brief article on page three announced that the investigation into the recent Sun City house explosion had concluded. The coroner ruled death by misadventure in Mildred's case. The investigators concluded that the gas had leaked from the stove after Mildred failed to disengage a burner. Later, a spark originating from a small appliance in the home caused the explosion.

Sax thought back to that night.

He hadn't expected to see Sondra so early; she was supposed to be at the theater with Milo, watching the opening night performance of *Hello, Dolly!* Yet she tottered in a little after eight. He prepared a whiskey sour and slid it in front of her. "You wanna talk about it?"

She inhaled the alcohol, a sure sign that all was not well in Sondra's world. "Not really."

They bantered back and forth; she requested a refill and he questioned her ability to hold her liquor.

"Look," she snapped, "I think I can handle a few drinks without falling off my stool."

He backed away. "Whatever you say, Sondra." While he mixed her second drink, the door swung open and a glum Bob stepped through. He slid the second drink in front of Sondra and approached him. "Bob! What are you doing here? Wasn't tonight the *Hello, Dolly!* opening?"

"So it was. Unfortunately, the whole performance carried the aroma of shit."

Sax gave a brief laugh before recognizing that Bob wasn't kidding. "I don't understand."

319

"Mildred went on stage smelling of diarrhea and flowers. She drove out half the audience. The actual production drove out the other half."

"I'm sorry to hear that," Sax said, sliding a beer in front of Bob.

"Me, too. Mildred's locked herself in her dressing room and refuses to come out. I thought I'd come here for a while and try to relax."

The next time Sax made eye contact with Sondra, she beckoned him over and asked about Bob. Sax told her the story, which only seemed to depress her further.

"Does this have something to do with your disappearing act last night?"

"It might." She winced.

He shook his head. "You've made a mighty mess, Carmella."

"I'm going to fix it right now." She pushed the drink away. "I don't suppose you'd take this off my tab?"

"Tell you what: if you plan on being back, I'll save it for you."

"Don't bother," she sighed. "This may take a while. Where is Mildred now?"

"As far as Bob knows, she's still at the theater. She wouldn't come out of the dressing room no matter what he said." Sax watched her totter toward the door; for only having one drink, she seemed surprisingly unsteady. "Sondra! You sure you're okay to drive?"

She waved him off and he returned to his duties without another thought. Less than an hour later, Bob called him over.

"I just got a message from Millie."

"Oh, yeah?"

"It says Sondra is driving her home. I saw her stagger out of here earlier. She barely looked able to drive, let alone make nice with my wife."

Sax told him about his earlier conversation with the glum woman. "And she wasn't drunk," he added when he had finished the rest of the story.

"I suppose you would know," Bob mused. "She does all of her drinking here, doesn't she?"

"Most of it," he allowed.

"Would you mind if I stayed with you tonight?"

"Shouldn't you go home and check on Mildred?"

"She'll be fine without me. And honestly, I just don't have the stomach for it tonight. If she still smells like she did earlier...let's just say I wouldn't be able to keep my dinner down. Besides, she's safely at home. Nothing to worry about."

Sax agreed to let him stay the night, against his better judgment; seeing Adam and Steve together the night before made him lonely.

Bob nursed his beer until closing. Sax gave him the key to his home and sent him on ahead. When Sax arrived home a little before midnight, Bob was in bed, but not asleep.

"Did you call Mildred to let her know you wouldn't be home?" Sax asked as he stripped off his white button-down shirt and black pants.

"Why are you so concerned about my wife, Sax?"

Sax shifted uneasily. "I just don't want to be the cause of anything bad."

"She'll never miss me."

"I'm sure you think that, but—"

"The only butt I'm interested in is yours," Bob smirked.

"Ha ha."

"Come to bed."

Sax's exhaustion had dragged him into oblivion quickly. He dreamt of sunny summer days and green grass and red kites against a blue sky. When the rumba ringtone of Bob's phone pulled him back into reality, the clock read four-forty-five. He nudged Bob awake. "Your phone."

"Wha—?" Bob rolled over and yawned. "Oh." Picking up the phone, he said, "Hello?"

Sax closed his eyes and tried to land softly on the grass of his dream, but it was not to be.

"Who is this?" Bob asked sternly. "This isn't funny."

Sax clicked on the bedside light and watched Bob's face pale.

"Of course...we'll be right there." He ended the call and stared blankly at the patio doors that led to the back courtyard.

"What's happened?" Sax asked. Images of Patricia Scoville with Mildred's face superimposed marched through his mind.

"Something happened at my house...no, to my house."

Inwardly, Sax felt relief flood through him. "What? Did a pipe burst?"

"No. The house did."

"The house burst?" Sax repeated. "Was that Mildred? Is she all right?"

"I don't think so, Sax. I think she might be dead."

The look in Bob's eyes had been wonder, not grief or remorse. Pushing the newspaper away, he tried to push the memory from his mind as well. He retrieved the broom and swept the floor, though there was nothing of much significance to sweep away. Finally, he leaned the broom against the wall, and went into his office to use the phone.

"Hello?" Milo answered.

"Milo, it's Sax."

"Hi, Sax. I'll get Sondra."

"No, I called for you."

"Me? Why?"

Sax shifted his chair to check the front door. He could see that the bolt was still in place, but he lowered his voice anyway. "Our conversation yesterday got me thinking about Mildred's death. Some things don't make sense."

"Like what?"

"I don't want to talk about it on the phone. Could you come by later?"

"I've got plans tonight. Claire and I are going out for dinner."

"Tomorrow morning, then. We could meet for breakfast."

"Okay. Denny's?"

"Sure. Seven?" Picking up a pen, Sax scribbled Denny's, seven a.m. on the back of a Chinese restaurant menu he had deposited on his desk.

"Works for me."

"Thanks. See you then." He ended the call and leaned back in his old swiveling desk chair, his hands folded behind his head. He went over the details again, mentally searching for any other clues he may have missed.

322

A while later, an insistent pounding on the bar's main door pulled him from his reverie. He stood up and walked out of the office, closing the door behind him. As he got closer to the front, he heard a woman's voice: "Sax! Are you in there?" She followed the question with three more insistent pounds.

"Sondra," he said as he opened the door, "long time, no see."

"I've been busy." She pushed past him.

"The bar doesn't open for another half hour."

"I'm not here for a drink."

He raised an eyebrow at her.

"Okay, maybe I would like a drink, but I'd also like to talk to you."

"About what?"

She moved toward her regular stool.

"Let's sit in a booth," he said, gesturing toward the one in the far corner. Reluctantly, she headed toward the booth he had indicated. He followed her there. "What's up?" he asked as soon as they were both seated.

"Did I tell you about my daughter Fanny?"

"That she wants to convert to Judaism? Yeah, you mentioned it."

"Adam told me I needed to get over my hang-ups and just support her."

"Seems like good advice to me."

"He also told me to apologize to Mildred."

"So?"

"You saw how well that worked out." She reached for a non-existent glass and frowned when her hand curled around empty air. "I really could use a drink."

"Twenty-five minutes. Listen, Fanny isn't Mildred Kovich. I'm sure Fanny wants to make up with you as much as you want to make up with her."

"I doubt that. She's never liked me much. And now I haven't talked to her in weeks."

"Why not?"

"I meant to call her...really I did. In fact, I planned to call her the Sunday Mildred died, but life got complicated and busy."

"You're just in a play, Sondra. It's not like you don't have at least twenty-two other hours in the day to call her."

She was staring at the table.

"What's going on?"

"I met someone," she mumbled.

"Now we come to the heart of it. You're dating."

"Yes."

"Who is he?"

"Ethan."

Sondra had mentioned Ethan before, when she talked about going to New Mexico for the science fiction convention. "The boy who offered you a lift to Albuquerque?"

"He's not a boy," she said irritably. "He's thirty-two."

"He's half your age! No wonder you haven't called Fanny – he's younger than she is."

"More than half my age."

"But younger than Fanny."

"Well...yes."

"How did this happen?"

"I called Ethan to tell him that I wouldn't be able to go to the New Mexico convention with him because I had to take over the Dolly Levi role in the play. He understood, but he said he really wanted to get to know me better. I was flattered. When he asked me to dinner, I said yes." She placed her hands flat against the table. "He's been at the theater every night since then. He texts me constantly." As if on cue, her phone indicated she had a new message.

Sax shook his head, exasperated. "What do you want me to say?"

A tear rolled down her cheek. "You don't know what it's like, Sax. I've been an actress so long that I feel like I need a script just to talk to my daughter."

"You just call her and say you miss her. That's all you need to do."

She wiped the tear away with the heel of her hand. "I've missed you, too."

"You know where to find me," he said, gesturing at the darkened bar.

"Yes, but I know you're busy with Bob these days."

"How does Bob seem to you?"

"You're the one living with him."

"I know. But I just wondered if he seemed ...different...since Mildred's death."

324

"He's like a new man. He's chipper and enthusiastic at the theater. The whole production feels lighter. Of course, he acts like it's all me, but he has played a large part in it."

"Does that seem odd to you?"

"Not really. It's not like Mildred was the love of his life. After all, she had the wrong parts to get his motor going." One of the regulars strolled in and planted himself at the bar. "It's noon. Will you fix me that drink now?"

"What are you going to do about Fanny?"

"Maybe I'll just let it ride until Christmas. She'll be more forgiving then."

"Does she even celebrate Christmas anymore? If she's truly converting…"

"Shit. Good point. I really need my whiskey sour."

"Fine." He stood. "Here or at the bar?"

"At the bar. Can I use your office for a few minutes?"

"Sure. It's not locked. I'll have the drink waiting for you."

Sondra disappeared. Sax attended to his patron, pulling the man a draft Guinness and sliding it in front of him. "How ya doin' today, Herman?"

"Pretty good, Sax, pretty good. That Sondra's a looker, ain't she?"

"That she is. You know her?"

"Yes, sir. She and I are on friendly terms, at least when I'm in my uniform."

"Oh? What uniform is that?"

"I'm the night watchman at the rec center."

"Really? I had no idea."

"Yep," the old man said proudly. "I've been doing the job for near on twenty years now."

"Must be relaxing work. I wouldn't imagine you have too many emergencies around here."

"You'd be surprised. Especially with those theater types. Although it's been quieter since the director's wife died."

"Mildred Kovich?"

"You knew her?"

"Not well," Sax equivocated. "I know Bob and Sondra better."

"You didn't miss much. She was a bossy thing. I used to feel so sorry for Mr. Kovich." He took a swig of his beer. "She tried to ban Ms. Lane from the rec center."

325

"Could she do that?"

"As long as Ms. Lane still had her rec center card, Mrs. Kovich would have had a hard time enforcing that one. As a matter of fact, I let Sondra into the theater against the Koviches' wishes more than once. I don't care how important you think you are – no one has the right to ban anyone else unilaterally."

The office door opened and Sondra walked to her stool. "I really need that drink, Sax," she said, slumping against the bar.

"Talk to you later, Herman." Sax mixed the drink and gave it to Sondra, who immediately polished off the top third. "What's wrong now?"

"When did you and Milo get so chummy?"

"What do you mean?"

"You're meeting him for breakfast, aren't you?"

"Yes. Tomorrow. How did you know?"

"He left a note on the pad next to the phone. 'Denny's at 7.'" She frowned. "I don't know if I like that."

"Why should it be a problem?"

"I don't know. I guess I just think of you two as living in different parts of my life."

"Contrary to your belief, the world does not revolve around you, Sondra." He slapped his hand on the bar. "You have got to be the most singularly self-absorbed woman I have ever known."

She leaned away from him, her eyes wide. "I-I-I'm sorry, Sax," she stammered before the fire of indignation ignited. "Wait a second here! All you've done is make me feel like crap. I thought we were friends!"

"Friends? Really? Every conversation we've ever had has been all about you."

She picked up her glass and drained it. "Fine! I'll never darken your doorstep again, Sax Ridley! I'm sorry for ever doing so in the past." She harrumphed off the stool and walked out of the joint, not even noticing Herman's wave as she swished past him.

Sax snatched the empty glass off the bar and took it to the sink, where he washed it vigorously before dropping it in the drying rack with a clank.

"Everything okay?" Herman asked.

"Yeah," he answered. "Can I get you a refill?"

Sax awoke early the next morning and snuck out of the house without waking Bob. When he arrived at the Denny's, Milo was already sequestered in a quiet booth at the far end of the restaurant. He strode back and took the opposite side of the table. "Thanks for meeting me."

"No problem. I didn't mean to stir anything up, though. The cops are probably right, you know."

"I saw the article, too. They say it was 'death by misadventure.' But I learned something that the cops didn't know: Mildred Kovich couldn't smell."

Milo's face twisted into a confused smile. "That's ridiculous."

"No," Sax confirmed, "it's more common than you'd think. It's called anosmia. Turns out there are lots of reasons why someone could lose their sense of smell. According to Bob, Mildred couldn't smell anything."

"That does make her more susceptible to dying the way she did."

"Exactly. But she was so vain that no one knew she couldn't smell except Bob. Milo, I'm starting to believe he killed his wife!"

Milo's eyebrows shot up and he pursed his lips.

"What?"

"Nothing much," he said slowly. "You say no one knew about her anos-whatchacallit?"

"Anosmia. No. Bob says she always acted like she could smell. If someone handed her a flower, she'd say it smelled lovely. She wore a lot of perfume, just in case she had a bad odor about her."

"Sondra knew."

"You fellas ready to order?" The waiter, a middle-aged swarthy fellow whose badge read Mike appeared by the table.

"I'll have a Grand Slam," Milo answered. "Coffee, too, please."

"Coming up. And you?"

"Moons Over My Hammy and an orange juice."

"Sounds good." The waiter walked away, but not before giving Sax a flirtatious smile.

Sax cleared his throat and redirected his attention to Milo. "What do you mean, she knew?"

"The night before the opening of the play, Sondra decided to pull a prank on Mildred."

"When Sondra and Adam came back to the bar, they had showered and changed clothes," Sax remembered. "What happened?"

"She borrowed my fart spray—"

"Excuse me," Sax interrupted, "Did you say your fart spray?"

"Yes."

"Why would you have fart spray?"

Milo grinned impishly.

"Never mind. Tell me what happened."

"She snuck into the theater and sprayed Mildred's costumes down with the stuff."

Adding Milo's story to Bob's account of the rapidly emptied theater on opening night, Sax understood. "Mildred couldn't smell, so she had no idea how horrible the odor was. She must have thought the others overreacted."

"That makes sense."

"Sondra went to the theater to apologize to Mildred. She must have realized that Mildred couldn't smell at that time."

"You don't think Sondra—?"

"What? Killed Mildred? No...no, of course not. That's ridiculous."

Milo didn't look convinced. "She can be...let's say, self-involved."

"She told me yesterday that she didn't want us to be friends – she said it was like two parts of her world colliding."

"Contrary to her opinion, the world doesn't revolve around her."

"That's exactly what I said!"

The waiter came back with their coffee. "Your meals will be here momentarily. Do you need any creamer?"

"Yes, please," Sax said, smiling at the man's retreating form.

"Aren't you with Bob now?" Milo asked.

"A man can look."

"Tell that to Claire," he muttered.

"Are things still bad with her?"

"I just don't understand what's wrong with her lately. One minute, she's happy as a lark; next thing I know, she's trying to peck my eyes out."

"Maybe it's menopause. Isn't that something women go through at her age?"

"I would have thought she was too young, to be honest. Dead Alice didn't start that until she was fifty."

The waiter reappeared with their food. "Can I get you anything else? Anything at all?"

"No, thank you," Sax said with a smile.

"Just wave me down if you change your mind," Mike said as he walked away.

"You should get his number," Milo commented.

"Somehow, I think Bob would object."

"Yeah, probably. But that would solve your problem."

"Which problem is that?"

"The one where you might be living with a murderer." Milo picked up a strip of bacon and bit into it.

"As it turns out, you might be living with a murderer, too."

They finished their breakfasts in a ruminative silence.

Squirm

The uneasiness in Sondra's stomach was constantly with her now, ever since the morning she had watched the police and firemen picking up pieces of Mildred spread across nearly two acres of ground.

While the play was running, she had pushed it out of her mind. Between acting and her budding relationship with Ethan, thoughts of dead actresses – both long dead and recently deceased – faded into the background.

On Thanksgiving morning, though, she was haunted by both Lianne and Mildred as she tried to steady her hand and apply eyeliner around her mossy green eyes. She was meeting Ethan's family today for the first time. She knew she was older than his mother – ten years older, in point of fact, though Ethan pretended he hadn't done the math. His father was the same age as she was.

Lost in thought, she didn't notice Milo standing just behind her at the bathroom's threshold until she shifted her eyes in order to apply the eyeliner to her lower lid. When she did see him, she jumped, creating an unappealing zigzag just below her eye. "Holy crap!"

"Everything okay, Sondra?"

"Why are you sneaking up on me like that?!"

"I just wanted to ask if you would like to come to Thanksgiving dinner at Brian and Marla's today."

"No, thank you."

"I don't think you should be alone for the holiday," Claire called from the living room. "No one should eat a T.V. dinner on Thanksgiving."

"Don't worry about me," Sondra responded loudly. She licked a finger and attempted to remove the eyeliner before it dried. "I've got plans."

"Oh? Are you going to Sax's house?" Claire appeared next to Milo in the hall.

"No. I'm going to my boyfriend's family dinner."

"Boyfriend?" the couple asked in unison.

"Yes, boyfriend. Haven't you noticed that I've been gone a lot more lately?"

Milo shrugged. "I just figured you were busy with the theater or spending extra time with Fanny."

330

She winced at her daughter's name. "Not so much. Fanny and I...we're not really speaking right now."

"Oh, Sondra," Claire said sadly, "you should always try to fix family rifts before the holidays. There's nothing worse than letting a Thanksgiving or Christmas pass in anger."

"I didn't say I was angry. We're just not talking."

"Who's this boyfriend?" Milo asked. "Why haven't you brought him around?"

"His name is Ethan. We haven't been dating very long."

"But your meeting his kids today?"

"No, his parents."

Milo's eyebrows shot up. "How old is Ethan?"

"Old enough. He's been married twice."

"A twice-divorced man?"

"No. He was widowed both times."

Now Claire frowned. "A twice-widowed man? That seems unlikely."

"He's had some bad breaks."

Claire folded her arms across her chest. "Sounds to me like his wives are the ones with the bad luck."

"We'll let you finish getting ready," Milo said, shooing Claire away. "Have a good time."

"I will. You too."

"Thanks."

The couple disappeared into the living room; for a few minutes, Sondra could hear them talking in hushed tones. By the time she finished blow-drying her hair, though, only Taz's soft snoring as he lay in the hall outside the bathroom disturbed the otherwise silent house.

Despite her recent happiness, Sondra didn't quite believe the charmed life she had suddenly fallen into: a starring role, a younger boyfriend, and the possibility of finally making some money off her Hollywood past. The occasional twinge she felt emanated from the apparent truth that all her newfound luck hinged on the death of another, albeit unlikeable, actress.

Done with her makeup, she left the bathroom and returned to her bedroom, followed by the rotund dog. She reached down and scratched Taz behind his ears; Taz grunted his appreciation.

She pulled a pair of black palazzo pants and a sequined red tank top from her closet, slipping out of her robe and into the clothes quickly. Once on, the top seemed too garish for the occasion. She pulled it off and located an olive-green angora sweater instead. "What do you think, Taz? Do I look good?"

Taz gave her a bark and she rewarded him with a laugh and a pat. "Good dog." Gathering her purse and keys, she left the house and drove to Ethan's townhouse. From there, he drove them to his parents' home as she fidgeted nervously at his side.

"You look beautiful," Ethan said reassuringly as they approached the front door. He took her hand, raising it to his lips. "Thank you for coming."

"Thanks for the invitation," she smiled.

"My sister and her husband aren't here yet, but Mom and Dad can hardly wait to meet you. Mom remembers you from Scions of Beauty."

Her stomach rolled uneasily. "Are you sure your parents won't be upset about our age difference?"

He laughed charmingly. "Of course not, Sondra. My parents raised me to value the inside of a person over the exterior features. Not that your exterior isn't flawless," he added.

"I just don't know if this is a good idea."

"Is that your heart talking, or your head?" His eyes darkened with seriousness; he set his square jaw forward as if to absorb a violent blow.

The warmth of his hand on hers traveled up her arm and into her heart. "My head," she said quietly. "My heart wants to believe in you."

He pulled her closer, until his lips were against her ear. "You have a very wise heart," he whispered before pulling back. "Come on. I want you to meet the folks." Grasping her hand tightly, he led her into the beautifully decorated home. A huge family portrait from at least ten years earlier hung in the living room over a massive brown-leather sofa. The walls were painted a muted green that matched the color of Sondra's sweater almost exactly. A surprising number of sculptures dotted the oversized room. Standing in the middle of all this were Ethan's parents, John and Rowena Tanner.

John was tall, with gray hair combed neatly to one side. His argyle sweater and pleated pants bespoke money. Rowena, a tiny woman, stood smiling at his side, an old-fashioned apron covering what looked to be a vintage 1950's pink-and-black-striped dress. "Welcome to our home," she said as soon as Ethan had made the introductions.

"Thank you, Mrs. Tanner, Mr. Tanner."

"Please, call us John and Rowena," the man said. "You're hardly a child. We're peers, aren't we?"

She pasted her most pleasant smile on. "I suppose we are."

"Dad, be nice now. Sondra is a wonderful woman."

His mother took Sondra by the hand. "Come and help me in the kitchen, Sondra. Ethan has told me so many nice things about you."

"Ethan?" Sondra asked, slightly panicked beneath her calm exterior.

"Go on, sweetheart. Have fun."

She allowed Rowena to pull her into the spacious kitchen behind the double doors beyond the massive living and dining rooms.

"Now then," Rowena said, smiling, "would you mind draining the potatoes?"

Sondra had limited knowledge of cooking. Over the years, she had mastered one meal: King Ranch Chicken Casserole. Bill's housekeeper had taught her to make it years before, and Sondra remembered it by rote. That one recipe had served her well; Fanny loved it, and so had every boyfriend she had dated in the years since Bill's death. Otherwise, she was useless. "What potatoes?"

"The ones in the big pot right there," Rowena said.

"How do I drain them?"

"Just pour off most of the liquid. Leave a bit in the bottom for the mashing."

Biting her lip much harder than she realized, Sondra picked up the huge pot, carried it to the sink, and attempted to drain some of the water off without losing any of the potatoes.

"No, no! That's not how you do it! You have to use the lid to hold the potatoes in!"

"What?" She set the pot in the sink and turned to look at Rowena.

"My goodness! You're bleeding!"

"I am? Where?" Sondra reached up but didn't touch her face – she wasn't sure where her injury was.

"Your lip is bleeding. What happened?"

She touched her fingers to her lip and they came away with a small amount of blood. She turned and rinsed them under the faucet.

"Oh, no! The potatoes!" Rowena moaned.

Sondra looked down and saw the pink tinge in the pan's water.

"Shit! I'm so sorry, Rowena! What can I do?"

She pointed sternly at a barstool on the other side of the kitchen's massive island. "Sit over there."

Sondra, hanging her head, went to the stool. "I really am very sorry. I didn't mean to—"

"Never mind," Rowena cut her off. "How ridiculous of me to think that an actress would know how to cook." She turned on the garbage disposal and dumped the ruined potatoes into the sink, pushing them ruthlessly toward the hidden blades.

Sondra winced, knowing Rowena wished she could do the same with her. She surveyed the kitchen, which resembled one of those cooking show sets she occasionally glimpsed as she flipped past the Food Network on television. The gleaming stainless-steel appliances, copper-bottomed pots, and Corian countertops told Sondra wordlessly that Rowena didn't actually need help in the kitchen – she had meant it as a bonding experience. "Your kitchen is lovely," she said as soon as the garbage disposal was off, trying to renew the warmth of their introduction.

"The whole house is a custom build for us." Rowena moved to the pantry, a walk-in closet lined with bins and shelves. She emerged with a small sack of potatoes. "Do you know how to peel potatoes?"

"Yes."

"Without cutting yourself?"

Sondra smiled apologetically. "If I do it slowly."

Rowena sighed and pulled two peelers from a drawer in the island. She pushed one peeler and a wooden cutting board toward Sondra, along with three potatoes. "Don't rush."

Sondra picked up the peeler and began to skin the tubers; Rowena did the same.

"How did you and Ethan meet?" Rowena asked, setting her first naked potato aside.

"I went to a screening of Siege of the Moon with a friend of mine. Ethan was there." Sondra turned her first potato in her hand, scraping another length of skin from its body.

"Siege of the Moon. That's the one where you were green, right?"

"It's the only major film I was ever in."

"To be fair, it wasn't really a major film, was it? I mean, I'm pretty sure that John and I saw it at a drive-in."

"Major films are shown in drive-ins all the time!"

"Of course. I'm sorry, I didn't mean to offend you." She set her second potato aside. "What I meant was that it was aimed at a younger crowd...a make-out film, some might say."

"Is that what you did?"

"What?"

"Never mind."

Rowena finished her fourth potato. "He seems very happy with you. More than with either of his first two wives."

"We're not married."

"Not yet."

Sensing an opening, Sondra asked, "What happened to his wives?"

"Just, you know, accidents." The petite woman focused on her current peeling project.

"What kinds of accidents?"

"Julia's chute didn't open and Astrid's rope broke."

Sondra shifted uncomfortably. "Was Ethan with them?"

"He was with Astrid. He was traumatized – he moved back home with John and me after her death."

"I had no idea."

"He doesn't like to talk about either of them. The marriages were...ill-advised. He and Julia had been considering a divorce when she went on that last base jump. With Astrid, he just didn't seem to be able to relax. She was remarkably beautiful. He worried she would leave him."

"But Ethan is so handsome!"

"That's what I told him, but he still thought it was just a matter of time before she broke his heart."

The kitchen door swung open and a dark-haired woman who could have been Ethan dressed in drag came through the door. "Mom! Happy Thanksgiving!" She gripped both of her mother's shoulders and squeezed before walking around the island to offer her hand to Sondra. "You must be Ethan's new sweetheart."

"Vivian, my dear, this is Sondra Lane. Sondra, my daughter Vivian."

Sondra met Vivian's hand. "Glad to finally meet you. Ethan speaks very highly of you."

"Does he? I hope he doesn't think I'm spreading lies about how great he is behind his back!"

Rowena trilled a laugh. "Don't mind her, Sondra. My daughter has always been a bit of a jokester. Where's Patrick, dear?"

"I left him with the boys, of course. They're playing pool in the loft."

"He always comes in to say hello to me, though," she pouted.

"Then go up and chastise him, Mom. I'm sure he'd love it."

"I have half a mind to do just that."

"Go on! Give me a minute with the next Mrs. Turner."

"We're not engaged!" Sondra exclaimed.

"Not yet. Ethan's quick, though. I think he's allergic to being single."

"Don't be too hard on her, Viv. I'll be right back." Rowena wiped her hands on her apron.

"How many potatoes do you need peeled, Mom?"

"Six," she answered as she disappeared through the door.

"One, two, three, four, five...and you're working on number six, I see." Vivian rinsed the five peeled spuds and retrieved a large knife from the butcher-block holder under a far cabinet.

Sondra finished the sixth potato.

"Toss it here, will you?" Vivian asked, holding out her free hand. Sondra's aim was a little off; Vivian caught the vegetable on the knife, sinking the sharp blade deep into its pale flesh. "Now, Sondra, may I ask how old you are?"

"Didn't anyone ever tell you that it's rude to ask a woman's age?"

"Sixty-three, right?"

Sondra crossed her arms defensively. "How could you know that?"

"You were born Sarah Lansky, the daughter of a Jewish accountant who worked for the mob, and his showgirl wife. You left Vegas, changed your name, and started appearing in commercials in the early Seventies. You were on Scions of Beauty for most of the latter half of that decade. You gave birth to your daughter – Epiphany, right? – not long after Siege of the Moon hit theaters. After that, you were effectively retired from show business, though you did get a few cameos on television – bit parts that were tossed to you by Hollywood acquaintances. You never married that big Hollywood star to whom you were engaged because he died before you two got around to it. When you moved to Arizona to live with your daughter a few years ago, you began actively seeking stage roles in community theater. Currently, you live with a man named Milo Crosby in Sun City. You also drink enough whiskey sours at the Brass Monkey that your insides are probably pickled."

"What is this?"

"You're dating my brother. I like to know as much as possible about anyone he finds interesting."

"Does he know you've had me investigated?"

She laughed. "Geez, Sondra – I got most of that off of Wikipedia! You're not exactly an unknown...even if your career never took off. Have a famous man's baby and you are, by extension, famous. At least in this wired world." The whole time she had been talking, she had also been dicing the potatoes. Now, she scraped them into another large pot, ran water over them, and put them on the stove to cook. "You're not his usual type, you know."

"What do you mean?"

"He usually goes for young, beautiful, and rich. You're attractive enough for your age, but you hardly fall into the same category as Julia or Astrid. I thought you must be rich, but if so, you're doing a damned good impression of a down-and-out actress. Not only that, but an alcoholic to boot!"

Sondra pushed herself off her stool just so she could feel the earth beneath her feet. "I don't know who the hell you think you are," she half-shouted, "but how I live my life is

337

none of your business! I won't even attempt to correct your assumptions because you've already decided I'm not good enough for your family! I thought that Ethan's family would be wonderful – after all, he is a remarkable man. You and your mother have proved to be bitchy, invasive, and rude. Have a good holiday – I'm going home!"

Vivian laughed. "You're still fiery, aren't you? Sit down, Sondra – I didn't mean to offend you."

Sondra reluctantly lowered herself back onto the stool. She kept a wary eye on the unpleasant woman.

"I think you could be good for Ethan – but you can't blame my mother for being leery of you. After all, she really wants grandchildren, and she's unlikely to get any from you." Vivian came around the island and sat on the stool next to Sondra's. "Do you know what you have that neither Julia nor Astrid had?"

Sondra shook her head, not trusting her voice.

"A spark. I saw it in your acting. Yes, I rented Siege of the Moon. It's a better film than it has gotten credit for being. I completely understand why it's gaining a reputation as a cult favorite. And I came to see *Hello, Dolly!* a few weeks ago. You were great in it, by the way." She took Sondra's hand affectionately. "I just wanted to see if you had that spark off the stage as well. I see now that you do – and that's a very good thing."

Rowena came back into the kitchen, smiling cheerfully. Vivian patted Sondra's hand and stood up. "What else can I do, Mom?"

"The sweet potato casserole needs to go in the oven. After that, if you'd just take care of the potatoes, I'll finish the rest up myself." She lifted the lid on the large turkey roaster and Sondra caught a glimpse of the golden-brown bird within. "Did you have a nice visit?"

Sondra opened her mouth to answer, but Vivian was quicker. "Lovely, actually. Sondra is as wonderful as Ethan has said."

"Lovely," Sondra echoed. "If you don't mind, I'd like to find Ethan right now."

"Up the stairs. You can't miss them," Rowena answered.

"Thank you." Sondra slid off the stool and walked from the room, fighting the urge to keep her eyes on them at all times; her inner voice was screaming that it would be dangerous to turn her back.

She took the stairs quickly and was surprised to see that Vivian's husband Patrick, a tall, gray-haired gentleman who resembled her own long-dead lover Bill, was at least as old as Rowena and possibly as old as Sondra herself.

"What's the matter, darling?" Ethan asked solicitously. "You seem distressed."

When she tried to answer him, she realized her jaw was hanging open. She snapped it closed. "I'm fine. I just...missed you," she answered, though she couldn't tear her eyes away from Patrick, who walked toward her with his hand extended.

"I'm Patrick, Vivian's husband. You must be the fascinating Sondra Lane."

She giggled and then reddened when she realized the noise she had made. Ethan looked at her strangely. Clearing her throat, she answered, "Yes. It's a pleasure to meet you."

"Likewise. I do hope my wife hasn't given you too hard of a time. She's very protective of Ethan."

"No harder than the CIA, I suppose."

"You've been interviewed by Central Intelligence before?"

"Not yet. But I believe I'm prepared for it now."

The men all laughed.

"Did you need something, Sondra?" Ethan asked.

"Could we talk for a few minutes?"

"Gentlemen, if you'll excuse me."

"Of course," John said, waving them off. "Use my office."

Ethan led her by the hand into a spacious room furnished with an oak desk and matching bookshelves; he pulled her down onto a plush blue loveseat. "What's wrong?"

"I don't think your mother and sister are too keen on me. This might have been a huge mistake."

"Don't be ridiculous, sweetheart. Thanksgiving is a very important holiday to me – I couldn't celebrate it without the one person I'm most thankful for this year."

"I'm much too old for you, Ethan," she pressed on.

His face lost all expression. "Are you breaking up with me?"

She looked away, unable to meet his eyes. "I'm afraid so. Yes."

339

"Please...not today," he said softly. "Wait until tomorrow. You may feel differently."

"I don't think I will."

He put both hands on her shoulders. "Just...wait. I know you don't want to ruin the day for us."

"Your sister had me investigated!"

"My sister is an investigator."

Sondra stopped pulling away from him. "Really?"

"Yes, really."

"Why didn't you tell me that before?"

"I didn't think it mattered."

"She seems to know every detail of my life."

"You are a celebrity, Sondra. Especially now that Siege of the Moon is gaining renewed attention."

"Okay. I'm sorry."

"You don't need to be sorry." He pulled her into his arms. "Just trust me. Trust what we feel for each other."

She laid her head against his shoulder, marveling at how his touch calmed her. Several minutes passed with them clinging to one another. When she opened her eyes, she saw another family portrait. This one had the Turner family plus two. "Is that Astrid in the picture?" she asked.

Ethan turned to look. "Which one?"

"The third shelf up."

"Yes."

The woman had coal-black hair and a wide smile. She was so thin she could have been a runway model. "She's gorgeous."

"She was."

"Who's the man next to Vivian?"

"That's Jean Claude, Viv's first husband." Ethan stood up, pulling her by the hand again. "Come on, my dear. Everyone will be missing us."

Downstairs, the family had already gathered for dinner. Rowena was carrying the turkey in from the kitchen as Sondra and Ethan descended the stairs. "There you two are! I was about to send up a search party!"

"Sorry, Mom. I was just giving Sondra a tour of the house."

"You have a lovely home," Sondra offered.

"Thank you. This is the home John and I always wished we could provide for our children."

"Mother," Vivian admonished, "it's not the building that makes the home, it's the warmth you find inside it."

"That's a wonderful sentiment," John said, patting his daughter's hand. "You know what your mother means, though."

"Of course. I just don't like for you two to think that there was anything wrong with the way Ethan and I were raised."

"How was that?" Sondra asked.

"We owned a carnival," John answered.

Sondra smiled at this couple who looked like the poster children for the Religious Right. "No, you didn't."

"Yes, they did," Ethan confirmed. "Vivian and I spent most of our childhoods living in tents and trailers."

"I was a fifth-generation carnival barker," John said proudly. "I inherited the whole shebang from my father. I planned to leave it to my kids, but neither Viv nor Ethan had much interest in it. So, when Rowena and I were ready to retire, I sold the show."

"Mom was a trapeze artist," Vivian commented as she spooned mashed potatoes onto her plate.

"I thought you said it was a carnival."

"We had a one-ring circus, too. A few animals, a few clowns. Nothing like Ringling Brothers, but then, we weren't performing in major cities, either."

Sondra couldn't help her bemusement. She was dating the son of circus folk – almost as rare of a breed as her own genetic heritage, and just as vilified by the general public. Her appetite restored, she filled her plate with sweet potato casserole, green peas, turkey, and mashed potatoes. "Tell me more about the carnival," she said.

The family spent the rest of the meal sharing anecdotes while she and Patrick listened with rapt awe. As Ethan drove her back to his place that evening, he held her hand. "My family loved you."

"I don't know about that." She watched as the Central Avenue scenery whipped past her window. "We should go to the art museum this weekend," she commented as they passed it.

"Good idea." He squeezed her fingers lightly. "I'm not kidding – my family really did love you."

She smiled at him. "I had a very nice time."

"I was wondering…would you like to stay over tonight?"

Unlike so many of her relationships in the past decades, she and Ethan were taking things slowly. She assumed his reticence was some sort of ill-placed respect; her own reluctance had more to do with their age difference. "Are you sure you want to be with me? I'm older than your mother."

"You're younger than me in some ways."

"And older than you in the way that society notices."

"Age is just a number."

She laughed. "So cliché."

"Yeah? There are clichés for a reason: they're true. Stay with me tonight."

"I didn't bring anything with me. I don't have makeup or clothes or…"

"None of that matters, Sondra. Just stay." He pulled the car into the garage of his townhouse and lowered the door. With one hand, he cupped the back of her head and pulled her into a deep kiss that made her remember every drive-in movie she had ever missed as a teenager. A thrill of arousal ran through her and she knew she would stay. When he reluctantly broke off the kiss, she got out of the car and followed him inside.

The soft fall sunlight streaming through the upstairs window the next morning seemed determined to show Sondra just how old she was. Her skin look thin and fragile to her, while Ethan's sleeping form looked thick and healthy. Staying with him was wrong; she should have known better. Ethan was right; she was younger than him in some ways – she was as selfish and spoiled as a toddler.

Slipping out of the bed, she gathered her clothes and tiptoed down the stairs. After she dressed, she found a spiral notebook on the counter and opened it up to rip a page from it. Once open, she saw that it was actually a sketchbook.

Ethan had drawn her as Sunrise Aeon and as Dolly Levi. Half a dozen sketches of her face followed, all of them showing her as she really was – lines and wrinkles included. Her finger traced around her lips, the surrounding pucker lines from too many years of smoking marring what was once her most striking feature. Despite their honesty, his drawing weren't cruel. She could see his affection for her in every stroke of his pencil. In the last image, she was sleeping. He must have drawn it just a few hours before. She saw an innocence and vulnerability in her face that she didn't even know she possessed anymore. She wasn't innocent, she knew. She had wished terrible things on people – Mildred. That night, as she stood in Mildred Kovich's driveway, she had wished the woman were dead. The next morning, her wish came true. A tear, equal parts regret and guilt, rolled down her cheek and splashed onto the sketch, leaving a splattered watermark on the pillow. She flipped the page and finally found a blank sheet. Picking up an abandoned pencil, she wrote: Dear Ethan, Thank you. Love, Sondra.

Flipping the sketchbook closed, she slipped off her shoes at the base of the stairs and climbed back up, stripping off her clothes as she went.

On the first Tuesday after Thanksgiving, Bob held auditions for The King and I. Sondra had spent most of Sunday running lines for her audition piece with Ethan's help.

Bob, who only two weeks ago had seemed to be bubbling over with happiness, greeted Sondra with an irritable growl.

"How was your Thanksgiving?" she asked, attempting to cheer him up before she had to perform in front of him.

"A disaster to rival the Hindenburg. Sax was god-awful to my son and his wife, asking all sorts of rude questions about our family. You know, I've got half a mind to leave him."

"Goodness, don't do that!" she exclaimed. "I know he's very fond of you, Bob."

He glanced around. A few others had arrived for the auditions. "I could really use someone to talk to, Sondra. Could you go for coffee with me after this?"

Not really wanting to but suspecting it might help her chances in the audition, Sondra agreed.

"Why don't you go last? That way, you have some more time to prepare and you won't just be sitting around waiting for me."

"Thanks, Bob. Do you mind if I go down to the green room?"

"Go ahead." He waved her away and called the first name on his list. A plump, bald man took the stage.

Downstairs, everything looked exactly as it had a few weeks earlier. No one had cleaned out Mildred's dressing room – the stench had lingered longer than Sondra could have anticipated. When she took over the Dolly Levi role, she hadn't worn the original costumes – Mildred was a much bigger woman than Sondra and the dresses wouldn't have fit her anyway. Luckily, a few costumes from a long-ago performance of Sunday in the Park with George were packed away in storage. They weren't exactly period-perfect, but the volunteer costume mistress had done a passable job of altering them to look right. They, along with all the other costumes from Hello, Dolly!, still hung along one side of the green room on the rolling metal rack a department store had donated decades earlier.

She settled into the sofa and reviewed her lines a dozen times or so before dropping the script and picking up an abandoned magazine – an ancient one, as it turned out. Inside, she found an article about herself.

The home Sondra Lane shares with her daughter in Beverly Hills is massive – much larger than the two need. A young man shows me into the living room and asks me to wait. This must be a trick she learned from her long-dead paramour; minor stars rarely use it. Ms. Lane is the exception.

While I wait, I study the room. A faux-Warhol painting featuring the actress hangs over the fireplace, looking out of place in this antique-filled mausoleum. The Art Deco furniture has seen better days – most of them more than fifty years ago. Some have said that Sondra Lane could have been the next Gloria Swanson if she had made better choices in the last decade. From where I'm sitting, she is more likely the embodiment of one of Gloria's best roles: Norma Desmond.

When she finally appears, Sondra is wearing a red-and-white wrap dress like the ones that were popular a few years ago. A cigarette dangles from one hand. "I'm so sorry I kept you waiting," she says as she sashays toward me. "Bud called."

I'm sure this is meant to impress me; a few days later, I will attempt to nail down the reference and come up empty.

Sondra stopped reading, closing the magazine. She remembered the interview. The reporter had been a young woman with a fake smile. She obviously had no idea who Sondra was prior to receiving the assignment. Of course, by the mid-1980's, Sondra was a nobody again to the public at large anyway. Only old Hollywood knew and cared about her.

Her agent had arranged the interview to promote what was to have been her second chance at stardom – a low-budget first attempt by a director who later struck it big in action films. A few days after her unpleasant encounter with the reporter, the project was shelved; the test audiences reviled it.

She had complained to her agent about the reporter. He had all but guaranteed that the interview wouldn't run – why would the magazine bother? After all, without the film, the article had nothing to promote. Until she picked up the magazine, Sondra couldn't have said for certain if the article was published or not. Burning bile rose up her esophagus, a combination of audition nerves and humiliation. She knew that she wasn't the greatest actress ever to live, but she was better than this girl had given her credit for being.

Chuck, a regular player, peered around the corner of the green room. "Bob's ready for you."

Swallowing down her nausea, she smiled and followed him up the stairs and onto the stage.

"Chuck, will you read the King's lines?" Bob called from the third row back.

"Sure thing." Chuck turned to Sondra. "You ready?"

"Yeah, let's go." The hours of practice paid off as they always did for her. She spoke the lines clearly and with character, with barely a glance at the pages in her hand. The few female audition participants who had stuck around to see the competition for the lead role groaned in despair, raising Sondra's spirits.

"Great. Thanks for helping out, Chuck. Thanks to everyone who came out and auditioned. I'll have the cast list posted in the rec center on Saturday morning."

The other would-be thespians filed out of the auditorium. Sondra walked down the steps at the front of the stage and over to Bob.

"You ready for that coffee?" he asked as he stuffed his notes into the brown leather briefcase he carried with him.

"Sure. Where to?"

"IHOP?"

"Works for me." They walked silently to the parking lot. She spotted Herman as she stepped into her car and gave him a short wave. Bob got into his car too, and they drove to the restaurant. She was already inside waiting for a table when he arrived.

"Let's get a booth," he said.

"Sure."

When the hostess came to seat them, she pointed to a booth in a nearly empty section toward the back. "Could we sit there?"

"The waitress assigned back there is about to go off shift."

"That's okay. We just want coffee."

She smiled tightly. "Fine." She led them to the booth Sondra requested, dropped the menus on the table and turned on her heel.

"Mildred was always pissing waitresses off, too," Bob said fondly.

"I think that's why we didn't get along – two pushy broads bumping our heads together."

"Yes. I'm sure you're right about that."

The waitress, a tired but pleasant-looking Hispanic woman, walked over with a coffee carafe. "My name is Esperanza and I'll be your waitress this evening. Would you like some coffee to start?"

"Just coffee tonight," Sondra answered. "If you'd just bring us a fresh carafe, we won't trouble you for anything else."

346

"Are you sure?" she asked looking from Sondra to Bob and back.

"Just coffee, thank you," Bob confirmed.

"I'll be back with a fresh pot."

As soon as she was out of earshot, Bob confided, "I've been thinking about Mildred a lot lately."

"That makes sense. You were married to her for – how long?"

"Almost forty years. I thought there were only a few people who knew how much of a sham our marriage was. But I guess there's just no hiding the truth, is there?"

"Well, you did move in with Sax before the fire department finished picking up the pieces of your wife."

"As far as the world knows, Sax is just a supportive friend," Bob answered staunchly.

"People will always assume the worst, Bob. You know that."

He slumped in his seat. "I suppose you're right. Besides, it's the truth."

"Are you going to tell me what went wrong over the holiday?"

"I don't think Sax is nearly as happy to have me staying with him as I am to be there."

"Sax has been single for a very long time, you know. There are bound to be some sticking points."

"That I can understand. What I don't follow is why he interrogated my son about my marriage."

Sondra shuddered, remembering Viv's intense interview. "What did he ask?"

"Did Millie and I fight a lot? Had he ever met any of my boyfriends?"

She frowned. "That must have made your son uncomfortable."

"Extremely. I mean, Kent knew his mother and I had our problems, but we always tried to keep our disagreements – and our affairs – away from the kids."

"Mildred had affairs too?"

"Of course, she did. She and Chuck had been going at it hot and heavy since six months after we moved to Sun City."

"Mildred and Chuck? Our Chuck?"

"No, Sondra, Chuck E. Cheese. Which Chuck do you think?"

"I'm sorry. I just...I had no idea. Mildred and Chuck. Huh. Were they in love?"

"I don't know. To hear Chuck tell it, they were the Romeo and Juliet of the senior set. I never got the impression that Mildred was that serious about him, though."

"Did you ever think about divorcing?"

"Of course not! We had a partnership. The difficulties involved in untangling our lives would have been nightmarish. Not to mention the trauma to the kids and the playhouse. Everyone knows that a theater troupe is like a family – our divorce would have ripped that family apart."

"But aren't you happier now? I mean, with her dead?"

Bob raised an eyebrow and lifted his cup halfway to his mouth before answering. "Aren't you?"

Charmed Life

Basket Case

Sondra's conversation with Bob echoed in her mind all week. She had walked away from IHOP with the uneasy sense that Bob may have killed his wife in order to prevent any ripples of trouble in his life. When she tried to talk to Milo about it, he blanched and hurried away with the excuse that Claire was waiting for him.

When Saturday morning rolled around, she half-heartedly dressed and drove to the rec center to see if she made the cut. Her name was at the top of the list, in the role of Anna.

It was time to repair some of the damage she had done in the last few months, starting with Sax. She knew the bar wouldn't be open yet, but she drove over anyway. The door was locked; she hammered her fist against it until she heard Sax shout in irritation, "I'm coming, I'm coming!"

As soon as the door opened, she said contritely, "I'm sorry."

He folded his arms and blocked her entry. "You should be."

"May I come in?"

"No. I'm closed."

"It's about Bob."

His mouth twitched. "Why didn't you tell me you knew Mildred couldn't smell?"

"It didn't seem that important. Besides, I only found out about it the night before she died."

"Exactly."

Her eyes widened in appalled innocence. "What are you thinking, Sax?"

He stepped back into the darkness of the bar. "Come in. I don't want to announce my theories to the world."

She stepped inside, he closed and relocked the door. "You want a drink?" he asked.

"You're not open."

"I think I owe you one."

"Probably." She headed for her regular stool and he went behind the bar to mix her favorite cocktail. "I had coffee with Bob the other night," she began, "and he was really upset with you."

349

"I think I stepped on his toes a bit with Kent and his wife."

"What were you thinking? Why would you question Kent like that? Bob felt like you were doing a post-mortem on his marriage."

"I know."

"You can't do that. He lives with you, Sax. Do you have any idea how much danger you could be in?"

Sax frowned. "What?"

"He killed Mildred," she stated emphatically.

"No. I don't think he did. They might not have been a love match, but Bob and Mildred had been partners for a very long time. He was loyal to her."

"Because of what a divorce would do to their family and the theater group."

"Where are you getting this from?"

"Did you know that Mildred was sleeping with one of the actors from our group?"

"She was?"

"Definitely."

"How do you know?"

"Bob told me."

Sax set the drink in front of her. "So she wanted a divorce?"

"Not according to Bob. But if he's guilty, wouldn't it be in his best interest to deny his marriage was on the verge of collapse?"

"True. But a lot of people had reasons to wish her dead. Including you."

"Okay. I admit I didn't mourn her loss deeply, but I only wished her dead. I didn't actually plot against her."

"The witnesses say you fought with her in the driveway."

"Yes, but I didn't go inside the house."

"Maybe not then, but did you go back later?"

"No. But then, I would say that if I did it, wouldn't I?"

Sax shook his head. "You're a lot of things, Sondra: selfish, egotistical, alcoholic. But I just can't see you as a killer."

"Thanks…I think. And I'm not a drunk."

He laughed. "Okay, I'll give you that one."

"What should we do about Bob?"

"I don't know that anything needs to be done. The cops don't seem to think so."

"I watched the police carry Mildred out in pieces. As much as I disliked the woman, she really didn't deserve what happened to her."

"Can you talk to Chuck without raising Bob's suspicions?"

"He's playing the King in The King and I. Oh! I got the role of Anna!"

"Congratulations! Why didn't you say?"

"Ever since my talk with Bob on Tuesday night, I just haven't been myself. I'm not even sure I want to be in the play."

Sax reached out and, with the back of his hand, felt Sondra's forehead. "You don't have a fever."

"Funny. I think you missed your calling."

"Are you afraid of Bob?"

"Yes," she confessed.

"But why? Even if he murdered Mildred, he has no reason to come after you."

"If he thinks I suspect him..."

"This is Bob we're talking about, not some mad serial killer."

Sondra sipped her drink. "What do you want me to do?"

"See what you can find out from Chuck about his relationship with Mildred. Maybe he'll shed some light on the whole thing."

She agreed.

"Have you talked to Fanny yet?"

"No."

"Sondra, she's your daughter. Christmas is less than a month away. You need to deal with this. Are you still dating Ethan?"

"Yes."

He picked up her now-empty glass and walked it to the bar sink.

"What, no comment?"

"Who am I to talk? I'm sleeping with someone I think may have murdered his wife."

"Milo's been acting really weird around me lately. And Claire isn't around as much as she used to be."

Sax winced. "That could be my fault." He told her about his breakfast conversation with Milo.

"So he thinks I could be a murderer?" she gasped.

"To be fair, he just didn't want to discount any potential leads."

"That's a crock of crap. I pulled one prank – and I felt guilty for it almost immediately afterward. I'd still feel badly about it, except Mildred proved just how much of a bitch she was when I tried to make nice."

"When do rehearsals start?"

"Tuesday."

"Let me know what you discover."

Even though they didn't have plans together until later that evening, Sondra drove over to Ethan's townhouse after she left the bar.

Vivian opened the door. "Sondra! What are you doing here?"

"Visiting Ethan. Is he home?"

"Of course." Vivian turned and called up the stairs, "Ethan! Sondra's here!"

As he padded down the stairs, he smiled. "There she is, the most beautiful woman in the world!"

"I'm sorry to drop by unannounced."

"No, you're not," Vivian said. "You've been cheated on before. This is a spot check, isn't it?"

Sondra blinked at her.

"There's no reason to lie. I've shared everything I learned about you with Ethan."

Vivian might as well have thrown a fastball at her sternum – her heart thudded painfully.

Ethan rushed to take her in his arms. "It's fine, baby. Nothing to be upset about."

She sank into his hug for just a moment before gently pushing him away.

She turned to face the younger woman. "What exactly is your problem?"

"No problem," Viv answered with a shrug. "I just believe in full disclosure."

"Fine. I'd like to disclose that you are a bitch."

"Actually, that's only 'disclosing' your opinion of me. Which, of course, says much more about you than me." The dark-haired beauty's eyes flashed with vicious humor.

"Now, ladies, let's just shake hands and go to our corners, okay?"

"Of course," Viv answered, holding out a hand toward Sondra, who refused to shake it. After a few seconds, she dropped it. "I'll just be going, Ethan. I'm sure you have a lot to discuss. Sondra, a pleasure as always." She breezed out the door, pulling it shut behind her as she went.

"Why does she hate me so much?"

"She doesn't. In fact, she's quite fond of you." His puzzled expression made her feel like a jerk.

"I'm sorry, Ethan. I don't know what's the matter with me. Maybe I'm reading too much into her behavior."

"That's probably true. Vivian is a very hard person to understand if you don't know her well. She has a dry sense of humor and a remarkably inquisitive nature. You should have seen the hours of research she did on Patrick before she married him."

"Did she do this to your wives as well?"

"She tried. I wouldn't listen to her when she attempted to warn me about Julia."

"Warn you? About what?"

He took her hands and drew her to the off-white modern sofa. "Julia had a death wish. She was always taking unnecessary risks. Vivian feared that she would eventually kill me."

"Murder you?"

"Not like that. Unintentionally kill me. Julie liked to base jump off buildings, bungee jump off bridges, and leap out of airplanes. I went with her most of the time. If she and I hadn't been separated, I would have been with her on her last base jump."

"How horrible! You would have watched her die."

"Not necessarily," he laughed. "She might have watched me die instead."

"I don't understand."

"I might have ended up wearing the improperly packed parachute instead of her."

"What is she warning you about with me?"

"Nothing. I swear to you, Viv thinks you're wonderful. Did she dig into your life? Yes. But she didn't find anything that alarmed her. Please forgive her interference. She's just trying to protect me."

Sondra turned away from Ethan and his beautifully chiseled cheekbones to stare at the empty hearth in front of them. Vivian's words floated through her mind. Once she had Ethan's explanation of them, they no longer seemed hateful. At last, she nodded. "I'm sorry. I'll apologize for being so defensive the next time we meet."

"Wonderful. Where would you like to go to dinner tonight?"

She glanced at the clock. "It's only one in the afternoon."

"I know," he said with a mischievous grin, "but our afternoon is all booked up."

Sunday morning, she arose early and went down to Ethan's living room, leaving him sprawled, exhausted, on the bed. Pulling her phone from her purse, she dialed Fanny's number. The phone rang five times; no one answered. At last, the voicemail started: "You have reached Fanny Dauber's phone. Thank you for calling. I'm not available at the moment. Please leave a message after the tone."

"Fanny, it's your mother. Listen, I know I've been horrible. I apologize. I'm sure you know that Adam and Steve were here a few weeks ago. Adam tells me Reuben is a good man who treats you like a princess – as he should. Can you ever forgive my foolishness? I've made such a mess of my own life, I can't imagine why I would think I should be allowed to run yours. I have some news I'd like to share with you. And I want to help you plan your wedding. I miss you, Fanny. Call me back." She clicked off the call and tried to put the subject out of her mind.

Back upstairs, she gathered her clothes and dressed silently before sitting next to Ethan on the bed. He roused enough to raise his head. "Where are you going?"

"Home. If I know you, you're going to sleep most of the morning away anyway."

He grinned impishly. "I planned to spend it in bed, but I don't have to be asleep."

She lightly smacked his bottom. "Bad boy. Get some sleep. I'll see you soon." She kissed him goodbye and left the townhouse.

At home, she found Milo and Claire at the kitchen table with Taz begging for scraps.

"I'm so glad to see you both. I wanted to clear the air."

Milo snickered at her wording.

"Oh, get over it, you overgrown teenager," Claire said testily.

"Are you okay?" Sondra asked.

"I'm fine. Geez. I don't know why everyone keeps asking me that." Claire stirred her coffee aggressively.

"Just checking." Sondra pulled out the third chair at the table and sat. "Just so everyone is clear on this, I didn't kill Mildred Kovich."

"No one said you did," Milo answered hastily, the guilt showing in lines around his mouth.

"I know about your conversation with Sax. I don't blame you for wondering, and I admit I wasn't exactly distressed when she died, but I didn't kill her."

"Okay. Whatever you say."

"No, really. I didn't do it."

"Yeah, we heard you," Claire said, her spoon clattering against the table.

"What do I have to do to convince you?"

"Relax, Sondra. The police already closed the case." Milo sipped his coffee.

"That's not the same as you believing me."

They both stared at her with concern.

"Okay. Fine. Let's drop it. By the way, I got the lead in The King and I."

"I'm sure you'll be wonderful in it," Milo offered.

"Thank you." She pushed away from the table and retreated to her room, wondering what she should do now.

Rehearsals started promptly at four on Tuesday afternoon. Chuck showed up with his head shaved and a gold hoop earring hanging from his right earlobe. Sondra thought he looked more like a pirate than a king.

"Right," Bob said as soon as they were gathered, "now, everyone grab a chair and let's form a reading circle."

For the next two hours, the cast sat, scripts in hand, and read the play aloud, including the lyrics to the songs.

"Very good," Bob said when the reading was finished. "Chuck, Sondra, you two need to work on your chemistry a bit. Why don't you go downstairs and run your lines? I'm going to work with the others for a while."

"Thanks," Chuck answered amiably. The two of them descended to the lower level and sat at opposite ends of the green-room sofa. "Shall we start at the beginning?"

"Before we do that, maybe we should get to know each other better."

He smiled slowly. "You like my new look."

"Not like that," she said, rolled her eyes.

He deflated. "Ah. Okay. What do we need to know about each other? We've been in half a dozen plays together in the last few years."

"True, but very rarely have we acted opposite one another. I think we can develop the right kind of chemistry by creating some intimacy between us."

"But the King and Anna barely know each other. There's an animal attraction to their relationship. You know: rawr."

"Was that a growl?" she winced.

His face turned beet red. "Yeah, well, it was supposed to be."

"Don't do that again." She turned toward him. "The best way to create chemistry is to share racy secrets."

"I've never heard that."

"Of course you have. You just didn't realize it at the time. Why do you think so many of the great Hollywood romances start on the movie sets?"

"I thought they fell in love because their characters fell in love."

She sighed. "In a way. Just trust me."

"I never had to work so hard with Millie," he said under his breath.

"Really? You had natural chemistry with her?"

"You could call it that." He grinned like the Cheshire cat.

"Okay. I'll share a secret first. When I fell in love with the father of my daughter, I was living with his best friend."

"Everyone knows that, Sondra. It's in your Wikipedia entry."

"Damned internet."

"Mill always said it was ridiculous that you had a page but she didn't."

"She was a stage actress in the era of movies and television. It stands to reason that she wouldn't have a huge presence on the web." She swiveled her head to look at him. "Wait. What? Did you call her 'Mill'?"

He blushed. "We were friends."

"Just friends?"

Sondra wasn't expecting the tear at the corner of his eye. "I loved her, okay? More than anyone in the world. She was my soulmate, and now she's gone forever."

"Did she feel the same way?"

"We were in love."

"But she was married to Bob."

He smiled wryly. "You know Bob is an old queer."

She couldn't deny it. "But they were devoted to each other."

"Millie and Bob met a very long time ago. The world was a different place and they both imagined themselves leading successful – not marginalized – lives. They wanted similar things: she wanted to be a star and he wanted to be a director. Millie showed me a few of the short films they did back in the Sixties. They were good – as good as Warhol, I'd say. Who knows why one succeeds and another fails?"

"Millie wouldn't have left Bob for you."

"She planned to leave him. We talked about it."

"When?"

"Several times. The last time was the night she died. I knew I should have taken her with me right then! What kind of husband leaves his wife alone after she has suffered such humiliation?"

"One who can smell. I drove her home that night, and she stank to high heaven."

"You told her she didn't stink at all," he accused.

"I was attempting to make peace with her. It hardly seemed like the appropriate time to tell her she smelled like shit." She folded her legs underneath her. "So you talked on the phone that night?"

"She needed help out of her costume. I drove over."

"Then you know she stank."

"Funnily enough, that was one of the things Mill and I had in common. I lost my sense of smell years ago – there was an accident in the factory where I worked and I breathed in some toxic chemicals. The doctors said I was lucky that my sense of smell was the only part of me that was killed."

One of the other actors came down the stairs and peeked around the corner. "Bob wants to run through the First Act once more before we call it a night."

Chuck didn't turn his head. Sondra answered, "We'll be right up."

The guy disappeared; they listened as his footsteps echoed on the stairs.

"You were right, Sondra. This was helpful. I haven't had anyone to talk to – I didn't want to tarnish Millie's reputation with all this. People can be so cruel."

"I'm glad I could help."

He walked to the lighted mirror at the back of the room. "My eyes aren't too red, are they?" he asked even as he checked them for himself.

"No," she said, standing. "You look fine. We'd better get up there."

"You go on. I'll be right behind you."

The first week of rehearsals went more smoothly than any of the previous productions had. By Friday, the whole cast had a good grasp on their blocking. Sondra, of course, had a knack for such things – she always knew exactly where to be and when to be there.

"Stop!" Bob shouted from his vantage point – three rows back. "Everyone, stop! I want to talk to you about this scene." He sidestepped out of the row and into the aisle, approaching the stage. "Sondra, Anna meets the king for the first time in this scene."

"I know that, Bob." She attempted to mask her irritation with him.

"I think you should look more awed."

"Odd? How so?"

"I don't know…maybe drop your jaw a little bit when you first see him."

"How is that odd?"

"Awed, awed…you know, impressed."

"Oh," she laughed, "I get—"

At that moment, Chuck shoved her roughly out of the way as a stage light plummeted to the spot where she had been standing.

"What the fuck!?" she shouted in fright.

The rest of the cast gasped, though she couldn't be sure if they were gasping because she was almost killed or because she had used the f-word.

"Chuck, you really are the hero, aren't you?" Bob quipped. "Aaron! I need you to check all the lights when you get a chance," he shouted back toward the control booth.

"Are you okay?" Chuck asked, kneeling next to Sondra, who hadn't quite recovered from the rescue.

"Yeah, I think so. That just came out of nowhere!"

"Lucky I looked up and saw something moving over your head! I couldn't really see what it was, but my old factory reflexes kicked in, I guess. Better safe than sorry."

"Thank you. Really."

"No problem. Glad you're okay." He held a hand out to her. "Let me help you up."

She smiled and he pulled her to her feet.

"Places, please," Bob called again. "Like I was saying, Sondra – give it a little more awe."

She called Fanny again after rehearsals that night. This time, she answered. "Hi, Ma."

"Fanny! Sweetheart! Thank you for answering."

"It's late, Ma. What do you need?"

"I had a scare tonight at the theater, and all I could think of was that you didn't know how much I really loved you."

"What kind of a scare?"

"A light almost fell on me."

"Oh, my goodness! Are you okay?"

"Yes, of course. I'm fine. It was just an accident."

"How does a light accidently fall in a theater?"

"Those things happen sometimes, Fanny. It's not that unusual." Except Bob did tell her to stop right there. She shook the thought away. "Did you get my messages?"

"Yes. I just don't know if I can trust that you aren't going to interfere with my life."

"Of course I'm going to interfere – I'm your mother."

"Reuben says you're toxic."

Sondra bit her tongue to stop herself from lashing out at him. "I'm sorry he feels that way. Give me a chance to prove him wrong. At the very least, meet me for a drink. I have something I want to tell you."

"I don't want to go to the Brass Monkey. How about a meal instead?"

"Okay."

They arranged to meet Sunday morning at the IHOP. When the call ended, Sondra tried to go to sleep. The events from earlier that evening refused to leave her mind, though. Bob had been so unconcerned about the falling light. If it hadn't been for Chuck, she certainly would have been hurt, if not killed outright. Could Bob have set her up for the accident? She didn't know why he would have – unless he feared she and Sax were on the verge of discovering something about Mildred's death.

Charmed Life

Charmed Life

Damnation Alley

Kent's loyalty and forgiveness toward Bob had surprised Sax, and he said so during the holiday meal. He had expected at least a small amount of anger that Bob hadn't been home on the night of Mildred's death – after all, had he been there, the explosion likely would have been averted.

"What do you mean?" Kent asked.

"You know your mother couldn't smell. If Bob had been there, he would have smelled the gas. Simple as that."

"Mom couldn't smell?"

It seemed impossible to him that Kent didn't know that. How could you live with a parent and not know something so basic about him or her? "She suffered from lifelong anosmia."

"That's impossible. She loved roses. She wore peony-scented perfume. She said the scent of coffee was the best thing about morning."

Bob, who had been fuming at one end of the table during the conversation, answered. "You know how vain your mother was, Kent. She didn't want anyone to know about her...flaw. She was an actress – she acted like she could smell. It's obviously much easier to fake than, say, sight or hearing."

Sax expected Kent to lash out in anger, but instead the man and his wife laughed.

"That sounds just like Millie!" Moira smiled.

"You know, I should have known that," Kent said. "Once, when I was a teenager, she burned a pan of brownies. I tried to tell her they were burning, but she said that must be how they were supposed to smell; after all, the package said to bake them for forty-five minutes. She wouldn't even check them. When the timer went off, they were so overcooked that they went straight into the garbage. It turned out that the forty-five-minute time was for a smaller pan than the one she was using."

The conversation turned to more memories of Mildred and her quirks; Sax's probing was quickly disregarded.

In the days following Sax and Bob's nearly disastrous Thanksgiving meal, the mood around the house was decidedly colder. Bob moved to the guest room as soon as his son and daughter-in-law left. Sax attempted to seem remorseful, but, in truth, he was relieved to be sleeping alone again. He hadn't enjoyed a good night's sleep in weeks, fearing that he was nodding off next to a murderer.

When rehearsals for The King and I finally began two weeks later, Sax and Bob were actively avoiding one another – Sax by going to the Brass Monkey early and staying late and Bob by staying in the guest room whenever Sax was home.

Sondra came straight to the bar after rehearsals ended on Tuesday night.

"How did it go?" Sax asked as he set her drink in front of her.

"Better than I could have hoped. Chuck wanted someone to confide in. He says Mildred definitely planned to end the marriage – they talked about it the night she died, in fact."

"When? Chuck wasn't in Hello, Dolly!, was he?"

"No. But he went to Mildred's house to help her out of her costume that night. He says she was infuriated by Bob's abandonment. She thought the whole cast had played a horrible prank on her, pretending that she had an offensive odor."

"He must have told her the truth – that she stank."

"That's the kicker: apparently, he was in some kind of factory accident years ago that left him unable to smell."

"Neither one could smell? That's just weird."

"According to Chuck, they bonded over it. I guess he's more open about his missing sense. Mildred confided in him after he told her about his own affliction."

Sax dropped both hands to the bar in front of them. "Wait. So Chuck was in the house on Saturday night. What if, on his way to my place, Bob decided to swing by and check on Mildred? Maybe he overheard their conversation and, knowing neither one could smell, turned on the gas before slipping out the door."

"Do you really think he could do something like that?"

He frowned. "Am I this afraid of being happy, Sondra? Am I turning Bob into a murderer to keep from having a solid relationship?"

She placed her own hands over Sax's. "I don't know. I've known Bob for several years – and I know he has been happier than ever before since he's been living with you."

"Yes, but is it me or his dead wife that makes him so happy?"

"Maybe...both? That still doesn't mean he killed her, though."

"I should let this go. The cops have already closed the case; I should apologize to Bob and just be happy."

"If you think so."

"You don't?"

"I don't know what to think anymore."

When a large group came in, Sax and Sondra cut off their conversation. Sax saw her leave a few minutes later.

That night, he woke Bob up when he got home.

"What?" Bob asked grumpily as he opened his bedroom door and squinted into the hallway light.

"Can we talk?"

"Can't it wait until the morning?"

"Not really."

Bob sighed heavily and opened the door, revealing his blue-silk pajamas and tousled gray hair. "Fine."

"Put your robe on. Let's sit in the back garden." Sax opened the nearest set of French doors and the two went out into the brisk late-night air. When they were settled in their chairs, Sax said, "I think I owe you an apology."

"You sure as hell do." Bob's eyes narrowed. "Which thing are you apologizing for?"

"I'm sorry about interrogating Kent during Thanksgiving dinner."

"Go on."

"That's all."

"One apology? You ruined my whole holiday!"

"You're right."

"How can you be seventy years old and never have been in a single relationship that lasted longer than a television season? You're a commitmentphobe, Sax! I don't know why I thought we could have a real relationship."

"Keep your voice down," Sax admonished. "The neighbors will hear."

"So? You think they haven't figured out that you're an old queer?"

"No, I think they're probably trying to sleep!" Sax pounded the table with one fist. "Like you're so much better! What kind of a gay man stays married for forty years to a woman like Mildred? When have you ever had a relationship that lasted longer than the run of whatever play you were working at the time?"

"With you!"

"This wasn't a relationship, Bob!"

"What was it then?"

Sax saw the pain in Bob's eyes and his heart softened. "You filled a need in my life. Intimacy without strings."

"I dreamt of leaving Millie and being with you," Bob said softly. "I imagined a life free from the constraints I myself put in place. I never considered leaving her for anyone before you."

"I'm sorry," Sax answered simply. "I didn't know."

"Well, you should have, damn it." He put his hand over Sax's. "Don't you see? We have a chance now – an opportunity to live the rest of our lives the way we should have done from the very beginning. It's fate or karma or whatever you want to call it."

The warmth of Bob's hand seemed to spread up his arm and into the rest of his body. "Okay. Let's start over." He stood and pulled the smaller man into his arms. "I don't want to be alone anymore."

The next few days were like a honeymoon for the two of them – they spent every spare moment together, getting to know each other's stories. Bob was a wizard in the kitchen and Sax appreciated the good food more than was necessarily healthy for him. They gazed at each other over plates of pasta, flank steak, chicken piccata, and even a scrumptious quiche. Sax packed his doubts away and took Bob at face value.

But on Saturday at noon, a visibly shaken and exhausted Sondra appeared at the bar. "I think Bob is trying to kill me."

"What? Why would he want to do that?"

"Because I've stuck my nose where it doesn't belong!" she wailed. "If it weren't for Chuck, I'd be dead already!"

"Sit down and tell me what happened. I'll fix you a drink."

"No drink, Sax. I can't afford to have my reflexes impaired."

Understanding the gravity of the matter, he came around the bar and sat down next to her. "Calm down, okay? Just relax."

"How can I relax?" She glanced nervously around the bar. "He's not here, is he?"

"Of course not."

"Last night at rehearsal, a stage light nearly fell on me."

He laughed.

"It's not funny, Sax. If it had hit me, I would be dead!"

"I'm sorry, you're right. That's scary. But you're fine and it was just an accident."

"That's what I thought at the time. Chuck looked up and saw it moving. He pushed me out of the way."

"So far, it still sounds accidental."

"Except that Bob stopped me right there. We were running through the play and Bob stopped me to give me an inconsequential piece of direction."

"How did he stop you?"

She rolled her eyes. "He said, 'Stop.'"

"So you think he had the light set to fall at a particular time?"

"That's the only thing that makes sense!"

"No," he said slowly, leaning away from her, "it doesn't make any sense at all."

"Don't you see? He knew I talked to Chuck. He knows we're onto him."

"But we're not. I mean, I don't think he did it."

"Did he tell you about the light falling last night?"

Sax thought back to the night before. Bob had made quiche for them, and they sat outside and ate it by the pool. Afterward, they took a swim and went to bed. Bob hadn't mentioned anything about the rehearsal at all. He shook his head.

"Doesn't that seem like the kind of thing worth noting?"

"You weren't hurt," he answered defensively.

"Still...a light falls from the stage rafters and he doesn't even get upset?"

"What did he do?"

"He called back to the tech people and told them to check the lights and replace the one that had fallen. Chuck helped me up – Bob barely blinked at my narrow escape. I got the distinct impression that he was disappointed!"

"Maybe he was distracted."

"By me not being dead!"

"I thought we had decided this was all in my head."

"That's not what I understood from our last conversation at all. I thought we suspected him more once we knew Mildred wanted to leave him."

Sax sighed. "I think you're wrong about this."

"Great. Go on, think I'm wrong – right up until I'm dead from a falling light or a fake gun or...or...poison!"

Her outburst drew the attention of the regulars at the other end of the bar, both of whom stared at her over their beers. Sax shot them a look and they both dropped their eyes. "Be quiet, Sondra. You're being a drama queen."

"I think a woman should be allowed to get emotional over her impending death," she stage-whispered.

"You don't have another rehearsal until Tuesday, right?"

"Yes."

"I'll do a little digging and see if I can find anything else to help us discover the truth."

"Dig fast, Sax, or instead you'll be digging my grave."

That night, after Bob fell asleep, Sax crept out of bed. He wasn't sure where Bob kept his mail; he was never home when the mail came. His own envelopes – whether bills or junk mail – were always bundled neatly and placed on one end of the kitchen counter. Sax was in the habit of carrying them and the daily newspaper with him to the bar.

Sax refused to have a computer in his home because those kinds of machines were meant for work. Therefore, the only desk in the house was the antique roll-top he had inherited from his mother years before. He never sat at it, instead relegating it to one corner of the infrequently used living room, where it looked distinctly out of place among the Asian artifacts and low seating. When Bob asked for a place to keep his papers, Sax had willingly given him the desk as his domain. As Sax crept silently away from the bedroom, he knew that desk was his last, best hope to learn the truth.

He slid the slatted wood slowly along its track, freezing as it clacked unexpectedly. He wished he had remembered to pull the bedroom door shut on his way out. After a few seconds, he pushed on; when the wood creaked again, he swiveled his head to be sure Bob wasn't sneaking up behind him. He continued in this manner, freezing and swiveling every few seconds, until the roll-top was safely open.

Bob's laptop sat on the flat surface, just begging Sax to turn it on; Sax resisted, though. He was unfamiliar enough with technology to wonder if Bob would be able to tell if he used the machine. Besides, he assumed that it would be password-protected; after all, Bob carried this computer with him to the theater rehearsals.

Instead, Sax pulled some opened envelopes out of the slot where Bob had stashed them. The first one was the final gas bill on the now-exploded home he had shared with Mildred: one-hundred-five dollars and forty-two cents. Sax didn't have gas in his house – everything had been converted to electricity long before he bought the place – but he suspected more than a hundred bucks for gas in a mild Arizona October was expensive. The gas must have been on for hours before the house exploded.

The next envelope contained a sympathy card from a theater troupe somewhere in the Midwest. The third envelope contained the claim forms for an insurance policy worth more than five-hundred-thousand dollars. Bob had started to fill them out, but only completed the first page and a half. Sax checked the postmark on the envelope: November eighth. Bob hadn't wasted any time in requesting the forms, that was for sure. It looked like he had stopped working on them because he needed Mildred's death certificate in order to finish.

The last envelope contained the most damning evidence of all: a "condolence" letter from an old New York friend that started by congratulating Bob on winning the marriage race. The friend went on to reminisce about events and people the two had known in the Sixties and Seventies, before Bob and Mildred left New York in search of friendlier audiences. The final paragraph noted that Mildred had confided years ago that she expected to be the last one standing; after all, Bob was a few years older than she was, and everyone knew that men died eight years younger, on average, than women. Mildred had expected thirteen years of widowhood at the end of her life, at minimum. The signature was illegible, and there was only a return address – no name – on the envelope.

Sax dropped into the chair, no longer aware of the creaks and groans that just ten minutes before had terrorized him.

"What are you doing?"

Sax jumped and turned to face Bob, who stood five feet away in his terrycloth robe, his arms folded over his chest. Sax swallowed hard. "Why didn't you tell me about Sondra's accident?"

"She wasn't harmed. I didn't think it was important."

"She thinks you're trying to kill her."

He laughed shortly. "If I wanted to kill her, she'd already be dead."

"That doesn't reassure me."

"I'm not trying to kill her. She's the only real actress I have left!"

He pulled out the envelope from the insurance company. "What about this? A half-million life insurance policy on Mildred?"

"We each have one...had one. We took them out years ago to protect each other, back when the children were small. If something had happened to one of us, the other one would have had a hard time surviving on one income with two children."

"I read the letter from your friend, too."

Bob shook his head. "She has no idea what she's talking about."

"Why did you keep the letter, then?"

"I've been working on a response to her. I don't want her to think I accept her take on events. She's a bitch and fool – she thinks she was Mildred's best friend, but Mill barely tolerated her."

"The night Mildred died, did you go by your house before you came over here?"

"Why would you think that?"

"I won't tell, Bob. The police are already done with their investigation. I just want to know the truth."

"Let's say I was there. What do you think happened?"

"I don't know. You tell me."

"You're the cop, aren't you? Go on."

Sax leaned back in the swivel chair, steepling his fingers as he thought. "Okay. I think you and Mildred had a big fight over the bad opening night. She refused to leave with you. You were angry and needed to cool down, so you came to the bar for a beer. You told me what happened, and I conveyed the information to Sondra. When you received the message from Mildred that Sondra was driving her home, you saw your chance to make Sondra the scapegoat in your wife's death."

Bob smiled quixotically. "Why would I attempt to frame Sondra for what would clearly be an accidental death?"

"I don't think you intended to use gas as the weapon originally."

Bob punctuated his surprise with his eyebrows. "Go on."

"When you got to the house, though, you found Chuck's car in the driveway. I think you had known for some time that Mildred was sleeping with Chuck, so that didn't surprise you too much. You were probably irritated at having to abandon your plan. What you overheard when you entered the house, though, made you formulate a Plan B."

"What did I hear?"

"Chuck cajoling Mildred to leave you and start a new life with him."

"He'd been doing that for months."

"Yes, but this was the first time she wavered in her devotion to you. She told Chuck she would think about it – and you heard her."

"So I turned on the gas and left the house?"

"Hoping to kill them both."

Bob met Sax's gaze with his own sad eyes. "I'm sorry you think so little of me." He turned and walked back toward the bedrooms.

"Where are you going?"

"If you don't mind too much, I'm going to finish getting my sleep in the guest room. I promise not to be here when you wake up. Feel free to lock your door."

Charmed Life

Sax pushed the envelopes back into their cubbyhole and closed the desk. His head hanging, he walked back to the bedroom. He stood with his hand on the doorknob for nearly a full minute before turning the lock and climbing into bed.

Charmed Life

Of Unknown Origin

Sondra dreamt of Bill Saturday night. In her dream, he was exactly as he was when she first met him at Bud Miller's house party: gray-haired, but dashing nonetheless. He took her hand and they walked along a forest trail – something that had never happened in their real lives together.

"I'm so happy, my darling," he said, swinging their arms together as they walked.

"Is this happiness? Where are the stores?"

The forest ebbed away and Rodeo Drive took its place, but they were still alone as they walked down the sidewalk. A photographer peeked out of an alley and a bulb flashed.

"I love you most of all my wives," he said. "You are the wife of my old age and the one for whom I've spent my life searching."

"We're not married."

"I wanted to marry you, remember?"

"We never got around to it."

"Because of you." He stopped in front of a Tiffany window and pointed at a ridiculously large diamond ring. "That would look beautiful on you."

"But you're gone."

"Not really. Because of you, I still live. Be good to Fanny." He bent his knees and jumped. The wind seemed to catch him under his arms and lift him toward the blue sky. "Let go of my hand, Sondra."

"No," she answered as her feet lifted from the sidewalk.

"You have to, my darling. If you don't, you'll fall."

"I won't." She raised her other hand to wrap around Bill's, her body dangling as they rose above the building facades. There were no buildings behind them – Rodeo Drive was just a movie set. The shock of the sight caused her to loosen her grip; a second later, she plummeted toward the earth.

She woke up gasping for breath. Light crept in around the window blinds, but she knew it was still early. She wasn't meeting Fanny for breakfast until nine o'clock. Rolling over, she tried to go back to sleep. The message light was flashing on her phone, though. She dragged the device onto the bed and, yawning, brought it to life. A text message from Sax said only Call me. The phone had received it at nearly two in the morning. She debated calling him, but decided that he was probably asleep by now. Instead, she sent him a text reply: I'm awake. Call me when you get up. She pushed the phone back onto her bedside table and closed her eyes, though she doubted sleep would come back to her. A few seconds later, the phone rang.

"Sax? What are you doing up at this hour?"

"I couldn't sleep."

"You mean you haven't slept all night?"

"Bob caught me snooping."

"Crap. What happened?"

"It's a long story, but I ended up accusing him of murder."

Sondra sat up in bed, fully awake now. "What did he say?"

"He didn't deny it."

"Is he still in the house?"

"He slept in the guestroom."

"I hope you're calling me from the bar."

"No, I'm at home. I'm in my bedroom with the door locked."

"Why the hell are you there?" She was on her feet now, looking for something to wear.

"I don't think he'll try to kill me. I told him I wouldn't turn him in."

"And you think he believed you?"

He didn't answer for a long minute. "Yes," he said finally.

"I'm on my way."

"I don't think that's a good idea, Sondra."

"Don't worry, I'm not coming to the door. Get dressed and I'll pick you up."

"I have a car, sweetie. I can leave whenever I want."

"Yet you haven't," she pointed out.

"Because I'm not in danger."

"Humor me. As your best friend, I think you need to get the hell out of there for a while."

"Bob said he'd be gone before I woke up this morning."

She sighed and sat down on the bed, her jeans pulled halfway up her legs. "Is he still there or not?"

"I don't know. I haven't heard him leave yet."

"Can you check?"

"Okay. I'll be back in a minute."

Before she could tell him to carry the phone with him, she heard the phone rattle against something solid. She waited, jittery, for him to return. Standing, she pulled her pants up, buttoning and zipping them with the phone still caught between her ear and her shoulder. She could feel her neck crimping uncomfortably. She lifted one hand to hold the phone and straightened her neck. She rolled her head from left to right and front to back gently, hoping to relieve the discomfort. Glancing impatiently at the clock, she wondered how long he had been gone. Was it one minute? Two?

At last, the sound of the phone scraping against a hard surface told her he was back.

"Sorry."

"Is he there?"

"I hear snoring from behind the door, so I'd say yes, he's here."

"I'll be there in five minutes." Cutting off any argument he may have had for her, she pressed the end button on her phone. She pulled a sweater from her dresser drawer and slipped it over her head. Grabbing her purse, she all but ran toward the kitchen door. Milo was already making coffee.

"Don't you ever sleep in?" she asked.

"Not really. Too many years of—"

"No time. I'm off to Sax's house to pick him up; I'm bringing him back here. Okay?"

"What's—?"

"We'll tell you later."

With Sondra's lead foot, she was in Sax's driveway in four minutes instead of five. Sax came through the front garden's gate, walked around to the passenger door, and got in. Sondra's wheels squealed as she pulled away from the house.

"You didn't need to do this."

Sondra glanced at her friend. For the first time since she had met him nearly five years before, he looked old. Purplish bags hung beneath his eyes and his normally steel-rod straight back seemed bent by the weight of the long night. "I couldn't leave you in that house with a murderer."

"What if we're wrong?"

"Better safe than sorry. Besides, you said yourself that he didn't deny it."

He slumped a little further down in the seat. "I don't want to go to the bar today."

"Should we swing by and hang a sign on it to say you're closed?"

With a sigh, he deflated further. "Maybe if I get a few hours of sleep…"

"Just relax. You can take a nap at my place."

They finished the short trip in silence. The sun was fully visible but still low on the horizon when they stepped out of the car at Milo's house. Inside, Milo sat at the kitchen table sipping his coffee. "You okay, Sax?"

"I've been better."

"I'm going to take him to my room so that he can lie down for a while," Sondra said. "I'll be back soon."

She helped the crumpled Sax into bed and stayed with him for just a few minutes. Before she left the room, he was snoring. She pulled the door closed behind her.

Back in the kitchen, Milo had poured a cup of coffee for her. She sat down in front of it, already exhausted at just past seven o'clock in the morning.

"So? What happened?"

"Sax confronted Bob with his suspicions."

"He's sure Bob killed Mildred?"

"I don't know all the details, but he thinks there's plenty of evidence pointing that way."

"Wow. That's too bad. It seemed like he and Bob made a good couple."

She shrugged. "He tried to kill me, you know."

"Who? Bob?"

"Who else?"

"What happened?"

She told him about the Friday night rehearsal and her close call with the falling light.

"That could have been an accident."

"Doesn't it seem like there are a lot of 'accidents' around him these days?"

"That doesn't prove anything."

"Sax said he found something, but he didn't tell me what. Whatever it was, it kept him wide awake behind a locked bedroom door all night."

Milo sipped his coffee thoughtfully. "Sax has never struck me as particularly panicky."

"Because he's not."

The click of Taz's nails against the floor alerted them to Claire's approach. Milo stood and walked toward the doorway, taking his girlfriend in his arms. "Good morning, sweetheart."

"Hi, babe." Peeking around the corner, she spotted Sondra. "Am I interrupting?"

Sondra smiled. "Of course not. We were just talking about—"

"The play," Milo inserted, cutting her off. "Sondra was telling me about rehearsals."

"That's right – how are they going?" Claire, released from Milo's embrace, crossed to the coffee pot.

Sondra glanced at Milo, who shot her a pleading, wide-eyed grimace. "Fine," she said brightly. "What's up with you?"

"Did you hear the good news? They finally sentenced Rafael Santos."

Sondra turned her head quickly to see Claire. "What? I thought you had to testify."

She shook her head. "The D.A. made him a deal. They took the death penalty off the table in exchange for Rafe's testimony against Solomon Parr. He pled out on Dorsey's murder, so the whole ordeal is finished."

"Are you okay with that? I mean, he did kill your husband."

She sat down at the table with her coffee. "I told Paul Orton that I didn't want revenge, I wanted justice. He says neither Rafe nor Parr will ever see the outside of a prison again." She lifted the cup to her lips, but paused before drinking. "The more time that passes, the more certain I am that neither Rafe nor Damon came to our house intending to kill us. They were just Parr's tools."

Despite her skepticism, Sondra couldn't help but admire Claire's forgiving nature. Life must be so much easier when one chooses to see the good instead of the bad. "I'm happy for you."

"It's time to move on and leave the past in the past. I know that's what Dorsey would have wanted."

"What are your plans for today?" Milo asked Sondra.

"I'm having breakfast with Fanny and Reuben this morning."

"Reuben?"

"Fanny's fiancé."

"I'm so glad to hear that!" Claire exclaimed. "You should be reconciled before Christmas – it's only right."

"They're Jewish, you know."

"No, I didn't realize." Claire face turned red. "How presumptuous of me."

"Don't worry about it. You couldn't have known."

"Is that why you've been fighting? Did she convert against your wishes?"

"Actually, Claire, I'm Jewish as well. I just don't practice."

Milo and Claire's jaws both dropped.

"Technically, I'm half-Jewish – and the wrong half at that." She gave a laugh to lighten the mood.

"There are right and wrong halves?" Milo frowned, puzzled.

"Judaism is matrilineal. You know that old saw, 'Momma's baby, Daddy's maybe'?"

"I've heard that before," Claire nodded.

"I think it might actually have come from the Torah." She laughed again, this time bitterly. "My father was Jewish, but my mother wasn't."

"Sondra Lane doesn't sound very Jewish," Milo pointed out.

"I couldn't very well pursue a film career with the name Sarah Lansky. So I changed it."

"So you weren't fighting because of that," Claire concluded.

"No, you're right. That's exactly why we were fighting. I didn't raise her with any of the old traditions. I wanted her to embrace her Hollywood heritage. She never would, though. I offered to pay for a nose job – she got my father's nose – but she wouldn't have any of it. She willfully chose to be her own person."

"Isn't that what we should want for our children?" Milo smiled gently, putting one hand on Sondra's arm.

Sondra nodded. "It just took me a few decades to figure that one out."

When Sondra left to meet Fanny and Reuben at the restaurant, Sax was still sleeping. "Wake him up a few minutes before noon if I'm not back."

Milo agreed, and she left the house. At the restaurant, her daughter already had a table and waved her over. She wasn't smiling, but she didn't seem angry, either.

"Hello, you must be Reuben," Sondra said, offering her hand to the nice-looking man.

"We've met," he said, but he shook her hand anyway.

"I know, but I admit to being abrupt in our previous encounter."

"You could say that."

"Fanny, you look lovely." Sondra meant it, too – her daughter had a glow about her that Sondra had never noticed before.

"Thank you," she answered, though her eyes narrowed in suspicion. "You're looking well."

"Thank you."

"Now that the pleasantries are done, perhaps we should order breakfast," Reuben said, picking up his menu.

"Of course." The three of them studied the offerings for a few minutes, then placed their menus on the table in front of them. The waitress arrived a moment later.

After their orders were taken, Sondra cleared her throat in preparation for her reconciliation speech.

"I think you should know," Reuben said before she could speak, "Fanny and I will be married on January first."

"I…I didn't think it would be…so soon," Sondra faltered.

"We don't see any reason to wait. Reuben would like children, and neither of us is getting any younger."

"You've already converted?"

Fanny flashed Sondra an expression that made her think of the fight they once had over rhinoplasty. "Two weeks ago. It's done, Ma, so any ideas you had about—"

Sondra raised a hand to stop her daughter's diatribe. "That's not why I'm here. I only wanted to apologize. I have tried to run your life as if you were an extension of me. I know now that I was wrong – you are your own beautiful creation. I would like very much to be a part of your life…of both your lives. I'm sorry it took me so long to realize that I was wrong."

Fanny sat across from her in stunned silence.

378

Reuben was the first to recover his voice. "Of course, Sondra. I believe I speak for both of us—"

Fanny's hand shot out from under the table and grabbed his arm. "What's the catch?"

"What do you mean?"

"There's always a catch, Ma. Whenever you do anything nice, there's always something I'm supposed to do to balance the scales. Aren't you the one who taught me that nothing in this world is free?"

"I'm sorry if you think that, Fanny—"

"Just drop the other shoe already."

Sondra picked up her glass of water and took a few swallows, attempting to fortify herself before sharing about Ethan.

The waitress arrived with their plates, sliding each one expertly in front of the three of them. "Enjoy your meal," she said with a bright smile.

"Doesn't this look wonderful?" Sondra said, relieved to have the distraction of food.

Fanny pushed her plate away. "Now, Ma. I want to know now."

"There's no other shoe, Fanny."

"I thought you had something important to tell me."

"She just apologized to you, darling. Don't you think—?"

"Reuben, you don't know her. Eat your breakfast."

He gave Sondra an apologetic glance and tucked into his food.

"I just wanted to tell you I'm dating someone, and I think it might be serious."

"That's it?"

"Yes."

Fanny smiled for the first time that morning. "That's good. I'm glad to hear that. Daddy's been dead for decades – it's time for you to move on. What's his name?"

"Ethan Tanner."

Reuben's fork clattered against his plate. "No way!"

"What's wrong?" Fanny stared at him, wide-eyed.

"Ethan Tanner is an effing genius! Everything he touches turns to gold."

"I'm sorry. I don't think we're talking about the same guy."

379

"He's an artist, right? Roughly, what – thirty?"

"Thirty!" Fanny exclaimed.

"I was going to mention that," Sondra sighed.

"He's responsible for three of the top-five comic franchises out today. His work is admired by everyone from the president to Hollywood screenwriters."

"Are you sure?" Sondra asked.

Fanny rolled her eyes. "He's a comic book geek and an entertainment lawyer. Trust him."

"He never told me any of that," Sondra said slowly.

"What did you think he did for a living?" Fanny pulled her plate to her and took a bite.

She shrugged. "I don't know…I guess I just didn't think about it. Everyone else I know is retired!"

"Yeah, but he's like half your age."

"Independently wealthy?"

"Well, yeah," Reuben laughed. "I suppose he qualifies as that."

"Why wouldn't he tell me?"

"Maybe he wants to be sure you're not a gold digger," Fanny said.

Sondra had trouble focusing on their conversation for the rest of the breakfast. When they parted, though, both Fanny and Reuben hugged Sondra; Fanny even invited Sondra to come with her to her final dress fitting later that week. Sondra's elation was somewhat muted by her preoccupation with Ethan's big secret.

Instead of going home, Sondra drove straight to Ethan's townhouse and knocked until he dragged himself out of bed. When he opened the door, he squinted against the brightness of the morning. "Sondra?"

"Ethan." She pushed past him into the living room. "I hope I'm not interrupting anything."

"Just my sleep," he answered grumpily. "What's going on?"

"I was just at breakfast with my daughter and her fiancé. I told you about that, right?"

"Yes, I remember. I guess it didn't go well, huh?"

"Why would you say that?"

He laughed. "Your mood, for one thing. What's up with you?"

She turned to look at him, her arms crossed over her chest. "My future son-in-law is a comic fanatic."

"Oh." He dropped into a chair.

"Yeah, oh."

"Okay, I probably should have mentioned that I was a comic artist, but I don't get why you're angry with me. It's not like you ever asked what I did for a living."

"I just assumed..."

"Yes?"

"I guess I thought you were...I don't know...."

"Rich?"

She grimaced. "I wouldn't have said that...."

"Obviously. Come here," he said, indicating she should sit on his lap. She reluctantly walked closer. He grabbed her hand and pulled her onto him, wrapping his arms around her. "I've got you now!" He tickled her playfully.

She slapped at his hand. "Stop that! This is serious!"

"How is this serious? You thought I was rich; lo and behold, I am! Where's the problem?"

"Why didn't you tell me you were famous, too?"

"If you didn't know who I was, I couldn't be too famous, now could I?"

"That convention in New Mexico – you weren't going as a fan, were you?"

He shook his head. "Caught me. If you'd gone, you would have known who I was. You also would have known something else I've been meaning to tell you."

"What's that?"

"Let me up. I have something to show you."

She stood and he launched himself out of the chair and sprinted up the stairs. A moment later, he stood before her with what looked like a comic book mockup. In the center was an image of her in green makeup and silver lamé. Emblazoned across the top was the comic's name: Sunrise Aeon.

Charmed Life

Charmed Life

Angel

Sax was relaxing in Milo's living room when Bob knocked on the door. Instantly, his heart rate increased two-fold, but he opened the door anyway. "How did you find me?"

"I stopped by the bar. Did you know Milo posted a sign that says 'Only Beer Today'?"

"I told him to do that. He doesn't know how to mix drinks."

"Why is he there at all?"

"I didn't feel like working."

Bob sighed. "Can I come in? It's a little chilly out here."

"I suppose. Just give me a minute." Sax shut the door and opened all the shutters in the front room so that anyone could see inside. Satisfied that the room was bright enough, he reopened the door. "Come in."

"That really wasn't necessary, you know."

"Just a precaution."

"I'm here to tell you exactly what happened the night Mildred died."

"Sit down."

"I'll stand, thank you," Bob said, his hands clasped behind him.

"I'd be more comfortable if you would sit."

Bob rolled his eyes. "You really don't get staging, do you?" He sat in the middle of the chaise longue end of the sofa.

"Thanks," Sax said, sitting back down in Milo's armchair.

"I didn't kill Millie."

Sax gave an exaggerated sigh of relief. "That's a load off. Why didn't you just say so?"

"Don't be an ass, darling. I knew you wouldn't believe me if I just told you that...so I didn't bother. However, now I have – if not proof – at least an alternative version of what actually happened."

"Okay. Go ahead."

"My witness isn't here yet."

"Your witness?" Sax squirmed uncomfortably.

"He ordered a beer at the Brass Monkey and didn't want to leave until he was finished. In the meantime, let me tell you what I was doing the night Millie died." He stood up again;

383

Milo bit his tongue. "As you may recall, after the terrible opening night of *Hello, Dolly!* I came to the bar to drown my sorrows in a drink. Around nine o'clock, Sondra tottered out of the bar and went, as you yourself told me, to make things right with Millie. Not long after she left, I received a message that told me Sondra was giving her a ride home. In the same text, she told me she was inviting a friend over for a nightcap. Millie and I had each used 'nightcap' for years to indicate that we were having a sleepover with one of our respective lovers. For instance, anytime I stayed with you, I would send her a note to say I was having a nightcap at your house. She would respond with 'Be safe.'"

"I remember that!"

"That was the equivalent of okay between us. We may not have had a traditional marriage, but we loved each other, nonetheless. She was my best friend, and I couldn't have picked a better person to spend my life alongside. In a different time, we wouldn't have married, but we still would have been lifelong friends."

A shadow passed over the room and Sax looked up in time to see Chuck approach the front door. "I think your witness is here."

"Ah! I'll get that." He opened the door and let Chuck inside. "Thank you for coming."

Chuck looked somberly greenish. "Of course. The least I could do."

"Chuck and I hashed over a few things at the bar and made some interesting discoveries."

"Interesting. Hah!" Chuck swayed slightly on his feet.

"You should probably sit down," Sax said to the man.

"Good idea." He dropped into the sofa, prompting an enormous belch from his body. "'Scuse me."

"It turns out," Bob continued with a wry smile, "that Chuck and Millie enjoyed a 'nightcap' after he helped her out of her costume. After their exertion, they were hungry, so he went to the kitchen to get them a snack. What was the snack again, Chuck?"

"Raisins."

"Oh, yes. Raisins. Millie and I always kept the raisins in the cabinet over the stove. Is that where they were that night, Chuck?"

"Like I told you, they were way in the back. I had to lean against the stove to get them out."

Sax's eyes widened. "Did you—?"

"Wait for it," Bob interrupted. "And after your snack, what happened?"

"Well, for a while, we both just nodded off. Then my head exploded."

"What?" Sax was on the edge of his seat now.

"He woke up with a migraine. So did Mildred, as it turns out. He got her a Vicadin from the medicine chest in the bathroom and took one for himself. Fearing that he wouldn't be able to wake up early enough to vacate the house if he took it there, he kissed Millie goodbye and went home."

"Didn't you notice the hissing of the gas as you went through the kitchen?" Sax asked Chuck.

"No," he sobbed. "I can hardly hear anything after working in factories all my life. Millie kept telling me that they made hearing aids so small no one would ever notice I had them on, but I was too vain! I killed her! My vanity killed her!"

"So, my darling Sax, you now see that Mildred's death was exactly what the police said it was: death by misadventure."

"I'm sorry, Bob. I was wrong."

"Yes, you really were."

"Can you ever forgive me?"

"I already have."

Chuck stood up, wobbled a bit, and fell back into the sofa.

"I'll give you a ride home, Chuck." Sax said.

"I'm fine to drive."

"No, you really aren't. I'll drive your car. Bob, would you follow me over there?"

"Honestly, Sax, I'm through following you anywhere. Chuck only lives a few blocks from your house. I think a good stretch of the legs may make all the difference in your outlook." With that, Bob turned and left the house.

Sax, still admiring his boyfriend's flair, helped the tipsy Chuck to his feet and out the front door, locking the handle and pulling it closed behind him. Bob's car was long gone by the time they made it that far. With Chuck's directions, Sax had the man home and inside of ten minutes. Bob was right –

Chuck's house was only a few blocks from his own. Feeling better than he had in weeks, Sax walked briskly toward home. He looked forward wholeheartedly to his future with Bob. For the first time, he could imagine a fully shared life with no secrets. Each breath felt like he was inhaling freedom for the first time since he was a child. Unable to contain his joy, he ran.

A few minutes later, he swung open the gate and sprinted to the door. "Bob! I'm home, Bob!"

The house echoed in silence.

Thinking he must be in the back garden, he walked to the French doors in the hallway and opened them. "Bob?" But the garden was empty as well. Fearing the worst, he peered into the pool; thankfully, it was empty. He checked the master bedroom, where he discovered the first sign of what had happened: the closet doors were open and Bob's clothes were gone. Sax dropped to the bed, his heart pounding painfully against his ribs. He took a few deep, calming breaths before investigating the rest of the house. When he rolled up the roll-top desk, he found the note.

Dear Sax,

When you get home, I'll be gone. My heart is broken beyond repair – to think that you believed me a murderer is too much for me to bear. I had dreamt of a second chance at life, but I see now that it was only a fantasy.

I forgive you for your distrust. I hope you will forgive me for thinking fate had put us together.

Sincerely,
Bob

Charmed Life

Walking Tall

Milo hadn't realized he was bored until he offered to tend bar for Sax that Sunday afternoon. He was disappointed when Sax walked through the door a few hours before closing time.

"I'll take over," he said, slipping behind the bar and taking the dishcloth off Milo's shoulder.

"You don't have to do that. Take the rest of the night off."

"The real drinkers start coming in around now. They'll be disappointed if they can't get their hard liquor." Sax balled up the piece of paper that had been stuck to the outside door – the one that said only beer was available.

Milo had been practicing a few different approaches to the conversation he wanted to have with Sax; he decided to try one of them out. "I bet it was nice to have the afternoon off, huh, Sax?"

"A bad day working is better than the day I had," he grumbled.

"I'm sorry to hear that."

"Yeah, well, Bob didn't kill Millie, so that's something."

"You must be so relieved."

The massive ex-cop grunted his response.

"Thanks for letting me try my hand at bartending."

"Why don't you take a stool. What can I get you? On the house."

"Beer's fine." Milo took Sondra's usual seat.

Sax pulled him a frosty mug of the stuff and set it in front of him. "I don't know what I'd do with myself if I just retired. Not much to life without someplace to be."

"I've been thinking about that today," Milo said, sipping his beer.

"Claire's got a job, doesn't she?"

"She's a zoo volunteer," Milo corrected.

"Yeah, but she's got somewhere to be."

"I suppose."

"Still, you must have been one of those guys counting the days until retirement."

"Not really. I would have stayed with the Border Patrol until the day I died if I'd been allowed."

"Yeah, but you like retirement now, right?"

"Actually, that's what I wanted to talk to you about."

"You wanted to talk to me?"

"Yeah."

"Okay. Shoot."

"I thought you might like to have a partner."

"I don't know, Milo, I think it might be a little soon for me to date again—"

"You and Bob broke up?"

"I thought you knew," Sax frowned.

"No. I'm sorry. I meant a business partner."

"Oh! You mean here at the Brass Monkey?"

"Unless you own another business," Milo said dryly.

"Heh, heh. No, just the one. Are you serious?"

"Serious as a bar fight."

"I don't know, man. I've been running this place on my own for a long time. I'm not sure I'm cut out to have a partner."

"Look, I don't know how long it takes to learn bartending—"

"Not long – anywhere from a week to a month, depending on which course you take."

"Okay. If I took the course, would you hire me on for a few shifts a week? We can see where it goes from there."

Sax stared at Milo as if his intentions were stamped, in reverse letters, on the back of his eyeballs. "You're serious. Okay. I'll give you two shifts a week after you pass bartending classes."

"I'm really sorry about you and Bob."

"It's for the best. I'm not really cut out for the domestic life."

"Maybe you should go to breakfast at Denny's more often. That waiter seemed interested."

Sax's laughter boomed out, causing conversations to pause while the patrons looked in his direction. "Maybe so, Milo."

Milo finished his beer and pushed away from the bar.

"Just a minute," Sax said, leaning over the counter. "Why do you want to be a bartender? You don't drink."

"Why not? At least you won't have to worry about me drinking up the profits."

"Good answer," Sax nodded. "See you around."

"I'll be back with my certificate."

"I'm sure you will."

Milo walked outside and inhaled the fresh evening air with a new sense of resolve. If he meant to stop treading water and start moving forward with life, he needed to have a few more conversations.

Sondra's car wasn't in the driveway when he got home, but Claire's was. As he opened the carport door, he saw her – the love of his life – standing in front of the stove. The scent of chicken and onions filled the air. "Where have you been?" she asked curiously.

"I filled in for Sax down at the bar."

She laughed. "But you don't know how to mix drinks!"

He told her about the sign and then about his idea.

"I thought you liked retirement."

"I do. But I think I'd be happier with a little less retiring and little more future." He wrapped his arms around her from the back, pulling her against him.

"This is new."

"This is me realizing that I need a new challenge in life."

She turned in his arms, wrapping her own around his neck. "I'm not enough for you?" she asked playfully.

"You are more than enough. Which is why I have something very important to ask you. Claire Combs—"

She gasped, her eyes wide.

"Don't worry – it's not that question. Not yet. I just want you to move in with me for now."

"Oh, Milo...I'm amazed you even want me around. I've been a raving lunatic lately, and, from everything I've read, you can't expect much improvement over the next ten years or so. Menopause will make me fatter and crankier with every passing day."

"You will never be fat in my eyes. And no matter how cranky you get, I can't imagine anything better than waking up next to you every morning for the rest of my life."

She took his head between her hands and kissed him, taking his breath away. "I love you, Milo Crosby."

"And I love you."

"But what about Sondra?"

The phone rang and interrupted their conversation. "You keep your eyes on dinner," Milo said. "I'll get that." He walked to the other side of the kitchen and picked up the receiver. "Hello?"

"Is Sondra there? This is Bob Kovich calling."

"Hi, Bob. No, I'm afraid she's not here."

"That's a shame. I wanted to give her this news personally. Do you know when she'll be home?"

"Sorry. Have you tried her cell phone?"

"She's not answering. I hope she's all right."

"I'm sure she's fine. Let me take a message for her." Milo found the grocery list notepad and pulled out a blank sheet. "Go ahead."

"Tell her I'm sorry, but I've cancelled The King and I."

"Can you do that? I mean, why would you do that?"

"It's complicated, but the upshot is I'm leaving Arizona. My daughter, who lives in Missouri, has asked me to come and stay with her for a few months. After that, I don't know what I'll do – but I won't be back here."

"Isn't there someone who could take over the theater troupe?"

"No," he answered bitterly. "There's no one qualified to do what I do. Besides, Millie and I had been the ones keeping the ship afloat – we never made a dime off any of the productions. In fact, we usually spent at least a thousand dollars on each show. I should have let the whole thing go after Millie died; she was the only reason I continued to direct. The theater was everything to her."

"I had no idea."

"No one did." Milo heard a sad sigh. "My life here is finished. Be sure to tell Sondra how sorry I am." The phone clicked in his ear.

"What was that about?" Claire asked.

"Bob Kovich is closing down the theater productions."

"Oh, no. Sondra will be devastated!"

"I'm afraid so."

Their dinner, which had promised to be so joyful, turned into a somber affair, each of them ruminating over how they would tell Sondra the good and the bad news.

At last, as Milo slowly took his last bite of chicken, Claire said, "What if I offer Sondra my condo?"

"That's so far from Sun City."

"But with the theater troupe defunct, she has much less reason to live all the way out here. There are three little theaters within a five-mile radius of the condo."

"She can't afford to pay much – you know I've been renting that room to her for almost nothing."

"What if I rented it to her for just the condo assessment fee? That's only a hundred and fifty a month."

"Are you sure you don't want to sell it?"

"In this market? It's barely worth what I paid for it. Besides, what if you get tired of me?" she teased.

"That's will never happen." He clasped her hand in his. "If you're sure you want to—"

"Yes. I'm sure."

They cuddled together on the sofa to watch a movie while they waited for Sondra to come home. Before long, they were both sound asleep.

When Sondra came in a little after eleven, she woke them. "Milo, Claire," she sing-songed, "wake up and go to bed!"

"Sondra! You're home!" Milo announced.

"Yes, Milo, I am."

"Could you sit down for a few minutes?" Claire asked, sitting up straight. "We have some news to share with you."

Sondra dropped into Milo's chair. "Uh oh. You're getting married and I need to move."

Milo and Claire exchanged worried glances.

"It's okay. I saw this coming. I just hoped I had a little more time to come up with a plan. I suppose I could ask Sax if I could stay with him for a while—"

"Wait. You're not quite right, but you are close."

"Do I need to make other living arrangements?"

"Yes, but—"

"Then whatever I'm wrong about is irrelevant."

"Not entirely."

She gazed at the pair skeptically. "Okay, fine. Tell me what I'm wrong about."

"Milo and I are moving in together – but we're not getting married."

Sondra started to speak, but Milo held up a hand to stop her. "I also spoke to Bob Kovich earlier tonight. According to Sax, Bob didn't kill Millie, but he and Bob are still through.

Bob called to tell you that he's pulling the plug on the theater troupe. He's cancelling The King and I and leaving Arizona for good." Milo gripped Claire's hand as they prepared for Sondra's meltdown.

Instead, Sondra laughed – at first just a giggle, but it grew into a body-shaking belly laugh in the space of a minute. Milo and Claire watched her in alarm. When the laughter subsided, Sondra gasped, "That's the best news I've heard in weeks."

"Really?" Milo and Claire asked simultaneously.

Sondra nodded. "Ethan and I have spent most of the day trying to work out a graceful way for me to quit the show."

"Why?" Milo scooted to the edge of the couch, intrigued.

Sondra's eyes sparkled. "Ethan created a comic book around me!"

"Around you?" Claire frowned.

"Well, not me, exactly...Sunrise Aeon. The character is testing well with males, ages fifteen to thirty-five. His publisher wants to release the first issue next month. I'll be travelling around the country attending comic conventions to promote her!"

"That's incredible!" Milo exclaimed.

"I know, right? I can't believe it either!" Sondra looked at them pensively. "So, you see, I won't be around much for the next few months anyway. And the publisher will be paying me to do the promotions, so when I'm back in Phoenix, I'll have plenty of money to move. Could I keep the room until then?"

"I have a better idea," Claire said with a smile. "I want to rent you my condo on Central."

Sondra blinked.

"I know it's a little far from Sun City, but without the theater troupe, there's nothing that requires you to live here."

Sondra smiled politely. "I appreciate the offer, Claire, but I can't afford to rent your place. I can barely afford what Milo's charging me right now."

"I only need a hundred and fifty a month – just enough to cover the condo assessment fee."

Sondra leaned back in the chair. "Wow. Really?"

"Absolutely. What do you think?"

"I think I'm moving to your condo on Central."

Claire stood and pulled Sondra to her feet, wrapping friendly arms around her. "You have been such a great friend to us, Sondra."

Milo watched as Sondra squirmed uncomfortably out of Claire's grasp. "Yes, well…You two have been lifesavers for me also."

"We'll help you move."

"I don't have anything but my clothing. I can take that in one carload." She gasped. "I don't own any furniture!"

"You can keep mine," Claire offered.

"I guess I'll have to." She turned thoughtfully toward the hallway. "I'll see you both in the morning. I need to call Ethan with the news."

Charmed Life

Beginning of the End

The condo, for all its amenities and views, was terminally beige. Claire told Sondra that her sister Beryl had furnished it for her; unfortunately, Beryl had little sense of what sort of furnishings would appeal to her much-older sister and stuck with a neutral palette.

"We'll get some art," Ethan said. "That will brighten the place right up." It was a few days before Christmas, and he had brought a small tree and some decorations over to add some seasonal cheer to the place.

"I won't be spending a lot of time here for the next few months, and who knows what will happen after that? Maybe I shouldn't make too much of a mark."

"Your home should be a comfortable place. I'm sure Claire would agree."

Claire and Milo had gone to Oklahoma for the holidays; Claire's father was still clinging to life despite his cancer-ravaged body. Claire wanted to enjoy Christmas with her family around her, and Milo could hardly deny her that.

"I know you're right, but I still feel like I should wait." She took the tree topper, a handmade angel, from the box of decorations he had brought with him and placed it on top of the tree. "How's that?" she asked, spinning around.

Ethan was on one knee in front of her. "I think I know what you're waiting for," he said, pulling a small box from his jeans pocket.

Her hands flew to her lips and her eyes filled instantly with tears. "Oh!"

"Sondra Lane, will you marry me?"

Charmed Life

No actresses were murdered in the writing of this novel.

Charmed Life

Acknowledgments

I am thankful to so many people every time I write a novel, and I usually forget to let them know. So, here it is, my list of invaluable people:

First and foremost, Daniel Bennett, you are my biggest supporter and the love of my life. Without you, I never would have written a single book. Thank you.

Christine Wells, I am blessed to have you for a grandmother and a reader. When I make you laugh or cry, I know I've written something great.

Maaijo Lowe, thank you for believing in my writing and publishing my work. Whenever I'm having a moment of doubt, all I need do is re-read some of the many encouraging notes you have sent me since you first accepted Circle City Blues.

Nikki McBroom, thank you for sharing your talents with me. Every book cover is a perfect reflection of the story inside.

My virtual writers' support group, the Book Junkies, make even the worst day better with their friendliness and humor. Thanks especially to Grace Guerra and Annarita Guernieri for volunteering to beta-read this novel.

Finally, thanks to my family and friends for reading my work. If you've read one of my books and enjoyed it, you are among my friends – even if we've never met.

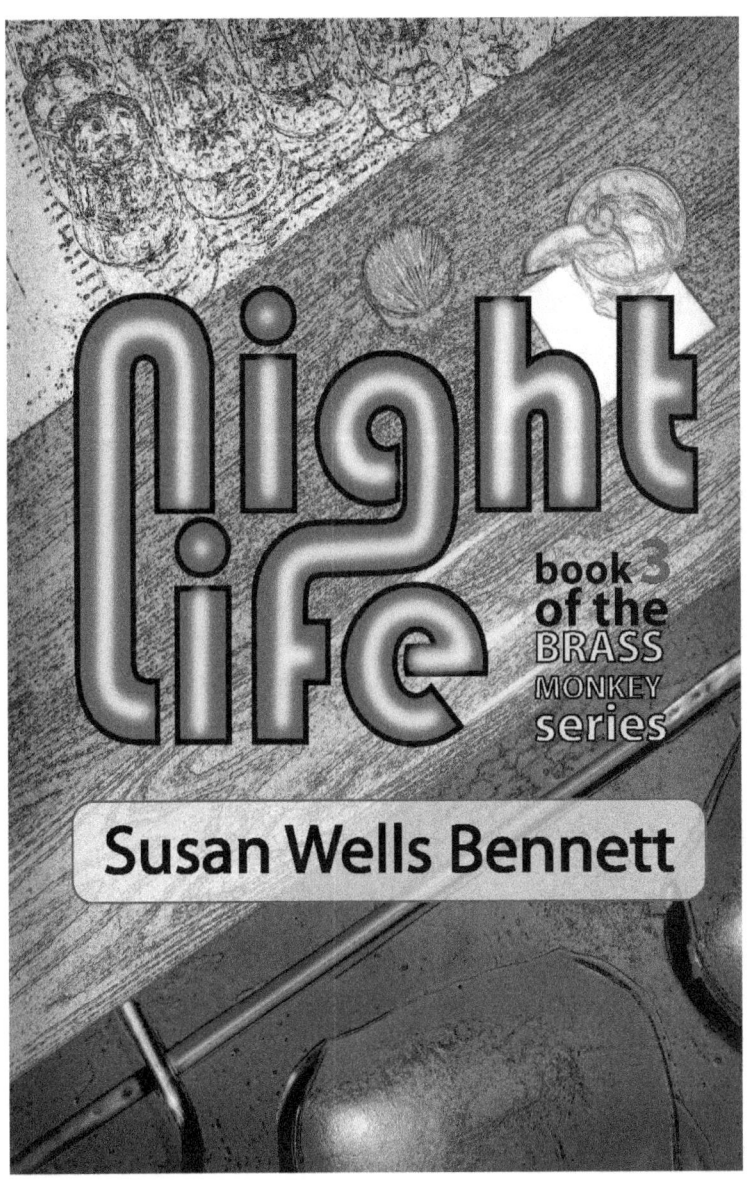

Things are changing down at the local watering hole…

Actress-turned-comic-book-muse Sondra is contemplating marriage to a man half her age. Already familiar with the seamy underbelly of Sun City, former cop Sax finds himself back on the job. Milo, lonely and bored, begins bartending at the Brass Monkey. But Claire may be making the biggest change of all…

And when Sondra's life is threatened, her friends come running to help.

Night Life
Book Three of the
Brass Monkey Series

Susan Wells Bennett

PUBLISHED BY:
Inknbeans Press

Night Life

Cara a Cara

Reuben Susser, wearing a tuxedo and a yarmulke, shook Ethan's hand enthusiastically. "This is the best day of my life!"

The thin line of Fanny's lips told Sondra Lane that her daughter was less than thrilled with her new husband's fawning adulation for Ethan Tanner.

Ethan politely broke off the handshake and smiled at the newlyweds. "I'm sure it is – to have such a lovely woman ready to spend the rest of her life with you must be invigorating."

Reuben cleared his throat and glanced sheepishly toward Fanny. "Indeed it is. Fanny is quite a prize – much like her mother." He dropped a nod toward Sondra, who smiled and pulled Ethan toward the reception.

"We'll see you inside, darling," Sondra said as they moved into the surprisingly large party. Sondra hadn't realized that her daughter knew so many people. She certainly hadn't suspected that the New Year's Day wedding – a second marriage for Fanny – would draw such a crowd. The music was already playing, and several couples were on the dance floor.

A young man with one of those haircuts that reminded her of the Beatles approached her. "How have you been, Sondra?"

"I'm sorry, have we met?"

"It's me, Sondra – Hunter."

"My goodness! You're so much taller than I remember!" Turning to Ethan, she said, "This is Fanny's son, Hunter."

"You mean your grandson?" he asked with a sly smile.

"Be careful," Hunter answered conspiratorially. "She hates those 'grand' words."

"No, I don't. I want you to call me grand--" She choked on the word. "Perhaps you could call me *Nonna* instead."

"We're closer to Acapulco than Naples. How about *Abuela*?"

She gave a short shake of her head. "Too many people know what that means. Let's go with *Nonna* and work up to *Abuela*."

"Then again, maybe *Savta* is better. It more accurately reflects our heritage, right?"

She rolled her eyes. "At least it's not Bubbe."

"*Savta* it is, then. And don't make that face – it's not like we see each other often. You don't even recognize me half the time."

"You keep growing!" she exclaimed defensively. "If you want me to recognize you, you should at least do me the courtesy of remaining the same from year to year!"

"I'm Ethan Tanner, your *savta*'s fiancé."

The younger man's jaw dropped open.

"Close your mouth, Hunter. You look like a simpleton." Sondra's own lips were a thin line now.

"You're getting married? When?"

"Not for a while."

Ethan flicked his eyes toward her. "I suggested a double wedding, but she vetoed the idea."

"Mom wouldn't have gone for that, either. Sharing the spotlight on her wedding day would have pissed her off." He took Sondra's arm. "I think she put us at a table close to the dance floor. Let me show you."

As they approached the table, Sondra was shocked to recognize two familiar faces: Adam and Steve Ross-Wright. "Oh, my goodness! What are you two doing here?"

"Are you insane, Sondra? We couldn't miss Fanny's big day," Adam said, standing to hug his old friend. His silvery silk scarf was pinned at the neck of his tuxedo with an onyx top-hat pin.

Steve, dressed in a more conservative tuxedo ensemble, stood and put his arm around Adam. "Hello, Sondra. Nice to see you again. You look lovely."

Sondra had purchased the silky navy-blue jumpsuit and the lacy white wrap specifically for the wedding; she beamed her appreciation to Steve. "Thank you. Fanny commanded I wear navy to match the rest of the bridal party."

"The blue-and-white winter theme was my idea," Adam gushed. "It came together beautifully, don't you think?"

Ethan stuck out his hand, interrupting the conversation. "I'm Ethan Tanner, Sondra's fiancé."

"When did this happen?" Adam asked, taking Ethan's hand but looking at Sondra for the answer.

"A couple of weeks ago." Ethan shook Adam's hand as firmly as he could, given Adam's limp hold. "I'm going to go out on a limb here and guess that you must be Adam and Steve."

Steve held out a firmer hand and Ethan took it. "Yes, we are."

"I wasn't aware that Sondra was dating anyone," Adam commented. "I'm surprised we didn't meet back in October."

"We weren't dating then." Sondra moved toward the chair with her name in front of it and Ethan pulled it out for her. The table sat six; she wondered who the last chair was for. The men sat down as well.

"What ever happened with that clunky Cleo from the Halloween party?" Adam asked, changing the subject.

"You'll never believe it – she died!"

"How awful! What happened? Was she allergic to the...you-know-what?"

Sondra felt the color of embarrassment rise up her neck. "No," she answered hastily. "She was in an explosion."

"*Quelle tragédie*! Did you get her part in the play?"

"Heartfelt, Adam. Yes. I did. Of course, now the Sun City Players are defunct, but at least I got to play Dolly Levi before the curtain came down for good."

"And she was magnificent in it." Ethan took her hand. "She really should be performing."

Sondra patted him affectionately. "Ethan has created a comic book around Sunrise Aeon. Can you believe that?"

"But she died at the end of the movie."

"He's worked around that – he claims Sunrise was merely unconscious at the end of *Siege of the Moon*, not dead."

"So you were a fan first." Adam turned to Steve. "Could you get us some drinks, darling?" Steve smiled and slipped away from the table.

"I was smitten with Sondra long before I met her in person. *Siege of the Moon* has a huge cult following these days."

"How did you meet?"

"Sax was trying to cheer me up, so he took me to a screening of the film. Ethan was there," Sondra answered.

"I don't mean to pry, but you seem considerably younger than Miss Sondra."

"Adam..." Sondra glared warningly at her flamboyant

friend.

"Only chronologically," Ethan replied. "At heart, we're both sixteen."

Adam's face melted into a sappy smile. He looked at Sondra under half-lowered lids. "He's a keeper."

Hunter appeared with the table's sixth occupant, a shapely but plain-faced brunette in a navy chiffon dress. "Livia, may I introduce you to Sondra Lane, Ethan Tanner, and Adam Ross-Wright. *Savta*, this is Livia Susser."

"This is your grandmother? The actress?" Livia asked.

Sondra cringed.

"Yes," Hunter answered. "This is Fanny's mother."

"A pleasure, I'm sure," the woman said, sticking her hand out to shake Sondra's. "I've heard a lot about you."

"I'm afraid I can't say the same."

"Not to worry. We'll have lots of opportunities to get to know each other now that Rube and Fanny are married. Have you met my parents?"

Steve arrived at the table with four flutes of champagne. "I'm sorry. I should have grabbed two more," he said, nodding toward Hunter and Livia.

"Hello there," Livia purred.

"Livia, this is Steve Ross-Wright."

"Brothers, huh? You two look about as different as night and day."

Adam met her eyes with a cold appraisal. "Steve is my husband."

Sondra saw the flash of surprise in her eyes, but Livia covered it quickly. "You must be from out of state. They don't allow gay marriage here yet."

"We prefer to think of it as just marriage," Steve commented. "Exactly the same as what your parents have."

"As far as I know, my parents only have one penis between them, so that's different."

The couple glared at her.

"Lighten up, fellas. No offense meant." She turned to Hunter. "I suppose that means you're my only real shot at getting out on the dance floor. Shall we?"

Hunter smiled apologetically at the other four. "We'll be back in a bit."

"What was Fanny thinking to put her at our table?"

Adam looked like he could rip out her throat with his bare hands.

"I doubt she expected to start a war in the middle of her wedding," Steve soothed. "Livia is probably a perfectly pleasant woman who simply got her foot caught in her mouth."

Adam pursed his lips but lowered his hackles.

The music stopped a moment later and the emcee announced, "Ladies and gentlemen, Mr. and Mrs. Reuben Susser!"

The lights of the room dimmed except for the spotlight on the dance floor where the happy couple appeared. For their first dance, they tangoed across the floor to the strains of "La Cumparsita," the tango from *Some Like It Hot*, a nod of the head to Fanny's Hollywood roots. A roar of approval came from the guests and the party was off at a gallop.

Livia was forgotten as Ethan, Sondra, Steve, and Adam joined in the festivities. Fanny had opted for a buffet to keep the party from stalling while the food was served, and it worked. Only the cutting of the cake – designed to look like a stack of blue-ribboned gift boxes – brought the party to a temporary halt.

"Sondra?" a white-haired woman in a navy pillbox hat approached her.

"You must be Mrs. Susser," Sondra said.

"Please, call me Naomi. I wish we had been able to meet prior to our children's wedding, but I'm so pleased to meet you now."

Sondra wondered how old this woman was. Other than the white hair, nothing indicated she was more than fifty. "My daughter should have arranged for us to have dinner."

"I'm afraid Isaac and I don't live in the valley anymore. We only visit occasionally."

"Where do you live?"

"Belize."

Fanny had told Sondra that she and Reuben were honeymooning in the tropical paradise. "They're going to spend their honeymoon with you?"

The woman laughed. "Hardly. We're going to stay in Phoenix and let them use the beach house for a few weeks."

An older man with a potbelly hidden ineffectively by a

cummerbund approached. Naomi reached out and pulled him close to her. "This is Isaac, my husband. Isaac, this is Fanny's mother, Sondra."

The lecherous gleam in the man's eye was impossible for Sondra to miss. "Sondra, it's a pleasure to meet you. I understand you're quite a firecracker."

Sondra smiled tightly. "I used to be. Have you met my fiancé yet?"

"The infamous Ethan Turner, I understand. My son and I share a fondness for graphic novels, as they call them now. In my day, they were just comic books."

"Mine, too, I'm afraid. I haven't been able to break myself of calling them that. If you'll excuse me."

"One moment. Naomi and I always invite the kids down for a week at the beginning of summer. We'd love it if you and Ethan would join us this year."

"I wouldn't want to impose--"

"No imposition! None at all! Our beach house is more than big enough – we'll even give you and Ethan the mother-in-law apartment if you'll agree to come."

"I'll think about it."

"Oh!" exclaimed Naomi. "Fanny's getting ready to toss the bouquet!"

Despite being a good ten feet away from the gathering of single women, Sondra turned around in time to see the white roses sailing toward her head. At the last second, Livia dove between her and the flowers, clutching them to her chest like a football. From the floor where she had landed, she exclaimed, "Got 'em!"

Fanny's face fell in disappointment.

Sondra turned back to see Livia's parents' reactions. Naomi appeared mortified, while Isaac chuckled proudly.

"She always has been the more athletic of my children. Rube would rather read a comic book than play football any day."

"She's getting rather old to be tackling bouquets at weddings," Naomi muttered. "Why can't she pin a man down instead?"

"When the right one comes along, she'll pin him down just fine."

"She was throwing herself at a *faygala* earlier...I saw her.

She has no sense, that one."

"You're too harsh, *bubbala*."

Sondra glanced to one side, looking for an escape route. Fanny was beckoning her. She smiled apologetically at the Sussers. "Fanny needs me. It was nice to meet you both."

"A pleasure. And think about coming to Belize this summer. You won't regret it!" Isaac and Naomi waved as she turned to follow her daughter.

She caught Fanny at the elevator doors. "Beautiful wedding, sweetheart."

"Thanks, Ma. I'm glad you've had a good time. Would you come to my hotel room and help me get ready to leave?"

"Of course! I just assumed you and Reuben – do they really call him Rube?"

Fanny giggled. "Yes. The whole family does. Odd, isn't it?"

Sondra shrugged and held her tongue, thinking it wasn't any stranger than her own daughter's decision to shorten Epiphany to Fanny. "Anyway, I assumed you would be staying here. After all, this is a beautiful hotel."

"We considered it. When we discovered there was a red-eye to Belize, though, we decided we didn't want to waste a single night in Phoenix."

"And this Belize thing – I thought you would go to Europe. You've never been much of a beach person."

"Reuben's work is so stressful, Ma – he just wants us to relax and spend time together during our honeymoon. Besides, the beaches in Belize are different from the ones in California."

If she and Fanny had a closer relationship, Sondra would have said what she was thinking: Fanny had made a lot of changes and sacrifices for this man. Instead, she changed the subject. "Thank you for including me in your wedding photos."

"You're my mother! I wanted you in them. Thank you for sharing my happiest day."

"I wouldn't have missed it for the world."

Fanny unlocked the door to her suite and they went inside. A beautifully wrapped present sat on the table. Fanny went straight to it. "Reuben already gave me my wedding present!" she exclaimed, fondling the sapphire drop earrings.

"I wonder what this could be."

"I asked Hunter to bring this up here for you. I thought you might like it."

Fanny shot a puzzled glance at her mother. "You didn't need to buy me anything, Ma. We told everyone no gifts."

"I didn't buy it. Go on – open it."

Her daughter swished across the room in her white silk gown, the navy-blue embroidered snowflakes on the bottom third of the dress moving like a surreal snowstorm. She pulled the silver ribbon off of the box and lifted the lid. "Ma! These are beautiful!" She gently lifted one of the two ornate silver candlesticks, staring at it in wonder. "I've never seen these before. Where did you get them?"

"They were your grandfather's. He told me once that my great-grandmother brought them with her from Russia. She sewed them into her petticoat to keep them safe on the journey here. He said he thanked God for each bruise they gave her on the journey because that meant they were still with her."

"Bruise?"

"She had to act like they weren't there, which meant she had to walk normally. Her legs were black and blue from these candlesticks."

Fanny smiled. "Acting is bred into us, isn't it?"

"I always thought so – but you never had much use for it."

She held out one hand, beckoning her mother to cross the room and take it. "I never told you, but I did some acting while I was in college."

"I would have flown to Missouri to see you! Why didn't you say?"

"I couldn't top you, Ma. You were a fantastic actress. And my father was one of the best actors of his generation. How could I pursue acting and not run the risk of being perpetually compared to my legacy?"

"Think of Drew Barrymore! Emilio Estevez!"

"I would have always come up short in the comparison. I'm not as good as you – not even close. But I loved acting."

"I had no idea." Sondra sat down on one of the chairs. "On the other hand, you must be quite a good actress – after all, I never knew you were dating until I moved out of your house!"

"Keeping secrets from you has never been a particularly difficult task," Fanny commented wryly.

"I'm so sorry, darling. I know I'm self-involved; I'm trying to change that. I don't want Ethan to think I'm shallow."

She lowered herself into the chair opposite Sondra. "Ethan loves you, Ma. I can see it in the way he looks at you."

"Do you really think so? I wonder what he sees in an old woman like me?"

"You're one of the youngest people I know! You always have been. You have a way of attacking life. I wish I were able to claim that trait for my own."

"But you have such a strength about you. I admire that so much, Fanny. You are an amazing woman, and Reuben is very lucky to have you."

Fanny's eyes welled up with tears and she cut her gaze away from her mother, clearing her throat. "So these were my great-great-grandmother's candlesticks?"

"Yes. You know what they are for, don't you?"

"Of course. For Shabbat. I'm surprised you kept them."

"Maybe I'm not the godless heathen you suppose."

Fanny laughed lightly. "Maybe you're just more sentimental than I thought you were."

"That could be it, too."

"Thank you for these. They mean so much to me."

"Maybe you could invite me over for Shabbat when you get back from your honeymoon."

"We will. Do you think Ethan would come?"

"He might. Though you shouldn't expect me to become devout or him to convert."

"We're not Judaism recruiters, Ma."

"I'm just saying."

They chatted amiably as Sondra helped her daughter out of the elaborate wedding dress. Fanny donned an attractive green pantsuit and a pair of slip-on flats.

"Will you take the dress and your present to my house?" Fanny asked her mother as Sondra zipped the gown into its plastic bag.

"Of course. I never asked: are you and Reuben going to live in Peoria?"

"No. With all the real estate bargains to be found these

days, we've decided to buy a place in the Central corridor."

"A house or a condo?"

"Reuben wants a place with a big yard for our kids."

"What if you don't have any?"

"We'll adopt. He wants at least three, so even if we have one or two naturally, we'll still end up adopting. The firm has a great attorney who specializes in adoptions. She's already put us in line."

"He's a successful attorney – I'm surprised he doesn't own a place."

"Oh, he does. It's a condo. He's going to rent it to Livia. By the way, what did you think of her? Nice, right?"

"She's a bit brash."

"True," Fanny admitted. "I was upset when she made the dive for the bouquet. I really wanted you to have it."

"I might as well tell you – she hit on Steve and pissed off Adam."

"Crap. I really thought she would be a good fit for your table."

Sondra glanced at the vanity. "Are you ready for me to pack up your makeup?"

"Just a second...I want to freshen my lipstick." Fanny bent in front of the mirror and picked up the tube. She caught her mother watching her. "What?"

"You really are a beautiful woman, Fanny. I'm sorry if I ever gave you any reason to doubt that."

"It's okay, Ma. It just took me a few decades to grow into my looks." She finished applying the lipstick and said, "The makeup bag is in the drawer. I'm going to check the suite over for anything I might have missed."

Sondra moved to the vanity and gathered the cosmetics while Fanny opened and closed every drawer in the place.

"Looks like I've got everything," Fanny said, standing behind her mother.

"So have I. Let's go."

"Do you want to leave the wedding dress and candlesticks here until after the party? I can give you my key. Maybe you and Ethan want to stay here tonight?"

"That's a lovely suggestion, darling. Would you mind?"

Fanny shrugged. "The room's already paid for; someone might as well use it."

408

Night Life

Leaving the dress hanging in the closet, Sondra followed Fanny back to the reception. The party was still in full swing. Steve and Adam were leading the crowd in a spirited rendition of "YMCA." Ethan was at their table, chatting with Livia, who fingered the prized bouquet with an air of self-satisfaction. Hunter was chatting up one of the servers, a girl with short blonde hair and only one flute of champagne on her tray.

As soon as Reuben spotted them, he excused himself from a conversation with his parents and strode toward Fanny. "Are you ready to go?"

"I am. Are you going to change out of your tuxedo?"

"I don't think so. It's not like I get a lot of opportunities to wear it."

"Won't you be uncomfortable on the flight?" Sondra asked.

"I'm sure I won't. This is probably the most comfortable suit I own." He smiled at his new mother-in-law. "Ethan is a great guy – just as I suspected."

"Sometimes I wonder if he's too good to be true," she answered.

"He's genuine, Sondra. I can tell when someone's pretending. He's definitely not."

"I'll take your word for it." She hugged Fanny and then Reuben. "Be happy, you two."

Reuben beamed at her. "We will. Your daughter is the best thing that's ever happened to me."

"Even better than meeting Ethan Tanner?" Fanny teased.

"Even better than that," he laughed, squeezing her tightly against him and tickling her side.

With his free hand, he signaled the emcee, who immediately stopped the music and announced, "Our hosts for this evening of revelry and celebration are leaving for their honeymoon and have decided not to take us with them! Please give Mr. and Mrs. Reuben Susser a warm round of applause as they take their leave."

The crowd turned toward the main doors, spotted Reuben and Fanny, and applauded loudly. A moment later, they were gone and the music started again. Sondra made her way to the table.

"Ethan was just telling me about the new comic book

409

series he designed around you," Livia said.

"Not around me, exactly. Around a character I portrayed in a movie."

"No need to be modest here, Sondra. The way Ethan tells it, he couldn't have fleshed out the character without your cooperation."

Sondra frowned.

Ethan took her hand reassuringly. "I merely said that having you around has been an inspiration."

"That's so sweet!" Livia batted her eyes at the couple. "I hope I find someone as devoted someday."

"I'm sure you will," Sondra said generously. "If you'll excuse us, I'd like to dance."

"Of course. Nice chatting with you, Ethan."

"And you, Livia." He took Sondra's arm and led her to the dance floor. "Thank you."

"For what?"

"The rescue. She's nice enough, but about as subtle as a baboon in heat."

A brief laugh escaped before she was able to shoot him an appropriately stern look. "Careful...that's my daughter's sister-in-law. We may have many more social encounters with her."

"You needn't worry. I'm nothing if not polite."

"So I've learned. Thank you for coming with me today."

"I wouldn't have missed it for the world. I only regret that it wasn't our wedding day, too."

"Ethan! We haven't even spent a full season together yet!"

"So? I know when something is right, and this is right."

"If we're still together in the spring--"

"How can you doubt us?"

"As I was saying, we'll set a date in the spring. I promise."

"Since when are you cautious?"

"I've always been a little gun-shy when it comes to weddings. You will be my first husband, you know."

"'Will be.' I like the sound of that."

"You're incorrigible."

He reached down and patted her butt. "And you love it."

"You're right. I do. We've been invited to Belize, by the way."

"By whom?"

"Reuben's parents. Apparently, they have the whole family down in early summer."

"See? You do believe we'll be together more than a season!"

"I never said I didn't." She leaned in against his chest as they swayed to the music, dancing in only the most simplistic definition of the word. "We have a room for tonight."

"What are we doing down here, then?"

Taking his hand, she led him out of the reception and up to the empty suite.

Night Life

The Natural

At eight o'clock sharp, Milo took a seat at the bar. To his right was a young woman with magenta hair, heavy eyeliner, and monochromatic clothing. To his left, a clean-cut man of roughly thirty sat, his elbows resting on the bar top. He turned to the man and held out his right hand. "Hi. I'm Milo."

The younger man gave Milo a long stare before taking his hand. "Buzz."

"Nice to meet you."

"Yeah. Whatever."

A woman in black pants and a white button-down shirt walked behind the bar. "Welcome to class. I'm Jenny Dallas, and I'll be your instructor." Milo noticed that she had a beautiful smile with strikingly white teeth. "Starting at this end," she said, indicating the far left of the bar, "please introduce yourselves. Give me your name, your favorite drink, and one fact about you."

As the Filipina at the far left introduced herself, Milo wondered just what he was doing. Everyone in the room was at least ten years his junior, including the instructor. He didn't have a favorite drink – hell, he didn't even like to drink! Just because he had fun serving beers to Sax's regulars one afternoon at the Brass Monkey didn't mean this was the right career for him. And why did he need a career anyway? He was retired, wasn't he? Damn straight. He was retired. He slid off the stool.

The instructor turned to him. "Are you okay?"

"I think I've made a mistake."

"You've already paid for the class, sir. You might as well stick around – the front office won't give you a refund."

Milo remembered signing the paper that said the same thing. He frowned, but sat back down.

Jenny looked at him expectantly.

Milo squirmed under her scrutiny. "Did I miss something?"

"It's your turn to introduce yourself."

"What about those two?" he asked, gesturing with his thumb toward Buzz and a woman who looked like a drug addict.

"They have already gone. Did you forget your hearing aids this morning, sir?" She said it in a gentle tone, but the words still smacked him across the face.

"No," he answered archly. "I guess I just wasn't paying attention. My name is Milo, I don't drink, and I used to be a border patrol agent."

"You don't drink anything?" Jenny asked.

"Nothing alcoholic," he amended.

"Then you must have a favorite non-alcoholic drink."

Milo felt the heat rise to his face. "I like coffee pretty well."

"And would you give us a fact that's true about you now instead of something from the past?"

He could feel the eyes of his classmates on him as he flicked through the Filofax of his brain, mentally pulling out and replacing various truths that he was unwilling to share. Finally, he said, "I'm an amateur photographer working with film instead of digital cameras."

The class seemed to be as relieved as he was, and Jenny was satisfied. "Thank you, Milo." She turned toward the Goth girl to his right. "And you are?"

"Morgana Fuscilli. I prefer blood...orange juice, and I am a social vampire."

Buzz gave a short laugh. "What does that mean? You suck the life right out of parties?"

Morgana arched a perfectly plucked eyebrow at him. "No. It means I feed on other people's energy."

Buzz smirked and rolled his eyes at Milo. Milo answered with a small shrug. Their man alliance was formed.

"It's a pleasure to meet all of you," Jenny said, resting her hands wide against the bar. "As you can see, bartending draws a diverse crowd. Even with classes this small, the diversity is evident." She went on to describe the noble history of bartending and its necessity to culture around the world. She asserted that no commerce-based society could function without a bar. Milo wasn't positive she was right, but she was certainly convincing. After an hour of lecturing, she taught them how to properly pull and serve a beer.

"Okay, let's take a short break. After that, we'll start learning some cocktails."

The other four students hopped off their stools and

headed for the nearest exit, cigarettes in hand. Milo stayed where he was.

"You should at least stretch your legs, Milo. I won't break for lunch until at least twelve-thirty."

"Don't worry about me."

She was drying the emptied beer glasses. "Why are you here?"

"Because this is where the bartending school is," he answered obtusely.

She hung the glasses on the rack and turned her full attention to Milo. "You know what I mean. You worked hard. You're a former border patrol agent, so I'm assuming you have a decent pension. You're what? Sixty?"

"Almost."

"What are you doing here?"

"Honestly? Looking for something to do. No one ever mentions how boring retirement is."

"Are you married?"

"Not right now."

She smirked. "I'm between husbands myself."

"I don't mean it like that. My girlfriend – her name's Claire – she was widowed less than two years ago. She's not quite ready to jump into marriage, but we're happy together."

"Why aren't you two spending your time traveling or something like that?"

"Claire volunteers at the zoo. She enjoys it, and I don't want to ask her to give it up. She's had too many bad things happen for me to go taking away a good thing."

"Why bartending?"

"I've got a friend who owns a bar. He says he'll give me a few shifts a week."

"I like you, Milo. Try not to let this next part freak you out."

The other students came back in from their smoke break, reeking of tobacco. The smell reminded him of Sondra; he made a mental note to give her a call later.

The next few hours flew by. Jenny passed out a packet of recipes and proceeded to demonstrate how to make each of the drinks listed on the sheets using the simulated alcohol behind the practice bar. During lunch, he studied the recipes. Afterward, each of the students – one by one – got their turn

414

behind the bar, with the other students and Jenny ordering drinks from the recipe list. Morgana went first, and wowed the group: she produced all five requested drinks without a glance at the packet. Buzz did well, too: he only used the cheat sheets twice. The Filipina – he thought her name was Malaya – was nervous and laughed a lot, but got the job done. Tammy, who was indeed a recovering meth addict, needed the cheat sheet for every drink and still messed up three of them. Milo needed the recipes too, but he consoled himself in knowing that at least he got the drinks right.

After the hands-on activity, Jenny passed out a multiple-choice test that asked the students to name the primary ingredients of drinks or missing ingredients from recipes. Milo answered thirty-three of the fifty questions correctly, resulting in a disappointing D on the test. Not surprisingly, Morgana aced it and Buzz got a high B. Jenny passed out another packet of drink recipes and dismissed the class.

Milo, exhausted, drove directly home, where he found Claire curled up on the sofa with a book. She didn't get up. "Hi, sweetheart," she said, barely glancing at him. "How was your day?"

"Miserable. I think I've made a terrible mistake," he whined as he dropped into his recliner.

She turned the book over and set it on the end table between them. "Why do you think that?"

"I used to be so good at remembering details. Did you know the other border patrol agents used to give me elephants as gifts because of my amazing memory? Someone could walk through my gate and I'd remember them forever. I caught more criminals--"

"What does this have to do with bartending?" Claire interrupted.

He sighed, annoyed. "If I can remember faces so easily, why can't I remember drink recipes?"

She smiled gently. "You've only spent one day learning drinks. Give yourself a chance."

"This should be child's play. The only one in the class doing worse than me is a burnt-out druggie. There's a girl – she can't be twenty – who is acing everything!"

"They say that the brain gets less flexible with age..."

"That's not helping, Claire."

"Geez! Sorry. I'm just trying to say that you might need a little more study time than a twenty year old."

"I should have quit."

"You already paid for the course. Why not finish?"

"You sound like Jenny."

Claire straightened. "Who's Jenny?"

"The instructor."

"What's she like?"

"Oh, fortyish, funny...a natural for bartending. She's like Sax – able to listen like she really cares."

"Are you saying I don't care?" Claire's face crumpled.

"No! Why would you think that?"

"Oh, I don't know...you come home talking about some woman who listened to all your problems today..." Tears threatened to fall, balancing on the ledge of her lower eyelid.

"Claire, sweetheart, I love you."

"For how long, though?" Two gushing rivulets formed vertically over her cheeks, both parallel to her nose, which instantly began running.

In his shock, he wondered that, too. This was not the same woman he met last summer. He didn't remember dead Alice going through this sort of change – then again, he had never paid a great deal of attention to dead Alice at all. Wisely, he moved to the sofa and took his sobbing girlfriend in his arms. "I will always love you, Claire," he said, thankful that she couldn't see his eyes from this position. He hoped this craziness was simply a passing phase as he rocked her against him.

She wrapped her arms around Milo and squeezed. "I'm sorry. I know I'm acting nuts these days. I know you aren't looking at other women that way."

"Let me get you a tissue, okay?"

She released him and he walked quickly to the bathroom while she fell back against the sofa like a latter-day Camille. "No one told me menopause would be so hard," she moaned.

"What about your mother?"

"I don't think she had started before I left Oklahoma – and, of course, she's well past it now. I just thought all those women were exaggerating." She hiccupped another sob.

"Maybe you should talk to someone who's been through it. Sondra could probably help you," he suggested.

"Oh, yeah, that's exactly what I want to do: talk to your ex-girlfriend about menopause." Just like that, the tears were gone, replaced with bitter sarcasm.

He handed her the tissues and backed away. "I'm going down to the Brass Monkey for a while."

"Go on. Run away." She harrumphed and crossed her arms under her breasts irritably.

"Yeah. I'll see you later. I can pick up dinner for us."

"Whatever." She picked up her book and drew her legs onto the couch.

Milo grabbed his keys and left the house. A few minutes later, he walked into the Brass Monkey. As soon as he saw Sondra's empty stool, he remembered that he meant to call her. He kicked himself mentally.

Sax waved. "Hey there!"

"Hey. Slow night?" Milo asked, glancing around the joint. Only a few old men were at the bar; two couples were playing cribbage at a table.

"Monday. This is how it usually is. What are you doing here?"

"Today was my first day of bartending school."

"Yeah? How'd it go?"

"Eh...not as great as I'd hoped."

"Don't worry about it. You're a natural listener, which is eighty percent of the job in a neighborhood joint like this one. Almost three quarters of the crowd won't ask for anything more taxing than a beer."

"It's the other quarter I'm worried about."

Sax chuckled. "Can I get you something?"

"What do you recommend?"

"For you? Seltzer water with a twist."

"Perfect."

Sax turned his back to pour the drink. "You heard from Sondra lately?" he asked, looking over his shoulder.

"I was about to ask you that."

"Nah. Haven't talked to her since before Christmas. I guess she's all wrapped up with that Ethan guy."

"What do you suppose he sees in her?"

Sax shrugged. "You'd know better than I would."

Milo laughed. "Yeah, I suppose I would. He's just so young."

"Sondra can be mesmerizing – I saw her work her magic on you once, you know." He set the drink in front of Milo. "Where's Claire tonight?"

Milo focused on the bar top. "At home."

"That doesn't sound good."

"I'm not sure what to do, Sax. Her mood swings are getting worse, and the only two I ever encounter are depression and anger."

"You gonna break it off?"

"No. I really do love her, and I know this isn't really her. It's her hormones making her nuts. If we can get through this..."

"Doesn't menopause last a decade?"

"Shit. Really?"

"That's what I've heard."

"If I were younger, I'd marry her and then join the merchant marines."

"How would that help?"

"I'd have a reason to be gone until she was past this."

Sax laughed. "You're not giving up on the bartending, are you?"

"No. I've already paid for the class. Maybe you'll give me some evening shifts to keep me out of harm's way."

"Deal. As long as you'll take a few morning shifts, too."

"We'll work it out."

Milo nursed his water for a few hours, watching one of the last football games of the season on the television over the bar. By the time he went home that night, Claire was asleep in bed. She had left a note on the kitchen table: *I'm sorry about earlier. I love you.*

The next morning, neither of them said a word about the fight as they prepared for their days: Claire at the zoo and Milo at school. They hugged and kissed on the way out the door.

Night Life

Milo's cell phone rang at noon on Friday, just after Jenny dismissed the class to study for their final exam. "Hello?"

"Hey, Dad. How's it going?"

"Not too badly. I don't really have time to talk, though."

"Oh? What's going on?"

"I'm prepping for the final in my bartending class."

"You're really doing that?"

"Yeah." Milo had told Brian about his plans during a Christmas Day phone conversation; Milo and Claire had been in Oklahoma with her family for the holidays. "Today's the last day, as a matter of fact."

"Good for you, Dad. I knew you were too young to just sit around for the rest of your life."

"You could have let me in on that a little sooner."

"Are you kidding? If I'd told you to get a job you would have told me to mind my own business!"

Milo conceded this was true. "What did you need, Son?"

"Are you and Claire available for dinner tomorrow night? Marla's making pot roast and she knows how much you love it. Tell you what – we'll make it a celebration dinner for you completing your bartending school."

Milo's chest swelled and his throat tightened. "That would be very nice, Brian."

"You okay, Dad?"

He cleared his throat. "Yeah. I'm fine. What time should we be there?"

"Six o'clock okay?"

"Perfect. See you then." Ending the call, he turned his attention to the multitude of recipes before him. The week, which had started on a worrisome note, had not turned out badly. Though he was clearly not an alcohol savant like Morgana, he wasn't at the bottom of the pack, either. The more practice he got behind the bar, the better he felt about his decision to stay in the class. Jenny assured him that using a recipe book or cheat sheets to make his drinks didn't mark him as a bad bartender. It was more important to produce the right drink than to look like he knew everything. His confidence rising, he found that the recipes began to make more sense and were therefore more memorable.

419

By the end of the day, he had received his final grade in the class: a respectable B. With his final test in hand, he drove directly to the Brass Monkey.

"Milo! How you doing?" Sax called out in greeting.

"Great!" He walked to the bar and handed the graded test to Sax. "When can I start?"

Sax grinned at his eager friend. "You remind me of what it was like to get my first job."

"I'm feeling pretty spry for a fifty-nine year old. I could be sixteen again."

"If that were true, you couldn't take the morning shift tomorrow – you'd be underage."

"Really? Tomorrow? What do I need to do?"

Sax walked to the drawer where he kept his office keys and pulled out a ring with two keys on it. Milo had followed him down to that end of the bar and sat on Sondra's stool. "Here you are. The keys to the palace," he announced, setting them in Milo's waiting hand. "One opens the front door and the other opens the office."

Milo's eyes widened. "Just like that?"

"It hardly makes sense for me to have to drive here to let you in or lock up at night. Besides, I trust you."

"I won't let you down, buddy."

Sax glanced around the bar. The usual Friday crowd hadn't arrived yet. "Let me run through the opening and closing procedures with you while it's quiet. By the way, do you clean bathrooms?"

On the drive to Brian's house Saturday evening, Milo and Claire barely spoke to one another. He turned on some music to cover the silence, tuning in a classical station. They had spent the week in polite avoidance; this drive was the first time they had been together without distractions.

"How was your week?" he asked as he merged his car onto the freeway.

"Fine. The zoo started a new program with the orangutans. They're letting them use iPads."

"For what? Frisbees?"

Her mood turned irritable. "No, Milo, not as Frisbees. You have no idea how smart orangutans are, do you?"

"They don't speak, so clearly they're smarter than I am."

She sighed.

He let the subject drop.

A few minutes later, she asked, "Why don't you come to the zoo anymore?"

"I don't know. I just haven't felt like it lately."

"It's because you don't want to see me, isn't it?"

"Don't be ridiculous."

"Just be honest with me, Milo. I don't blame you – I'm a raging bitch these days." She was looking away from him, but he could hear that she was on the verge of tears.

"Don't cry, darling," he said, reaching his free hand toward her. "I promise to visit the zoo more often. I love you very much."

She crowded the door to keep out of his reach. A sob escaped.

Milo sighed. "Do you want to go home?"

"No," she said, her voice thick. "This is your night. We're celebrating your success."

"I can make an excuse. I could tell them I have a headache."

"No," she said again. "I'll be fine. I promise."

He turned up the music, allowing Vivaldi's violins to drown out the possibility of further conversation.

As soon as they pulled into Brian's driveway, Milo's granddaughter burst from the house and launched herself at him. "Grampa!"

"Alice Marie! My, but don't you look pretty tonight."

He set her down and she twirled to show off her dress, which featured a fine pink gossamer over-skirt. "This is my costume for the dance recital next month. Are you coming, Grampa?"

"Of course I am," he answered, though this was the first he had heard of the event.

"What about you, Gramma Claire?"

"Alice Marie," Marla said sternly. "We call Grandpa's friend Miss Claire, don't we?"

The girl frowned. "I'm sorry."

"It's all right," Claire said. She smiled and hugged her. "Maybe someday you can call me that."

Milo shifted uncomfortably. Marla caught the movement and tilted her head with concern. He gave her a weak smile. "Where's Brian?"

"He's in the backyard tossing the baseball with Eric."

"I'll just go around back, then." He left the two women and his granddaughter and found his son and grandson in the grassy yard.

"Hey, Dad! Grab that mitt and join us!"

A well-used catcher's mitt sat on the patio table. Milo picked it up and jogged into the yard, forming a triangle with Brian and Eric.

"Hi, Grampa."

"Hi, Son. You going out for baseball this spring?"

"That's the plan. You ready?"

"Sure. Toss it here."

Eric wound up and tossed a fastball at Milo, who caught it with ease. "Nice one. You going for pitcher?"

"I'm thinking about it."

"You should do it. You've got a good arm." Milo tossed the ball to Brian, who threw toward his son. They continued in this manner for the next half hour or so, chatting idly about Brian's work, Eric's schooling, and Milo's new career, until Marla sent Alice Marie out to announce dinner was ready.

Inside, Milo was pleased to see that Claire's mood seemed much improved. He gave her a quick squeeze at the waist and she smiled at him for the first time in days.

"Eric, will you say the blessing?" Marla asked.

"Heavenly Father, thank you for this food Mom has prepared. Thank you for this family and especially thank you for bringing Claire into my grampa's life. Bless this food to the nourishment of our bodies. In Jesus' name, amen."

"Amen," Milo echoed. He was impressed with his grandson's eloquence. In just a few short months, Eric had blossomed from sullen child to likable teenager. In fact, he felt closer to his son and his son's family than he ever had before – and at least part of that was because of Claire. Her relationship with her own family, especially since her father's cancer diagnosis, had gradually improved in the time since she and Milo began dating. She encouraged him to seek

Night Life

Brian out and mend their fractures as well. He reached under the table and squeezed her hand. She squeezed back.

Night Life

Morning Breeze

Claire moaned when the alarm went off Monday morning. No matter how much sleep she got these days, it never seemed to be enough. If she weren't expected at the zoo, she would have rolled over and slipped back into her dreams; unfortunately, she had responsibilities.

Milo, who didn't need to be up for another two hours, was already out of bed and making their morning coffee. The scent, which usually made her smile, tipped her stomach on its side instead. She ran to the bathroom, turning the faucet on as she passed it. She barely made it to the toilet before what was left of the previous night's dinner emptied itself into the bowl. The bitter bile made her spit again in an effort to clear the taste.

This wasn't the first time she had thrown up in the last few weeks. At first she thought it was the flu, especially when coupled with her exhaustion. She never developed a fever, though. Instead, her stomach was bloated and she was uncomfortable most of the time.

"Are you okay?" Milo was knocking on the bathroom door.

"Fine," she answered, wiping her mouth with the back of her hand. "Don't worry about me."

"I have your coffee ready. What time do you need to be at the zoo today?"

"Nine."

"It's seven-fifteen."

"Thanks. I'll be out in a few minutes."

He walked away. She flushed the toilet and went to the sink, examining her face in the mirror. She had bags under her eyes and looked every day of her forty-five years. She pressed her stomach gently, wondering how much more bloating it could take. Everything she read about menopause told her she could expect to feel like crap for many more years. Some of her symptoms didn't line up, though; the nausea, in particular, was a problem.

She splashed some water on her face and brushed her teeth before turning off the faucet. She pulled her brush through her thick blonde-gray hair, gathering it into a low ponytail. In the bedroom, she pulled on her purple zoo shirt and a pair of khaki pants.

When she walked into the kitchen, Milo looked up at her and smiled. "Good morning."

"Yeah," she said, grabbing the mug. When she got it close to her nose, though, she couldn't drink it. She set it back on the table.

"What's wrong?" Milo asked. "Do you need more creamer?"

"No. I'm just not in the mood for coffee these days."

"Do you have time for some breakfast? I could fix you some toast."

She sat down in the chair and nodded.

He stood and went about preparing the toast. "Sweetheart," he said hesitantly, "have you considered seeing your doctor? I've done a bit of research, and I understand there are several treatment options that could help you through menopause."

"Great. Now you want me to take something that might give me cancer or some other crappy disease, just because I'm a little moody?"

"Of course not. But there's no point--"

"In what? Taking it out on you?"

"I was going to say suffering." The toast popped up from the toaster and Milo turned to apply the butter.

"What's the point in going to the doctor? I know what's wrong. All he can do is confirm it and send me on my way, because there's no way I'm letting him pump me full of drugs so that I'm more fun to be around."

"I'm sorry I brought it up." Milo slid the toast in front of her.

She picked up one of the slices and bit into it half-heartedly. It tasted like cardboard in her mouth. Nothing tasted right anymore. She sighed. "I'm sorry, Milo."

"Do you know how often you say that to me these days?"

"Every time we talk?"

"At least. I know you aren't feeling like yourself, but I'd really appreciate it if you wouldn't take it out on me so often."

"You're right." She reached across the table and took his hand. "I'm so...glad I have you in my life."

"Better," he answered.

"You're working at the bar today, right?"

"Yes. Morning shift again."

"How's it going?"

"So far, I love it. I didn't realize how bored I was before."

"I guess we should have kept square-dancing. At least we would have made some friends."

"Not after I had the caller arrested," he smirked.

"True."

"What's really going on with you, Claire?"

"It's just menopause, babe. I promise."

He gave her a stern nod. "If you say so."

"I do." She took another bite of the toast before pushing the plate away. "I'd better go or I'll be late."

"Okay. Have a good day."

"You too. Love you."

"I love you, too." He stood to hug and kiss her and she walked into his arms.

"I'll make a doctor appointment," she promised.

"Good. I'm just worried about you."

"I'm worried about me too."

At the zoo, she walked directly to her post in Monkey Village, giving Zareb a cursory wave. The muscular black man was already engaged in conversation with one of the young mothers who strolled the zoo with her progeny on a daily basis. That was one of the things she loved about the zoo – it was like a small town. Sure, there were strangers around, but a familiar face was always just around the bend. The fresh air seemed to remove the nausea that had plagued her since she woke up, and the squirrel monkeys were already chittering away at one another. Claire loved animals, but she adored monkeys. Monkey Village and the orangutan enclosure were her favorite assignments.

"Hey, Claire," said Isabel, the young Hispanic woman with whom she frequently worked.

"Good morning. How was your weekend?"

"Busy! The weather was so nice, I think every family in

the valley decided to visit the zoo!"

"It's definitely that time of year." Claire shielded her eyes and looked up. "Today's going to be beautiful, too."

"I'm sure we'll see a lot of the regulars," Isabel commented.

Zareb let the first group of visitors inside: a harried young mother surrounded by six youngsters, all of them about seven or eight years old. Each one had a name tag, but that didn't help the woman when one of the boys broke into a run.

"Kevin! Kyle! Whatever your name is, stop running!" the woman shouted.

"Field trippers," Claire said as the boy ran to the center of the village. Addressing the child, she said, "You need to stay with your group, son."

The boy turned around and stuck his tongue out at Claire. "You can't make me!"

The urge to slap the child was almost overwhelming. She raised her arm.

Isabel stepped between her and the boy. "Go back to your group now," she said in a low tone.

"No!" The boy kicked her in the ankle just as the field-trip chaperone arrived.

"What did you just do?" the woman asked, her nostrils flaring and her eyes wide in that expression every child has sense enough to fear.

"N-nothing."

"Don't you lie to me, Kai. I know your mother." With one hand around the boy's upper arm, she looked up at Claire and Isabel. "I am so sorry about this."

Claire, who still couldn't believe she had considered striking the child, was mute.

"Don't worry about it. I have tough ankles," Isabel answered.

The woman laughed weakly. "Children! Come on. Kai has cut this trip short with his behavior."

The other five children immediately began to whine and cry as, slump-shouldered, they followed her and the condemned Kai from the exhibit.

"Are you all right?" Isabel asked when she turned to look at Claire.

"I'm...not sure. I don't feel..." The world went from bright to

427

black in seconds.

The last time Claire passed out, she had good reason. She had been pushed down a flight of stairs. This time, she was embarrassed to realize, nothing precipitated the collapse. Opening her eyes, she saw Zareb's face hovering over hers.

"Just lie still, Miss Claire. The paramedics are on the way."

"Paramedics? Don't be ridiculous," she pushed herself up on her elbows. "I'm fine."

"Obviously, you aren't," Isabel said worriedly. "You collapsed!"

"I haven't been feeling well. I think I've got the flu," she lied.

Zareb and Isabel both took a step back.

Claire took the opportunity to push herself into a sitting position.

"You should go home," Zareb said.

"I'm fine. Really, I am."

"If you've got the flu, you are not fine. You will spread your germs to everyone else here."

Immediately, she regretted her lie. "I don't think I'm contagious..."

They all turned at the sound of an ambulance making its way through the zoo on the asphalt walkways that led to the Monkey Village. The short wails of its siren scattered the people in front of it, causing the procession to look like a parade.

"No point in arguing with us," Zareb said. "Let the paramedics check you out."

Her lips thinned to a grim line. "At least help me up. Don't make them bring a gurney in here."

Instead, Zareb looped one arm under her legs and wrapped his other arm around her back, lifting her easily from the ground. "Get the gate, Isabel."

Isabel scurried ahead of him and, with one eye on the tricky monkeys, opened it for Zareb and Claire to pass through.

The paramedics only hesitated a second. "Is this the patient?"

"Yes," answered Zareb.

"No," said Claire at the same moment.

"I see we have a stubborn one," commented the second paramedic.

"I'm fine, really." Claire squirmed, trying to get Zareb to set her down.

"She passed out." Zareb gripped her more tightly.

The first paramedic pulled the gurney from the back of the ambulance. "We'll take her from here."

Zareb lowered her and then quickly stepped out of her reach.

Claire stared at him with narrowed eyes as the paramedics began their ministrations.

"Feel better soon, Claire!" Isabel called from behind the gates of the village.

Claire, her mood now completely black, flipped her off.

After checking her vital signs, the paramedics concluded that she wasn't in any immediate danger. Still, they wanted to take her to the hospital. She refused.

"You could be dehydrated."

"I'll drink some water."

"Look, we can't force you to go," the younger of the two paramedics said. "At the very least, don't drive. Call a friend."

She agreed, but she couldn't think of anyone to call. Milo was at the Brass Monkey and she didn't want to disturb him. She knew Sax, but not well enough to ask him to drive across town to get her. At last, her mind settled on Sondra. She dialed her number.

"Hello, Claire! How are you?"

"Not so great, actually. I have a huge favor to ask." The slight hesitation on Sondra's end made Claire's stomach flip and her nausea return.

"Sure. What can I do for you?" she finally asked.

"I just fainted--"

"Oh, my God! What's wrong?"

"It was nothing," Claire soothed. "I might have a stomach bug or something. The paramedics--"

"Paramedics!? Why are you calling me? Where's Milo?"

"Milo's at the bar. He's working today."

"Milo's working at the bar? Since when?"

"Sondra. Please focus. I need someone to drive me home. I'm at the zoo."

"We'll be right there."

The phone went dead in Claire's hand. She walked to her car and leaned against its trunk, wanting to be able to spot Sondra's red convertible when it came through the parking lot. While she waited, she looked up her doctor's phone number and dialed it. She listened to five minutes of elevator music before the receptionist answered. Finally, a voice said, "Good morning. How may I help you?"

"I need to schedule an appointment."

"Is this an emergency or a checkup?"

Claire had mostly recovered from her fainting spell. "A checkup."

"The earliest I can schedule an annual physical is the first week of February."

"That's fine."

"Will February third at ten o'clock be all right?"

"Yes."

"We'll see you then."

Confident that she had at least fifteen minutes before Sondra arrived, Claire walked back into the zoo to see the volunteer coordinator.

"What are you still doing here?" the woman asked. "You should be on your way to the hospital!"

"I'm fine, Donna."

"You most certainly are not! You fainted! In front of guests!" Donna looked scandalized, as if the worst part of Claire's behavior was that she'd had the nerve to distress the patrons of the zoo.

"The paramedics checked me out. I'm okay...I've just got a stomach bug."

Donna backed up.

"They don't think I'm contagious," she added.

"You never can be too careful. Why are you here?"

"I wanted to be sure you didn't put me on the schedule for February third."

Donna quick-stepped around to the back of her desk

and pulled up the volunteer schedule on her computer. "February third. That's a Friday."

"I know. That's why I'm here. I know you normally put me with the orangutans on Fridays."

Donna frowned, thinking. "Hmm. I guess I'll have to work around you."

"Yes, I'm afraid you will. I have a doctor appointment that day," she volunteered.

"Not a problem. Thanks for telling me. Now, go home."

"I'm going. I'm just waiting for my ride." Claire didn't move.

Donna seemed to vibrate with jitters. "Was there anything else?"

"Hmm? No...that's it." She didn't usually take pleasure in other people's discomfort, but today it gave her a warm fuzzy feeling.

"I was on my way to lunch," Donna said pointedly.

"At ten-thirty? That's early."

"I have a meeting downtown." She gathered her purse and various electronic gadgets before asking, "Will you be here tomorrow?"

"I plan to, but if I'm still feeling poorly this afternoon, I'll let you know."

"Fine." She moved toward the door, attempting to herd Claire the same direction.

At last, Claire relented and left the office, much to Donna's obvious relief. She walked back out to her car to wait for Sondra. Almost immediately, the vintage convertible rolled up in front of her, with Sondra at the wheel and a handsome young man in the passenger seat.

"Hi, Sondra. Thanks for the rescue."

"No problem." She stepped out of the car and the man slid over to take the wheel.

Claire gestured to the man. "I haven't met your boyfriend before."

"And you still haven't. This is my daughter's son, Hunter."

Claire reddened. "I-I'm sorry."

"Don't worry about it. Hunter and I were preparing his mother's house for the newlyweds' return. They're flying home on Wednesday."

"Where are we going, *Savta*?"

"Can you take me to the condo, Sondra? I don't want to

431

go home yet. Milo will know something is wrong if I'm home before he is."

"Sure." She turned back to Hunter. "Meet me at the condo. You remember how to get there, right?"

"I was just there this morning. I think I can find it."

"And watch the sarcasm, young man!"

He revved the engine and pulled away with a sly grin.

"I'm starting to sound like a grandmother," she sighed.

Claire handed her the keys to the car. "I'm sorry about...you know."

"Don't worry. Ethan's not that much older than Hunter! A little more than a decade, actually." She pressed the key fob and unlocked the doors. "I could get used to this."

"What?"

"All the little luxuries cars made after the turn of the century provide."

They both ducked into the car and put on their seatbelts. As she put the key in the ignition, Sondra asked, "Why don't you want Milo to know you're not feeling well?"

"He's just started working at the bar, and I know starting a new career has got to be stressful. I don't want him to worry about me on top of everything else."

"What's this about Milo working at a bar?"

"He's working at the Brass Monkey."

"Why would he do that? The man hardly drinks! More importantly, why would Sax allow him behind the bar?"

Claire filled her in on Milo's recent bartending education and Sax's willingness to give him a few shifts a week.

"They really seem to have hit it off, don't they?" Sondra mused.

"I think it's great. I know Milo didn't really have any friends out here before."

They settled into a comfortable silence. Claire drifted off to the rhythmic sound of the tires against the freeway.

Sondra woke her a few minutes later. "We're here."

"Thank you. I promise I'll be out before sundown."

"Don't worry about it. Hunter and I will be busy at my daughter's place until the late afternoon. If you leave before I get back, just lock the door handle." They rode the elevator up to the condo, where they found Hunter sitting by the door.

"You could have stayed in the car," Sondra said as the

432

Night Life

young man pushed himself to his feet.

"I was hoping for a glass of water. I'm parched."

"It's the dry winter air – makes everyone want a drink. Speaking of which, are you old enough to go into a bar?"

"I'm only eighteen, *Savta*."

"What's the drinking age in this town?"

"Twenty-one."

"Well, shit. I guess you'll have to wait in the car."

Claire yawned. "I'm going to lie down for a while. If you drop by the Brass Monkey, don't mention today."

"I won't. Feel better, Claire."

She slipped into the rarely used second bedroom and closed the door behind her. She was asleep before Hunter and his grandmother left.

Night Life

Nordic Dragon

Sax breathed in slowly and deeply, his back straight and his focus on the jade dragon figurine a friend had sent him from Japan years ago. He exhaled with control – only his diaphragm showed any movement. He practiced this controlled breathing, attempting to empty his mind of all thoughts.

When the ice maker dropped a new batch of ice and broke his already weak concentration, he exhaled in irritation, his shoulders slumping. A moment later, his left calf shot through with a burning pain that forced him to break his position completely. "Damn it!" he exclaimed as he pulled his foot into a ninety-degree angle, attempting to quell the pain. He rolled off of the cushion and onto his back, thankful once more for the high wall that surrounded his front garden. No passerby would see him rolling around like an idiot.

When he agreed to give Milo a few shifts at the bar, Sax planned to use the extra time to re-center himself. The end of his relationship with Bob Kovich had been sudden and final. For a man rapidly approaching the end of his seventh decade on earth, it didn't bode well for his remaining years – no matter how good he looked for his age.

So far, though, peace was difficult to achieve. The meditation habit he had abandoned during Bob's brief stay in his home was proving elusive to reacquire. In his mostly silent home, even the smallest sound stalked him, waiting to catch him off-guard.

The pain subsiding, he pushed himself to his feet. Even the sound of his own footsteps was distractingly loud as he walked to the back garden. Standing at the edge of the heated square-shaped pool, in which he had intended to swim that morning, he reconsidered his plans. Perhaps it would be better to go to the gym after all. A little noise to drown out the silence might be exactly what he needed.

Abandoning his black silk kimono in favor of a light-blue tank and a pair of sports shorts, he drove to the gym.

"Hey, Sax!" the enthusiastic desk clerk greeted him. "I'd given up on you!"

The clock over the guy's head reminded Sax that it was already eleven o'clock – nearly four hours later than his normal

434

workout time. "Yeah...I intended to take it easy at home this morning, but--"

"The exercise bug caught you!" The clerk laughed.

Sax managed a polite smile. "Something like that." Not interested in further conversation, Sax swiped his card and kept walking. As usual, the cardio room was full of women, most of them retirees. Though he knew Sondra wouldn't be there, he still gave the room a cursory scan. He opted for a treadmill – the only piece of cardio equipment that really made his heart pump. He set it for running/walking intervals and began his workout. The noise and activity of the gym distracted him, at least momentarily, from his internal angst. The row of televisions hanging in the middle of the room were all tuned to CNN, and Sax watched it disinterestedly, the sound of his feet pounding on the treadmill soothing him in a way that meditation had failed to do.

"Excuse me!" a woman called from a few feet to the right.

Sax ignored her, assuming she was addressing someone else.

She moved closer to his treadmill and called again: "Excuse me!"

He was in the middle of a running interval and didn't want to stop. He grunted an acknowledgment.

Satisfied that she had his attention, she asked, "How do you get the machine to do that?"

"Do what?"

"Change pace. You're walking, then suddenly you're running. How does it do that? Does it sense what you want to do?"

"Lady...I'm running here...ask a trainer."

She bristled. "It's a simple question, isn't it?"

"Do I look...like a trainer?"

"As a matter of fact, you do. Whatever happened to common courtesy?"

"I don't know...where did you leave it?"

The woman huffed and walked away, leaving him aggravated and wondering why he didn't just stay home and swim. No longer soothed by his rhythmic feet, he tried to concentrate on the news, but soon found that aggravating as well. It seemed to him that nothing good had happened in the country since 2001 – as if the whole nation had been crippled

435

by one terrorist attack.

That's how he felt now – as if he had suffered a personal terrorist attack. His existence was as lifeless as the twin towers after the collapse. He didn't hold out much hope of finding anything worth nursing back to health. He was single – that was the end of it. Realistically, what did he have to offer anyone? He worked all the time – well, most of the time now. And who knew how long Milo would want to play bartender? He could wake up tomorrow and decide he preferred retirement.

"You okay, Sax?" The desk clerk stood in front of the treadmill.

Startled, Sax jumped and missed a step, stumbling briefly before regaining his stride. He wondered how the clerk had snuck up on him like that. "Yeah, I'm fine. Why?"

"Well..." the younger man hesitated.

The treadmill adjusted back to walking pace. "Spit it out, son."

"You're not...you look like you could spit nails."

"Maybe I could."

"It's scaring some of the patrons."

"It's a gym, not a social club."

"True," he agreed. "But I just had a woman tell me you were rude to her."

"Look, I don't work here, I work out here. What difference does it make if I'm polite to the old biddy?"

"You violated Number Four." The young man pointed at the gym rules, which were painted in large letters on the far wall. Number four read: *Treat others as you wish to be treated.*

"That's a matter of opinion."

"How do you figure?"

"If I were being rude to another patron, I'd want to be told about it."

"You were rude to another patron."

"She was rude first."

"But she complained about you."

"Why am I at fault simply because she tattled? What is this, kindergarten?"

"Sax, I just wanted to let you know that you violated one of our rules." The man drew himself up as if he had real authority.

"So? What happens now?"

"Um...what do you mean?"

"I mean, what is my punishment?"

His eyebrows scrunched together. "There's no punishment, per se..."

The treadmill returned to running speed. "Great. Then I'll just continue to treat others...as I prefer to be treated."

"As long as you're not rude."

"The rule doesn't say that."

"It's implied."

"Not to me."

"Sax, you've been coming here a long time without any trouble at all. I wouldn't want to lose your business."

"Is that a threat? Are you threatening to terminate my contract?"

"If I must."

Sax hopped off the treadmill, resting his feet on the edges of the machine. "Do you think you have that kind of power? You think your boss is going to let you kick a client to the curb because he wouldn't interrupt his workout to help an old woman learn how to use a machine? Isn't that why your boss employs trainers?" He stopped the machine and stepped off of it.

"Now you've violated two rules," the man said as he backed nervously away from the advancing Sax.

"Oh? What did I do now?"

"You didn't wipe down the machine when you left it."

By now, the room was nearly silent as all of the women and the smattering of men stopped their cardio workouts to focus on Sax and the much smaller desk clerk.

"I was planning to return to it."

"What if someone takes it before you do? You've left it wet and dirty. That breaks rule Number One."

Sax stepped toward him threateningly. "And what is the punishment for that?"

"N-nothing, by itself. But with the f-first violation, it means I c-can kick you out. P-please leave."

The audience at first gasped in shock. However, the woman who had started the problem in the first place led a round of applause that was quickly joined by random shouts of "Get outta here!" and "Jerk!"

437

Sax, shocked to realize that the gym had turned against him, took a step back from the smaller man and surveyed the room. No one was in his corner on this. He held up his hands in surrender. "Fine, I'm going." His words were drowned out by the angry mob.

He drove home in despair. He dropped his sweaty gym clothes in a pile by the washing machine and took a hot shower. Standing in front of the mirror, he lamented his falling jowls and wondered if shaving off his mustache might make him look younger. He shaved his other whiskers and applied some aftershave. He picked up the scissors to trim the mustache and found himself whacking it away, one clump of gray hairs at a time. Shaving the remaining stubble, he saw himself without the whiskers for the first time in decades. Immediately, he wished he could glue the hair back on.

Turning away from the mirror in disgust, he stalked to the kitchen to make himself some lunch. He turned on the radio; the noise made him jumpy, so he turned it off again. He considered making himself a hamburger, but when he saw the head of lettuce slowly wilting in the back of the vegetable drawer, he pulled it out instead. Stripping away the outer leaves, he shredded the rest. He grated a carrot over the lettuce and chopped up a bell pepper too. At last, he poured some poppyseed dressing over it and carried the bowl to the back patio. The day was crystal clear and just slightly chilly – perfect winter weather for Arizona. If Bob were still around, this would have been a good day to go to a park or even the zoo.

The zoo made him think of Milo and Claire, who had met at a zoo. He worried that Milo would decide the relationship was too hard and throw in the towel. He chewed his lettuce thoughtfully. He couldn't let Milo make that mistake. One never knew when they were in the last relationship they would ever have. He was certain now that Bob had been his last chance at love – and he had screwed it up with his suspicious nature. Just because Claire was going through menopause – and taking it out on Milo – didn't mean that she didn't love him.

A hummingbird buzzed into the garden and headed straight for the red-glass feeder Bob had hung a few months ago. Bob liked birds. The liquid was almost gone. Sax realized he would have to figure out how to fill it or take it down permanently.

What would Sondra do if Claire and Milo broke up? Claire would probably want her condo back, he decided. Perhaps Sondra would move back to Sun City, he thought hopefully. But no, that wasn't likely. She had her boyfriend in the city – that young fellow, Ethan. Sondra had too much sense to abandon that relationship. The only way it would end was if Ethan broke it off or she died.

He finished his salad and wandered back into the house, where he rinsed the fork and bowl and scraped the discarded vegetable scraps into the garbage. He decided to give meditation another shot and, shuffling into the dining room, lowered himself onto a cushion. Since the dragon wasn't working as a focal point for him today, he sat facing the front garden instead. He crossed his legs and rested his arms, palms up, on his thighs. Straightening his spine, he inhaled slowly.

Maybe Sondra missed Sun City. If he invited her to live with him, she might accept. She wouldn't be a bad roommate to have. She was funny and relatively sane. He imagined she would probably even meditate with him...

Which was something he seemed incapable of doing alone anymore. Frustrated, he pushed himself up, grabbed his keys, and drove to the bar.

Milo did a double take as he came in. "Sax?"

A few of the regulars swiveled their stools to wave; transfixed by the sight of a mustache-less Sax, their hands seem to hover uncertainly.

"Hey, Milo." He walked to the stool next to Sondra's regular spot and sat. "Give me a beer, will you?"

"Everything okay?" Milo asked as he pulled a Guinness for his friend and employer.

"Not great, actually." He glanced at the empty stool to his right. "Don't suppose she's been in."

"You just missed her. The seat's probably still warm."

"Damn it! This just isn't my day."

Milo backed away slightly. "What's wrong?"

Sax shook his head. "I don't know. Everything, I think."

"Sax, you can talk to me, buddy."

"I don't share well," he answered. "Why was Sondra

here?"

"She just stopped in to see everyone."

"Was her boyfriend with her?"

"No. And she didn't stay long – her grandson was waiting in the car."

"I really could have done with seeing her today."

"Yeah. I needed to see her myself. Claire and I had another fight this morning."

"Listen...I wasn't going to say this, but you shouldn't get too upset with Claire. She seems like a really good woman to me...not that I'm a great judge when it comes to the fairer sex, but...well, you know. She's good."

"That's nice of you to say, Sax, but you haven't seen her lately. I'm starting to wonder if she's in a bad mood because of me instead of in spite of me. Maybe she would be happier on her own."

An older man Sax had never seen before slid onto Sondra's seat and signaled to Milo.

"That seat's taken," Sax said gruffly.

"There's another seat on the other side of you," the man pointed out.

"Seat's taken," Sax repeated.

"Listen, buddy, I just want to drink my beer in peace."

"Then move to another seat." Sax inhaled, flaring his nostrils at the guy.

"If you'll just move down here," Milo suggested in an appeasing tone.

"This is a public space and I can sit where I want."

"Actually, this is a private business and, no, you can't sit wherever you want," Sax said.

"You're going to let this drunk treat your customers like this?" the guy asked, addressing Milo.

The regulars in the bar held their collective breath. No one had ever seen Sax angry, but considering his bulk and his well-known workout regimen, no one doubted his strength.

"He's the owner." Milo said simply. He backed up a few paces, just in case he was about to be caught in the crossfire.

Sax stood up and leaned down toward the man. "Get out."

The stranger, recognizing his mistake, stuttered, "Yeah, man. I'm g-going."

Night Life

"Don't come back."
"I w-won't." The guy all but ran from the bar.

Night Life

Sweet Heat

Despite her initial misgivings about Claire's totally taupe condo, Sondra had to admit it had a lot of pluses. One was the view from the balcony, where she stood watching the sun sink into the western sky. She sipped the whiskey sour Ethan had thoughtfully prepared for her and pulled her wool wrap closer to her body. Inside the condo, just a few feet away, Ethan was chopping vegetables and tenderizing meat, filling the place with the comforting scent of cooking – a skill Sondra herself had never really gotten the hang of. Having made her famous King Ranch Chicken Casserole for him, her kitchen repertoire was exhausted. And, though he seemed to enjoy it, he wasn't interested in a steady diet of the rich dish. Therefore, he had taken over the home-cooked meals portion of their relationship.

"You okay out there?" Ethan called when he caught her looking at him. "Do you need a refill?"

She held up her glass and shook it from side to side, causing the ice to clatter in the glass. "In a few minutes. I'm still working on this one. How long until dinner?"

"Twenty minutes or so."

The sun was gone now, leaving the lonely pink and orange sky in its wake. The night was still young, though. Judging by the traffic below, it couldn't have been much past six. She leaned on the railing and listened to the street noises that floated up: an occasional car horn, a particularly loud shout, a siren in the distance. She straightened and took another swallow of her drink. Ethan's arms slid around her from behind and she leaned into him, relishing the warmth his substantial form offered. "Mmm."

He kissed her neck. "You're cold."

"Not now."

"Shall I stay and be your personal heater?"

"Sounds nice."

He stepped backward, pulling her with him, until they dropped together into the wicker loveseat they had purchased especially for the condo balcony. "Are you happy?"

"Why wouldn't I be?"

"Answer, please."

"Of course I'm happy!" She turned in his lap, throwing

442

her legs over his, and kissed him softly. "You are a perfect boyfriend."

"Fiancé," he corrected.

She broke eye contact, glancing toward the kitchen. "Is our dinner safe without you watching it?"

"Why are you changing the subject?"

She sighed. "I've never been the marrying kind."

"Maybe you weren't in the past, but I'm here to change all that."

"Haven't you ever heard how hard it is to teach an old dog new tricks?"

He arched an eyebrow. "It's a good thing that you're not a dog."

She laughed and slapped his arm. "Watch it!"

"Come inside and keep me company while I finish dinner."

"If you insist."

"I do."

As they walked into the condo, he took her glass to refill it. "Another whiskey sour, right?"

"Have you ever seen me drink anything else?"

He didn't answer; instead he added sugar and a new lemon slice to the glass.

"So, are we staying in tonight?"

"On a Friday? That sounds boring."

"As you just confirmed, I'm old. A night in sounds lovely to me."

"Alas, I am young. And so is the night. I'm taking you to a gallery opening."

She sat down at the table. "Where?"

"Not far. The gallery belongs to an old friend's girlfriend. She invited us because she wants me to be the next artist in residence." He slid the new drink in front of her and returned to cooking.

"Really? With your comics?"

"Some of the comic stuff...some of my pencil drawings too. You'll like her...Arlo tells me she's not the marrying kind either."

She sucked on the lemon, dropping the rind back into the glass. "That usually means the guy doesn't want to get married, not the other way around."

"Trust me, Easter is the one controlling the direction of that relationship."

"Easter? Odd name."

"It fits her." He lifted a pan lid, and the scent and sizzle of searing steak filled the room. "Have you spoken to Fanny since she got back?"

"She called to thank me for delivering her dress and the candlesticks to her house. She sounds good...happy."

"Have they found a house yet?"

"They just got back a few days ago, Ethan!"

He shrugged. "I thought they might be in a hurry."

"You mean because they want kids? I don't think she's pregnant yet."

"Just wondering."

"How is the comic book coming?"

"You mean the Sunrise Aeon graphic novel?"

"Sorry."

"It's okay. It's the same thing, really. Just fancier packaging. And it's coming along brilliantly. You're going to love it. As a matter of fact, my publisher says it should be ready for its debut in February at the MegaCon."

"What's that?"

"It's this huge comic and sci-fi convention in Orlando."

"When were you going to tell me?"

"I just heard the news this morning," he answered. "I wanted to tell you over dinner. The publisher is springing for a costume designer to come and create your outfit, too."

"I've got to wear silver lamé?"

He smiled apologetically. "Yeah, I'm afraid so."

She sighed and sipped her drink. "All because I let the producers dress me like a space-age hooker thirty years ago."

He plated the food and carried their dinners to the table. "For madam."

"When is the costume designer coming?"

"Toward the end of the month – the date's not set yet."

"This will be my last steak dinner. Beef makes me carry water-weight."

"Then I hope it's delicious."

"Me, too. Orlando, huh?"

"Yep."

"Are we driving?"

"Not this time. The company's springing for first-class flights."

"Well, hallelujah...at least there's a cloud lining to match my costume."

As they ate their dinner, they chatted about the last few days. Ethan, hard at work on the graphic novel, had been too busy to spend much time with Sondra. He never failed to turn up in the evening, though, and he usually stayed the night in her bed. She had forgotten how sexually energetic a young man could be. Perhaps she had never known – all of her lovers before Ethan were older than her, with the exception of Milo who didn't count because she had thought he was older when she first went to his bed. When Ethan left every morning, she always slept an extra two hours to make up for the late-night exertions.

"Did I tell you I stopped by the bar earlier this week?" she asked idly, spearing one of the last bites of steak with her fork.

"On Monday, right?"

"Yes. I'm still surprised Milo is working there."

"You shouldn't be. Technically, I don't need to work anymore – I've made more than enough to keep me in modest comfort for the rest of my life. Yet I can't stop working."

"But you're thirty years younger than Milo," Sondra pointed out.

"It's a man thing. We must keep working or we die."

"You sound like Bill."

"Fanny's father?"

"Yes. He retired from acting, but then couldn't keep himself busy enough. That's why he went into producing."

"That's a natural enough progression."

"Exactly! Actor to producer makes sense. Border patrol agent to barkeep doesn't."

"I think his decision to become a bartender was more about the opportunity than the desire."

"And you don't see anything wrong with that?"

Ethan's fork stopped halfway to his mouth and he shrugged. "Not really, no. Have you talked to Sax?"

"He hasn't called me."

"Maybe you should call him."

"I feel so guilty about the thing with Bob – I never should have pushed him to dig deeper."

"Listen, if you really thought the guy was a murderer, you didn't do anything wrong."

"Maybe not, but I was mistaken and it cost Sax his boyfriend."

"From what you've told me about Sax, he's probably happier alone anyway."

Their meals finished, Sondra gathered the dishes and put them in the dishwasher. Cleaning up was her contribution to dinner. "What should I wear tonight?"

"Nothing too fancy. Black is a good choice. That black sweater with the cowl neck and a pair of jeans would be perfect."

She smiled, thinking about how similar to Bill this young man was: Bill had always picked her clothes when they were going out. "Okay."

When she straightened from putting the plates in the dishwasher, Ethan was in front of her. He wrapped his arms around her and said, "Have I told you lately how much I love you?"

"Yes, but you can tell me that as many times as you want."

"Let's get married, Sondra. We can go to the courthouse and get a certificate Monday."

"And start our honeymoon on Tuesday?"

"Yes. And our honeymoon will be for the rest of our lives."

"Sweet talker."

He laughed huskily. "Maybe we should skip the opening."

She danced out of his arms. "No! I want to go. I'm going to change right now."

He gave an exaggerated sigh. "Fine. The opening doesn't start until seven, though."

"You can take me for my last dessert first."

"Last dessert?"

"Costume fitting," she reminded him. "I'll have to cut the sweets from my diet, too."

"Ouch. No fun." He followed her into the living area and plopped down in one of the beige armchairs. "Where do you want to go?"

"I feel like ice cream. Mary Coyle's?"

"Okay. Get ready."

As she dressed, she smiled to herself. Ethan made her feel as young as he was – and it was a very good feeling. She located some long silver earrings in her jewelry box and added them to the casually elegant outfit Ethan had suggested. As she gazed in the mirror, she thought she didn't look too bad for a woman past sixty. Her dyed red hair might be a bit too bright for her increasingly pale skin. She made a mental note to discuss the problem with her hairstylist. Perhaps a slightly lighter red would balance her out better.

"Wow, babe. You look fantastic," Ethan exclaimed as she came back to the living room.

"Thanks. Are you ready?"

"Let's go." He hopped out of the chair and pulled his car keys from his pocket.

Mary Coyle's was a Phoenix landmark – an ice cream parlor that first opened its doors in 1951. As a transplant, Sondra wasn't aware of the place until Ethan took her there on one of their early dates. Since then, she had come to appreciate its old-fashioned pink-and-black décor and homemade ice cream. Even the perky young waitresses looked like they were going to a sock hop instead of serving sundaes.

Sondra and Ethan were led to a booth and given menus. The place was busier than normal, with several families enjoying a Friday-night treat. Sondra decided on a cashew caramel sundae and pushed her menu aside. Ethan grinned at her.

"What are you smiling about?"

"I'm just looking at the most beautiful woman in the world."

"You can stop with the flattery, you know. You've already got me."

"It's not flattery. It's the truth."

She blushed. "What are you having?"

"My usual: two scoops of the honey banana."

"For such a creative guy, you certainly are set in your ways."

"I just know what I like."

The waitress came over and took their order.

When she left, Ethan stretched an arm across the table.

She settled her hand in his.

"So, where do you know Arlo and Easter from?"

"We met in college. You know that tattoo on my left shoulder?"

She pictured it in her mind: a superhero logo from the comic series that had made him wealthy. "Yes?"

"Arlo did that for me."

"He's a tattoo artist?"

"Yeah. A really talented one."

She couldn't help smiling at him. "You are an amazing person, Ethan."

"Why, thank you, babe! What did I do to earn your accolades?"

"The way you just accept people into your life, no matter where they are from or what they look like...you're fantastic."

"To be fair, Arlo and Easter look relatively normal. I mean, he's not covered head to toe in tattoos or anything like that."

She waved his words away. "I didn't mean they were circus freaks. But you pursued me even though I'm twice your age. At the wedding, you even talked to Reuben's sister!"

"Not my favorite person, but still...I believe in reading the book, not just looking at the cover. My parents taught me that by raising me in the carnival."

"It seems like the same upbringing taught your sister to be suspicious of everyone, no matter what they look like."

He shrugged. "Viv and I are very different from one another. I was always much more accepting than she was. She's a lot like Mama Constance."

"Who?"

He smiled lopsidedly. "Damn. I haven't thought of her in years. She was our great-great-grandmother."

"So your father told you Viv reminded him of his great-grandmother?"

"No. I saw the resemblance for myself. She was still around when I was a kid. Viv spent a lot of time with her -- that's probably why she turned out so much like her."

"She must have been ancient!"

"She was in her nineties, I think. She barely noticed me, but she doted on Viv."

The waitress returned with their ice cream treats and they were silent for a few minutes as they ate.

"Have you told your family that you proposed to me?"

"Of course," he answered. "I even told them you said yes."

"Are they all okay with that?"

"Mmm-hmm," he mumbled, his mouth conveniently full of ice cream.

"Let me guess: Viv isn't thrilled."

"You two definitely have some issues to work through."

"She doesn't like me!"

"She liked you fine until you called her a bitch."

"She deserved it." Sondra's anger reignited in her belly; she pushed the ice cream away.

"Don't get upset, babe. I understand that Viv can be hard to take, but she's my sister and I'd like for you two to get along. Maybe you could call and apologize?"

"Of course. The next time it snows in the valley."

He shook his head. "You're both stubborn as mules. Don't waste your ice cream."

"I'm not hungry anymore."

"Fine." He pulled the glass toward him and dug in.

"Can I taste the honey banana?" she asked after he had eaten a few bites of her cashew caramel sundae.

"Sure," he said, sliding it toward her.

She dipped her spoon into what looked like vanilla ice cream but tasted like sweet bananas. "Mmm. I understand why you stick with this."

"Are we changing the subject?"

"Yes, we are. And I recommend you go along with it."

He chuckled. They finished their ice cream without further discussion of Viv.

The gallery was in an old red-brick strip mall with huge plate-glass windows. As they drove past it and into the rear parking lot, Sondra saw a collection of retro dresses on tattooed women holding wineglasses standing just outside of the gallery.

"Did you see the woman with the blue hair?" Ethan asked.

"The one holding court in front?"

"That's the one. That's Easter."

"She looks like a Big-Band-era Marge Simpson."

He laughed. "Tell her that. She'll love you for it."

"God, no. I couldn't."

"I'm serious. She'll think it's hilarious."

She shook her head as he parked the car. "Are you ready?"

"As ready as I'll ever be. I think I might have fit in better in my wrap dress."

"You look fantastic. Besides, you don't want to blend, you want to stand out." Folding her arm over his, he led her to the back entrance of the shop and down the long hallway that led into the open space of the gallery.

Some remarkable portraits hung on the nearby walls; they reminded Sondra of the paintings found in museums. "Who buys portraits of other people to hang in their home?" she asked Ethan, gesturing toward the paintings.

"Good question. Maybe that's why these are at the back of the gallery." He led her into the crowd, taking two glasses of wine from a passing tray. "For you, my lady."

"Why, thank you, kind sir." She took the glass and sipped, wrinkling her nose. "It's not the good stuff," she whispered to Ethan.

"Of course it's not. It's free," he whispered back. He walked toward a lanky man standing next to a fantasy world of clouds and butterflies on canvas. "Arlo!" he said, just loud enough to cut through the crowd's noise.

Arlo looked up and, smiling, waved. "Ethan! You made it!"

"Wouldn't miss it," he said when they were closer. "I'd like you to meet--"

"Sunrise Aeon!" the tattooed man said, his jaw dropping. "I'd know you anywhere!"

His exuberance caught Sondra off-guard and she took a step backward even as he stepped toward her. She stuck out a hand to forestall the hug she feared was coming. "Nice to meet you."

Arlo stopped and assessed her body language with a grin. He met her handshake. "It's an honor to meet you. Wait until Easter sees you're here. She'll be thrilled. Where is she?"

"She was standing outside when we drove up. When I

450

pointed her out, Sondra said she looked like--"

Sondra elbowed him in the side.

"He'll think it's funny, babe!"

"Please," she said, her eyebrows raised worriedly.

He laid a comforting hand on her shoulder. "Okay. I won't say it."

"Fine. Keep your in-jokes to yourself," Arlo mock-pouted. "Let's find Easter, you two." To the others gathered around him, he said, "Excuse us." He led them through the throngs and out the door, where Easter, in all her blue-haired glory, stood, still surrounded by Betty Page wannabes. "Bunny!" he called. "Come here!"

"Bunny?" Sondra whispered to Ethan.

"Pet name."

"Figures."

"Yeah, honey?" she asked, extracting herself from the crowd. "Is everything okay?"

"Fine. Ethan's here and he brought a date."

The girl, who Sondra noted was actually quite attractive despite her vivid hair, looked toward Ethan and Sondra for the first time. "Oh, my God! Ethan! You came!" She bounced into his arms and Ethan swung her around.

"Of course I came! You invited me!"

"If I'd known it was that easy to get a celebrity like you, I would have invited you sooner!" She pounded her tiny fists against his back affectionately. "So, what do you think?"

"So far, it's great. I want you to meet my fiancée, Sondra." He hooked his hand around Sondra's arm and pulled her closer.

Easter's face registered mild surprise. "I didn't even know you were dating!"

"We've only been together a few months," he answered, "but she is definitely a catch."

"And here I was planning to leave Arlo for you," she teased.

"If only I had known." He gave her a playful bow and she laughed.

"It's a pleasure to meet you, Sondra," she said, holding out her hand.

"Likewise."

Her hand still in Sondra's, she cocked her head to one

side. "Have we met? You seem really familiar."

"No, I don't believe we have."

"And your voice...it's so melodic. Say 'You are so much more powerful than the men of my world. You will make in me a great warrior.'"

"Do I really have to?"

"Oh, my God! You're her, aren't you? Girls!" she called to her friends. "Look who's here! It's Sunrise Aeon!"

Three of them whipped their heads around and squealed. The whole group migrated to form a half-circle around Sondra, who smiled in spite of herself. "Yes, I'm Sondra Lane, the actress who played Sunrise in *Siege of the Moon*," she confirmed.

"I thought you were dead!" one of the girls said, awestruck.

"No. Not yet, anyway."

"Shut up, Megan," Easter reprimanded. To Sondra, she said, "Thank you so much for coming to my gallery opening. I had no idea you lived in the valley."

"I told you I saw her in Tempe," another girl said. "At the showing, remember? You never believe me!"

"Maybe if you didn't lie so often," Easter chided.

Sondra shifted uncomfortably.

"Leave us alone, ladies," Easter instructed. All of the women backed away until they had formed a circle a short distance from them. "I'm sorry about that." She aligned herself beside Sondra and looped an arm through hers. "Let me give you a personal tour of the gallery."

Before the evening was over, Sondra had selected a fantastic painting featuring a candy cathedral, and Ethan had made lunch plans with the couple.

Sondra and Ethan were a few minutes late to lunch the next day. Easter and Arlo were already in one of the booths along the windows. Sondra had seen the place a few times, but she had never stopped in to eat at Mel's Diner, fearing it was just trying to profit from tourists seeking the original place featured in the old *Alice* television show. If that was their goal, they were doing a damn fine job of it: she could have sworn their waitress was Flo.

"Thanks for coming last night," Easter said as soon as they sat down. "And for buying a painting! Megan was thrilled!"

"Megan? The girl who thought I was dead?"

"That's the one."

"She's M.D. Carlyle?"

"The one and the same. She's quite talented, don't you think, Ethan?"

Ethan, who had been pleased with Sondra's choice, nodded. "Incredible work. She's got a real eye for absurdism. That's unusual in female artists."

"That's sexist," Sondra said.

"No, it's true," Easter confirmed. "Most of the absurdist artists are men -- at least the well-known ones. That's one of the reasons Megan uses her initials and didn't make a point of introducing herself as the artist."

"How sad."

Easter shrugged. "I don't know...I think being the mysterious artist is fun for her."

Arlo picked up his menu. "We'd better decide what we want to eat. They don't like non-paying customers in here."

"What's good?" Sondra asked the others.

"The pork tenderloin sandwich is amazing," Easter answered. "Just like back home."

"Where's home?"

"I'm from Missouri originally. I came here right out of high school -- I couldn't wait to get away."

"And now all she does is moan about how much she wants to go back," Arlo laughed.

"I just didn't appreciate all that greenness as I should have. And knowing everyone -- that was pretty great, too."

"Small town, huh?"

"Yeah. I thought it would be great to disappear into the crowds of a big city, but I was wrong."

"Is that why you color your hair?"

Easter frowned. "Color it? This is natural."

Sondra laughed and shook her head.

"Can I tell them now? Please?" Ethan begged.

"Tell us what?" Easter asked.

"I said something snarky last night before I met you," Sondra confessed. "I keep telling him to forget it, but he thinks it's funny."

"If Ethan thinks it's funny, it must be freakin' hilarious!"

"I don't want to hurt your feelings," Sondra protested.

"What feelings? Do I look like I have feelings? Does a woman with feelings have this many tattoos?" she joked, lifting her shirt to flash a full-stomach tattoo of the Italian countryside, complete with a villa in the distance.

"Oh, my goodness!" Sondra exclaimed. "That's gorgeous!"

Easter beamed. "Thanks! Arlo did it for me. You should see the painting one of my friends did -- she took the tattoo as her source material and then painted me into it. It's gorgeous. Did you see the portraits at the back of the gallery last night?"

"Yes."

"The same artist did those paintings. She's got a talent for portraiture that rivals any of the Dutch masters, in my opinion. Now, tell me the joke."

Ethan glanced at Sondra, who nodded and shrugged her acquiescence. "She said you looked like a Big-Band-era Marge Simpson."

Arlo and Easter both burst into laughter.

In an obvious attempt to quell the noise coming from their table, the waitress came over to take their order. "What would y'all like today?"

"I'll have the pork tenderloin," Sondra said as Arlo and Easter worked to regain control.

"Same," said Ethan.

Arlo, still unable to speak, signaled the waitress for two more.

The waitress arched a warning eyebrow and walked away.

Easter calmed herself with deep breaths.

Arlo cleared his throat. "That's so much better than what I told her the first time she went blue."

"He called me Cookie for a month." When Sondra and Ethan stared at her blankly, she continued, "As in Cookie Monster."

Ethan and Sondra worked to contain their giggles.

454

The four of them talked about art some more, segueing into a discussion of Ethan's latest project, the Sunrise Aeon graphic novel.

"I don't suppose you have any pencil drawings of your early concepts for the book," Easter said hopefully.

"A few," Ethan conceded.

"Those would fly off the walls. You know my crowd is full of sci-fi geeks."

"I've never really thought of myself as that kind of artist."

"What kind is that? Someone who actually sells their work to hang on walls?"

"Exactly."

"But you should be. You've seen his work, Sondra. What do you think?"

"I think you're right, Easter. His work is amazing." She told them about the morning she had considered breaking up with Ethan and how his artwork had sent her back up the stairs instead of out the door.

Ethan took her hand and gazed into her eyes. "You never told me that."

"They are so cute together, don't you think, Arlo?" Easter said, fluttering her eyelids at her boyfriend.

"Adorable," he agreed.

"Okay, cut it out, you two." Ethan broke away from Sondra and rolled his eyes at his friends.

"Was he this way with his first two wives?" Sondra asked, only half joking.

The silence was palpable. Sondra looked down, embarrassed.

Ethan cleared his throat. "It's okay. You can tell her whatever you want. We don't have any secrets."

"It's not our place to say," Easter answered quietly.

The waitress slid their plates in front of them and set the ketchup on the table with a loud clunk. "Enjoy."

They ate in silence. Sondra tried to think of something that might lighten the mood, but couldn't. Finally, Ethan announced, "I want another tattoo, Arlo."

"Really? I thought you said the super-hero thing was all you would ever need."

"I've changed my mind." He pulled out his wallet and

removed a piece of paper, sliding it across the table to the tattoo artist. "This is what I want."

Arlo unfolded the picture and gave Ethan a queer smile. "Are you sure about this?"

"As sure as I'll ever be."

"Then I guess we'll go to the shop after lunch."

The tattoo parlor's walls were lined with images, some simple and some ornate. Sondra, who had never been tempted to get a tattoo before, found herself drawn to some of the more beautiful designs.

"You want one?" Easter asked from behind her.

Sondra, startled, turned quickly around. "I think I'm a little old for this trend."

"Not really. We get all kinds. We have such a great reputation that we get young and old, wild and conservative, rich and poor in here."

She had to admit that the place was very nonthreatening for a business that challenged the cultural norms -- sort of like the Mary Coyle of tattoo shops. "Where did Ethan and Arlo go?"

Easter turned her gently in their direction. "He's right there, don't worry."

Sondra gave her a weak laugh before confiding, "I feel so uncool right now."

"Don't worry about it. You're sure you don't want a tat of your own?"

"I'm going to say yes, I'm sure."

Easter laughed. "Come sit in the break room with me while Arlo does his magic." She took Sondra by the hand and led her past the row of tattoo stations and into the back, where a small kitchenette, complete with a hot plate and old-fashioned refrigerator, awaited.

Sondra sat down at the old aluminum table as Easter pulled two sodas from the fridge, setting one in front of Sondra.

"Do you have anything diet? I'm about to be fitted for a

Sunrise Aeon replica costume -- I need to be trim."

"Diet soda is bad for you. Trust me, the calories in that soda are better for you than anything in the fake stuff." She sat down, crossing her legs and leaning forward. "So...spill."

"Excuse me?"

"Oh, come on! I want to know the deets! How did you snag that gorgeous hunk of talent?"

"I'm not sure, to be perfectly honest."

"Where did you meet?"

"You know that screening your friend mentioned last night? Ethan was there, too. He tracked me down online a few days later and suggested that I go to a sci-fi convention with him. He even got someone interested in sponsoring my appearance."

"Wow. So you went on a road trip together?"

Suddenly parched, Sondra popped the top on the soda. "No. I wound up with some prior engagements that couldn't be avoided. But Ethan was persistent. How long have you known him?"

"We went to college together."

"But Ethan's--"

"A few years older? Yeah. He got a late start. He and Arlo met in an art class; they were already tight before I came along. I was an art history major. Arlo and I met when I volunteered to be the nude in his life study class."

"Interesting choice."

She shrugged. "I'd read about all the greats and I thought, hell, how can I end up as an artist's muse?" She laughed and sipped her soda.

"But now he's a tattoo artist."

"Admittedly, that's not what I expected him to be, but he's damn good at it. Wait until you see his work."

"He did the one on Ethan's shoulder, right?"

"Yeah, but that one didn't take a lot of skill. I mean, it's just a superhero logo. The one he's doing today is real art."

"What is it?"

Easter pressed her thumb and forefinger together and drew them across her lips. "Sorry. I'm sworn to secrecy."

"If you won't talk to me about that, what about his wives?"

"I never liked the first one."

"Why not?"

"Julia was a spoiled little girl who was always looking for the next big thrill. I never understood her."

"But Ethan loved her, right?"

"Too much, if you ask me. He would follow her anywhere -- even off buildings."

"They were split up when she died, though."

"That's what he told us. He kind of faded out of our lives after he met her. Like I said, I didn't like her. That makes couples' dinners uncomfortable."

"What about Astrid?"

"I introduced them. Astrid was a friend of mine." Easter's face was instantly etched with lines of regret. "I can't help thinking she would still be alive if I hadn't brought them together."

"You blame Ethan for what happened?"

"Oh! No! Of course not! But they were together when she died -- mountain climbing."

"Vivian told me--"

"You've met the queen bitch, huh?" Easter smirked.

"You're not a fan?"

"Don't tell Ethan. He idolizes her. He's such a good person that he can't imagine Viv has bad intentions."

"How do you mean?"

"She's like a stalker chick when it comes to Ethan's relationships. Astrid told me it was creepy how close they were."

"But she married him anyway."

"What can I say? Ethan's a charmer. Besides, I think the creep factor comes from Viv's behavior, not Ethan's." Easter shook away the memories and said brightly, "Let's talk about something else. Tell me about Hollywood."

Sondra told her stories, at first hesitantly. She wanted to get more information from Easter about Ethan's past, but she knew better than to pry. Soon, she was swept away by her own past, sharing the romantic tale of her life with Bill.

Hours must have passed, though neither of the women thought to look at a clock. When Arlo appeared in the doorway and cleared his throat, Sondra felt closer to Easter than she did to her own daughter.

"What's up, honey?"

"Ethan's tattoo is done. He wants Sondra to see it."

Both women stood, though Sondra moved a bit more slowly, her knees stiffened from so much time in the same position. Easter took her by the hand and led her back to the parlor.

Ethan's smile was like a bolt of lightning to her heart. "Did you have a nice visit?" he asked, holding a hand out to her.

"Of course. So, where's this fantastic new tattoo?"

He pulled her closer and turned his other arm toward her. From his elbow to his shoulder, a miniature Sunrise Aeon stood with her hands on her hips and a smile on her lips.

Night Life

Frost

Milo, who had never been a late sleeper to begin with, woke up even earlier these days. Normally, he left the bedroom quietly to let Claire continue sleeping. Just because his body could function on less than six hours a night didn't mean hers could.

Today, though, he propped himself up on one elbow and watched her sleep in the dim, pre-dawn light. When she was asleep, none of the worry lines creased her face. She looked like a perfect doll, her blonde hair spread out beneath her head. She was more beautiful than dead Alice or Sondra -- the only other women to ever occupy his bed. Her beauty radiated from deep within her. Even when she was angry or depressed, he couldn't help but consider the moods no more than clouds passing over the sunshine of her soul. God help him: he loved her.

She stirred beneath his gaze and her eyes opened. She smiled up at him with tenderness and he leaned down to kiss her. "Good morning, sweetheart."

"Good morning." The smile disappeared and, even in the gloom, he saw that her skin took on a ghostly greenish pallor. She pushed out of bed, muttering, "I have to use the bathroom." The door slammed closed behind her. The water faucet was turned on full blast, but that didn't hide the sound of her retching.

He pushed himself out of bed and shuffled from the room, wanting to give her privacy. Whatever was wrong with her, she wasn't ready to share it with him. In the kitchen, he started the coffee and dropped a couple of bread slices into the toaster. From this part of the house, he couldn't hear her being sick, which both relieved and worried him all the more.

If they were younger, he would think Claire was pregnant. Though he had missed most of dead Alice's pregnancy, he wasn't a complete idiot. He knew that morning sickness was a common side effect. But Claire was in her mid-forties. She had been married for more than twenty years to her first husband, and they had wanted children desperately. She had told Milo herself that she was infertile.

Ruling out the obvious, Milo was left only with more frightening diseases to consider. Cancer was his first thought,

460

but he dismissed it. Cancer didn't cause nausea, did it? His thoughts were interrupted by the sound of toast popping out of the toaster. He buttered it and dug around in the fridge for some jam, finally pulling out some of his daughter-in-law Marla's homemade peach preserves.

Claire appeared in the doorway, still pale but less greenish. "Good morning again."

"Good morning, darling. Can I get you anything?"

"Just toast. No butter."

Milo dropped two more slices in. "I don't mean to irritate you, but have you made a doctor's appointment yet?"

"Yes. But the appointment isn't until February third. Are you working today?" she asked as she sat down at the table.

"No. I have the day off."

"Will I see you at the zoo?"

He turned and looked at her with surprise. "You're not going in, are you?"

"I'm on the schedule. And I feel okay now."

"Maybe you should stay home and rest."

She rolled her eyes. "Yes, Father."

"Stop that. I'm just trying to look after you."

"Don't worry about me, babe. I'll be fine. Are you coming to the zoo or not?"

"Maybe. I'll call you if I decide to come by." He put the dry toast on a plate and carried it to the table before sitting down with his own toast across from her. "Where are you working today?"

"It's Friday, right?"

He nodded.

"I'm scheduled with the orangutans."

"Good. At least you'll be inside and out of the cold."

She smiled sweetly, giving him a glimpse of the woman with whom he fell in love. "Of course, that's still hours away. Maybe we should go back to bed."

"You're not feeling well," he reminded her.

"I'm well enough."

"Flirt."

The smile disappeared, replaced by a worried frown. "What's wrong?"

"I'm not attractive to you anymore, am I?"

"Don't be ridiculous, Claire! You are just as beautiful as

461

the day I met you. More, actually."

She sneered, looking down at her slightly plump body. "Yeah. Right. These fat rolls are so sexy."

"That's not a roll, babe. It's barely a bump."

"You do see it!" her eyes flashed and Milo recognized he had been snared by an angry mood again.

Deciding to be honest, he answered, "Yes, you've gained a little weight. But you are not fat -- not even close. Please, sweetheart...stop beating yourself up."

She dropped the half-eaten slice of bread and left the kitchen. A second later, he heard the bedroom door slam.

Sighing, he stood. He took half a dozen steps toward the bedroom before changing his mind. Turning back, he poured himself a cup of coffee and sat back down at the table.

Milo knocked on the front door of Brian's house. Marla's van was in the driveway, so he was certain she was still at home.

"Milo! What a surprise! The kids aren't home..."

"I didn't come to see them," he said. "I came to talk to you. Do you have a few minutes?"

"Of course." She stepped to one side. "Come in."

He walked past the formal living room and into the family room, sitting down at the large dining table that separated the kitchen from the television.

"Can I get you something to drink? I could make some tea for you."

The aroma of coffee was heavy in the air. "If there's any coffee, I'll have that."

"I think there's a cup left." She detoured into the kitchen and poured him a mug. "Do you need sugar or cream?"

"No, thank you. I like it black."

She carried the cup over and sat down kitty-corner from him. "What's up?"

"It's Claire."

"What's wrong?"

462

"She's in menopause and I don't know how to deal with it."

Marla colored slightly and leaned away. "I don't think I'm--"

"You're the only person I can talk to about this," he pleaded.

She sat up straight and pursed her lips, thinking. "I'm not really qualified to tell you much. I haven't experienced -- that -- for myself yet."

"I know. But I'm just looking for a woman's insight."

"You've been through this before, Milo. You probably know more than me."

"What? You mean with d...Alice?" He looked down at his cup guiltily. "I don't remember much of that."

She narrowed her eyes. "You lived with her -- how can you not remember?"

"I was working a lot back then."

She stared hard at him. Finally, she relaxed back into her chair. "Fine. You don't remember. I had a few conversations with her about it."

"You talked to Alice about menopause?"

"She would call in tears asking to talk to Brian. She told me it felt like her life was ending...at least the important part of it. She regretted only having one child -- she wanted more, but told me that you didn't. She advised that I have at least two children."

"And you listened to her?"

"Brian and I already knew we wanted two children. Do you remember when Alice Marie was born and Alice came out to stay with us for a few months?"

Milo remembered those two months of peace well. He had been free to watch what he wanted, eat what he wanted, and wear what he wanted. After Alice died, he felt the same way, at least for a while. "Yes."

"She was right in the middle of it then -- hot flashes that made her look like she was melting, sudden mood changes, uncontrollable emotions. Every time she looked at the children, she burst into tears. She could only hold it together when Brian was home. She didn't want him to know anything was wrong."

"I wonder if she hid it from me, too," he said hopefully.

463

"Not likely." She folded her arms across her chest. "She told me that you seemed oblivious to her pain."

Milo, fearing he had damaged his only recently repaired relationship with Marla by asking this question, drank the rest of his coffee. "I'm sorry I bothered you with this. Please forgive me."

She dropped her arms to her sides and widened her eyes. "I'm sorry I haven't been much help, Milo. Listen -- I like you. I never heard your side of the story when it came to your relationship with Alice. Alice was so good to me, it's hard not to think of her as the wronged person in your marriage."

Milo smiled kindly at his daughter-in-law. "Alice was a good woman. We just weren't meant to spend our lives together, and we both paid for our mistake."

"Don't give up on Claire, Milo. She really loves you. What she's going through...it's not easy. It's probably twice as hard on a woman who never had children -- if she wanted children, menopause must feel like failure. Heck, even if she never wanted them, it's probably enough to make a woman think twice about her choices."

"Thanks, Marla. You've been a lot of help." He pushed away from the table and stood up.

Marla stood too, wrapping her arms around him. "You're a wonderful grandfather. Alice Marie loves you more than anyone else...including her father and me. Because you are good to her, I will always be here for you."

Claire was watching Duchess, the oldest of the zoo's orangutans, play with her granddaughter when Milo walked into the enclosure. He slipped up behind her and put his hands over her eyes. "Guess who?"

"I thought you were going to call before you came."

"I wanted to surprise you."

"I'm not doing so well with surprises these days."

He wrapped his arms around her from the back. "How are you feeling?"

"Better than this morning."

"I'm glad. I want to take you out to dinner tonight."

"You don't have to do that."

"I know. I want to."

Duchess switched her focus from the small orangutan to the people inside the building. She put one long-fingered hand against the window that separated the two species. Claire broke away from Milo and walked to the window, pressing her hand against Duchess's. Milo could almost swear that the animal smiled at them.

"She was raised by humans for a while when she was young," Claire said. "I think she misses the contact."

"What must we look like to her?"

"Family, I think." She straightened and turned back to him.

"You seem so calm here."

"The animals make me feel more normal. I don't know why."

He hadn't planned to have this conversation at the zoo, but the moment felt right. "Are you happy?"

"Right now? Yes, of course."

"No. I mean, are you happy with me?"

She gave him a half-smile. "Well, there are still things I plan to improve, but overall--"

"You know what I mean, Claire," he said softly.

"Yes, Milo, I am happy with you. The way I've been lately...it has nothing to do with you. This is all me."

"Are you sad because you never had children?"

"Where did that come from?"

Not wanting to admit he had talked to Marla about her, he said, "I'm just guessing here."

She sat down on the bench and he sat next to her. They both stared straight ahead; Milo didn't want to risk looking in her eyes.

"I wanted a child. Just one would have been enough -- no point in getting greedy. I envy Beryl and her flock of children," she admitted.

"But you wouldn't want one now, right?"

She shrugged. "In theory, I wouldn't be upset about it. But then I think about how old we would be when he or she finally graduated from high school." She laughed. "Can you imagine, Milo? You'd be in your late seventies! That's an old dad."

He laughed along with her. "Ancient."

"So no, even though I wish I'd had children, I know that having them at this age would be...difficult, to say the least. Besides, I'm infertile. Twenty years of marriage to Dorsey proved that."

"You're sure it wasn't Dorsey who was infertile?"

She looked at him sharply. "What are you thinking?"

"I was just curious."

"Don't worry, Milo. I'm not going to trap you into marriage with a baby," she said bitterly.

"You wouldn't have to trap me, Claire. I love you."

She looked away from him again. "I know. Did you bring a camera today?"

He patted the lower pocket of his Guayabera. "Of course."

"Go take some photos. I'll meet you on the bridge at four-fifteen."

He wrapped an arm around her and squeezed, kissing her cheek. "Sounds good." He left her sitting on the bench and willed himself not to look back as he left the building.

Night Life

The Forbidden Fruit

"Sorry about the short notice," Claire said as Sondra opened her door.

"No problem. It's the first day of the month; I was expecting you. Come in!"

"Thanks, but I don't want to intrude." Claire stepped inside despite her words.

"You're not intruding. I have a fresh pot of coffee and some hazelnut creamer waiting for us." Sondra ushered her further into the condo. "Sit down. Make yourself comfortable, okay?" She went into the kitchen.

Claire stepped into the living area. Spotting the large painting of the hard-candy cathedral, she went to stand in front of it. "This is beautiful," she commented when she heard Sondra approaching from behind.

"Thank you. Ethan and I bought it at a gallery opening we attended a few weeks ago."

"It adds so much to the room. I should have bought some art when I lived here."

"You had other things on your mind."

"True." Claire took the cup of coffee Sondra held out to her. "This smells wonderful."

"Are you hungry? I have some bagels too."

"I had breakfast already," she lied. The dry toast she made for herself that morning had turned her stomach. She fed most of it to Taz, who seemed more than happy to play garbage disposal for his mistress.

Sondra settled herself into one of the armchairs. "How is Milo doing at the bar?"

"He loves it," Claire answered. She lowered herself into the sofa.

Sondra gave her a strange half-smile. "What's going on with you?"

"What do you mean?"

"I don't mean to insult you, but you've put on a few pounds. I mean, I only saw you a few weeks ago, and I could swear--"

"I'm in menopause. All I have to do is look at a cookie and I gain a pound."

"You should start exercising. It will make you feel better

and help your body metabolize the food you eat more completely."

"I've never had this problem before." She sipped the coffee, frowned, and set it on the nearby end table.

"Naturally thin, huh? You poor thing," Sondra said sarcastically.

Claire laughed. "It's not like I could control my genes."

"Now your hormones are in control. Welcome to the rest of your life."

"Thanks." She picked up the coffee cup and took another sip. Her stomach lurched as if it alone were at sea. "Excuse me for a moment," she said, awkwardly pushing herself off the couch and quick-stepping to the bathroom. She just managed to lift the seat on the toilet when the coffee and the few bites of toast expelled themselves from her body.

A soft knock came from outside. "Are you okay in there?"

"Just a little nauseous," she called back. "I'll be out in a minute." She let herself sink to the edge of the bathtub as she tried to calm her nerves and recover her strength. She flushed the toilet and rinsed her mouth out at the sink before exiting.

Back in the living room, she found a small plate of saltines and a Sprite waiting for her. "Thanks," she said, smiling weakly and sitting back down.

"Have you been to the doctor, Claire?"

"No, but I have an appointment on Friday."

"So how do you know you're in menopause?"

"I'm forty-five, I can't stop eating, I'm gaining weight, and everything seems off. My body feels weird. And my periods have stopped."

"And, apparently, you're nauseous."

"Off and on."

Sondra moved to the sofa and took one of Claire's hands in both of hers. "Sweetie, you're pregnant."

"Don't be ridiculous!" she laughed. "I'm forty-five!"

"Yes, you are. Which is why you need to get to a doctor as soon as possible."

"What makes you so sure?"

"Um...your symptoms?"

"All of them could be related to menopause," Claire

answered staunchly. "I looked them up on the Internet."

"Fine, Dr. Combs. Whatever you say."

"There's no need to be snide. You're not a doctor either."

"True. But there's an easy way to test my theory: buy a pregnancy test."

Claire swallowed hard. Her hand shot out and took one of the saltines. "What if you're right?"

"Then you tell Milo and live happily ever after."

"I couldn't."

"What do you mean? Of course you could! Milo has every right to know if he's going to be a father."

"After what dead Alice did to him?" Claire reached for the Sprite and took a swig to wash down the cracker. "I won't force him into a marriage."

Sondra leaned away from Claire. "Are you crazy? He loves you. I'm sure he wants to marry you."

"If I'm pregnant, how can I know that for sure?" She felt her stomach roll again.

"You're turning green. Calm down. I'm going to get my checkbook."

Claire took a deep breath. In her mind's eye, all she could see was the look of horror Milo would wear if she were pregnant. It was out of the question; she couldn't have a baby now. The hard-candy cathedral drew her eye and she focused on that. Every time she blinked, though, a horrifying glimpse of the future inserted itself behind her eyelids: an unplanned wedding, the disapproval of Brian and his family, a small mountain of dirty diapers, Milo growing old trying to support a family he never planned to have, Milo dying while their child was still young, her own death before the child was grown. She couldn't catch her breath; she sucked in air, but it didn't seem to reach her lungs.

"Oh, my God! Claire! Calm down!"

Claire could hear Sondra but, still struggling to breathe, she couldn't answer her. What if they had a child with medical problems? Wasn't that more likely with older parents? She had read somewhere that old fathers were more likely to produce offspring with autism. Older mothers were more likely to have Down's Syndrome babies. She would be trapping them both in a life of regret, worry, and fear.

"Breathe into this," Sondra said, forcing a bag into Claire's hands. When she didn't respond, Sondra slapped her. "Claire! Breathe into the bag!"

Startled, Claire lifted the bag to her mouth and breathed. Her mind torn from the litany of terrors, she focused on the sound of the air rushing into her lungs and out again.

"I know this is scary. I could be wrong -- but you need to find out sooner rather than later. Trust me, waiting isn't going to make the situation any better." Sondra was making comforting circles on her back with one hand. "This could be a good thing, you know."

"This is a disaster," Claire said flatly.

When her breathing returned to normal, she took Sondra's check and left.

Her stomach continued to roll as she drove toward Sun City. She almost went straight home, but Sondra's words compelled her to stop at the drugstore. She felt like a fool as she walked to the back of the store and picked up the pregnancy test off the bottom shelf.

A clerk walked by and gave her a sympathetic smile. "Daughter problems?"

"What?"

"You think your daughter is...you know..."

She closed her eyes and sighed.

The clerk patted her on the shoulder and said quietly, "Don't worry. Every parent goes through it." She walked away, leaving Claire holding the test.

"This is ridiculous," she muttered. But Sondra had a point: her symptoms did line up with pregnancy. She wanted to call Beryl and confer with her about the problem, but she knew her sister already had her hands full, what with her husband and kids as well as their critically ill father, who remained, teetering, on the edge of death. If Beryl had an inkling of Claire's situation, it would be just like her to drop everything and fly to Phoenix. No -- Claire would have to weather this storm on her own. She turned to walk to the front of the store, only to see Sax standing at the end of the aisle, looking over some slipper socks in a bin. She jammed the test between her hip and her purse. Deciding that trying to dodge out of his line of sight might only serve to raise his suspicions, she walked toward him. "Hi, Sax."

"Claire! What a surprise! How are you?"

"Oh, you know. Same old, same old. How are you? Are you enjoying your time away from the bar?"

He shrugged. "Not as much as I thought I would. But I'm getting better at this 'relaxing' thing. I'm surprised you aren't at the zoo."

"I usually have Wednesdays off."

"I didn't realize that. I'll schedule Milo off on Wednesdays too from now on."

"No," she said quickly, "don't do that. I run errands and do things Milo doesn't like to do. I saw Sondra this morning, as a matter of fact. I had to pick up the rent."

"How is she?" he asked, leaning against the nearby shelves, clearly settling in for a longer conversation than she wanted to have.

"Good. She looks good. Hey, I hate to do this, but I really need to run."

"Oh. Sorry about that. I didn't mean to hold you up."

The sadness in his expression made her regret her words. "You know what? I'm not doing anything that important. You want to get some coffee or something?"

"I'd like that. Ever since Sondra moved to town and Bob...well, you know, I've been lonely." He went back to the socks bin. "I came in here just to kill a little time. I couldn't stand my empty house one more minute." His face lit up. "Hey! Why don't you come to my house? Do you like tea? I'd love to have you over."

Not seeing the harm in it, she answered, "Yes, I'd like that."

"Great. Do you know where it is or do you need to follow me there?"

"I'll follow you. First, I need to pick up some prescriptions back at the pharmacy," she lied. "Wait here for me?"

"I'll be around here. Let me know when you're ready to leave."

She walked to the pharmacy checkout, where the same clerk who had talked to her earlier now stood.

"May I help you?"

"Yes, please," she said, slipping the pregnancy test out from between her purse and her hip. "I need to pay for this."

"This is the pharmacy, ma'am. If you don't have any medicine to pick up, I can't help you."

"Please." She bit her lip for a moment, hoping the woman would relent. Unfortunately, she seemed stalwart in her position. Claire lied again. "Please help me out. My daughter's father is in the store, and I don't want him to know about the test. He's got a terrible temper and I'm afraid of what he will do to us if he finds out."

The clerk looked over Claire's shoulder and asked, "Is that him?"

Claire turned her head as far as she could without changing her body position. Sax was thirty feet away, in front of the sleep aids. "Yes," she whispered.

"My goodness! Do you need help? I have a friend--"

"No," Claire cut her off. "Right now, all I need is to get out of this store without him finding out about the test."

"He's walking this way."

"Help me, please." She shoved the test hard and it slid across the counter and onto the ground at the clerk's feet.

She felt Sax's hand touch her shoulder lightly. "Sorry to interrupt, but could you tell me which sleep aid is best?" he asked to the clerk.

"I'm sorry, sir, but you'll need to wait your turn," she answered, her eyes narrowed.

"It's all right. I can wait a moment."

"Thank you, Claire. I have a friend who swears by Tylenol PM, but I don't know anything about these drugs. I've never needed them before," he explained apologetically.

"I'm not surprised," the clerk answered, rolling her eyes at Claire.

Sax, who had been gesturing toward the drugs, didn't notice her disgust. "Yeah. Up until a couple of months ago, I slept like a baby."

"Tylenol PM is a pain reliever and a sleep aid. If you don't have any pain, I recommend Unisom."

Sax saluted her with the box. "Thanks. I'll try that.

Claire, I'll be up front when you're done."

"Okay."

"I'll just get those prescriptions for you," the clerk said loudly. As soon as Sax was out of the area, she leaned down and picked up the box. "Let me just ring that up for you."

Claire had seen the high-walled patio homes from the street a number of times since she moved in with Milo. The recluse in her found them intriguing. As she walked through the garage and into Sax's kitchen, she was delighted to find the house was bright and airy, with plenty of garden-view windows. "This is lovely!" she exclaimed. For the first time all day, her thoughts were turned outward and her worries seemed to disappear.

"Thank you, Claire!" Sax opened his arms widely and said, "Let me give you the grand tour." He led her into the living room filled with low Asian-style furniture and one conspicuous roll-top desk. "This is the living room, of course. I don't spend a lot of time in here, though. I've never been a living-room kind of person." He walked on, leading her to a tatami-matted dining area filled with Asian pottery and sculpture.

Claire crossed the room to the jade dragon figurine. "This is beautiful, Sax. I had no idea you were a fan of Japanese culture."

"I fell in love with Japan years ago. I always thought I should have been Japanese; I think there was a cosmic screw-up."

Claire laughed. "Maybe there's a Japanese woman who dreams of bartending in Arizona."

He looked at her sideways and smiled broadly. "I think we're going to be great friends." He folded her arm over his. "Let me show you the rest of the place." He led her through the house and out onto the back patio, where the swimming pool gleamed in the bright winter sun. "Shall we sit out here?"

"That sounds wonderful," Claire agreed.

"Have a seat. Relax. Are you hungry?"

473

Her stomach grumbled at the words. "Actually, I am."

"I'll make us a light lunch and some tea. You just sit there and soak up the sun. You could use some -- you look pale."

He disappeared into the house and she allowed herself to relax into one of the wicker lounge chairs near the pool. She loved the high walls; all she could see above her was the square of blue sky. This home could have been a hundred miles from its nearest neighbor. She wished that Milo's home felt as remote.

She pushed her hands along her expanding stomach, attempting to discern by touch alone whether the bulge was caused by menopause or pregnancy. Having never been pregnant, she had no frame of reference. Despite the many breakfasts she had lost in her morning bouts with nausea, she still managed to consume more than her fair share of calories. The craving for kettlecorn overwhelmed her almost every time she worked at the zoo. In recent months, she had developed the habit of eating cookies and milk before bed. The likelihood of the bulge being anything other than the result of her poor eating habits was laughable. She forced out a chuckle at her own ridiculousness.

"What's so funny?" Sax asked, appearing at her side with a tray of fruit, crackers, cheese, and tea. He set it in the middle of the small table to her left and dragged another of the wicker chairs over to the other side of the table.

"Nothing. Sondra suggested something this morning and I just realized how completely ridiculous it is."

"Sondra is nothing if not unique. What did she suggest?"

Claire shook her head. "No. It's too silly. Besides, I want to get to know you better. Tell me all about you."

"I don't share well."

"Come on," she cajoled. "You were a cop, right?"

"Back in Jersey. A lifetime ago."

"Did you know you were gay then?"

"Honey, I've known I was gay forever. Some people just know -- like we came out of the womb knowing we weren't the same as the other little boys."

"Why did you choose to be a cop?"

"I couldn't think of a better place to hide."

She put a few slices of apple and cheese on her plate and set the small plate on her lap. "That's sad."

Sax shook his head. "Not really. When I was young there were only two choices: hide and be safe or be a flamboyant victim."

"Weren't you lonely?"

"Sometimes. I wasn't always alone, though. I had lovers over the years."

"No one permanent? Steve and Adam seem so happy together..."

"I never found anyone I wanted to spend forever with."

"What about Bob?"

"Yes," he admitted. "I thought maybe, for a minute, I'd found that person. But it didn't work out. Let's talk about something else. How are you and Milo doing?"

She shrugged. "Up and down. It's no pleasure cruise living with me these days."

"Milo mentioned that you've been moody lately."

Frowning, she picked up her teacup. "I don't want to bore you with my troubles."

"Your husband was a Navajo, wasn't he?"

"Half-Navajo," she corrected.

"How did you meet?"

She smiled, remembering the tanned soldier who followed her from rodeo to rodeo. "I was a barrel racer back in Oklahoma. He asked for my autograph after a rodeo about a hundred years ago."

"Not that long ago."

"No, maybe not. But it seems like it."

"You still miss him."

"I'll always miss him." She sipped her tea. "But if you're asking if I really love Milo, the answer is yes. I do. Dorsey was the other half of my soul, but I want to spend the rest of my life with Milo."

Sax nodded slowly. "I understand. I've never had that, you know. I look at guys like Steve and Adam and wonder what I did wrong. Why didn't I find that kind of love in my life?"

"You just haven't found it yet. There's still time."

"Not much," he grumbled. Before she could counter his comment, he asked, "You're not a native Arizonan either?"

"No, though sometimes it seems like I've been here

forever."

"I've never been on a horse," Sax commented.

"I haven't been on one in decades."

"Were you any good?"

"My grandfather was sure I was going to be the top barrel racer in the country," she smiled.

"Why did you give it up?"

She shrugged and looked toward the sky. "Life had other plans for me."

Their conversation meandered through the years of their lives as they sampled different combinations of fruit, cheese and crackers.

"Why did you agree to hire Milo?" she asked as their afternoon wound to a close.

"I don't know," he admitted. "I think he just caught me at a weak moment. I know what it's like to think your life has lost all purpose."

"What do you mean?"

"When I had to leave the force, I was sure my life was over. I seriously considered eating my gun. My partner -- the one guy who had always known my secret -- talked me out of it. He reminded me that life is a journey and the road sometimes gets bumpy or takes a detour. Milo needed a detour."

She left Sax's house about an hour before he was supposed to be at the Brass Monkey to relieve Milo. For the first time in weeks, she felt at peace. Talking with Sax had brought her to a mellowness that had been absent for a while. She glanced at the pregnancy test, still wrapped in its Walgreens plastic bag, and considered returning it to the store. Some little doubt stabbed through her tranquility and insisted that she take it home instead.

Thanks to Sax's never-ending pots of tea, she wasn't going to have any trouble peeing on the stick. At home, she carried the package with her to the bathroom and opened it. Inside were two tests and a sheet of instructions. The sheet said the tests worked best in the mornings, but she disregarded that advice and pulled the cap off one of them.

Within a few seconds, she stood in front of the bathroom mirror watching the test develop. When the unmistakable plus sign appeared in the window, she dropped the stick, which rattled around the sink before coming to a rest upside down. With one finger, she flipped it over, praying that her eyes were playing tricks on her. There it was, though: a plus sign. Desperate, she picked up the directions and read them over again, just to be certain she hadn't done the test improperly. Maybe taking the test in the afternoon sometimes resulted in false positives.

Just the opposite, of course, was true. The paper fluttered to the floor as she leaned on and slid down the bathroom wall. Taz pushed the door open and came to sit next to his mistress, who was pregnant and unmarried at forty-five.

Night Life

Beer and Bite

Running into Claire at the drugstore had been a stroke of luck, as far as Sax was concerned. As much as he had wanted to give Milo a sense of purpose, he hated having his schedule -- the one he had kept almost since the day he moved to Arizona -- disrupted. At least Claire kept him occupied for a few hours.

After escorting Milo's girlfriend out of the house, he changed into his bar uniform of black pants and a white button-down shirt. Even though he was alone again, the lingering joy of having company cheered him as he gathered the dishes and carried them to the sink. Glancing at the clock, he decided to head to the bar early and test Milo's bartending knowledge.

The regulars greeted him with smiles and waves as he pushed through the swinging door.

"Sax!" Milo exclaimed, smiling. "You're early."

"Not very. How was the day?"

"Slow but steady."

"Why didn't you tell me Claire had Wednesdays off?"

Milo ducked his head and gave him a sheepish grin. "Does it matter?"

"Maybe if you spent some time together, your relationship would improve."

Milo stiffened. "If you don't mind, I could do without the relationship advice."

"Fine. Get me a Sake Bomb." Sax sat down on Sondra's stool.

Milo turned away to pull the beer. Over his shoulder, he asked, "You ran into Claire today?"

"At the Walgreens. She was picking up a prescription."

Setting the beer on the bar, he picked up the bottle of sake from the liquor selection behind him. He frowned as he poured a shot of the rice wine. "Claire's not on any medication."

"Maybe she was picking it up for you."

"Yeah. That must be it." He dropped the shot glass into the beer and slid the concoction toward Sax.

Sax sipped it. "Nice. Thanks."

"If that was a test, you're going to have to come up with

478

something more challenging."

Sax did his best to look indignant. "This happens to be my favorite drink."

Milo shrugged his eyebrows disbelievingly. "Are you any better?"

"What do you mean?"

"I mean, are you adapting to your new schedule?"

"Well enough," he lied. "Why don't you go home? That's where Claire was headed."

"Why are you so worried about us, Sax? You hardly know Claire."

"We spent the afternoon together," he said casually.

"You and Claire?"

"Yes. She came to my house and we had lunch."

"Is there something I should know?"

"Don't be ridiculous." Sax sipped his drink. "I was lonely and she didn't have anything important to do -- since you were working."

"Don't lay that on me. She's the one who likes to run errands on Wednesdays. Just because I don't want to do that doesn't make me a bad boyfriend."

"Whatever you say."

Milo pulled the dishcloth off his shoulder and laid it on the bar. "I'm going home."

"Good." Sax took one more sip of his drink and stood up. "Have a good night."

"Yeah," Milo said, grabbing his keys out of the drawer, "you too."

Sax slid the drink into the fridge and took his place behind the bar, happily picking up the abandoned towel.

No longer welcome at the gym, Sax was forced to change another habit. Luckily, as a resident of Sun City, he was pleased to discover he had access to a state-of-the-art gym just a mile and a half from his home. He soon replaced his old routine with a twenty-minute jog to his new gym, a vigorous hour-long workout, and a quick walk from the gym to the Fry's, which was only five minutes away. He walked the aisles of the grocery store, dodging old men and women with the graceful agility of a much younger person.

He bought fresh fruit and vegetables and watched for other men shopping alone. One day he ran into the waiter from Denny's -- Sax thought his name was Mike -- but he was shopping with another man. He greeted them both and moved on with his day.

When he finished shopping, he walked home and put away his groceries. He changed out of his gym clothes, made his bed, and fixed himself breakfast, which he ate by the pool.

Afterward, he dressed and went to one of the nearby strip malls, wandering in and out of the thrift shops, boutiques, and small markets. That was how he had run into Claire -- he had been exploring the L-shaped strip mall that framed the Walgreens. Most of the time, though, he didn't talk to anyone on these solitary jaunts. Not surprisingly, there were more women than men in the shops, and the women tended to shop in pairs. Occasionally, he would have a conversation with a store manager or owner.

Sometimes -- maybe once a week or so -- he would see someone who drank at the Brass Monkey. He never initiated a conversation with them, though -- not many of his regulars were anxious to be friends with their bartender.

About a week after running into Claire, he dialed Sondra's number. Even though they were friends, he feared intruding on her happiness, especially in his current state of mind.

"Sax! Where have you been?" she answered cheerily.

"I could ask the same. I've missed you."

"Are you okay? You sound unhappy."

"I'm fine. Do you have time for lunch today?"

She hesitated.

"If you don't, that's okay. I know this is short notice--"

"Of course I have time for you. Where?"

They made plans to meet at a Greek place located close to halfway between them. Sax had never been there; he was shocked to find it was located in a rundown strip mall. Inside, a brusque waitress seated him at one of the few tables and brought him a menu and a glass of water. He glanced over the menu before allowing his eyes to take in the restaurant as a whole. The place was a dive -- not the sort of restaurant he would have chosen at all. But the smells coming from the kitchen convinced him to wait for Sondra.

A few minutes later, Sondra sashayed through the door in tight jeans and a beautiful green sweater with a belt around the middle. The waitress greeted her with enthusiasm. "Miss Sondra! So good to see you again! Where is Mr. Ethan?"

"He's working, Melina. I'm meeting a friend."

Melina, smiling now, led Sondra to his table.

"I bring you bread right away. You want hummus?"

"Yes, thank you," Sondra smiled brightly at the woman, who hustled away. "It's so good to see you, Sax!" she said, taking his hands between hers. "I've missed you."

"Not enough to come to the bar," he answered, immediately regretting his reproachful tone.

"I've been busy. I just had a fitting for a new Sunrise Aeon costume last week." She inflated her cheeks. "I look like a balloon animal in it."

"That couldn't possibly be true."

"I promise you," she answered, raising one hand in oath.

"How are things with Ethan?"

"Good," she answered, though her voice seemed a bit too high for it to be true.

"You can tell me the truth."

She sighed. "To be honest, I'm a little worried."

"About what?"

She waved the thought away. "It's nothing important." She told him about meeting Ethan's friends and the new tattoo Ethan had Arlo ink on his bicep. She blushed when she talked about that.

Sax told her about running into Claire and having lunch with her.

"How did she seem to you?"

"Fine. I don't know her that well, but she was relaxed and chatty."

"When was this?"

"The same day you saw her, I think. She said she'd seen you that morning for the rent."

"I guess I was wrong."

The waitress set a basket of homemade pitas and a

481

bowl of hummus on the table along with their drinks.

Sax picked up one of the round pieces of bread and asked, "Wrong about what?"

Sondra laughed and shook her head. "Nothing. It was a ridiculous thought, anyway."

"Now I'm curious. Come on -- share. I won't tell anyone."

She looked around exaggeratedly, as if she expected the paparazzi to be following her every move. "You know how Claire told Milo she was in menopause?"

"Yeah?"

"I had another theory -- as a matter of fact, the opposite of what she thought."

"You thought she was pregnant?!" he exclaimed.

"Shush! Geez, Sax, let's just announce that to the whole world."

"Sorry about that," he half-whispered. "She's a little old for that, isn't she?"

"She's only forty-five. It's not unheard of."

"Did you tell her what you thought?"

"Yeah. Actually, I thought she was going to run home and take a test right away."

Sax chewed a piece of the bread thoughtfully before remarking, "I did run into her in a drugstore. But she was picking up a prescription, not buying a test."

"Are you sure?"

The waitress came back to the table, interrupting their conversation. After placing their lunch orders, Sondra repeated her question: "Are you sure she didn't have a test?"

"I didn't inspect her purchases. I suppose she could have."

"But she was calm at your house?"

"Yes. Completely."

"Then I must have been wrong." Sondra changed the subject, talking about the upcoming trip to Orlando with Ethan for the convention.

"First class? The publisher must think they have a real winner on their hands," Sax commented, impressed.

"Ethan is their golden boy -- he can do no wrong as far as they're concerned."

"Why do they want you involved? Wouldn't it make

more sense to hire a younger actress to play Sunrise at the conventions?"

"The film has such a following that they are hoping to capitalize on its popularity -- a built-in audience, if you will."

"Ethan's idea?"

She smiled. "I'm pretty sure he's the one who sold them on it." She sipped her drink and dipped a piece of bread in the hummus. "Are you dating anyone new?"

He shook his head. "I think I need to adapt to being single."

"Sax, you've spent your life alone. How much adapting could you need?"

"I know it's bizarre, but just those six weeks with Bob altered everything about my life. What if he was my last chance at a real relationship?"

"Don't be ridiculous. You're not even seventy yet!"

"That's the thing about love, Sondra -- you never know who will be your last lover."

"Bob is not that guy," she said resolutely. "I'll find you a date and all of last year will be a distant memory before you know it."

"Don't, please. I'm not ready."

The waitress returned with their plates of moussaka and spanakopita. "Everything good, Miss Sondra?"

"Delicious, as usual. Thank you, Melina."

"Wave if you need anything," she said, walking away from the table. She never made eye contact with Sax.

"Strange woman," he commented.

"They're nice enough once they get to know you."

"This is a restaurant. Shouldn't they be pleasant to all of their customers?"

She shrugged. "They've always been nice to me." She inhaled deeply over her plate. "My God, I swear this is the best Greek food outside of Athens."

Sax had to admit, it smelled delicious. He dug a fork into the savory eggplant dish before him and let the slightly sweet, slightly bitter flavor overwhelm him.

"Have you ever considered getting a tattoo?" Sondra asked.

"How do you know I don't have one?" he teased.

"Do you?"

483

He smirked. "No, I don't."

"They're very popular with the younger crowd these days."

"Do you have one?"

"Not yet," she said, "but I'm considering it."

"Really?"

She nodded. "Ethan's friend Easter pointed out some lovely designs when I was there."

"What does Ethan think?"

"He likes the idea. The only thing I worry about is what it will look like when I get old."

"You're already--"

"Don't even think it," she warned, her eyes flashing.

"If you're worried about the elasticity of your skin, I think it's less of a problem than you imagine."

She wobbled her head from side to side. "I might do it. Maybe after I've thought about it some more."

Sax tried to stay out of the Brass Monkey, especially after his terse conversation with Milo. He liked the guy and he liked Claire, too. With Sondra enmeshing herself even more deeply into Ethan's world, Sax suspected he would need Milo and Claire's friendship all the more.

A day or two after his lunch with Sondra, he made a point of apologizing to Milo.

"What for?"

"The other day when I put my nose where it didn't belong. Your relationship with Claire is just that -- your relationship. I shouldn't have interfered."

"Forget about it, Sax. You want a drink?"

Sax glanced at the clock; he was fifteen minutes early for his shift. They had settled into a routine: Milo worked from opening until five and Sax worked until closing during the weekdays. Milo came in for a few hours on Saturday night, just to help out with the crowd. Otherwise, the weekends were Sax's exclusive domain. "Nah," he answered.

The next day though, he found himself at the bar

earlier. Milo pulled a beer for him and he settled in to watch *Jeopardy* with the Professor.

And so it continued, every day a little earlier, until, at last, Sax could be found nursing a beer on Sondra's old stool from three until five every weekday, matching wits with the other regulars and keeping Milo company.

Night Life

Royal Flush

At a little before ten o'clock on February third, Dr. Reynart's nurse called Claire from the waiting room to have her vital statistics taken. Stepping on the scale, she watched as the nurse edged the weight higher than she could ever remember it going. She paled.

"Are you all right, Claire?" the nurse asked as she wrote the impossibly high number on her chart. "You look like you're going to be sick."

She swallowed the nausea down. "I'm fine. I'll be fine."

The nurse led her to a treatment room and closed the door. "Now, are you here for a specific complaint today or an annual checkup?"

"I'm pregnant," Claire blurted.

The nurse looked at her, then back at the paperwork. "Women often think that when they first start menopause."

"I took a home pregnancy test two days ago. It was positive."

"False positives are more common than you might think. Let's take your blood pressure."

Irritated, Claire submitted to the nurse's probes and prods in silence, including a blood draw.

"The doctor will be in shortly."

Claire nodded and the nurse closed the door. She wasn't sure why, but the nurse's words had answered one question: if in fact she was pregnant, she would be keeping the baby. As soon as she acknowledged that fact to herself, she felt better than she had in weeks. Her only worry now was Milo.

"Claire!" Dr. Reynart said as he came through the door. He was tall and thin with a fatherly face and gray hair. His hair had always been gray as far as she knew -- he must have been in his seventies by now.

She smiled. "How are you?"

"Quite well. That's not why we're here though, is it?" He took one long step into the room and sat down on his rolling stool. "Lorita tells me you think you're pregnant."

"I took a test, and it was positive."

"Well, we'll just take a few more," he said in his best bedside manner. "You're how old now?"

486

"Forty-five."

"How are you doing? I know what you went through had to be terribly hard. Have you finished grieving for Dorsey?"

She felt the sting of tears behind her eyes. "I'll never stop grieving. But I've met someone else."

"Were you trying to get pregnant?"

"God, no," she laughed. "I thought I couldn't!"

He nodded. "I have to tell you, Claire, I believe you have a better chance of being dealt a Royal Flush at a casino poker table than you have of being pregnant. And if, by some miracle, you are with child, your troubles have only just begun. Carrying your first child to full term in your forties is no picnic. You run a higher risk of Down's Syndrome, did you know that?"

"Of course. I don't care about that, though."

"You're saying you would want to raise a mentally impaired child? At your age? Who will take care of it when you're gone? Is the father substantially younger than you?"

"No. He's nearly sixty."

"Sixty! There are studies that suggest autism is more common in children with older fathers. Have you ever seen a severely autistic child, Claire? They're practically vegetables!"

"I've done some research. They're making great strides in learning to teach autistic children. Technologies, like the tablet computers, seem to be offering new hope."

"But they'll never be normal," he scoffed.

Claire looked at her feet and took a deep, calming breath. "I've had a few days to think about this, Dr. Reynart. I honestly believed I was in menopause until a friend pointed out that my symptoms looked like pregnancy to her. After years of dreaming of motherhood, I thought that particular dream was out of reach. Now it turns out I have this one chance. And I'm going to take it."

His lips thinned to a line as he rolled to the supply cabinet and took out a small cup with a lid. "Give me a urine sample and we'll do a quick hCG test before we go any further."

She took the cup without another word and went to the restroom to fill it.

A few minutes later, she was back in the exam room, waiting for the doctor to return. She shifted on the exam table, the paper crinkling noisily beneath her.

Dr. Reynart pushed open the door, his forehead creased. "When was your last period, Claire?"

"Around the first of October."

"You waited nearly four months to see a doctor?"

"I thought I was in menopause. I didn't need a doctor to tell me that."

He sighed and dropped onto the rolling stool again. "Lie back on the table and pull up your shirt."

She did as he requested. A moment later, she felt his hands probing her expanding middle.

"Am I pregnant?" she asked, worried that something else might be wrong.

"Yes," he answered. "And if you're really four months along, we need to schedule you for a number of tests to check on the baby's and your health."

Joy flooded through her.

"You've already gotten a Royal Flush. Let's hope you're on a winning streak."

Filled with both exhilaration and terror, Claire drove home from the doctor's office alternating between laughter and tears. She wanted to tell someone -- anyone would have been fine. Anyone, that is, besides Milo, Sondra, or Sax.

Pulling into the driveway, she nearly skipped into the house. Looking around at her home, she realized with a start that, in less than six months, she would have to move. Sun City had strict rules about children -- they weren't allowed. No one under the age of eighteen could live in Sun City year round. The thought sobered her. She sat down in one of the kitchen chairs. Taz came to her and rested his chin on her foot sullenly, as if he knew life was about to change and he didn't approve.

"Don't worry, boy," she said, ruffling his fur with her other foot. "I won't let anything happen to you."

Milo wouldn't be home for a few hours. She decided she could safely call her sister Beryl.

"Hello?"

"This is Claire," she said.

"I can see that. Your picture came up on the phone," Beryl answered, sounding frazzled. Claire knew she had been stretching herself thin since their father was diagnosed.

"Is everything okay?"

"As fine as it ever is. I tried to call you the other day. You didn't pick up."

Claire remembered. She hadn't answered because she hadn't wanted to worry Beryl. "I've been busy."

"What if I had been calling to tell you Dad was dead?" she scolded. "How can I get hold of you if you won't take my calls?"

"Send me a text," she quipped.

"Not funny."

"No, I guess not."

"Next time, at least call me back."

"You didn't leave a message." Claire tapped her nails against the table, anxious for the conversation to move forward.

"But you knew I called." Beryl sighed. "Why are you calling now?"

"I was returning your call from last week."

"Very funny. You're a regular laugh riot today."

"I have some news."

"You're getting married?!"

"No. I don't think so."

"Oh. Sorry. Is everything okay with you and Milo?"

"For now."

"What does that mean?"

"Sit down, Beryl." Taz sat up and looked at her with accusation in his big, round eyes.

"Okay. I'm sitting. What's going on?"

"I'm pregnant."

"What? Oh, my God! What? Really? Are you sure?"

"Relatively."

There was a pause on the line before Beryl asked warily, "Have you seen the doctor?"

"I just came from Dr. Reynart's office. They did a urine test and it was positive. He told me the blood test would be more conclusive."

"I've never had a urine test be wrong. You're pregnant. I can't believe it! That's such great news! I'm so happy for you and Milo."

"Milo doesn't know."

"But you're telling him tonight, right?"

Claire paused. "I don't know."

"Claire," Beryl said sternly, "you've got to tell him."

"I don't know if I can," Claire admitted. "His first wife trapped him into marriage when she got pregnant with his son. I don't want him to resent me the way he still resents her. Did you know he calls her 'dead Alice'? I mean, if I die tomorrow, will I become 'cremated Claire'?"

"Probably not," Beryl reasoned. "You'd just be 'dead Claire.' You have to tell him about the baby, though. It's not something you can hide long term. At some point in the next eight--"

"Five."

"You're four months along? And you just realized you're pregnant?"

"I thought I was in menopause."

"Sometimes I wonder what it's like on your planet."

"Now you're funny."

"Of course I am -- I have plenty of material to work with. Speaking of which, Dad seems to be a little better these days. I think he's holding out for spring."

"What do the doctors say?"

"Not much. One of the hospice nurses told Mom that it's normal for a terminal patient to rally before the end."

"How is she doing?"

"She's Mom. She'll deal with everything in her own way and without ever saying a word about it to either of us."

"Maybe she won't say anything to you, but when he dies, it'll be my fault."

"How can it?"

"If I'm there, the stress of seeing me will kill him. If I'm not, the sorrow of not seeing me will break his heart."

Beryl chuckled. "You've got to let this go, sis."

"It's harder than you think."

"I know. I thought you were infertile."

"So did I. I guess it was Dorsey all along."

"You wanted children, right?"

"Yes. I just didn't want them to be graduating from college at the same time I was applying for Medicare." Claire watched as Taz wandered away, no doubt in search of one of his beds. "Plus, I can't stay in Sun City. They have rules against children."

"Sounds like China."

"It's worse. At least in China you can legally have one child. And they don't throw you out of the country if you have two."

Beryl laughed again. "Hey, I hate to do this, but I need to fix dinner or I'm going to have children gnawing on my ankles while I cook."

"Understood. Love you, sis."

"Love you, too."

Claire ended the call. Overwhelmed with exhaustion, she walked to the bedroom and lay down on the bed, not bothering to take off her clothes. She was asleep within minutes.

Mink Coat and No Manners

Sondra didn't recognize the number, but with Ethan out of town, she didn't want to risk missing his call. "Hello?"

"Sondra, this is Vivian."

Wishing she could hang up, she said, "If you're looking for Ethan, he's in New York this week."

"I know. Could we meet for a drink and a chat?"

"Gee, Vivian, I'm kind of busy..."

"With what?" the woman laughed. "Lounging around your condo drinking coffee? Don't forget, Sondra, I know you better than you know yourself. You haven't left the condo since you drove Ethan to the airport two days ago."

"Why are you spying on me?"

"I have my reasons. I'll tell you what: just to make sure you're comfortable, I'll meet you at the Brass Monkey."

491

"That's a long drive for a chat."

"Trust me, this is a conversation we need to have. Three o'clock."

The audible click told Sondra the call was over.

She dialed Ethan's cell phone. After five rings, his voicemail picked up. "Ethan, call me when you have a few minutes."

She set the phone on the coffee table in front of her and willed it to ring. After an hour, though, she couldn't wait any longer. She showered, dressed, and left the condo to meet Vivian.

Sondra ran into Sax in the Brass Monkey's parking lot. "I'm so glad to see you," she said, throwing her arms around the muscular man.

"Hey! What are you doing here?"

"I'm meeting Ethan's sister."

"All the way out here?"

"She suggested it."

Sax's eyes narrowed. "What's going on?"

"I don't know exactly, but I'm awfully glad you and Milo are close at hand."

Sax hesitated at the door.

"Are you going to open that?"

His mouth set in a grim line, he pulled it open; Sondra stepped inside, waiting a moment for her eyes to adjust to the gloom. In the back booth, she saw the outline of Vivian. Slowly, the details came into focus. In defiance of political correctness, she wore a fur coat and a predator's smile. Sondra moved toward the table cautiously, not taking her eyes off the woman.

"I went ahead and ordered for you," Vivian purred as Sondra slid into the booth. "You're a whiskey sour girl, right?"

Sondra ignored the question. "Why are we here?"

"We need to talk."

Milo walked over and slid their drinks in front of them. "Hi, Sondra," he said. "It's great to see you."

492

"You, too, Milo. How's Claire?"

His face crinkled, suggesting worry even as he said, "She's well."

"You can do old home week after I leave, can't you?" Vivian said pointedly.

"Excuse me." Milo turned away.

"Don't be rude to my friends."

"Oh, I'm sorry. Did I look like I gave a shit about your friends?"

Sondra clenched her teeth.

"I'm here to tell you to break it off with Ethan."

Sondra laughed. "Why would I do that?"

"You'll do it because you love him and you don't want him to go through the pain of being widowed a third time."

"Is that a threat?" Sondra whispered harshly.

A slow smile spread across Vivian's deceptively beautiful face. "Of course not. I'm only speaking of the large age gap between the two of you. With Julia and Astrid, it was reasonable to expect they would live as long as Ethan. With you..."

"Where is this coming from?"

"You haven't heard about poor Patrick?" A crocodile tear rolled down one cheek. Sondra had to admire the artistry of her manufactured grief. "He's in the hospital. On his deathbed, I'm afraid."

The handsome image of Vivian's husband filled her mind. He had so reminded Sondra of her own long-dead love, Bill, that she had stuttered in Patrick's presence. "What's wrong with him?"

"It's his heart. But no matter -- I always knew our time together was -- limited." She sipped her martini delicately. "I can see why you come here. The bartending is more than adequate and the atmosphere has a certain...ambiance. I'm thinking Prohibition-era gin joint. Your mother danced in one of those, didn't she?"

"Don't be ridiculous." Sondra stared at Vivian with hard eyes.

"Oh...that's right. Your mother was a Las Vegas showgirl. And your father was a dirty Jewish accountant."

Sondra's hand flew off the table, hitting the martini glass before her nails scratched across Vivian's face. The

493

drink shattered against the floor.

"Let's face it, Sondra...when it comes right down to it, you aren't worth that ring--" she gestured at the large diamond on Sondra's left hand "--or the risk. Break things off with Ethan. You'll still get your share of the earnings for the Sunrise Aeon books. And Ethan will be free to find someone more suitable." She calmly pulled a compact from her purse and examined the damage Sondra had done: two angry red scratches ran diagonally across her left cheek. She applied a small amount of makeup over the lines and they all but disappeared. "No lasting damage done, now is there?" Flashing Sondra another predatory smile, Vivian scooted out of the booth gracefully and walked out the door, her heels clicking loudly in the silence that surrounded her.

Sax came to her side as soon as the door swung closed. "You okay?"

"I've been better."

Milo, cleaning up the spilled drink, asked, "What was that about?"

"I'm so sorry, Sax, Milo. I didn't mean to break the glass."

"It's okay. Accidents happen." Sax wrapped an arm around her waist and led her to her regular stool. He left her for a moment, soon returning with her barely touched whiskey sour. She picked it up from the bar and tossed it back. The burn of it made her gasp a little, but it also returned her to the present. "You going to tell us what's going on?" Sax asked as Milo came around the end of the bar.

"I think Ethan's sister just threatened my life," she said wonderingly.

"You're not sure?" Milo asked.

"Tell us exactly what she said," Sax requested.

Sondra recited the conversation to her friends. When she finished, she gave a despairing laugh. "This just isn't my year, is it? Or, maybe it is...if I'm not done in by falling lights, I'll end up as just one more in a long line of dead women who loved Ethan."

"How long is that line, exactly?" Sax asked.

She gave them a dry laugh. "Only two deep so far. Of course, Vivian makes a good point: I am a lot older than he is. It's almost a guarantee that I'll be taking a dirt nap long before he will."

"Do you think that's what she meant?"

"It must have been, right? I mean, she couldn't seriously be threatening my life."

Sax and Milo looked at each other.

"Come on now. We have to stop hearing hoof beats and looking for zebras. If it looks like an accident, it probably is one. We all should have learned that lesson last fall." Sondra's brain chose that moment to replay a particularly grisly scene from last November: a cop carrying part of Mildred Kovich's skull as he walked past her. She shivered involuntarily and finished her drink, pushing the empty glass toward Milo.

Milo asked, "Another?"

"Yeah. One more. Don't let me talk you into a third, though; I've got a long drive home."

Milo walked a few steps away to mix the drink, while Sax leaned in conspiratorially. "How many times has Vivian been widowed?"

"How did you know--?"

"It was a guess."

"Once, I think."

"Was he old, like her current husband?"

"No. I saw a picture of him. He was her age."

"What do you know about him?"

"Not much. I think he was foreign. At least, he had a foreign name -- Andros or Carlos, something like that. He looked Mediterranean."

"So, these two siblings have somehow managed to have three dead spouses between them?"

"Four, soon, if you believe what she just told me."

Milo placed the new whiskey sour in front of Sondra. "So, what are we thinking?"

Sondra pursed her lips and stared at her friends. Finally, she said, "Nothing. We aren't thinking this. I can't believe Ethan ever would have harmed his wives. You two don't know him. He is the most charming man I've met since I lost Bill decades ago -- no offense, Milo."

Milo shrugged. "I never claimed to be anything other than a pain in the ass."

She sipped her drink. "Viv and I simply don't get along well. She probably is trying to protect Ethan from who she perceives me to be. If she really meant me harm, why would she have offered to meet me here -- where I have friends and she doesn't? No. That would be a dumb move. I mean, what if something happens to me now? You two would immediately point at her."

"She has a point, Sax," Milo said.

"I have a bad feeling about that woman," Sax answered grumpily. "It's almost like she thrives on danger. Who wears a mink coat these days? We live in Arizona, for God's sake. It's not even weather-appropriate."

Sondra's phone rang and she pulled it out of her purse. "It's Ethan," she said, sliding off the stool. She gestured toward the office, asking with her eyes if she could take the call in there.

Sax turned and grabbed the keys out of the drawer behind him, tossing them to Sondra, who said, "Hello?'

"I just heard your message. Is everything okay?"

She turned the key in the lock and entered the privacy of the dingy office space, closing out the noisy bar behind her. "I'm fine."

"You didn't sound fine. What was wrong?"

She hesitated, not wanting to tell him what his sister had said. "Your sister wanted to meet me for a drink. Patrick is in the hospital."

"I know. Mom called me this morning. How is she holding up?"

"Surprisingly well," she answered, dropping into the old recliner Sax kept in the room. "Considering her husband is on his deathbed..."

"She married him knowing he had a heart condition. They were determined to enjoy the years they were given."

"You're talking like he's already dead."

"I don't mean to sound unfeeling, darling, but he's unlikely to recover."

"That's a shame. I really like Patrick. He seems like a wonderful man."

"Not more wonderful than I am, though, right?" he wheedled.

She giggled. "No, you are too wonderful for words."

"Did you two play nice today? Tell the truth now."

"She rattled me," Sondra admitted. "She told me to

496

leave you because of our age difference."

"That's just the grief talking. Viv doesn't wear her emotions on her sleeve, but I know how much she loves Patrick. When she first met him, Mom and Dad tried to tell her that dating someone so much older guaranteed she would be widowed again."

"Your parents are right, Ethan."

"About Viv and Patrick? Probably."

"No, I mean they are right about big age differences -- like you and me."

"Please. You'll outlive me -- I guarantee it!"

"Be serious." She tapped her fingers against the desk. "You are thirty years younger than me, and I've been a heavy drinker for most of the last two decades."

"You're also a fanatical exercise nut and a woman. Both of those facts would suggest you will live a long time."

"But you exercise too, and you never had a drinking problem."

"Fine. I'll give up exercise and start drinking. I'll shave years off my life. But I'm not giving you up."

She burst into laughter. "You can't do that!"

"Who says so? Listen, Sondra: you're stuck with me."

"Okay," she surrendered. "But don't start drinking or stop exercising. I might just be pickled enough to be the first modern woman to see the far side of a hundred and thirty."

"That's the spirit. I love you madly, Sondra Lane. I'll see you in a few days."

"I love you, too." She ended the call and exited the office, returning the keys to Sax. "Where's Milo?" she asked, glancing around the barroom.

"I sent him home. No point in both of us being here. Did you tell Ethan what Viv said?"

"Yes, and he put me at ease."

"How?" he asked, knitting his eyebrows.

"He says it was her grief talking."

"She didn't seem to be grieving to me."

"She's...different. She hides her emotions well."

"No one is that good at hiding their emotions, Sondra. If she is, then she should have been an actress."

Sondra rolled her glass on its edge, tilting the liquid inside back and forth, before pushing it away. "I'm going home."

"You're not mad at me, are you?"

"For what? Giving me your opinion of a woman I already dislike?" she asked, smiling wryly. "No, Sax, I'm not mad."

"I know you're not too worried about this, but do me a favor. Be careful."

"I will." She stepped off her stool and exited the bar.

Night Life

Sundown

Saturday nights were exhausting, as far as Milo was concerned. How Sax had ever handled them alone, he had no idea. With both of them working, it seemed they could barely keep the glasses filled. Glancing toward Sax, who was gathering the empty glasses from the various surfaces around the barroom, Milo steeled himself for the worst part of this job: latrine duty.

As he headed for the men's room door, Sax called out, "Why don't you just leave that?"

"Are you kidding? I told you I'd clean the bathrooms when you hired me to bartend."

"I know, but it's late and we're both beat."

"If I don't do it now, you'll have to deal with it tomorrow." Milo waved him off. "Go home. I'll take care of this."

Sax yawned. "Thanks, Milo."

As soon as he heard the bolt turn in the lock, Milo remembered that he had meant to talk to Sax about Sondra. Despite his own misgivings about their dulled crime-fighting instincts, he feared Vivian was a true threat to their friend's safety. Next time, he thought.

Pushing open the bathroom door, he groaned. Crumpled paper towels, poor aim, and too many patrons conspired against him. He spent the next two hours cleaning the bathrooms. By the time he locked up and drove home, it was well after midnight. He opened the door quietly, but Taz's bark shattered his attempt at silence. He bent down to pet the elderly pug, who had stopped barking and started snorting happily as soon as he saw Milo. "You're an alarmist, Taz," he said, scratching behind the dog's ears. Taz looked at Milo with something verging on awe, his large eyes wide and his mouth curved into the doggie equivalent of a smile.

Milo loved Claire's dog. Because dead Alice had been a cat person, he hadn't owned a dog since he was a child. Though he wouldn't have selected a pug as a pet, he had to admit that Taz had an excellent personality. "Let's go see if your mom's awake," he said to the dog, who wiggled his tail and followed him into the bedroom. After Taz's barking, Milo had expected to find her with her eyes open; however, he could see her still form under a pile of covers without turning

499

on the lights. To Taz, he whispered, "Bark louder next time."

Sitting on the end of the bed, he sighed. Claire hadn't said more than two sentences at one time to him all week. Every time he looked at her, she averted her eyes, as if she were afraid even that much connection would be dangerous. He knew talking to her tonight would have been pointless, but he still wished that she were awake. He missed the connection they used to share. He listened for her steady breathing, seeking at least that comfort. When he tried to pick it out from the rattling fan and the pug's heavy breathing, though, he couldn't. His eyes now adjusted to the gloom, he turned to look at Claire. A flash of reflected light told him her eyes were open. "Claire?"

Silence. A moment later, the sound of steady breathing reached his ears, but it was false -- he could tell. The rhythm was too studied, too perfect.

He said her name again, hoping to shame her into admitting she wasn't sleeping. "I know you're awake."

The steady breathing continued. Giving up, he stripped out of the sweaty white button-down shirt and soiled black pants and rolled into bed, purposely bouncing on the mattress. He turned his back to her.

He slept late on Sundays now. He couldn't help it -- Saturdays took their toll on him. Claire never woke him up before leaving for the zoo. At first, she let him sleep out of courtesy; now, he suspected she did it to avoid talking to him. When he pulled himself out of bed at nine-thirty the next morning, she was, of course, already gone. Claire had stopped drinking coffee, claiming it upset her stomach. With no one to share in a full pot, Milo also gave up the beverage. The morning breakfast ritual died away.

He poured himself a bowl of Cheerios and sat down at the table. As was the routine, Taz sat just a foot or so from his leg, begging silently with his popped-out eyes. Milo tossed him one of the circular bits of cereal that had managed to avoid contact with the milk.

Night Life

The house felt colder lately, and it wasn't because of the weather. He remembered living with a similar chill when he shared a home with dead Alice. He didn't like it. Finishing his cereal, he rinsed the bowl and spoon, setting them upside down in the dish drainer.

Deciding on his next move, he selected one of his vintage cameras, threw on a Guayabera and a pair of chinos, and headed for the zoo.

Unlike some of the other days of the week, Claire didn't have a permanent assignment on Sundays. Sometimes she was with the baboons, sometimes the horses. Milo, uncertain of her whereabouts, chose to head toward the Monkey Village, where he had first met her as he was trying to get a close-up of a squirrel monkey. When one of the smart little creatures figured out that he had a store of dried peas in his pocket and attempted to steal some, Claire had sprayed Milo and the monkey with her water bottle. He chuckled at the memory as he walked through the crowds of families. Not surprisingly, Zareb stood at the gated entrance to the village.

"How are you, Zareb?" Milo asked, clapping the man on the shoulder.

"Milo! Long time, no see! How are you, sir?"

"Not bad, not bad. Have you seen Claire today?"

"She's not working here."

"I can see that. I was hoping you knew where she was stationed."

He shook his head. "You don't understand me. She is not working at the zoo."

Milo, stunned, stepped backwards. "Of course she is, Zareb."

"No. Not since the beginning of the month. After she fainted a few weeks ago--"

"Claire fainted?"

"Yes, sir. I thought you and she were living together."

"We are. At least, I thought we were. Her dog is still at the house." Zareb's low chuckle brought Milo back to the conversation. "Did she say why she was quitting?"

"I don't think she has quit the program," Zareb answered. With one hand, he held open the gate and ushered a family inside. "She told me she was just taking some time off."

"Did she say when she would be back?"

"Shouldn't you talk to her about this?"

He smiled at the bigger man. "What makes you think we talk?"

"I don't think I should tell you anything more. Find your woman and talk to her, Milo."

Milo turned and walked slowly back along the lake, barely aware of the crowd around him. Were things really so bad between them that she was hiding from him? That was the only explanation he could think of for her not telling him something like this. Finding a bench, he sat down and dialed her number.

After three rings, she picked up. "Hello, Milo."

"Hi. I was thinking of visiting you at the zoo today. Where are you working?"

"Today? It's so busy, Milo. I won't have time to take a break."

"That's okay. I'll just come see you for a few minutes. I'll bring a camera with me to keep me busy."

"I'd rather you didn't."

"Why not?"

She sighed audibly. "Just stay away, Milo. I'll see you at home tonight."

He ended the call and dropped his hands to his lap in despair.

Milo sat in the backyard, watching the sunset and sipping a soda. Taz, already exhausted from a tour around the yard, lay at his feet. Except for the dog's panting, the world around him was silent -- one of the benefits of living in a retirement community, he supposed.

He had spent the afternoon thinking about his relationship with Claire. Just a few months ago, he had anticipated spending the rest of his life with her; now, he was certain he had to end their relationship, for his own good as well as hers. The thought of returning to the lonely state he had only recently left made his heart beat too quickly and his arms feel numb. He doubted that Sondra would want her room back; besides, he had reclaimed it for his photography hobby. At least he had a job to bury himself in.

The sound of Claire's engine roused the drowsing dog, who ran to the side of the house to bark his greeting to his mistress. Milo wondered if Claire might let him keep Taz. After all, he had a yard for him to play in. Not anxious for the conversation to come, he stayed seated and waited for her to find him.

Ten minutes later, she opened the back door and walked to the patio set. "What are you doing?"

"Watching the sunset."

"The sun is down, Milo. Why don't you come inside?" She turned to go back in the house.

Instead of following her, he asked, "Why are you lying to me?"

He watched her freeze for a moment before facing him. "Lying to you? About what?"

"I was at the zoo today."

Biting her lip, she closed her eyes and sighed. "I didn't want you to know."

"That much seems clear. When were you planning to tell me?"

"I was afraid you would think you had to quit your job at the bar to entertain me."

"Where are you spending your days? Or, should I ask with whom are you spending them?"

Her forehead creased with anger. "I'm not cheating on you, if that's what you think."

"It crossed my mind."

"I would never do that, Milo. I know that we have our problems, but--"

"I think we should consider ending our relationship." He said the words steadily, in an even tone, though inside his heart was fractured.

"Consider ending it? Or end it?"

He broke eye contact with her. "We aren't married--"

"So I've noticed," she spat.

"Wait...what? When I asked you to officially move in with me -- not more than two months ago, Claire -- you nearly had a heart attack because you were afraid I was proposing!

Now you're angry that we're not married?"

She sank into one of the chairs and dropped her face in her hands. "I love you, Milo. I know I'm not good at showing it -- especially lately. But you are the only person who has made me laugh since Dorsey died. Please...give me another chance."

"Why did you lie to me?"

"I didn't want to worry you."

He reached across the corner of the table and took her hand. "What aren't you telling me? Are you sick?"

She met his eyes. "I'm...waiting for some test results."

"What kind of tests?"

"A little of everything," she averred. "The doctor isn't sure what's wrong with me."

"Does this have to do with your fainting spell?"

She widened her eyes, startled. "Who told you? Sondra?"

"Sondra knows?" He shook his head. "I ran into Zareb today and he told me about it."

"The paramedics didn't want me to drive, so I called her for a ride."

"Don't blame her. She kept your secret. Though I think I'll be giving her a call."

She squeezed his hand. "She only did what I asked her to do. I'm her landlady -- you can't expect her to rat me out."

"So you aren't working at the zoo because you're having fainting spells. So what have you been doing instead?"

"I went to the art museum. I spent the whole week studying the paintings." She smiled. "The collection is quite large, you know."

He laughed.

"Do you really want me to leave?"

He released her hand. "You have to be honest with me from now on, Claire. This relationship won't work, otherwise. And I want to go with you when you go back to the doctor."

"You don't need to do that."

"I want to be there to support you. Please."

She agreed.

He pulled her to her feet and wrapped his arms around her. "I love you, Claire. I just want us to be happy."

"Don't say anything to Sax or Sondra, okay? I don't want to worry anyone unnecessarily."

"That's ridiculous! They're our friends."

"Just...not yet. After we know what's wrong, we can tell them."

He agreed.

On Monday, Milo waited impatiently for Sax to show up at the Brass Monkey. When the Hulk Hogan lookalike strolled in at just a few minutes after three, Milo met him at his barstool. "I meant to ask Saturday night: what happened with Sondra?" He slid Sax's beer in front of him.

Sax shrugged. "She says she's not going to worry about it. Ethan reassured her that Vivian is just grieving the only way she knows how."

"By threatening her brother's girlfriend? Where does that fall in the seven steps of grief?"

"I'm not sure." The left side of Sax's mouth twitched upward. "We need to honor Sondra's wishes, though. I would hate to screw up her chance at happiness like I did my own."

"Someone needs to look out for her. And we're the only ones who can."

"Milo, you have to admit our crime-solving skills are a bit rusty. And we don't even know if there's been a crime."

"Three dead spouses between two thirty-something siblings? A fourth spouse on the verge of death? Either these two are cursed or they're guilty."

Sax sipped his beer thoughtfully. "We can't do it. We can't investigate what we've been told to leave alone."

"At least do a little research. Heck, it'll give you something to do during the day -- think of it as an exercise of the mind."

"You're determined to get involved, aren't you?"

"It's just a little research. Brush off the top layer of dust and see if there's anything interesting underneath."

"Fine. I'll do it. But if Sondra catches us, this was all your idea."

Night Life

Bloodhound

Though Sax had been reluctant to dig where Sondra had asked him not to, after his conversation with Milo he approached the project with curiosity. If for no other reason than she seemed like she might be up to no good, Vivian warranted investigation. The problem was that Sax had no idea what Vivian's last name was. He had to start with Ethan.

Instead of going to the bar and using the computer in his office there, he opted to use the library, where the internet speed was bound to be better than the bare-bones dial-up service he had. Securing a computer for half an hour, he started his search at Google, typing in Sondra's boyfriend's name. Instantly, pages of website listings appeared. Surprisingly, the first one referred to Ethan Turner as a Bluebeard who killed two wives for their money. Stunned to see that Milo's and his suspicions were already being promulgated on the Internet, he clicked on the link. Instantly, a blurry picture of a young man on a sailboat appeared. He pulled his phone out of his pocket to call Milo; then his eye was drawn to the garish red splatters at the left edge of the page and the word "Dexter" at the top. A closer investigation of the page showed that Ethan Turner was a fictional character -- a murderer who was himself murdered by the fictional anti-hero, Dexter Morgan. Realizing that he had typed the wrong name, Sax groaned, closed his eyes, and wondered again what he thought he was doing; his investigatory skills were so rusty that his fingers should be dripping orange sweat.

Starting back at the search, he typed *Ethan Tanner artist*. A much smaller selection came up, but almost all of them dealt with the man to whom Sondra was engaged. He found an Internet magazine that had profiled him two years before and he read through it, learning that Ethan was the son of carnies. At the time of the interview, Ethan's second wife had only been dead a few months. The writer referred to him as "a tragic figure whose own life rivals those of the greatest superheroes." The details of both wives' untimely deaths were summarized. The first one, Julia, had died in a base-jumping accident when her parachute failed to open properly. Astrid -- dead wife number two -- had fallen to her death in a climbing accident. Even if everything else in Ethan's life had been perfectly normal, those two deaths would have seemed too coincidental to Sax. He wrote the women's names on a scrap of paper. He also copied down the carnival information from the article, as well as his parents' names: John and Rowena Tanner.

Returning to the Google search, he found Ethan's Facebook page. In a rare stroke of luck, Ethan's page had no restrictions on it -- Sax could see everything, including his friends. He scrolled through the list and soon found a Vivian Bradford. Her page was completely closed to him, but from her resemblance to Ethan and the rarity of her first name, Sax was reasonably certain this was Ethan's sister. He Googled her name; half a dozen web-page listings appeared. Most of them were death notices for much older women. Only three were related to Ethan's sister: her Facebook page, a business page advertising her services as a private investigator, and a wedding notice from *The Arizona Republic*, the only major newspaper in the valley. Sax now understood how Vivian knew so much about Sondra: it was her business to know the details of other people's lives. The wedding announcement was brief, but it told him something he wouldn't have otherwise known: Vivian's previous name -- the one she carried before Bradford -- was Guyon.

He searched for Vivian Guyon, and found an obituary from two years before the wedding announcement, in which she was listed as the surviving spouse of Jean Claude Guyon, who had died of a previously undetected heart problem. He leaned back in the chair, threading his fingers behind his head. That was interesting -- wasn't Patrick dying of something similar right now? His critical mind found it difficult to believe that Vivian would marry two men with the same ailment. The common denominator was Vivian. But if that were true, why hadn't Ethan's wives also died of heart-related complaints?

With no way to find more information without paying for a records search, he glanced at the clock. His half hour was up. Gathering his notes, he left the library.

Night Life

Sax knocked on Sondra's door and she flung it open enthusiastically, jumping toward him with her arms wide. "I'm so glad you came to see me!" she exclaimed, hugging him tightly.

"I'm sorry for the short notice," he said. "If I'm interrupting your plans--"

"Don't be ridiculous. Ethan is working and I'm bored out of my mind. If it weren't for the conventions we have to go to for the Sunrise Aeon promotions, I'd be auditioning like mad just to have something to do!" She pulled him into the condo. "Have you had lunch? I know a good place we could go. Or I think there are some leftovers in the fridge. Ethan's a great cook."

Though Ethan's wives hadn't died of poisoning, Sax was reluctant to eat anything he had prepared -- just in case. "Let's go out."

Sondra shrugged in acquiescence. "Can I get you anything to drink or do you want to go right away?"

"I'm not thirsty right now. Sit down. Let's talk for a few minutes."

"What's going on?"

"Nothing," he reassured her. "I just thought we could chat for a few minutes before we go."

Sondra lowered herself into the chair across from his seat on the sofa.

"I love that painting," he said, indicating the fantastical candy cathedral.

"That's the one Ethan and I bought at his friend's art gallery."

"I've never seen anything like it before."

"Every time I see it, I smile." She shifted toward it, craning her neck back. "What do you want to do today?" she asked again.

"I've been thinking about that tattoo parlor," he said casually.

"Really?" Her eyes widened. "You want to get a tattoo?"

He hadn't completely thought this through; he had

508

hoped he could convince her to get the tattoo, since she had said she was tempted. "Actually--"

"This will be great!" she interrupted. "We can both get one. What do you want? Ooh, you should get a monkey! No-- one of those Chinese symbol tattoos that are supposed to mean 'happy life' but actually mean something completely different like 'stupid round eyes.'"

"Why would I want that?"

She smiled mischievously. "You like all that Asian stuff."

"What do you want to get?"

"I'm thinking about a Star of David."

"Where?"

"Probably right here," she said, indicating the outside of her right ankle. "Easter had one with a flowering vine threaded through it."

Sax frowned. "Easter is Jewish?"

Sondra laughed. "Sorry. No. I meant she had that design on the wall of the shop."

"Ah. Gotcha." He tilted his head in confusion. "Sondra, not six months ago you were having a fit because Fanny was converting to Judaism. Now you want a Star of David on your ankle?"

"If you can't beat them, join them. Think of me as a modern-day Rahab."

"I have no idea who that is."

"Look it up."

"Wait...will that interfere with your Sunrise Aeon costume? I'm pretty sure no one has ever claimed there were Jews on Mars."

"Disco boots, remember? No one will ever see it when I'm in costume."

"I guess you've thought of everything." He took a chance and turned the conversation toward Vivian and her dying husband. "How is Patrick doing?"

"Better, actually. Well enough to go home, in fact. I think Ethan was right about Vivian -- she was just grieving her husband when she warned me away from Ethan. You should see how devoted she is to him. She won't even let hospice come in and take over some of the nursing duties. She says she wants to take care of him herself."

Sax shivered visibly at the words.

"What's wrong?"

"Nothing," he answered. "I think I'm hungry."

Sondra drove them, in her usual confrontational style, to a nearby bistro. After a relaxing and satisfying lunch, they headed to the tattoo parlor owned by Ethan's friends. Sax, who had seen his share of shady tattoo parlors back in New Jersey, was suitably impressed with the overall atmosphere of the place -- clean and bright, with tattoo-covered but smiling artists, two of whom came over to hug Sondra as soon as they saw her.

"Oh, my God! Sondra! What are you doing here?" asked the thin but pretty girl with the now-multicolored hair.

"I want a tattoo, Easter. Are you busy?"

"For you, I'd clear my schedule." She laughed. "If I had one to clear!"

"I'm glad you're here. I thought you might be at the gallery."

"It's closed on Mondays and Tuesdays, so I hang out with the guys instead. Are you sure you don't want Arlo to do your art? I'm a bit rusty."

The thin, rangy man next to her said, "Don't let her modesty fool you -- she's the only one I trust to work on me."

Easter smiled up at the guy adoringly, confirming in Sax's mind that he was Arlo.

"My friend wants a tattoo as well," she said, grabbing his wrist and pulling him closer. "This is Sax Ridley."

"Hey, man," Arlo said, holding out his fist to bump.

Sax had seen younger men do this and thought it was ridiculous. Why couldn't they just shake hands? The greeting was tried and true and didn't confuse anyone. Nevertheless, in the interest of the investigation, Sax raised his fist and bumped. "Hey."

"I was hoping you could do Sax's tattoo. I love the work you did on Ethan."

"No need to butter me up," Arlo said. "I have an appointment at five-thirty, though. If it's going to be a larger work, you might want to opt for one of my other artists."

"If you don't have time today, I'll make an appointment and come back then," Sax offered.

Arlo rubbed his neck, considering. "What do you have in mind?"

"When I meditate, I focus on a small jade dragon a friend brought me from Japan years ago. I think I would like something similar in a tattoo."

"So, you're looking for a green serpentine dragon?" He walked to the counter and crouched, searching for something on the shelves below. When he stood, he had an old photo album in his hands. Setting it on the counter, he flipped the pages until it was open to a collection of dragons. "Like this?" he asked, pointing to a fierce, fire-breathing dragon.

"Sort of. Only I want one that is peaceful."

"A peaceful dragon. Easter? Do we have anything like that?" To Sax, he said, "Easter knows our art archive like the back of her hand."

Easter, who had been talking with Sondra, walked behind the counter and asked, "What are you looking for?"

"A peaceful dragon," Arlo repeated.

The woman frowned, looking up and to the right. "I know just what you want!" She dropped out of sight below the desk.

Sax gave Sondra a worried glance; she smiled encouragingly.

Easter reappeared with a smaller, slightly feminine-looking album. She opened it and pointed at a serpentine dragon with a calm, knowing smile. The only problem with the image as it existed was its color: it was done in blues and grays.

Sax nodded, warming to the idea of wearing this tattoo for the rest of his life. "You can do this in green?"

Arlo looked at him like he was an idiot. "Of course."

Having the good sense to blush, he said, "I'm sorry...stupid question. I've never done this before."

"Not a problem."

"Do you have time before your appointment?"

"Where do you want it and how big?"

Sax touched his right pectoral and said, "I want it here. Four or five inches high."

Arlo looked at the clock, which read two-thirty. "I'll tell you what: we'll start on it. If we run out of time, you might have to come back tomorrow. I have an opening at noon then."

Sax agreed, and Arlo led him to a chair.

"Take off your shirt. You can hang it on that coat hook." He indicated a hook just to the right of his equipment.

Sax, never one to be shy about showing off all his hard work, shed the shirt quickly and sat in the chair.

"How old are you, man?"

"Why?"

"I thought you were around sixty, but your physique says forty, max."

His ego stroked, Sax admitted, "I'll be seventy this year."

Arlo nodded. "I hope I look this good at your age."

"Start working on it now," Sax said, eyeing the thin man.

Another artist a few feet away laughed. "Ouch. Burned, Arlo! That had to hurt."

Arlo rolled his eyes and said, "Shove it, Burris." He removed a clean razor blade from the station's stack of drawers and inserted it into the razor.

"What's that for?" Sax asked nervously.

"I've got to shave the area where the tattoo will be."

Sax glanced down at his relatively sparse chest hair. He didn't have much, and he hated the thought of losing any of it. "Maybe we should put it on my back instead."

"Don't do that. You put art on your back when you run out of space on the front," Arlo advised.

"Is that what you did?"

"Naw. No one told me that when I was getting my first tattoos. But if you're paying for art, you should put it where you get to enjoy it."

"I see your point." He relaxed into the chair and Arlo shaved his pectoral.

"How do you know Sondra?"

"She used to be a regular at my bar."

"You're a bartender?"

"I own the Brass Monkey in Peoria. It's a neighborhood joint."

"That's cool. I couldn't believe it when Ethan told me he was engaged to her. I'm a huge fan."

"You think it'll last?"

"If Ethan has his way. He's devoted."

"I understand he's a widower. Is he ready for a new relationship?"

"Have you met him?" Arlo asked rhetorically. "Ethan was born to be a married man. He's never really happy without a wife."

"What was his wife like?"

"Which one?" laughed Arlo.

"How many have there been?" he asked, feigning ignorance.

"Three...but the first one didn't last long."

"What happened?"

Arlo was prepping his equipment as they talked. "Bad match. I think they actually had it annulled."

That meant there was one ex he could talk to -- if he could find her. "You've been friends for a long time, I take it."

"About ten years now. We met in college."

"So you knew all of his wives?"

"Yeah, of course. Easter didn't like Julia too well, so we kind of lost touch for a while. But Easter introduced him to Astrid. You ready?" he asked, holding the tattoo needle poised over Sax's chest.

"No time like the present." He braced himself for the pain.

"Try not to tense up. Relax."

Sax took a deep, calming breath. "How long have you been a tattooist?" Sax asked, changing the focus so that Arlo wouldn't get suspicious.

"Easter and I opened this place right after college -- about the time both of us realized we didn't want to live like Van Gogh. We preferred an easier life, and tattooing was on the rise. I already had four or five myself and Easter had two, I think. Anyway, it seemed like a lucrative field. We bought this house at a bargain price, fixed it up, brought in a few experienced artists, and learned the craft."

"That must have cost a pretty penny."

Arlo laughed. "Yeah, Easter's trust fund saved the day. Her father just about fell over when we told him what we were doing. Easter has a degree in Art History -- tattooist didn't sound like a great career move to him."

"Her parents are rich?"

"Her father is," Arlo corrected. "Her mother's been MIA since before we met."

"You said Easter introduced Astrid to Ethan. How did

she know her?"

"They grew up together in the Phoenix Country Club. Astrid was the epitome of the perfect daughter: beautiful, obedient, and smart. I think their friendship was the ultimate proof that opposites attract."

"How do you mean obedient?"

"Where Easter would go out of her way to irritate her dad, Astrid would go to extremes to please her parents. I think marrying Ethan was the first thing she'd ever done that pissed them off."

Sax let the conversation wander as Arlo worked on the outlines of the dragon. Arlo talked about the shop, Easter's gallery, Ethan's remarkable talent. Occasionally, the conversation would lull and Sax would turn his head toward Easter tattooing Sondra. The pain was subtle -- more like an irritation than a penetration, despite the needle. When it seemed like it was going to overwhelm him, he would take a few deep breaths and attempt to meditate his way through it.

"Time to add the colors. Do you need a break?"

"Just a few minutes, maybe. How are we doing on time?"

"I think we'll be done around four-thirty at this rate. You've been an easy client so far." Arlo stepped back. "Stretch your legs."

He walked over to Easter's station, where Sondra's Star of David tattoo was progressing nicely. Sondra was on edge, though: her jaw was clamped tightly shut and her eyes expressed the tension in her body. He laid a hand on her shoulder. "Take a deep breath, Sondra."

She glanced up at him irritably, but did as he said.

"Another."

Her ragged inhale was followed by a calmer exhale.

"One more."

She patted his hand gratefully. "I'm glad you're here."

"How's the dragon coming?" Easter asked, looking up from Sondra's ankle. "Looking good! You're going to be really pleased with that."

"I like it so far." He bent down to examine Sondra's tattoo more closely. "This is beautiful. Do you paint, too?"

"No," she blushed. "I'm not that good with a brush."

"I saw the painting Sondra bought at your gallery. I was

thinking of buying a few pieces for my home and bar."

Sondra glanced up sharply.

Pressing on, he asked, "What's the name of your place?"

"Easternalia," she said. "Why don't you grab one of my business cards? They're up front on the desk."

He walked over and found the cards, taking one. On it, printed in a Gothic font, was the name of the gallery and Easter L'Oeuf, proprietress. Recognizing her last name as French for "egg," he asked incredulously, "Is this your real name?"

She smiled broadly. "My father has an interesting sense of humor."

"What am I missing?" Sondra asked.

"Do you know any French?"

"Not really. Why?"

"Easter's last name means 'the egg.'"

Sondra's jaw dropped. "And you didn't change it?"

"Actually, I like it. Not many people make the connection. And it's so much more interesting than if I married Arlo. I mean, Easter Jones? What's the fun in that?"

Sax laughed as he slid the card into his wallet. With a name like that to lead him, he was certain he would be able to track down Astrid's parents. He walked back to Arlo and sat down, satisfied with the information he had obtained. The rest of the tattoo was done well before Arlo's next client arrived. He hugged both Arlo and Easter when he and Sondra left the shop. His right pectoral felt like it had a sunburn, but the art was top-notch.

In the car, Sondra said, "What was that all about?"

"What?"

"You're buying art for the bar?"

"Maybe," he answered defensively. "What's wrong with that?"

"Nothing, except the place is so dark no one would ever see it."

"I could use something for my house."

"Fine. If you say so."

Night Life

Easter's name proved to be the key to finding Astrid. Knowing that Arlo and Easter met in college about ten years before, he estimated that she had to be around twenty-eight. From there, he made a reasonable guess as to her graduation date, give or take a year. After determining which high school the girls would have attended if they didn't go to private school, he stopped by and examined the yearbooks. Within an hour, he had found her: Astrid Dresden, a strikingly beautiful girl with alabaster skin and blonde hair.

A quick search of the telephone directory turned up only one Dresden household in the surrounding area. Provided they weren't unlisted, that had to be her people. Hoping his luck would hold, he drove to the address and knocked on the front door. A sad but beautiful woman, looking very much like an older version of Astrid, opened the door. "May I help you?"

"Mrs. Dresden?"

"Yes."

"I'm sorry to bother you. I'm here about Astrid."

Her eyes widened slightly and she started to close the door.

"Please, Mrs. Dresden. I really need to talk to you."

"No comment."

Realizing she thought he was a reporter, he stuck his foot in the door. "I'm not with the press. Please."

She hesitated. "Who are you?"

"My name is Sax Ridley. A good friend of mine is engaged to marry Ethan Tanner."

The woman seemed to consider his words carefully. Finally, she opened the door again. "Can I see your driver's license?"

Sax pulled out his wallet and showed her the I.D.

"Come in." She stepped further into her home, unblocking the entrance. "Forgive my rudeness. About every six months someone doing a story on Ethan shows up on my doorstep looking for a comment from my husband or me."

"I understand. That must be very painful."

"Excruciating. No parent should outlive their child. The

fact that mine was married to a minor celebrity at the time of her death just means that someone is always looking for a way to peel the scab off our wounds."

"I'm afraid I will be doing the same thing by talking to you," he apologized.

"But you have a good reason!" She led him into a sitting room that looked like something out of a Renaissance-era palace. "Please, have a seat." She indicated toward a maroon brocaded sofa. "Would you like something to drink?"

"Just water, thank you."

"Malia!" she called out.

A middle-aged Hispanic woman appeared in the archway through which they had just passed. "Yes, Mrs. Dresden?"

"Would you bring us two glasses of water, please?"

"Right away."

"I don't know what I'd do without Malia," she sighed as she lowered herself into the throne-like armchair across from Sax. "She's been with us forever -- she practically raised Astrid. I know she was just as heartbroken as we were when...she fell."

"A friend of Astrid's told me that you and your husband opposed her marriage. May I ask why?"

She wrinkled her nose, distorting her face into a mask of ugly disapproval. "How much do you know about Ethan?"

"Not much. He only met my friend in October. He proposed at Christmas."

"That's just like him. He always wants to rush into the marriage before his potential bride starts to sniff out the danger."

"You think he's dangerous?"

"My daughter is dead, isn't she?" Mrs. Dresden arched an eyebrow at him.

The maid appeared with iced water in crystal glasses. "Anything else, Mrs. Dresden?"

"No, thank you, Malia."

"My biggest concern is that his sister threatened my friend recently."

"Oh, yes. The sister. What was her name? Victoria? Viola?"

"Vivian."

Her face puckered. "Vivian. Yes. The merry widow. That's what Astrid called her."

"Her first husband was already dead?"

"Astrid told me he died of some kind of heart problem. I don't think Astrid ever met him, but he hadn't been dead very long when Ethan and she started dating. She came home from a date--"

"Astrid lived at home?"

"Why wouldn't she?" Mrs. Dresden asked, gesturing to the massive structure they were sitting inside. "The house is much too large for my husband and me alone." She seemed to lose her place, staring instead at the room around them. "It is lovely, though, isn't it? So hard to imagine living somewhere else."

"I'm sorry I interrupted. You were saying she came home from a date?"

Mrs. Dresden sat motionless for a few moments and Sax wondered if she would continue. Finally, she said, "Yes. She came home from a date rather disturbed by her first meeting with Vivian. Ethan had told her that Vivian had recently lost her husband -- a young Frenchman from a successful family, as I recall. He said Vivian wasn't herself at all since his death. Astrid took that to mean that the woman was sullen or morose. Instead, she told me that the girl was all but giddy! She flirted outrageously with the waiter at dinner and later, at a nightclub, she disappeared with a strange man for forty-five minutes."

"Was that when you decided that Ethan wasn't a suitable match for her?"

"Hardly. I didn't realize how quickly their relationship would progress. Her father and I didn't hire the private investigator until after they were engaged. They eloped before we received the final report."

Sax straightened and asked, "May I see the report?"

"I'll have Malia make you a copy. Malia!"

The woman appeared a second later; she must have been standing just out of sight, listening to the conversation. "Yes, ma'am?"

"Please go to Mr. Dresden's office and make a copy of the Ethan Tanner file."

"Right away." The woman disappeared.

518

"Did you show the file to your daughter?" Sax asked.

"She wouldn't look at it. She was determined to make her marriage to Ethan work, and she all but cut her father and me out of her life."

"After she died, did you go to the police?"

"Of course. But they told us there was nothing they could do. He hadn't been present when his first wife died, and, as far as they were concerned, there was nothing suspicious about Astrid's death."

"What about Vivian's husband's death?"

"We didn't have that investigated. All we were interested in was Ethan." She glanced at the diamond-encrusted watch on her wrist. "I'm sorry to do this, but I'm late for a charity luncheon. Do you mind if I excuse myself?"

"Of course not. Thank you so much for seeing me. You have been so much help."

"I hope you are able to convince your friend to leave him. It may save her life." She reached out, offering her hand in a manner that made Sax think he should bow and kiss it; instead, of course, he merely shook it.

"Malia should be down shortly with the copy. She will see you out."

The file was a treasure trove of information: in it, he found Julia's last name -- Moritz -- and the name of Ethan's first wife: Emlyn Kopczynski. He also discovered that Ethan's parents lived in a home that was in their daughter and son's names.

With several new leads in hand, he first searched for Emlyn, who, thankfully, had not married again. He sent her a note on Facebook and hoped he would hear back from her.

With only Julia's name to go on, he wasn't able to get very far. Unlike the surname Dresden, hundreds of Moritzes lived in Arizona. And, of course, he had no idea if her family even lived here. The file gave him everything he needed to know, though: Julia had been an experienced base jumper who packed her own chute. However, a friend who regularly jumped with her told the investigator that he suspected Julia's chute had been switched with another one. He claimed the canopy was wrong: Julia swore by Fox canopies, but the one that she was wearing the day she died had been a Flik. Since Julia's death had been a few years before, the investigator wasn't able to prove or disprove the friend's claims.

The investigator had tracked down Emlyn, but she hadn't provided much information. She claimed she had only known Ethan a few weeks when they married. She told the investigator they had both known immediately the marriage was a bad idea, and they had it annulled. Sax was less interested in her take on Ethan than in her opinion of Ethan's sister. She was likely to be the only one who could tell him something about Vivian's relationship with her first husband.

He flipped back to the page that talked about John and Rowena Tanner. The carnival had been more than games and rides -- it had featured a small, one-ring circus as well. Rowena Tanner had once been billed as The Remarkable Rowena, an acrobatic high-wire artist who was the star performer. Some of the old-timers the investigator tracked down remembered that she had been engaged to David "Duke" Tanner, the first son of the circus's owner, as well as the magician. John Tanner had been the second son. Duke, the Tanner Traveling Circus heir, had died in a magic trick that went awry. Their father, an elderly widower himself, was broken-hearted by his favorite son's death. He, too, soon passed away. After their deaths, John married Rowena and stepped into the leadership role. To Sax, it read like a Greek tragedy: John had eliminated the competition and married his brother's girlfriend.

More out of curiosity than any real need to interview them, he drove to their house and knocked on the door. A pixie-like brunette opened the door wearing a Fifties-style apron over her dress. "Yes?" she asked, her eyes sparkling in the sunlight.

"I'm sorry to bother you ma'am, but I was referred to you by--" he pulled the name of one of the circus performers out of his head "--Jan Cabbage?"

"My goodness! Really? I haven't seen Jan in years! Come in, come in!"

Pleased that his luck was still holding, he stepped into

the house. "Thank you, ma'am. You see, I'm writing a book about traveling circuses of the Twentieth Century, and I was hoping to interview you and your husband for it."

"How wonderful! Of course, we'd love to talk to you, I'm sure." Turning toward the staircase, she called out, "John! We have a visitor!"

A thin man in a cardigan walked down the stairs. Together, Mr. and Mrs. Tanner looked like parents straight out of a pre-Vietnam television show. It struck Sax that they were "acting normal."

"John, this is...I'm sorry. I didn't catch your name."

"Call me Ridley," he said. If their daughter had investigated him, he knew his first name would be a dead giveaway.

"This is Ridley. Jan Cabbage sent him."

John tilted his head slightly and gave him an odd smile as he shook his hand. "Jan Cabbage? Really? I thought she was in a nursing home."

"Yes," Sax lied. "That's where I found her. Very nice lady. Happy to talk about her years with the Tanner Traveling Circus."

"That's probably all she remembers, the poor dear." John's face cleared. "Senility, you know."

"I'll get us some drinks," Rowena said. "Would you like tea? A soda? Water?"

"Whatever you are having is fine," Sax answered.

"Have a seat." John pointed at an overstuffed leather armchair, and Sax obliged. "Where would you like to start?"

"I'm interested in documenting the history of as many circuses and carnivals as I can. The Tanner Traveling Circus seems to have been neglected by other historians in the field. I understand it was started by an ancestor of yours."

He nodded. "The circus was founded just after the Civil War, as a matter of fact. My great-great-grandfather, who happened to be a dwarf, was one of the original attractions as well as half-owner with his brother."

"Very interesting. So, was it always a one-ring show?"

"Yes. We added the carnival and sideshows as we went along."

Rowena appeared with three glasses of ice and a bottle of cola. "I was the main attraction," she boasted as she sat down next to her husband on the sofa. "You probably can't tell now, but I was once a great acrobat and tightrope walker."

Sax looked suitably impressed. "After having it in the family for all those years, why did you sell it?"

"A combination of things, really." John opened the bottle and poured the soda. "We tried to raise our children with the idea that the circus was their future. Our daughter even apprenticed as an acrobat under Rowena and studied the healing arts with Mama Constance. Ethan -- our boy -- was never interested in the carnival, though. He was a natural-born artist, but there's not much call for that kind of talent in a traveling show."

"Ethan was meant for something better," Rowena said with conviction. "He's a well-known figure in the comic art world."

"Rowena's rather proud of the boy," John smirked.

"Why didn't you let your daughter take over the circus?"

"I wanted her to do just that, but she wasn't interested. And, to be fair, it was time for us to sell it. There were a lot of tragic memories associated with it." He frowned.

"I heard your older brother died during a magic performance."

John looked away, brushing at his eyes.

Rowena smiled graciously. "It was a terrible accident, but I can't be too sad about it. Bad things happen, but out of the bad grows the good." She patted John's hand and he grabbed it and squeezed.

Sax heard a key turn in the front-door lock and a woman exclaimed, "I'm sorry! I didn't know you had a guest!"

"Come in, sweetheart. This nice man is writing a book about our circus."

Sax swallowed down his surprise and turned to smile at Vivian, hoping she wouldn't recognize him.

Vivian blinked at him for a moment before smiling. "Wonderful," she said. "And you are?"

"Just call me Ridley."

"Of course, Mr. Ridley. I hope my parents have been helpful." Her lips were curved in the semblance of a smile, but they forgot to tell her eyes.

"Oh, yes. Very helpful." He raised his glass and drained it. "Well, thank you folks for the conversation. I think I'd best get on my way."

"So soon?" questioned Mrs. Tanner. "We would love to share some of our stories! Wouldn't we, John?"

"Of course! Please don't rush off."

"I have a few other stops to make today. Maybe we could set aside a day to talk later. Could I have your phone number?"

"Sure." John stood up and dug a business card out of his wallet. It read *John Tanner, Retired*. "My son had those made up for me after I sold the show. Not that I have much call for them. I think that's the first one I've given out this year."

"I'll call you," Sax assured the couple and turned toward the door.

"I'll just walk you out, Mr. Ridley," Vivian said, coming to his side. "Back in a moment, Mom." Once they were outside, she said in a low voice, "I could have you arrested, you know."

"For what? Asking questions?"

"Investigating without a license. That's illegal, you know."

"I have recently become interested in twentieth-century circuses. There's no law against me tracking down people who know about them."

"What else are you interested in these days?"

He turned to look at her, hoping to gauge her reaction. "Poisons."

A slow, amused smile spread across her face. "Is that so?"

He nodded. "How is Patrick today?"

"He's back in the hospital. I don't think he'll be coming back home again -- unless, of course, we're talking about his ashes."

"You really are a merry widow, aren't you?"

"We always knew our time together would be limited. I'm just so happy we had these few years. Patrick wouldn't want me to be sad." She reached out and took his hand in an unwilling shake. "If I were you, Mr. Ridley, I'd be encouraging Sondra to move on -- without Ethan." She dropped his hand and turned her back on him, returning to her parents' home. Sax shivered as a chill ran through him. Pulling out his phone to turn the ringer back on, he saw that he had a message waiting on Facebook. It was from Emlyn: she was willing to meet him.

Emlyn Kopczynski was a somber, round-faced woman who looked like she had absorbed a whole country's suffering in her short lifetime. Her cheery scrubs did little to change that impression. "Sax Ridley?" she asked, approaching his table at the Denny's where they had agreed to meet.

"Thank you for meeting me, Ms. Kop--"

"Ca-CHIN-ski," she pronounced. "But please, call me Em. Everyone does."

"Thank you, Em. Just call me Sax. I'm glad you recognized me."

"You're the only Hulk Hogan lookalike currently in the restaurant." She slid into the booth across from him. "How can I help you?"

"My best friend is engaged to marry Ethan Tanner."

She smiled wistfully. "How wonderful for her."

"Why do you say that?"

"Ethan is a truly amazing man. Such a gentleman. So talented."

Confused, Sax asked, "Why did you divorce him?"

"I didn't. We had the marriage annulled."

"Why?"

"It wasn't working out."

The waitress came to the table; Sax ordered coffee and the young woman ordered a lemonade.

When the waitress retreated, Sax said, "I don't want to pry. I just need some insight into his family."

Her eyes widened and she pressed into the booth. "You're here about Vivian, aren't you?"

"Yes. How did you--?"

"Who else could it be? Ethan is a dream and his parents are Ward and June Cleaver. That only leaves Vivian."

"Do you remember an investigator talking to you about the Tanners a few years ago?"

She shook her head. "He never asked about the Tanners. He asked about Ethan -- just Ethan."

524

"So you didn't tell him about Vivian."

She looked around before leaning forward and whispering, "I've never told anyone about Vivian."

"Will you tell me?"

The waitress came back with their drinks. Em smiled and thanked her. She smelled her drink before sipping it. "Yes," she said, "I'm going to tell you. But you have to promise me that no one will ever know where you got your information."

"I promise."

For the next hour, she spun out the tale of her romance with Ethan Tanner. She had been a nursing student at Arizona State University when they first met. He swept her off her feet and made her feel like a princess. However, because she had a boyfriend back home in Chicago, she resisted dating him. After several months, he persuaded her that his intentions were honorable. She broke off her relationship with her high-school sweetheart; from there, it was a short trip to the altar. She met her sister-in-law after the wedding, when Ethan took her with him to share the happy news. "I'd met his parents before, but somehow Vivian and I had avoided an encounter. I like to think that if I had met her before, I would have known better than to fall so deeply in love with Ethan. Their relationship -- it's not normal. At least, not from her side. I think Ethan sees her as just his sister. But Vivian seemed -- at least to me -- to have a more visceral connection to him."

"Do you mean they were physically involved?"

"No!" she hastened to answer. "Though I think Vivian wouldn't be opposed to it. She insisted that we stay for dinner with Jean Claude and her."

"So you met her first husband?"

"She's not with him anymore?"

"He died a few years ago."

She shuddered visibly, her eyes widening. "Maybe this isn't a good idea."

"Please, Em. My friend could be in danger."

She bit her lip and looked down as if she were going to stop talking. Finally, she leaned forward again. "She threatened me."

"When?"

"That night. She called me into the kitchen to 'help'

prepare dinner. It was a galley kitchen with only one exit, I remember that. She paced me back against the wall and told me in a low voice that I'd better get the marriage annulled. What she said...it was so hurtful. Ethan had given me a gorgeous wedding ring -- he told me it was his paternal grandmother's ring. She said I 'wasn't worth the ring or the risk.'"

"What did you do?"

"I was shocked, you know? I couldn't imagine why she thought she could threaten me like that. I told her I would tell Ethan what she said, and she just laughed. She said he'd never believe me over her. I didn't know what to do, and when we went back to the living room, she was as pleasant as she had been before the threat. I would have looked like a fool."

"So you had the marriage annulled?" he asked, incredulous. "On the basis of that threat?"

She shook her head. "There's more. She finished preparing the meal alone -- fettuccine Alfredo. Before we even made it home, I was in severe gastrointestinal pain -- like the worst case of heartburn and gas ever. Ethan was so worried! I mean, this was our wedding night! Not long after that, the diarrhea started. Terrified that I was going to die, he took me to the hospital. The next day, Vivian brought me flowers and told Ethan she would sit with me while he went and ate something. Then she..." The memory seemed to overwhelm her. She was breathing quickly, as if she were still frightened after all these years.

"Calm down, Em," he said, reaching across the table to touch her arm. "She's not here. She's not coming after you."

She closed her eyes and took a deep breath, blowing it out slowly. "Ever since that day, I've been prone to these panic attacks." She drew a bottle of pills from her purse. "Paxil," she said. She opened the bottle and popped one into her mouth, washing it down with the lemonade. "I don't sleep well. I wasn't sleeping before my doctor prescribed these, so I don't know if the medicine is making it worse or not. Before all this happened, I wanted to be a surgical nurse. The panic attacks took that away from me. Vivian took that away from me. I work in a hospice. Can you imagine? All I ever wanted to do was help people, and now I just watch them die."

526

Night Life

"What did Vivian say to you?"
"She asked me how much more rat poison I thought my body could take."

Night Life

Snap, Crackle, Drop

Sondra's phone rang, filling the living room with an instrumental version of "Y.M.C.A." Sondra, who was enjoying the view from her balcony, barely heard it. She considered letting it go to voicemail, but, after a few bars, stood and went to pick it up. Sax's face was on the screen. "Hello, sweetie. How's your tattoo healing?"

"Right now it looks like hell. I'm taking it on faith that the end result will be more attractive."

"It will be. I've seen Ethan's, and it looks fantastic." She settled into her sofa with a sigh. "What's up?"

"I was wondering if you had time to see me tonight."

"It's already five o'clock. You must be at the bar."

"I am," he acknowledged.

"So you want me to come to you."

"If you don't mind."

Glancing around her empty apartment, she shrugged to herself. "Sure. Why not? Ethan's out of town anyway."

"Where did he go?"

"His publisher's again. Something about problems with the final proofs...a color issue."

"Pack a bag. Instead of driving home, you can stay with me tonight."

"With an offer like that, how can a girl resist?"

He laughed. "You're easy."

"You been talking to Milo?" she shot back. "I'll be there in an hour or so."

"Okay. Drive carefully."

She fixed her makeup, refreshing her lipstick and making sure her eyeliner wasn't smudged. Gathering her toiletries into a travel bag and collecting a change of clothes for the morning, she packed a small suitcase and headed down to her car. On her way out of the garage, she noticed that her brakes seemed a little soft. She made a note to take the car to a garage tomorrow and have her brake fluid checked.

Flipping on her radio, she tuned in to a pop station and turned onto Central Avenue. At the next corner, she turned left on Camelback and drove toward the Black Canyon Highway. A few minutes later, she merged into rush hour traffic and slipped into the middle lane. Irritated by the slow pace of traffic, she tried to find a way around the slowpokes ahead of her. Finally, she accepted that forty was going to be her maximum speed for the afternoon. With no one to honk at and not seeing the point in flipping off the other drivers -- who were just as stuck as she was -- she settled into the pace.

Traffic started to break up as they reached Bell Road, and Sondra found a hole big enough for her to make her escape. She floored the pedal to slip into the gap and slid into the far lane. Knowing that her brakes were spongy, she tried to leave a big enough gap between herself and the car ahead of her. She was able to accelerate to almost fifty miles an hour.

Two cars ahead of her, a tire blew on an SUV. The driver directly in front of her hit his brakes to avoid the flying rubber. Sondra, pressing down on her brakes, had only a split second of panic when the pedal went all the way to the floor with no resistance. The sounds of twisting metal and shattering glass were the last sounds she heard.

The lights were too bright, Sondra thought as she attempted to open her eyes. She squeezed them shut. Someone was holding her hand, and she squeezed it in response.

She heard Sax's voice. "She's awake!"

She almost answered him, but someone else answered first. "That's a good sign. I'll let the doctor know." The sound of rubber-soled shoes left the room.

"Sondra? Can you hear me?"

She tried to answer, but her tongue wouldn't loosen itself. She tried to nod, but pain shot through her like bolts of lightning. As a last resort, she squeezed his hand again.

"Can you open your eyes?"

She willed her eyelids to open, but as soon as the light penetrated her lashes, she squeezed them closed again.

"Do you know what happened? One squeeze for yes, two for no."

Night Life

She remembered getting in her car to drive to the Brass Monkey. The brakes were spongy. She remembered getting on the freeway. Traffic was slow. Something happened. Something loud and unpleasant. Metal-twisting, glass-breaking unpleasant. A car accident. She squeezed his hand.

"You're in the hospital. The police found your phone in your purse. Did you know that you still have me listed as your emergency contact?"

She squeezed.

"I called Ethan. He's catching the first flight he can out of New York."

Frustrated by her inability to speak, she grunted angrily.

"You can't talk because of the ventilator, Sondra. Don't worry -- it's not permanent. The nurse tells me they will pull it out before you wake up from surgery."

She forced her eyes open and squeezed his hand as hard as she could, holding on until he looked at her. She could hear the heart-rate monitor beeping more quickly.

"You're going to be all right." He passed a soothing hand over her forehead. "Your hip was broken in the accident. You've also got a few fractured ribs and bruised kidneys. If you had been traveling any faster, you might not have survived. They are taking you in for surgery soon. Oh, and I used your phone to call Fanny and Hunter. They'll be here when you wake up."

Squeaky soles entered the room again. "The surgeon is ready. We need to move her now."

"Okay. Thank you." He released Sondra's hand. "I'll see you afterward. Remember, you've got a lot of people praying for you."

She closed her eyes again, nauseated at the sight of the fluorescent lights flashing by overhead. When the bed stopped rolling, a middle-aged man in a gown and mask introduced himself as her anesthesiologist and pumped something into the IV. She felt a warmth roll through her and she fell asleep.

Fanny was next to her when she woke up.

"You're okay now, Momma," she said reassuringly.

Sondra reached for her daughter's hand; Fanny took it and, smiling, raised it to her lips. "I think you're going to have to get a new car, though."

Sondra chuckled weakly and was surprised to hear the sound. She reached up with her free hand and felt around her mouth, relieved to realize that the respirator was gone. "You are so beautiful, Fanny," she croaked. Her voice sounded like her throat had been scraped across a cheese shredder a few times and then scalded for good measure. "I love you."

"I love you too, Momma." Fanny teared up.

"Is my face okay?"

She wiped the tears away and laughed. "Yes. The doctor said you must have thrown your arms up to protect your face, because the undersides of both of your forearms needed stitches. They look like a patchwork quilt."

"That's okay. No one ever looks at the underside of my arms."

"Is she awake?"

Sondra turned to find her grandson in the doorway. She held her arms out to him and he crossed the room to hug her. "Let's forget all that 'savta' nonsense. I'm your grandmother. You should call me that."

"Did the accident jar your brain or something?"

She whacked his arm and immediately regretted it. "Ouch! I must be bruised from stem to stern!"

"The doctors say it will be a while before you feel entirely yourself. You're going to need physical therapy to strengthen your hip. Do you remember what happened?"

"My brakes gave out and I couldn't stop the car."

"I knew you should have replaced that thing years ago! This was bound to happen."

"Don't be ridiculous, Fanny. Ol' Red served me faithfully for thirty years!"

"Ol' Red?" questioned Hunter.

"Sure. She deserves a name after so many years, don't you think?"

"Yes, but it should have been something better than old red. What was Adam's stage name?" Hunter mused.

"Why?"

"It was a convertible," he smirked.

"That was so cheesy," Fanny said, rolling her eyes at her son.

Someone knocked on the door frame. Hunter moved to one side and Sondra saw Ethan.

"I came as quickly as I could," he said, striding to her bedside and taking her free hand.

"You should have stayed in New York. I have lots of people to take care of me."

"Don't be ridiculous. I belong at your side, especially when something like this happens."

Fanny released her other hand and said, "Hunter and I are going down to the cafeteria. Do you want anything, Ethan?"

"No. Nothing at all. Thank you."

Her daughter and grandson slipped out of the room, leaving the couple alone.

"What happened?"

"Car accident."

"Did you fall asleep? Could you not see well? How did this happen?"

"I noticed the brakes were spongy when I got in the car. I should have stayed off the freeway, but I thought they would be okay. The last thing I remember is pushing the brake pedal all the way to the floor and the car not stopping."

"My God, Sondra. I almost lost you." He dropped his head to the bed next to her hand. "I just...I can't lose you, too."

"I'm going to be fine. Outside of needing a few months to recover, I'll be okay."

"As long as it takes. I'll get you the best physical therapists we can find. You'll be back on your feet before spring."

"That may be pushing it a bit. I'll settle for before summer."

He kissed her hand. "And I'm not leaving you by yourself again. We'll just pay for the extra ticket and you can come with me wherever I need to go."

"Now who's being ridiculous? I'm just as safe here as I would be if I went with you to New York or anywhere else."

"Clearly, that isn't true. If you'd been in New York with

me, you wouldn't have just been in a car crash."

"Now, Ethan, you can't roll her in bubble wrap to keep the world at bay," Vivian said, striding in with a bouquet of yellow roses and baby's breath. "Sondra, you're looking better than I thought you would be."

"Thank you."

"These are for you." She dropped the bouquet on the rolling u-shaped tray on the far side of the bed. "I'm a wreck when it comes to arranging flowers, so I'll leave them for Sax or Fanny to deal with."

"Thank you for coming," Ethan said, looking up appreciatively at his sister. "I know you are busy with your own problems these days."

"What's wrong?" Sondra asked.

"Patrick's back in the hospital. This is probably the end. If they try to send him home again, I'm going to ask them to move him to hospice." She said the words as casually as one might talk about putting down a stray dog.

Ethan didn't seem to hear the callousness in her voice. "I'm so sorry, Viv. I do think it's for the best that you don't try to nurse him yourself. The hospice will be able to make him much more comfortable than you would."

Sondra, with no energy to start a fight, let the comments pass. "Thank you for the flowers. They're beautiful."

"A token of friendship," Vivian answered. "Ethan, dearest, I'm so thirsty. Would you be a sweetheart and find me some water?"

"You can use the cup here," Sondra said, gesturing to the rolling table. "I haven't used it yet."

She wrinkled her nose. "Ethan knows how much I hate tap water."

"Of course, Sis. I'll be back in a few minutes." He leaned in and kissed Sondra on the forehead before leaving the room.

As soon as he was gone, Viv moved from the foot of the bed, where she had been standing, to Sondra's side, adjusting herself so that she could keep an eye on the door. "So, how much damage did you take?"

"A broken hip and a couple fractured ribs."

Viv gave a low whistle. "You must be in some serious

pain."

"Not really. The painkillers are taking care of that."

"Good to know." Viv smiled and leaned close to her ear, whispering, "How much more damage do you think your body can take?"

Sondra leaned away, her eyes wide. "What do you mean?"

"A woman your age has all kinds of potential problems when it comes to broken bones. Are you taking anything for osteoporosis? Judging by the way your bones broke, I'm guessing no. Of course, if you'd been caught in a cross-traffic accident in that old car, you might not have survived -- no side airbags, you know. So, what I'm asking is this: how many times do you think you can avoid dying if someone is really trying to kill you?"

Sondra stared back at her would-be sister-in-law. "Are you saying--?"

Vivian stood up straight and moved to the bedside chair, relaxing into it like a sated lioness after an antelope dinner. "It's a real shame about your Mercedes, Sondra. That car was a classic."

"As long as she's alive, who cares about the car?" Ethan entered the room with two bottles of water, handing one to Vivian and opening the other for Sondra. "Besides, it always bothered me that you were driving such an old car. The safety features of a newer model really make your car look like a death trap."

"Death trap might be overstating it, Ethan," Vivian commented as she opened her bottle.

"When you're ready to buy a new car, we'll pick out something great for you, babe. I guarantee it will be ten times safer than your old car and probably get four times as many miles to the gallon."

Vivian stood. "I suppose I should go on up to ICU and make sure Patrick is comfortable. I do hope you have a speedy recovery, Sondra."

"I wish you didn't have to rush off," Ethan said. "Is there anything I can do for you? I know you're having a rough time -- with Patrick sick and everything."

"I'll be fine. Just take care of Sondra." She patted one of Sondra's legs. "You've got months of physical therapy ahead of you. It's a good thing you have been so faithful in your workout routine. You'll probably be back to normal by next Christmas."

"Thank you for stopping by," Sondra said coolly. "Give Patrick my regards."

"If he regains consciousness, I'll be sure to do that." The younger woman sashayed out of the room.

Ethan took Sondra's hand and sat down in the chair Vivian had just abandoned. "Do you need anything?"

Sondra considered telling Ethan about the conversation she and Vivian had just shared, but Vivian hadn't said anything that could be considered a confession. Instead, she squeezed his hand. "Just you, Ethan."

Night Life

The Vamp

After everything Sax turned up about Vivian and Ethan, he and Milo agreed that they would rather irritate Sondra with their constant presence at the hospital than risk leaving her vulnerable to an attack. Therefore, the two men decided to alternate between manning the bar and staying close to Sondra's bedside.

With Sax on guard duty, Milo found himself behind the bar alone on a long Saturday shift. The place was busy, but most of the drinkers were regulars who cut Milo some slack when they realized he was on his own. Therefore, though he had a steady stream of activity to attend to, he wasn't too busy to notice the gorgeous brunette with the almond-shaped eyes who slid onto a stool in the middle of the bar. Her pullover sweater was clinging in all the right places and his eyes were torn between focusing on her words and her cleavage.

"I said, I'd like a dry martini," she repeated.

Milo cleared his throat. "Of course. Coming right up."

"I'm new around here," she said to his back. "A neighbor told me this was the place to come if I wanted to meet other singles."

"I think most of our eligible bachelors might be too old for you," he said looking over his shoulder. She couldn't have been forty-five -- Claire looked older.

"I could lie and tell you that I prefer older men," she laughed, "or I could tell you the truth."

"What's the truth?" He turned back to her and, dropping in the olive on its toothpick, set it in front of her.

She smiled, tilting her head to the side. "I'm like a fine wine -- I've aged well."

Though the lights were dim in the bar, he gave her a closer appraisal. Hiding between the supple plumpness of her lips and the inviting crease of her breasts, her neck revealed the age lines of an older woman. "What's your secret?"

"A carefree life and lots of sex."

Milo, caught off guard, laughed. "Sounds wonderful."

"It has been. I'm Sonia Belcourt, by the way." She extended her graceful hand across the bar.

He shook it. "Milo Crosby."

"Milo. That's an unusual name. I don't think I've ever met a Milo before."

"What a coincidence. I've never met a Sonia."

She laughed huskily. "How long have you been a bartender, Milo?"

"Just a few months. I needed something to keep me occupied."

"Retired?"

He nodded. "I was border patrol for thirty-odd years." Out of the corner of his eye, he saw one of the regulars hold up an empty glass. "Excuse me. Duty calls." He refilled the regular's beer as well as a few other glasses. He made change so that a woman could play a few songs on the jukebox. When he came back around to Sonia, she was still nursing her martini.

"I thought I'd lost you." She smiled at him.

"Where are you from originally?"

"What makes you think I'm not from Arizona?"

"You did say you were new around here."

"It's a big valley. I could have meant I was from Mesa originally."

"I suppose that's true." Mesa was on the far eastern edge of what was known as the Metropolitan Phoenix area. Milo knew people who had never been there, despite having lived in Arizona for decades. Claire, who had lived in the east valley during her long marriage, had never been west of Central Avenue before Dorsey's death.

"You must have lived along the border. Nogales? Douglas?"

"You certainly know your Arizona geography," he commented. "Actually, I lived in International Falls."

She frowned. "I've never heard of it. In fact, I didn't know there were any waterfalls along the Mexico-U.S. border."

"There aren't. I'm from Minnesota."

Another fog-covered laugh rolled across the bar at him. "I was a geography teacher once upon a time."

He popped his eyelids up. "If you'd been my geography teacher, that would have been my favorite class."

"Maybe I could give you a lesson sometime. I'd love to escort you across some borders."

"I'm kind of in a relationship right now."

537

Night Life

"Is that like sort of being single?"

He hesitated, but shook his head regretfully. "Let's just say I'm caught in customs at the moment."

"I'm not in a hurry. Maybe I'll still be around when you've got everything worked out."

The bar had an influx of customers and Milo spent the rest of the night filling and refilling orders. Sonia and her dark-blue sweater sat at the bar for another hour, nursing her drink and taking in the crowd. Before she left, she slipped a tip under her glass: a dollar bill with her name and number written on the edge.

Taz started barking the moment Milo pulled into the driveway. When he opened the door, he was surprised to hear Claire shushing him from the living room. Walking around the corner, he found her lounging on the sofa in a very un-sexy pair of sweatpants and an old, stained t-shirt. She muted the television and asked, "How was your day?"

"Busy. I wasn't expecting you to be up."

"I missed you. I thought I should stay awake."

He tried to picture Claire in Sonia's dark-blue sweater, but it was impossible. "You should be getting more sleep. Have you heard from your doctor?" He was still waiting to learn the results of the dozens of tests Claire said the doctor was running.

"No. I'll call on Monday."

"I asked you to call a week ago."

"Milo, these tests take time. It's not like the movies, you know."

"They don't take this long, Claire. If the doctor suspects there is something seriously wrong--"

"If he thought that, I'd be in the hospital and we'd already have the results. I'm okay, Milo. I'll be fine."

"I hardly see you eat, and yet look at you: you're bloated like you've been gnawing the house down."

She pulled the afghan over her bulging middle. "Do you think we'll ever get married?"

"What?"

"Do you want to marry me...someday?"

"I don't know. I thought that's where we were headed, but honestly...Claire, it's like you've given up. Are you just going to lie on that sofa for the rest of your life? Walk around here in t-shirts and sweatpants? What happened to the woman I met at the zoo? The one who sprayed me with a water bottle? That's the Claire I fell in love with. You're not even close to the same person. As a matter of fact, you're starting to remind me an awful lot of dead Alice."

By the time he finished his tirade, tears were rolling down her cheeks. Silently, she pushed the blanket off of her and walked to the bedroom, closing the door behind her.

Defeated, he dropped into his chair. His cell phone chimed. Flipping open his phone, he read a note from Sax letting him know that Sondra was fine. He replied, telling Sax that he would be at the hospital as soon as visiting hours started the next morning.

Pushing himself out of his chair, he dragged himself to the bedroom door. It was locked. He pounded on the door. "Claire, let me in."

"No," she answered.

Milo looked down to find Taz at his feet. "Your dog would like in."

"You can both sleep in the living room. He likes you better, anyway."

He stumbled back to the couch, crash-landing against the remote control sitting where Claire had left it. He turned the volume up and stewed as a couple of has-beens tried to sell the insomniacs of the world a collection of 1970s easy-listening music. What the hell was going on around here? Wasn't this his house? Why was he the one sleeping on the sofa with the dog? In the last few months, his life had gone pretty seriously awry.

T.L.C.

Bad dreams chased Claire all night. More than once, she woke up and reached for Milo, only to find herself alone in his bed. It was his bed; though she had lived with him for months, everything in the house -- with the exception of her clothing -- was his. Even the dog was more his than hers now.

In her last dream, her body began inflating. Soon, she was floating down the street like a Macy's Thanksgiving Day parade balloon. Unable to control her body, she watched helplessly as she drifted into a radio antenna on the top of a building and popped.

Unable to lull herself back to sleep after the terror of exploding, she rolled out of bed, unlocked the door, and padded to the living room to apologize to Milo. It was time to tell him what was really wrong with her. Another two weeks, and she wouldn't be able to hide the pregnancy any longer.

On the sofa, Taz lay wrapped in the afghan alone. Milo was already up. She continued on to the kitchen, but he wasn't sitting at the table, either. She peeked out the back window, expecting to see him on the patio. Only a few quail scavenged through the yard, undisturbed by human activities. Finally opening the carport door, she saw that his car was already gone.

Taz, now at her feet, licked her ankle, reminding her that she needed to fix his breakfast. She closed the door and poured some food in the dog's bowl before walking back to the bedroom and calling her sister.

"Hi, Claire. How are you feeling?"

"Like a sperm whale. How are you?"

"Fine. Have you told Milo yet?"

"No. I was going to this morning, but he's not home."

"It's only a little after nine here. Where would he go so early in the morning?"

"I don't know. The bar doesn't open for hours. I suppose he might have gone to see Sondra."

"His ex?"

Claire fiddled with an abandoned spoon, spinning it on the table. "She's in the hospital. Car accident."

"This is the woman who was living with you both, right?"

540

"Yes, of course."

"You should track him down," Beryl urged. "If you planned to tell him today, don't let anything stop you."

"Maybe it's a sign. Maybe I'm not supposed to tell him."

"Since when are you into signs and wonders? When was the last time you were out of the house?"

"When I went to the doctor."

"Hang up this phone and go directly to the shower. Get dressed, put on some makeup, and find Milo."

"Nothing fits!" Claire wailed. "All I have to wear are sweatpants!"

"You have to do this. You can't let this situation continue as it is. Don't you have a loose-fitting dress somewhere? Go to your closet."

Claire walked to the bedroom and opened the closet door. "There's nothing here."

"Have you even looked yet?"

"I'm standing at the door and I'm telling you, there's nothing but khaki pants and zoo shirts."

"Don't be ridiculous. I know for a fact you have more clothes than that. You weren't even working at the zoo when I moved you to the condo, and you had two closets full of clothes then."

Claire stepped deeper into the closet, pushing the familiar khakis and shirts out of the way. She pulled out a hanger. "I have a denim dress with an empire waist."

"That would probably fit you. What else?"

Listlessly, she moved a few more hangers. "A pair of elastic-waist pants."

"Any blouses?"

A blue-and-white-striped smock top presented itself. "One," she said, describing it to Beryl.

"Good. Anything else?"

She flipped through some more hangers, but couldn't find anything else that looked comfortable. "No."

"You'll probably be most comfortable in the dress," Beryl recommended. "When I'm pregnant, I can't stand anything that cinches in around my middle. Now, go find Milo. Tell him what's going on."

"He doesn't want to marry me," Claire sobbed.

"You know that for sure?"

"I asked him last night if we were going to get married, and he said he didn't know."

"What did you say?"

"Nothing. I locked him out of the bedroom."

Beryl sighed. "Your hormones have got you by the tail. Put yourself in his shoes for a minute."

"I'd be more understanding," she pouted.

"No. You wouldn't. I love you, Claire. Be careful getting ready. Call me later."

"Okay. I love you, too." She clicked the end button and went to the shower.

It took Claire two hours to get ready. She needed to rest after every stage of the process. Pulling up her underwear required a two-minute break afterward. Finding a bra that didn't bite into the abundant flesh of her growing breasts took ten minutes. She finally settled on a sports bra that made her look like she had a uni-boob. Five minutes of sitting on the bed followed.

She had to apply her makeup four times. Every time she got to the point of applying the mascara, she would burst into tears that would cause the makeup to run and make her face splotchy. She would then wash it off and wait until the splotches faded. On the fourth attempt, she skipped the mascara.

The dress, while snug, was relatively comfortable. She located a pair of flats to complete the outfit, grabbed her purse, and drove to the Brass Monkey. If she had been in her normal, logical state of mind, she would have scanned the parking lot for Milo's car. Logic wasn't her strong suit these days, though. She parked her car and marched into the bar, barely noticing her surroundings at all.

"Claire!" Sax called, waving her over.

"Hi, Sax," she smiled. "Have you seen Milo?"

"He's at the hospital with Sondra."

Feeling tears spring to her eyes for the umpteenth time that day, she cursed herself.

"What's wrong?" Sax asked, taking her hand.

"Nothing. Everything. Why is he spending all this time with Sondra?"

"Didn't he tell you?" Sax looked genuinely shocked.

"Tell me what? Is he leaving me?"

"Claire! Get hold of yourself! He's not leaving you. We think Sondra's life may be in danger."

She hadn't expected to hear that. She slumped onto the barstool. "What are you talking about?"

Sax related the sordid tale he had pieced together about Vivian and Ethan's spousal death toll. "We don't want to leave Sondra alone, just in case Vivian decides to try something."

"Do you think she had something to do with Sondra's car malfunctioning?"

"We don't know for sure. Sondra told me that Vivian made some veiled threats regarding Sondra's ability to heal, but she didn't come right out and threaten to kill her."

"She should tell the police," Claire asserted.

"She doesn't want to throw accusations around willy-nilly. She's afraid of hurting Ethan."

"So she's just going to keep quiet?"

"I'm trying to change her mind, but you know Sondra. She's not that flexible when she's got something set in her mind."

"You could go to the police."

"Everything I've got is circumstantial. They would laugh me out of the station."

"You're thinking like a cop. If you are a citizen who suspects something is wrong, you don't have to provide the proof, do you?"

"You must have something that is at least suspicious."

"I'd say three dead spouses is suspicious."

"Maybe," he allowed. "Say, I don't want to butt in where I'm not welcome, but...are you pregnant?"

"Are you saying I look fat?"

"No, no," he backpedaled. "You just have a...glow?"

She rolled her eyes. "I can neither confirm nor deny that rumor at this time."

"You haven't told Milo yet, huh?"

"I've been holding off."

"How far along are you?"

"Far enough. Don't mention it to Milo until he mentions it to you, okay? I don't want him to know other people knew before he did."

"I don't think you should wait much longer. Your condition is becoming obvious."

She slid off the stool with a small grunt. "I know. Thanks for the information, Sax."

"Anytime."

She smiled and gave him a short wave before waddling toward the door.

Deciding that a visit to Sondra wouldn't seem too odd, she drove to the hospital. Inside, she received directions from an elderly woman in an aqua smock who was ensconced behind the welcome desk. "Just take that elevator to the twelfth floor, honey. Turn right, walk past two hallways, and turn left at the third. You can't miss it."

The halls were busy, full of families visiting broken-hipped grandmothers or cancer-stricken uncles. She imagined Sundays were always like this in the hospital -- the one time of the week when everyone remembered to visit their not-quite-dead family members.

She followed the greeter's advice and easily found the unit where Sondra was recuperating. At the doorway of her room, Claire paused to listen for movement within the room. Milo's voice drifted out to her. "...beautiful woman. No one ever flirted with me before."

She could hear Sondra answering, but she couldn't make out her words.

"Is this what the rest of my life is going to be like? I haven't felt this awful since dead Alice..."

Heartbroken, Claire backed away from the door -- and into a handsome young man. "Excuse me," she said, wiping the tears from her eyes with the palm of her hand.

"Are you all right?"

"Fine, thank you."

"Were you visiting Sondra?"

"What?" She focused on the face swimming in front of her. She straightened and pinned on a smile. "You must be Ethan."

"Yes. Are you Claire?"

She nodded.

"Have you been in yet?" When she didn't answer immediately, he continued, "I know she would love to see you. And please don't cry -- she's going to be fine."

"I'm really not--"

"Don't be ridiculous. You came all the way here, didn't you?" He linked arms with her and all but dragged her inside. "Look who I found loitering in the hall, babe."

Milo looked up and ducked his head. "Claire. What are you doing here?"

"I came to see Sondra."

"Of course. I wish I had known. We could have come together."

"You might have told me your plans," she answered sullenly.

"Perhaps if you had been more amenable to conversation last night..."

Ethan cleared his throat uneasily. "Milo, why don't we take a walk down to the cafeteria and let the ladies talk alone for a few minutes."

"Yes, that's a lovely idea," Sondra concurred.

"Fine. You'll stay until we come back?" Milo asked Claire.

"Yes, of course."

The men left the room.

"Come sit down. How are you doing?"

"Not great," she admitted.

"I see the pregnancy test was positive."

Claire crossed her arms over her body, horrified. "Is it that obvious?"

Sondra shook her head. "Not really. But you've definitely gotten bigger since I saw you last."

"I don't know what to do," she confessed. "I was going to tell Milo today, but..."

"How much did you hear?"

"He's planning to break up with me, isn't he?"

Sondra sighed. "You haven't made it easy for him, you

545

know. He thinks you are as miserable as he is. He doesn't want to end up in a loveless marriage again. And, honestly, can you blame him?"

"But I love him so much!"

"Of course you do. But how can he tell? He knows you're hiding something from him."

"But if I tell him, won't he just feel obligated to marry me?"

"This isn't 1969, Claire, and you aren't Alice. Have enough faith in Milo to believe that he won't do something he doesn't want to do."

Claire leaned back in the chair and took a few deep breaths. She thought about Milo and how he had lived his life up to this point. Shaking her head with a sad smile, she said, "I know you haven't met very many men like him, Sondra, but Milo is an honorable man. He will want to marry me, even if he doesn't love me. At the very least, he will believe he has to support this child for the rest of his life. He never planned to have another child -- I can't put him in a position that forces him to be a father."

"You're being ridiculous! The man adores you! He just doesn't know what to think of your craziness in the last few months!"

"He was flirting with someone else, wasn't he?"

Sondra dropped her eyes.

"I'm going to have this baby, because it is a miracle that I conceived at all. But I'll raise it on my own."

"You don't know what you're saying. Take it from me: being a single parent is a miserable, lonely job."

"Your daughter came out fine, though, didn't she?"

"Through no fault of my own."

"They'll be back soon. I'm asking you not to say anything to Milo."

Sondra frowned. "I won't."

"Ethan seems like a nice man."

"He's a gem. And I'm going to have to break up with him."

"Why?"

"It's a long story...and it's one I'd prefer he didn't walk in on."

"What about all your gigs as Sunrise Aeon? What will

happen to them now?"

"The publisher is hiring an actress. The doctors say I won't be able to walk without assistance for at least six weeks."

"I'm so sorry."

"Why? You didn't do anything. I'm just glad that I'll be able to walk again someday. This could have been so much worse -- I might have been dead."

"Knock, knock," a woman's voice called from the doorway. "Mom, are you decent?"

Claire looked around the side of the curtain and saw a Romanesque beauty. Fanny was definitely not what Claire had expected. "Come on in. I was just leaving."

"Don't rush off on my account. I'm Fanny Susser, Sondra's daughter."

"Claire Combs." She pushed herself out of the chair. "Really, I was just leaving." She took Sondra's hand. "Thank you for listening. I'm praying for a speedy recovery."

"You and me both, sweetie. Come back soon."

Claire smiled, already knowing she wouldn't.

As she walked out of the hospital that crisp late-February morning, Claire was going through some logistics in her mind. Outside of a single outfit that she had left laying across their bed, none of her clothes fit her at this time. Everything else she might need -- a toothbrush, some makeup, a curling iron -- could be replaced at any drugstore. Long-term parking for her car could be an issue.

Digging around in her purse, she found the spare key for the condo. Driving directly there, she parked in the empty space that Sondra's car would no longer be filling. She took the elevator to her floor and entered the condo. The computer -- the one she had left for Sondra's use -- was exactly where she had left it. She pressed the on button and went to the kitchen to pour herself some water. Opening a drawer, she found a scratch pad and a pen. *Dear Sondra,* she wrote, *I have decided to go home for a while. As you know, my father is very ill and likely to die within the next few months. I hope to put our relationship right before he is gone forever. Also, I believe that Beryl will be a great comfort to me in my current situation. The keys to my car are next to this note. Please feel free to use it anytime you would like. I know it will be weeks before you read this, but if Milo doesn't already know by then, be sure to tell him that I am fine and that he can keep Taz. The dog likes him best, anyway. Much Love, Claire. P.S. Don't forget to pay the association fees.*

She pushed the note to the center of the counter in what she hoped would be a prominent place. Glancing around the apartment, she spotted a few green plants. Ethan would probably be by to water them; He would find the note first. That was fine. With her glass of water, she walked back to the computer and pulled up a travel website. Within a few minutes, she had a seat on a flight leaving Phoenix at six o'clock that evening and arriving in Oklahoma around midnight. She booked a cab online, too, asking for it to pick her up outside the building in twenty minutes.

She pulled out her cell phone and dialed Beryl's number. "It's me. Can you pick me up at the airport at midnight?"

Night Life

Rusty Nail

On Monday morning, Sax was up early and on his way to the hospital at the same time he normally would have been working out. He was feeling rusty in more ways than one -- his brain and his muscles needed some extra lube. He and Milo hadn't been in the same room together for more than a few minutes since Sondra's accident, so the investigation was, for all intents and purposes, stalled. The bit he had shared with Sondra had made him feel like he was wasting his time anyway. She was right -- he had nothing in the way of solid evidence.

Vivian had yet to make another appearance outside of her first one. She was supposed to be tending to her nearly dead husband, but when Sax visited ICU, Patrick, who looked more like a pincushion than a man, was alone. He was also unconscious, which was not what Sax had been hoping to find. He intended to try again that morning.

Sondra was awake and taking her first steps with a walker when he arrived at her room. A physical therapist stood on one side while Hunter stood on the other.

"You're doing great, Grandma!" Hunter offered as she took another step.

"Fantastic. All I need are my tap shoes and I'm back in business," she grumbled.

"I'd dance with you," Sax said, smiling.

"Only because you think you'd look better than me on the dance floor these days." She stopped and raised her eyes. "You don't have to keep showing up, you know. I get it -- you and Milo care about me. Now, go tend your bar."

"What can I say? We have a soft spot for old actresses. And we need you back at the bar. Revenues have really fallen off of late."

"Ha ha, you old fairy. Get over here and take Hunter's place -- he's about to crumple under the pressure."

"Grandma, I'm stronger than I look," he whined.

Sax had to admit the boy looked to be lacking in the muscle department. But that was how the girls like their dates to look these days: malnourished and stick thin. He was probably getting a lot of action in college, which reminded Sax that he should be there. "What are you doing here, Hunter?

549

Aren't you in school?"

"I took emergency leave. Mom thought this was going to be a lot more serious than it is."

"When do you go back?"

"I'm driving back on Sunday."

"Why don't you take a break? Give me a few minutes with our glamour girl."

"You got it," he smiled. "I'm going to the cafeteria. You want anything, Grandma?"

"No, that's okay. I might as well eat what they bring me...they're going to charge me an arm and a leg for it anyway."

"Sax?"

"I'd love a water." With his free hand, he pulled his wallet out of his pocket. "Open this up and take a five out."

The boy waved him off. "Naw, I got this, Sax."

"That's a nice boy you've got there, Sondra," he said as soon as Hunter was gone.

"I like him pretty well. Hell, I'm just glad the kid still wants to talk to me."

"Are you kidding? His grandmother is Sunrise Aeon. All the bad shit gets washed away with a rep like that."

"Let's take some more steps, Ms. Lane," the business-like physical therapist said.

Sax and the woman spotted Sondra as she moved a few more feet.

"Just like riding a bicycle," Sondra joked.

"You're making great progress, Ms. Lane. Let's try to make it to the door."

Slowly, they moved forward.

"I saw Claire yesterday," Sondra said between steps.

"So did I. She stopped by the bar."

"She was really distressed. I'm worried about her."

"She'll be all right, won't she?"

"I don't know. I don't envy her, being pregnant at her age. It's hard enough when you're a young woman. To have to deal with those kinds of hormones at her age -- that sucks."

"Let's turn around now." The therapist guided them through a turn and they started the slow journey back to the bed.

"Why are you really here, Sax?"

"I just can't shake the thought that your car accident wasn't so accidental."

"Stop it. Just...stop. I've been giving this a lot of thought over the last few days. I'm going to end things with Ethan, so there will be nothing for you old busybodies to worry about."

"I don't think you should do that."

"Why not? He's three decades younger than me! When I'm eighty, he'll only be fifty. And what happens when he realizes he wants children after all? Thirty-two is too young for a man to make that kind of a decision."

"I have to admit I had my doubts about him, Sondra, but I've been watching him around you for the last few days. He absolutely adores you. You may never find a man who looks at you like that again."

"Turn," the therapist instructed. They helped Sondra sit down on the bed. "That's all for today, Ms. Lane. I'll be back in the morning."

"Thank you, Salena," Sondra said.

"I can't believe you're walking already."

"It's the titanium. I guess when you're as old as I am, they don't even mess with trying to mend the bones. Kind of an 'out with the old, in with the new' mentality."

Sax laughed. "Whatever works."

"The doctors still say it will be weeks before I'm anything close to normal again. But, as they say, *c'est la vie*."

"When are they releasing you?"

"No later than Thursday. After that, I'm going to a rehab center for a few weeks at least."

Hunter appeared, carrying a fountain drink in one hand and a bottle of water in the other. "Catch," he called, tossing the water bottle at Sax.

"Thanks."

"Anytime. How'd the old biddy do?"

"All the way to the door and back," Sax answered.

"Hey! I told you that Grandma was okay, but I can do without the improvisation, buster," Sondra said indignantly.

Hunter chuckled and gave Sax a conspiratorial grin.

"What's going on in here?" Ethan boomed as he came through the door, catching all of them off guard.

"Ethan! Good morning," Sax answered, recovering as gracefully as possible from his girlish hop.

"Sondra, you look lovely this morning," he said, sweeping past Hunter and Sax with a nod to them. "I brought you this lovely bloom from your gardenia plant."

"Oh! Thank you, darling," she said, smiling and taking the flower.

"I have something else that's a little less pleasing, I think," he said, perching on her bed. It's from your friend Claire." He handed her a note.

Sondra read it. "Oh, my God!" she gasped. "She's left Milo!"

"Left him? Are you sure?"

"You tell me," she said, handing it to Sax.

"She says she's going home to make peace with her father. She'll be back."

"But read the end -- she asks us to tell Milo to keep the dog! She's not coming back."

"She's pregnant, though -- she has to come back. Milo is the father."

"She isn't going to tell him. She thinks it's better if he doesn't know."

"But we know!" Sax exclaimed. "What are we supposed to do, keep our mouths shut?"

"I believe she wants us to act like we don't know." Sax leaned forward to argue, but Sondra held up a single finger. "If we want to call ourselves her friend, we need to do as she asks."

"Let's give these two some privacy, Hunter," Sax said, putting an arm around the kid's shoulder. "I want to talk to you for a minute anyway."

"Thank you," Sondra called as they rounded the corner.

"What's up?" Hunter asked.

"Follow me." Sax led him to the intensive care unit where Patrick Bradford lay. "You seem like a bright kid. What are you studying?"

"French literature."

Sax grimaced. "Really? Why?"

"Because when it comes right down to it, unless I'm planning to be a lawyer or a doctor, my undergrad coursework is completely irrelevant. And my classmates are almost all female," he grinned.

"What are you planning to do with your life?"

He shrugged. "Based on the current economic situation, I'd say a long-term stint in the fast-food industry."

"That's a good one, kid." He pointed toward the room with the gaunt, sleeping Patrick. "You see that guy?"

"Yeah?"

"That's Vivian's husband."

"You mean Ethan's sister? Why would she marry a man that old?"

"To hear her tell it, theirs is a love match."

"Okay. Why are we here?"

"I'm going to tell you something important because I need your help. But I'll need you to keep it to yourself. You okay with that?"

Hunter stared hard at Sax before nodding slowly.

"Here goes: I think Vivian has killed three people and is currently working on her fourth and fifth victims."

Hunter pulled back and gave a short laugh. "No way."

Sax nodded grimly.

"So you're saying...she's the reason Grandma is in the hospital? But the police say the accident was just that. Besides, who would try to cause an accident by impeding the brakes in a city as flat as this one? It just doesn't make sense."

Hunter had a good point -- one that hadn't occurred to Sax. His brain, still lacking the necessary lubricant for a smooth train of thought, ground out a theory: "Maybe the car accident was about something other than killing her. It might have been a warning. Or it could have been a way for Vivian to gain access to Sondra. One of Ethan's wives told me--"

"Wait a second. Both of Ethan's wives are dead."

"I did some digging and discovered he was married to another woman briefly. She had the marriage annulled after Sondra poisoned her and threatened to finish the job later. Vivian's first husband and the one currently dying share a number of symptoms and diagnoses." He lowered his voice to a whisper. "I think she is poisoning him. And she might be planning to poison Sondra as well."

"We've got to stop her. Can't you go to the police?"

"I don't have enough evidence. I was still investigating when Sondra ended up here. Milo and I have been switching off for days now just to make sure someone was with her during visiting hours, but that meant I had to put my research on hold."

"I can stay with her," Hunter volunteered. "At least, until Saturday," he amended.

"That should be plenty of time. Thanks for the help."

"No problem. She may not have won any grandmothering awards, but I'm pretty fond of the old gal. And she's finally starting to soften up a bit."

After saying goodbye to Sondra, Ethan, and Hunter, Sax went to his car to plot his next move. As he flipped through the file of information he had gathered, Easter L'Oeuf's card slipped out onto the passenger seat. Sax picked it up, fingering it thoughtfully. He hadn't intended to talk to either of the tattooists again. However, if he could get her alone...

He pulled out his cell phone and dial the number on the card.

"Easternalia -- where art and magic come together. I'm sorry, but the muses are dancing at the moment. Leave us a message and we'll cast our spell around you soon." A low tone followed.

"Um, Easter, this is Sax Ridley calling. Sondra Lane's friend, remember? I was just wondering if I could get a private showing at the gallery today. I know you aren't usually available on Monday, but I hoped you could make an exception." He left his phone number and hung up. That was probably a waste of time.

Astrid was a cheerleader in high school. He knew it was a long shot, but he had copied down the names of all the other girls on her squad in hopes that a few of them had kept in touch with her. He would need a computer to track them down. He headed for the main library on Central Avenue. As he walked from the parking lot to the building, his phone rang. "Hello?"

"Sax? This is Easter. As it happens, I'm setting up for a new show today at the gallery. If you'd like to stop by--"

"Thanks so much. Can I bring you anything? Lunch? A drink?"

She laughed. "Just bring your wallet. I have the perfect piece for you."

"Great. See you soon." Ending the call, he glanced regretfully at the library before returning to his car.

The building, an older strip mall with most of its parking in the back, was well-suited to the sorts of businesses that called it home now. Easternalia, in particular, took full advantage of the huge plate-glass windows to draw in customers. Sax had the advantage of parking in one of the three spaces right in front of the store. Facing the window on three free-standing white walls were two paintings in a style similar to the hard-candy cathedral in Sondra's living room and, on the middle wall, a particularly evocative portrait of a middle-aged woman. He could see the folding metal gate, a necessity in this part of town, pushed to one side of the shop. On the other end, the door was propped open with a wooden wedge.

He stepped out of his car and locked it behind him. At the entrance, he called, "Easter? You here?"

He felt someone tap his shoulder; he jumped.

Easter laughed, her bright yellow hair looking like a cotton-candy confection piled on her head. "Didn't mean to startle you." She held out a drink in a styrofoam cup. "I got this for you."

He took it. "What is it?"

"The place next door makes killer Italian cream sodas. That one is vanilla -- everyone likes vanilla, right?" She moved past him and into the gallery.

He followed, sipping the drink. "Yeah, I suppose so."

"How's the tattoo healing?"

"It looks good."

"Mind if I take a look?"

He blushed slightly. "Um..."

She rolled her eyes. "Oh, come on, Sax. I'm practically a married woman and you're gay. I just want to see the tat."

Chagrined, he unbuttoned his shirt far enough that she could see it.

Nice," she said, nodding her approval. "Arlo's such an artist. If you'd given him a little more notice, he probably would have created something unique for you. But as long as you're happy..."

"I am. It's just what I wanted."

She smiled widely. "Perfect. Now, I want to show you this new piece that came in recently--"

"Before we talk art, I'd like to ask you a few questions."

"About what?"

"Is there someplace where we can sit and talk for a few minutes?"

She led him further into the gallery to a grouping of tufted black ottomans. She lowered herself onto one and gestured toward another. "Please. Have a seat."

He squatted onto an ottoman and leaned forward, balancing his elbows against his knees. "Do you know Sondra is in the hospital?" he asked.

She nodded. "Ethan called Arlo a few days ago. She was in a car accident, right?"

"That's what it looks like."

"But you don't think so."

"No, I'm afraid I don't. Arlo told me you were a good friend of Ethan's last wife."

"Yes, Astrid and I were very close." She blinked, and Sax had the impression that she had just pulled the shades on her internal thoughts.

"I want you to be honest with me," he probed.

"Honesty doesn't pay well, especially when it comes to Ethan and his sister."

"What do you know about Vivian?"

"Other than that messing with her is a really bad idea?" Easter arched a well-plucked eyebrow at him.

"Do you think she killed Astrid?"

She gave a brief shake of her head. "What do you think of the soda?"

"Very good. Please...I'm just trying to protect my friend."

"I really think you're going to love the piece I've got in mind. You're a fan of Asian-themed art, aren't you?"

He sighed, recognizing that he wasn't going to get any further with her. "Yes."

"Let me show you this lovely piece. The artist is working in traditional ways, using rice paper and inks, but creating modern works." She led him toward the far right wall, where a collection of the artist's works were gathered. She pointed at a long, narrow one that featured a dragon scaling a skyscraper, its body twisted around the modern edifice.

"That's beautiful."

"Toya calls this one *Eastern Values*."

"Toya? The artist?"

"Toya Mizokuchi. She's talented, isn't she?"

"Very."

"I think you should meet her."

"Really? Why?"

"You have a lot in common. She's originally from Japan...and I met her through Ethan."

He nodded slowly, hoping that she was saying what he thought she was saying. "Okay. I'll take it."

"Excellent choice, Sax. I'll just roll it up for you."

He handed her a credit card, praying that the thousand-dollar price tag was worthwhile. She slid the rice-paper painting into a wide tube and rang up the purchase using her smart phone. "Do you have a pen?"

He patted his pockets before remembering that he had left his pen and notepad in the car. "I can get one. Give me a minute." He took the painting with him, securing it in the backseat before gathering his writing implements. Back inside, he handed them to her.

"This is Toya's phone number. I think she'll be glad to hear from you -- she appreciates knowing who is enjoying her work. Just let her know I told you to call."

"Thank you, Easter." He took her hand and clasped it warmly, making eye contact with the woman.

She blinked and looked away. "Just...be careful."

Toya Mizokuchi, a thin woman with striking eyes, opened the door to her red-brick Willow District home and, bowing slightly, invited Sax inside. "I am honored to welcome you to my home."

"Thank you. I appreciate your hospitality."

"Which of my paintings did you purchase, if I may ask?"

"*Eastern Values*."

"Ah! That is a personal favorite of mine. Please, follow me. I have prepared tea for us."

She led him through the arched hallway to the dining room, which featured a black lacquered table and ornate armchairs with low backs. He settled in the chair to which she directed him. She poured the tea before sitting down across from him.

"You have a lovely home," he said with a smile.

"Thank you. It is much different from the home where I was raised. I have been very blessed. America has been good to me."

"Easter tells me she met you through Ethan Tanner."

"Yes."

"How did you meet him?"

"Ethan's parents were my host family when I first came to Arizona."

Sax sipped his tea and waited for her to continue.

"I chose to attend Arizona State University in order to obtain a degree in Art Studies. My pastor at the church I attended in Kyoto arranged for me to have a place to stay."

"You lived with them while you were in college?"

"During the holidays and summers only. I did not fly home because of the cost for tickets. And Americans take so many holidays! I never knew that before I came here."

"So, Ethan introduced you to Easter?"

She nodded. "We would have met without him, though. She was an art history major. We took classes together later. Easter has been one of my best friends."

"Do you know Vivian?"

Toya smiled. "Of course. Vivian is very good to me."

"Are you still close to all of the Tanners?"

"Yes. They are like family to me."

"Did you know any of Vivian or Ethan's spouses?"

"Of course. My husband is Julia's brother."

Sax, shocked, sat back in the chair and surveyed the walls for pictures. There were none. "I had no idea. So, you were once Ethan's sister-in-law?"

"Indeed."

He was stumped. He knew for certain that Easter had sent him here for a reason, but he wasn't at all sure what questions he should be asking. Knowing that Toya was fond of the Tanners, he trod carefully. "How long have you been married?"

"Joe and I were married nearly ten years ago. Ethan met Julia at our wedding."

"How did you meet Joe?"

"Joe was my ceramics teacher." She smiled and looked down at the table. "More tea?"

"Yes, please."

She poured the refills.

"Were you close to Julia?"

For the first time, her smile faltered. "She was a difficult woman to like."

"May I ask why?"

"She was dangerous."

"I don't--"

"No, that isn't the word. Why is English so imprecise?" Her beautiful eyes narrowed in frustration. "Impulsive. Yes, that's better. But dangerous impulsive."

Remembering what others had said about Julia, he supplied, "She took risks?"

"Yes. Big risks. I never understood why."

"You and Joe must have been upset when Ethan and Julia separated."

She nodded. "We tried to talk to them. They still loved each other -- anyone could tell that. Ethan wanted her to see a doctor. Vivian even tried to talk to her. I thought Vivian would fix it. No one can resist her."

"What do you mean?"

"She is very persuasive. Charming, too. When she said she would talk to Julia, Joe and I relaxed. We knew she would fix everything. But then Julia died."

"So Vivian didn't have a chance to talk to her?"

Toya shook her head slightly. "No, she did."

"But she wasn't successful?"

"No, she was."

"I don't understand."

"Vivian told me that Julia agreed to see a doctor."

"When did Vivian talk to her?"

"Right before that last base jump." She shook her head, full of sorrow. "Vivian carries so much guilt about Julia. If only

Night Life

she had not convinced her to go ahead with that last jump."

Night Life

A Hole in One

"Now that I know you are in good hands here, I need to return to New York," Ethan said, holding one of Sondra's hands in both of his.

"No...really?"

"I'm afraid so. I cut the trip short to be at your side, but my publisher desperately wants me to talk to some producers about the Sunrise Aeon project."

"What kind of producers?"

"Television."

Sondra's eyes widened. "They're going to make a television show?"

"Possibly. Let's not get our hopes too high."

Standing in the doorway, Hunter cleared his throat.

"Come in," she called to her grandson.

"I'm sorry to interrupt."

"You're not interrupting," Ethan said. "As a matter of fact, I need to go. I'm supposed to be on a plane in two hours."

"Good luck," she said, squeezing his hand and smiling at him.

"As long as you are okay, I have all the luck I need." He bent over and kissed her warmly. To Hunter, he said, "Take good care of her."

Hunter shook his hand. "You know I will."

When Ethan was gone, Sondra asked, "Where did Sax go?"

"He had some errands to run."

"Did he say when he would return?"

"No, but I'm here to keep you company."

"You don't need to do that."

"But I want to, Grandma." He sat down in the empty chair next to her bed. "How are you and Ethan doing?"

She smiled wistfully. "Well enough, but I think our May-December romance may have run its course."

"How can you say that? He obviously loves you very much."

"Maybe. But his sister hates me and I can't help thinking that it isn't fair for me to hold onto him -- especially now that I'm crippled."

"Don't be melodramatic. With a few months of physical therapy, you'll be back to normal."

"Maybe. But over-sixty normal and thirty-something normal are at different ends of the normal spectrum."

Hunter frowned. "Wait...isn't Ethan's sister married to an older man?"

"How did you know that?"

He shrugged. "Sax and I went upstairs to look in on the old guy."

"You know where he is?"

"Yes. He's in ICU."

Sondra pushed the button that would raise her to a sitting position in the bed. "Find a wheelchair, Hunter. We're going to be neighborly."

"Grandma, he looked pretty out of it--"

"Maybe so, but that's no reason not to visit." She swung her legs over the side of the bed.

Hunter, deciding not to argue with her, retrieved the wheelchair sitting outside of her room and helped her into it.

"Where's my brush? I need to do something about this hair."

He opened the drawer in the bedside table and retrieved it, as well as the few cosmetics his mother had thought she might want. "Here you go," he said, handing her the brush and the cosmetic bag.

"Thank you, sweetheart. Roll me into the bathroom so I can fix myself up a bit."

Sondra hadn't looked in a mirror since the accident. The first glimpse was shocking -- her hair desperately needed recoloring and her skin had gone from ivory to pallid in just the few days she had been in the hospital. "My God, Hunter! I look like death!"

"You look fine. It's the fluorescent lights -- they aren't doing you any favors."

She grumbled, but pulled the brush through her hair until it looked reasonably styled. She thanked the heavens for the natural curl she had spent most of her life cursing. With lipstick and mascara, she succeeded in improving her overall appearance to the point where she felt she could leave the room. "Let's go!" she announced. Hunter appeared behind her and guided the wheelchair out of the room and past the nurses' station.

"Where are you going, Ms. Lane?" asked the nurse assigned to her that day. She stepped out from behind the station and blocked Hunter's progress.

"A friend of mine is in ICU. My grandson is going to take me to see him."

"I don't think that's wise. Why don't we go back to bed?"

"Are you planning to join me?" Sondra asked.

"Why, no, of course not!"

"Then I think we'll--" she waggled her finger between herself and her grandson "--just take a little walk."

"You shouldn't bother the other patients!" she said, exasperated.

"I promise not to cause any problems. I just want to look in on my friend. Please," she said, widening her eyes and turning down the corners of her mouth, "he's very ill. I might never see him alive again."

The nurse relented, stepping to one side. A nicotine breeze wafted past Sondra's nose. "Don't be gone too long."

"Thank you. By the way, can I bum a ciggy off you? I'm dying for a smoke."

The nurse pulled a pack from her pocket and slipped a single cigarette to her. "There's a smoking area on the far side of the building."

"Thanks. Forward ho, Hunter," she said, slipping the cigarette into the pocket of her robe.

"Are you really going to smoke that?" he asked as they rolled toward the elevator.

"Yes, of course. Why not?"

"I just thought you'd given them up."

"Not likely."

"You know they'll kill you."

"Only if nothing else beats them to the punch."

Hunter pressed the button for Patrick's floor and stood silently behind her.

"I can actually feel the waves of disapproval coming off of you, son."

"Not much I can do about that."

"I wish I had spent more time with you when you were young."

"Why?"

"Because then I'd have some idea of your imperfections. As it is, I feel like you have the advantage."

He laughed. "Good. I should have the advantage in something."

The doors slid open, and Hunter pushed her toward the room. As they rounded the corner, Hunter pointed and said, "There he is."

Sondra barely recognized the gaunt man in the hospital bed. As she rolled closer, her eyes locked on his face, his eyes opened and the corners of his mouth twitched upward. When they were in the room, he said hoarsely, "Sondra Lane."

"Yes, Patrick, it's me. How are you feeling?"

"I've been better."

She took his hand. "What's wrong?"

"The doctor thinks it's my heart."

"He's not sure?"

"I was originally admitted because of dangerously low blood pressure readings and an irregular heartbeat. Dr. Thakkar put me on Florinef to raise my blood pressure and it worked. He sent me home. Once I was home, though, the Florinef stopped working and my blood pressure fell again. Dr. Thakkar raised my dosage. The next thing I knew, I was back in here. Vivian tells me I was in a coma for a few days."

"Has Vivian been here today?"

"Not yet. She usually comes in the afternoon." His gaze shifted to just over her head. "Who is this young man?"

"This is my grandson, Hunter."

"A pleasure to meet you, son. I don't get many visitors. Vivian is my only family, you know."

Sondra was startled. "You don't have children?"

"I'm afraid not. My first wife didn't want any. Vivian and I talked about having one or two, but I'm past seventy. I don't want to leave her with the burden of raising children alone."

She smiled, remembering Bill. "My first love was considerably older than I was. He died when our daughter was young, but I've never regretted having her."

Hunter let out a disbelieving guffaw.

She swiveled to look up at him. "It's true -- even though your mother and I haven't always gotten along, I still love and cherish her."

Hunter studied his grandmother for a minute before allowing himself a short nod. "Yeah. I guess you do."

She looked back at Patrick, whose eyes were drifting shut. "We'll go now, Patrick. Feel better soon."

He squeezed her hand. "Come back again. I'd love to see you tomorrow."

Hunter wheeled them back to the elevator and pressed the button for the ground floor. As the car glided smoothly down the shaft, he asked, "What do you think is wrong with him?"

"I'm not sure, but it sounds serious. Vivian told us that he was at death's door. Clearly, it's even more serious than Patrick suspects."

He rolled her out of the hospital and toward the far corner of the building. It was a beautiful late-winter day in Phoenix, the kind of day that all the tourism brochures brag about: warm, but not hot, with a slight breeze and a blue sky. The gardeners had planted colorful flowers along the sidewalk border, and Sondra was cheered by the sight of them. As they rounded the corner, they found a row of wheelchair-bound smokers polluting their bodies as well as the air.

Sondra retrieved the cigarette from her robe pocket and asked the old man in the chair next to her for a light. As she drew in that first hit of nicotine in almost a week, she sighed with pleasure.

Hunter coughed and realigned himself out of the drifting smoke. "Sax thinks Vivian might be trying to kill him."

"I wouldn't put it past her."

"Shouldn't we do something to help him?"

"What can we do? We don't have any evidence."

"If Sax comes up with something--"

She turned her head sharply. "What do you mean?"

"Sax is doing a little detective work."

"I asked him not to do that."

"I didn't get the impression that he was much for taking orders -- from you or anyone else."

"He's going to get himself killed if he's not careful."

"Who would kill him?"

She bit her lip and stared out across the parking lot, flexing her hands in frustrated impotence. Finally she grasped Hunter's wrist and pulled him closer. "I think she did something to my car," she whispered.

"Grandma! Did you tell the police?"

"Tell them what, exactly? I don't know what she did or how she did it! All I know is that my brakes went from spongy to non-existent in the space of a few miles."

"They could check the car--"

"And what if they found something? Just because I say Vivian threatened me doesn't mean the cops will be able to link any tampering back to her. And I don't want to destroy my relationship with Ethan -- he's my link to the Sunrise Aeon franchise. Without him in my corner, I won't reap any of the financial benefits."

"If you break up with him," Hunter reasoned, "won't you lose the benefits anyway?"

"I'm working my way around that." She sucked deeply on the cigarette and tapped away the ash. "I want him to think our breakup is what he wants."

Hunter frowned. "You'll never pull that off."

"Have a little faith in your grandmother." She took one more drag and stubbed out the butt. "Take me back inside. I'm chilly."

"Mrs. Lane?" A curvaceous brunette knocked on the hospital room door.

"Miss Lane, if you please," Sondra corrected.

The woman glanced at her clipboard. "Oh, my goodness. I'm so sorry. May I come in?"

"Of course."

Hunter stood up and offered the woman his chair.

"My, aren't you polite?" she said, smiling graciously as she sat.

"Good manners are the mark of good breeding," Sondra said, smiling at Hunter.

"Indeed, they are." The woman had a sweet Southern drawl that reminded Sondra of her long-dead friend Lianne. "My name is Devanna Hennon, and I'm here to discuss your rehabilitation needs."

"It's a pleasure to meet you."

"Likewise, I'm sure. Now, Dr. Getz tells me you'll be released from the hospital tomorrow."

"So soon?" Hunter asked, concerned.

"I know it seems premature, but most hip replacement patients are moved to a rehabilitation facility within a week of their surgery."

"But she can barely walk."

"That's why she needs to be in a rehab center," she said to Hunter. "Maybe we should speak privately, Miss Lane."

"Hunter is my grandson. I want him here."

"Fine," she answered, her silky voice barely concealing the steel beneath her words. She proceeded to describe the benefits of the Greenleaf Rehabilitation Center in detail, right down to a discussion of how much Medicare would pay. "Now, of course, the balance would be your responsibility, but what is money for if it can't buy you a healthy recovery?"

"You're right," Sondra agreed.

"I can guarantee you a place at our facility if you'll just sign here..." Devanna, pointing at the bottom of the form, handed her clipboard to Sondra.

Sondra pulled the pen out of the space behind the clip.

"Grandma, I think we should talk about this first."

"Hunter, what am I going to do if not this?"

"Ms. Hennon, please give us a moment."

The woman flashed angry eyes at the young man, but stood. "Of course. Please, take a few moments and talk it over. Just remember, we don't have a lot of beds available." She swished out of the room, leaving her clipboard behind.

"Hunter, what are you thinking?"

"You need to go home."

"What are you talking about?"

"Grandma, we can arrange for a physical therapist to come to the condo. What we can't do is protect you from Vivian if you're at the rehab center."

"This is ridiculous. She's not going to kill me -- I'm breaking up with Ethan."

"Why do you think she threatened you?"

"Because I'm engaged to her brother."

"You said yourself that you want to preserve your relationship with Ethan because of the potential money involved. What if that's the real reason she threatened you?"

She laughed. "You think she threatened me out of greed?"

"That's the only motive that makes sense!"

Sondra remembered Vivian's words from their argument at the Brass Monkey: she wasn't worth the risk. What risk was she talking about? Hunter could be right. "Okay," she said. "I'll go home."

"Good. I can stay with you until the weekend. I'm sure Mom will be happy to--"

"Your mom has to work."

"Reuben makes more than enough to support her. She can take family leave from work."

She sighed. "Don't get me wrong, Hunter, but your mother and I would kill each other if we were left alone for days on end."

"I thought you two were getting along."

"We are -- in the same way that Israel gets along with its neighbors."

"I haven't seen an array of missiles in either of your homes," he joked. When she didn't laugh, he sobered. "Okay. I get it. Who else could help you?"

"I don't have a lot of friends."

"What about Sax and Milo?"

"Sax is wonderful, but he needs to take care of his bar. Milo's been on auto-pilot since Claire took off. He's broken, but he doesn't know it yet. Besides, he's not much of a caretaker type."

"I'll take another week of emergency leave and we'll figure something out."

Devanna knocked on the door frame. "Have you made a decision? I need to get your application in right away if you're going to be staying with us."

"Thank you for taking the time to go over my options, Devanna, but I've decided to go home instead."

The woman stiffened and shot Hunter an irritated glare. "I think you are making a terrible mistake--"

"Nevertheless, it's my mistake to make."

"Yes, I suppose it is." She nodded curtly at Sondra. "Thank you for allowing me to talk to you." She turned on her heel and left the room.

Night Life

"Well, now we've done it," Sondra sighed, taking her grandson's hand. "You're stuck with me."

Just before noon the next day, a transportation attendant rolled Sondra out of the hospital. Hunter brought his car around, reminding Sondra that her oldest and most reliable friend -- her red convertible -- was no longer with her. The wave of loss that rolled over her was only mildly less than the one she had felt when Bill died. After all, her car had been with her decades longer than he had.

"You okay, Grandma?" Hunter asked as he opened the door of his weathered Toyota sedan. The car had belonged to his mother before him and showed all the signs of her ownership. It was a single woman's vehicle of choice. Boys -- especially teenage ones -- were much more interested in sports cars or trucks. Nevertheless, Hunter didn't seem particularly bothered by his car's lack of style. His was a personality ruled by function over form: the car was free and it ran, two selling points he couldn't overlook.

"I'm fine," she sighed, allowing him to hook his arm under hers and guide her into the passenger seat. "Did you tell your mother I was getting out today? I thought she might be here."

"She had to work," he said, pushing the hospital-owned chair toward the attendant, who took it and disappeared inside. "Are you buckled in?"

She nodded and he closed the door, walking around to the other side. "Are you hungry? Should we stop and get some lunch?"

"I'm hardly able to get into the car. How am I going to get inside a restaurant?"

"Not to worry -- I picked up a wheelchair for you this morning."

"I'm not using one of those in public," she answered archly.

"So, you're planning to stay in your condo for the next six weeks?"

"I'm already walking."

"Make up your mind, Grandma. Either you're an invalid or you are self-sufficient -- you can't be both."

She pressed her lips together firmly, already regretting her decision to go home. Hunter started the car and headed toward the condo. "Why did you get me a wheelchair? I would rather have a walker."

"Actually, I have both. The walker is already at your place."

"You've been busy this morning. I wondered why you weren't at my bedside."

"I had to risk that you would be okay until I could get there."

"I wanted to visit Patrick again before I left. He's going to think I broke my promise."

"Should I stop for lunch or not?"

"Let's just drive through," she answered, staring out the window. The dingier part of Camelback Road flew past. The west side of the valley just wasn't as nice as the central and eastern portions. The condo, located close to the corner of Central and Camelback, was right on the fashionable edge of the divide. She wouldn't have chosen that particular building, but Claire had different taste than she did. And, of course, Claire also had the money to buy whatever she wanted -- within reason. Would Claire be selling the condo now that she wasn't living in Phoenix? Sondra worried that she might soon find herself without a place to call her own.

Hunter pulled into a fast-food restaurant and ordered a couple of burger meals for the two of them. Sondra dug in her purse, extracting a twenty to pay for the food.

"I can buy, Grandma."

"I know, but I don't want you to," she answered, pressing the money into his hand. "You're doing more than enough already."

In the condo garage, Hunter parked in a visitor space, since Claire's car was in the space assigned to Sondra's unit. Sondra waited while he extracted the wheelchair from the trunk and wheeled it to the passenger side, opening her door for her. Together, they maneuvered her into the chair. Hunter leaned back inside the car and retrieved the bag of food, settling it in her lap.

Night Life

He rolled her to the elevator and they rode up in silence. Once inside the condo, he pushed her up to the dining table and went to the kitchen to get plates for their meals.

Sondra surveyed the condo. The furniture had been rearranged to provide wider pathways between the rooms. She supposed that was also Hunter's doing. The walker, red and shiny, stood by the armchair.

Hunter returned with the plates and sat down across from her. "How are you doing, Grandma? Can I get you anything else?"

"No. I'm fine."

"Sax is going to stop by later."

"That's nice of him."

"Yeah. I like him -- he seems like a real mensch."

"You've been spending too much time with Reuben's family," she accused.

He chuckled. "Maybe so."

After lunch, he rolled her to the armchair and helped her transfer out of her wheelchair.

"How's that feel?" he asked, pushing the chair to the far side of the desk.

"Great. Especially after spending so long in bed."

He sat down on the sofa. "When is Ethan coming back?"

"Not until the weekend. Have you set up my physical therapy appointments?"

"Yes. The therapist will be here for the first one this afternoon."

"Today? I don't even get a day to settle in?" she whined.

"You need to keep on schedule with this, Grandma. If you don't, you might never have the mobility you had before the accident."

She frowned and rolled her eyes. "You just don't want to take care of me."

"Don't be ridiculous. I'd stay forever, but I don't want my tuition to go to waste." He walked back to the table and gathered the wrappers and bag from their lunch. "Do you need a pain pill?"

She rolled her head from shoulder to shoulder, assessing her pain level. "If I take a pill, can I still have a whiskey sour?"

"No."

"Then just make your granny a drink and we'll call it good."

"I've never made one of those," he cautioned. "I might not get it right."

"I think you'll figure it out. Ethan keeps a recipe book next to the whiskey bottle. Give it your best shot."

He shrugged. "The pill would be easier."

"Yes, but the drink will be more appreciated."

A few feet away, her phone vibrated in the bottom of her purse. She leaned forward, attempting to snag the shoulder strap with her outstretched hand. It only took her a moment to realize that she wasn't going to be able to do it. She pulled the walker in front of her and attempted to maneuver herself into a standing position. The wheels of the walker rolled away from her and she was forced to choose between following it or falling back into the chair. She chose wisely, and the walker rolled forward, clattering loudly to the floor a moment later.

"Grandma!" Hunter called, running around the end of the kitchen.

"Relax. I'm fine."

"What were you doing?"

"Trying to reach my purse."

He arched an eyebrow at her. "By launching the walker at it?"

"No, smart ass. By standing up and walking to it."

"Why didn't you just ask me to bring it to you?"

"You aren't going to be here all the time. I need to be somewhat self-sufficient, don't I?"

"Not yet. You've still got full-time help."

She sighed. "Maybe we should spend the next few days interviewing caretakers."

"Seriously? You'll let some stranger come and take care of you?"

"It will only be for a few weeks."

"Months."

"Whatever. Clearly, I'm not going to be mobile for a while."

The doorbell rang.

"I'll get it," Hunter said.

"Of course you will. Hand me my purse first, okay?"

He picked up her bag and carried it to her before heading toward the door. Sondra dug around in it, finally retrieving her phone. A text message from Ethan was waiting for her: *Hope you are home safely. Will call tonight. I love you.*

Hunter and a tall, muscular blond were a few feet away when she looked up. "Grandma, this is Lucas Loewenberger, your physical therapist."

"How do you do, Miss Lane?" asked the man, who looked like a prototype for the master race.

"Well, aren't you...something. Where did you find him, Hunter? Germany?"

The man gave a good-natured chuckle. "Very good, Miss Lane. My father's family emigrated from Germany a few generations ago."

"Grandma, the agency assigned him."

"Stop calling me that," she admonished. "Lucas will think I'm older than I am." She batted her eyelashes at the man. "Please, call me Sondra."

Hunter cleared his throat. "If you're going to be a while, I need to run out to the store for a few minutes."

"I'll be here for about an hour. Take your time."

Sondra, whose attention was thoroughly absorbed by the handsome therapist, barely heard the door close. "How long have you been doing this?" she asked as he massaged her calves.

"A few years. I always wanted to help others, so this seemed like a natural fit." Holding one hand flat against her knee, he pushed her leg up.

"What are you doing?" she asked, alarmed.

"Checking your range of motion." He moved her through several more stretches before helping her to her feet. "What is your goal?"

"What do you mean?" She was flustered -- her mind had been occupied by some of her baser instincts as she watched the strong man manipulate her body.

"Your goal? For therapy?"

"Oh. I want to be able to do everything I could do before the accident."

"What could you do?"

Her mind involuntarily flipped through an impressive array of sexual positions that had once been in her repertoire. She feared the Seventh Posture of *The Perfumed Garden* was permanently out of reach now. "You know...walking unassisted would be nice."

"What sort of hobbies did you have?" he persisted. "Were you a cyclist? A hiker? A runner?"

"I'm an actress," she answered. "I only pretend to sweat."

"You're in great shape for someone who doesn't exercise," he commented.

Obviously, the man had no sense of humor. "Fine. I used to work out at a gym. I liked to use the stationary bike. Since I moved here, I've been using the swimming pool."

"We'll have you back in the pool before you know it."

Sondra stopped trying to flirt and allowed him to guide her through a series of exercises. When the doorbell rang, she was thankful for the break -- her muscles were much achier than they had ever been before the accident. "Would you mind getting that for me, Lucas? Hunter must have forgotten his key."

"Of course, Ms. Lane."

As he walked to the door, Sondra couldn't help but admire the view.

"Oh! I'm sorry," Sax said as Lucas swung the door open. "I must have knocked on the wrong door!"

Sondra leaned to one side so that Sax could just see her over Lucas's massive shoulder. "I'm here, Sax! Come on in."

Lucas stepped aside and Sax passed him, making a discreet appraisal of the other man's form. Sondra, catching the expression, nodded and fanned her face. Lucas turned and caught the gesture. "I think you've had enough for today, Ms. Lane. I'll be back in two days."

"Don't rush off on my account," Sax offered.

"No, of course not. But my hour is almost up anyway."

"Thank you, Lucas," Sondra said. "Would you mind locking the handle on your way out?"

"Not at all." The brawny blond gathered his equipment and, throwing the bag over his shoulder, left the condo.

"Sorry I interrupted," Sax said, smiling slyly. "Or perhaps I should say lucky I interrupted."

She shook her head. "Nothing is going to happen there. He's either too dense to recognize flirting or very good at ignoring it."

"He could be gay."

"No. Definitely not. He didn't seem to have any clue who I was."

"That's not exactly a definitive marker of young gay men."

She shrugged. "Trust me -- you don't have any better shot with him than I do."

Sax laughed. "Where's Hunter?"

"He went to the store."

"Will he be back soon?"

"I think so. Why?"

He sat down on the sofa and leaned forward, putting his elbows on his knees. "I've got some information to share with you. And I'm not sure you want Hunter in on it."

"On what?" She tilted her head to one side and knit her brow. "Is this about Vivian again? I told you to drop it. I'm breaking things off with Ethan anyway."

"Do you love Ethan?"

"Of course I do. Which is exactly why I need to end the relationship. He's much too young for me. Vivian may be a bitch, but when she's right, she's right."

"If you love him, then you want him to be happy, right?"

"Yes."

"He'll never be happy as long as Vivian is around," he pronounced.

"Why not?"

"She killed Julia." He told her about his interview with Toya Mizokuchi. "She had motive and opportunity, Sondra. What's more, I think she may be poisoning Patrick right now."

Sondra leaned back in her chair, considering her friend's words. "If what you are saying is true...." She shook her head. "It doesn't make sense. And how could we prove that she's doing anything at all? If the doctors haven't seen any reason to suspect her..."

"Maybe they just aren't looking for anything suspicious. I think it's more than coincidental that her first husband and Patrick seem to have such similar symptoms."

She shook her head. "That doesn't make any sense. A

murderer who tampers with a chute doesn't seem like someone who would have the patience to deal with a slow-acting poison."

"You've watched too much television, Sondra. Not all murderers stick to the same methodology. Besides, tampering with a chute will only work on anyone foolish enough to strap one on in the first place. Neither of her husbands participated in high-risk sports."

"What about Astrid's death?"

"I think it was truly an accident, despite what her parents might believe."

"Her parents?"

He related the details of his meeting with Mrs. Dresden.

"You have been busy, haven't you?"

"You're more important to me than I think you know," he admitted. "You're the best friend I have, and I don't make friends easily. It's in my best interest to keep you alive."

She gave him a lopsided grin. "Thanks. Now what do we do?"

When the knock at the door came, Sondra sent Hunter to answer it. From her seat in the living room, she could see Vivian give her grandson a lascivious once-over.

"Sondra invited me," she said, stepping toward the boy.

"Of course. Come in." Hunter had been instructed to be polite when he greeted her and practically invisible after that. "Grandmother is in the living room." He directed her with a wave of his arm and disappeared into the second bedroom, where Sax also awaited, just in case.

Viv, smirking, strode across the room to loom over Sondra.

"Thank you for coming," Sondra said graciously, craning her neck to see Viv's face. "Please sit down."

"I don't plan to stay long. I'm only here to accept your concession speech."

"Is that why you think I invited you?"

"Of course. Why else? You've seen what I can do..."

"So you admit that you tampered with my Mercedes?"

Viv smiled widely. "Think what you want. As long as you end things with Ethan."

"No."

"That's not acceptable."

"I'm sorry you disapprove, but I love your brother and I won't be breaking his heart."

Viv's eyes narrowed. She stalked away from Sondra, dropping irritably into one of the dining chairs. "How can you be so selfish? You will ruin his life by staying with him."

"How is Patrick?"

She waved her hand dismissively. "The doctors still can't diagnose him correctly."

"Maybe you should tell the doctors about Jean Claude. Perhaps they could find a link."

She blinked silently.

"Are you all right?" Sondra asked. "Do you need a drink?"

"What do you know about Jean Claude?"

"Only that he was your first husband and that he also suffered from a mysterious heart problem. That's quite a coincidence, don't you think?"

Viv stood. "Perhaps I'll have that drink after all. Would you like one?"

"Hunter?" Sondra called. Her grandson appeared. "Could you fix us some drinks? A whiskey sour for me, and..."

"I'll have the same." She lowered herself back into the chair. In a whisper, she asked, "How did you find out about Jean Claude?"

"Is that really important?"

"What do you want?"

"I want you to leave Ethan and me alone. Your brother's relationships are not your business."

"Someone has to take care of him."

Hunter handed a drink to each of the women.

"Thank you, sweetheart," Sondra said, sipping the drink. "This is perfect."

He nodded and smiled before disappearing again.

"Maybe he should leave." Viv swiveled to glance toward the now-closed door.

"No. I feel more comfortable with him here. For obvious reasons, I should think."

577

She shrugged and took a slow pull on her drink.

Sondra turned the conversation back toward the subject at hand. "Ethan is a grown man, Vivian. I'm sure he can take care of himself."

"He's too trusting. If you'd met his wives, you would understand."

Sondra laughed. "It's not as if they married him for his money. From what I understand, he was something of a struggling artist when he married Julia."

"True enough. But money isn't the only thing that can ruin a marriage."

"I don't understand."

"And you never will -- I can see that. But Ethan gives his heart away too easily. Just look at how quickly he latched onto you. You started seeing each other in, what -- October? Here it is February and my brother is pushing you to set a date. Surely you can see the problem with this."

"If his wives didn't keep dying, he'd already be a happily married man."

"Ha! As if he could be happy with any of you."

"Geez, Viv...I'm starting to think you believe you are the only woman good enough for him!"

She inhaled, her eyes wide.

Sondra couldn't help the small laugh that escaped her. "That's it, isn't it? You're in love with your brother!"

"Don't be ridiculous. That's sick!"

"And he doesn't feel the same way. How sad for you."

"Stop it!" she spat. "Stop saying that!" Intending to set her drink on the coffee table, she instead fumbled the glass, spilling its contents onto the rug. "I don't know who you've been talking to, but...but...."

"I haven't been talking to anyone but you, Vivian."

She stumbled to her feet and backed away from Sondra, never taking her eyes off her rival. "Keep your nasty thoughts to yourself, Sondra Lane! None of this...fiction had better ever reach Ethan's ears!"

Sensing that she was losing her opportunity to discover the truth, Sondra said hastily, "At least tell me what you've been doing to Patrick. Are you poisoning him? How?"

But Viv was at the door now. Flinging it open, she fled down the hallway. Before her own door swung shut, Sondra heard the stairwell door open and bang heavily closed. That's a long run down, Sondra mused.

The door to the spare room opened and Hunter and Sax joined her in the living room.

Sondra sighed as she reached for her phone and turned off the recording app. "No confession. Now what?"

"Maybe not," Sax said, "but I think we can safely assume she is doing something to Patrick to cause these symptoms."

"If we go to him with our suspicions, he'll just tell her what we've said."

"If I go to him, you're right. But if you go to him, maybe not."

She laughed. "You expect me -- with my broken hip, no less -- to seduce a dying man?"

"Not seduce, exactly...just...finesse."

The next morning, Hunter drove Sondra to the hospital and rolled her up to Patrick's bedside to wait for the man to open his eyes. Hunter left the room with the understanding that his grandmother would call him when she was ready to leave.

She studied her rival's husband as he slept. Patrick, with his white hair and still-tan skin, reminded her of the love of her life. When he was awake, she found the resemblance even more startling. In a perfect world, this man would be her boyfriend -- not Ethan.

"Sondra?"

"Yes. How are you feeling?"

"Better now that you're here." He smiled wistfully. "I thought you were released. That's what Vivian told me."

"I was, but I had my grandson bring me back to visit you."

"That was sweet of you. Say, could you get me a little water? I'm parched."

She poured some water from the maroon pitcher on the side table into a small cup. A straw sat on the rolling tray. She plopped it into the water and held it up to Patrick's mouth; he sucked on it gratefully. "You look better today."

The straw reached the bottom of the cup and he sucked in air. "More, please." While she poured the water, he glanced around his room. "Have you seen Viv today?"

"No." She held the straw to his mouth again and he took a few sips before waving her away.

"Thank you, Sondra. You're so sweet." He glanced at the clock, frowning.

"What's wrong?"

He met her eyes with sadness. "I think Vivian is tired of being married to a sick old man."

"Why would you say that?"

"She used to be so much more attentive, when I just had aches and pains. She used to apply a special pain rub that worked wonders on my arthritis."

"What brand was it? I'll buy you some."

He shook his head. "It was homemade. Something she learned years ago when her family owned the carnival."

Sondra pulled herself closer to the bed and leaned forward. "Who would have taught her to make medicine?"

"Her grandmother, I would imagine. Hasn't Ethan told you about the carnival at all?"

"I guess I haven't asked the right questions."

He shook his head. "I guess you haven't. Their grandmother -- actually, from what I understand, she was John's great-grandmother -- lived with them right up until they sold the carnival."

"That can't be right," she laughed. "The woman would have been a hundred years old."

"One hundred and five, to be exact. She was raised in the Appalachians by her widowed mother, who supported her family by working as a healer and a midwife to her neighbors. Anyway, the old woman -- her name was Constance -- ran away with the Turner circus when it came through her neck of the woods. Making use of what she had learned from her mother, Constance served as the show's doctor throughout her long life. Eventually, she chose to pass her secrets on to Vivian."

"What happened to her?"

"She died when John sold the carnival."

580

"How sad."

Patrick shifted and frowned. "I always thought it was rather poetic -- she spent her whole life -- most of the twentieth century -- traveling the country. It was too late for her to settle down."

"How did you and Vivian meet?"

"I came to her for professional services -- I needed an old business partner tracked down."

"That's right! I keep forgetting she's a P.I."

"A damn good one, too. She found the guy I was looking for in no time."

"Did you ask her out or was it the other way around?"

He smiled. "Vivian isn't the kind of woman who sits around hoping that life will happen."

"When did she start giving you her special rub?"

"Oh, about a year ago. I had a flare-up of bursitis in my shoulders, and she mixed up a batch of this herbal rub Mama Constance used to apply to the acrobats."

"What's in it?"

"I don't know, exactly."

"Does it work?"

"Oh, yes! It warms and numbs the area. It's a great relief."

"Maybe I should ask her for some of it. My hip is really sore these days."

"Why don't you check the drawer in the bedside table? I bet she's left some for me to use."

Sondra rolled to the drawer and pulled it open. "What would the container look like?"

"It should be in a light-blue jar."

Sondra pulled it from the drawer and opened the top. A minty odor drifted up from the purplish-gray concoction. "Do you mind if I take it with me?"

"Not at all. I don't have much use for it these days -- I'd have to slather my whole body with it to get any relief!" He yawned.

"I'm going to let you get your rest, Patrick."

Smiling gratefully, he patted her hand. "Thank you for visiting a sick old man, Sondra."

"You're not that much older than I am!" she reminded him.

Night Life

"Too bad we didn't meet sooner," he sighed.

His eyes closed and she rolled out of his room. Calling Hunter, she said, "Come and get me. I think I've finally got what we need."

Night Life

Envy

Since Claire's departure, Milo had thrown himself into his work, picking up the slack for Sax while he investigated Vivian. Outside of sleeping in his own bed, his house offered him no comfort. Everywhere he looked, he saw traces of Claire. Having Taz at his feet didn't help, either. Using the bar as his excuse, he talked Brian and Marla into taking the dog for him.

It wasn't a complete lie -- the dog was alone most of the time. Milo spent every moment he could at the bar, which was where Sax found him that Monday morning.

"What are you doing here so early?"

Milo looked up from sweeping. "What does it look like?"

Sax held up both hands to ward off Milo's anger. "Not that it's a problem. Have you heard from Claire?"

"She won't answer her phone."

"How often have you tried to call?"

"I stopped trying a few days ago."

Sax sat on a barstool as Milo continued sweeping. "Maybe you should give it another try."

"Nah. No point. And, in the end, isn't it better that we make a clean break of things?"

Sax gave him a dubious stare.

"What?"

"Nothing. It's your life. You can ruin it however you see fit."

"Thanks for the support."

"On a better note, the cops took Vivian Bradford into custody this morning."

Milo dropped the broom in surprise. "What?"

Sax, grinning from ear to ear, nodded. "We were right about her, Milo! And we solved our first paying gig!"

"Now you've lost me. 'We' didn't solve anything. And who is paying you?"

"Oh, come on, Milo! I couldn't have done it without you!"

"I didn't do anything. I just took care of the bar."

"Exactly. Without you, I would have been stuck behind the counter, unable to help our Sondra."

Milo shrugged, deciding to drop the argument. "Who is paying you?" he repeated.

"Patrick Bradford. He says I saved his life."

"I thought we were trying to prove she tampered with Sondra's car."

It was Sax's turn to shrug. "It turns out it was easier to prove she was poisoning Patrick."

Dumbfounded, Milo sank into a chair. "What in the hell did you uncover?"

"Vivian was using an aconite-laced lotion to cause Patrick's heart problems."

"What's aconite?"

"Have you ever heard of monk's hood?"

Milo shook his head.

"It's a flowering plant that just happens to be poisonous. It's also a folk remedy for pain. When Patrick started complaining about shoulder pain, Vivian mixed up a batch of the stuff, using monk's hood -- Aconitum -- from her garden."

"She's smart. They'll never convict her -- she'll just say it was an old family remedy."

Sax smiled. "That might have worked," he agreed, "if she hadn't used the same stuff on Jean Claude Guyon, her first husband. He suffered from the same symptoms as Patrick before he died. His body is being exhumed this morning."

"Amazing." Milo shook his head.

Sax moved to the table where Milo was sitting and took the chair across from him. "I need to talk to you about something."

"This sounds serious."

"It is." He raked his thinning blond hair back with one hand. "This investigation has made me realize something: I'm a good detective."

"Of course you are! You were an officer."

"Yeah, but I was just a beat cop. I never thought I had it in me to actually solve crimes. After what happened last fall -- with Bob -- I was sure any skills I once had were long gone."

"But they aren't."

"No." Sax glanced around the bar. "You know the lease on this place is up in April."

"No, I didn't realize." Milo guessed where Sax was going. "You're not renewing, are you?"

"There are a lot of problems with this place, not the

least of which are the bathrooms. When you first approached me about the bar, you offered to be my partner."

"And you said you weren't comfortable with that idea."

"I'm comfortable now," he said with a half smile. "And I think we should move."

"Are you kidding? This is a great location!"

"It's been fine. But the place I have in mind is bigger."

"What place?"

"Come with me and I'll show you."

Milo glanced at the clock.

"Please. The bar doesn't even open for another two hours," Sax said, rolling his eyes.

They locked the door and Sax drove them two miles north, pulling into the weedy parking lot of a long-empty building. Though the signage was long gone, the establishment's former name was outlined in a quarter-inch of paint.

Milo looked at Sax skeptically. "I thought this place was scheduled for demolition."

"That was before the real estate market took a dump. The current owners are in no position to wreck the place."

"So they want to rent it?"

"No. They want to sell it."

Milo's jaw dropped.

"Now, before you get too excited--"

"That wasn't excitement, Sax; it was disbelief."

Sax dug around in his pocket until he came up with a key. "Before you veto it, let's at least have a look around. Could you grab the flashlights from the backseat?"

"There's no electricity?"

"Not right now. As soon as it's ours, we can have it turned back on."

"You're nuts."

Sax shrugged and went back to the car to get the lights. "Wait until you see it."

Milo took one of the flashlights and followed Sax into the building, which was, shockingly, fully furnished in old but apparently functional wooden booths and tables. The nautical-themed barstools and chairs had seen better days -- probably sometime in the 1980s, by Milo's estimation -- but otherwise, the place seemed promising.

"This was a bar before -- why did it go out of business?" Milo asked.

"That's the best part: the bar did well, but when the real estate market hit its peak a few years back, the barkeep sold the property and retired. The current owners figured this would be a prime spot for a commercial development. They were wrong."

"Wish I could see it better."

"I was in here once before it closed, back when I was checking out the competition. The best part of the place is the floor space. We're talking twice as big as our current location, with two offices in the back."

"Why do we need two offices?"

"Let's go back outside." The men carefully skirted the furniture and emerged into the bright winter light.

"What aren't you telling me?"

"I want to start a detective agency."

"In Sun City? Seems like there wouldn't be much call--"

Sax's laughter cut him off. "Are you kidding? Cheating spouses, suspicious deaths, drug dealers...and those are just the cases we've run across. The residents may be old, but the sins are the same."

"How much did Patrick pay you?"

"Enough to make me think this could be lucrative."

Milo leaned against the car, his arms folded across his chest. "So, when you say 'partner,' what you're really saying is you want someone to run the bar for you."

"Not all the time," Sax answered defensively. "I'll still take a few shifts a week -- when I've got time between cases."

"I'll tell you what," Milo said, negotiating, "right now I'm fine with working as much as I can. However, if I get another girlfriend or my grandkids need me around more, we may need another bartender to help out. Plus, this place is going to need at least one waitress -- twice as much space means twice as many drinkers. Let me hire a waitress and a bartender, and you've got yourself a partner."

Sax frowned worriedly. "Another girlfriend? You're not giving up on Claire, are you?"

"She left. I'd say she's the one who gave up on me."

"Didn't she say she just wanted to fix her relationship

with her father before he died?"

"Yes, but--"

"I think you're being a little shortsighted here, buddy."

Milo rubbed his stubbly chin, thinking he really should have shaved this morning. "That ship has sailed, Sax. There's no point in my pining over a woman who doesn't want to be with me."

"Don't you think you should give her one more chance? Anyone who would put up with you--"

"Let's just drop it, okay?"

"Fine."

"What do you say about the partnership?"

"Okay. You've got a deal."

On the way back to the current Brass Monkey, Sax filled Milo in on Sondra.

"She's really going to break things off with Ethan?" Milo asked.

"Yeah, but he's in a bad place right now, what with his sister going to jail and all. She hasn't figured out exactly when or how she's going to do it."

"I'm shocked that she would do it at all. She seemed so happy with him."

"Vivian may be insane, but she was right about one thing: an age difference is hard to overcome."

"This may be a sign that she's becoming less selfish."

"Maybe, but I wouldn't count on it. I'm sure she has already mapped out a plan that will see her land firmly on both feet with a fortune in her arms."

Milo laughed. "She's one of a kind."

"Thank the gods." Sax pulled into the parking lot and came to a stop alongside a gold sports car with a woman sitting in it. "I think our first customer of the day is waiting for us."

"I'd better unlock the door before she decides it's too early for a drink." Milo stepped out of the vehicle; when he turned to close his door, Sonia was leaning against the gold car, smiling. "Good morning!"

"Good morning to you, too."

"We don't open for another hour, but for you I'll make an exception."

"Actually, I was just checking to see if you'd made it

across the border."

"Excuse me?"

She smiled. "To put it more bluntly, are you single yet?"

Sax stepped out of the car and shot Milo a questioning look.

"Sax, this is Sonia. She's new to town."

"Nice to meet you," Sax said.

"Likewise." She walked to the end of her car, revealing a navy cashmere dress that clung in all the right places. "So, Milo, am I being too aggressive here? When we talked, I got the impression you were almost free."

"Not at all," he said with a smile.

"Good. Are you interested in an early lunch? I thought we could go before the bar opened."

"Now isn't a good time," Sax inserted. "Milo and I have some business to work out."

"Can't that wait?" Milo arched an eyebrow at his friend.

"No. Not really."

"I'm sorry, Sonia. Maybe another time."

"Dinner?"

Milo gave Sax a hard stare; Sax shrugged, frowning. "I can do that. I'll be done here around five."

"Perfect. I'll pick you up."

Despite Sax's grumbling objections to Milo's dinner plans, Milo left the bar promptly at five.

Sonia, the keys to her sports car dangling from her hand, was waiting in the parking lot. "You drive," she said. "I like to know how a man handles a beauty like this one."

He could feel the blush rising to his face as he took the keys. Clearing his throat, he asked, "Where are we going to eat?"

"I know a great little Italian place. You like garlic?"

"Yeah. Sounds good."

They got into the car. Milo marveled at the soft lushness of the leather seats as he strapped himself in. "This is quite a car for a geography teacher."

"Oh, it's been a few years since I taught...geography."

Her voice was an aphrodisiac -- Milo felt its effects all over his body. He swallowed hard. "You know a lot about me and I know almost nothing about you."

"There's not much to know."

"You never told me where you were from."

"Most recently, I'm from Washington."

"Beautiful state. Lots of rain."

"Yes, it is. But I meant D.C."

"What took you there?"

He felt her eyes on him. "I was a lobbyist."

"Fascinating."

"Not really. I was good at it, though. Then again, any woman with a good figure and a tight sweater would be good at lobbying."

"What were you lobbying for, if I may ask?"

"The National Rifle Association."

He coughed.

"Don't worry -- I'm not packing."

"Good to know. I'll definitely avoid irritating you, though."

He parked in front of the restaurant and went around to the other side of the car to open her door.

"I love a man with old-school manners," she purred.

"I believe in being a gentleman whenever possible." He offered her his arm, and she wrapped a hand around it.

Inside, the host found them a table near the window and they settled in across from one another.

"I can't believe a woman like you is single."

"I was married a few times. From what I've been told, I can be difficult to live with." She smiled deprecatingly.

"I'm sure you're a sweetheart compared to my ex-girlfriend."

"I don't know about that. I've spent most of the last thirty years more committed to my career than my husbands. But I'm retired now." She sipped her water. "Was that your business partner I met today?"

"Sax Ridley. Actually, we just became partners today."

"Retirement wasn't for you?"

"I needed something to do. Since things went south with Claire, I needed something to keep me out of the house."

"Claire." She pursed her lips. "The ex?"

"Yeah."

"How long were you two together?"

"Only a few months." He sighed and shook his head. "I haven't had great luck with women. My first wife and I should never have married, and now I've had two girlfriends in less than a year."

"How long were you married?"

"Too long. She died a few years ago."

Her eyebrows shot up. "A lifer, huh?"

"I suppose," he said glumly.

The waiter appeared, placing fresh bread and preparing a small plate of oil and balsamic vinegar for them. They ordered their dinners and each of them picked up a piece of bread.

"Have you ever considered that maybe you aren't ready for a serious relationship? I mean, a long marriage like that..."

"Alice and I didn't have much of a marriage for the last decade or so. She lived her life, and I lived mine."

"But you were still together."

"We still lived in the same house, but we avoided each other."

"Like you were avoiding Claire."

"That was different."

"How?"

Milo dredged his bread through the oil and vinegar, thinking. "Alice and I didn't have anything in common. I really thought Claire was the woman I would spend the rest of my life with."

"What changed?"

"She did. It was as if her whole outlook changed overnight. She said it was menopause, but..."

"You thought it was you."

He nodded. "My friends seem determined to push us back together. Sax was furious with me all day because he knew I was going out with you tonight. I don't understand why they can't just let the idea of Claire and me together go."

"Maybe they know something you don't."

"Like what?"

Sonia leaned back in her chair. "Look, just so you know, I never had any long-term plans for us. You seem like a nice guy, and you are handsome enough. But, ultimately, I'm not ready to commit more than a week or two into the future."

Milo winced. "You're dumping me before the main course?"

"No. I can't dump you, because you weren't free to be picked up in the first place."

"That's not true," he protested. "Claire packed up and left a few weeks ago."

"True. She left you. You didn't leave her -- and I'm not certain she won't be back. If she comes back, I have no doubt that you will happily pick up where you left off."

"But I'm single now."

"You may not realize it, but what you are is on a break. It sounds like she needed a little space -- and so did you. But you still love her. It's obvious every time you say her name. If I were to take advantage--"

"You wouldn't be," he inserted.

She cut her eyes at him irritably. "As I was saying, if I were to sleep with you now, you would go back to her with so much guilt that your relationship would never be the same. Trust me on this; I've been down this road in both directions."

The waiter returned, setting their dinners in front of them. As soon as he retreated, Milo said, "She won't answer my calls. What am I supposed to do about that?"

"Do you know where she is?"

"Oklahoma. Her father is dying of cancer. She left a note saying she wanted to spend some time with him."

Sonia, who was in the midst of raising her first bite of lasagna to her mouth, dropped the fork back to her plate. "Wow. And you don't think this woman has a right to be a little on edge? She's menopausal and her father is dying. You just proved you're a man."

"Hey," he answered defensively, "I tried to be supportive. She kept pushing me away."

"I'm sure she did. What was your last argument about?"

He looked down at the fettuccine before him. "She wanted to know if we were getting married," he mumbled.

"And you said no?"

"Be reasonable, Sonia. Why would I marry a woman who was already so unhappy?"

She shook her head. "You're hopeless."

"What?"

"If she was that unhappy with you, why would she be asking for a ring?"

"Oh." He twirled some pasta around his fork, but didn't lift it off the plate. "I'm an idiot."

"No. You're just a man. Do you still love her?"

He took a bite of the pasta and chewed it slowly before answering. "Yes," he admitted, as much to himself as to Sonia. "My God. What am I going to do?"

"How should I know? I just met you." She took a sip of the house wine, a heavy red of indeterminate origin.

"Should I go to Oklahoma and propose?"

"Wow. That was quite a leap."

"I don't want to lose her. How could I have been so insensitive?"

"Look, let's finish our meal before things turn too maudlin."

He pulled out the smart phone he was only starting to understand. "Can I buy a plane ticket from this thing?"

"When you're done with a date, you're really done, aren't you?"

"I'm sorry. I just...I need to fix this. I've been an idiot."

"I don't suppose you know any other guys I could date, do you? What about that Sax guy?"

"You aren't his type. But I'll introduce you to a few of the regulars when I get back from Oklahoma."

"I'm going to hold you to that." She took the phone from him and rapidly accessed a travel site. "Where in Oklahoma?"

"Not too far from Oklahoma City. I'll need a rental car, too."

"Get your credit card ready."

He pulled out his wallet and slipped a card across the table.

"Tomorrow morning is the soonest you can leave. Should I book it?"

"Do it."

The waiter approached their table. "Is everything all right with your meals?"

"Fine, thanks, but we need boxes," Sonia said.

Milo, chagrined, said, "We can finish our dinners."

"Are you kidding? We have to find you a suitable ring if you're going to propose!"

Night Life

Night Life

Port in a Storm

The maternity-wear store in the local mall had a surprisingly small selection of black dresses -- at least as far as Claire was concerned. As she slipped the last of three choices over her head, she heard Beryl tap on the door.

"Anything work?"

"Not really," she answered, eyeing herself in the mirror. She could have been a linebacker for the L.A. Raiders in this one.

"You've got to make a choice, Claire. We're supposed to be at the chapel in less than an hour."

She stepped out of the dressing room to show Beryl the outfit. "This is the best of the three."

"Nothing you wear for the next few months is going to be super-flattering. That's just how it goes."

Claire could still see the most-recent tear tracks on her sister's face. Neither of them were doing a great job of keeping their emotions in check. Only their mother seemed as steady as a rock. In the past, Claire would have chalked her mother's lack of tears up to a lack of human warmth. Only the past few months -- particularly the last couple weeks -- had helped her to see her mother as strong rather than cold. "Do you think Mom will like this?"

"Yes. Probably. It's hard to tell. On the plus side, she's not going to be focused on your lack of fashion sense."

"Thanks."

"Is that your phone?"

Claire stopped and listened. "Yeah," she said, but made no attempt to answer it.

"You've got to talk to him sometime," her sister sighed.

"Not right now. I can only handle one disaster at a time." She tried to laugh, but the sound came out like a sob.

Beryl put her arms around her. "I know you miss him. I do too. But Dad is at peace now."

Hugging her tightly, Claire nodded against her shoulder. She had held her father's hand as he breathed his last just yesterday. She could honestly say nothing but love was left between them in the end -- she had seen to that. Coming to Oklahoma on her own had been the best decision she could have made.

Beryl pulled away first. "The dress is fine. Buy it," she commanded.

Smiling, Claire wiped the slight wetness away from her eyes. "Yes, ma'am." She turned and went back to the dressing room. She retrieved her phone from the bottom of her purse, surprised to see that the name showing on the screen was Sondra's. Frowning, she dropped it back in her purse and made a mental note to call her back after tomorrow's funeral.

Her childhood home had never been so full of people. After the funeral, everyone who had ever done business or shared a meal with her father came to the house. In typical fashion, her mother had hired a caterer, whose somber staff floated silently through the crowd offering up canapés and drinks.

"Your father was a great man."

"Thank you."

"I hadn't seen him in a few years, but I remember him well."

"So nice of you to come."

"He was always a gentleman."

"Yes, he was."

"His death is a great loss to the community."

"Yes, it is."

"You have my condolences."

"Thank you again."

She had the same conversation at least two dozen times; she overheard Beryl following the same script at least a dozen more. Their mother, smiling and gracious, accepted the gentle hand clasps and sympathetic pats, but didn't seem able to form words.

"Are you all right, Mom?"

Her mother looked up at her blankly.

"Mom?"

"Yes, dear?"

"Are you okay?"

Her mother looked down at her hands and then at Claire's. "You have my fingers. Look, Claire. Look at how they taper so elegantly. Your father always said any daughter of ours would be lucky to have such beautiful hands." She glanced in Beryl's direction and sighed. "Beryl's hands are more like your father's. Did you ever notice?"

"No, I didn't."

"You should see. You should put them next to each other and--" Her mother stopped talking, looked up at her, and blinked.

"Do you want to lie down for a while?"

Olivia Turner, her plain face pale, nodded and took Claire's hand.

Claire led her mother up the stairs to her bedroom. The room had been Olivia's alone since her father fell ill.

"I should redecorate," her mother said, gazing at the warm yellow walls and the Italianate furniture. "I never liked this look, but your father loved it. He said it made him feel like a Medici."

"Dad loved luxury." She guided her mother to the bed. Carefully lowering her ripened body to her knees, she removed her mother's shoes. She felt her mother's hand on the side of her face; the affectionate gesture surprised her, despite the strides they had made toward repairing their relationship.

"You turned out so lovely, Claire. Your grandfather would have been proud."

She blinked several times to push the tears away. "Thank you."

"You certainly prove the case for nature, my dear. I'm afraid you didn't receive much in the way of nurturing."

She wanted to tell her mother that was okay, but the words got stuck in her throat.

"I know you will do so much better with your daughter than I did with you."

This was the first time her mother had mentioned Claire's condition, though Claire and her father had discussed it. Her father had advised her to return to Milo, whom he had referred to as "that crusty gentleman in the Guayabera shirts." He was surprised when he learned that Milo hadn't proposed; apparently, he had asked for her father's approval during their

Christmas visit. "I don't know, Mom. I don't know if I can do this."

"Of course you can! You are going to be a wonderful mother. And Milo will be a fine father."

"Milo doesn't want to be a father."

She laughed. "He should have thought of that before."

"I'm going to raise the baby alone," she said, her voice faltering.

Her mother's gaze seemed to cut right through her. "We were lucky, you know."

"Who? You and me?"

"No...your father and I. We were already married when we fell in love. It made all the difference."

She lay back on the bed and closed her eyes, dismissing Claire, who walked softly out of the room, pulling the door shut behind her. She felt her cell phone -- which she had slipped into the dress's only pocket -- vibrate. "Hello?"

"Claire? Oh, my God! I can't believe you answered!"

"What's wrong, Sax?"

"You've got to come home. Right away."

"Is something wrong with Milo?"

"Yes."

"What? What's wrong?" She felt the panic rise up from the depths of her body, overwhelming the heavier grief that had taken up residence in her stomach.

"He's dating!"

A sob escaped, carrying the panic up and away from her, like a helium-filled balloon. "My father just died, Sax. I can't come home yet."

"Please, sweetie. I swear to you, this is an emergency. He misses you so much that all he does is work. He's so desperate that he's about to make a huge mistake. At least call him!"

"Sax, he stopped calling me days ago. I think it's too late. I need to go. People are looking for me," she lied.

"Okay. I'm sorry about your dad."

"It's okay," she said; for the first time, she meant it. She disconnected and was about to slip the phone back into her pocket when she remembered she owed Sondra a call. Clicking her number, she waited as the phone connected.

"Hello?" a young man answered.

"Ethan?"

"No, this is Hunter. Claire?"

"Yes. Hello. I was returning your grandmother's call."

"She didn't call you. I did. She needs a favor and I didn't know who else to call."

"Are you sure you don't want me to go in with you?" Beryl asked for the third time as they drove toward Will Rogers World Airport.

Sighing, Claire answered, "I'm getting the impression you'd prefer to come in."

"Allow me my mother-hen tendencies," she said, smiling.

"Okay. Come in with me. We'll find a place to get coffee."

Beryl glanced at her sideways. "Is this what you want to do?"

"No. Yes. Probably." She shook her head. "Oklahoma isn't my home anymore. I miss Arizona."

"You mean you miss Milo."

"No. I don't mean that. As a matter of fact, I'm going to make sure he doesn't know I'm back."

"How? Isn't he friends with Sondra?"

"Sax told me he works all the time. And now he's dating someone new..."

"You didn't tell me that."

"Oh?" She slid her eyes away from her sister. "Must have slipped my mind."

"Yeah. Must've." Beryl found a parking space and the sisters stepped out of the vehicle. "I'll get your bag," Beryl said, opening the back of her SUV.

"I can get it. I'm not an invalid."

"You'll have plenty of time to be on your own soon enough. Let me help you."

Claire shrugged.

"Have you got your ticket?"

She opened her purse and flashed the printout at Beryl. "Right here."

"I can't believe you're leaving already. We just buried Dad."

"Will you be okay? I mean, with Mom and everything?"

"Yeah. I've always got Rory to fall back on."

"You're a lucky woman."

"Don't I know it."

They bought a couple of coffees and found a bench to sit on. Neither of them had much left to say. They chatted idly about the people who had come to the funeral. Most of them were only vaguely familiar to either of the women -- their parents had never mixed family with social or business circles.

"I think this is all going to hit Mom hard in a few days." Beryl stared straight ahead.

"She was already cracking yesterday. She started talking about our hands -- right in the middle of the wake, as if no one were around but us."

"I think I'll head over there. She probably needs some company."

Claire searched for a clock; when she found it, she stood up. "I've got to go. I need to get through TSA."

Beryl blinked; Claire couldn't help but see their mother in her for just a moment. "Of course." She stood up and hugged her. "I love you. Be careful."

"I love you, too. I'll call you later." She threw her coffee cup, still a quarter full, into a nearby trashcan and walked toward the gate. When she looked back, Beryl was sitting on the bench again, her own coffee cup between her hands as she watched the crowds of people pass by.

Night Life

Very few drinks were spilled in the writing of this novel.

Book 4
of the
BRASS
MONKEY
series

Susan Wells Bennett

Forty-five and pregnant, Claire is playing a high stakes game of hide and seek with her baby's father. Milo, distracted by his new business venture, has a blind spot when it comes to figuring out why Claire is avoiding him

Meanwhile, his partner Sax is relishing his new profession, even as it drags him into the disturbing world of the Goth scene. And Sondra is attempting to calculate her way out of a marriage to a much younger man and into a generous cash settlement.

What they all wish for, in one way or another, is a NEW LIFE - and this may be their last chance to start over.

New Life
Book 4 of the
Brass Monkey Series

By Susan Wells Bennett

Published by
Inknbeans Press

New Life

For Duchess.

New Life

Frog Went A-Courting

"Welcome to Oklahoma, y'all," the stewardess announced. "We will be landing in just a few minutes now, so please return your seats to their full upright position. Donna will be making one more pass..."

Milo tuned her out as he stretched and rolled his neck and shoulders.

His seatmate, a rather large woman who had claimed the armrest between them as her own early in the flight, looked down her nose at him. "You've got quite a snore, you know. You should have that checked."

"That's funny," he retorted, "I didn't hear a thing." He felt the pocket of his Guayabera, reassuring himself that the box -- containing a one-and-a-half-carat diamond ring -- was still safely ensconced within.

A stewardess, presumably Donna, was advancing down the aisle holding a white plastic bag. "Cups? Napkins? Trash?" she asked, holding the bag out in his direction. Extending her arm across Milo's face, the fat woman deposited her trash in the bag. Irritable from the flight, he momentarily contemplated biting the fleshy upper arm that presented itself a mere inch from his nose. The stewardess, however, gave him a sympathetic smile and Milo decided not to create a dental imprint on the unpleasant woman.

"I'm visiting my mother," the woman volunteered, suddenly chatty. "Why are you flying in?"

"I'm visiting my fiancée and her family." She would be his fiancée, right? Of course she would say yes -- marriage was what she wanted.

"Aren't you a little old to be getting married?"

"Aren't you a little fat to be on an airplane?"

She huffed. "Don't be rude!"

"You first."

Her mouth dropped open, creating an upside-down staircase of chins.

He focused on the back of the seat in front of him and bit down on the insides of his cheeks to keep from laughing.

When the plane had landed and finished its long taxi to the terminal, Milo jumped out of his seat, grabbed his bag from the overhead compartment, and joined the slow but steady line of passengers working their way toward the exit. Before long, he was free of the crowd and striding down the long hallway that led out of the structure. Sonia had reserved a rental car for him; he had only to find the rental company's shuttle to make his getaway. He knew the drive to Claire's parents' home would take the better part of an hour. He calculated that he would arrive in mid-afternoon, the perfect time -- neither so early that he would catch the household sleeping nor so late that his visit would be seen as an intrusion. He stopped at a courtesy map and scanned it, looking for the rental company's check-in booth.

"Milo?" asked a familiar voice to his left.

Turning, he saw Claire's younger sister standing a foot away. He scooped her up in a joyful hug. "Beryl! How did you know I'd be here?"

As soon as he released her, she took a step away from him and straightened her clothes. "I didn't. I just dropped Claire off."

"Where is she?" He whipped his head around, searching for her familiar face in the crowd.

"She's already at her gate."

"Where is she going?"

"Back to Phoenix, where else?"

"Thanks!" He took off at a sprint toward security.

"Milo!" Beryl shouted.

He stopped and looked at her, holding his hands out to his sides. "What?" he mouthed.

Shaking her head, she walked to him. "They won't let you back through without a ticket."

She was right. His shoulders slumped in disappointment.

"Why are you here, anyway?"

He pulled the jewelry box from his pocket and popped it open.

"Milo! That's gorgeous!"

"Thanks. I had some help picking it out. Do you think Claire will like it?"

"Of course she will." Beryl tilted her head to one side and knit her eyebrows. "There's no reason for you to stay in Oklahoma...why don't you try to get a ticket on her flight back to Phoenix?"

"When does it leave?"

She turned his wrist so that she could see the time on his watch. "Less than an hour, but if you hurry--"

"Lead me to the ticket counter."

The line wasn't too long, considering it was Saturday. As they waited, Beryl filled him in on recent events.

"I'm sorry about your father," Milo said. "He was so nice to me at Christmas."

"I'm just glad he and Claire were able to mend their relationship before he died. Even she and Mom are on good terms these days. I think that has a lot to do with you. You've filed down a lot of her sharp edges."

He laughed disbelievingly. "I doubt that! Beryl, I love her more than anyone or anything in this world, but she's been in a bad mood for months now."

"There's a good reason for that--"

He held up a hand to stop her. "I know, I know. She's in menopause."

Beryl bit her lip.

"What?"

"Just...give her a little more leeway. I have a feeling she's going to be in a happier place very soon."

One of the ticket agents waved Milo and Beryl over. "How may I help you today?" the young man asked pleasantly.

"I need a ticket to Phoenix on the flight leaving at eleven."

"I'm sorry, sir. That flight is full."

Milo looked at Beryl.

"Maybe you can catch her at the gate." Beryl turned to the agent. "Give him a ticket on the next flight to Phoenix."

"It doesn't leave until three o'clock," he warned.

"That's fine," Milo confirmed, handing his credit card across the counter.

The agent printed the ticket and handed it and his card back to him with a smile. "Good luck, sir."

"Thanks," he said, waving. He and Beryl hustled toward security.

As they approached the line, Beryl grabbed him in a quick hug. "You're a good man, Milo. I'm glad Claire found you."

"I'll make sure she calls you when she gets to Phoenix."

She walked back down the hall toward the front of the airport where she had found him.

He stood in the line as patiently as he could, though the minutes remaining before the flight took off were draining away. Shifting from foot to foot like a child in need of a bathroom, he peered over the shoulders of the slightly taller man in front of him. A couple traveling with three small children was causing an unexpected delay.

"Kids!" said the man ahead of him over his shoulder. "I'm so glad I'm past that stage in life."

"You and me both, buddy. I only had one, but the wife and I never tried to travel with him when he was small."

"Lucky man. My ex and I took our five kids -- all under ten at the time, mind you -- to Disney World one year."

"How many of them did you leave there?"

"Ha!" burst the guy. "That might have been the right solution! Or maybe leaving all of them there -- along with the ex."

The line started to move again and both men busied themselves with preparing their items for scanning. Milo's scan went smoothly and he was off at a quick pace to try and reach Claire's gate before the plane boarded. He dodged one of the children from the harried couple's caravan and wove his way between and around the crowds he had previously raced past in the opposite direction. Milo spotted the woman who had been his seatmate still lingering at one of the airport shops. He deliberately moved to the other side of the concourse. Looking up, he saw the gate number. The tail-end of a line was disappearing through the boarding doors. He thought he saw the back of Claire's hair and called out, but she didn't turn around. Desperate, he approached the attendant who had been taking tickets at the door. "Excuse me, I think my fiancée is on this plane, and I need to catch her."

"Do you have a ticket?" the older woman asked.

"Yes." He handed her the ticket he had just purchased.

"I'm sorry, sir, but this is for another flight."

"I know. But I just need to--"

"Sir, you're going to Phoenix, too. Can't you just wait and talk to her there?"

"This is very important," he pleaded. "She needs to know something right now."

"She probably still has her cell phone on, sir."

He heard the echo of the airplane door closing. Sighing, he said, "Thanks. I'll try that." He turned and walked slowly away.

"Have a good day," added the attendant.

New Life

This Old Man

A few weeks later, Sax and Milo, business partners, found themselves patiently waiting to sign the paperwork completing their purchase of the new location for the Brass Monkey.

"Has she answered any of your calls?" Sax asked, referring to Claire.

"No," Milo answered. "I know she's at Sondra's, but Sondra told me not to stop by. Claire doesn't want to see me."

Sax shook his head sympathetically. "She'll come around -- give her time."

"I've given her nearly three weeks already, Sax! I think it might be time for me to step away completely. It's like you said: you never know you're with your last love until it's over."

"I believe she is your last love, but I don't think it's over. I know you two belong together."

"Mr. Ridley? Mr. Crosby?" asked the plump secretary at the escrow company's front desk.

"Yes?" they answered in unison.

"Mrs. Brown will see you now. Go down this corridor to the third door on the left," she instructed, pointing the way.

"Thank you," Sax said, and the two men walked down the short hall to find the escrow officer.

"Good afternoon," said a woman with a pleasant smile and an overly tight hair bun as they came even with her doorway.

"Mrs. Brown?" Milo asked.

"Yes. Please come in and have a seat."

Mrs. Brown patiently walked them through the paperwork, which included a fifty-thousand-dollar bank loan. Both Sax and Milo had come up with a quarter of the asking price in cash; together, they had easily secured a loan for the other half of the necessary funds. When they finished signing everything, Mrs. Brown said, "As soon as everything is recorded, I can give you the keys."

"When will that be?" Sax asked.

"Tomorrow after ten."

The men both shook her hand and thanked her before exiting the office.

"You want to have coffee?" Sax asked, glancing at his watch. The bar didn't open for a couple of hours yet.

"I should probably get to work." Milo looked toward the parking lot as if he couldn't wait to get back to the bar.

"Come on. We should go over some of the details regarding the partnership anyway."

Milo rubbed the back of his neck. "Yeah, okay. You're right. There's a Burger King on the way back toward the bar."

"Meet you there."

At the fast-food joint, they found seats as far away from the other diners as they could. An uncomfortable silence fell and they both fidgeted.

Sax cleared his throat and attempted to ease the situation. "I'm sorry about what I said earlier."

"What did you say?"

"You know...about Claire."

Milo waved his words away. "Don't give it another thought. I know you like her." He sipped at his cup. His brow furrowed and he looked up sharply at Sax. "Have you seen her lately?"

"Yep."

Folding his arms over his chest, the smaller man leaned back in his seat. "You might have mentioned that."

"I didn't think it was relevant."

"How does she look?"

"Good. Really good, actually." When he had seen her a few days ago, she had been glowing; the morning-sickness phase was over, and she seemed calmer and happier than she had in months. "Maybe you should just drop by one day...you know, unannounced."

Milo grimaced. "I don't want to upset her. Let's talk about something else."

"Like what?"

"Business?"

Sax laughed weakly. "Yeah, okay. So, are you having any regrets?"

"About...?"

"The business?"

"Oh! No, of course not. I'm glad you decided to make me a partner. I appreciate the trust you have in me."

New Life

"And I appreciate your faith in the Brass Monkey. I'm sure this move will be great for the bar."

Milo took a sip of his coffee. "I think we'll lose some of our regulars."

"Really? Who?"

"The professor, for one. He doesn't like to cross Grand Avenue in his golf cart."

"He's what? Ninety-three? I don't think he's likely to be a regular for many more years anyway."

"You have a point."

"Anyone else?"

"I don't know for sure. I have a feeling our demographic will change, though, especially since the new place is near so many apartment buildings."

"I think that's a good thing. If we can get a good mix of young and old--"

"You think the Sun City people will still come if the place is overrun with the barely legal set?"

"If we handle it right, the younger party crowd won't be hanging out at the Brass Monkey anyway."

"You have a plan?"

"Of course I do. Don't worry -- the crowd won't be changing that much. When are you going to start looking for the new bartender and waitress?"

"Soon. I want to have them in place before we move to the new building, if possible."

Sax finished his coffee. "That's a good plan. Will you advertise online?"

Milo shrugged. "Maybe. I think I'll start my bartender search at the school I attended. If my instructor was anything to go by, I don't think we could go wrong hiring a graduate."

"It's your call. Just make sure he or she understands that our clientele aren't big tippers."

Milo laughed. "You got that right."

Sax slid out of the booth and gave his friend a little salute, which he immediately regretted.

Milo smirked. "You know who you reminded me of just then?"

Sax rolled his eyes. "John Inman?"

"Spot on, old boy," Milo answered in an atrocious British accent.

"Just forget I ever did that."

"If you weren't twice the size of the guy, I'd say you should dress as him for Halloween. I'm sure we could find you a suit like the one he wore in *Are You Being Served?*."

"You're not that funny, you know. I'll see you later."

"Wait up, I'll walk out with you."

Sax crossed his arms over his chest and leaned on the booth while Milo drained his cup. "I wouldn't have pegged you for a big Britcom fan."

"Dead Alice hated them," he answered, smirking again.

A few days later, Sax entered the new Brass Monkey and flipped on the lights, seeing the whole place without the aid of a flashlight for the first time in more than a decade. The nautical theme -- featuring a lot of red, white, and blue -- looked even more dated under the dim fluorescent glare. A ship's wheel stood in one corner; the brass plate attached to the base claimed it was salvaged from the *Thomas W. Lawson*, a schooner that sank near the isle of Annet in 1907. Sax didn't know much about nautical history, but he sensed the plaque was a lie.

He walked down the hallway at the back of the building and opened the men's room door. As he remembered, the bathroom was larger than the one at the old bar; it even had two urinals. However, years of neglect had left hard-water marks in the toilets and layers of dust on the floor, sink, and every other surface. He shuddered in disgust.

On the left side of the hallway were two doors marked "private." Trying the keys in the locks, he soon had both doors open. The rooms were empty, save a few empty crates in one and a broken desk chair in the other. Someone had glued a wallpaper border featuring anchors along the upper edge of the walls in both rooms. Years without proper temperature regulation had caused the paper to come loose at the seams. The bigger office was the one with the chair. Sax mentally claimed it as the home of his new private-eye business.

Walking back out to the bar, he dropped himself onto one of the barstools and surveyed the large space. He wouldn't need to visit the gym for the next few weeks; he would be getting his workouts painting walls, scrubbing toilets, and refinishing furniture. The parking lot was a mess, too -- weeds had long since overwhelmed the asphalt. Part of the deal he had made with Milo dictated that renovation of the building was his responsibility; Milo would run the existing business and hire the help. He slumped against the bar top, recognizing he had made a fool's bargain. Maybe it was worth considering a professional maid service for the initial cleaning. Rather than admit to Milo he was overwhelmed, Sax decided he would pay for the service himself -- after all, his partner was already doing his share of the work. Nodding to himself, he stood up, dusted off his pants and headed back to his office at the Brass Monkey to look up a few cleaning companies.

New Life

If Wishes Were Horses

"Have I said thank you today?" Sondra asked from the passenger side of Claire's car as Claire flipped the right-turn signal on.

"You can stop that anytime now, you know," Claire answered. "I'm happy to help you. It takes my mind off my own problems." She rested one hand against her ballooning middle and felt the baby's foot or hand drag across the interior of her body. The sensation still sent shivers through her.

"I still can't believe that you left your family to come take care of me."

"Why not?"

"I didn't realize we were friends."

"Of course we are!"

"Well, yes...now I know that. But when Hunter told me you agreed to come and take care of me, I was upset. I thought we were only acquaintances because of Milo."

"I admit we got off to a rocky start," Claire said, remembering her first tense encounter with Sondra, "but I thought we became friends before you moved from Milo's house to here."

"You're the only female friend I have. Did you know that?"

Claire had suspected as much, but she managed to keep her face neutral. "No, I didn't realize."

"I've never gotten on well with most women. I think they find me threatening."

"That could be because you're an incorrigible flirt."

"Ya think?" Sondra laughed. A moment later, she sobered. "What if this is it, Claire? What if I never have another lover for the rest of my life?"

"Ethan's still around--"

"Not for long."

"Why not?"

"He needs to be with someone younger. Now that his criminally insane sister is locked away, I think it's time for him to find someone more suitable."

"I know you've been talking about breaking up with him--"

Sondra shook her head. "I'm not leaving him. He's going to leave me."

"Don't be ridiculous." Claire had watched Ethan with Sondra -- the man fell all over himself to make sure Sondra was happy.

"Trust me -- he will."

"If you think he's the last lover you'll ever have, why would you want him to leave?"

"Let's call it a sacrifice. I've never done anything that wasn't motivated by selfishness -- except this. I've taken and taken and taken from the universe. Now that I'm nearly midway through my seventh decade, I think I should try to balance things out a bit."

"You're being a little harsh, aren't you? After all, you brought up a beautiful daughter--"

"She might as well have raised herself. I was so busy trying to be the center of attention that I never gave her a chance to shine."

Claire, glancing toward Sondra, saw tears roll down her friend's cheeks. This wasn't the first time Claire had seen them; Sondra had been pretty low for weeks now. She patted Sondra's hand and smiled. "I have a feeling Ethan's not going to be the last love of your life. There's someone out there for you -- someone who will make you as happy as you make him."

"You mean like you and Milo?"

"I'm doing the right thing, Sondra."

"You can't possibly believe that. Especially after what Beryl told you."

Claire frowned and drove silently, remembering her sister's story about Milo showing up in Oklahoma with an engagement ring the same day she left. If it was true, why didn't Sondra or Sax know about it? Both had been shocked when she told them what Beryl had said. She turned into the parking lot and found a handicapped space. "Ready?"

"I suppose."

"I'll get the walker." She got out of the car and opened the trunk, removing the cherry-red device from it. Sondra was already putting her feet on the ground by the time Claire had the walker ready for her. "You're getting too quick for me," she joked.

"Just call me Speedy." She steadied herself on its handles and pushed herself to a standing position. "Don't think you're going to get out of talking about Milo and the baby that easily," Sondra scolded. "I'm not senile yet."

"I'm doing what I think is right," Claire answered stubbornly. "Now move. We're going to be late."

"Do you want me to go with you?" Sondra asked the next morning as Claire rushed around the condo.

"No, I can do this on my own. It's just a blood test." She glimpsed herself in the mirror and couldn't help running a hand over her belly. "Dr. Slotnick says this is just a precautionary thing."

"What's it called again?"

"A quad test. It's a screening test to determine if the baby is at risk for Down's syndrome and a few other problems."

"I wish Milo were going with you."

"If wishes were horses..."

"You're a laugh riot."

Claire grabbed her purse. "I'll be back soon."

After she came back to the valley, Claire did some research and discovered that Dr. Slotnick was well known in Arizona for guiding high-risk pregnancies to successful deliveries. Dr. Reynart, her primary physician, happened to be acquainted with Slotnick. He had pulled some strings to get Claire under the obstetrician's care.

Dr. Slotnick reminded Claire of every absent-minded professor she had ever read about or seen on television. He dressed like someone who never actually turned on the light in his closet, and he frequently seemed on the verge of dozing off. His nurse had explained that, though he could use a wife, he was married to the job. She also told Claire that he had been in attendance at every one of his patients' labors, save five, in the last five years. With a track record like that, Claire knew she had found the right doctor.

Today, though, she would only be seeing the phlebotomist. She waited patiently, flipping through a three-year-old *Parenthood* magazine and sipping water from a paper cup. Around the edges of the room, other pregnant women -- some alone and others with partners -- also waited. Most of them were older mothers like Claire. One of the men looked to be as old or older than Milo. He was gently caressing the side of his wife's belly and smiling. A pang of sadness and guilt went through her. She wondered if she was depriving Milo of something that would have made him happy. Even if Beryl were telling the truth about the engagement ring, Milo didn't know she was pregnant. She knew he would still propose if he saw her belly, but she doubted that he would be as thrilled to become a father as she was to become a mother.

"Mrs. Combs?" the nurse called, peeking around the edge of the door.

"Coming," Claire said, pushing herself out of the seat.

"How are you this morning?"

"Hungry."

"This won't take long, and I can recommend a few great restaurants nearby." She led Claire down the hall to an exam room featuring a special chair with what looked to Claire like an abbreviated desktop attached to it. "Have a seat," the nurse said.

She settled into the chair and laid her right arm lengthwise across the desk, veins up. "You must do this all day long."

The nurse shrugged. "Pretty much. Are you comfortable?"

"I'm fine."

"Ball your fist and try to relax."

Claire looked away as the nurse tied her arm off and prepared the needle.

"Is this your first baby?" she asked as Claire felt the prick of the needle.

"Yes."

"You must be excited. I have two little ones myself."

"I am. How long before I know the results of the test?"

"A few weeks -- two or three at the most."

"I always wanted children...I just wish--"

"No point in that," the nurse said abruptly. "As my granny used to say, God watches us make plans and laughs."

Claire rolled the words around in her head and smiled. How true, she thought. How very true.

New Life

Ding Dong Bell

With a three-woman cleaning crew dusting, sweeping, mopping, and polishing the barroom and the bathrooms, Sax set about tearing down the wallpaper border in the offices. Though the edges of the paper were easily separated from the wall, the rest of it clung stubbornly, leaving a strip of anchors around the room. Borrowing a bucket and a sponge from the cleaning crew, he began the arduous task of wetting the remaining paper and scraping it off the wall.

The new signs for both the bar and Sax's detective agency had been put in place the day before, so he shouldn't have been surprised when a young man -- apparently an escapee from the Goth movement, judging by his half-grown-out black hair -- appeared in the doorway of the office. Nevertheless, Sax jumped when he saw him, nearly falling off the overturned liquor crate he had been using as a step stool.

"Sorry about that, sir. Didn't mean to sneak up on you."

Sax, clearing his throat and regaining his composure, stepped carefully off the crate. "Don't worry about it. I'm fine."

"You really shouldn't be doing that, you know. You should get a real ladder."

"May I help you with something?" Sax asked, studying the boy. He had the slimness of youth, as if his hormones hadn't fully kicked in yet. Sax estimated him to be about the same age as Sondra's grandson, Hunter.

"Uh, yeah. The sign outside says there is a private detective agency here?"

"Yes. I'm Sax Ridley. How can I help you, Mr...."

"Heber. Don."

"Heberdon?"

The kid shook his head, reddening. "No. I'm Don Heber. I need help."

"As you can see, I'm not set up to take clients just yet--"

"Oh. Yeah, I guess not." He shrugged. "I probably couldn't afford your help anyway."

Sax glanced around the room. "Are you any good with your hands?"

"What? You mean, like manual labor?"

"Helping me get this place in working order."

"What'll you pay me?"

618

New Life

"Let's talk about your case before we make any decisions." He clapped the young man on the shoulder and guided him out of the office and into the bar, where the three women in blue uniforms were scrubbing the walls.

Don crinkled his nose. "This place is rough."

"It's been empty for nearly a decade." Sax walked around the end of the bar top, which had already been wiped down. He gestured at the nearest barstool. "Have a seat and tell me your troubles."

He sat down, his body forming two sharp right angles. "You're a bartender too?"

"Former cop and barman. Now, what seems to be the trouble?"

"I met a girl a few months ago in a club. I need to find her again."

"Why?"

He frowned and looked down at the bar while he formulated his words. "She took something of mine...two things, actually. And I think she might be pregnant with my kid."

"What makes you think that?"

"A pal of mine said he saw her a few weeks ago and she's pregnant."

"What's her name?"

"That's the problem. She didn't give me her real one."

"How do you know?"

"My friends laughed when I told them her name. Turns out it's historical: Elizabeth Bathory." The kid chuckled. "Pretty creative of her, actually. Bathory liked to drink and bathe in blood. It's a perfect Goth name."

"Okay. What did she take?"

"A coin. I think she stole it out of my dresser."

"What kind of coin? A half dollar? A wheat penny?"

"I don't know, man. It was special. My great grandfather brought it back from Italy after the war. It was really old -- you know, like Roman-times old."

"Why would she take it?"

"Because it was priceless?"

"How did she know it was there?" Sax leaned his arms against the bar.

Don looked away and mumbled.

"Speak up, son."

"I showed it to her. I was trying to impress her."

"With a coin? Son, I think you may be a little confused as to what girls like."

"No, really. She had a cool coin on a ribbon around her neck. It looked old, too. When I asked her about it, she said she'd had it forever and that it was Italian."

"So you showed her your coin."

"Yeah."

"Then what happened?"

He shrugged and said, "You can guess."

"And the next morning she was gone?"

"Exactly. And I didn't even think about the coin for, like, a week at least. Then, one day, I was looking for something else in my drawer and realized the coin was gone."

"What else is missing?"

"Nothing."

"You said she had two things that belonged to you."

Don reddened and dipped his head. "I don't know how she did it -- and I know this sounds stupid -- but she's got my heart. Who falls in love with a thief, right? But she made me want to grow up...just so I can take care of her."

That explained the hair. Sax nodded. "I'll see what I can do. You have a regular job?"

"I work the graveyard shift at the gas station across the street."

"What time are you off?"

"Six."

"I'll meet you here. You give me three hours a day for a week, and I'll consider that your retainer."

"You think you can find her?"

"Sure," he answered with more confidence than he felt.

The kid reached across the bar top, offering his hand. "Thanks, Mr. Ridley. I'll see you tomorrow morning."

The next morning, Sax approached Don with a list of questions regarding the so-called Elizabeth Bathory, including contact information for the friend who claimed to have seen her and the bar where he had first met her. He took down a detailed description of her as well, including a note about a strawberry-shaped tattoo in an unusual place. Sax knew there was very little chance that the tattoo detail would come in handy unless he had to identify her body in a morgue.

When all of his questions were answered, Sax put the kid to work stripping the wallpaper from the offices. Alone in the barroom, he pulled out a blank sheet of paper and began listing the items he would need for his new office.

1. New computer. The one at the current Brass Monkey was old -- so old that, even with a better internet connection, loading a single image could take as long as ten minutes. If he were going to be an efficient investigator, he would have to abandon his Luddite ways and invest in some of the modern conveniences.

2. New desk. His old one was a flea-market find. Its all-metal construction might be sturdy, but it wasn't comforting to anyone, least of all distraught clients. Also, it was clearly built to be pushed against a wall. He needed one that would impress a client. In his last few months of rambling through second-hand shops around Sun City, he had seen more than a few handsome, wooden desks that would fit the bill.

3. New chairs. Not just for him, but for the clients too. He pictured a brown-leather high-back chair for himself and a couple of matching armchairs on the other side of the desk. He would have Don paint the office. He wondered what color would be most soothing for his clients. Green? Brown?

His cell phone rang, pulling him out of his decorating reverie. "Hello?"

"Sax, darling, it's Sondra."

"Hello! How are you doing?"

"Wonderfully. I saw the doctor a few days ago, and he's ecstatic about my progress. How's the new bar coming along?"

"Pretty well. The place isn't quite as much of a wreck--"

"That's great," she interrupted. "I have a favor to ask."

Sax chuckled silently and shook his head. "What do you need?"

"Do you still have the contact information for Ethan's first wife?"

"You mean Emlyn Kopczynski?"

"Yes, her."

He scratched his chin thoughtfully. "I think so. Why?"

"I need to reach her."

"And again I ask: why?"

621

"Let's just say she's the lynchpin in a plan I've made."

"Look, Sondra, this poor girl has been through the wringer. Vivian tried to poison her, she was forced to give up the man she considers the love of her life--"

"I won't hurt her, Sax," Sondra answered irritably. "I want to help her."

"She's really fragile. Your kind of help might be too much for her." He waited for her to answer, but heard only silence. "Sondra?"

"Will you give me her number or not?"

"I don't have it with me. I'll call you later."

"Please do."

Sax ended the call and laid his phone on the counter. He already knew he'd be giving his friend Emlyn's number. For the sake of the plump, timid nurse, he hoped he was making the right decision.

New Life

The Queen of Hearts

When the doorbell rang, Sondra called out to Claire, "Could you get that?"

"Sure. Just give me a minute." A moment later, Claire, wearing a pink-polka-dot smock, appeared. "Are you expecting someone?"

"Yes." When she didn't elaborate, Claire shrugged and went to the door.

Sondra could hear a younger woman asking if she was at home.

"Yes, of course. Follow me," Claire said. When she turned to face Sondra, the puzzlement was apparent on her face. "Sondra, your guest has arrived."

Sondra stretched out to shake Emlyn's hand. "Thank you so much for coming, my dear."

Emlyn smiled. "It's a pleasure to meet you."

"Please, have a seat." To Claire, she asked, "Would you mind bringing us drinks? I'd love a whiskey sour. Emlyn, what would you like?"

"Oh! Um...just a soda would be fine."

"What kind?" Claire asked.

"Sprite?"

"Of course." Claire smiled and disappeared around the corner into the kitchen.

"I suppose you're surprised to hear from me," Sondra began, "seeing as how I'm Ethan's fiancée."

The woman was staring at Sondra. "You're not exactly what I expected."

"You, on the other hand, match my imagination perfectly."

"You said Sax Ridley gave you my number?" She pulled herself to the edge of the sofa and leaned forward. "You know...about Vivian?"

"Yes, I'm afraid I know all too well. She won't be hurting anyone again, though. The doctors have diagnosed her as a narcissistic sociopath. Ethan tells me her lawyer is recommending that she take a plea to avoid the death penalty in her first husband's murder."

Claire handed the two women their drinks and retreated to her room.

Emlyn popped the top on her soda, but pushed the glass of ice to the middle of the coffee table. "Do you think she will?" She sipped from the can.

"It's likely. Even though she denies any wrongdoing, she's not a stupid woman. I have a feeling staying alive is more important to her than risking everything on a trial."

She seemed to relax and even smiled at Sondra. "I'm happy you and Ethan are okay. Is that why you called me here? To tell me about...her?"

"I felt it was important to thank you for sharing what you knew with Sax. I know you did so at great personal risk -- Vivian was a dangerous woman to cross."

"I appreciate that. As I've said, it's a great relief to know that she didn't harm you."

"Oh, she tried...Sax was just a bit quicker than she was."

Emlyn cleared her throat and pushed off the couch. "It's been a pleasure to meet you."

Sondra glanced nervously at the clock. "You're not leaving already, are you? I was hoping you would stay for dinner."

"My shift at the hospice starts at five," she answered. "And, to be perfectly honest, I don't eat food prepared by anyone other than me."

Sondra remembered Sax telling her that Vivian had fed Emlyn poisoned fettuccine. "I understand your hesitance, but--"

"I appreciate the offer. Really, I do. But, as I said, I need to get to work." She tipped back her head and drained the soda can. "Thanks for the drink."

Sondra heard a key turn in the lock and breathed a sigh of relief.

"It's me, Sondra!" Ethan called. She could hear the dry whisper of plastic grocery bags; he was planning to make enchiladas for dinner.

Emlyn, looking very much like a rabbit uncertain of which way to run, blocked Sondra's view of her gallant boyfriend.

"I'm in the living room, Ethan," she called.

But he didn't answer her. "Emlyn?" he asked softly.

"Hello, Ethan."

"My God...what are you doing here?" His voice, finely wrought with intricate emotions, caught in his throat.

"I invited her," Sondra said. Despite knowing she was doing the right thing, Sondra felt regret shredding her heart.

"I'm sorry about your sister."

Emlyn fidgeted, moving to her right just enough that Sondra could see around her. Ethan was pale and motionless; the grocery bags clung to the ends of his fingers like mountain climbers on the verge of losing their grips. The tremor of his bitter laugh caused one of the bags to lose its purchase and fall to the floor.

A clatter of tin cans shook him from his shock. "Don't be. She deserves whatever she gets."

"I know you were close."

His face hardened.

"I'm afraid I need to go. My shift starts at five, and I really should get there a few minutes before--"

"You're a nurse?" he asked, interrupting her.

"Yes."

"Good for you. I have often wondered--"

Sondra interrupted. "Are you sure you can't stay, Emlyn? I know Ethan would like to catch up."

She turned, blocking Ethan once again, and smiled at Sondra wistfully. "I appreciate the offer, but no." She reached out and Sondra took her hand. "Again, it was a pleasure meeting you." Emlyn released her and walked toward the door, pausing in front of Ethan for just a moment before placing her hands on his shoulders and stretching up to kiss his cheek. She whispered something Sondra couldn't hear and disappeared out of the door.

Ethan was frowning at her. "How did you find out?"

"About Emlyn? Sax found her when he was looking into your past."

He set the groceries on the hallway floor and walked to the couch, sinking into it with exhaustion.

Claire, who must have heard the exchange outside her door, appeared and gathered the grocery bags, taking them into the kitchen.

"I feel like I've just seen a ghost."

"I'm sorry. I didn't mean to upset you."

"I'm not...upset." He stared straight ahead, his gaze trained on the glass doors that overlooked the city. After a few minutes, he asked, "Is she still single?"

"According to Sax, yes."

"She's the sweetest woman I've ever known."

Sondra saw Claire cross back into her room, trying to give the couple privacy.

"Why did you annul the marriage?"

"That was what Emlyn wanted."

"That's not what she told Sax."

He whipped his head toward her. "No?"

"Vivian threatened her, too."

A sob escaped him and he dropped his head into his hands. "How could I have been so unaware of what my own sister was doing?"

"You trusted her, Ethan. You didn't do anything wrong."

"I could have been happy with her." The words seemed to slip from him. They weren't directed at Sondra, though she heard them.

Gingerly, she moved from her chair to the couch, where she pulled him against her and rocked him comfortingly. She was certain that the future had been changed.

The next morning, after Ethan had departed, Claire brought Sondra a fresh cup of tea and settled on the sofa. Though tea wasn't Sondra's preferred morning beverage, she accepted that Claire's condition made coffee an anathema.

"That was quite a scene you orchestrated yesterday," her pregnant friend commented.

"Merely a coincidence." Sondra dropped a sugar cube into her cup.

"I'm starting to think you don't actually know what that word means."

She rolled her eyes and changed the subject. "Have you heard from the doctor about the test results?"

"Not yet. They said it would take a few weeks."

"What about Milo? Have you talked to him?"

Claire stiffened. "No. And you better not pull a stunt like you did yesterday with the two of us."

"Hey, you want to screw up your life? It's your call."

"You aren't the Queen of Hearts, you know. You don't get to run everyone's romantic lives."

"I was only making a course correction to my own life yesterday."

"What do you think is going to happen? Ethan is too honorable to leave you for that girl."

"You forget that he loved her first, and it wasn't his decision to end the relationship." Sondra sipped her tea, a wistful smile on her face.

"What if Emlyn isn't interested?"

"Not interested?" Sondra scoffed. "What red-blooded woman wouldn't be interested in Ethan?"

Sondra's phone began playing "Y.M.C.A." Holding up a single finger to Claire, she reached over and picked it up from the end table next to her. "Hello?"

"Hi, Sondra," Sax said. "I just wanted to let you know that he called."

"As I expected. Did you give him her number?"

"Yes. I hope you know what you are doing."

"I'm making things right -- that's the best I can do for him."

Sax grunted a goodbye. Sondra clicked the end button and set the phone down.

"Ethan called Sax for Emlyn's number?" Claire surmised.

"Emlyn is going to get the happily ever after she deserves."

Claire wagged her head from side to side. "I just hope you don't regret this."

New Life

Wind the Bobbin Up

While Sax worked on the new building for the upcoming relocation of the Brass Monkey, Milo kept the current bar running smoothly. He was happy to have something to occupy his time, since Claire refused to see him. He spent his days -- from eleven in the morning until eleven at night -- tending bar and talking to the regulars. As he had promised, he introduced Sonia to a few of the bachelors and she made herself comfortable on Sondra's old stool. She was a *Reader's Digest* version of Sondra -- refined, but still sexy, and a lighter drinker. She confided in Milo that she had decided to get her real estate license -- retirement wasn't for her. When the bar was quiet, she studied for her exam.

With the opening of the new place a little more than a month away, Milo made a special morning trip to the bartending school, where he was pleased to run into his former instructor, Jenny Dallas.

"How have you been?" she asked, pulling him into a half-hug.

"Terrific, thanks. I'm actually here to post an open position for my bar."

"You own a bar already?! That's unbelievable!"

"I'm half-owner, actually. And we're getting ready to move the business to a bigger building, so we need another bartender and a waitress."

"You might do better to hire two bartenders," she advised. "That way, when it's really busy, you have extra help making drinks."

"Not a bad idea, except bartenders usually make more than waitresses, don't they?"

She shrugged. "A little, but on slow nights, why should you have two people standing around? This way, you can alternate shifts for the two of them."

"That's a good idea."

"I guess you're enjoying the profession."

"It suits me better than I realized it would."

"Great to hear!" She glanced at her watch. "I've got to get back to my class. Good luck on finding a couple of talented bartenders!"

"If they were trained by you, they're guaranteed to be great."

"Aw! Sweet talker." She kissed his cheek and disappeared down the hall.

Milo made his way to the office and filled out the paperwork to start the search for his new bartenders.

The following Monday, Milo scheduled a block of interviews back to back from nine until noon, each one half an hour long. He had pre-screened all of the applicants with telephone interviews; these six represented the best of them.

Of the six, he had met only one before -- though she didn't seem to recognize his name or his voice during the preliminary interview. And when Morgana Fuscilli walked through the door, Milo didn't recognize her either.

"I'm sorry, miss, we don't open until noon today." He looked down to review his paperwork. The last applicant, an older man, had seemed promising on the phone, but his personal hygiene left a lot to be desired. The body odor was still dissipating as Milo marked the interview notes with a large NO. When he looked up again, the young woman with the pixie haircut was still there.

"I'm supposed to have an interview--" she glanced down at a piece of paper in her hands "--with Milo?"

Milo frowned. "I'm sorry. I must have double-booked. I'm expecting another candidate any minute now."

The girl smiled brightly. "Hey...don't I know you?"

"I don't believe so..."

"Yeah, I do! We were in the same class at bartending school!"

He studied the girl again. Gone were the long black hair and vampire-like wardrobe, but, even without the burgundy lipstick, her heart-shaped lips and perfectly tweezed eyebrows were recognizable. "Morgana?"

"Oh, my goddess! I knew there had to be a reason why this job sounded so perfect!" She practically skipped to the chair, plopping herself down across from him. "That palm reader was right! The universe is guiding my steps!"

The last time he'd seen the girl, she'd been so thin that he imagined she would disappear if she turned sideways. That wasn't true anymore -- not entirely anyway. She had the slightest hint of a protruding bump in her mid-section. "You look terrific," he blurted.

"Thanks. I've decided to make some changes in my life...for the baby, you know." She patted the bump affectionately.

"I have to say I was shocked when you applied for this position. You were such a great student, I assumed you would be employed."

"When I decided to change my hair, the bar manager said I didn't fit the customer demographic anymore."

"You know that's illegal, right?"

She laughed. "He didn't say that to me. That's what I heard later from some of my ex-coworkers."

"What did he say?"

"'You're not working out.' I was still on probationary status."

"Probation?"

"Not that kind of probation." She rolled her eyes. "No. The job market is so tough that no one hires straight away anymore. I was there on a two-month on-the-job audition."

"Their loss is my gain," he said, surprising himself. He had chosen to interview her because he knew she was a talented bartender, but he hadn't expected to like her. Yet here she was, an altered young woman. He went down the list of questions, and was pleased with both her answers and her attitude. Finally, he asked, "You understand what kind of a bar this is, right?"

She glanced around the place, then gave Milo the once over. "I'm not prejudiced. I have a lot of gay friends."

"No. This isn't a gay bar."

"Oh. With the name and all--"

"The name refers to George," Milo said, hitching his thumb toward Sax's brass monkey statue, reigning over the room from its place behind the bar.

She reddened. "How embarrassing. Sorry about that. I just assumed--"

"That I was gay?"

"Well...you're really old and you aren't wearing a wedding ring and you dress kind of...I don't know...." Her voice trailed off.

"No. This is an old-fashioned, drink-to-get-drunk bar with lots of older patrons. Some of them are even older than me," he commented wryly.

"Please, Milo, I need this job. I'm sorry for my mistake. I'm not that bright. The only thing I'm really good at is mixing drinks, and without a job me and my baby are going to starve to death--"

"Don't you have a family?"

She shook her head. "My parents are divorced, and my dad's a complete asshole. Mom's remarried and her new husband is an even bigger jerk than my dad."

"What about your boyfriend?"

"You mean the baby daddy? He's just a sperm donor. I'm not with him."

"Does he know you're pregnant?"

She shrugged. "Doesn't matter. I'm not interested in him messing up my kid."

"He has a right to know, Morgana."

"You don't get it," she huffed. "He wasn't interested in more than fu--" she stopped and cleared her throat. "He only wanted to mess around, not make a family."

He grimaced.

Her shoulders fell. "That's okay, Milo. I understand. Why would you want some messed-up girl like me working for you?" Without making eye contact, she pushed herself to her feet and turned to leave.

"You're hired."

She turned back to look at him. "Are you kidding?"

"Not at all. I think you'll be a great addition to the team."

Her mouth spread into a wide grin and she flapped her arms as if she were resisting the urge to hug him. "That's amazing, Milo! Thank you so much! When do I start?"

"Can you come by tomorrow around eleven? I'll show you the ropes."

"See you tomorrow! Oh! What should I wear?"

"We like to see white shirts and black pants. Beyond that, the style is up to you."

"Got it!"

631

She bounced out the door. Milo smiled.

The rest of the interviews were less successful. Of the other candidates he interviewed that morning, only one of them was remotely acceptable. He decided to talk to Sax before making a decision.

Morgana arrived on time and properly dressed, encouraging Milo to believe he had made a good choice where she was concerned. He walked her through the opening and closing procedures, though he intended to be at the bar for both events for the foreseeable future. "Oh, and you'll need to clean the bathrooms."

Immediately, her nose wrinkled. "I can't do that."

"Why not?"

"The cleaners. They give me morning sickness."

"Then clean them at night."

"Morning sickness isn't actually limited to the morning, you know."

"I'm sorry, Morgana. This is part of the job. If you can't do it, then--"

"No, no! I'll work it out. Just the ladies', right?"

He had intended to give her the full latrine duty, but said, "Fine. You do the women's and I'll do the men's."

The front door swung open and Sax strode in. "I got your voicemail, Milo. What do you need?"

"Hey, Sax! How's the remodel coming along?"

"Pretty well. I got me a helper down there now. I'm thinking of keeping him around after the place is up and running. Not sure what he'll be doing for us, but I like the kid."

Milo waved Morgana over. "I wanted you to meet our new bartender, Morgana. Morgana, this is Sax, my business partner."

"Nice to meet you," she said.

"Likewise. Say...you're a young thing. You been bartending long?"

"As long as Milo has...we were in the same class."

"She was the star pupil," Milo put in.

"Good to hear." Turning to Milo, he said, "I thought you were hiring two people."

"I interviewed six candidates yesterday. Morgana here was the cream of the crop. Unfortunately, the others weren't what I was looking for. What about the guy you found? Is he a bartender?"

Sax pulled on the corner of his recently regrown mustache. "I doubt it. He's working as a convenience store clerk and handyman right now."

"If you like him, maybe you want to suggest bartending school."

New Life

Tweedledum and Tweedledee

Sax glanced up at the clock. "Do you have time to chat before the bar opens?"

"Sure," Milo said, stacking clean glasses behind the bar.

He looked pointedly toward the new hire, who had busied herself straightening chairs and wiping down tables. "In private?"

"Morgana, why don't you stack the glasses for me and wipe down the bar? Sax and I will be in the office."

"You got it, boss," she said.

Sax closed the office door behind them and cleared his throat.

Milo frowned. "You don't like her."

"What? Oh, no...she seems fine. A little young maybe...."

"She's young, I'll give you that. I don't think she's even old enough to drink yet."

"But she's old enough to bartend?"

"Nineteen's the legal age for that in Arizona. Plus, she won't be sneaking any drinks when we're not around -- she's pregnant."

"Really?" Sax asked, incredulous. "How can you tell?"

"She was a rail when I first met her. Plus, she told me. I think she's going to be a perfect fit for us."

"I trust your judgment." Sax moved toward the desk chair and pointed Milo toward the old recliner. "Let's sit down."

"What's going on?"

"I want to talk to you about this boy I've got working for me."

"You said his name is Don?"

"Yeah. Don Heber. Young kid...not much older than Morgana. He's actually a client."

"The first official Brass Monkey Detective Agency client?"

Sax laughed. "I was just going to call it the Ridley Agency."

"Your call," Milo said with a shrug. "Doesn't have much of a ring, though. So, what's the kid's story?"

"He says a one-night stand stole a valuable coin from him."

"Why doesn't he go to the cops?"

"He doesn't want her punished because he's in love with her."

"After one night?" Milo rocked in the chair.

"He's young."

"Where did he meet her?"

"A club. I've got the name of it in my notes, but I don't think that's going to help."

"Why not?"

"Well, she was one of those girls who dresses all in black. She had black hair, too. And it's not like I have a picture of her."

"Did he get her name?"

"She told him it was Elizabeth Bathory."

"Well!" exclaimed Milo. "What's the problem? That can't be a common name."

Sax picked up a pen and tapped it against the desk. "It's not. Unfortunately, it's a fake. Elizabeth Bathory was a mass-murdering fiend a few centuries ago."

Milo rocked the chair again as he stroked his chin. "Is there some reason you don't want Morgana to know about this?"

"She's a bartender, not a detective."

"True. But when I first met her she was one of those Goth girls -- you know, the all-in-black type."

"So you think she might know Don's Elizabeth?"

"Maybe, maybe not. But she could be able to give you some insight into where you could start looking for her. Have you got anything else to go on?"

"Not really, except she might be a coin collector."

"Seems unlikely."

"I thought so, too, but Don told me she was wearing an ancient coin around her neck."

Milo leaned forward. "Who else knew that this kid had the coin?"

"I don't know," Sax answered, frowning. "I didn't ask him that."

"You may want to. What if this girl set out to seduce him just so that she could get her hands on the coin?"

"I hadn't thought of that."

"And another thing: I don't buy his story that he's in love with her. I can't help but wonder if he stole the coin from someone else, and that's why he doesn't want to report the theft to the cops."

Sax shook his head once, firmly. "No. This kid has clearly made some serious changes to his life in recent weeks. I talked to a friend of his who said he saw the girl buying a pregnancy test; Don thinks she might be carrying his kid. Yesterday, he showed up with a buzz cut that took off what was left of his dyed-black hair."

"Wait...she's pregnant?"

Sax's jaw dropped. "You don't think...?"

"That would be a hell of a coincidence." Milo walked to the door and called Morgana over. The girl folded her bar towel and laid it next to the sink before crossing to the office doorway.

"Yeah, boss?"

"Morgana, do you know anyone named Elizabeth Bathory?"

She laughed lightly. "Of course. Several."

"What do you mean?" Sax asked.

"That's like asking if I know anyone named John Smith. It's an alias. Goth chicks use it all the time."

"Have you ever used it?" Milo went back to the recliner and let the girl step further into the office.

"No...never felt the need. Most people who meet me assume Morgana is my Goth name anyway."

Sax leaned forward, his elbows on his desk. "Where do you meet other Goths?"

"Besides the conventions?" she asked, smirking. "It's not a super-tight community."

"Is there a particular nightspot where one might find them?"

She pursed her lips and stared at the two men before answering. "Why?"

"I'm sorry?"

"Look, I don't mean to be difficult, but I'm having a hard time understanding why two old guys are interested in how today's youth spend their time."

"Sax is a private investigator," Milo answered.

"I thought you said he was your business partner."

"I'm both," Sax said. "And right now, I'm working on a case that involves young people who are part of the scene."

She rolled her eyes. "It's hardly a 'scene.' After all, we are in Phoenix, Arizona, not New York or L.A."

"The place you worked before...what was that called?" Milo asked.

"Villa Medici," she answered begrudgingly. "I'm only telling you that because you can find it on the resumé I gave you."

"Do you know a place called..." Sax hesitated, searching his memory, "Drac? My client said he met Elizabeth Bathory at Drac."

"First of all, what kind of Goth is he? Was he so stupid that he didn't know Elizabeth Bathory was an alias? Sounds to me like he's a poser -- he just wanted to get it on with a freaky girl."

"So he's not who he says he is?"

"If he's saying he's hardcore, then no -- he's not who he says he is."

"What about Drac? Ever heard of it?"

"Of course I have. That's what Villa Medici calls its Friday night party -- Club Dracula."

After getting a little more information from a reluctant Morgana about the Goth scene in Phoenix, Sax left the bar and returned to the building in renovation. Outside, Don was sanding down and re-gluing the old chairs in preparation for refinishing them.

"Good morning, Mr. Ridley," the boy said.

"It's noon. Let's take a break. I brought you a hamburger," he said, waving the Jack in the Box bag in his direction.

"Thanks, man!" Don followed him inside. They sat down at the bar and Sax distributed the food.

"I met a girl this morning who is familiar with the Goth scene," Sax said casually, watching the boy in the mirror behind the bar for his reaction.

Don stopped chewing for a second, then gulped. "Yeah? Where?"

"My partner hired her as a bartender. For a second, I thought I'd found your girl."

"But she's not."

"No. Definitely not. However..."

"Yeah, I need to get something out of the way right now." Don set down his hamburger and turned slightly on the stool. "I'm not really a Goth. I mean, I tried to be, but I just didn't fit in. I thought it was all about horror-movie shit and sexy girls, but I was so wrong, man. I tried to blend in by acting like I understood what everyone was talking about, but you just can't fake understanding all the Goth references the crowd throws around. I tried to just stay quiet -- you know, seem like a brooder. But I sucked at it."

"So, why did you give me that song and dance about changing your life for this girl?"

"I have! Honest to God, Sax, I'm a different guy. I don't want any more random hookups or to be someone I'm not. I just want a normal life with a girl and a kid or two."

Sax frowned and concentrated on his burger. The kid did the same. They ate in silence for a few minutes. Finally, Sax asked, "How many people knew you had the coin?"

He shrugged, not making eye contact. "A few," he mumbled.

Intuitively, he knew Don had told everyone about the coin -- he had made himself a target. He patted the boy on the back. "Hey -- it's okay. Had you ever seen the girl before the night you slept with her?"

"She was around. She hung out with a different crowd, though -- the VIP types. She would walk through and people would step out of her way."

"Didn't it strike you as odd when she showed an interest in you?"

He sagged on the stool. "Yeah," he admitted, "I wondered if I was being punked. I kept looking around for her friends to come out, to point and laugh at me. A lot of them had called me names before."

"What kind of names?"

"You know...poser, baby bat, that sort of thing. When Eliz...when she showed an interest in me and no one got in my face, I thought I'd finally made the scene."

Sax pulled on the end of his mustache. "Don, we're going clubbing on Friday night. I need you to point out who's who."

He looked up, aghast. "I can't go now! Look at me -- I'd just be proving their point! I was a poser."

"They won't even recognize you. We're going in looking as normal as their parents."

"They won't even let us through the door."

"We have a special pass named Morgana Fuscilli."

New Life

"This is illegal, you know," Morgana complained, pursing her lips angrily.

"That's it!" exclaimed Milo. "That's exactly how you looked in bartending school. Except your hair was longer."

"You could have said no." Sax took in the girl draped in a black-silk dress and thought she looked like a young widow. He caught a glimpse of himself in the mirror and cringed inwardly. Morgana had insisted that Sax at least wear black for their Friday-night excursion. The color made him look like he had spent several months underground. He wished he had taken the time to go to a tanning salon.

Milo waved good night to the last of the Brass Monkey patrons and locked the door. "When's the kid supposed to be here?"

"He's late," Sax answered.

"It's ten-thirty. We need to go soon. The place usually fills up a little after eleven. If we aren't there in time, I can't guarantee I'll be able to get us in." She fidgeted with the black flapper-style wig with which she was covering her brown pixie cut.

"Is all this really necessary?" Sax asked, watching her.

"That depends...do you care if we get inside the club?"

Someone knocked on the door.

"We're closed!" Milo called.

"I'm looking for Sax?"

"That's Don, Milo."

Don walked in stiffly, his hair slicked back and blackened with some kind of goop.

"Seriously? This guy?" Morgana asked.

"Yeah." Sax turned to Don and said, "Glad you could make it."

"Sorry. I overslept. Hey...aren't you one of the bartenders from Drac?"

"I used to be," she sighed. "Come on. We have a long drive."

They said goodbye to Milo and headed for Morgana's car, which she deemed most appropriate for the excursion. The ancient, oxidized-black Toyota was plastered with bumper stickers for bands and ink shops. Sax was amused to see one for Arlo and Easter's place plastered prominently in the back window.

For a rebel, Morgana was a cautious driver. Sax wondered if that was due to her pregnancy or an actual respect for the rules of the road. In any case, he was able to relax with her behind the wheel.

Unfortunately, Don couldn't. Sax heard the guy fidgeting in the back seat. He leaned forward and looked over Morgana's shoulder. "You could probably go faster."

"Sit back. I'm driving," she growled.

"I'm just saying...we need to get there soon, right?" He slid back in the seat, pouting. A few minutes later, he asked, "Do you recognize me?"

"No."

Sax had a gut feeling she was lying, but he wasn't at all sure why she would.

At a quarter past eleven, Morgana parked the car and headed toward the front of the line. The two men followed her. Sax surveyed the crowd as they walked; he was the oldest person within sight by at least two decades. He hoped his youthful physique would hide his true age.

"York!" exclaimed Morgana, bumping fists with the burly young man at the door.

Sax strained to hear the conversation over the aggressive beat of the music spilling out into the street. He moved closer, until he hovered just over the shoulder of the small woman.

"Morgana! Haven't seen you around in a while."

"Yeah...I decided to broaden my horizons."

"Welcome back into the dark and satiny folds," he said with a smirk.

She rolled her eyes and laughed. "These are my bodyguards," she said, indicating Sax and Don.

York gave them a quick once-over. "Building an entourage, huh? I didn't think you were the social type."

"I can be...when I want to be."

York lifted the rope and said, "Don't do anything I wouldn't do."

"I'll keep that in mind."

The three of them moved into the club. The interior reminded Sax of an Italian villa, with frescoed walls and dark wooden furniture. The low lighting enhanced its luxurious feel.

New Life

Just like the line outside, the clientele seemed to have a median age of twenty-four. Most of the revelers wore black, though a few -- girls, mostly -- broke the rules and wore deep reds and purples, too.

"Okay. You're in. Don't make too big of a spectacle of yourselves -- I don't want to end the evening with a permanent ban."

"Thanks, Morgana." He slipped her the fifty-dollar "bonus" they had previously agreed on and she disappeared into the crowd.

Don scanned the room like a rookie cop looking for a criminal. "I don't see her," he said.

"Stop that," Sax said sharply.

The kid looked at him. "Isn't that why we're here?"

"Not exactly. I'm more interested in who would have put her up to stealing the coin. You said she hung out in the VIP room?"

"Yeah." Don pointed discreetly toward a doorway with another bouncer guarding it.

"Did you tell anyone else who hangs out there about the coin?"

Don shrugged. "Probably. There's this one emo guy who talked to me a few months ago. I think I mentioned the coin to him."

Sax frowned. Morgana had given him a short course on the latest slang. He knew "emo" referred to kids who portrayed themselves as particularly sullen or angst-ridden. "How does a Roman coin come up in conversation, exactly?"

"I don't know," Don said defensively. "I just, you know, needed something to talk about. So I carried it with me."

"You had a valuable, ancient coin in your pocket?"

He shrugged.

"I'm surprised you made it home with it. What happened after that?"

"The next Friday, the emo guy found me and said someone wanted to meet me. He pulled me into the VIP room and dragged me in front of this guy sitting on a throne."

"What did he look like?"

Don shifted his weight and grimaced. "You know...good-looking. I'm not gay, but I could definitely see his appeal, if you know what I mean."

"Was he white? Black? Hispanic?"

"Oh! Uh, Hispanic, maybe?"

"What was his name?"

"Trevor, I think."

"Okay, so what happened?"

"When?"

"When the guy dragged you in to meet Trevor."

"Oh." Don squinted. "He bowed down to the guy."

"Trevor bowed down to the emo?"

"No, the other way around. The emo guy bowed down to Trevor. I think he called him Lord Trevor."

"How did he introduce you to this Trevor character?"

"He said I was the guy with the coin. He asked to see it, but I didn't bring it with me that night."

A girl in a red corset bumped against Sax. He felt for his wallet, just to be safe; it was still there. "Was there anyone else in the room?"

"Six or seven others. All of them seemed to be with Trevor. That was the first time I saw Elizabeth. She was one of the two girls sitting on either side of the throne at his feet."

"At his feet?" Sax repeated.

"Yeah. They had leather leads around their necks, too." Don shook his head. "You know, now that I'm saying all this aloud, it sounds bizarre. Doesn't it?"

"Yeah," Sax agreed. "What happened when you couldn't produce the coin?"

"He asked me how long I'd been a Goth. I told him a few years. The others laughed at me, but he gestured for them to stop and they did. He kept asking questions: did I know this or that band, was I into bondage, what did I think of Poe's work. I think it was a test or something."

"I take it you didn't pass."

He shook his head mournfully. "He dismissed me and the rest of the group heckled me from the room."

"We're going in there."

"In the VIP room?"

"Yes. We need to have a word with Trevor."

"How are we going to get in?"

"A little luck and a lotta balls." Sax led Don to a table not too far from the VIP entrance. Sax studied the bouncer. He didn't look too bright -- he'd probably fried his brain with steroids to get his muscle-bound look. "Find Morgana. We need her again."

Don nodded and headed toward the dance floor.

The bouncer didn't look like he would be a patron when he wasn't working. He had earphones on, which meant he probably wasn't a big fan of the music the DJ was spinning. Sax watched his foot and, sure enough, it was tapping to a different beat than the song blaring through the building. His music must have been turned up full blast for it to block out the noise around him. Sax smiled to himself -- his plan could work. Even if it didn't work for long, he only needed a minute or two to establish contact. He pulled out his wallet and extracted a business card. He had his story now.

Don arrived back at the table with Morgana in tow.

"What do you want now?"

"Do you know who Lord Trevor is?"

"Yeah. He's one of the owners of Villa Medici. He hangs out in the VIP room."

"What's his full name?"

"Trevor Vallejo."

"Thanks. Now I need you to distract the bouncer."

"How?"

"Flirt with him."

"I think he'd be more responsive to Don than me," she answered with a straight face.

Sax looked at the guy again and decided she might be right. "Don, distract the guy."

"Hell, no. I ain't no fag!"

"Yeah? Well, I am, but I've already got an assignment in this little scenario."

Don, his eyes wide, looked at him and backed up a step. "Sorry, man. I didn't know."

Sax shrugged and said gruffly, "Good to know. I hate it when my choice of bed partners is the first thing people notice about me."

Morgana, apparently unfazed by Sax's revelation, suggested, "Don and I could have a fight in front of him. The club doesn't condone violence and the bouncer would have to step in or risk losing his job."

"Just yelling at each other? We could do that," Don agreed.

"Okay, we'll start with that," Morgana said, dragging him by the wrist.

Sax positioned himself to one side of the VIP entrance and attempted to look casual. Meanwhile, Morgana and Don began performing what appeared to be a dramatic pantomime of a fight just inside the bouncer's line of sight. When Morgana reared back and smacked Don across the face, the bouncer took two steps to the right and caught Morgana by the wrist. Sax slipped into the VIP room and walked swiftly toward a man sitting on what appeared to be a throne. Two women were at his feet, just as Don had described.

The man stretched and yawned, as if bored with his surroundings. "Where is Bruno? Shouldn't he be watching the door?"

One of his male acolytes scurried past Sax; Sax kept advancing. "Trevor Vallejo?"

"Fool! Address him as Lord Trevor!" commanded another of the men surrounding him.

"Stand down, Damien. I don't think he's one of my subjects." Trevor smirked as he ran his eyes up and down Sax. Sax stood his ground, though the younger man's gaze made him both nervous and somewhat aroused. "Who might you be?"

"My name is Sax Ridley. I'm a private eye." He produced the business card from his pocket and held it out toward the man. One of the girls took it.

"Of what am I being accused now?"

"Nothing. On the contrary, I believe I may have something of yours."

"Okay, I'll bite." He snapped his teeth and the women at his feet purred. "What, pray tell, do you have?"

"This isn't the place or time to discuss the matter. Call the number on the card tomorrow, and we'll arrange a meeting."

"Very mysterious. What if I don't call?"

"Then it's your loss." Sax turned on his heel just in time to greet two large men -- one of whom was the aforementioned Bruno, the guy Morgana and Don had distracted. Positioned on either side of him, they each looped an arm under one of his and prepared to drag him from the room. "It's okay, boys...I was just leaving."

Nevertheless, the men escorted him to the exit, giving him a rough shove a second before the door closed behind him. When he turned around, he saw Morgana and Don, who were leaning against the outside wall.

"Yeah, so, thanks. You got me permanently banned," Morgana groused.

"Look at it this way: you won't be tempted to go back."

"Just because I was taking a break from the scene doesn't mean I wanted to completely leave it behind."

"Trust me, Morgana," Sax answered, "once that baby comes, you won't have time for clubbing."

"You're pregnant?" Don exclaimed.

"So?"

"You should have told me! I almost socked you when you slapped me."

She smirked. "You're too much of a gentleman. That's the real reason you never would have blended with this crowd: you're not scary." She pulled her car keys out of her tiny bag and jingled them. "Let's go home, boys."

As they followed her to the wreck of a car, Don asked, "What happens now?"

"We wait. In a day or two, I expect to hear from Mr. Vallejo." Sax lowered himself into the passenger seat and let himself nod off as Morgana drove them back to the Brass Monkey.

New Life

Did You Ever See a Lassie?

Saturday morning, Milo was up early. The weather was beautiful this time of year, so he took his newspaper outside and spread it out on the patio table. On mornings like this one, he missed Taz, the pug dog that Claire had left in his care. When he flew off to Oklahoma City to propose, Milo had asked his son's family to look after him for a few days. When he came home, he asked them to keep him. Milo told himself it was wrong to leave the poor animal alone for twelve hours at a time, and Taz was better off with Brian, Marla, and the kids. In truth, he felt guilty every time Taz looked at him with his big, brown, bulging eyes; Milo knew it was his fault Claire wasn't with them.

His cell phone rang and Milo, startled by the loud noise in the quiet morning air, grabbed it. "Hello?"

"Hi, Dad." Brian sounded glum.

"What's the matter, Son? Why are you calling so early?"

"I have some bad news."

Milo sat up straight. "What's happened?"

"Taz is sick."

Milo pulled into Brian's driveway less than an hour later to find Alice Marie sitting on the front steps, waiting for him. Her ivory skin seemed even paler and her eyes were rimmed with red. Instead of throwing herself into Milo's arms -- as was her habit -- she stood and waited for him to get to her, her head bowed in sorrow. He picked the girl up and cradled her against his shoulder.

"Daddy says Taz is real sick, Grampa."

"I know, sweetheart. I'm sorry."

"You can fix him, right?"

He knew better than to lie to this intelligent little girl. "I don't think so. Taz has lived a long, full life. It's time for him to go to heaven."

"Are animals allowed in heaven?"

"I think so."

"My friend Emma says they aren't."

"Has Emma been to heaven?"

Alice Marie shook her head against his shoulder.

646

"Then I doubt she knows that for certain."

"I love you, Grampa." She kissed him on the cheek and squirmed to get down.

Milo set her on her feet. She took his hand to lead him into the house, but stopped short a moment later. "Grampa?"

"Yes, Alice Marie?"

"You're a lot older than Taz."

"That's true."

"Are you going to die soon?"

He bent his legs so that he was eye to eye with her. "I will die someday, but not too soon."

"When?"

"I don't know for sure. No one knows when they will die."

"I want to live to be a hundred!" she stated firmly.

"That sounds good. I'll try for that, too."

"How old will I be when you are a hundred?"

"Oh, you'll be older than your mom is now."

She nodded solemnly. "That's old."

He winked at her. "Don't say that to her, okay?" Straightening, he took her hand and they went inside the house.

Taz lay in his bed. His breathing sounded even more labored than usual. His eyes opened and he looked up at Milo, who knelt next to the old dog.

"I'm sorry, boy," he said, stroking Taz.

Taz wagged his half-curled tail weakly.

"The vet gave him something to ease his pain so that I could bring him home," Brian said. "He's coming by the house to...you know..."

"What time?"

"We set the appointment for eleven-thirty."

"I've got to call Claire." He pulled out his cell phone and dialed. She didn't answer, as usual. "Claire," he said to the voice-mail recorder, "I need you to call me right away. It's important." He ended the call and looked at his son and Marla, who had wandered in and sat on the sofa nearby. "She won't call me back."

"Are you sure?" Marla asked. "You did say it was important..."

"I'd better try Sondra." He dialed again; Sondra answered.

"Milo! How are you?"

"Not great. Is Claire around?"

She hesitated. "No...I think she went...to the grocery store."

"For an actress, you're a lousy liar. Look, it's about Taz. Would you tell her that?"

"Just a second." He heard her slide her hand over the phone and muffled voices talking. "Here she is."

"Milo?" Claire asked.

Hearing her voice flooded him with warmth. His voice cracked as he said, "Yeah, it's me."

"What's wrong?"

"I need you to come to Brian's house right away. Can you do that?"

"No! I can't! I thought this was about Taz--"

"It is. Brian and Marla have been taking care of him for a while now."

"You gave my dog to your son?"

He bristled at her accusatory tone. "I was working long hours at the bar. It seemed like they could give him a better life." He waited for her to respond; when she didn't, he continued, "Taz has congenital heart failure. He's dying, Claire."

"No..." She sobbed loudly.

"I'm so sorry, sweetheart. The vet gave him a sedative and pain reliever so that the family could say goodbye to him at home. He's going to be here to put him down at eleven-thirty."

She was still sobbing. He heard a loud clatter and held the phone away from his ear. "Hello? Hello, Claire? Can you hear me?"

"Milo, it's Sondra. What's going on? Claire can't tell me -- she can't catch her breath."

"Taz is dying. She needs to get to my son's house as soon as possible."

"I don't think she can drive in her current condition! And I certainly can't."

Milo looked at Brian and Marla. "Claire's too upset to drive."

"I'll pick her up," Marla said, pushing herself off the couch.

"You don't have to--"

648

"Nonsense. She'd do the same for anyone. Where does she live?"

"Near Camelback and Central. Camelback Towers. I don't know the address."

"I know where that is. I'll be there in twenty minutes."

"Sondra, my daughter-in-law is coming to get her. Send Claire downstairs in twenty minutes."

"Shouldn't we make sure she wants to go?" Sondra asked.

"She needs to come. Tell her she'll regret it if she doesn't. Goodbye." As he ended the call, he heard a door close as Marla went to her SUV.

Alice Marie was next to Taz's bed, petting him gently.

"You want a drink, Dad?" Brian asked.

Catching the scent of fresh-brewed coffee in the air, he said, "I'll take a cup of java." He followed his son toward the kitchen.

Brian pulled a couple of bright-red mugs from the cabinet and filled them both. He slid one in front of Milo, who pulled out a stool at the counter. Milo watched as his normally tough son sagged against the counter across from him.

"I'm sorry about this, Son," Milo said.

"It's been a rough day," Brian admitted, sipping his coffee. "But the kids are handling it pretty well. I thought Alice Marie would be a mess -- she loves him so much. And I think the affection is mutual. He slept in her room, you know."

"If I'd thought there was any chance he was sick, I never would have given him to you."

"Don't beat yourself up. The vet said it's difficult for the average pug owner to recognize the signs of congenital heart failure in their dog because the dogs have such terrible breathing problems to begin with." He took another sip. "On the bright side, having Taz around convinced Marla that a dog isn't such a horrible idea. Both the kids really stepped up and took care of him. In fact, Eric is the one who woke me up this morning to tell me there was something wrong with Taz. He was up way too late playing video games when he heard Taz coughing."

"Where is he now?"

"Sleeping. He went to the emergency vet with me, so he hadn't gotten any sleep at all."

"Did he make the baseball team?" Milo asked, remembering a recent game of catch he had shared with his son and grandson.

"He did! The team's doing great, too."

"Why didn't you tell me? I would have been at the games!"

Brian smiled. "No, you wouldn't have. I know you're spending every day at the bar, Dad."

He grimaced but nodded. "I hired another bartender this week, though. I'll be at all the games from here on out."

"Great. I'll get you a copy of the schedule."

They sipped their coffee in silence for a few minutes before Brian asked, "Do you want to watch the news while we wait for Marla to get back?"

"No. I think I'll just go in and sit with Alice Marie and Taz." He stood and carried his mug into the living room. Funny name for a room, really: living room. Milo knew his son's family didn't do much of their living in here, preferring the cozy family room. The living room was reserved for guests and, apparently, dying pets. He set his mug on the end table with the duck-decoy lamp and lowered himself to the ground next to Alice Marie and the sweet pug.

"I think he's sleeping," the little girl said, still stroking his fur.

Milo held his hand in front of Taz's nose and the dog responded by licking his palm. Milo sighed with relief. "Yes, honey, he's just resting." He ran his fingers over the peach-fuzz hair that stretched from just above Taz's eyes to just behind his ears.

Alice Marie scooted closer to Milo and rested her head against his shoulder. "I don't want him to die."

"I know."

They stayed like that for a long time, until Milo heard the SUV pull back into the driveway. Alice Marie straightened and said, "Miss Claire's here."

Milo patted her on the cheek and rolled to his knees, using the sofa to help himself back to his feet. When he turned around and saw Claire for the first time in months, his knees buckled and he dropped back onto the sofa.

"Hi, Milo," she said, awkwardly folding her arms over her belly.

New Life

Out of the corner of his eye, Milo saw his son's jaw drop as Marla wrapped a supportive arm around Brian's waist. "You're pregnant," Milo stated.

"Yes. I am." Using the arm of the sofa, she lowered herself to her knees and turned to where Taz was lying. "Taz?" She stroked his fur and his eyes opened. "It's okay. I'm here now."

Taz whined for the first time and Claire pulled his head into her lap. She was murmuring to the dog now, no longer paying any attention to the people surrounding her. Milo could see huge tears rolling down her face. He wanted to go to her, to kneel next to her and offer her comfort -- but he might as well have been a pillar of salt for all the movement he was capable of.

Alice Marie moved closer to Claire and wrapped her arms around her. Claire put her free arm around the girl, and together they petted the ill pug.

He wasn't sure how long he sat there in stunned silence, but when Marla and Brian each took one of his arms, he allowed them to lead him away. In the family room, they placed him in Brian's recliner.

"How far along is she?" Brian whispered.

"She told me she's just about at the end of her second trimester," Marla answered.

"You didn't know, Dad?"

"No. No, I didn't. What in the hell--?"

"Shush!" Marla glanced toward the living room. "You want her to hear you?"

More softly, he said, "What in the hell was she thinking? Why didn't she tell me?"

Marla shifted her eyes, avoiding Milo's face.

"You need to tell me what she said."

"I can't. It's between the two of you."

Milo took her hands and begged, "Please, you have to tell me. She hasn't spoken to me in months."

Marla met his eyes and bit her lip. Finally, she sat down next to him. "She doesn't want to trap you into marriage."

"That's ridiculous," he said, even as he recognized the kernel of truth in her words.

Marla shrugged. "That's what she believes."

New Life

Despite the obvious disapproval of his son and daughter-in-law, Milo slipped out the side door. In a daze, he drove to the Brass Monkey.

"Milo! I wasn't expecting you to show up at all." Sax was stacking glasses behind the counter.

"You knew she was pregnant, didn't you?" Milo slumped onto a barstool.

"Who? Morgana? Yeah, you told me."

"Not Morgana, you asshole. Claire!"

"Careful now, buddy. You don't want to say something you'll regret." Sax set the glass in his hand on the bar top with a thump.

"How long have you known?"

"Listen, she asked us to keep her secret."

"I can understand why Sondra didn't tell me -- she's a woman, and she's renting from Claire. But you?"

"In my defense, I..." Sax pulled on one end of his mustache as he thought.

"What?"

"Never mind. I don't have a good defense."

"I could have told you that." Milo sagged lower, his adrenaline draining away. "Why didn't she tell me?"

"You're nearly sixty years old. You can't blame her for thinking you might not be interested in starting a new family."

"But she's carrying my baby! I don't really have a right to-_"

"And that's exactly why she didn't tell you."

Milo stared blankly at his friend.

"Because she didn't want to trap you into marriage," Sax said slowly, as if he were talking to an idiot.

"That's ridiculous. I wanted to marry her!"

"Wanted?"

"I mean...I want..." His head dropped to the bar. "Holy shit. I'm sixty. That means this kid won't be out of my house until I'm nearly eighty. What if I don't live that long? What if something happens to Claire? This kid could be an orphan! My son could end up raising it!"

Sax patted him on the shoulder. "I think you've got some soul-searching to do."

New Life

Milo shook his head. "None of that matters. She's pregnant, it's mine, and we're getting married."

"Good luck with that."

Bye, Baby Bunting

Sax was surprised when he didn't hear from Trevor on Saturday. When he didn't receive a call on Sunday, he was disappointed. By Monday, he had the sinking feeling that Mr. Vallejo wasn't missing anything he cared to recover.

As Sax contemplated where to turn next in the labyrinth of his case, Don appeared, carrying in a recently refinished chair. The kid definitely had some skill when it came to refinishing furniture; the bar was nearly in good enough condition to open now. "Excellent work, Don."

"Thanks. Has Trevor called yet?" He pulled off his cap and pushed the accumulated sweat from his head down the collar of his shirt. Sax could see the residual black hair dye coloring both the boy's hand and around his neck, making him look considerably dirtier than he was.

Sax shook his head. "What about that friend of yours? The one who says he saw Elizabeth buying a pregnancy test?"

"I can call him. But he thought her name was Elizabeth, too."

"At least we could find out where she shops."

"That's easy. My friend works at the Walmart up at the old Christown Mall."

"He saw her there?"

"That's what he said."

"Okay. Do you think you could describe her to an artist?"

"You mean, like a sketch artist?"

Sax's phone chimed loudly and he held up a finger to Don as he answered the call. "Sax Ridley."

"Mr. Ridley," said the smooth-as-brandy voice. "Trevor Vallejo. I believe we spoke on Friday night."

New Life

He raised his eyebrows and Don sat down to listen to Sax's side of the conversation. "Mr. Vallejo. I was wondering if you'd lost my number."

"Weekends are my busiest time, I'm afraid. Villa Medici is...a lifestyle, shall we say."

"So I saw."

"So, Mr. Ridley, what is it you have that belongs to me?"

"I'd rather not discuss it over the phone."

A warm trill of laughter bubbled over the line. "So secretive. Are you sure you aren't part of the scene? Everyone always wonders where the original Goths disappeared to...maybe you're here to lead us home?"

The question sounded just sincere enough that Sax was unable to formulate a response, afraid that he might offend this possible "true believer."

Another laugh wiped away the tense silence. "No, I suppose not. I'm afraid you're going to have to give me something more if you expect me to meet you, though."

"I understand you have an interest in coins." Sax looked at Don, who shrugged uncertainly.

"Certain coins. But I'm not missing any."

"That's too bad. You see, I have one from the Roman Empire--"

"Anno domini or before Christ?"

"I'm no expert. It fell into my possession through a client. I got the impression she lifted it from your collection."

"How interesting. What was her name?"

"As I said before, I'd be more comfortable discussing this matter in person."

"Why don't you come to me?"

"I'm not really comfortable with that."

"Please, Mr. Ridley, indulge me. My acolytes find it disconcerting when I break character. Leaving my lair during the day...that's practically blasphemous in their world."

"What are you, a vampire?" Sax asked incredulously.

"Of course not! How ridiculous would that be? Let's just say...I burn easily."

"Fine. Where should I meet you?"

He gave Sax an address on Central Avenue, then said, "You can't miss it. I'm in the corner home. Bring the coin with you."

"You'll understand if I'm not comfortable with that."

"I'm starting to think you don't trust me, Mr. Ridley." Another rolling trill of laughter bubbled out of him. "I'll look forward to your visit."

The phone clicked to silence in Sax's hand.

"You lied to him," Don said, his eyes wide.

"Yeah. So?"

"What are you going to do about the coin?"

"Do you think your Elizabeth stole your coin and turned it over to him?"

Don propped his elbows on the chair's arms, bringing his fingers to a steeple beneath his chin. "I doubt it. Like I said, she seemed to know more about coins than I do."

"If she's Trevor's pet, he could have trained her to recognize valuable coins, couldn't he?"

Don shook his head. "I doubt it. My grandfather tried to teach me the hobby when I was young, but it's more complicated than you'd think. He gave up eventually. He said I didn't have the knack for it."

"What did he mean by that?"

Don shrugged. "I couldn't tell the difference between real and fake coins, no matter how many times he tried to teach me."

"From just one night with her, you think Elizabeth could?"

"I know it sounds weird, but she reminded me of my grandfather."

"Then maybe she was hanging around with Trevor for more than the role-playing." Sax laid the towel he'd been polishing the glasses with on the bar top and headed for the bathroom. Don followed him.

"Should I go with you?" Don asked, watching Sax brush his hair back and groom his mustache.

"No. I don't want Trevor to associate the two of us in his mind."

"Don't you think you should take someone with you? You know, for backup?"

"You think this guy is dangerous?"

Don frowned. "A full-grown man who pretends to be a vampire? I'd say he's unpredictable."

"Point taken." He pulled his phone out of his pocket and dialed the Brass Monkey.

An hour later, Sax pulled up in front of a massive, four-story building that resembled a medieval castle.

Milo, who was riding shotgun, whistled. "Impressive."

"Overstated."

"This guy fancies himself a vampire?"

"It's more like he play-acts as a creature of the night. I don't think he really buys his own bullshit."

Milo shrugged his eyebrows. "Who knew being a freak could be so profitable?"

They stepped out of the car and followed the pathway to the front door. "Remember, I need you to look threatening," Sax said before he rang the bell. "Poker face."

Milo, who was a full six inches shorter than Sax, rolled his eyes. "There's no way they're going to believe I'm your bodyguard."

"Just pretend you're wearing a sidearm."

The door swung open and a ridiculously thin young man with coal-black hair and large gauges in his ears stood before them. The kid had either perfected his blank expression or he was, in fact, brain-dead. "Yeah?"

"Sax Ridley. Trevor is expecting me."

The kid ran his eyes over them, though nothing resembling curiosity creased his expression. "Follow me."

As soon as the kid turned his back, Milo arched an eyebrow at Sax, who shrugged in response and stepped into the home. Their guide stepped through an archway to the right of the foyer. An elevator waited for them. The interior featured a dark-wood wainscoting and a golden pressed-tin ceiling with recessed lights in the corners. The kid pushed the button for the third floor. A moment later, the doors slid open. Stepping out of the elevator, they walked to the left through a Gilded-Age dining room with red-brocade-draped French doors and into a formal living room with purple velvet sofas that would have been at home in a whorehouse. Despite a multitude of windows, the room was twilight-dark, thanks to wooden shutters. Trevor Vallejo lounged elegantly on a scarlet-red chaise longue. On the floor in front of him sat a young, waif-like woman wearing a leather collar and lead -- and not much else. She didn't raise her face to look at them, but Sax didn't see any signs of abuse on her over-exposed body. Sax tried to take his own advice, but he could feel his poker face slipping.

"Eric," Trevor said, holding out the lead attached to the girl's collar, "please take Alicia to her cage."

The boy took the lead and the girl followed him, on her hands and knees, to the elevator. Sax glanced at Milo, who was successfully holding his blank gaze in place. Clearing his throat, he said, "Thank you for agreeing to meet with me."

Trevor waved the thanks away like a pesky fly. "You left me little choice. Besides, I think I may have a use for you."

"A job?"

"Possibly. I assume since you brought a companion, you also brought the coin?"

"No. But I've got a picture." He pulled out his phone and brought up the photo he had snapped of a coin on the internet; Don swore it looked just like the one he was missing. He held the device out to Trevor, who made no attempt to reach for it.

"Bring it closer, please."

Sax inched forward and stretched toward the man.

With a smile that showed nearly every tooth in his head, Trevor said, "I don't bite."

Sax laughed nervously and stepped closer.

Trevor reached out and took the phone with his manicured hands. Sax noted that he wore a sparkling black polish on his sharpened nails. A second later, he handed it back. "That's not mine."

"Really?" Sax asked. He had expected Trevor to claim it, even though he knew it couldn't possibly belong to the man.

"No," he answered sourly. "Who was this person who claimed to have stolen it from me?"

"Obviously, she was lying." Sax decided to play his last card. "She claimed her name was Elizabeth Bathory and that she was close to you."

Trevor lowered his eyelids and smiled slyly. "You have been taken for a fool."

"Yes. A little research into the scene soon revealed that it holds as many Elizabeth Bathorys as the morgue holds Jane Does."

"She didn't give you her real name, yet she left a valuable coin in your care?"

"She was desperate, that much was clear. I don't know why she would have lied about its origins."

"Nor do I, Mr. Ridley." The handsome younger man gracefully stood and glided to a wet bar that occupied the three-quarter circle of windows in the corner. "Would you or your man like a drink?"

Sax glanced at Milo, who gave a discreet shake of his head. "No, thank you."

"As you wish." He poured himself something viscous and red. Sax hoped it was tomato juice -- the alternative was far too disturbing to contemplate. He strolled back to Sax, standing a little closer than Sax would have preferred. "At least your trip over won't be a total loss. I would like you to find someone for me."

Sax shuffled backward half a step. "Who?"

Trevor laughed and waved his hand dismissively. "Another of the trifling 'Elizabeths.' This one actually did take something of mine -- a bronze Etruscan coin with a double head. It's worth a small fortune."

"You said you weren't missing anything when we spoke earlier."

His eyes flashed. "Good memory. I wasn't alone when I spoke with you on the phone. I prefer not to let my acolytes know such details."

"If the coin was worth so much, how did she get her hands on it?"

"Almost everything I own is worth a small fortune. It makes no sense to encase my dwelling in a mesh of security." He turned and walked back to his chaise.

"Seems risky."

"My companions are high-school dropouts and runaways with little understanding of the riches surrounding them. I am their rescuer -- their foster father, if you will. Most have been trained not to bite the hand that feeds them. I keep them warm and fed, and, in return, they serve me."

"How exactly do they serve you?" Milo asked. Sax shot him a surprised glance.

"So, your eunuch speaks! What a lovely surprise. Not that it's any of your business, but they provide me with an entourage -- people to fawn over me and help me present the proper image to the world."

"You're very self-aware for an egomaniac," Sax commented, smiling.

"I'm a businessman, Mr. Ridley. In today's world -- filled with all its gadgetry and speculation -- it is necessary to present the proper image at all times. You never know who may be watching. I own part of every Goth business in this town. I can't very well walk around in a t-shirt and shorts and expect to have the respect of the scene."

"So, it's an act."

Trevor smiled again, but didn't confirm or deny Sax's assertion. "I made a mistake recently."

"How so?"

"I took in a young woman who was...different...from the others. Smarter. Quite attractive, though not as beautiful as Alicia," he said, waving a hand in the direction of the elevator. "She intrigued me. She played the role of submissive well, but I could always see something in her eyes that suggested she was a natural dominatrix." He sighed, and Sax shivered involuntarily. "At first, I spoke as freely in front of her as I did the others under my wing. When I realized she was listening to what I said and even learning from me, I became more cautious. However, I did help her obtain her GED and even sent her to a few college classes."

"How long was she with you?"

"Almost a year." He pulled a cell phone from the pocket of his blue-silk smoking jacket and sent a text message. "Eric is bringing a picture of her now."

"You keep pictures?"

"I thought we had established that I was smart," Trevor said, raising an eyebrow.

"What do you want from me?"

"As I said, she took a coin when she left."

"How do you know she was the thief?"

"I suppose it could be a coincidence, but she slipped out of the house and never returned on the same day the coin disappeared."

The elevator doors slid open and the malnourished young man reappeared, carrying some kind of computer tablet. He took it directly to Trevor and retreated in silence.

Trevor turned on the device and held it out to Sax. "Alicia is on the left. Thora is on the right."

Sax took the tablet and studied the picture. The girl on the right looked taller than average; her legs appeared several inches longer than Alicia's. Since they were both sitting at Trevor's feet in the photo, it was hard to tell just how tall she was. She had black hair, though he could reasonably assume that it was dyed. The dark spot on her leg drew his eye. "What is this?" he asked, turning the tablet back toward Trevor and pointing. "On her inner thigh?"

"Very good, Mr. Ridley. That is a tattoo of a strawberry."

Sax remembered Don telling him about the same tattoo on his Elizabeth Bathory. "That seems fairly unusual," he commented.

"I'd have to agree -- especially among the Goth crowd. We tend to choose more morbid subjects for our body art. With a girl like Thora, though, I guarantee it meant something. She was very...deliberate."

"She looks much larger than Alicia."

"She was." He stood again and held his hand about an inch below his head. "I'd say she was about five-ten."

"You keep referring to her in the past tense. Is she dead?"

"Only to me, as far as I know," he deadpanned.

"Where do you think she went?"

"If I knew that, Mr. Ridley, I wouldn't need you."

"Was she close to anyone in the house?"

"I usually took her out with Alicia, as you see here. And, of course, Eric was familiar with her. I encourage a free-love environment, so I wouldn't be surprised if a few others in the house were friendly toward her."

"How many kids do you have living here, Mr. Vallejo?"

"Right now? I'm not sure exactly. Eric could tell you."

"Your valuables would be safer if you didn't take in runaways, you know."

A slow smile slid across his face. "It's a big house, and I hate cold beds." He sent another text. "Eric will return momentarily. Ask him any questions you like. He'll also take you to the others you might want to talk to." He waved his hand, indicating Sax and Milo should move toward the elevators.

Sax cleared his throat. "There is the small matter of a retainer."

660

New Life

"Of course. Eric will see to that as well."

"We haven't discussed the amount," Sax persisted.

"I assume three-thousand dollars will be enough to get you started."

Trying not to look overjoyed, Sax scratched his nose nonchalantly. "Yeah. That's a good start."

"And you'll let me know if and when Thora shows up?"

"Yes, Mr. Vallejo. One last question: is there any chance your girl could be pregnant?"

The younger man laughed quietly. "Not by me. I don't take chances like that. The others...may not be as careful."

Sax heard the elevator ding and the doors slide open. "Thank you, Mr. Vallejo. I'll be in touch."

Eric was waiting, his hands folded in front of him in a near-perfect military at-ease stance. Sax and Milo stepped into the car and Eric followed them, pressing the basement button. A silent moment later, they followed him out of the elevator and into a short hallway, stopping in front of a door clearly labeled "Business Office." Eric tapped on the door, and a woman answered, "Enter!"

Eric opened it and Sax saw a plain woman with a brown pixie-cut sitting behind an efficient-looking metal desk. Sax thought it looked a lot like the ones that had populated the New Jersey police station where he had worked years before. "Ah, Mr. Ridley," the woman said in a clipped English accent. "Please have a seat."

Only one chair sat in front of the desk; Milo moved to one side and stood silently while Sax eased into it.

"My name is Gwendy Mosby, and I'll be your liaison with Mr. Vallejo from now on." She signed a check with a flourish and passed the slip of paper across the desk. "I understand your retainer is to be three thousand, correct?"

"Yes." Sax pulled his wallet out and slipped the check inside.

"When you have information to share with Mr. Vallejo, simply call this number--" she held a business card out to him "--and leave a message, day or night. I will get back to you just as soon as I am able."

"I need to question--"

"Yes, of course. I'm heading out for lunch right now. Why don't you use my office to conduct your interviews? Eric will

661

retrieve anyone you think may have valuable information to convey."

"Um...thanks. You don't have to--"

"Understood. However, as Mr. Vallejo's business manager, I do feel strongly that certain parts of the manse be restricted to residents only." She stood, and Sax observed her tailored, ecru linen business suit. Without Sondra's eye for fashion he couldn't be sure, but he thought it must have cost a few hundred dollars at the least. "I'll be gone for a little more than an hour, so take your time." She held out a hand and Sax met it, noting the firm strength the woman exuded. Under different circumstances, he would have thought she was quite admirable. As she was Vallejo's employee, though, he couldn't help being a little disgusted by her.

She exited the office without another word and Eric asked, "To whom would you like to speak first?"

Sax, surprised by the proper grammar of the sullen boy, asked, "How well did you know Thora?"

The boy, frowning, studied Sax and Milo before answering. "We were friends."

Sax moved around to the leather executive chair behind the desk and gestured for Eric to take the seat he had emptied. "Close friends?"

"We're all close here."

"Forgive me for saying this, but you're very well spoken for a runaway."

"We're not all runaways. But Master is exacting when it comes to our education."

"Master?"

Eric looked down and away. "Mr. Vallejo, I mean."

Despite his curiosity, Sax drove the conversation away from Trevor Vallejo and back to the missing girl. "When was the last time you saw Thora?"

"Around the end of February."

"Mr. Vallejo suspects she stole something valuable on her way out."

The boy's eyes shot up and met Sax's for the first time. "She wouldn't dare."

"Why not?"

"The Master..." he hesitated.

New Life

"Please, go ahead. Call him whatever you are comfortable with calling him."

"You don't steal from the Master. He is generous and kind as long as we are obedient and subservient."

"And if you aren't?"

The boy shook his head quickly and broke eye contact.

"How long have you been here, Eric?"

He puffed up slightly. "I've got seniority now. I'm the Master's right hand."

"How long did it take for you to get there?"

"Five years."

"When did Thora first arrive?"

"About a year and a half ago. The Master picked her out at the Blue Moon Harvest."

"How do you mean?"

The boy sighed and rolled his eyes. "You know what a blue moon is?"

"The second full moon in a given month?" Milo volunteered.

"Not even. It's the third full moon in a season with four full moons," Eric said.

"I've never heard of that." Sax shifted forward, leaning his arms against the desk.

"You've heard the expression 'once in a blue moon,' right?"

"Yeah. As in something that happens rarely."

"The Blue Moon Harvest is like a holiday for Master."

"What happens?"

"Lots of stuff," Eric said with a shrug. "But it's also when Master fills the empty beds."

"I don't understand."

"Master has space for twenty people here. Lots of people want to live with us, but not everyone is comfortable once they get in. So, to weed out the unworthy, Master only selects new residents on the Blue Moon Harvest."

"How often is that?"

"Every couple of years."

"How does he pick the new residents?"

"On the night of the blue moon, the applicants are invited to a party."

"At the club?"

"No, here."

"And?"

"He picks the winners."

Sax leaned back in the chair, balancing his elbows on the chair's arms and clasping his hands together. "Mr. Vallejo said he made a mistake with Thora. Do you know what the mistake was?"

Eric shook his head. "She was a beautiful girl. She got along with everyone well."

"I can't help but notice that you are referring to her in the past tense. Do you think something happened to her?"

"Once you leave the protection of Master, you are dead to the clan."

That was clearly the party line around here. "I'd like to speak with Alicia next."

Eric stood and moved to the door. "I'll just retrieve her." He left the room, closing the door behind him.

"What do you think?" Sax asked Milo.

"I think we'd better wait until we're elsewhere to talk. I wouldn't be surprised to find this office is bugged."

Sax nodded. "You have a point."

They waited in silence for the next few minutes. When the door pushed open, the same young girl who had been at Trevor's feet appeared, this time wearing a demure skirt and blouse. She smiled sweetly and slipped into the chair across the desk from Sax.

"Your name is Alicia?" Sax asked.

"Yes, sir."

"Alicia what?"

"I'd prefer not to say."

"Afraid I'll report you as a runaway?"

She smiled again, this time with teeth showing. "I'm old enough to know what's best for me. Eric said you had questions about Thora."

"Did she ever tell you her last name?"

"It was a dorky man's name."

"What do you mean?"

"You know -- like Horace or Filbert..."

"Wendell? Edwin?" Sax suggested.

"Herbert?" Milo offered.

"Yeah! That was it!"

"Thora Herbert."

"Exactly," she said proudly.

"How well did you know her?"

"Well enough. We were cage-mates."

"You actually live in cages?"

She laughed. "That's just what we call them -- you know, for the outsiders." She raised an eyebrow ironically.

"Like me, you mean."

"Like you...and anyone who doesn't live here."

Sax leaned forward and cleared his throat. "What can you tell me about Thora?"

The girl scanned the room, her eyes coming to a stop along the edge of the ceiling.

Sax looked in the same direction and saw the camera lens nestled discreetly in the moulding, replacing one of the cherubic faces.

"Thora was smart. And she was older than a lot of us, too."

"How old?"

"Twenty-one or -two, maybe. She knew a lot about history."

"Did she have a particular friend here?"

She shook her head. "Not that I knew of."

Sax leaned back. He wasn't going to get anything of value out of the people here. They were too dependent on Trevor Vallejo for their survival. "Thanks for talking with me, Alicia. If you think of anything else--"

The girl leaned forward and shielded her mouth from the camera above. "Talk to Bruno," she whispered. She stood up and smiled sweetly again. "Sorry I couldn't be more help." She let herself out and Eric reappeared.

"I think that will do it for today, Eric. Thanks."

"Of course. I'll see you out."

Neither Sax nor Milo said a word until they were driving down Central Avenue. "What did she say to you?" Milo asked, breaking Sax's silent rumination.

"She told me to talk to Bruno."

"Who's that?"

"The only Bruno I know is a bouncer at Villa Medici. And I'm not sure I'm going to be able to get him to open up. He helped escort me out the other night."

Milo laughed. "Figures."

A few more buildings flew past. "I've never felt so old," Sax confessed. "How did I get so out of touch?"

"I don't think these kids are representative of the whole generation."

"I hope you're right."

"What's next?"

Sax shrugged. "We go back to the Brass Monkey and you concentrate on Claire. I appreciate your help, but I'll take it from here."

"Are you sure? This situation seems dangerous."

"I don't even know how I'm going to find this Bruno character. And Thora Herbert is in the wind, as far as I can tell."

"So why did you take Vallejo's money?"

"Can't hurt to try. Maybe Morgana will have an idea or two."

"Great. Now you're relying on our pregnant bartender for help."

Sax smiled. "She's been a wealth of knowledge so far." He turned on the radio, signaling the end of their conversation. He had forgotten to ask for a copy of the girl's photo. He would have to call Gwendy when he got back to his office. Milo cleared his throat, and Sax turned the radio down. "Something on your mind?"

"I don't want to burden you, but...I could use someone to talk to about Claire."

"Oh." Sax snapped the radio off. "Have you heard from her since Saturday?"

"No. I called Sondra this morning. She said Claire hasn't been out of bed since Taz died."

"Are you getting back together with her?"

Milo shook his head. "I don't know."

"Really?" he asked, incredulous.

"I'm too angry with her right now."

"You do seem a little irritable."

He let out a frustrated sigh and pushed his hand through his hair, ruffling it in a way that made him look much younger than his nearly sixty years. "Less with her than with me, to be honest. How stupid am I, Sax? In my lifetime, I have now managed to impregnate not one, but two women out of wedlock. Not only that, but I did it forty years apart!"

"What does Brian think?"

"I'm not sure. He was almost as shocked as I was when Claire walked through the door. I don't know if he has even considered the ramifications."

"A baby brother or sister younger than his own children...that's got to be disconcerting."

"To say the least. Alice Marie is so young, I doubt she'll understand why the baby is getting more attention that she is."

Sax smiled. "From what I know about the girl, I don't think she'll have that much trouble adjusting. She'll probably want to babysit."

"Maybe so."

Out of the corner of Sax's eye, he saw his friend's form relax slightly. "What do you think Claire will want?"

"I wish I knew. What if she doesn't want us to be together? How can I be a father if I'm not with her?"

"I guess you would take the baby some days, and she would have it others."

"Sounds awful."

"If that's not how you want things to be, you'd better lose your anger and try to win her back."

Milo fell silent and turned his face away.

After several minutes, Sax said, "Maybe you should let her leave you out of this completely."

"How can you say that?" Milo swiveled and glowered at his friend.

"Be realistic. You're fast approaching sixty. You'll be nearly eighty by the time he or she leaves high school -- if you live that long. Are you willing to give up the rest of your life to raise another kid?"

"I'm in good health," Milo said staunchly.

"Maybe so, but twenty years--"

"What about Claire? She's in her mid-forties."

"Women live longer than men."

"So that makes her raising the baby alone okay?"

"Milo, she loves you. Get past your anger and make things right between you." Sax turned into the parking lot of the Brass Monkey and found a space. A few golf carts and cars were in the lot. Sax figured they had half a dozen patrons at the moment. "Why don't you ask Morgana to work the rest of today? Go home and figure out what you want to do next."

"I can do that here as well as at home," Milo answered. "Besides, I don't want Morgana to exhaust herself in her condition."

"Fine. But really think about it, okay?"

"Yeah."

They walked inside, Milo in front. Sax waited at the front of the room for a moment while his eyes adjusted to the light. Morgana was behind the bar, smiling as she rinsed and dried some glasses.

"Hey, Milo! Sax!" The girl seemed more cheerful than ever.

Sax decided now was the time to talk to her about Bruno. "Morgana. How are you?"

"Well enough. No morning sickness today, so that's a plus." She had a lovely smile, which surprised him. He hadn't seen her give more than an ironic grin before.

"Good. Glad to hear it." He turned to Milo. "Would you take the bar for a few minutes? I'd like to speak with our girl."

"Of course," Milo said, pulling the bar rag from Morgana's hands.

Instantly, her expression changed to one of suspicion. "I am not your stool pigeon for my generation."

"Sure you are," Sax answered, walking toward the corner booth.

She walked slowly around the bar, her arms folded over her chest, and stood at the end of the table. "What now?"

"Sit down."

"I'd rather stand."

"Fine. I went to see Trevor Vallejo this morning."

Her eyes widened. "He actually called you?"

"Yes. He wants me to find a girl who used to live in his house."

Morgana slid in across from him and leaned forward on the table. "Wow. Why would he want that?"

"She took something from him, and he wants it back."

"So now you're looking for two Goth girls?"

Sax shook his head. "I don't think so. From the picture he showed me, I'd say I'm looking for one girl."

Her jaw dropped.

"Now is the time to tell me: do you know Thora Herbert?"

Morgana looked at the table. "Not well."

"Did you know that was who Don was looking for?"

"I suspected," she sighed. "But Thora's not the kind of girl you really want to find."

"Why not?"

"She's...untrustworthy."

"What does that mean?"

Morgana's eyes rolled. "She takes things that don't belong to her."

"Like what? Come on, Morgana, I feel like I'm pulling teeth here."

"She steals boyfriends, for one thing. And according to Don, she steals coins, too."

"Do you know anyone she might still be in contact with?"

"If I had to guess, I'd say your best bet is one of the bouncers at Villa Medici."

"Bruno?"

"How did you know that?"

"One of Vallejo's slaves suggested I talk to him. What's the connection?"

She shrugged. "They were friendly."

"Didn't you say he was gay when we were there the other night?"

"Yeah."

"Okay. How do I talk to Bruno now that we've been removed from the club?"

"If Vallejo hired you, you're probably not banned anymore."

Sax mentally kicked himself. She was right. "Thanks."

"If you want to get a rapport going with Bruno, you might want to put your queer foot forward, so to speak."

"I'm not completely without a brain, Morgana."

"I'm just saying. Talk show tunes or whatever."

Sax pushed himself out of the booth and waved at Milo on the way out the door. He had some work to do, not the least of which was writing an email to Gwendy requesting a copy of Thora's photo.

New Life

One for Sorrow

Taz's death put Claire in bed for the rest of the weekend. Her energy, which had been waning in recent weeks because of the pregnancy, drained from her completely. Sondra, who was once more ambulatory, if a little slow, brought her chicken soup and cups of tea. She sat with Claire and listened to her talk. The dog's death had brought old memories of Claire's murdered husband to the surface, and she related the harrowing story of the day he was killed but Taz was spared.

By late Monday morning, she was somewhat recovered. Wearing an ancient terrycloth robe, she wandered into the main room of the condo and lowered herself onto one of the dining chairs.

Sondra glanced up from the magazine she was perusing. "Nice to see you up and about."

"I couldn't lie there any longer. I think the baby is using my bladder as a pillow." She turned and looked out the balcony doors. Gray clouds hung heavily over the valley. "Looks cold out there."

"I think it's supposed to be in the sixties today. Might rain later."

"At least the gloom matches my mood. Have you heard from Milo, by any chance?"

"No. But then, I would guess he's not talking to me after what he just found out."

Claire shook her head. "He can't blame you."

"Why not? He was my friend before you were."

"But what about female solidarity?"

"I generally don't have that particular allegiance, and Milo is aware of that." Sondra dropped the magazine into her lap. "Don't worry, though. He'll forgive me."

"I don't regret not telling him," Claire said staunchly. "Look at how he reacted!"

"Geez, Claire. Give the man a few days to process! He'll be around before you know it."

Ethan, wearing a tight pair of black pants and still drying his hair from the shower, came out of Sondra's bedroom. "If you had told him when you first found out, he would have already adjusted."

671

"I'm sorry, Ethan. I didn't know you and Sondra were experts on relationships," Claire sniped.

"We're just trying to help," Sondra said.

"No. You most definitely are not trying to help. You two walk around acting all holier than thou. Why don't you try talking to one another instead of commenting on my relationship?" Claire pushed herself out of her chair and exited the room for the balcony, where she sat down on the wicker loveseat. The cell phone in her pocket began to vibrate. She pulled it out and answered it.

"May I speak with Claire Combs?"

"This is she."

"Claire, this is Adena from Dr. Slotnick's office."

"Yes, of course. Hello."

"We need to schedule a high-def ultrasound for you."

"I'm sorry? Why?"

"The quad test came back with some abnormal results," the nurse said breezily. "The ultrasound will help us figure out what, if anything, is wrong with the baby."

"There's something wrong with the baby?" Claire could feel her heart beating against her ribs.

"Not necessarily. We just need to do a little more testing."

"What could be wrong with the baby?"

"Don't dwell on this, Claire. Can you come in today?"

"Please tell me. I need to know."

"Why don't you talk to the doctor when you are here? Can you be here at twelve-thirty?"

"Yes. Wait! Can we make it for tomorrow instead?"

"Better sooner than later. You don't need to worry -- this is a non-invasive procedure."

"Fine."

"Wonderful. We'll see you later, then."

She ended the call and walked back into the living room, interrupting Ethan and Sondra mid-conversation. "Something's wrong."

"What? What do you mean?" Sondra asked, alarmed.

"I have to go for a test. Will you go with me?" Claire asked.

"Of course! Ethan, darling, can we talk about this later?"

Claire looked at Ethan, registering for the first time that she had interrupted a serious conversation. "I'm so sorry. I never should have said--"

"Forget it." Ethan offered her a forgiving smile. "You're under a lot of stress these days. I need to get going, anyway. I'm meeting with Easter about that gallery exhibit she wants me to put together."

"I'm glad you're moving forward with that." Sondra pulled her walker in front of her and heaved herself to her feet. Ethan leaned toward her and kissed her cheek affectionately. "Off you go. We'll finish our chat later."

Ethan disappeared into the bedroom, no doubt looking for his shirt.

"I'm going to take a shower. We need to leave here in about an hour."

"I'll be ready. Are you going to call Milo?"

"There's no point in worrying him yet. Everything could be fine."

"Claire, now that he knows--"

"I'll tell him when there's something to tell." She went into the bathroom and closed the door behind her.

The two women arrived just before twelve-thirty and the nurse put them in a room with a lot of medical equipment. Handing Claire a gown, she said, "Put this on with the opening in the front. The doctor will be in shortly." She left, pulling the door closed behind her.

Sondra turned to face the wall and Claire took off her top.

"Sorry about earlier," Claire said for the fifth time that afternoon.

"Would you forget it already? Like I said, Ethan and I are still working up to a split."

"I don't know how you can be so calm about it. Don't you love him?"

"Of course I do...though not as much as he thinks he loves me, which is why this is taking so long."

"Okay, I'm covered," Claire said, perching on the edge of the examination table.

Sondra turned around and, using her walker's seat, sat down. "Think of it this way: It's like I've opened the cage door but the pigeon hasn't decided to fly yet."

Claire chuckled. "Somehow I don't think Ethan would like the comparison."

"Then do me a favor and don't tell him. With Vivian locked up in that psychiatric hospital and his parents adjusting to reality, Ethan will soon realize that he is free to pursue the woman who will make him the happiest: Emlyn Kopczynski."

"How do you know he will be happiest with her?"

"She was his first love. If Vivian hadn't interfered in the first place, Ethan and Emlyn would have been happily married for the last decade and I never would have met him. It's like I've got a chance to rewrite history."

"Not exactly," Claire frowned. "You can't erase his two dead wives from his life. Or the torment Emlyn went through."

"So it's not a fairy tale...it's as close as I can get to one." She scooted the walker closer to the table. "Let's talk about something else. Did you call Milo?"

"No." Catching Sondra's disapproving gaze, Claire added hurriedly, "I thought about it, I really did. But why should I drag him into this right now? If there is something seriously wrong with the baby, it might not even make it to term. If not, why should I worry him? He's got more than enough worry on his plate right now."

"I really think you're being foolish here. Milo loves you more than anything in the world."

"The same could be said of how Ethan feels for you."

Sondra rolled her eyes. "Not even close. Milo has lived long enough to know what real love is, and he knows he's got the real thing with you."

The door opened and Dr. Slotnick, his tie askew, appeared. "Good afternoon, Claire. How are you feeling today?"

Sondra slid unobtrusively toward the far wall.

"A little nervous, Doctor," Claire answered, rubbing her belly. "Does the quad screen come back with questionable results often?"

"More often than not with older mothers. But it's nothing to be alarmed about. Normally, we'd run the quad screen again before we moved on to the high-def ultrasound, but since you were a little further along than most mothers are when we ran the first test, I thought it would be prudent to move forward sooner rather than later. Go ahead and lie back on the table. Try to relax." He squirted a jelly-like substance into his hands. "This will be a little chilly," he said a moment before he applied it to her abdomen. She shivered in response. "Is this your first ultrasound?"

"Yes," she answered. "I was supposed to have one a month ago, but I missed the appointment because my father died."

"I'm sorry to hear that." He picked up the machine's wand and said, "This won't hurt a bit. You'll just feel some pressure." He pressed the instrument against her belly.

Sondra gasped and Claire, alarmed, looked at her. "I'm sorry," Sondra whispered. "Look at the monitor."

Claire turned and glimpsed her child for the first time. Her heart seemed to swell within her and her eyes filled with tears. "She's beautiful!"

The doctor laughed. "That's a pretty big assumption. It could be a boy, you know."

"Oh...yes, I guess it could."

"You want me to check?"

Claire looked at Sondra again, who shrugged and asked, "Why not?"

"Yes, please."

He floated the instrument around until he got a view of the baby's genitals. "You're right! It's a girl!"

"Hooray!" Sondra exclaimed. "Girls are so much more fun than boys. No offense, Doctor."

"None taken," Dr. Slotnick answered with a smile.

"What could be wrong with her, Doctor?"

"Well, the good news is there are no physical abnormalities that I can see."

Sondra squeezed Claire's hand encouragingly.

"What's the bad news?"

"Nothing, yet. But I do recommend that you have an amniocentesis just to be on the safe side."

"Isn't that risky?" Sondra asked. "Don't amnios cause spontaneous abortions?"

Claire tensed.

"Very rarely," Dr. Slotnick responded.

"How rarely?" Claire asked.

"About once in every sixteen-hundred pregnancies. And the benefits far outweigh the potential downside. We will be able to diagnose a number of chromosomal problems as well as spina bifida. It will also allow us to predict when her lungs are mature enough for a safe delivery."

"But I'm going to full term, right?"

"Ideally, yes. However, it doesn't hurt to be prepared for the worst. After all, you are forty-five years old. With mothers your age -- even first-timers -- it isn't unusual for the baby to come early."

Claire took a deep breath. "When can we do it?"

"I can perform the test now."

"No!" Claire answered. "I want the father to be here for this."

"That's fine," the doctor said. "You do need to have it done soon, though. I'll send the nurse back in to help you clean up. Schedule an appointment before you leave, okay?"

"Yes, Doctor. Thank you."

Smiling kindly, the doctor left the room.

"I guess I'd better call Milo," Claire said. "Hand me my purse."

Sondra reached around the walker and pulled Claire's purse from the basket on the front of the device.

Claire retrieved her phone and dialed Milo's number. "Milo? Do you have time to talk?"

"I'm pretty sure I've been available for a chat for months now."

Claire ignored his tone and pushed forward. "Good. I need to talk to you about the baby." Silence drifted through the airwaves. "Milo? Are you still there?"

"I'm listening."

"The doctor says I need to have an amniocentesis done. Do you want to come with me for that?"

"What is it?"

"It's a test where the doctor sticks a long needle--"

"Got it," Milo interrupted, sounding upset. "What's wrong with it?"

"The test?"

"No, the baby. What's wrong with it?"

"N-nothing...at least, the doctor isn't sure..."

"Do you want me there?"

"If you want to be."

"I'll think about it. Look, I gotta go. I've got customers waiting." He hung up.

Claire spent the afternoon alternately crying and sleeping. Her tears must have upset the little girl she was carrying, because she seemed to be turning cartwheels in her uterus. At a little after seven that evening, she heard a knock on the door. Rather than force Sondra to answer it, Claire rolled out of bed and left her room for the first time since arriving home from the doctor's office.

Sondra, who was already pushing herself up with the walker, said, "I would have gotten there."

"I know, but, even in my current condition, I'm nimbler than you are." Claire put her eye to the peephole and saw Milo waiting patiently in the hall. Her heart dropped to her stomach and the baby rolled again. She stepped backward and took a deep breath.

"Who is it?" Sondra asked.

"It's Milo," she answered, her voice barely above a whisper.

He knocked again.

"Are you going to open it?" Sondra was moving toward the door now.

"I haven't decided."

"You must. You need to talk to him."

"He was so angry earlier."

"I can hear you two talking," Milo commented through the door. "Is someone going to let me in?"

"Just a minute!" Sondra called. "Hold your horses." She reversed herself and headed toward the bedroom. "I'm going to give you some privacy."

Sighing heavily, Claire opened the door. "Hi, Milo."

"Claire." He leaned forward as if to hug her, but stopped. He put out a hand for her to shake instead. She ignored it and he let it drop to his side.

"Come in. Can I get you anything to drink?"

He shuffled past her into the living room. "No. I don't think I'll be staying long."

"Okay." She followed him in and watched him settle into the beige sofa. She took Sondra's chair. "You didn't have to drive across town tonight. The appointment isn't until tomorrow morning."

"I thought we should talk before then."

The baby kicked again and Claire, rubbing her abdomen, let herself recline into the chair. "She's been really active today."

He met her eyes with surprise. "It's a girl?"

678

"That's what the doctor said."

His expression lost its hard edges and he smiled. "I always wanted a girl."

"Really? You never said."

"Why would I have? To tell you I wanted something I didn't think you could have...." He frowned. "Besides, who starts a new family at sixty?"

"You're not sixty yet."

"I'm a damned sight closer to that than forty. Or fifty, for that matter." He rubbed his forehead. "Why didn't you tell me, Claire?"

She thought back to that first moment of realization -- the day she bought the pregnancy test. "I...At first, I was in shock. All I could think was that there had to be a mistake. After all, I was married to Dorsey for twenty years, and I never even missed a period."

"You and Dorsey never talked to a doctor?"

"What would have been the point? We were barely scraping by in the beginning. And by the time we had money, we were used to our life the way it was."

"Didn't you regret...?"

"To be honest, I never thought too much about it until Beryl came back into my life." She studied her hands and remembered a long-ago conversation with her murdered husband. "When I told Dorsey I thought we should look into fertility treatments, he said he didn't want us to go nuts trying to have children. In his opinion, if children were in God's plan for us, we would have had them already."

"But if you wanted--"

"What could I say? I loved him more than I wanted children."

Milo looked down. "Okay, so you didn't tell me after the pregnancy test. What stopped you later?"

"You have to admit we weren't happy. I held out hope that you would propose--"

He grumbled irritably.

"I know," she said, holding her hands up to stop him. "To say I was sending mixed signals is an understatement."

"I wanted to marry you, Claire. I flew all the way to Oklahoma to propose."

"And if you'd seen me that day, you wouldn't have."

"You don't know that!" he snapped.

"Fine. Are you saying you want to marry me now?"

"Yes," he answered, though he shifted his gaze. "You're carrying my baby."

"It's the twenty-first century, Milo. My pregnancy is not a valid reason for marriage."

"Of course it is."

She reached out and took his hands in hers. "No. It really isn't. As angry as you are with me right now, why would you want to be my husband? Why would I want to be your wife? If we can't be happy together, it's better for all of us -- including our daughter -- if we just try to be friends."

He winced. "You won't marry me."

"Not now."

"I don't know if I can do this. How can I be a father if I'm not there for her and for you?"

"That piece of paper saying we're married isn't a contract that promises you'll support me."

"Yes, it is. That's exactly what it means."

She smiled. "Okay. But I don't think we need it. The appointment is tomorrow morning. Do you want to meet me there?"

"I'll pick you up. That way, if you don't feel up to driving home, you won't have to." Milo stood and took a deep breath, as if he were breaking the surface of a pool after swimming underwater. "It's good to see you."

"And you," Claire answered. Milo put his hands out to help her out of the chair and she accepted them, allowing him to pull her to her feet. "I hope you'll forgive me for my deception."

"I'll try. What you did..." His voice trailed off as he looked into the distance. "This hurt more than what dead Alice did."

His words took the air out of her as completely as a blow to the chest would have. Gasping, she said, "I never meant to--"

"I know you didn't," he interrupted. "But that doesn't change the fact that you did." He dropped her hands and walked toward the door, leaving the condo without another word.

New Life

New Life

Humpty Dumpty

Sondra missed her red Mercedes convertible. The car accident that had left her with a broken hip had also taken her old friend away from her. The weeks of recovery needed for her hip to fully mend had given her far too much time to brood over the car's absence, despite the fact that she was currently incapable of driving. Every time she was loaded into Claire's practical beige sedan, she remembered that she would never again sit behind the wheel of the only tangible thing she ever owned as a result of her acting career.

She was scouring the internet for her car's doppelganger when Milo arrived to pick Claire up that Tuesday. Knowing that her friend was still in the shower, Sondra grabbed her walker and went to answer the door.

"You're looking well," Milo commented, wrapping one arm around her and kissing her on the cheek.

"Thank you!" she cooed. "You're early. Claire's in the shower."

"I know. I was hoping to catch you alone for a few minutes."

"You have my full attention." She led him back to the living area, where he made himself comfortable on the sofa. She sat down in her chair.

"That's a beautiful painting," he commented, looking at the surreal hard-candy cathedral hanging above the mantel of the electric fireplace.

"Thank you. Ethan and I picked it out together."

He frowned. "I heard from Sax that you were breaking up with him."

"No! He's going to break up with me."

"But you're still together?"

"For now." She shifted toward him. "But surely this isn't what you wanted to talk about."

"No," he admitted, "it's not. I wanted to talk to you about--" he dropped to a whisper "--Claire."

"I suspected as much, but I can't help you."

"Of course you can! You were my friend first."

"Milo, she's the only girlfriend I have! I won't ruin our friendship--"

New Life

"Do you really want to live with her and a screaming baby?" Milo interrupted.

Her eyes widened at the thought. When she had her daughter Fanny all those years ago, she had been blessed with a large home and a nanny. She never suffered a single sleepless night, and she handed the baby back to the nanny when she needed food or her diaper changed. By comparison, the condo was minuscule -- and it belonged to Claire. Of course she would be bringing the baby back here. And Claire would probably need help. "What do you need from me?"

"Just some gentle persuasion on your part. If everything goes the way I hope it will, she'll be out of your hair before the baby comes."

"I'll do what I can."

They shook on their verbal agreement as Claire, wrapped in her terrycloth robe, opened the bathroom door. She narrowed her eyes at the pair suspiciously. "You're early," she said to Milo.

"I wasn't sure what kind of traffic I would run into coming across town so early in the morning."

"Hmm. I'll get dressed and we can go."

"Can I get you something to drink?" Sondra asked, pulling her walker toward the chair.

"Don't get up. I'll get my own beverage."

"There's a pot of tea next to the stove." Someone knocked on the door. "And would you be a dear and get that?" Sondra asked Milo.

"Of course."

A moment later, Ethan stood awkwardly in front of her, like a child who had done something wrong and was being forced to confess. "Hi, Sondra."

"Good morning, Ethan. Is everything all right? When you didn't show up last night, I was worried."

"Yeah," he answered, "about that...we need to talk. But first I want you to come with me."

"Where are we going?"

He smiled brightly, his boyish enthusiasm shining through. "You'll see!" He placed the walker in front of her and steadied it as she got to her feet.

"Where are you two going?" Milo asked, wandering out of the kitchen with a cup of tea in his hand.

"I have a surprise for Sondra. We'll be back in a few minutes."

"Claire and I will probably be gone. It was nice to see you again, Ethan."

"Good to see you too, sir." He opened the door and held it while Sondra pulled herself over the threshold.

"Where are we going?" Sondra asked again.

"Patience, now." He pressed the elevator button. "I talked to my agent yesterday. The production company is moving forward with the pilot for the Sunrise Aeon television show."

"That's wonderful news!" Sondra exclaimed.

"And...my publisher wants at least two more graphic novels for the series! My agent has the contract in hand, and she says it's golden."

The elevator doors slid open and he waited while she stepped into the car. Once inside, he pressed the button for the parking garage.

"I wish you'd told me we were leaving the building. I would have put on my makeup." She reached up and fluffed her hair with one hand, leaning heavily on the center bar of the walker with the other.

He didn't answer her; instead, he just smiled. The elevator doors slid open and she followed him down the row of visitor spaces, stopping in front of a cherry-red sports car. "What do you think?" he asked, holding up his arms as if he were one of the *Price is Right* models.

"You bought a new car?"

"I bought a fully loaded Mercedes SLK to be exact. Do you like it?"

She gave a low whistle and proceeded to circle the hard-top convertible. Its low profile and racy style were exactly what she would want. She could tell the backseat was practically non-existent, but that wasn't really an issue. The tinted glass roof looked like something out of a science-fiction novel. "It's beautiful, Ethan. That contract must be platinum! Are you taking me for a ride?"

He came to stand in front of her and put his hands over hers on the walker. "I bought it for you," he said softly.

She allowed a slow smile to stretch across her face and bugged her eyes out just a touch. "Really? This is too much--"

"It's no more than you deserve. But if you don't like it--"

"No! I love it! It's absolutely gorgeous!"

He grinned. "Do you want to sit in it?"

"I'll probably need help getting in and out of it right now."

"Don't worry...I'm here to help."

They moved around to the driver's side of the car, and Ethan opened the door for her. She backed up to the seat and let go of the walker, which Ethan deftly moved out of the way. Taking her hands, he steadied her as she lowered herself gingerly into the leather seat. Sondra inhaled deeply, and the new-car scent filled her with joy. As much as she missed her old car, she had to admit the lingering scent of fart spray had never completely vanished. She immediately vowed to never allow a single bottle of the foul stuff inside this beautiful vehicle.

"Ethan, this is the most incredible present anyone has ever given me."

"You deserve it." He smiled, but she could see that he was working up to telling her something he feared wouldn't make her happy at all.

"I have the strangest feeling another shoe is waiting to drop."

He pulled the walker back toward the car and sat down on its seat. "Yeah. About that.... First of all, I want you to know that I am going to stand by my promise to take care of you. Just consider this car an earnest deposit on that. I have also gone to my lawyer and had him draw up some papers regarding the Sunrise Aeon franchise."

She struggled to keep a neutral expression. "What sort of papers?"

"From now on, you own thirty percent of the proceeds. I think that's a fair number for being my muse, don't you?"

"Of course, darling," she said, allowing herself a tentative smile. "But if we are married--"

"That's what I need to talk to you about."

"Oh." She thought about dead puppies and teared up.

"Please don't cry, Sondra," he begged. "I honestly do love you very much. But seeing Emlyn again...she's the love of my life, and my sister had the gall to drive her away from me. As much as I care about you, I think marrying you when I have a chance to pursue a future with her would be a huge mistake -- not just for me, but for all three of us."

Sondra wiped her tears with the back of her fingers. "I can't believe this is happening. You swore you loved me!"

"I know, and I'm so sorry. Look, I know it's nothing when compared to a life together, but I'll have the lawyer change the percentage to forty. You'll never want for money again, darling."

She lifted her eyes to his. "Do you think your lawyer could come to the condo right now?"

Ethan and his lawyer were long gone before Lucas, her physical therapist, arrived that afternoon. In the weeks that had passed since she first met the brawny blond, she had moved from lusting after him to hating him with a dark passion. The man seemed to relish making her cry out -- and not in a good way.

Today, though, she found the pain tolerable. Every time she felt a muscle threatening to revolt, she envisioned her beautiful red convertible and the fat quarterly checks she would be receiving for the foreseeable future. Not that she wouldn't miss Ethan -- with his muscled young body, his unparalleled skill in the kitchen, and his *joie de vive*, it would be hard not to miss him. But, in all fairness, she had barely been able to keep up with him in the bedroom before the accident. She held him at bay as her hip healed, but she had felt well enough to resume a normal sex life a few weeks ago. However, the difference between a thirty-year-old man's normal and a sixty-plus-year-old woman's normal is, roughly, two western states apart. And, for the first time in decades, she was seriously considering discontinuing her monthly bikini waxes -- an expense she had always included in her budget, even when it meant she might not eat a square meal that month.

"You must be doing your exercises faithfully, Sondra," Lucas said. "You're very limber today."

"Am I?" she mused. "I guess I'm just relaxed."

"That's excellent. I think you are doing well enough now that you can start swimming again. Won't that make a nice change?"

"Lovely."

Lucas indicated it was time to roll onto her stomach, and she did so happily. He manipulated her legs and feet. Sondra thought how good a massage would feel.

"Lucas, do you know any massage therapists who do home visits?" she asked.

"Of course. I'll leave you a few names."

"Thank you, darling."

The door opened and she heard Claire say hello to Lucas.

"Good afternoon, Claire. How are you and the baby today?"

"Fine, thank you, Lucas. How has our patient been?"

"She's had a very good session. I was just telling her that it's time for her to get back in the pool."

"Wonderful. I'll make sure we go for a swim tomorrow."

"Don't I get a say?" Sondra groused from her face-down position on the table.

"Not really," Claire answered.

"Did everything go all right at the doctor's office?"

"So far, so good. I won't get the results for a few days, though. I'm going to lie down for a bit."

Sondra heard Claire's door shut.

Lucas finished stretching her muscles and helped her from the table to her chair. He sat down on the sofa and pulled out his phone and a business card. "Do you have a pen?"

Sondra found one on the end table next to her chair and handed it to him.

"Thanks."

As he scrolled through his contacts looking for a few massage therapists to refer her to, Sondra asked, "How many more therapy appointments will I need?"

"If you keep up the good work, only a few more weeks' worth. Your range of motion is quite good. In fact, it's close to normal for a woman of your age."

Sondra grimaced. "I was a reasonably talented dancer before the accident."

"I don't think you'll be doing many fan-kicks, but you should be able to return to dancing."

Fan-kicks? Until he said that, she had been relatively certain the man was straight. Now she wondered if she should try to set him up with Sax. "Are you a musical theater fan?" she asked with a smirk.

"I suppose so. My girlfriend is a regular player at one of the local playhouses." He handed her the business card. "I'll see you on Thursday. Don't forget to take a swim tomorrow."

Sondra used her walker to stand and follow Lucas to the door, closing it behind him. At least her "gay"-dar hadn't let her down. Across the room, her phone started playing "Who Can It Be Now?", the ring she had designated for all unrecognized phone numbers. "Of course," she said aloud, scooting herself across the room as quickly as she could. She bent down to pick up the phone just as it stopped ringing. Irritated, she dropped back into her chair and waited for a voicemail to arrive. A couple of minutes passed before she gave up and set the phone back on the end table. Almost immediately, it began playing the song again. Snatching it up, she answered with an exasperated "Hello?"

"Oh, I'm terribly sorry. I must have the wrong number."

"What number did you dial?"

The man on the other end recited the digits, which matched hers exactly.

"That's my number. Who were you trying to reach?"

"Sondra Lane."

"You didn't mis-dial. I am Sondra."

"Goodness! You don't sound like yourself at all."

"Who is this?" she snapped, offended.

"How rude of me. Of course. This is Patrick Bradford."

Sondra inhaled sharply and her heart jumped. Patrick, Vivian's estranged husband and erstwhile murder victim, was the one man she knew who made her feel like a schoolgirl with a crush. Instantly, her voice went an octave higher and turned breathy. "Patrick! My goodness! How are you?"

"I'm well, thank you for asking. And how are you?"

"Healing. My physical therapist just told me to dig out my dancing shoes!"

"Ethan must be so pleased."

"I guess you haven't heard."

"What's wrong? Did something happen to him?"

"No, no. He's fine. I'm afraid we've parted ways, though."

"I'm sorry to hear that."

But, from the lilt in his voice, Sondra could hear he wasn't too sorry. "Yes. I think it's for the best, though. As a result of this nasty business with Vivian, he has reunited with his first love."

"Ethan's a good man. He deserves happiness after what Viv did to him. But I'm very sorry for you."

She hesitated just a moment. "I'm sure I'll be fine."

"Let me take you out...to cheer you up."

"You don't have to do that, Patrick."

"But I want to! You and your friend saved my life. The least I can do is buy you a meal."

"I know very well that you have already paid Sax for his detective work. You don't need--"

"Don't be ridiculous!" he scoffed. "I can't think of anything I'd rather do."

"Well...if you insist..." She rattled off the address of the condo.

"I'll be around at six o'clock. Good afternoon, my dear."

"Bye, Patrick." She clicked the end button. If she'd been able to, she would have done a series of fan-kicks across the living room. Instead, she settled for a victory cheer from the comfort of her chair.

Sondra experienced something like *deja vu* as she attempted to pick an outfit for her dinner date, remembering an afternoon more than forty years before when a party invitation changed the direction of her life and career forever. As much as she loved her vintage red-and-white wrap dress, it just didn't have the same oomph without the strappy red fuck-me pumps she normally wore with it. Heels were definitely off the table at this point, despite the fact that the walker could easily be adjusted to the proper height. Claire absolutely refused to consider any shoes higher than an inch, no matter how much Sondra whined.

"No! What if you fall and hurt yourself? You've been wearing flats or tennis shoes for the last month and I've seen you nearly fall at least once every other day. If you'd been in heels, you might have broken your other hip!" Claire lined up a selection of flats from Sondra's closet.

"Flats simply aren't sexy. I need to look fantastic tonight."

"You know what else isn't sexy? A walker."

Sondra frowned, considering. "I can probably walk without it. I might be a little slow, but--"

"No! Who's going to catch you if you fall? Patrick? He's not exactly the robust type."

"I'm light enough," she answered obstinately.

"Forget it." Claire dug another dress out of the closet, this one jade green. "I bet this looks great on you with your red hair."

"Why do people always want me to look like a Christmas tree? Put it back. I think I have a pair of palazzo pants in there. At least they will look okay with the black flats."

"What will you wear for your top?"

"Somewhere in there is a black-and-silver blouse with butterfly sleeves. Find it."

Claire disappeared back into the closet. Sondra dug through her jewelry box until she found a pair of wide silver hoops. She briefly considered sweeping her hair into an updo, but one glimpse of her lined neck in the mirror was enough for her to drop the red strands back down to obscure it. Claire emerged with the top she had been sent to find.

"Thank you!" Sondra said, snatching it from her hands. "This will be perfect, don't you think?" She held it in front of her.

Claire nodded. "It's beautiful. Do you know where you're going?"

"No, but I can pull this off no matter where we go. It's glitzy enough to blend well in a fancier place, but casual enough for Chili's."

"You'd look a little overdressed at Denny's or IHOP."

"I don't think we're going to a diner, dear."

"Isn't it a little soon for you to be dating? What if Ethan finds out?"

"You forget -- he broke up with me, not the other way around."

"This morning. And you're not exactly acting heartbroken."

690

New Life

The doorbell rang. "He's here!" Sondra exclaimed. "Would you answer it for me? I'll be out in just a few minutes."

Claire, shaking her head, left Sondra alone in her room. She managed to dress with little difficulty. Before long, she would be back to her old self. Standing in front of the dresser mirror, she applied a fresh coat of red lipstick, fluffed her hair with her fingers, and made sure every part of her body was in its assigned place.

From the living room, she could hear Claire talking to Patrick as they moved further into the condo, but she couldn't make out the words. Hurriedly, she grabbed her walker and exited the bedroom.

"There she is!" Patrick exclaimed. Sondra was pleased to note that he was dressed in a suit with a tie. He had regained at least fifteen pounds since she had last seen him. It was hard to believe this was the same man who had been wasting away in a hospital bed only a few months ago.

"It's wonderful to see you, Patrick!" Sondra answered, steering the walker toward him. If it weren't for the occasional loss of coordination, she would already be free of it. She leaned over it to hug the older man warmly.

"Shall we go? I made reservations."

"Of course."

"Have a wonderful time," Claire said, following them to the door.

"I'm sure we will," Patrick answered.

They fell into an awkward silence as they waited for the elevator and rode to the parking level. He had a space not too far away, thanks to the handicapped placard hanging in the front of the car -- a silver Jaguar. He opened the door for her and took the walker to the trunk. A moment later, he returned and closed her door before making his way around to the driver's side. As he sat down, he smiled at her. "You look lovely tonight, Sondra."

"Thank you." She was surprised to feel heat rising to her cheeks; she turned away so that he might not see her blush.

"I have a confession to make," he said.

"Really?" She continued to stare out the passenger window at nothing in particular.

"The first time I met you -- at Thanksgiving, remember? -- I was instantly jealous of Ethan."

Forgetting her embarrassment, she swiveled her head to look at him. "Why? You were married to Vivian."

"True. And she is...even now...a beauty. But she was a hard woman to please, to say the least. I could tell that you were not only gorgeous, but also tenderhearted and compassionate."

When compared to a callous serial killer, Sondra supposed that was true. She took Patrick's hand and squeezed. "You remind me of someone I cared very much for many years ago. From the first moment I saw you, I felt like I knew you."

"Perhaps fate has thrown us together." He started the car. "You aren't a vegetarian, are you?"

"No."

"Excellent." A few moments later, they were driving down Central Avenue. "When did you and Ethan split up?"

"Recently," she answered vaguely.

"How has he been handling Vivian's arrest?"

"He's furious, of course. And he feels like a fool. He had no idea what she was doing."

"I'm sure he didn't. Ethan's a nice kid, but he's always seemed a little distracted."

"His art can definitely sweep him away," she agreed. "But clearly, there weren't a lot of signs that Vivian was a murderer."

"A pretty exterior can hide a multitude of sins -- at least for a while."

"I think your vision of the past may be clouded by what you know now."

He nodded slowly. "Yes. I'm sure you're right." He made a quick left and pulled onto a side street next to Durants, a steakhouse even Sondra knew was legendary in Arizona. "I hope this is all right."

"Wonderful." She flashed her most charming smile at her escort and waited patiently as he made his way around to her side of the car, opening her door with a flourish. She took his hand and eased her legs out of the car and onto the pavement. "Perhaps you should get my walker now," she suggested.

"It's just a short walk inside the restaurant. You can lean on me." He held out his other hand for her to pull herself up.

New Life

She hesitated. "I'm not sure you can support my weight. You're only just out of the hospital yourself, you know."

"You needn't worry, my dear. I'm much sturdier than I appear to be."

Deciding to trust him, she took both his hands and pulled herself to a standing position. He wobbled slightly, but regained his footing quickly and offered her his arm. "Patrick, don't be foolish. The walker--"

"Nonsense! I will take any excuse to have you draped on my arm."

Smiling, she wrapped her hands around him and they made their way slowly through the kitchen entrance. At the host's podium, Patrick slipped the middle-aged man some money -- Sondra didn't see how much -- to put them in a secluded booth. He led them to one of the horseshoe-shaped red-leather booths furthest from the bar. Patrick helped Sondra onto the bench before sliding around to the middle of the booth from the opposite side. Sondra scooted toward Patrick until only six inches of seating separated them. The host slid a menu without prices into her hands. She couldn't remember the last time she had held a menu without prices; it must have been a long time ago, when everyone knew her -- either from television or as Bill's lover.

"What are you thinking about?" Patrick asked, giving her a quizzical look.

"A long time ago, in a galaxy far, far away."

"When you were a star?"

"I never really made it past starlet, did I?"

"You still shine brightly in my galaxy."

She rolled her eyes and laughed. "Cheesy."

"Maybe so, but I don't believe the stars could have aligned any better than they have tonight. I think the universe always meant for us to be together."

"I thought this was a friendly dinner." She lowered her lashes coyly, peeking at him from her peripheral vision.

"Of course." He put his menu on the table and took her left hand in both of his own. "I'll be your friend, if that's what you want. I'll be anything you need."

His words were so sincere Sondra began to wonder if this plan were truly her own or if some greater force was indeed at work. Not wanting to seem too callous -- especially since she and Ethan had only just broken up -- she answered, "Just help me put the pieces of my heart back together and we'll see where we go from there."

New Life

Needles and Pins

For Claire, the next few weeks passed as slowly as the last bit of honey drains from a bottle. Now that Sondra was more self-sufficient and embarking on a new romance with Patrick, she seldom called on Claire for help. Claire was more of a roommate than a caretaker at this point, which was probably just as well. Her energy level had plummeted in the last couple of weeks. She felt nearly as bad as she had after her husband's death; she suspected she was depressed.

Beryl kept calling and leaving messages. Claire knew she should pick up, but she just couldn't talk to her sister -- the mother of a brood of children, all perfectly healthy. Instead, she called her mother and told her everything was fine. She didn't mention the tests or the fight with Milo or the unsettling position she now found herself in: a single, middle-aged, first-time mother carrying a potentially damaged fetus.

To keep from crawling into bed and hiding, she forced herself to dress and visit the zoo every third or fourth morning. She missed working there more than she ever would have thought was possible. But she didn't miss her fellow volunteers nearly as much as she missed the black swan, the orangutans, and the coyotes. She sat and stared back at Duchess, the oldest of the orangutans, for hours. She imagined they were sharing a telepathic conversation on the difficulties of motherhood. Duchess was so much more sympathetic than Sondra. The elderly primate's granddaughter would try to distract her, but she would remain calm and focused. Claire wondered if perhaps she were a Zen master in a previous incarnation.

She found herself noticing children more now, especially those with obvious disabilities or Down's Syndrome. She watched their parents for signs of regret, but she rarely saw any. And, for the most part, the children seemed oblivious to their differentness. They were fascinated by the animals and completely without guile. They seemed more innocent than the so-called normal children. She wondered if Milo would be able to accept their daughter if she were less than perfect.

Milo. He haunted her, day and night. Just thinking about him made a throbbing pain spread across her chest.

New Life

She pushed herself to her feet, feeling the dull ache across the middle of her back. Her feet, swollen and tired, moved her out of the orangutan exhibit and onto the wide asphalt path that led to Monkey Village. She let herself travel in that direction, hoping to see Zareb. Not so long ago, the muscular African had carried her to a waiting ambulance. For his trouble that day, she had flipped him off. Claire had since apologized, and their relationship hadn't been damaged by her rash behavior.

Stationed by the door, Zareb spotted her and waved. Claire waved back and walked a little faster.

"Miss Claire! You look lovely today."

"Liar." She smiled as she hugged him. "How are you?"

"I am fine, as always. How much longer until the baby arrives?"

"We've still got a few months to go."

"Milo must be so excited." He took a tin of Altoids from his pocket and popped it open. "Would you like one?" he offered, taking two for himself.

"Yes, please." She had read somewhere that peppermint would ease a queasy stomach. "What's been happening around here?"

"Not so much. We miss your face, though. I think the monkeys wonder where you are."

"Don't be silly," she laughed. "They barely notice us humans."

"I would not be so sure."

"How is Isobel?"

"Quite well! She is leaving us soon, though. She has a real job at a zoo in Chicago!"

"How exciting! Is she here today?" Claire peered through the foliage, attempting to spot the volunteers on duty in the village.

"No. But you must come to her going-away party. It is next Monday afternoon."

"I'll try to be here."

They chatted for a few more minutes. Zareb caught her up on some of the other volunteers' lives and the revolt Donna, the volunteer coordinator, had narrowly averted after attempting to limit the number of hours each volunteer was allowed to spend at any given exhibit. Claire, who had never been particularly fond of Donna, enjoyed a laugh at the woman's expense. When a large group approached Monkey Village, Claire parted with her friend and slipped inside ahead of them. She always had a soft spot for monkeys and apes. The squirrel monkeys who resided within the village were of particular interest to her. They were bright little creatures with a knack for mischief. The first time she met Milo, one of them attempted to steal dried peas from his pocket. She chuckled silently at the memory of the water spot on his pants.

The two volunteers manning the exhibit were familiar to her, but she didn't know either one well. They recognized her and smiled. She returned a grin and turned to watch the monkeys, who were working intently to free strawberry jam from the blue rubber treat dispensers the zookeeper had hung for their amusement. One of the monkeys dangled from a tree branch just a few feet away. Claire could have sworn the animal was watching her; when she met its eyes, it chattered and swung away. Maybe Zareb was right.

Her feet were beyond aching now. With the energy she had left, she headed toward the parking lot. As she approached the koi pond near the exit, she heard her phone ring. Sitting down on the bench, she dug it out of her purse and answered.

"Claire? Are you all right?" Milo asked.

"I'm fine."

"You sound upset."

"No, really, I'm fine. I'm just a little out of breath."

"What are you doing?"

"Just leaving the zoo." Now that she was sitting in the sun, she realized just how hot the day was. She wished she had brought a hat.

"You're there by yourself?" He sounded irritated.

"I'm not an invalid, Milo. Exercise is good for the baby and me."

"Maybe so, but--"

"I'm fine. What did you want?"

He sighed audibly. "Have you heard from the doctor?"

"Not yet. I promise I'll call you as soon as I do."

"I'd like to see you."

697

"That's probably not a great idea." Two little boys ran past her while a little girl stopped short and peered into the pond.

"Please. I'll take you out to dinner. How about the Abacus Inn?"

The mention of the Chinese restaurant made her stomach grumble hungrily. She supposed the baby was in the mood for snap peas and egg rolls. "You don't have to do this..."

"I want to. We need to talk about the future."

Remembering her earlier thoughts, she nodded. "All right."

"Great. I'll pick you up at six."

"See you then." She flipped the phone closed and dropped it back into her bag. As she pushed herself up, her feet protested, sending hot prickles up her legs. She hobbled toward her car.

"Come in!" Claire called in response to the knock on her bedroom door.

"Hey, what do you want for dinner?" Sondra asked.

"I'm going out."

Sondra pushed the door fully open and put her hands on her hips. "With whom?"

"Who do you think?" Claire was examining her reflection in the mirror. She was wearing the black dress she had worn to her father's funeral.

"In that?" Sondra looked aghast.

"It's the only dress I have."

"Then wear pants!"

"I want to look nice," Claire protested with a frown.

"Honey, this dress looks like a funeral shroud."

Claire rolled her eyes.

Sondra went to her closet and flipped through the clothes. "What about this?" she asked, holding out a flowery smock.

Claire winced. "I look like a walking botanical garden in that."

Undeterred, Sondra pulled it from the hanger and held it in front of her friend. "Better that than a dead woman."

698

"I'm wearing the dress. I paid way too much for it to only wear it once."

Sondra pursed her lips. After a few moments, she returned to the closet and rehung the blouse. "Can I at least dress it up a bit?"

"How?"

"What about a scarf?"

"I don't have any."

"That's not a problem. I have several." She headed out of the room.

Claire noted that Sondra's walk was almost back to normal; the walker stood abandoned in the living room, despite Claire's repeated admonition that she should still be careful.

She studied herself in the mirror again and grudgingly admitted that Sondra was right: the dress did make her look dour, to say the least. She opened her jewelry box and shifted its contents, looking for a pair of earrings to frame her face.

"Here we are," announced Sondra, sweeping back into the room with half a dozen scarves draped over her arm.

"I don't know about this..."

"Trust me. You'll look fabulous with a scarf." She pulled the first one, a huge square with pastel butterflies, off her arm and wrapped it around Claire's shoulders.

Claire wrinkled her nose. "I look like a football player."

"Hmm. You're right -- that does make the eye focus on your shoulders too much." She pulled the scarf off and let it float to the ground, replacing it with a long, brightly colored abstract rectangle of silk. "This is much better."

"But what do I do with it? Just let it hang there?"

"Of course not." Sondra moved in front of her and tied the scarf into an elegant bow.

"Seriously?" She felt like a clown.

"It's perfect, Claire! Just lovely!"

"I vaguely remember this look from the Eighties."

Sondra untied the bow, allowing the second scarf to litter the ground as well. She held out a solid blue scarf.

"I'll look like a walking bruise."

The fourth scarf: "Another floral disaster?"

The fifth scarf was a gauzy red number with tassels that was wide enough to wrap around Claire's belly. Sondra wrapped it around her and tied it at the side; Claire smiled for the first time.

"You like it?" Sondra asked.

"It certainly brightens the whole thing up!"

"I think it's perfect."

Claire turned from side to side. "It's not exactly slimming."

"Sweetie, when you're seven months pregnant, nothing is slimming. Might as well show off that baby bump!"

Claire laughed and nodded. "It's more like a baby zeppelin. But okay, I'll do that."

Someone knocked on the door and Claire glanced at the clock. "That's Milo."

"I'll get it. You find some silver earrings -- they'll be perfect with the dress."

Sondra disappeared; a moment later she heard the door opening and Milo and Sondra exchanging pleasantries. Digging in her jewelry box again, she found some small silver hoops her mother had given her on her last trip home. She was pretty sure she had worn them to her father's funeral as well.

"How's Sax?" Sondra asked.

"Busy. He's getting the new building ready and working a case at the same time," Milo answered.

"When do you move?"

"The lease is up at the end of the month."

"Would you like a drink?"

"Just water would be fine."

As she finished a last-minute touch-up to her lipstick, Claire heard the clink of ice cubes in glasses. Sondra would be mixing herself a whiskey sour. One last glance in the mirror told her she looked as good as a pregnant forty-five-year-old woman was likely to look. She walked toward the door, turning out her bedroom light as she passed through it.

Milo, who was sitting on the sofa, lit up when he saw her. Claire, in turn, felt the warm glow of his adoration and smiled. "You look beautiful. Now I think I should take you somewhere better than Abacus Inn."

"Don't you dare," she answered. "I've been looking forward to Chinese food all afternoon."

New Life

Sondra came out of the kitchen with Milo's water and gave Claire an approving wink. "Here you are, sir! Claire, why don't you get yourself a drink and sit down for a few minutes. I was just catching up with Milo."

"All right. Do you need anything?" she asked Sondra.

"No. I'm going to mix myself a drink at the bar," she answered, rattling the ice cubes in her glass.

Claire rounded the corner into the kitchen and fixed herself a glass of tea while Milo and Sondra visited. When she came back into the living room, they were discussing Alice Marie.

"She's still dancing," Milo said. "And I think she's got Brian and Marla talked into a puppy."

"Really? Marla seems much too uptight for pets."

"She's not that bad, really. I think she was pretty attached to..." Milo looked up and frowned.

"It's okay," Claire said. "I know they loved Taz. I'm glad they were able to give him such a good home for his last few months." Rather than sit next to Milo, she moved to the dining room table and pulled out a chair, lowering herself gingerly onto it. "I'm afraid I let him down," she confessed.

"You had a lot going on," Sondra said.

Claire saw Milo roll his eyes. "Anyway," she hurried on, "I'm glad they were able to bond with him."

"He was an easy dog to like." Milo sipped his water. "I was sorry to hear about your broken engagement. Ethan seemed like a nice guy."

"He is," Sondra answered. "He's wonderful, in fact. I don't have any hard feelings toward him. I was pleased that he decided to reunite with his first wife. And, of course, he was very generous with me."

"I thought his wives were dead."

"Not all of them. He and Emlyn had their marriage annulled back when they were in college. Emlyn's a sweetheart. I think they'll be very happy together."

"And you're dating someone new?"

"Patrick Bradford...Vivian's husband."

"That sounds dangerous," Milo said, frowning.

"Not really. Vivian is never going to see the outside of that psychiatric hospital. We'll be perfectly safe."

"I hope you're right." He drained his glass and set it on the coffee table. "Are you ready to go, Claire?"

Claire smiled and put her glass on the table. "Of course."

"You two have a great time!" Sondra exclaimed, a little too enthusiastically.

Claire grimaced. "We will."

Milo extended a hand toward Claire and she accepted his help getting to her feet. She walked ahead of him to the door and out into the hallway. "Have a good night, Sondra. Are you staying in?"

"I'm expecting Patrick later. Don't hurry home," she said, grinning slyly.

"I'll keep her out for a few hours at least," Milo answered. "Good night."

The door closed behind them.

"You really do look beautiful," Milo said, pressing the elevator button.

"Thank you. I guess I'm overdressed."

"Possibly," he answered with a smile.

"I just...I guess I wanted to look good for you. Even though this isn't a date...right?"

"It's a little late for dating." The elevator arrived and he ushered her inside. They rode down silently. When the elevator opened again, he led them toward his car, opening the door for her when they arrived.

"Thank you."

"Of course."

When he was settled in the driver's seat, she said, "I guess we need to talk."

"Let's save the serious stuff for later. Tell me about your day."

She described her visit to the zoo and told him about her conversation with Zareb.

"Are you going to the party?"

"I don't know. I probably should. After all, I worked with Isobel a lot. I consider her a friend."

"Then you should go."

"It's going to be hot on Monday. I'm not sure I can take the temperature in my current condition."

He shrugged.

"What have you been up to lately?"

"Running the bar, mostly. Do you remember me mentioning Morgana? The social vampire from my bartending class?"

"Yes. The strange girl with a talent for mixing drinks."

"Right. I hired her."

"Really?! She doesn't seem like a good fit for the Brass Monkey."

"To be honest, when she came to interview for the job, I didn't recognize her. She's lost the black hair and clothes. And she's pregnant."

"Wow. Still, don't you think it's odd that a girl so young would want to work near Sun City?"

"She says she's trying to change her life so that she'll be a good parent."

Claire smiled. She, too, felt the urge to make serious course corrections before her little girl arrived.

The sky in front of them was streaked with orange, pink, and blue as the sun disappeared behind the White Tank Mountains. Milo whistled low. "You don't get sunsets like that in Minnesota."

"Nor in Oklahoma. I remember how amazed I was by the sky when I first moved here. Dorsey and I used to sit on the porch and watch the sun go down every night." Remembering those early conversations about their future, she felt an unexpected tear gathering in the corner of her eye. She wiped it away surreptitiously.

"Dead Alice never went outside much, particularly in the summer," Milo laughed. "She was terrified of mosquitoes. She never failed to get bitten; even just a walk to the car could result in two or three bites."

"That's terrible! Mosquitoes have never bothered me much."

Milo parked in front of the restaurant and turned off the car. "Wait there. I'll come around and help you out."

"I'm not an invalid," she protested.

"I know that. But your center of balance is more than a little askew these days." He stepped out of the car before she could argue.

She opened her door and he was already there waiting. He must have jogged around, she thought. She wanted to be annoyed, but she could use his help -- standing up had recently become more challenging. She took his hand, and he steadied her as she stepped out. She noticed that his hand seemed firmer than it had only a few months ago -- no doubt a side effect of working at the bar. "Thank you."

"You're welcome." He squeezed her fingers before releasing her hand. Holding the door to the restaurant open, he ushered her inside.

A smiling Chinese woman bowed slightly and led them to one of the booths that lined the windows. Bowing again, she left menus for each of them. Claire liked the Abacus Inn. Its traditional interior -- including a bamboo screen and two three-dimensional Asian wall hangings -- brought the final scene of *A Christmas Story* to her mind. She wondered if they prepared duck.

"What are you thinking about?" Milo asked.

"I don't know...not much, really. What about you?"

"Let's order first."

They studied their menus for a few minutes. When the waitress came back, Milo ordered the Mongolian beef and Claire ordered the lemon chicken. When the waitress walked away, they looked at each other awkwardly.

They spoke at the same time: "I guess I'll--" "I'm sorry--"

Milo laughed nervously. "Go ahead."

"No. You first."

Looking down at the table, he cleared his throat. "I still love you."

"I'll always love you, too, but--"

"No. I'm still in love with you. Pregnant, not pregnant...it doesn't matter."

She pressed her lips together and broke eye contact with him.

"You don't love me anymore."

"No," she answered slowly, "that's not true. But I don't know if love is sufficient to our needs. Have you really thought about what it's going to be like to be a parent again? At your age?"

"Of course I have! This is my chance to get it right -- to have a child who likes me."

"Brian likes you."

"Now. But we spent decades at odds. All because of my bad relationship with dead Alice."

704

"What if there's something wrong with this child?" She met his eyes again.

He didn't look away. "There won't be."

"You can't know that. What if she has Down's Syndrome? Or something worse? There's no guarantee--"

"This baby will be perfect, even if she has Down's Syndrome." He reached across the table and took her hand. "This little girl is our child, and she is a miracle. I'm not one to question God; I'll accept our little miracle no matter what."

Claire squeezed his hand, but frowned. "You say that now."

"I'll always say that."

The waitress slid two bowls of soup in front of them and they released their grip on one another. "Hot tea?" she asked.

"Yes, please," Claire answered.

Milo flipped both of their cups upright, and the waitress poured the steaming liquid into them and left the stainless-steel pot on the table.

"I wish you would move home," Milo said as he emptied a packet of sugar into his cup.

"I don't think I'm ready for that yet. Besides, in a few months, I would have to leave."

"I want us to be a family! Why would you leave?"

"Well," she laughed, "we can't very well send the baby out to live on her own!"

He blinked at her, clearly confused.

"You live in Sun City," she reminded him. "Children aren't allowed, remember?"

"But I'm fifty-five, and she'll be my child!"

"Doesn't matter. No children are allowed to live in Sun City permanently. You know that."

"I hadn't realized--"

"I'm sure you hadn't. Don't worry about it. We should take things slowly anyway. The baby and I can live in the condo."

"What about Sondra?"

"I suppose she can move out if she doesn't like it." Claire slurped a spoonful of the egg drop soup, savoring the salty flavor. Lost in thought, Milo ate his soup as well. Claire took the silent interval as a chance to scan the restaurant, which had filled up since they arrived. Probably a quarter of the tables had college students around them; the restaurant offered their meals at a good value and the students from the nearby college clearly recognized that. A few families, including both children and grandparents, were scattered around them as well, most of them at the round tables in the middle of the room. She found her eyes drawn to a little boy with the distorted features of a Down's Syndrome child. He was smiling widely, and the woman next to him smiled back adoringly. Claire inclined her head toward them. "Look at them." Milo turned just enough to glimpse the family. Though he covered it quickly with a smile, Claire still saw the brief flash of terror in his eyes. The seedling of hope she had allowed to germinate in her heart withered.

"He's such a happy child," Milo said.

"Yes."

The waitress returned with their dinners, limiting their conversation for the next few minutes. That was fine with Claire -- she didn't have much left to say to him now.

"I'm tired of calling her 'the baby.' Since we know we're having a girl, we should name her."

Claire had given some thought to the subject, but hadn't come to any firm decisions yet. "What do you think of Barbara?"

"I've never liked it."

"Deirdre?"

"People will call her Dee Dee. How about Megan?"

Claire shook her head. "Too popular. I don't want our daughter to be one of half a dozen children with the same name."

Maybe something unique? Xandra?"

"Sandra isn't unique."

"No, Xandra. With an 'X.'" He sighed. "You're right. No one will get it."

"Alexandra."

Milo smiled. "I like that."

"Okay. We'll put it on the short list." She dug around in her purse and pulled out a pen. Folding over a corner of the Chinese Zodiac place-mat, she jotted down the name. "How do you feel about Sherry?"

"It's a lousy drink."

"But a great name for a bartender's kid." She smiled in spite of herself.

New Life

"I was a border patrolman much longer than I have been a bartender. By your logic, we should name her Customs."

"Or Tijuana."

"Very funny."

Claire giggled. The baby kicked. "Oh!"

"What's wrong?"

"Little Tijuana just kicked."

"Really?" Milo slid out of the booth and around to sit next to her. "Where?"

She took his hand and held it against the spot. The baby obliged and kicked again. "Feel that?"

Milo had tears in his eyes as he held his hand against her. "That's our daughter."

Claire allowed herself to smile at him.

"I never got to do this with Brian," he said softly. "I was in Vietnam, you know. I missed all the expectant parent stuff. Not that dead Alice would have..."

"She must have loved you once, Milo."

"If she did, she'd forgotten why by the time I came home. She and Brian formed a clique of two and there was no room for me." He wiped the back of his hand across his eyes and moved back to the other side of the booth.

"I'm sorry."

"For what? You didn't ruin my marriage. Dead Alice and I did that all on our own."

"I'm sorry I didn't tell you about the baby sooner. I was wrong."

He nodded once, firmly. "I forgive you." He pushed his plate away.

"Not hungry?"

"I've had enough." He wiped his mouth with his napkin. "My mother's name was Beatrice. I know it's old fashioned, but--"

"I like it. Beatrice Alexandra."

He smiled lopsidedly at her. "Yeah. Let's call her that for now."

When Beryl called the next day, Claire picked up.

"I've been so worried about you!" her sister exclaimed. "Where have you been?"

New Life

"I asked Mother to let you know I was fine," she whispered, stepping out onto the balcony. Sondra's bedroom door was still closed, so Claire figured she was asleep.

"She has trouble remembering her own name these days. She can't be counted on to relay messages."

"What's wrong with her?"

Her sister's sigh traveled through the airwaves. "Grief, mostly. She's not snapping out of it, Sis."

"Our parents were together for nearly fifty years. I'm not surprised she's still mourning."

"I just thought--"

"You've never been through it, Beryl," Claire snapped.

"I'm sorry. You're right."

"How's Rory?" she asked in a softer tone.

"He's fine. He's been a real help with the kids lately. I'm spending a few days a week with Momma. How's the baby?"

Claire sat down on the wicker loveseat, enjoying the warm morning sun. "We're waiting for some test results."

"We? As in, you and Milo together?"

"We're talking," she acknowledged. "But we're not a couple again."

"Why not? What are you waiting for?"

It was Claire's turn to sigh. "The doctor thinks there might be something wrong with Beatrice."

"Who's Beatrice? Oh! The baby, right?" There was a long pause. "What's wrong with her?"

"We don't know. Possibly Down's Syndrome."

"Oh, no. I'm so sorry." Beryl's voice thickened and climbed an octave.

"It's okay. Really."

"But it's so horrible--"

"No, it's not. Down's Syndrome children are as sweet and honest as angels. If God chooses to send me an angel, I'll take her." She stared out at the northern half of the city, willing herself not to tear up. Beryl had healthy children and a reliable husband. She was not allowed to feel sorry for Claire -- especially when Claire had spent hours convincing herself there was nothing for anyone to be sorry about.

"What does Milo think?"

"He says our child is perfect, no matter what."

"That's good. He's a good man."

New Life

He's a liar, Claire thought. She knew what his terrified glance at the Down's Syndrome boy meant -- *please, God, not our child.* "Yes, he is."

"When will you get the results?"

"Next week, probably."

"You don't know for sure?"

"I just had the test last week. I'm sure the doctor will get back to me as soon as he can."

Claire heard one of her nephews talking in the background; Beryl, her voice muffled, answered him before returning to their conversation. "Let's talk about that name."

"Milo and I are trying out Beatrice Alexandra."

"Wow. That's a mouthful."

Claire bristled. "I think it's beautiful."

"Beatrice? It's so old, it's moldy."

"It was Milo's mother's name. And anyway, we'll probably call her Alex."

"Be-a-trice Al-ex-and-ra Cros-by. Nine syllables, Claire."

"What does that mean?"

"It's so long! She won't be able to pronounce her own name until she's ten!"

"Don't be ridiculous."

"Fine. Don't listen to me."

"Fine. I won't."

Another of her sister's long-suffering sighs floated through the airwaves. "Call me when you hear from the doctor."

New Life

It's Raining, It's Pouring

These days, Milo found that he did his best thinking behind the bar, usually while washing glasses or wiping down the smooth, polished surface of the bar top. He hadn't talked to Claire since their dinner out, despite his repeated attempts to get in touch with her. He knew she was fine; he left voice messages and she sent him texts. But she wasn't talking to him, and he had no idea why.

"What are you doing?" Morgana asked, slipping onto a stool in front of him.

"Working. What does it look like I'm doing?"

"Polishing this spot on the bar to a high gloss."

Milo flipped the rag over his shoulder. "What are you doing here?"

"I'm working the night shift, right?"

"But it's only--"

"Four?" she said, raising her eyebrows and looking pointedly at the clock.

"Wow. Where did the day go?"

"Have you eaten?"

"No," he said, realizing that the pains in his stomach weren't just related to his current distress over Claire and Beatrice.

"You should take a break -- go get some food before the Friday-night rush starts."

She headed to the end of the bar. She was starting to show in a way that others -- those who had not known her when she resembled a broomstick -- would notice. She had the slightest potbelly pressing against her white button-down shirt. He was surprised her pregnancy wasn't more obvious, considering how slight a girl she was. He suspected she would look like a broomstick with a pot hung in the middle by the time she reached full term. "How are you feeling these days? Are you past the morning sickness?"

"Oh, yeah," she answered cheerfully. "I feel great -- except that my clothes are starting to chafe. Too bad this isn't a nudist bar."

"Don't even think about it, Morgana. You'd give the clientele heart attacks."

She rolled her eyes. "Get out of here."

710

"I'm going." He pulled the bar towel off his shoulder and handed it to her before walking around the end of the bar. "I'll be back by six."

"Take your time -- I've got it covered."

After spending the day in the dim twilight of the bar, the brightness of the sun temporarily blinded him. He stood blinking just to the side of the door. A few of the regulars passed by him, saying hello. Milo, unable to distinguish facial features, answered them with generic greetings.

"Hi, Milo."

The distinctive, smoky female voice was familiar to him. "Sonia! How are you?"

"Terrific."

"Haven't seen you around lately."

"I was visiting friends in Florida. How are you?"

"Well enough."

"How's Claire? Are you engaged yet?" Sonia had helped him pick out the ring for Claire and even driven him to the airport when he flew to Oklahoma to propose.

He shook his head. "We're not."

"What's wrong with that woman?"

"Nothing. Except that she's pregnant."

Sonia took his hand. "I'm so sorry."

"Don't be," he said, pulling away as he felt the heat of embarrassment rise through his chest. "We're happy about it."

"The baby's yours? Then why aren't you--?"

"She doesn't want to marry me."

"But you're happy about the baby?"

Milo's eyes had adjusted enough that he could see her confused expression. "Of course. Why wouldn't I be?"

"Forgive me if I'm not convinced."

His phone rang. Glad to have an excuse to get away from Sonia, he pulled it out of his pocket. "This is her. Please excuse me." He smiled apologetically and walked toward the parking lot. "Hi, Claire."

"Hi. Am I interrupting anything?"

His head swiveled guiltily on his neck, searching for her car. If she was nearby, he couldn't see her. "No. I was just stepping out to grab some food."

"Good. I know how busy the bar can be on Fridays. The doctor's office just called."

"And? Do we need to go in for an appointment?"

"No. It's good news, Milo. Dr. Slotnick says Beatrice is fine. Perfectly normal."

"That's wonderful!" His heart swelled with relief.

"Yes."

"What's wrong?"

"Nothing."

Milo had been with dead Alice for too many years not to know that nothing always meant something. Still, he didn't press her. "Do you want to go out to celebrate?" he offered.

"You can't do that now, can you? It's Friday night--"

"Sax and Morgana can handle it."

She hesitated. "No. Not tonight. I'm tired."

"Okay...if you're sure. You take good care of yourself and our little girl."

"I will. Goodbye, Milo."

It was time to make an appointment with a real estate agent -- Milo had a house to sell.

"This is a very nice duplex," Sonia complimented as she moved through his home.

"Thanks," Milo answered. After months of living alone and working long hours, it had taken him the better part of a day to get the place back from the edge of condemnation. The newspapers and dishes had piled up to alarming heights, and the master bathroom had been disgusting.

"How much did you pay for it?"

"A little more than $120,000."

She whistled low. "It'll be hard to get that much out of it now."

Milo had been pleased to learn that Sonia had passed her real-estate licensing exam, and he had immediately engaged her services because she was a friend. Looking at her now, though, he saw the cold, appraising look that every house salesperson seemed to possess. "I understand. I bought the place as the market was in free fall. I had no idea how low the prices would drop."

New Life

"Maybe you should hold onto it for a while. The market is climbing these days...given another year, you might get your full investment out of it."

"But we have a baby on the way--"

"You're not living with the mother," Sonia pointed out.

"That's the problem I'm seeking to rectify."

Sonia led him into the kitchen and sat down at the table. "Have you considered keeping the place as a rental? You'd be surprised how well you could do with a place like this. I mean, the homeowners' dues keep the outside maintained, right? This is exactly the sort of place winter visitors clamor for."

"That's all well and good, but how am I going to afford a new place if I don't sell this one?"

"Just take a mortgage," she suggested. "You make more than enough at the bar--"

"I'm not comfortable with that." He placed his hand flat on the table. "Look, just tell me what you think you can get for the place."

She glanced around the kitchen before peering back into the living room. "If you want to sell it fast, I'd price it at $90,000."

He shook his head and grimaced. "What if I want to sell it a little slower than that?"

"I might get fifteen thousand more if you can wait for the right buyer."

"List it. I'm in no position to quibble."

"At ninety or one-oh-five?"

"The latter. I've got a few months before my situation becomes impossible."

"Whatever you say." She jotted down some notes. "I'll bring the listing agreement by in the morning, okay?"

"Sure." He walked her to the front door and shook her hand. "Thanks for doing this."

"Thank you for the opportunity. I appreciate you trusting me with this."

"You've more than proven your honesty. I know you'll do right by me."

She smiled and waved goodbye.

New Life

Stepping back into his house, he heard his cell phone ringing from the kitchen table, where he had left it. He rushed to answer it. "Hello?"

"Dad? Are you okay?"

"I'm fine, Brian," he said, dropping into the kitchen chair. "I just had to run to catch your call."

"Geez, Dad. Let it go to voicemail next time. You need to be careful."

"What? Why?"

"I'm just worried about you."

"Don't be. I'm perfectly all right."

"How's Claire?"

"She's well."

"And the...my..."

"Your sister?"

Milo could picture Brian anxiously raking a hand across his military-style haircut. "Yeah. How is she?"

"Also great."

"No problems with...anything?"

"Claire just called me yesterday to tell me the good news -- all the tests indicate that Beatrice will be normal."

"Beatrice? You're naming her after Grandma, huh?"

"I think so. We're still trying out the name, but I think it will stick. Why are you calling?"

"Can't a son call his father?"

"Of course. But you don't usually call for no reason."

"I suppose you're right. Marla told me to call. We haven't seen you since Taz died."

Milo ducked his head, remembering that he had promised to go to Eric's baseball games. He hadn't made it to one yet. "We've talked, though."

"That's not good enough for my wife. She wants you to come to dinner -- tonight, if possible. She's making a brisket."

"That sounds lovely, but you don't have to--"

"We know, Dad. Do you think Claire would come?"

"I don't know. I could call her."

"Why don't you do that. We'll see you around six, okay?"

Milo frowned, uncertain of when he agreed to come. "Yeah, I guess that's fine."

"Great." Brian disconnected.

Milo dialed Claire's number.

714

"Hello, Milo," she answered.

"Hi, Claire. How are you feeling?"

"Fine. What's up?"

"Brian just called to ask us to dinner tonight."

"I don't know if I'm ready for that."

"I can pick you up. I think they would really like to see you."

"I haven't even showered yet today."

Milo glanced at the kitchen clock, which read just ten-thirty. "It's still early. We don't need to be there until six."

He waited in a long silence. When she answered, she sounded worried. "I don't know if that's a great idea. I'm sure Brian is less than thrilled to discover he's going to have a sister."

"Actually, he seems comfortable with it. He even asked after you and Beatrice."

"About the name--"

"You don't like Beatrice anymore?"

"It's not that. But my sister pointed out that we were giving her quite a mouthful for a moniker. I think Alexandra may have to go."

Milo smiled in relief. "That's fine. We'll find something better."

"Six, huh?"

"Yes. Marla's making a brisket."

"She is a good cook..."

"...Especially for such a skinny gal," Milo laughed.

"Okay. I'll see you around five-thirty."

"Great. Thanks, Claire."

Milo and Claire arrived at Brian and Marla's right at six. As usual, Alice Marie was the first to greet them. She was holding something in her arms.

"Look, Miss Claire, we got a puppy!"

Marla, who wasn't far behind her, frowned and said, "Honey--"

"No," Claire said quickly, "It's fine." She leaned down to pet the soft, wriggly creature in the girl's arms as Milo went around them to greet Marla with a hug.

"Thank you for inviting us," he said.

"I wish you'd come around more often."

"When did you get the puppy?"

"Last weekend. Alice Marie kept asking for one until Brian just couldn't stand it anymore. He found a pug puppy on Craig's List." Marla looped her arm around Milo's and led him away from Alice Marie and Claire and toward the house. "I'm sorry I sprang Claire's condition on you."

"That wasn't your fault."

"As soon as I saw her, I wanted to call and warn you. I was terrified you'd have a heart attack!" she said with a nervous laugh.

"It was a shock," he admitted, "but I've adjusted. How has Brian been with it?"

"He wasn't thrilled at first, but he's warmed up to the idea. We both like Claire a lot, you know. And, of course, Alice Marie adores her. When are you getting married?"

He shook his head discreetly. "Best not talk about that."

"Haven't you proposed?" she whispered.

"More than once now. But Claire is determined not to rush into anything."

"What about you?"

"Can you keep a secret?"

Marla nodded solemnly.

"I put my house up for sale today."

"Why...? Wait. Sun City. You can't live there with the baby, can you?"

"Nope. And I'm determined to live with Claire and Beatrice. I want us to be a family."

Alice Marie skipped up alongside Milo and took his free hand. "Grandpa, did you see the puppy?"

"I did! What's his name?"

"Her name," she corrected, "is Stella."

"A girl, huh?"

"Yes. Just like me!"

Claire, holding Stella, caught up. She held out the puppy, and both Marla and Alice Marie released him. He took the furry, short-nosed, big-eyed creature and nuzzled her. "Aren't you a cutie!"

"Aw!" his daughter-in-law and granddaughter said simultaneously.

New Life

"Are you coming in the house or what?" called Brian from the doorway. "We're letting all the cold air out!"

Milo, puppy in hand, followed the rest of the group inside. Eric and a teen-aged girl with blue hair sat on the rock-hard sofa in the living room holding hands. "Hello, Eric. Who's your friend?"

The girl stood up and put a hand on one hip. "I'm Diva."

She certainly was, Milo thought as his eyebrows shot up.

"This is Eric's girlfriend," Marla said. Her tight-lipped smile told Milo everything he needed to know.

"Nice to meet you, sweetheart."

"I'm not your sweetheart. Please call me Diva."

Milo stared at the girl with a bemused smile on his face before turning away from her and Eric and following his son into the family room. Was this what the next twenty years of his life held? Wheedling children and rude teenagers? Remembering that he and Claire were expecting a girl, he groaned inwardly. No, he decided, his future was worse -- horny boys and a sullen, hormonal daughter. Suddenly dizzy, he put the puppy on the floor and made his way to the sofa.

"Take the chair, Claire," Marla said, waving her toward the easy chair she normally sat in. "That will be less trouble for you to get out of later."

"Thank you." Claire lowered herself into it with a sigh. "I'm looking forward to this being over. Pregnancy is definitely a younger woman's game."

Marla laughed. "That's why I'm so glad my childbearing days are over! Excuse me, please. I need to check on dinner." She crossed the long room to the kitchen at the other end.

"How has work been, Brian?" Milo asked.

"Busier than I'd like. I wish criminals were snowbirds. I could do with a quiet summer. How's the bar?"

"Great. Sax has just about got the new place ready. Just in time, too -- the lease on the old place is up at the end of the month."

They chatted back and forth about small things for the next fifteen minutes or so while Claire listened and studied the backyard through the sliding-glass doors. Alice Marie, carrying Stella, came in and sat on the floor next to her. The pup curled up in her lap and napped.

"Dinner is ready!" Marla sang out. "Alice Marie, put Stella in her cage and go wash your hands."

Milo stood and walked to the chair where Claire sat and held out his hands. "Let me help you up," he offered.

"No, that's okay," she answered, placing her hands on the armrests. "I think I can manage."

Brian shot his father a sympathetic glance and headed toward the table that separated the family room from the kitchen. Eric and Diva made it to the table just before Milo and Claire, causing him to sit across from Claire instead of next to her as Milo would have preferred.

"Smells wonderful," Claire said, smiling at Marla.

"Thank you! Brian, would you carve the meat? I need to get the salt and pepper."

"Of course, sweetheart." He took the carving knife and fork and began cutting.

Milo looked at his grandson and asked, "How's baseball been going?"

"We've had a decent season," he answered. "Our first-string pitcher graduates next month. The coach says I'm in the running for the spot next year."

"Excellent! I'm so proud of you!"

"I don't think he should play," Diva said.

"Of course he should!" Marla finally sat down. "If he keeps playing, he'll have an excellent shot at a scholarship."

"Who needs one of those?" she said, rolling her eyes. "College is just a big waste of money. We're going straight into the military. Aren't we, Eric?"

He shifted uncomfortably and shrugged. "Maybe. I'm still thinking."

Brian set the carving implements down and looked at Eric as if he were contemplating carving him instead. "What is there to think about?"

"Like Diva says, college doesn't seem to be much of a boost these days. And I don't really know what I want to do yet. The military could help--"

"The service isn't all it's cracked up to be," Milo said quietly.

"Oh, yeah?" Diva was glaring at him. "My dad was in the service, and he says it's the best place for any young person to go after high school."

"With a name like yours, I'd imagine it would be hell on earth."

She rolled her eyes again. "I'm not going to serve. I'm going to be a military wife."

"How long have you two been dating?"

"Almost two months," Marla answered for them.

"Sweetheart, you'd best dig your claws into another boy, because I won't let you ruin my grandson's life."

"Grandpa..."

"Eric, you don't need this girl, no matter what you think right now."

"Dad," Brian said, "we think it's best if Eric make his own decisions about the people in his life."

"Brian, I know I was a lousy father, but at least I kept you out of the military. I consider myself lucky that you found a jewel like Marla to marry. But I'll be damned if I'm going to sit here and listen to your son talk about imploding his life for this...tartlet of a girl." With everyone staring at him, he pushed back his chair and marched out the front door. Once he was there, he realized he couldn't leave -- not without Claire. He sat in his car and turned on the air. Deciding to rest while he waited, he lowered the seat and closed his eyes. Angry thoughts kept him from sleeping, though.

A few minutes later, a tap at the window startled him. Claire was waiting for him to unlock the door for her. He flipped the latch and she lowered herself in. "You okay?"

"Yeah," he sighed, raising his seat back to a sitting position. "I'm sorry I went off the rails in there."

"I believe you were provoked."

"Really?"

"Definitely. That girl is just about the most unpleasant person I've ever met."

He wondered briefly who qualified as more unpleasant before thinking of the two thugs who had murdered her husband and nearly killed her less than two years before. The baby she carried now was more than an inconvenient detour -- Beatrice was a miracle. This woman -- this amazing, beautiful creature who made him feel more than anyone ever had before -- might have been dead long before he met her. If he hadn't moved here from Minnesota...if he hadn't taken up photography as a hobby...if he hadn't fed the squirrel monkeys dried peas.... "Claire, you are my destiny. You are everything I want for the rest of my life. Please, marry me."

Claire's eyes popped and she leaned away from him as if he were threatening to skin her alive instead of put a ring on her finger. "No."

"Why not? Why won't you marry me? I love you!"

"I saw how you looked at that Down's Syndrome child in the restaurant. I saw the pity and horror in your eyes."

Closing his eyes, he sighed. "But there's nothing wrong with Beatrice."

"Right now. But what if she is autistic? What if she gets sick later on? I'd rather know that I am on my own as a parent than think I have someone beside me and find out I'm wrong when the chips are down."

"I'll be there--"

"How can I know that for sure?"

"I'm selling my house. I want to buy something for us...for our family."

"It takes more than a house to make a family, Milo." He saw his own sadness reflected in her eyes.

"Do you not love me?"

She blinked in silence for a long moment. "That's not it."

"Just tell me the truth, Claire."

"I love you. I didn't know I could love anyone after I lost Dorsey; I can't believe I found you. But I love someone else just as much as I love you." She caressed her belly. "If you hurt her, I don't know how I could go on."

"I never would," he answered, his voice raspy. "I wouldn't hurt either of you, ever."

"I want to believe you."

"Then do."

"Let me think about it."

With nothing left to say, he drove her back to the condo in silence.

New Life

New Life

Roses are Red

Sondra was feeling almost like her old self again. She wasn't likely to be running any foot races, but then again, she hadn't been a marathon runner to begin with. As long as she could waltz across a dance floor with Patrick, that would be good enough.

She glanced up at the massive bouquet of red roses that filled the dining-room table, leaving little room for actually eating at it. She hadn't counted them, but she was certain there were at least a hundred of them -- a trinket of Patrick's love. The arrangement had been so heavy she had asked the deliveryman to place them on the table for her.

There were times when she wished she were able to give herself a proper pat on the back, particularly when things fell into place just the way she envisioned they would. Ethan may be an artist with a pencil or a paintbrush, but she painted with actions and emotions.

Just a few days ago, Ethan had called to tell her the good news: he and Emlyn had eloped, thereby correcting the grievous wrong Vivian had done them. Sondra had happily congratulated him. He had also shared with her that Vivian was officially committed to the Arizona State Hospital for "rehabilitation." Sondra hoped the sociopath wouldn't be able to talk her way out of the hospital anytime soon, especially now that she herself was dating Vivian's soon-to-be ex-husband.

Just thinking about Patrick made her smile. He was her first love reborn in so many ways -- a debonair, indulgent, stylish man who adored her every expression. She hadn't felt so beautiful or spoiled in years.

A knock at the door drew her out of her reverie. Alone in the apartment -- Claire and Milo were out to dinner -- she answered it herself. "Fanny! What are you doing here?"

"Can't a daughter visit her mother?" She reached out and hugged her tightly.

Sondra pulled her inside. "Is everything all right?"

"Of course. Why do you ask?"

Holding her at arm's length, Sondra studied her. The awkward girl had long since given way to the poised

Romanesque beauty before her. Yet something unhappy lingered behind her eyes. "What has happened?"

"I don't want to talk about it. Let's talk about happy things."

Sondra let her arms drop and Fanny took her hand and led them into the living area, where the scent of roses filled the air.

"My goodness, Ma! Who sent these?"

Sondra beamed in spite of herself. "Patrick Bradford."

"Your new beau has excellent, if showy, taste." She leaned forward and sniffed one of the flowers. "When do we get to meet him?"

"Soon, I think."

"Why don't you bring him to Shabbat?"

"He's not Jewish. I'm afraid he might feel out of place. Besides, I don't want him to feel like I'm forcing my family on him."

"Then have Reuben and me over for dinner."

"You know I don't cook."

"Make King Ranch Casserole -- I know you can make that!"

Sondra smiled. "Aren't you tired of that? You must have eaten two-hundred pounds of the stuff over the years."

"I haven't had any in forever."

Sondra sat down in the armchair and gestured for Fanny to sit on the sofa. "I'll talk to Patrick about it. He might prefer to take us out somewhere instead."

"I think we'd get to know each other better over a home-cooked meal." Fanny moved across the room and looked out the glass doors instead of sitting down. "This place has a great view, doesn't it?"

"The best part of living here," Sondra agreed. Thinking of her grandson, she asked, "How is Hunter?"

"Fine. He sends his love."

"I hope he didn't fall too far behind in his studies while caring for me."

"It was early in the semester, and Hunter is nothing if not a diligent student. He was caught up in just a few weeks' time."

New Life

"Tell him to call his grandmother." Sondra, tired of talking to her daughter's back, walked to the doors. "What's so interesting?" she asked as she approached.

"Nothing." Fanny raised a hand to her face and turned to avoid her gaze.

Sondra took her hand and, pulling it back, saw Fanny was crying. "Tell me what's wrong," she cajoled.

"I just came from the doctor. Reuben and I had some tests done to make sure we were healthy enough to start a family. My results..."

"Fanny, you're scaring me. What's wrong with you?"

Her silent tears became body-wracking sobs. "I'm in menopause!"

"How is that possible? You're not even forty yet!"

"The doctor told me to ask when you started menopause."

"Oh, sweetie...I had a hysterectomy, remember? When you were small."

"Oh my God...I completely forgot. What about your mother?"

"I'm sorry, but those were different times. I don't remember my mother ever talking about female issues with me other than when she taught me how to use a sanitary belt."

Fanny looked puzzled. "What?"

"It's what you had to do before they developed the adhesive strips on the back of sanitary napkins."

"Okay. So, no idea what the family history for menopause is, then."

"I'm sorry, sweetheart."

Pulling a chair away from the dining table, she dropped heavily onto it. "Reuben will be heartbroken."

Sondra sat at the table too. "I thought you were planning to adopt anyway."

"We are. The lawyer says it's going to be a few months yet, but we should have a child by the end of the year. It won't be a newborn, though. If we want a baby, we'll have to wait longer -- maybe three or four years."

"Getting a child who is already potty trained seems like a perfect situation to me. I hated changing diapers."

New Life

Fanny rolled her eyes. "As if you ever changed a single one."

"I did!" she protested. "At least one. Maybe two." Fanny laughed in spite of herself and Sondra smiled in triumph. "There now. You see? This isn't the end of the world."

"But Reuben will never have a son or daughter of his own."

"Your husband is a good man. I can tell these things -- I'm a very good judge of character, as you know. I'm willing to bet that he cares a lot more about being married to you than he does about being the natural father of any child."

Fanny bit her lip worriedly.

"Why do you doubt me?"

"It's not that. What if...Ma, what if I can't love a child that's not my own?"

"Nonsense."

"It's not! I adore Hunter, but he's mine. He grew inside me. I loved him before I ever saw him!"

"Fanny, you are one of the most compassionate people I've ever known. I don't know how you grew inside me -- you must have gotten an extra dose of your father's goodness, because Lord knows I didn't have any to spare. You may not bond with an adopted child in exactly the same way you did with Hunter, but I have faith that you will bond to him or her."

"I just don't understand. How come Claire is able to have a baby at forty-five and here I am, only in my thirties and barren? It's not fair."

Sondra couldn't help but smile -- her daughter had always been particularly concerned with the unfairness of life. To keep her daughter from misconstruing her expression, Sondra stood and walked behind her, wrapping her arms around the distraught woman. "Life still isn't fair. Things don't always even out. But you and Reuben have the chance to make life fairer for a child without parents."

As her sobs subsided, Fanny stilled. Sondra moved back to the chair and saw that her daughter was smiling. "Thank you, Ma. You just clarified this issue for me."

"I'm glad I could help."

Fanny reached out and took her hand. "You know, you're pretty wise for an old actress."

"It's all those scripts I've read. I learned to be a real person from writers."

She shook her head. "I doubt it." Standing up, she said, "I need to go home. Did I tell you we found a house?"

"No, you hadn't mentioned it."

"You'll love it. It's not far from here -- right around Third Street and Northern. It has a big yard and five bedrooms."

"Sounds big for just the two of you. I guess you'd better get moving on those adoptions. Are you already moved in?"

"Not yet. We're having it renovated. It's a little outdated -- I think it was last decorated in the Eighties."

"Lots of mauve and antique blue, huh?"

She laughed. "I'm afraid so. It should be ready by the time we're back from the family trip to Belize in June. Which reminds me -- are you coming? Ike and Naomi asked me to check with you."

Remembering Reuben's quintessentially Jewish parents from Fanny's New Year's wedding, Sondra winced.

"Come on, Ma, they're not that bad."

"I got the distinct feeling that Isaac was flirting with me."

"He flirts with everyone -- it's just his way."

"And Naomi seemed...well..."

"Like a pushy Jewish mother?" Fanny said, one eyebrow arched.

Sondra bristled slightly. "I'm not like that at all."

"Did I say you were?" She smiled imploringly. "You'll have a great time. Belize is just beautiful. You'll get a tan--"

"I'll burn. The red hair is real, you know."

"So you'll slather yourself in sunscreen. Even better -- bring Patrick along to do it. That should keep Ike at bay."

"I'll think about it."

"I hope so. Hunter's going, and I know he wants you to come as well." She leaned toward her mother and gave her a tight squeeze. "Thanks for talking to me."

"I'm always here for you, darling."

Smiling sweetly, Fanny gave a quick wave and was out the door.

"I think it's time we got you out in the fresh air," Patrick announced a few days later. He was wearing plaid pants and a pink polo shirt, clear signals that he was a golfer -- a detail Sondra had previously failed to glean.

"Isn't it a little warm to be outside?" Sondra asked. She never lingered in the Arizona sun. Even though she was no longer technically a natural redhead, her skin still burned. Just the thought of eighteen holes in the bright spring sun was enough to make her skin red.

"It's a beautiful day! Sunny and breezy, barely over eighty degrees...perfect golfing weather."

"I'm not sure Lucas would approve," she said, invoking her physical therapist's name.

"I talked to Lucas while you were in the pool the other day. He thinks it's a great idea. You're all but done with therapy at this point anyway."

"It's too bad I don't have anything to wear on the green--"

He held out a bronze plastic bag emblazoned with his country club's logo. She recognized it from the one time he had taken her to dinner there. Now she remembered how he had talked about all the amenities of the place: a weight room, a sauna, a bar, and -- oh, yes -- a world-class golf course. Somehow, she had received the impression that he only joined for the Thursday-night poker games. "I took the liberty of selecting a suitable outfit for you, my dear."

She faked a smile and took the bag. "I hope it fits me..."

"I'm sure it will. Now, get dressed."

Reluctantly, she carried the bag into her bedroom and pulled out the new garments: a sleeveless aqua polo shirt and a startlingly white skort. A box containing a pair of white-and-aqua golf shoes was under the clothes. In addition, a large bottle of SPF +100 sunblock spray was rolling around at the bottom of the bag. He had covered her every objection; she smiled and shook her head. He might be the perfect man for her, if she were truly willing to let him manage her life.

Stripping down, she sprayed the sunblock thoroughly over her body. The new clothes were a perfect fit; she looked as if she belonged on the green.

"You look beautiful!" Patrick enthused as she emerged from the bedroom.

"All that I'm missing are a sun visor and golf clubs."

"They're waiting for you in the car," he said with a grin. "Shall we?"

"I suppose we shall." She linked her arm through his and let him lead the way.

Outside, a slight breeze kept the day from being too hot, despite the bright sun. Patrick had booked a ten o'clock tee time -- as early as he could reasonably expect Sondra to leave the condo. As they walked through the club toward the green, several members waved their greetings at Patrick. Sondra was pleased to note that at least a few of the older women did double-takes as they passed her. The men, of course, simply took one long stare -- also gratifying. Nearly three months of enforced seclusion had bruised her ego just a bit. After all, Lucas, Milo, and Sax -- her main visitors -- weren't romantically interested in her. Only Patrick had been around to make her feel beautiful, and that was a job for more than one man.

Patrick leaned down and balanced a golf ball on the tee box. "Would you like to take the first swing?"

"You know, of course, that I've never played this game."

"Really? You spent your life in Nevada, California, and Arizona, and you've never played golf?"

"The hair color might not be entirely natural these days, Patrick, but I am a redhead. I burn in direct sunlight."

"Not with that sunblock spray I bought you. The clerk guaranteed me that not a single ray of sun would penetrate it."

"And that's the only reason I'm willing to give this a try."

"The only reason?"

"Well...the second reason," she said, smiling at him.

"Golf can be a very romantic game, you know."

"How so?"

"We're out here together, just the two of us...there are tiny balls involved--"

"Patrick!" she exclaimed, shocked and pleased at the same time.

He laughed huskily. Selecting a club from his bag, he approached the ball and swung, sending it sailing toward the first hole. He leaned down again and placed another ball on the box. "Your turn, my dear."

"What do I do?"

"Grab the driver from your bag and bring it here."

"Which one is it?"

"The longest one."

She stood over the bag for a moment, determining which club was indeed the longest. It had a thick head and looked like it would make an effective weapon for clubbing a baby seal. Carrying it over to Patrick, she held it out to him.

"No, you're going to need that, not me."

"You don't really expect me to hit that little ball, do you?"

He sighed, showing exasperation for the first time.

"Maybe we should just head for the nineteenth hole now and save ourselves the trouble," she suggested.

"No, Sondra, you're going to earn your drink today."

"I can think of better ways to earn a drink," she said, smirking.

"You're incorrigible," he said, but he smiled too.

"Fine. I can see I'm not getting out of this. How do I use this thing?"

"Come here. I'll help you with your swing." He spent the next few minutes attempting to shift her body into the proper stance. The foursome with the ten-fifteen tee time arrived during the lesson. One of them, a younger man with rakish stubble, kept glancing at his watch. The other three, all of whom were closer to Sondra's age, seemed quite content to study her form as Patrick worked to shape it.

After a few practice swings, Patrick positioned her in front of the tee box. To her surprise, she connected with the ball and it flew in the direction of the first hole, though not as far as Patrick's had. The three older men applauded, and Sondra turned and bowed as the younger man rolled his eyes.

"Come on, dear girl," Patrick said, stepping into the golf cart. "We need to finish this hole so that these gentlemen can start their game."

"Thank you for your patience," she said with a wave.

She hopped into the cart and Patrick drove her to her ball, where he recommended she use the driver again -- "with just slightly less force," he suggested. Her ball landed close to the green. They drove to where Patrick's ball lay. Taking careful aim, he landed the ball within a few feet of the hole. A few minutes and four strokes later -- one his and three hers -- they were on to the second hole.

New Life

And so the game went, with Sondra averaging six strokes a hole and Patrick usually finishing in three or four. She hoped it wasn't indicative of their anticipated sex life, and said so jokingly just after the tenth hole.

"It's been awhile since I played that game," he answered, stroking his whisker-less chin. "I seem to recall a higher average."

"Maybe we should give me a handicap when we decide to play," she suggested.

He shrugged, and she noticed he was blushing. "That could be arranged."

Though she lost -- something the intensely competitive Sondra found irritating -- she still had a good time, if only because of the companionship. Patrick had been right: a day in the fresh air was just what she needed. And now she needed a drink.

"Wait here, darling," Patrick said, seating her at a table by the window. "What would you like to drink?"

"A whiskey sour, of course." As he turned toward the bar, she added, "And a glass of water. I'm a little dehydrated, I think." She wasn't sure that he heard her, but didn't want to follow him. She adjusted her chair so that she could look out the window onto the man-made lake. Half a dozen ducks were paddling in the water, and a few rabbits were foraging near the edge. When she had lived in Sun City with Milo, she had loved to look out the window and see the small creatures playing in the yard. Though she had never been the outdoorsy type, she understood the appeal of watching animals. She had even invested in a block of birdseed specifically for quail in order to attract more of them into her view.

"Excuse me," said a woman dressed in what Sondra took for a tennis dress, "you look so familiar, but I'm afraid I don't recall your name."

Sondra smiled and held out a hand. "Sondra Lane. And you are?"

The woman gripped her hand tightly. "Your biggest rival. Listen, sister, I've had my eye on Patrick for months now. Just back off, okay?"

Sondra pulled her hand away from the crazy woman. "I think Patrick can decide for himself who he wants to date."

"Who do you think you're kidding?" she snarled. "With your dye job and your painted face -- you aren't even in the same realm as Patrick and me."

"Dr. Glew! What a surprise to see you here on a weekday!" Patrick said as he approached with their drinks in hand.

"Hello, Patrick," the nut job cooed. "I always take Wednesday afternoons off for tennis. And, please -- I've told you before -- call me Naomi."

"Naomi is my dentist," he said to Sondra, who was doing her best to hide her complete disgust.

"I was just telling Sally here--"

"Sondra."

"Whatever, that I've known you for years. Even before you married Vivian, as a matter of fact. God rest her soul."

Sondra, shocked, said, "She's not--"

"To be forgotten," Patrick cut her off. "We don't want to keep you, Naomi."

Naomi hesitated for a moment before flashing her shiny, white teeth at them. Sondra wondered if they were bleached or just sharpened. "Of course. Call me anytime you feel like talking, Patrick. Consider me a friendly ear." She walked away slowly. When she heard Patrick resume talking to Sondra, she looked back over her shoulder and shot her a deadly glare.

"...marigold hotel?"

Frowning, Sondra realized she had missed nearly every word Patrick had said in the last minute. "I'm sorry."

"For what?"

"I was distracted. Is that nutball really your dentist?"

"Dr. Glew? Yes! She's one of the best in town. She specializes in cosmetic dentistry, but she also takes on a lot of the club members as regular patients." He smiled curiously. "What did she say to you?"

"She thinks she has dibs on you."

"How flattering!"

"Wrong answer." Sondra took her drink from his hand and swallowed a quarter of the drink before slamming it down on the table.

Flustered, Patrick took the seat opposite her. "I'm so sorry. I'm just not used to being a desired commodity."

"How can you say that? You're as handsome as a movie star and rich to boot!"

"Please. I'm not a good-looking man -- never have been."

Sondra, who was less adept at giving compliments than receiving them, stumbled over her words. "What mirror...are you blind? You're...distinguished and...perfect!"

"Now I know you're just blowing smoke. I'm not perfect."

"You're right. Perfect may have been an overstatement. But you really are very handsome."

He laughed disparagingly. "In my mind, I'm still a gawky teenager with a bad case of acne." Taking her hand, he added, "And I feel like a teenager around you. You're the most beautiful woman who has ever looked at me twice."

"Prettier than Dr. Glew?"

"No comparison."

She smiled warmly at him. "I think we make a wonderful couple."

"As do I. And as soon as my divorce is final, I intend to make our relationship more permanent."

A five-carat diamond ring floated through her mind's eye. "Really?"

"Absolutely."

Remembering her conversation with Fanny, she said, "My daughter and her husband would like to meet you."

"I would love that. Why don't we meet them for dinner?"

"When?"

"I'm free tonight."

Sondra took another swig of her drink. "Fanny's husband is a lawyer. I'm sure they would need more notice--"

"Fine...let them pick the date. My schedule is clear. That's one of the benefits of retirement."

Sondra spotted her daughter at a table toward the back of the Havana Cafe and waved. Fanny lifted her wine glass in response as the hostess led them toward the table. Reuben stood and pulled out Sondra's chair, kissing her cheek as she slid around the front edge of it.

The restaurant, a strip-mall find of Reuben's, was far below Patrick's usual standards, in Sondra's estimation. "This is...kitschy," she said as brightly as she could.

"It reminds us of Belize," Fanny said, wrapping her hand over the top of Reuben's. "We just love it there."

Patrick, who looked uncomfortable in the plastic chair, pulled himself closer to the table. "This is Cuban food, right?"

"Yes. I hope that's all right with you."

"Yes, of course. I visited Cuba once."

"Really?" Fanny and Sondra asked in chorus.

"Indeed. Beautiful country. Amazingly warm people. Of course, I haven't been there in decades -- Castro and the bad relations, you know. But I remember loving the food."

Reuben smiled and lifted a pitcher of deep-red liquid. "I took the liberty of ordering sangria."

"Wonderful!" Patrick said as he pushed his and Sondra's glasses toward Reuben.

"So, Patrick -- I saw the roses you sent to Ma," Fanny said.

"Just a small token of my affection."

"There must have been a hundred of them!"

"And they all pale in comparison to your mother." He sipped the fruited wine and said, "This is excellent. Great choice."

"I also ordered tapas -- tostones and maduros fritos," Reuben said.

"I find plantains are wonderful in any form. Though I am fan of seviche as well."

"I wasn't sure how adventurous your palate was. Their seviche is excellent. Would you like to order it as well?"

"What's seviche?" Sondra asked.

"Seafood in lime juice," Fanny answered, wrinkling her nose. "Not a favorite of mine."

"You've never been much of a fish person," Sondra commented. "Just like your father that way -- Bill wouldn't eat fish even if it were the highest-quality salmon. I swear that's why he left the Catholic church."

"Your father was Catholic?" Reuben asked, his eyebrows shooting straight up.

"That's news to me. I barely remember him, and Ma never talked about him much."

"I may know more about him than you do!" Patrick joked. "I read his biography years ago. You look a lot like him, you know."

Fanny shook her head. "I thought about reading the book, but it seemed like an odd way to learn about him."

"What do you want to know?" Sondra set her wineglass down and looked straight at her daughter. Her resemblance to Bill was suddenly so obvious that it took her breath away -- Fanny's nose, the feature Sondra had always blamed on her Jewish heritage, was actually more like her father's Roman features.

"Were you happy together, you and Dad? Or was that just what you told the magazines so that you didn't look like a gold-digger?"

Reuben placed a hand on Fanny's shoulder and gave her a warning look.

"It's a fair question, Reuben," Sondra reassured him. "Yes, I did love your father. He truly was the love of my life and we were very happy together."

Turning toward Patrick, she asked, "Is that what the biography says?"

"Yes, as a matter of fact, it is. From what I read, he believed that Sondra was his soul mate. He stole her from a friend of his, you know."

"He did? You never told me that."

Sondra smiled, remembering the sleazy producer with whom she had lived before Bill swept her off her feet. "It wasn't much of a theft. I think Bud was just as happy to see me go as I was to leave."

"Bud?" asked Reuben.

"George Miller," Sondra clarified.

His jaw dropped open.

Fanny didn't seem to notice. "He was so old when you got pregnant. Did he really want children?"

"Absolutely. He was thrilled when you came along."

"So I didn't ruin your last years together?"

"Not at all." Sondra took a sip of her sangria. "In fact, you were supposed to have a little brother or sister."

"What happened?"

"A good friend of mine died unexpectedly. My doctor put the spontaneous miscarriage down to stress."

"I'm sorry, Ma."

Sondra smiled and waved the apology away. "That was a long time ago."

"You're talking about Lianne Morris, right?" Patrick asked. "The one who exploded on a domestic flight to Texas?"

"Oh, my God! You were friends with a terrorist?" Fanny exclaimed. The waitress, who had been on her way to their table with the appetizers, wheeled around and headed back to the kitchen.

"I think you scared the server, sweetheart," Reuben said.

"No, I wasn't friends with a terrorist." Sondra zeroed in on Patrick. "All this was in Bill's biography?"

"You know how it is -- the more salacious the details, the better the biography sells. Bill made some odd decisions in the Seventies."

"Didn't we all?" she answered wryly.

He nodded. "I've always thought my polyester suits were particularly tasteless."

"Can we get back to the exploding friend?"

"Lianne Morris was one of your mother's costars in *Siege of the Moon*."

"She was a starlet -- not much of an actress, but she had an appealing, innocent look about her. She was the girlfriend of the primary investor in the film, which is how she got the part."

"I don't know...I thought she was pretty good, myself," Reuben commented.

Sondra rolled her eyes. "Anyway, we ended up becoming good friends. I even considered naming you after her, but she told me not to -- she thought her name sounded too hillbilly."

"It's better than Epiphany," Fanny said.

"Not as far as she was concerned."

"Are you going to tell me what happened to her, or do I have to Google it?" she asked, pulling her phone out of her purse.

"Of course I'm going to tell you! I told you I'd answer your questions," Sondra sighed. "Lianne was very self-conscious about her small breasts. She went to a cut-rate doctor and got implants. Unfortunately, they were faulty. The next time she flew, her breasts exploded."

"Wait...she was killed by her breasts?" Fanny frowned.

"In a nutshell, yes."

"That...can that really happen?"

Reuben shrugged, Patrick nodded, and Sondra said, "Of course it can happen! It happened to Lianne!"

"Sounds to me like she just wanted out of Hollywood. I bet she faked her death."

"Don't be ridiculous," Sondra said, exasperated.

A different server returned to the table and set their appetizers before them.

Reuben nodded his thanks and the young man retreated. "Try the tostones, Sondra. I think you'll really like them."

"How is that more ridiculous than death by implant?" Fanny asked, refusing to abandon the conversation.

"Lianne wouldn't have just...left me! She was my best friend!"

"You can be more than a little self-centered. Maybe you just didn't notice--"

Patrick slapped his hand on the table, rattling the silverware and startling Fanny into silence. "That's enough. I'll not have you talk to your mother that way in my presence."

"It's fine," Sondra soothed, rubbing the back of his hand.

"No, it most certainly is not." Turning to Fanny, he said, "Now, I don't know what all has passed between you two in the past, but it's all water under the bridge these days. Your mother has been through the wringer in the last few months -- Vivian tried to kill her, Ethan left her, and, just a few days ago, a woman at my country club threatened her."

"What? Why?" asked Fanny.

"Do you need an order of protection, Sondra?" Reuben asked.

"Of course not. She's just a jealous woman who had her eye on Patrick." Sondra took one of the tostones and bit into it. It tasted nothing at all like a banana -- more like a particularly crunchy tater tot.

"I don't think Dr. Glew will actually hurt her--"

"The dentist?" Reuben's jaw dropped again.

"You know her?" Patrick asked.

"Yes. She's one of my clients. I have to say I never would have imagined her threatening anyone."

The young waiter approached their table again. "Are you ready to order?"

"I haven't even looked at the menu," Sondra said, wondering if they were even going to make it to the main course.

"Let me order for everyone," Reuben offered. "I've had everything on the menu."

The other three agreed and he rattled off four different entrees. "That way, we can all sample a little of everyone else's dish."

"This isn't Chinese food, Reuben," Fanny admonished.

"I think it's a great idea. Since I've never had Cuban," Sondra added.

The conversation veered away from Bill and the past. Sondra sipped her wine silently, wishing she had a couple whiskey sours in front of her. The sangria wasn't doing much to take the edge off her memories. Fanny was as silent as she was -- probably smarting from Patrick's rebuke. Though he shouldn't have done it, Sondra was thankful that he had. No one had ever defended her like that. And even if she didn't deserve the defense, she still felt a welling of warmth toward him.

When the food arrived, the table fell silent, except for the occasional "try this" or "wow." The food was, as promised, delicious. Unfortunately, it was soaking up the alcohol and eliminating Sondra's buzz. The pitcher of sangria was empty. She waved down the waiter and ordered a whiskey sour, even though Fanny shot her a dirty look. Sondra didn't care what her daughter thought -- she was aiming for a level of drunkenness to which she didn't usually aspire.

Thankfully, Reuben and Patrick seemed genuinely interested in talking to one another; their conversation masked the fact that Sondra and Fanny were fuming at each other.

By the time the plates were cleared away, Sondra was onto her third whiskey sour and her mind was a tabula rasa. She could even look at Fanny again without feeling the heat of anger rise within her. "You know, I nearly aborted you," she slurred in a matter-of-fact tone.

"What?"

She repeated herself: "I nearly had an abortion. I called Lianne and asked her to drive me to the clinic, but she wouldn't."

Patrick placed a cautionary hand against her shoulder.

"No, don't stop me. She wanted to know the truth, the whole truth, and nothing but the truth. If *Siege of the Moon* had been a hit, I never would have had you. I wanted my career more than I wanted children."

Patrick stood up and lifted Sondra to her feet. "Forgive her, Fanny, Reuben. She's had a little too much to drink."

"No need to shield me from that. She's been a drunk my whole life."

In a fit of pique, Sondra grabbed a full glass and doused her daughter in water and ice. Patrick, grasping her by the shoulders, steered her from the restaurant.

When she opened her eyes the next morning, Sondra's head felt like it weighed a hundred pounds. Even the silence of her bedroom seemed too loud to her. Groaning, she rolled away from the door, just in case Claire decided to check in on her. She couldn't remember the last time she drank so much in so short a time, but she definitely remembered why she hadn't. She wracked her brain trying to remember how to cure a hangover. The only thing she could think of was having "a hair of the dog" -- a wake-up whiskey sour -- but that would require her to stand up, walk to the living room (which was guaranteed to be too bright), and fill a glass. Failing to see how she could even get out of bed, she let her eyes close again.

The image of Fanny doused in water appeared on the insides of her eyelids; her eyes popped open again in horror. She had only just made amends with her daughter. And what had she done to her budding relationship with Patrick? She imagined Dr. Glew would get her shot at him after all. More than sixty years on the planet, and she still hadn't learned a thing.

She fervently hoped that reincarnation was a myth; if it wasn't, she feared her next life would be much more unpleasant.

New Life

New Life

There was a Crooked Man

When Sax showed Don the photo of "Elizabeth"/Thora Herbert, he recognized her immediately, eliminating the need for him to sit down with a sketch artist. A few days later, he managed to stop Bruno on his way into Club Medici. One pair of tickets to *Wicked* later, Bruno shared that Thora was definitely pregnant and still in the valley. He had also pointed her in the direction of a coin collector willing to buy black-market goods. Though he wouldn't give him Thora's phone number, he promised to call her and convey Sax's request that she contact him.

Sax tracked the coin collector down at an antique fair that weekend. With Don at his side, he scanned through several cases of coins before the young man pointed excitedly at a familiar piece.

"That's mine!" Don stage-whispered, drawing the attention of the dealer.

"You find something you like, son?" asked the salt-and-pepper-bearded man.

Sax flashed his PI credentials. "Sax Ridley. How are you today?"

"Fine," the man answered warily. "Can I help you two?"

"Could you pull that coin out of the case, please?"

"That's a rare piece. I'd just as soon it stay protected."

Don looked like he was going to object, but Sax held up a hand to silence him. "We have reason to believe that you obtained this coin and another one from a thief."

"Listen," the man said, puffing out his chest, "all of my sources are reputable--"

Sax whipped out the photo of Thora and slid it across the glass toward him. "She sold you two coins, didn't she?"

The man hesitated before saying, "I never saw her before."

"Interesting. How coincidental that you ended up in possession of two rare coins she is suspected of stealing."

"Two? You only found one."

Sax pushed his finger along the glass until it came to rest over a coin that looked exactly like the one Trevor Vallejo was missing. He tapped his finger meaningfully over it. "Shall we try this again?"

"You can't prove I knew they were stolen." He glanced around furtively.

The place was packed; Sax was certain the guy didn't want his business ethics called into question in the midst of so many potential customers. He peeled a thousand dollars -- part of Vallejo's money -- out of his money clip. "I could call the police and cause a hassle, but no one wants that, do they?"

The man gave him one quick head-shake.

"How about I give you $1,000 for the pair?"

"That's less than half of what I paid," he whined.

"I guess that would be the price of doing business. Might even be a lesson for you to remember in the future."

The man scowled. "I'm too old to be learning any new lessons. I need at least two thousand."

"That's a shame. Don, keep an eye on the coins. If he tries to take them out of the case, give a shout." He turned slightly away from the dealer and pulled out his cell phone with a flourish.

"Okay!" the guy half-screamed. "Okay. I'll take a thousand."

Sax, smiling to himself, considered dropping his offer to nine hundred before shrugging and saying, "Wrap 'em up."

He and Don were out the door in minutes. The younger man turned and asked, "Were you really going to call the cops?"

"No. I didn't have any way of proving he was dealing in stolen merchandise."

"What if he had called your bluff?"

"We would have walked away."

Don shook his head incredulously.

"Hey, we got the coins, didn't we?"

"Yeah. Thanks for that. I'm glad Eliza...I mean, Thora...won't get in any trouble."

"How can you be so forgiving of a girl who stole from you?"

"If what you told me about Vallejo is true, she must have been desperate to get away from him. Plus, she's pregnant, and the baby might still be mine. We don't know for sure yet."

Sax sighed. "Don't get your hopes up, Don. I think you were just a mark for her."

New Life

Sax spent the next few days staking out the Walmart where Thora purchased the pregnancy test. It was a long shot, but it was still the only lead he had. He sat on a bench just inside the store and stared at every possibly pregnant pale-complexioned shopper who passed by. Some of them hurried past him, averting their eyes in discomfort. One tattooed young woman stopped and stared him down, giving Sax ample time to determine that while she was pregnant, she certainly was not Thora Herbert. Finally, a harried manager approached him and asked him to leave.

"Why? I'm not doing anything wrong."

"You don't appear to be a customer," the woman answered. "Therefore, you are loitering on store property. We don't allow that."

"Fine." He stood up, towering over the blue-vested authority. "I'll just go buy something."

"I think it would be better if you just left, sir." She straightened up and put her hands on her hips like a stern mother.

"But why? I haven't done anything wrong."

"You've made a number of young women uncomfortable."

"How?"

"By staring at them like a lecherous pervert."

"Perhaps they would be less uncomfortable if I wore something that identified me as gay. I think I have a rainbow sticker in my car..." he said, smirking.

"If you're gay, why are you staring at women?"

He pulled out his wallet and showed her his PI license. "I'm looking for a pregnant woman who is known to shop here."

She dropped her arms. "Oh. Is she in trouble?"

"Nothing serious. I just need to contact her -- a friend asked me to make sure that she was all right."

"Do you have a picture of her?"

Sax held his phone out to her so that she could see Thora's face. A moment of recognition altered her features. "I'm sorry, but I don't know her."

"You don't need to lie for her. I promise you, I'm no threat."

"I don't know who told you they had seen this girl, but I'm sure they were mistaken."

"Now you're just being ridiculous--" he glanced at her name badge "--Joy. This is a huge store; there is simply no way that you can guarantee me she has never been here."

"I have a really good memory. And you need to leave." He saw her look over his shoulder and push her chin up, no doubt calling the security guard from the mall entrance of the store.

"Fine." He pulled a business card from his wallet and handed it to Joy. "When she shows up again, ask her to call me."

"I already told you--"

"Maybe she'll magically appear." He turned on his heel as a fat man in a rent-a-cop outfit approached him. "I'm going," Sax said, holding up his hands. "I can find the exit."

"Did you find Thora, too?" Vallejo asked as he turned the coin over in his hand. Though Eric had been dismissed, Alicia, dressed in something made of strips of leather, remained sitting on the floor next to the chaise longue where the elegant man had been resting when Sax arrived.

"I'm afraid not. She seems to have vanished."

Trevor gave Sax a knowing smile. "We both know that's not exactly true. Still, you did recover the coin without involving the police. And you did it in remarkably good time."

"May I ask why it was so important to keep the police out of it?"

Trevor chuckled as he glided toward the bar and poured two glasses of brandy. "Gwendy is such an efficient business manager. She reported the coin stolen as soon as the theft was discovered." He held out one of the glasses to Sax and glanced at the glassy-eyed leather-bound girl. As far as Sax could tell, she didn't seem aware of her surroundings -- nevertheless, Trevor pulled out his phone and called for one of his minions to lead her away. "There are some things best discussed in private," he said, gesturing toward one of the tufted purple sofas.

Sax sat down and the two men waited in silence for less than a minute before another starving-thin young man appeared and led Alicia away.

"That's better," Vallejo said, relaxing back onto the chaise. "Sometime I forget they're even around...especially the girls."

Sax, who had been rolling the Gothic would-be prince's words around in his mind, said, "You already collected the insurance money for the coin, didn't you?"

He nodded slightly. "In the end, I'm glad Thora was able to pull off the theft. I'm proud of her -- she's as clever as I suspected."

"How did you get her to do it?"

The dead-eyed stare of a man Sax was beginning to believe was soulless was the only answer he received. "Did you bring your final bill with you?"

"Don't you want me to find Thora Herbert?"

"Now that I have my coin back, I consider that matter of no consequence."

"The retainer Ms. Mosby gave me more than covered the investigation. I can get you a money order for the balance."

"Keep it. Consider it a bonus for a job well done. I'll be holding onto your card, Mr. Ridley. A man like me can always use a good PI." He sipped at his brandy, which reminded Sax that he was holding a glass too. He set it on the small table to the right of the sofa. "You really should have some of the brandy -- it's of the finest quality."

"Thanks, but I'm driving."

"You look like a man who can hold his drink just fine. You own a bar, too -- correct?"

"Nothing like the one you own -- just a neighborhood joint."

"I own clubs, Mr. Ridley. Do you know the difference between a club and a bar?" He didn't wait for an answer. "The cover charge. People pay to see and be seen at my venues. Any money I make on the sale of alcohol is incidental." He drained his glass.

Sax stood. Vallejo reached for his phone but Sax said, "I can see myself out."

"I'll be in touch," the man said to Sax's retreating back.

Sax hoped it was an empty promise.

New Life

When the phone call finally came, Sax was caught off-guard.

"May I speak with Mr. Ridley?" asked a young woman with a clarion voice.

"Speaking," Sax answered. With the grand opening of the new Brass Monkey only a few days away, he was checking the alcohol inventory, leaving room for the open bottles he and Milo would be transporting from the old location the next night.

"Mr. Ridley, my name is Thora Herbert. I understand you've been looking for me."

Sax stopped counting and turned toward Don, who was arranging the last of the newly refinished chairs around their tables. "Yes, Ms. Herbert, I have been."

Don looked up, his eyes wide.

"May I ask why?"

"I was hired by two separate clients to locate you. However, one of them has recently called off the search."

"That wouldn't happen to be Trevor Vallejo, would it?"

"Yes, it would."

"Can I safely assume that he recovered his lost coin, then?"

"Yes, he did."

"I'm afraid you have me at a disadvantage regarding the second party."

"His name is Don Heber."

She didn't respond.

"You stole a coin from him?"

"Oh! You mean the baby bat I let take me home?"

"He would like to see you."

"I'm sure he would," she laughed. "I don't think so. I don't have what he's looking for."

"I recovered his coin as well, Ms. Herbert."

"Aren't you thorough? Still, I don't think seeing me is a great idea."

"Because you're pregnant?"

"Joy told me you thought I was PG. I'm not."

"If you won't see Don, would you meet with me?"

"You're not some kind of perv, are you? Joy and Bruno both said you were gay. True?"

"Yes, that's true."

"Okay. Come to my apartment."

She gave him an address near old-town Glendale. Sax imagined it was one of the small complexes that he had stumbled across in his exploration of the valley. He was disappointed to find himself at a cracker-box complex tucked behind the more picturesque bungalows and long-standing shops and restaurants of the area. Her apartment was a sunken first-level unit. He had just tapped on the door when it opened.

The girl was even taller than Sax had imagined -- at least six feet. Her hair was no longer black; in fact, she had dyed it platinum blonde and gotten a buzz cut. The effect on her looks was startling: where she had once appeared feminine and attractive, she now gave off the vibe of a bull dyke. In addition, she was rail-thin -- if she was pregnant, she hid it well.

"Mr. Ridley?" she asked.

"Yes. Thora Herbert, I presume."

She nodded and stood aside, silently welcoming him into her home. The apartment had a moldy smell and dark-brown carpeting that could hide a multitude of sins. The landlords probably hadn't replaced it in years. Otherwise, the place was neat, if sparsely furnished. If she had made money on the sale of the coins, she certainly hadn't spent much of it on her new place.

"Thanks for agreeing to see me."

"It's the only way I'm going to get the baby bat to forget about me, isn't it?"

"You're still using Goth terminology," he noted.

She rolled her eyes. "Goth isn't just a look, you know. It's an attitude...a way of life. I'll always be Goth." Turning sideways, she said, "As you can see, I'm not pregnant."

"Why did you buy the pregnancy test?"

"To see if I was."

"Were you?"

"Don't you know about female reproductive rights?" she spat. "Oh, wait...I guess you probably don't. All that matters is that I'm not currently with child."

She was still standing. Sax decided to sit down, hoping to pry some more information out of the surly young woman. He took the blue swivel chair and turned it to face her. "So, if you're still a Goth, why did you leave Trevor Vallejo? I'm sure he would have paid for your abortion."

She smiled slowly, narrowing her eyes. "You don't want to mess with Vallejo, old man. He'll tear you up."

"Believe me, I'm not going to. But for my own edification, I'd like to understand."

"Let me see your phone."

"Why?"

"Because I don't want this coming back on me -- ever."

Frowning, he handed her the device. She manipulated it for a minute before determining what Sax already knew: he wasn't recording. "Satisfied?" he asked.

"Yes." She put the phone on the half-wall that separated the kitchen from the living room. "Trevor knew I was leaving -- I never hid anything from him."

"Why were you leaving?"

She shrugged and dropped into the well-worn black sofa, pulling her legs underneath her. "I'm going to be a writer someday."

Sax frowned at the non sequitur. "You couldn't be a writer and live in Trevor's manse?"

She rolled her eyes again. Sax wished they would get stuck. "All the great writers say that in order to write about life you have to live it. Think of Hemingway: he ran with the bulls, documented a war, slept with anyone and everyone, and generally wasn't afraid to experience life."

"So, you lived in the manse because you wanted the experience," Sax surmised.

"That, and to finish my thesis. I'm finishing my Masters in Social Work." She smiled with self-satisfaction.

"Why did you steal the coin from Trevor? Was that just another experience?"

"Everything is experience."

"Why did you take Don's coin?"

"For the thrill, of course. That felt so much more authentic than taking Trevor's coin. With Trevor, it was a business transaction."

"Don really wants to pursue a relationship with you."

"He won't when you tell him I'm not pregnant. Besides, I'm not ready to settle down with anyone yet. I have way too much to accomplish before that happens."

"May I give you a piece of advice?"

She looked at her nails and began casually digging dirt out from beneath them. "If you feel you must."

"Be careful who you hurt with your adventures. Not everyone looks at life the way you do, and you could end up on the wrong side of someone much more dangerous than Trevor Vallejo." Leaning forward and reaching into his back pocket, he pulled out a battered business card. "Call me if you ever need help."

She took the card and examined it. "Saxon, eh? That's a great name. Why'd you shorten it?"

It was his turn to shrug. "It always weighed too heavily on me." He stood and shook her hand before leaving the apartment. Sitting in his car a few minutes later, he remembered a time in his life when he didn't worry about who he hurt. A phantom pain twanged in his broad chest.

New Life

A Wise Old Owl

Sax, knowing that Don was waiting for him, dawdled on the way back to the bar. He liked the guy -- he was earnest and hardworking, if a little misguided. He wished that Thora had broken Don's heart directly instead of using him to do it.

When he finally pulled into the parking lot, he was surprised to see Claire's car. He hadn't seen her in a few weeks -- not since Milo found out about the baby. Hoping he might be able to put Don off, Sax strode into the polished and pristine new business. "Claire! I'm so glad to see you!" he boomed enthusiastically.

She pushed herself out of the chair across from the kid and hugged him. "The place looks fantastic! When do you open?"

"Two days from now. Are you coming to the Grand Opening?"

"Milo invited me -- I haven't decided yet."

"You really should come, ma'am," Don inserted. "It's going to be a great party!"

She smiled and rubbed her hand across her belly. "I'm not in any condition to drink."

He hitched his thumb over his shoulder. "Then come for the games," he said, indicating the two pool tables and the dartboards behind him.

"I'll think about it," she answered.

Shrugging, he turned to Sax. "Will Thora see me now?"

"I think we should talk about that later."

"At least tell me: is she pregnant?"

He shook his head. "False alarm. We'll talk later."

Don frowned, creasing his forehead. "My friend was so sure..."

"He was wrong. Why don't you take off for a while? I'll call you later."

"He doesn't need to leave on my account," Claire said.

"That's okay. I'm hungry anyway. Can I bring you anything?" Don stood up and headed toward the door.

"No, thanks," Sax answered, taking his seat.

Claire sat down across from him as the door swung closed. "You could have talked to him -- I would have waited."

Sax pushed a couple of fingers against his temple. "I'm not ready to have that conversation yet."

"Bad news, huh?"

"It'll seem bad to him right now. Someday, though, he'll have the good sense to be relieved. Now, why are you here? Not that I don't appreciate the visit..."

"...But I don't come around much, do I? Especially not lately." She glanced pointedly at her midriff.

"Milo says you won't marry him."

"Always the pessimist, isn't he? I told him I'd think about it."

"I'm going to tell you a story," Sax said.

"What?" She frowned as if she hadn't heard him right.

"Don't worry, I have a point."

"Sax, I didn't come here for advice."

"Yes, you did. Why else would you come all the way out here, to an empty bar, when you are seven-months pregnant?"

"You're my friend?" She squirmed uncomfortably in her chair.

"Thank you for that, but you have other friends who are closer at hand -- Sondra, for one."

"Okay," she said, nodding, "you're right. But it's not advice I need so much as a clearer perspective. I feel like this pregnancy has clogged my intuition."

"I'm going to tell you a story," he repeated, "and this time, don't interrupt."

She pulled her fingers across her lips, miming a zipper, and smiled, closed-mouthed, at him.

"I was in love once, a long time ago. He was my soul mate."

Sax knew he was different when he was only five years old. It wasn't that obvious -- after all, the other boys his age weren't chasing girls yet. But when Tommy moved in next door, Sax felt as if his world had shifted on its axis.

Tommy was lithe and handsome in a way that would, decades later, be called androgynous. He was a few years older -- eight to Sax's five -- but he was kind to his younger neighbor. Sax followed him around like a lost puppy for years, watching as his friend stayed thin and grew taller while he himself broadened into his football-player build. By the time Tommy was eighteen, Sax knew he was what the other guys accused Tommy of being: a fag, a homo, a queer. There was no name for it that sounded good or polite; even "gay" was a word people whispered back then.

"How do you stand it?" Sax asked Tommy one Indian-summer day after school. They sat on the short retaining wall that surrounded their lawns, breathing in the sweet smell of dying leaves and admiring their colors.

"I'll be gone soon," Tommy said. "In just a few months, I will graduate and leave this town behind. Those words they throw at me hurt about as much as one of those leaves landing on my shoulder." The talented young musician had a number of schools vying for him -- college was in his future.

"They aren't right, are they?" Sax asked. "You're not...?"

"What if I were? They're still just words."

Sax reddened. He felt eyes on him and looked up to find Tommy studying him.

"Saxon! Come inside! You need to do your homework!" his mother shouted from the doorway of their small home.

"I didn't know," Tommy whispered urgently.

Sax's eyes widened. He stood up and backed away, shaking his head. "No! You don't know." He broke into a run, allowing the demon specter to chase him inside and away from Tommy.

Sax avoided his friend for weeks after that, walking to school early and staying late nearly every day to practice with his teammates. When his fellow football players threw hateful words at Tommy, Sax would avoid his friend's penetrating gaze and snicker with the rest of them. When Sax did look at Tommy, he had to ignore the pain he saw there and push down his empathy until it didn't bother to come back up.

A layer of snow covered the ground before they spoke again. Hoping that their last conversation had been forgotten, he greeted Tommy with a non-committal "hey."

"Hey," he answered. He was sitting on the front steps of his home, watching his little sister try to build a snowman out of the scant white stuff that barely covered the dead grass beneath.

"Hi, Saxon!" squealed the little girl, a motormouth of a child with red pigtails. "Where have you been? We've missed you a lot, haven't we, Tommy? You wanna help me build a snowman? I think there's just enough snow to do it, but Tommy says I'm wrong. Am I wrong, Saxon? You tell him I'm not wrong."

He patted the girl's hair and climbed the stairs to sit next to Tommy. "Keep trying. I'll watch."

She shrugged and busied herself with her impossible task.

"You're a coward," Tommy said bluntly, staring straight ahead, ostensibly watching his sister.

"No, I'm not."

"You let those guys call me names and you just stand there, laughing."

"You said that the words hurt you less than a leaf falling on your shoulder."

"Maybe so, but if you stand under a tree long enough, you can get buried in leaves." The pain etched itself across his face, aging him.

For a moment, Sax caught a glimpse of his friend as an old man. "I'm sorry."

"Boys like us should stick together." Tommy reached over and took his hand.

Sax felt a bolt of lightning fly through his body, quickening his spirit. "I think about you all the time," he whispered.

They both heard the squeak of Sax's house door -- it was always louder in the winter -- and they quickly pulled away from each other. "Saxon! Come help me with the furnace! It's acting up again."

"I've gotta go," he said unnecessarily.

"Come over later. My parents are going into the city to see a show tonight. It'll just be me and my sister."

He didn't answer aloud, just nodded.

After dinner, he told his mother he was going to one of the football players' homes for a party.

"Do you need to take a gift?"

"It's not that kind of party, Ma," he said, kissing her on the top of her head.

"Don't stay out too late. We have church in the morning."

He slipped out of the house and stole across the yard. Snow was falling again, and he felt the flakes land and melt against his cheeks. The little girl had managed to create the tiniest of snowmen; the gnome-sized creature stood forlornly in the middle of the yard, its knit doll's hat drooping under the weight of the fresh flakes. Standing on the porch, he experienced an aftershock from his earlier lightning bolt as he rapped softly on the door.

Tommy opened it. "I didn't know if you would come."

"I needed to see you." He walked into the familiar home; he had been invited in many times over the last ten years by Tommy's sweet, redheaded mother. The home felt so different from the one he'd been raised in. It was full of instruments, exotic art, and comfortable furniture, but Sax had always thought the real difference between this home and his own was the presence of a man. Tommy's father was a composer, though he frequently made light of his profession. "I'm a jingle writer," he had once told Sax. "None of my compositions are more than thirty seconds long." Sax's own father had never come home from the war.

"I already put my sister to bed. She won't bother us," Tommy said, taking Sax's hand and leading him into the living room.

Sax felt himself harden; embarrassed, he sat down as soon as he was near a chair and crossed his legs.

"Are you all right?" Tommy asked.

"I'm fine. I just...wanted to sit."

"Of course." Tommy lowered himself gracefully onto the couch. Sax had never seen anyone as graceful as Tommy -- not even the movie stars compared in his mind. "I wanted to tell you...I think about you all the time, too."

"But it's wrong, isn't it, Tommy? The church says it's a sin!"

"I'm sure if God had written the Good Book himself instead of farming it out to a bunch of scribes, that bit wouldn't have even been in there. If God really hates fags so much, why isn't there a commandment that says so?"

Sax leaned back in the chair. "Are you saying the Bible got it wrong?"

"I think the Bible was written for God by men, and men sometimes get things wrong. But we were made by God, and

He never gets anything wrong." He knelt in front of him and pulled Sax's face toward his, their lips touching for the first time. If his hand was like a lightning bolt, his kiss was like an electrical storm. Sax knew, without a doubt, that he loved Tommy.

They didn't hear the door open; instead, Tommy's mother's gasp was what broke them apart. His father, just a moment behind her, shouted, "What in the name of all that is holy are you doing to that boy?!" He flew across the room, dragging Tommy to his feet and punching him hard across the cheek. Sax watched as Tommy's neck snapped like a rubber band.

"No! Don't hit him! God, please don't hit him!" Tommy's mother cried out as his father continued to pummel him.

Sax, true to his cowardly nature, crept from the house, leaving the family in turmoil. He never saw Tommy again.

"I have never let myself trust in love again," Sax concluded. "I have spent my life going from one meaningless relationship to another, getting involved with men who weren't free to be with me. Tommy was right when he called me a coward. And I'm right when I say I see a lot of me in you."

She sat up straight. "I'm not--"

"Yes, you are. Look at what you're doing: you are threatening to deprive your daughter of an intact family because you are afraid of being hurt. I know what it feels like to lose the most important person in your world. But you can't let that stop you from being happy again."

She slumped against the back of the chair. "You're right. I love Milo."

"And I know for a fact that he adores you. Let's make a pact: I'll stop running away if you will."

She smiled and held up her hand, her pinkie sticking out toward him. "Pinkie swear?"

"You got it, babe." They linked fingers and Sax grinned at his friend. "Now, I've got a bit of a crush on someone you know. Any chance you could help me out with that?"

New Life

With only one day left until the new Brass Monkey opened, Sax knew he should be taking care of the final details at the bar. Nevertheless, he was strolling through the zoo with Claire at his side and a tin of Altoids in his pocket. "Are you sure this is a good choice?"

"Trust me. The man eats them like candy."

"You're sure he's single?"

"He was the last time we talked about it," she shrugged. "Of course, there are no guarantees."

Sax stopped and took a deep breath, attempting to exhale his nerves.

"What's wrong?" Claire asked, rubbing his back like an experienced mother.

"I've never asked anyone on a date before."

"Never? How did you...?"

He smiled wryly. "I was younger, I worked out, and men hit on me."

"What about Bob?" she asked, referring to Sax's most recent lover -- the one whose wife had been accidentally blown to bits.

"He flirted with me."

"It's going to be fine," she soothed. "You are still a handsome guy. You're in great shape, you're a business owner, and you look two decades younger than you are."

"But how long will that be true?" he asked, latching onto her last few words. "I'm seventy years old! How much longer am I going to be a fit companion for anyone?"

"Look at Jack LaLanne -- he was in great shape right up to the day he died! In his nineties, no less! You take great care of yourself...who knows how long you'll live?"

"Once you're past seventy, you're living on borrowed time. The Bible says man gets three score and ten years."

"It's amazing how much and how selectively you remember that book," she said, grinning. "As I recall, there's also a character named Methuselah who lived nearly a thousand years."

Sax laughed and the panic lifted. He straightened and smiled at Claire. "You're right. Let's do this."

They walked toward Monkey Village and Zareb, the handsome African gatekeeper.

New Life

Girls and Boys Come Out to Play

On the first Friday in May, the new Brass Monkey opened. George, the eponymous brass statue, was ceremoniously inserted into his place of honor behind the bar; the event was documented in a number of photographs taken with cell phones, digital cameras, and one antique box camera with Milo behind the lens.

"Everyone, hold still!" he commanded from under the black draping. In the frame -- upside down of course -- he could see everyone who mattered to him. To the right of the monkey stood Sax, Sondra, and Claire. On the left, Brian, Marla and Eric smiled at the camera. Peeking over the edge of the bar, Alice Marie was sticking her tongue out at him playfully. "Pull your tongue in, young lady, and don't wiggle! This will take about a minute."

"Invest in a digital camera, Dad!" Brian said, causing the whole group to laugh.

"Film is more permanent," Milo insisted. "Now, on the count of three, hold your pose! One...two...three!" He exposed the film and waited, watching through the viewer as his family and friends tried to stand still and hold their expressions in place. It seemed to Milo he could see the children growing, Brian getting older, and even Claire holding -- instead of carrying -- their daughter. In that long minute, he imagined their future. Glancing down at his stopwatch, he closed the flap on the film and released them from their poses.

When he extracted himself from the black drape of fabric, Claire was beside him, smiling. "I'm glad you came."

"Thank you for inviting me," she answered.

"I will always want you with me." He folded in the wooden legs of the tripod and prepared to move the apparatus to his office -- an uncluttered space that Sax had thoughtfully furnished with an old desk and a comfortable chair, as well as a relatively new computer.

"I believe you," she said, putting her hand on his upper arm and stopping him in his tracks.

"You do?"

"I do."

He stared at her for a moment; she just smiled at him.

New Life

The door at the front of the bar swung open, temporarily blinding him. By the time he could see again, Claire had turned away to talk to Zareb, who had tapped her on the shoulder.

"I'm so glad you could make it!" she said, hugging the imposing monkey-house bouncer.

"Thank you, Miss Claire, for introducing me to Sax. He is a very charming man." Zareb's smile was beautiful to see -- Milo couldn't remember ever seeing him light up so completely when he'd seen him at the zoo.

Sax appeared at Milo's side. "Great day, isn't it?"

"So far, it's perfect. Listen -- I need to run home for a minute. Could you cover for me?"

"Is something wrong?"

"No. Don't worry. Everything's fine."

The crowd was thickening. Holding the bulky camera out in front of him, he made his way toward his office.

"I've been looking for you!" exclaimed Sonia, his real estate agent. She was wearing one of her tight-fitting sweaters, this one a pleasantly fuzzy aqua-blue number.

"I'm kind of in a hurry right now," he answered over the buzz of voices.

"But I got an offer on your house! Full price! Can we talk in your office?"

"I really need to--"

"The only catch is that they need your acceptance by five o'clock today!"

"As soon as I get back--"

"It's four-thirty, Milo."

He glanced at his watch: four-twenty-five. "Look, I've got a similar window of opportunity to propose," he said apologetically as he pushed past her. "Put the papers on my desk -- I'll sign as soon as I have the ring on her finger!"

"Milo! The housing market sucks right now! You might never get another offer like this!" Sonia scolded, her fists resting angrily on her hips.

Hesitating, he realized he was putting more than just her commission at risk -- the house had to be sold for him, Claire and the baby to have a secure future. But there would be no future to secure if Claire didn't marry him. "Sorry," he said with a shrug.

He trotted down the hall, stowed his camera in the office, and exited the building through the back door. He threw himself into his car and peeled out of the parking lot toward his duplex. Inside the house, he ran to the bedroom and dug the small jewelry box out from beneath a layer of underwear. He dropped it into the big pocket on the front of his Guayabera.

He glanced at his watch as he drove back into the bar parking lot -- the trip home and back had taken twenty-five minutes, leaving only ten minutes to secure Claire's hand and sign the paperwork. He searched the crowd, hoping to spot her based almost exclusively on the amount of room she currently required. No such luck. Morgana was behind the bar, slinging drinks as fast as she could. Milo headed straight for her. Catching her attention, he asked, "Have you seen Claire?"

Morgana shook her head. "Sorry -- it's been busy around here, in case you haven't noticed. Help a girl out?"

He shook his head. "Can't right now." Don, looking lost and forlorn, sat on a stool next to where he stood. Nudging him on the shoulder, he said, "Hey, hop behind the bar and give Morgana a hand."

"But I'm not a bartender."

"You're over eighteen, right? That's all we need for now. Clear empties and take payment. Morgana can handle the rest."

"Thanks, Milo!" she shouted at his retreating back.

Seven minutes left. He spotted Sonia waving frantically from the entrance to his office. Turning deliberately away, he found Sondra sitting at a small table with Sax and Zareb. "Have any of you seen Claire?" he shouted.

"She's in the bathroom," Sondra answered.

"Could you get her for me?"

"Relax -- I think she's too big around to fall in these days!"

"No," he said, pulling the box from his pocket, "I'm on a deadline!"

They all smiled at him as if he were a lunatic.

"Really! I need to make sure she'll marry me before I sign the papers to sell the house!"

"You're selling your house?" Sax asked.

"Do I look like I have time to talk about this right now?"

"I'll get her," Sondra said. "Sax, get this crowd to shut up; I want to hear Claire say yes! Follow me, Milo."

As it always did for Sondra, the crowd parted and let her pass. Milo followed in her wake. When they reached the hallway, Sondra ducked into the ladies' room.

"Milo! Come on! The clock's ticking!" Sonia nearly screamed.

"I've got something I have to do first." Carefully, he lowered himself to one knee and opened the box. The diamond ring inside fairly glittered under the hallway's track lighting. As he held it out in front of him, the bar crowd fell silent. One by one, they turned to watch Milo and wait for Claire to appear. Glancing up, Milo saw that someone -- probably Brian -- had lifted Alice Marie onto one of the tables so that she could see him. He winked at his granddaughter, who winked back at him and giggled.

"...know how strange you are being, Sondra?" Claire asked as she was pushed into the hallway. "What's going...." She stopped talking when she realized the entire crowd had been waiting for her to emerge from the restroom. Her eyes widened in silent shock. When she looked down, her expression softened.

"Claire, my love, I don't want to spend another moment without you by my side. Please do me the honor of agreeing to be my wife." He pulled the ring out of the box and held it toward her.

She nodded.

"What was that?" yelled someone in the crowd. "We didn't hear you!"

"Yes!" she shouted hoarsely. "Yes, I'll marry him!"

A shout of celebration went up from the bar patrons as she held out her hand. Milo slid the ring onto her finger, only to have it stop just above the middle. He looked up in horror.

"Pregnancy bloat," she said, smiling. "It will fit perfectly in a few months."

"Sign this," Sonia said, shoving the paperwork between them and holding a pen out to Milo.

Milo looked at his watch again. "It's already too late, Sonia. We'll have to wait for another buyer."

New Life

"We've got a few months," Claire said. "I'm not due until the beginning of June anyway."

Sonia, her eyes closed, shook her head in frustration. "Congratulations to you both. I need a drink."

New Life

Oranges and Lemons

Sondra marveled at the speed with which Claire moved out of the condo and back in with Milo. One might think they were in love, she mused as she sat in the now-silent apartment. All but the heartiest of her massive rose bouquet had died; the last three, which she had removed to a smaller vase a few days before, were looking droopy now.

Patrick hadn't called since their disastrous dinner with Fanny and Reuben. Sondra now thought of it as her very own Cuban Missile Crisis. She had shared this *bon mot* with Sax at the Brass Monkey's grand opening, but he had been less amused by it than she had hoped. Instead, she had received sympathy from both him and his handsome date, which had driven her to the bar. There, she met Sonia Belcourt; the two of them had traded rounds and war stories until they were loaded bodily into Sax's car and driven to their respective homes by the happy new gay couple.

She suspected she was becoming more like Norma Desmond than that bitchy interviewer of thirty years ago had ever envisioned. Like that unhappy character, her beauty had faded and her ability to catch and hold a man through her mystique was an illusion. It didn't help that she was prone to similar temper tantrums. Of course, after what she had said to her daughter, she feared Patrick and Reuben were likening her to Joan Crawford. Sondra had met Joan once or twice; Bill and she had been co-stars years before. She was an unpleasant, jealous woman. Being compared to her was infinitely worse than being compared to a delusional -- and fictional -- character.

At least she had an easy living. The money from the Sunrise Aeon franchise was more than enough to keep her comfortably in the condo -- though she feared Milo and Claire would ask her to leave after the baby came. She kept her fingers crossed that they would receive another offer on Milo's place soon.

She wanted to sit on the balcony, but the blast of heat from an unseasonably warm May day kept her inside. Instead, she fixed herself a drink. So what if the clock said it was only ten -- it was noon on the East Coast.

New Life

Someone rang her doorbell. "Just a minute," she called, sipping the drink and gliding toward the door. Looking through the peephole, she found Patrick standing on the other side, his arms behind his back. Quickly setting the drink just around the corner in the galley kitchen and smoothing her hands over her hair and down her loose-fitting dress, she called out again, "Just a minute!"

She was sure he said for her to take her time, but she didn't want to risk him changing his mind and disappearing. She took one deep breath, exhaled slowly, and opened the door.

"Hello, Sondra," he said, a gentle smile on his face.

"Patrick! What a surprise to see you here, today."

"I was in the neighborhood. May I come in?"

Realizing she hadn't moved to one side, she blushed. "Yes, of course. Please."

He stepped inside and wrapped his arms around her, catching her off-guard. She hesitated before hugging him back. "I'm sorry," he whispered against her hair.

"I'm the one who should apologize. I said such horrible things--"

"You didn't say them to me, though. I never should have disappeared like I did." He squeezed her as tightly as he could against him before pushing her back, his hands on her shoulders. "I wasn't prepared for how much anger a child can have for her mother. I thought she must have a reason -- more of a reason than I perceived, you see."

She broke away and went to the living room, wishing she hadn't put the drink in the kitchen. "So you thought I was a monster." She swept across the room dramatically and lowered herself into her armchair.

"I thought...I don't know exactly what I thought. I guess I worried that you weren't showing me the real you."

"So why are you here? Did you miss me so much you decided the monster in me didn't matter?"

He sat down on the sofa, leaning forward with his bony elbows balanced on his long legs. "I went to see my former brother-in-law and your ex-fiancé."

She leaned back in the chair. "Why would you do that?"

"To ask his opinion of you."

She laughed. "Ethan isn't much of a judge of character."

"On the contrary, I find his taste in women impeccable."

"Vivian was a serial killer!"

"You can't pick your relatives, Sondra. I'm sure Fanny would agree." He arched an eyebrow and smiled playfully at her. "Speaking of your daughter, have you heard from her?"

"No, and I don't expect I will."

"Don't be so sure about that. Reuben tells me she's terribly embarrassed about what she did."

"You've talked to Reuben, too?"

He nodded. "He called me the next day to apologize for Fanny's behavior and to invite me to play golf with him."

Her eyebrows shot up. "He apologized for her?"

"Apparently, when she sobered up the next day, she was appalled by what she had done. She knew she pushed you into a corner. Reuben said it would probably take her a few weeks to get around to apologizing to you, but she knows it wasn't your fault."

The relief was physical -- it knocked the wind out of her and made her lungs and eyes burn. A sob tore its way through her body and out of her mouth. Patrick moved closer and took her hand. When she regained her breath, she said, "Thank you."

"I haven't done anything but cause you additional pain!"

She squeezed his hand. "You just gave me the best news I've ever gotten: my daughter doesn't hate me!"

He laughed in amazement. "No, of course she doesn't! You may not be perfect, but you've always been there for her -- anytime she needed you."

"What did Ethan say about me that changed your mind?"

"He said he is and always will be profoundly grateful to have known you. If it weren't for you, he and Emlyn never would have gotten their second chance at love. And he was overwhelmingly happy that I was seeing you."

"He's a goodhearted boy," she said, leaning toward him. "But I need a man."

"Flatterer."

"I try."

He sniffed her breath and frowned. "Have you been drinking already this morning?"

"I had a sip of a whiskey sour two seconds before you knocked on the door."

"It's ten o'clock."

"I was pretending I was in New York."

"Let's both pretend we're someplace a little more romantic."

"How does Belize sound?" she asked, leading him toward the bedroom.

"Perfect."

That afternoon, while Patrick recovered his strength with a nap, Sondra wrapped a satin robe around herself and silently left the bedroom to call Fanny. Her daughter picked up after just one ring.

"Ma? Are you okay?"

"I'm fine. I just wanted to apologize to you for...what happened."

"It wasn't all you," Fanny sighed. "I provoked you, I know. Reuben says it sounded even worse than I remember."

"That was still no reason for me to say those things to you. I wanted you, baby. The only reason I considered an abortion at all was because of a misunderstanding between your father and me. When he realized I was pregnant, he went out and bought me the biggest diamond ring I'd ever seen."

"Why didn't you get married?"

"It was the Seventies. Everyone my age thought marriage was an old-fashioned institution."

"So it wasn't because you wanted to be able to leave him if someone better came along?"

"Listen to me: I never would have left Bill. I loved your father more than I ever have or ever will love anyone. Though I'm pretty fond of Patrick."

"He looks a lot like Dad."

"Yes," Sondra answered wistfully, "he does. But it's more than that. It's the way he looks at the world -- and at me. I think I could be happy with him."

"Happier than you were with Ethan?"

"I was always waiting for him to leave me. What does a young man want with an old woman? I couldn't give him children, and our time together was guaranteed to be shorter than a more evenly matched couple."

"Reuben says you and I are more alike than we are different."

"He's probably right -- we're both ridiculously stubborn."

"He says we're like oranges and lemons -- sometimes sweet, sometimes sour, but always acidic."

Sondra, caught off guard, let out a belly laugh that caused the snoring in the next room to miss a beat. She whispered, "What a perceptive man."

"I sometimes think he prefers you over me. You should have heard how he defended you!"

"Smart son-in-law, but not such a wise husband. You tell him thanks, but that next time he should back you one-hundred percent. After all, he's sleeping next to you."

"I'll let him know. Are you and Patrick coming to Belize next month?"

"I just talked to him about that a little while ago," she said, remembering the conversation they had shared just before he sank into that coma-like state most men seem to experience after a rambunctious bout of lovemaking. They had determined that if pretending they were in Belize was half as fun as actually visiting the country, they should buy their tickets immediately. "As long as we're still invited, we'd love to come."

"Of course you are. Ike and Naomi are looking forward to seeing you."

They chatted a few more minutes. She asked her daughter how their progress toward adoption was proceeding, and Fanny was positive they would have a child soon. Sondra asked about Hunter, too, and was pleased to hear he would be home from college in just a week.

At the end of the call, she said, "I love you, Fanny."

"I love you, too, Ma."

She hung up the phone and went to the kitchen, retrieving her watered-down whiskey sour. Cheers, Norma Desmond, she thought to herself. She knocked back the drink and smiled.

New Life

New Life

Nuts in May

The day after their engagement, Milo helped Claire move back into Sun City, even though they both knew it was only a temporary solution. While Milo worked at the bar, Claire carefully packed his cameras, his collection of elephants, and other mementos of his life. With every piece, she felt she knew him better.

Occasionally, she would hold out an item, leaving it on the table as a reminder to ask Milo who had given it to him or where it was from. Since he almost always arrived home after she was sleeping -- he still worked until at least eleven most nights -- she would ask him the next morning as they lay in bed: "Where did the tiny white elephant come from?"

"It's from India. Years ago, a friend of mine wanted to go on an exotic vacation. He chose India as his destination. This was probably thirty years ago now -- people didn't travel then like they do today. His wife was reluctant to go, but eventually he talked her into it. They tried to get Alice and me to go with them--"

"You didn't call her dead Alice!" Claire said with surprise.

"Huh...you're right." He pulled Claire closer, and she felt her roundness press into his side. "As I'm sure you can guess, Alice wasn't getting on a plane to India for anything."

"Did you want to go?"

"I always wanted to travel overseas. The only country I ever visited was Vietnam, though." He paused. "Do you like to travel?"

"I've never done much of it, but I'm sure I would."

"Might be difficult with the little one," he said, patting her belly affectionately. "Maybe in a few years, though. I bet Marla would watch her if we asked."

"So, your friend..."

"Oh, yes. They went. Had a great time. Brought me back that little ivory elephant."

His life was full of aborted adventures and missed opportunities, things delayed and eventually forgotten. When she came to the abstract orange ashtray that reminded her of her childhood, she set it on the table.

"Did you smoke?" she asked the next morning.

"In Vietnam, everyone smoked. We didn't know it was bad for us yet -- they used to give us smokes as part of our rations, you know."

"But when you were home, did you smoke?"

"Not before I joined the service. Afterward, when I came back to Alice and Brian, I had a half-a-pack-a-day habit. I convinced Alice to take it up; she was having trouble losing the baby weight and everyone was saying they were great for weight loss."

"When did you quit?"

"I don't know...a few years after I was back. It was more of a hassle than a joy by then. Running out of cigarettes in the middle of a Minnesota blizzard was like Dante's seventh circle of Hell. Finally, I just quit."

"What about Alice?"

"She never did. I always felt guilty for starting her down that path. I used to think she refused to quit because she wanted me to suffer. I think that's why people really get divorced -- they can't stand being with someone who knows all of their mistakes."

When she found Brian's baby book, she spent an hour looking through it and neglecting the work waiting to be done. He was a plump, Scandinavian child with pale skin and blue eyes. The photos -- all taken in the early Seventies -- had discolored, making everything look redder than it should be. Or maybe the light is redder in the north. She wondered if this were likely or even possible. She calculated how old she would have been when the photos were taken. Her heart skipped a beat when she realized she would have just been starting school when Brian was born. The handwritten notes and captions were neatly scribed in a rigidly upright script that she assumed was Alice's hand. "B's first tooth" under a pouch with a hard nugget inside. "B's first haircut" over a snippet of blond hair tied with a blue ribbon. Claire wondered if "B" was for "Brian" or for "baby."

Toward the end of the book, she found a studio portrait of dead Alice and Brian. She didn't know what she had been expecting, but it certainly wasn't this bouffant blonde with cat's-eye glasses and a round, still-girlish face. Her smile was hopeful, and she held her son like he was the most important person she had ever met. All the stories about the shrew Milo described evaporated. But hadn't Milo already confessed that the bad marriage wasn't entirely her fault? He had stayed out of a sense of responsibility, not because he loved her. She closed the book and dropped it in the bottom of the box she had already marked as "misc."

Around the third week of May, Claire was startled awake by a bad dream. In it, she was buried underground and the pressure around her middle was unbearable, as if her body were being crushed by a one-ton pickup truck. She was gasping for breath when she finally came to, but the pain evaporated. She turned on her side and checked the time on her phone: just after three in the morning. Reaching behind her, she found Milo's arm; he had made it home.

With a familiar pressure in her bladder, she hoisted herself from the bed and walked blindly toward the bathroom, her hands stretched in front of her to find the door. Once inside with the door shut, she flipped on the light and sat down on the toilet.

A second later, Milo tapped on the door. "Are you okay in there?"

"I'm fine. I didn't mean to wake you."

"It's okay...I'm having a hard time sleeping anyway. I think I'll sit up for a while."

"Go back to bed. I'll be out in a second. You can talk me back to sleep."

"Are you saying I'm the human equivalent of Ambien, darling? If so, I've heard better compliments."

"That's not exactly what I meant," she answered with a small laugh.

"Fine. I'll be waiting for you."

She finished up in the bathroom and went back to the bed, beaching herself next to him. "How was work?"

"Good. It was a busy night. I think business is up considerably. Those two apartment complexes across the street have certainly changed the demographics of the clientele, though. Seems like we have more of an under-fifty crowd these days."

"Any of the regulars still showing up?"

"A few. The professor shows up for Jeopardy every day. He and Sax sit at the bar and compete with each other. The weekends belong to the kids, though. Sax and I have all but decided to pay for Don to go to bartending school. He's a great server, and Morgana seems to like him pretty well."

"What are you two old men doing down there? Playing matchmakers?"

Even in the dark, she was certain he was blushing. "Can you blame us for wanting everyone to be as happy as we are?"

"I take it he and Zareb are still getting on fine."

"Better than, I think. Sax is happier than I've ever seen him, and Zareb is in the bar two or three ti--"

Claire's unexpected screech of pain cut him off.

"What's wrong? Is it the baby?" Milo was on his feet, his arms spread wide in panic. "What's going on?"

Claire couldn't answer him. The bands of pain had rendered her temporarily speechless. By the time she could speak again, Milo had guessed the problem.

"You're having a contraction, aren't you? Wait...you aren't due for another few weeks! What is happening? Is this bad? Are you in danger? Is the baby?" He seemed unable to stop blathering and focus on the issue at hand: her intense labor pains.

"Stop!" she shouted when she caught her breath.

Her fiancé rooted himself to the ground and closed his mouth.

"My bag is in the closet. You need to get me to the hospital."

He frowned. "You already had a bag packed? Why didn't you--"

"Milo, let's discuss this later."

"Of course, darling."

Claire rolled herself out of bed as soon as the pain had fully subsided. She sent up a prayer that she would be forgiven for ever thinking that, after everything she had already been through in her life, childbirth would be as painless as a mosquito bite.

"Do you want to get dressed?"

She considered it for a moment; then her water broke, making the decision for her. "Grab a towel from the bathroom to put over the seat. We need to go now." She picked up her phone and hit the speed dial for her obstetrician's office. The answering service picked up. "This is Claire Combs. I'm in labor!"

"Who is your doctor, ma'am?" asked a preternaturally calm operator on the other end.

"Slotnick."

"Which hospital are you going to?"

She put her hand over the receiver and asked Milo.

"Boswell," he answered, guiding her toward the front door.

"Boswell," she repeated.

"I'll notify him immediately." The line disconnected and she handed the phone to Milo, who had just finished spreading the towel over the passenger-side bucket seat of his car.

"You're doing great," he said, helping her into the car.

As she sat down, another contraction started. "Time them!" she shouted at Milo, who gave her a thumbs-up as he crossed in front of the car, glancing at his watch. Closing her eyes, she pushed back in the seat, doing everything she could not to bear down. By the time the wave had passed, she could see the hospital looming ahead. Thank God they lived so close!

Milo wasn't talking anymore, she noticed. She reached out and took his hand and he smiled at her.

She suddenly regretted not taking Lamaze more seriously. She and Milo had made it to only two classes -- just enough for her to decide an epidural seemed like a great idea. She wasn't ready. How ridiculous was that? Sixteen-year-old girls were more prepared than she was -- not for motherhood, of course, but for the actual experience of giving birth. She had imagined every part of motherhood: holding her child, dealing with possible genetic complications, teaching her how to be a good and honorable person, drying her tears when her heart was broken, and celebrating her successes. What she hadn't thought about was how this beautiful little girl was going to come into the world.

"Claire? It's time to get out of the car now," Milo said gently. He was standing at the passenger door with a wheelchair.

New Life

She shook her head.

"What are you doing?"

"I'm fine. Just take me home."

"Claire, you're having contractions. It's time to have the baby."

"I'm not ready."

"I think Beatrice is."

"She can wait. Let's go home."

The emergency-room doors slid open and a young man in scrubs walked toward the car. "Do you need help getting her to the wheelchair?" he asked Milo.

Milo threw up his hands in frustration. "Yes. Do you have a psychiatrist available?"

"Excuse me? I thought she was pregnant."

Milo turned to face the orderly. "She is! But she's apparently lost her mind. She won't get out of the car."

Claire took the opportunity to push the wheelchair out from between the door and the rest of the car and pulled the door shut, hitting the locks a second later.

"Claire!" Milo shouted, hitting the car window with the side of his fist. "You've got to..."

She didn't hear the rest because another wave of squeezing pain hit her, causing her to roll forward in her seat. She didn't even know she was crying until she felt the wetness on her hands. When she opened her eyes, she saw Milo's hands against the window. He was holding up six fingers. Six minutes apart.

The orderly had disappeared, leaving her baby's father to stand helplessly outside of the car. Six minutes wasn't very long. When did the opportunity for an epidural slip away?

The hospital doors slid open again. This time, a familiar, kindly face appeared -- Dr. Slotnick. He approached Milo, shook his hand, and knocked on the window. She rolled it down. "Claire, it's time to come inside."

"I'm not ready," she repeated.

"Now, we talked about this."

"About what?" queried Milo, fear shadowing his face.

The good doctor placed a comforting hand on his shoulder. "Nothing to worry about, but with Claire's advanced age I suspected she might deliver a few weeks ahead of schedule."

"You knew this could happen? And you didn't tell me?" Milo sounded incredulous.

Claire shrunk away. "I was sure I wouldn't be early!"

Milo's jaw dropped as he stared at her. Then he started laughing. At first, it wasn't much more than a giggle, but it grew from there until he was doubled over and tears were streaming from his eyes. His laughter proved contagious -- though she hadn't thought anything was funny a few minutes earlier, Claire found herself laughing almost as hard as he was. Even Dr. Slotnick chuckled, though not with as much enthusiasm as the couple.

When the laughter subsided, Dr. Slotnick said, "We should get you into that wheelchair before you have another contraction."

"Okay. Can I have an epidural?" she asked, unlocking the door.

"I'll do my best to make that happen."

By eleven o'clock the next morning, Claire was alone with her daughter for the first time. Milo, exhausted, was finally sleeping on the second bed in the room. The baby, who was in a portable crib next to her bed, opened her big blue eyes and waved her arms and legs tentatively, as if she were exploring the limits of this new and larger space. Claire reached out with one finger and brushed Beatrice's palm; the tiny hand wrapped tightly around it and Claire smiled.

She was perfect -- ten fingers, ten toes, and no signs of anything abnormal. Her skin, which had been bright red at birth, had faded to ivory. The wisps of hair on her head were blondish red and fine.

Milo had called everyone before he fell asleep: Sax, Sondra, Brian, and Beryl. Beryl wanted to get on a plane and come to Arizona immediately, but Milo talked her into waiting a few weeks -- until the small family had a home with a third bedroom. Sax was covering the bar and Brian was at work; Marla would bring the children after school. Only Sondra was likely to make an appearance before then -- but probably not much before. Claire knew from months of rooming with her that Sondra wasn't usually dressed to leave the condo before noon. And -- based on the fact that Milo heard a man's voice in the background -- she wasn't likely to change her habits and rush over.

A Hispanic nurse peeked around the corner of the door. "Is she awake?" she asked, indicating the crib.

Claire nodded, laying a finger across her lips and pointing toward the other bed. "But he's not," she whispered.

"Yes, I am," Milo said with a groan.

"You need to sleep!" she scolded. "You won't be getting much more of that once we're home."

"Is this your first one?" the nurse asked in a neutral tone that Claire appreciated.

"Yes," she answered.

"Congratulations," she said, stepping into the room and looking down at Beatrice. "She's beautiful. Since you haven't nursed before, do you want some help?"

"Is it difficult?" Claire hadn't considered that feeding her child might be a challenge.

"Let's just say there's a learning curve. More for you than for her, to be truthful. Babies are born with the instinct to suck when something small and round is inserted into their mouths. If she could get your finger to her mouth, she'd suck on that -- at least until she figured out she wasn't getting any milk from it."

Milo and Claire both laughed and relaxed.

The nurse, smiling, leaned over the crib and picked up Beatrice, reading the tiny hospital bracelet. "Lovely name," she commented. "I have a cousin named Beatriz...though the whole family calls her *Abeja*."

"Why?" they asked in unison.

"Because she buzzes around like a busy little bee!" She stood next to the other side of the bed with Beatrice now. "Just unsnap the snaps along one shoulder or the other so that your breast is exposed."

Despite the knowledge that half a dozen people had been between her legs in the last twelve hours, she blushed. However, she reached up with one hand and did as the nurse instructed. The nurse helped her position her breast so that her nipple would be easily accessible to the baby; then she laid her in Claire's arms. The child latched on immediately and Claire felt a rush of happiness and pride.

"I'll leave you to it," the nurse said.

"Wait! How will I know when to quit?"

"Don't worry...she'll stop when she's full." The nurse pulled the door closed and disappeared.

Milo dragged a chair close to the bed and watched his daughter and his fiancée.

"Have you ever seen anything so amazing?" Claire asked, marveling at their daughter.

"No. I never have."

New Life

Star Light, Star Bright

If one is to plan a July wedding in Phoenix, Arizona, there are only two choices: you can either have it inside or you can have it at night. Technically, three, thought Sondra as she admired herself in the mirror: inside and at night. Though lime green wouldn't have been her first choice, she had to admit that the color suited her well. She was thankful she had avoided a sunburn in Belize. The dress looked nice on Beryl too, Sondra noted, though Beryl's figure was decidedly more matronly than her own.

Sondra had tried to convince Claire to push the wedding back to the fall, arguing that the stress of a newborn would be all that she and Milo could handle for a while. Milo, however, had wanted to marry Claire as soon as she and the baby were released from the hospital. July was the compromise, so July it was.

Sax, who had volunteered to pick up Claire's family from the airport, had told Sondra that every one of them had wilted the moment they emerged from the air-conditioned terminal. Claire's mother, in particular, seemed to think of the weather as a personal assault on her senses.

Beryl bustled into the room, her dark curls drooping. She hadn't taken Sondra's suggestion to use more hair spray. "Is Claire ready? Everyone's here!"

"It's barely past seven -- the ceremony isn't supposed to start until seven-thirty," Sondra answered calmly.

"Why wait? It's not like those folding chairs are particularly comfortable, you know. Our mother is already complaining."

When Sondra moved in with Patrick right before their trip to Belize, Milo and Claire vacated the Sun City duplex, selling much of Milo's furniture. The house was empty now, save the twenty-four rented white folding chairs, arranged in four rows of six with an aisle down the middle, which filled the living room. At the front, where the couch used to sit, Beryl used an abundance of lime-green tulle and white flowers to turn the window into something that closely resembled an arch. The woman was a whiz with tulle.

"But--"

New Life

"It's all right," Claire interjected, emerging from the bathroom. Morgana, who followed her out a second later, had proved to be quite a talented hairdresser -- she had woven Claire's blonde hair into a crown and decorated it with baby's breath. "Help me into my dress. Morgana, please let Milo know that I'll be ready to start at seven-fifteen.

"Ten minutes?" Sondra whined as Morgana left.

"Plenty of time."

Sondra retrieved the garment bag from the otherwise-empty closet. She had helped Claire shop for it, so she knew what was inside: a simple, white-silk, sleeveless dress with a V-neck and an empire waist. It truly was the perfect gown for Claire, emphasizing her well-toned arms and long, elegant neck, while hiding the remaining baby fat under a flowing, floor-length skirt. At first, Claire had resisted wearing white, citing tradition. But the dress and Sondra had changed her mind.

Milo had given Claire a white-gold necklace with a heart-shaped, diamond-encrusted pendant as a wedding gift the night before. As Beryl helped her with the clasp, Sondra unsheathed the gown, unzipping the long zipper at the back of it. A moment later, she was zipping it up again, this time on Claire. The two women stood back as Claire admired herself in the mirror.

"You look amazing, Sis," Beryl said, her hands clasped under her chin.

"Gorgeous," agreed Sondra.

"I just need some earrings."

"I've got them." Beryl went to the folding table where her purse sat and pulled a small satin bag from it. "Mom wants you to wear these," she said, holding the bag out to Claire.

Claire emptied the bag into her palm. Two round diamond-and-pearl earrings, each the size of a penny, shone under the light. One pearl sat in the center of each, with diamonds swirling out from them. "These were our grandmother's," she said quietly.

"More importantly, Grandpa Harry bought them for her. Mom thought you would appreciate that. They can be your something old and something borrowed."

New Life

"She's got the something new," Sondra said, indicating the necklace. "And I've got the blue." She held up a garter, waving it between two fingers.

"I should have put that on before the dress."

"Hold out a leg. I'll help you out." Claire hiked up her skirt and lifted her foot off the ground while Sondra pushed the garter to just above her knee. "Perfect. With any luck, it won't slide down your leg halfway through the ceremony."

Claire's eyes widened. Beryl laughed first; Sondra joined in. All mirth ceased as the music started in the living room.

"This is it," Beryl said. "Put on the earrings. Let's go."

Each woman took one last look in the mirror and smiled.

Sax sat in the third row back, behind Beryl's husband and two of their brood. He wasn't too surprised to see that Zareb was already tearing up. After a few months of dating, he knew what a softy his boyfriend could be. He pulled the handkerchief from the inside pocket of his jacket and handed it to Zee (as Sax called him), who smiled gratefully.

Don, the Brass Monkey's newly christened fourth bartender, started the music before sitting down next to Morgana and right behind Sax and Zee. Soon, Sondra appeared in her lime-green dress -- a garment for which there could be no possible use after this event. Still, Sax knew if anyone could find a use for it, Sondra would. She stood on the right, next to Milo; she was his "Best Man." Behind her came Beryl, the Matron of Honor, looking a little more ragged than Sondra but still lovely. Finally, Claire appeared in her elegant, flowing gown. Zee gasped and Sax took his hand.

Across the aisle, Sax could see Milo's son and his family as they happily watched their soon-to-be stepmother and step-grandmother glide toward Milo. Even though Beatrice would never remember being at her parents' wedding, Marla, who held the baby in her arms, tilted her up so that she could see her mother walk down the aisle. Or maybe she did it so that Claire could see her daughter.

Claire reached the front and handed off her green-and-white bouquet to Beryl. Milo took her hand and they turned to face the preacher, a middle-aged man with a warm, friendly smile and a tenor voice. "Milo and Claire asked me to start by thanking you on their behalf for all of the friendship, love, and support you have given them over the years. They truly believe that without each and every one of you, they would not be standing here today. They look toward the future with joy and expectation, knowing that you will all continue to walk alongside them and their newborn daughter, Beatrice Marie."

Zee squeezed Sax's hand; Sax squeezed his right back.

As she stood before the preacher with Milo holding her hand, Claire marveled at how perfect and complete the moment felt. She couldn't remember feeling so wonderful since she won her last barrel race on Dorian. Her life had been bittersweet, if not sour, ever since. Her horse's death, her grandfather's death, her estrangement from her family, even Dorsey's death -- all of that misery had led her to this place.

"Do you take this man to be your lawfully wedded husband?" the preacher intoned.

"I do."

"Place this ring on his hand."

She slid the golden circle onto his finger and smiled.

"Do you take this woman to be your lawfully wedded wife?"

"I do," Milo said.

The preacher handed him her ring with the same words he had spoken to her. The ring slid on easily, now that she wasn't swollen from pregnancy.

"Friends and family, I am pleased to present Milo and Claire Crosby!"

Everyone stood and applauded, gathering around the happy couple.

"Best wishes," her brother-in-law Rory whispered against her cheek before kissing it.

"Grandma!" shouted Alice Marie as she launched herself toward Claire, hugging her tightly around the waist. Claire smoothed the girl's hair affectionately.

The others offered congratulatory hugs and best wishes to them as well. In the kitchen, Beryl and Sondra were already pouring champagne, while Don and Morgana were rearranging the chairs and setting up folding tables in the living room. Morgana looked up and Claire caught her eye, mouthing "thank you" to her.

Marla handed Beatrice off to Milo and gave Claire's hands a good squeeze. "I'm so pleased to have you for my new mother-in-law."

"That means the world coming from you. I know how much you loved Alice."

"Alice was a goodhearted woman. But I've recently come to the realization that even the best people have faults."

Sondra appeared in the doorway between the kitchen and the living room with the cake -- a modest affair with a smooth, white ganache glaze and lime-green decorative flowers. Sax and Zee had provided the cake topper, a pair of monkeys dressed in wedding attire. "Everyone find a seat! It's time to cut the cake."

The guests scurried to sit down as Milo and Claire joined Beryl and Sondra at the table closest to the kitchen. Somehow, while everyone was milling around, Sondra and Beryl had managed to place four flutes of champagne on every table. Claire watched as Marla removed the glasses from Alice Marie's and Eric's hands, much to their disappointment.

"A toast!" announced Sondra. "To one of the most honorable men and the single sweetest woman I have ever met. May their happiness be eternal! Cheers!"

"Cheers!" shouted the crowd.

Milo, still holding the baby, raised his glass and clinked it against Claire's.

Beryl stepped forward and held her glass up as well. "One more and we'll get to the cake. I would like to toast my sister -- a true survivor. A woman with more strength of character in her pinkie than most people have in their whole bodies." She turned to face her and said more quietly, "I know fate has dealt you bad hand after bad hand. But I'm sure that you're on a winning streak now. Cheers."

The party toasted and drank. Sondra handed Milo the knife, and together he and Claire cut the cake.

Milo, Claire, and Beatrice cut the cake as a family, since Milo wouldn't hand her off to anyone. Someone -- he thought it had been Marla -- had given them a baby sling right after Beatrice was born. He had considered wearing it during the wedding ceremony, but first Sondra, and then Beryl, nixed the idea, both arguing that he was marrying Claire, not their child. Though Claire had liked the idea, they bowed to the pressure.

Almost as soon as the ceremony ended, though, he had his daughter back in his arms. He was infatuated with her -- that perfect blend of his and Claire's features. All of the fears he had about being a father at sixty had vanished the moment the doctor placed the red, squirming, angry creature in his arms.

They had chosen a Sunday night for the wedding, because Sundays were the slowest night at the bar. Sax even agreed to close the place for the occasion. But the problem with a Sunday-night wedding was that most of the younger guests had to go to work the next day and the older guests were up past their bedtime as soon as the clock tolled nine.

As the crowd thinned out, Eric sat down next to his grandfather. The two hadn't seen each other since the disastrous dinner where Milo had called Eric's girlfriend a "tartlet." Milo, feeling unusually magnanimous, apologized.

Eric shrugged. "You were right, Grandpa."

"You're not with Ditzy anymore?"

"Diva," he corrected, laughing. "No, we broke up a few weeks ago."

"I'm sorry to hear that."

"No, you're not."

"What do you think of your aunt?" he asked, changing the subject.

"Aunt Bea? She's adorable. Watch out though -- Alice Marie might try to smother her in her bed," he joked. "She's stealing you away."

Milo frowned. "Don't even joke about that."

Looking properly chastened, he said, "Sorry. Bad joke. I just came over to say goodbye. Dad has to work tomorrow, so we're leaving."

"That's okay, son. Thanks for coming."

"I wouldn't have missed it." He grinned. "Claire is great. I'm glad you found someone." The lanky kid stood up and hugged Milo around the shoulders.

New Life

Before long, Brian, Marla, and Alice Marie -- who kissed Beatrice on the forehead -- had all said their goodbyes. Sondra, who had indulged in one too many glasses of champagne, said goodnight as well. Patrick guided her out of the house. He was a good match for her, Milo thought.

Don and Morgana were folding up tables as they emptied and loading them into Don's pickup truck. Before he knew it, his chair was the only one remaining in the living room. Claire came up behind him and wrapped her arms around his neck. "Thank you," she whispered.

"For what?" he asked, startled.

"Everything." She stood up straight and rubbed his shoulders lightly. "I guess we should go home."

"What about the stuff in the bedrooms?"

"Already packed up. The house is empty again."

"I'm going to miss this place," he sighed. "Do you think we should keep it?"

"Why?" she laughed. "We won't be able to live here for eighteen years!"

"What if you decide to dump me? I might need a home."

"I'm never going to divorce you. You're stuck with me, as far as I'm concerned. Are you planning to leave me someday?"

"Of course not."

"If neither of us plans to escape, why do we need an escape plan?"

He stood up and she took the chair, folding it and setting it against the nearest wall. She had changed out of her wedding attire; she stood before him in a summery red-and-yellow sun dress. "Have I told you lately how beautiful you are?"

She blushed, warming her skin to a rosy pink. "Sweet talker." She held out her arms, and he laid Beatrice in them. She pulled her daughter close and smiled.

He put an arm around her. "Come on, girls," he said, "it's time to go home."

New Life

No hearts were broken in the writing of this novel.

New Life

Author's Note

And finally, we reach the end of the Brass Monkey series...for now at least. I have loved writing these characters – I hope you have loved reading about them.

I would like to thank my publisher, Inknbeans Press, for encouraging me along the way. Having spent more than a year with Milo, Claire, Sondra and Sax, I find that I miss them. But, of course, I am already well on my way with a new set of characters and my first foray into science fiction.

A special thank-you goes out to Grace Guerra, who has faithfully beta-read and offered her thoughts on all four of these novels. She is truly the best reader a writer could ever hope for.

One more note: not long after I finished writing this novel, one of the series' real-life muses died. Duchess, the matriarch of the Phoenix Zoo's orangutan family, passed on as a result of cancer. I will miss her wizened face and knowing eyes when I visit the zoo in the future.

If you would like to know more about Arizona and my life, I hope you'll follow my blog at
http://brightlightsbigcacti.wordpress.com/.

Happy reading!
Susan Wells Bennett

New Life

About the Author

A third-generation native Arizonan, Susan Wells Bennett was born and raised in Phoenix. As a child, she wrote a letter to then-President Carter that was published in a local daily newspaper. From then on, she wanted to be a writer when she grew up – that, or President. At sixteen, she left Arizona to attend Cottey College in Nevada, Missouri, for two years. Returning to Arizona, she attended Arizona State University as an English major. She spent a fair amount of the next decade trying to escape the Southwest, but never succeeded. Susan worked in and around the real estate and home-building industries for the majority of the last two decades, a career that evolved into a position as a writer and editor for one of the nation's largest homebuilders. In 2009, with the support of her husband, she began writing novels fulltime. To date, she has completed ten novels and is working on her eleventh.

She has no plans to run for political office in the near future.

New Life

If you enjoyed this book, look for her other titles from Inknbeans Press:

Circle City Blues
Thief of Todays and Yesterdays
The Prophet's Wives
An Unassigned Life and
Forsaking the Garden.
The Brass Monkey Series:
Wild Life
Charmed Life
Night Life
New Life
Available at Amazon, Barnes & Noble,
Smashwords.com and other fine booksellers.

Contact Ms. Bennett at SWB@inknbeans.com.

Fresh Books Brewed Daily